PART ONE
JACK AND N

THURSDA

When the teacher called out, "That's it, stop writing please," Jack had already been sitting with his arms folded for twenty minutes dreaming of sunflowers. The pencils went down one by one, and when the last of them hit the desk, he and his classmates were no longer schoolboys; because it wasn't just the end of this exam, it was the end of all exams, the end of school, forever. In Jack's case, at least, the transition to adulthood is going to be hard, not an unqualified success; but perhaps I am getting ahead of myself.

The boys remained seated for a few seconds while the papers were collected, then variously sighed and mildly cursed before rising as one and filing out into the corridor to try to work out how well or badly they'd done. As you may have experienced yourself, discussing performance with peers can only lead to bluffing and disillusion, so Jack and his best friend Milo decided to avoid the group post-mortem and conduct a private dissection instead.

"How did you do?" asked Milo.

"Smashed it, mate."

"Annihilated it?"

"Obliterated it."

"Exterminated it?"

"Eradicated it."

"Excellent work! Aren't you going to ask me how I did – I mean,

5

before we run out of crushing superlatives."

"Sorry, Milo. How did you do?"

"Not as well as you, by the sound of it."

And there you have it.

They wandered out of the building and into the playground, where, suddenly liberated, they shouted at the tops of their voices, maybe even louder than that, a variety of well-crafted swear words, the last sacred mantra of fleeting childhood. Let's not sully our opening page by listing body parts and sex acts, there is plenty of time for that later. Let's just observe a passing teacher failing to hide a grin as he pantomimed an exaggerated finger wag, 'You have been very very naughty.' The final reprimand of seven long years.

They had no bags or coats to collect, so, dressed in the last-ever wearing of their blue uniforms, the whole class strolled out of the gates for the ultimate time, completely neglecting, as boys do, to mark, or even notice, the portentousness of the occasion. They meandered across the road to the pub, forcing a few irritated cars to slow down. It was late spring, three hours of light were left, and working people were still at work. Jack had two more hours to cling to boyhood before the event that would change him forever.

The class entered the saloon bar of The King's Hind. Other exam- inations were also emptying out, so the pub was quickly swelling with more and more dark blue blazers. And infiltrating the dark blue of the boys there were increasing numbers of bottle green uniforms as the girls from their school next door began to enter, hesitantly. Those young ladies would baulk at being described as proper, but still would never normally come to the pub like this, certainly not straight after school wearing their blazers. However, in the excitement, on this the shared last day, they had decided col- lectively to mark the moment and the memory. A first daring three put their heads around the door, shyly; then a slightly furtive four, then two pairs boldly, and finally a whole form with linked arms

For my mother Brenda and my father Len,
who are ultimately responsible

Published by Lorenz Books
an imprint of Anness Publishing Ltd
www.annesspublishing.com
info@anness.com

First edition: 2025
Printed in China

Copyright © Paul Anness 2025

Publisher: Joanna Lorenz
Cover Illustration: Ivan Hissey
Cover Development: Peter Bridgewater
Jacket Design: Nigel Partridge
Editor: Joanna Lorenz
Typography and Production: Ben Worley

A CIP catalogue record for this book is available from the British Library.

Although every precaution has been taken in the preparation of this book,
the publisher and author assume no responsibility for errors or omissions.
Neither is any liability assumed for damages resulting from the use of
information contained herein. Don't try this at home. Nothing is real
except the fantasy.

ISBN 9780754888888

CONTENTS

PREAMBLE   4

PART ONE: JACK AND MILO   5

PART TWO: A LAUNCH AND A SWAN   288

PART THREE: DOWNHILL WITH LETTERS   562

PREAMBLE

I am old now, and this story is about a summer I had more than sixty years ago. This account of those few weeks has been constructed slowly over decades; first I had to make the time and then I had to find the confidence to tell it.

Memory does not fade in a straight line, it undulates: images that start out sharp and vivid can lose their focus and their colour for a time, but then come back, suddenly, brighter and more vibrant than ever. Perhaps the trick is to pick them at the right moment.

The narrative itself, and the way I've told it, has also evolved and developed. I see in my notebooks that a dozen different inks and pencils have been used, some pages are torn out, others are inserted, and the handwriting has changed beyond recognition.

Earlier on, I had the recollections of the others who were there, to help me, but they're gone now. They left me a dozen letters, and one of them sent me an article cut out of a newspaper, but I can't hear their voices anymore. Recently I rediscovered a small black and white photograph of us all together, gathered around a tree stump by the lake.

In all honesty, I might have had to create or shape some passages here or there to fit an empty space or join some ragged dots together; in which case, not everything might have happened exactly the way I've said. But that doesn't make it any less true.

laughing, each taking courage from the other. And so the greens mixed with the blues, like the merging colours of the changing tides, and formed a single swelling sea of hope and apprehension.

The King's Hind was a proper cathedral of antique boozing, soaked in drink and smoke all the way down from the stained-glass windows to the malted plush banquettes and the sticky fleur-de-lys carpets. This faded alcotectural magnificence was nothing unusual in the East End back then; there were another nine similar pubs within twenty minutes' walk, some even more shabby and lavish. That night each of those nine saloons was welcoming its own groups of girls and boys dressed in their own blazers: purple, black, light blue, mauve; all of them celebrating the end of childhood. The end of exams, the last-ever day of school, the first night of the long summer holiday – this was heady stuff.

These seventeen- and eighteen-year-old girls and boys were on the brink of the new. The majority were already looking for jobs and many would be starting work the following week …. For them it was hard not to feel that youth had passed already, and adulthood in the form of baking, banking or bricklaying was frighteningly close.

For a few, the bright ones, or the kids whose parents had pushed them, there was the possibility of university or art school or teacher training college in three months' time, subject to results. For them, there was the prospect of a break beforehand, maybe filled with a temporary job to get a bit of money, or perhaps a gap month or two, nothing grand or middle class or in the Far East or on a bootstring, but perhaps a few wet weeks on a budget in a caravan in a place that looked better on the map than it did out of the window. Jack is one of these lucky ones, if that's what we're calling it.

For now, he has found a corner table for himself and some friends; it's not hard for him to get a top spot because he's a regular, and Milo is the owner's son. You need to know more about Jack because he is possibly our hero. He is a mid-sized youth of pleasing appearance to some (good hair, moody brown eyes, nose probably slightly bigger than strictly necessary, expressive lips, teeth mainly straight) and, as we meet him more intimately for the first time, he is holding forth on one of the exam papers of the day, and the questions he had answered on The Great Gatsby. He's very confident, annoying the four friends with him, because as ever with Jack, the confidence doesn't guarantee he's right, just that he doesn't want to be challenged. Jack has been a prince of childhood; for him the next stage will be harder.

The other two boys at the table are Bob and Mike, friends with each other for fifteen years; they were born in the next street and travelled together through all the ages of school. Bob is small, quick and drinks too much. Mike is huge, and plays rugby for the school, which makes him a local celebrity; but now, thinking about it, that's all over for him.

Jack is bound for university (subject to results) but Bob and Mike are not; where they are going to work is also as yet unspecified, primarily undetermined because all three boys, along with friend Milo, have rucksacks in the boot of a car outside, with clothes, passports, francs and tickets for the night ferry.

The two girls at the table in their green jackets, very old friends, are totally unaware of the plan, the tickets and the getaway. One is Maggie, extremely pretty in an unkempt way, hair askew, collar in and out, not one to exhaust the looking glass, gentle, tolerant and very bright. And her loyal and much beloved friend Joan, clumsy and uncomfortable in her skin right now, going through some years she will try hard later to forget. But this is not her story; she's great, but don't get too fond of her because she's disappearing soon.

"And at the end of each section," Jack is saying (yes, he is still talking, uninterrupted), "I brought it back to the green light across the bay. It was so elegant."

"What does the green light mean?" asks Joan, who has done Twelfth Night instead, and whose interest in Jack's Fitzgerald monologue is entirely feigned by now.

"It is the distant light that represents hope and salvation. It is the green neon," Jack purrs, aiming for charming but hitting cheesy pretty hard, "bouncing off the betting shop window onto Maggie's blazer as she waits for me longingly at the bus stop."

The line crashed and burned, especially with Joan. Mike and Bob, barely outside Jack's line of vision, mimed putting their fingers down their throats to induce vomit. Joan noticed and laughed. Maggie just looked mortified for Jack, while he quickly fashioned a wrist-and-hand waving gesture indicating he was being ironic; a good effort but too late to save himself.

If you had asked Maggie and Jack at any time in the past four or five years if they were girlfriend and boyfriend, Maggie would probably have said yes, and Jack would probably have said no – it was that kind of relationship. And right now, Jack is feeling a little caught out, a little uneasy. That's why he's trying too hard.

Maggie is booked on a summer course for the next two weeks; she has to pass a language exam specified by one of the fancy universities if they offer her a place. Jack and Maggie joked it was a test they gave the poor kids to make sure they weren't going to embarrass everyone when they got there. "It will probably include a module on what cutlery to use." "There's a paper on what bonnet to wear for the rowing". What larks, Pip. But the main point is, because she is going to be away, he hasn't actually revealed the French flit to her. His upcoming adventure as a continental drifter remains either a closely guarded secret, or merely unmentioned, depending on which side you favour.

Previously this could have been considered a matter for a future conscience, but Jack is disconcerted right now, because Maggie has just announced (she said "reminded him" but he was denying that) that some time ago the course had been rescheduled to the middle of the vacation. Therefore, he must recall, she is available through-out the coming weeks for escapades, from covert kisses at Kew to cockling at Canvey Island. This is a little joke between them – like a McGill postcard – shared knowingly, because of course there are no cockles in June; they will have to wait till they are older.

What to do, therefore? He had the choice between:

- Giving up France without telling her he had been going, and thereby letting down his three friends, in order to stay clean with Maggie and get those tiny kisses

- Coming clean about the French trip, explaining why he hadn't told her, and exerting maximum moral blackmail to let him go anyway ("It is only a few weeks, and I did think you were going to be away...")

- Telling her to go home quickly and get her passport and come with them (but... a 'girlfriend' on a bloke's trip?)

- Coming clean about the French trip, giving it up for her, maybe trading up the sacrifice for some bigger kisses

- Taking the coward's way, slipping away at the end of the evening, getting in the car, and heading to the ferry port with the lads, then calling later. That's a risky route, but the stakes are high

What would you advise? Let's leave him considering the options.

The general frivolity in the pub evolved gradually into something more frenetic, as alcohol played its role, and kids began to realise where they had come from and wonder where they might be going. Tension continued to mount for an hour or more as it grew darker. The drinks flowed, the crisps rustled in the bags, and back then, you may remember, we also smoked, so, five hundred cigarettes were lit, and many of them were inhaled.

Milo, working behind the bar, watched as the air became dense, the carpet soaked, and movement to the bar or washroom or between groups could now only be achieved by jostling, nudging or by politely tapping the shoulders of intervening bodies. He had worked in the pub for several years by now, he was raised in it, and could sense that the atmosphere, driven by excitement, fuelled by anxiety, powered by drinkers unused to drinking, was in danger of tipping over. The laughter was happy in places, still, but felt cruel or mocking in others. Gradually in the mix were odd discordant grunts, slurred shouts, and, particularly from the boys with no girls in their groups, bad language, bad jokes, and offensive comments as a means of making themselves feel better for the loss they've not yet acknowledged. In the background, playing on the jukebox, Dion is crooning The Wanderer. It is timeless; ageless.

Also behind the bar was the landlady Alice, Milo's mother, four feet seven inches tall with arms thicker than Jack's thighs. She moved back and forth behind the counter on a specially raised platform that allowed her to reach the pumps and go eye to eye with the customers. In the height of the current crush she was pulling three pints a minute and hooting with the adrenaline.

Alice's husband Herbie held the pub licence for twenty years before dying of his own poison, and she and her three boys had taken up the lease a few years back, revolutionising the business with the magic jukebox, some experimental flavoured snacks, a new-found reluctance to guzzle the stock, and a blind eye for the ever-decreasing age of their clientele. Sadly, on the night in question, two of the three sons, Milo's brothers Bruno and Sholto, were out doing their weekly church charity work, or we might not have ended up where we arrived an hour later. The Kelly family were intensely Catholic: Alice had all the boys in church every Sunday, and they each devoted an evening or Saturday morning every week to one of the parish's charitable enterprises.

Initially Milo slid out occasionally from behind the bar to briefly join Jack and the group in the alcove at the far end of the room. But as it got busier, he stayed close to his mother – they hadn't anticipated quite the level of business, and they were understaffed for the night. Milo wasn't in the same situation as his friends, although this was his last day at school too: his future was theoretically a bit more carved in, being the son of the landlady, and thereby expected without discussion or consultation to work for the family business.

While Jack's table was exhaustively discussing The Modern American Novel (or he was, at least), outside on the street fate had gathered itself ready to snare Jack and Milo. Six drunk boys from far away, at least a mile, tall and entitled, wearing maroon blazers, were flipping a coin to see whether they would come in to The King's Hind or not.

The blazers belonged to prefects from St Francis, the fee-paying school across town, who were on a celebratory pub crawl, randomly deciding as they progressed where they would drink and where they would pass. This group, bonded for years and spoiled by their petty powers, had also finished school that day, and to them it meant the end of glory days in which they'd walked as Gods. At the entrance to The King's Hind the coin fell heads, dread destiny on which our tale turns; and so they opened the door and pushed in as a phalanx through the throng to the heaving bar now hung with soaking towels.

Their leader, Bart, called out, "Six Light and Bitters." Waiting till they had been poured, and distributed, his sidekick Richie shouted loudly enough for everyone in the bar to hear, "Why the hell are we in this shit hole." Minion one, Rodge, six foot two, sniggered, waiting for it all to kick off, downing his pint in one.

Conversations up and down the room slowed and ceased, heads turned, turned back, and turned again – some nervously avoiding eye contact, and some ostentatiously staring. Beer stared at beer and decided this was not the time. The noise flared up as quickly as it had stalled, and the maroon cadre found themselves in the very unusual position of being ignored.

"Six more," shouted Damian, who was wearing a fuchsia waistcoat under his maroon blazer; he tried out a Flashman sneer, but as he had no moustache to twirl, he only succeeded in looking like a badly colourised plate in a cheap edition of Tom Brown's Schooldays. Maybe it was just the inebriation, but all the indicators are that no-one had told these boys they were dicks in a very long time. If ever. And now it was simply too late for positive criticism to be taken on board productively.

"No more for you, boys," called back Alice. "If this is a shit hole, you don't want to drink here, and we don't want you – off you go." Alice's word had never been denied.

On the jukebox, Peggy Lee launched jauntily into Ain't We Got Fun, the lyrics dancing confidently above the perky tones of the Nelson Riddle Orchestra. Laughter broke out, and the maroon boys, floating like a woefully windless vessel adrift in a blue green sea, looked stupid, and knew it.

"We'll go when we're ready," shouted Richie, lamely. No-one was taking them seriously. Is this what the future looked like?

"You heard her," shouted Milo rising to the protection of his mum. "Back where you come from if this is beneath you. Let's be moving, boys." He called out strongly and confidently as he had done often before, backed up by the presence of his two big brothers. Possibly he had forgotten this time that they were out delivering toys to the orphanage.

So then of course it happened. In every fatal event there is a single moment that switches anger, fear, embarrassment or envy from posturing and bluster to a physical action that cannot be undone. And on this occasion it was the humiliated drunken prefect pulling back his arm and throwing a heavy pint pot hard at Milo.

The thick glass missed Milo by a very long way but clipped Alice on the side of the head as it flew past her, tearing her ear before shattering against one of the mirrors that lined the back wall of the bar and bringing down half a dozen bottles of spirits. It was the first time Alice had been frightened since her husband died. On another night, this could have turned out differently; it was not unusual in the Hind for aggravation to occur, in fact it had a great tradition. It wasn't even that rare for Alice herself to be offered violence. But generally her family's history and reputation either persuaded troublemakers to curb their instincts or nipped the violence in the bud very quickly.

On another night, all the sons and bar staff would have leapt the bar, smacked the ringleader, and rushed the perpetrators out of the saloon with their feet trailing, long before the situation could escalate. Perhaps, if they believed they had just cause and sufficient provocation, they might lay into them a little bit in the alley outside, just to make sure they wouldn't come back. On this night, without thinking, but maybe for family honour and school bravado, perhaps from the excitement of the day, possibly the fizzing nerves of an uncertain future, Milo went over the bar and straight into the posh boys, flailing away, before suddenly realising, cartoon-style, that he was perfectly alone. No-one was following him. Like the trench Lieutenant leading the way over the top shouting "Come On, Lads" only to realise, a moment too late, that his platoon had thought better of it.

What you need to know about Milo is, he's not a fighter. He's a dreamer, a thinker, a joker. His main claim to fighting fame was when he was summoned for a ruck outside the gates by one of the school bullies for some unintended slight. "When you're called out, you have to go," Jack had said, shaking his head regretfully. There was no getting out of it. At the appointed time Milo nervously raised his fists, the very model of a Victorian pugilist, but the bruiser pulled out a highly-sharpened compass. Milo fumbled in his pocket and found only a protractor. "Sucker," he shouted, waving it menacingly, "it looks like you've brought a compass to a protractor fight." The crowd creased up, even the bully laughed, and they mutually stepped back from the brink of asymmetrical warfare. Later Milo would tell you that charm, wit and superior geometry had won the day, without realising what everyone else knew – that the thug had spotted Milo's very big brothers cracking their knuckles menacingly four feet away.

So, not a fighter, but no-one could doubt Milo's courage, this night or any other. He did his best to take on the six, spinning, barging and throwing punches; but he was quite a lot smaller than them as well as being vastly outnumbered. Around the melee the ground cleared, the crowd pushed back and girls screamed. The packed bar suddenly found the space to centrifugally compress and a twenty-foot circle materialized, revealing the boys in the middle. Dozens of other kids began pushing at the doors to get out in case the police came and caught them in their uniforms; tables and chairs were kicked across the room, and for some reason the lights went out, leaving the pub illuminated only by the last of the crimson sun and the streetlights shining in through the blood-toned glass.

Milo was smashed down in seconds, and the boots began to go in. Around the circle, no-one moved, frozen in shock or just not wanting to get involved. Then breaking in through the perimeter charged Jack, closely followed by Mike and Bob. Jack acted impulsively out of care for his friend, not thinking what he hoped to achieve by leaping in, his first instinct to cover Milo, to prevent the kicks landing and to stop the horrible thumping noises. As he flopped down on top of him he began to take some kicks and punches himself, and briefly contemplated getting up to fight, but decided to curl up and protect Milo and himself as best he could. Then Mike and Bob did enough to hit the ruck and break the rhythm, and for a moment it looked like the momentum was gone and the fracas would dry up. Jack, eyes to the ground, arms around his limp friend, blood pulsing hard in his temples, chest heaving, thought these words, or versions of them: 'Thank God it's done. Now they'll step in; maybe the police will come.'

But a scream went up "blade," and the fuse relit. Above Jack, standing astride him and Milo, one of the maroons was flourishing a knife. The circle widened further around them, a circumference of fear overriding curiosity amongst even the most hard-line spectators. It was Bart who was waving the steel in front of him; Mike and Bob and a few others thought better of it and backed off. A couple of the other maroons were looking worried, thinking 'This is not what we signed up for,' and casting around for a possible way out. But Bart, Rodge and Richie were in it all the way.

15

"You OK, Milo?" whispered Jack, and at least got a grunt in reply; so he's alive. Apparently, they were between the legs of a drunk and dangerously demeaned ex-prefect with a sharp implement; so they could be stabbed, cut or sliced at any moment by a boy with hurt feelings. What to do?

Deciding on balance that some form of action, even if it wasn't exactly attack, was the best defence, Jack braced himself, brought his knees up under his chest, and then, with a bellow, thrust himself up in a kind of desperate star jump, forcing the power in his arched spine upwards through Bart's groin and into his diaphragm. Jack never saw it, but Bart went flying, the knife still gripped tight in his fist. Everyone else watched as he seemed to hover in the air, then twist, trying to break his fall with his hands in front of him, before flopping flat on his belly five feet away, bucking and yelping once, then not moving.

Silence. Then chaos. Shouts and screams broke the stillness and the St Francis boys started swinging again, this time to protect themselves against the crowd that was beginning to wake up and menace them. The prefects tried to surround Bart and lift him, or drag him, to safety, but he was a dead weight, stuck in the beer-soaked carpet like a boot trapped in mud. They couldn't shift him.

In the confusion, Jack grabbed Bob, they pulled Milo up between them, and with Mike running in front of them clearing a path, they pushed through the swing door and into the street, not the first to get out because a general fearful exodus was already accelerating. The boys gave an automatic sigh of relief to be out in the cold and had a few quiet mistaken seconds of feeling free, of having escaped, while propping Milo up against the pub wall to see if anything was broken.

Then crashing out behind them came the five still-standing maroons, beating a retreat now from the hostile mob, deserting their prone and heavy comrade, and ready to run for home. The two groups confronted each other, hating each other and embarrassed to be drained of fight. The maroons shouted at Jack and

Milo, wild eyed.

"You killed him, you stupid tossers. Bart's fucking dead."

"His uncle's a detective, dickhead. The cops are going to be all over you. You guys are in a shit-heap of trouble."

A half-hearted kick went out, a desultory and pointless punch, and then the sirens started three streets away, the police were coming. The maroons reacted fastest and shot off down the side road, back towards their side of town. Clearly there was no code at St Francis about never leaving a man behind; it was obvious that notwithstanding their fallen leader's family connections – if that was even true – they were no keener on mixing it with the police than The King's Hind boys.

The doors to the pub, four of them, two sets at the front, two down the side, opened wide and as the sirens got louder the evacuation got swifter, kids scattering hurriedly down alleys and back roads, all desperate to flee without getting involved, without having their names taken, without having to give a statement. Within thirty seconds, hardly anyone remained inside: the last thing Jack saw in the darkened room as the door swung shut for the final time was a small group of anxious people hovering over the body on the ground, and Milo's mother crying and nervously wrapping and unwrapping a tea-towel round her wrists.

As the street cleared, Jack's breathing and pulse calmed and he grasped a semblance of composure, shaking Milo and asking twice, "Where's the car, mate, where did you park?" Milo raised his hand gingerly and pointed down the sideroad to his grey four-door Morris Minor in the shadows fifty yards away. "There, where we left it earlier."

Of course it was, they had been in it a couple of hours ago, hiding their luggage in the boot. Jack got his hand in Milo's pocket and fished out the keys as they were scurrying towards the car. He unlocked it and jumped in on the driver's side. Bob and Milo were in the back, with Milo mainly lying across the seat and Bob squeezed up against the passenger side. Mike hunched up his outsized frame into the passenger seat next to Jack. "You can't drive." said Mike. Jack didn't bother to answer right away; he got the key in, started the car and pulled away with his best driving-school clutchwork, eventually remembering, when they were a hundred and fifty yards up the road, to switch on the headlights. He threw a sharp left, down into the estate, just as a police car, sirens blaring, lights flashing, turned into the main road and screeched up outside the pub.

"I've got a provisional licence, and I'm on my ninth lesson. I can keep us going till Milo gets his breath. Bearing in mind what else has happened, driving without a licence feels like the least of our worries. But given that Milo has a full licence, I think our best bet if we get stopped is to say this is a driving lesson– I am sure that'll be a winning strategy."

"Jesus, Jack," muttered Bob in the back. "Jesus Jesus Jesus Jesus Jesus."

"What are we going to do now?" said Mike. "What's bloody happened, and what are we going to do?"

Milo was groaning and shifting around.

"Check him out, Bob, see if there's any blood."

By now Jack had driven through the estate, taking the car quite slowly up the pedestrian path at the end with the missing bollard that the locals used as a vehicular shortcut in times of need. Turning right, he took the back route to the bypass, and in three minutes they were heading out of London, gradually gathering velocity as Jack gained confidence. "At this rate you'll get us all the way up to the speed limit in an hour or so," Mike commented sarcastically. Morale was low: Jack made a mental note to organise some team-building activities when they had an opportunity. Clearly their All For One And One For All needed a little bit of nurturing, but even the Musketeers must have had the odd bad day.

"There's no blood or broken skin," said Bob from the back, running his hands over and under Milo's shirt and trousers. "But where I can see, there's a lot of bruising and grazing, some of that is going to be quite nasty."

"I am right here, you know," said Milo without opening his eyes, and definitely without smiling. "I'm not dead."

"You're a crazy bastard," said Jack, "and you need to stop doing that stuff. We don't care about you, obviously, but you'll get the rest of us killed". The joke dropped flat. Maybe gallows humour is not so funny when you've just been hung. If it was meant to raise their spirits – always a risky objective – it had the opposite effect, and suddenly they all felt utterly exhausted, as the truth hit them.

"Jesus, Jack, what happened in there, are you not taking this seriously?" Mike repeated. "What are we supposed to be doing?"

"I think we are on the run, Mike," said Jack. "That seems to be what's happening. How we quite got this far I don't know, but in the greater scheme of things it feels like it would be counterproductive to turn back, having made it this far. Right?"

As ever, only Milo knew if Jack was being facetious or sincere, and he lacked the energy to translate.

Jack's wits were beginning to reassemble themselves in roughly the right order. It didn't make for pleasant reflections, but it gave him the chance to try to come up with a plan. To help his mulling he turned on the radio, which was tuned to a jazz station Milo loved, and they got the start of Just One of Those Things, with Ella letting it swing.

"Jesus, Jack," said Bob. "Jesus Christ, man, are we dancing now?" He came from a family that demonstrated respect through abstinence and solemnity. There was a superstition about joy or pleasure during trying circumstances. There should be no song, then the boy might live.

19

"Listen up, guys," Jack spoke calmly now. "I am as scared as you. To be perfectly truthful I am completely fucking terrified. But hang on to a few facts. We were in a pub having a celebration. Whether we should have been there or not is beside the point. A bunch of troublemaking hoodlums came in and threatened everyone, with weapons. Various people tried to protect themselves and others. In fear of their lives, people defended themselves with a little force, less even than equal force – that must be allowed, right? Surely everyone saw that nothing was our fault, and everything that happened was either their fault or an accident. I do feel we're morally entitled to proceed."

['Jesus,' thought Bob in the back, 'listen to it!']

"OK so we've run," Jack continued, "that might not help, but we've done it. I do admit, it could look bad, we could be in real trouble, we could end up arrested – we could get railroaded, especially if the posh kids really do have relations in the police station and get good lawyers. And the cops always have it in for Milo's family and the Hind, that's one thing I am thinking.

"But in terms of real guilt, we don't even know what's happened. When I looked back through the door it definitely looked like people were working on him, it could have been mouth-to-mouth and so on. They wouldn't be messing with him if he was dead, right?

"As it happens, not only are we already on the run, like it or not, but we also have the perfect getaway. The four of us have packed bags in the boot, with passports and money. We're halfway to Dartford; once we're through the tunnel, it's an hour to Dover, and we're on the ferry.

"And the key point – no-one knows. We told no-one we were doing this trip, not parents, not friends, right? And Milo only just got the car, hardly anyone has seen him in it.

"As we all agreed, I left the postcard on my pillow for my mum saying, 'Surprise, mum – to celebrate final exams I've gone to Yarmouth for a few days with the boys, in a caravan. Thanks for being the best mum ever xxx.'

"Let's face it, no offence, Milo, but in terms of hot pursuit, the police are not going to get any change from your mum and anyone else around the Hind. Being honest, this is where you belonging to a prominent local crime family comes into its own: your tribe is forbidden by the criminal code of conduct from co-operating with cops, they know that.

"The St Francis tossers scattered as quickly as they could, they never looked back, and they won't be putting up their hand to anything till they're forced, or until the Bill come knocking. There's no more school, so they are not going to go in tomorrow and spill their guilty tale to a friendly master or classmate.

"And remember all this only matters if that boy is really hurt – if he is just winded or scratched, there's no reason for a massive hoo-ha. With any luck, if anyone does decide to take an interest, they'll start by looking locally, which should buy us a full day. And we'll be halfway down France by then.

"The key is getting through Dover, on the ferry, and off – once we are clear of the Port of Calais, we're home free on the empty French roads…"

The other three were quiet, a bit stunned – and worried – by Jack's coolness and calculation.

"Jesus, Jack," said Mike, "are you actually trying to sound like a criminal mastermind? I never intended to join a gang of desperate crooks, but as we all seem to have done that, I suppose I should be grateful you're our leader.

"But back in the real world, what about that lad, for Christ's sake, mate, he could be dead."

"Or he might not. And if he is, does it help him if we go back? And can I just remind you, he started the insults and shouting; he chucked a glass that could have severed a vein or pierced an eye; he got out a knife and waved it in your faces; and he was leaning over me and Milo, presumably ready to cut our throats or gut us......

"All I did was stand up unexpectedly to throw him off, let us get up, and stop him sticking us with weapons.

"Having a good plan and some logical conclusions doesn't make me evil, or cynical, it just makes us well prepared. And actually, as you ask, by pretending to be all cool and grown-up I am only trying to give you all some courage, because, truthfully, we are almost certainly going to get stopped at Dover. I just thought it might help you all to believe we won't."

That ended the lesson; there was no more to say, so they withdrew into their own thoughts. Milo's head was clearing, and as it did he began to feel the soreness, scrapes and bruises all up and down his body, thankfully not too much on his face due to Jack protecting his head. But he just wanted to rest, to sleep if possible.

They drove on without talking for the next half hour, the others looking out of the window into nothing, while Jack focused on the road ahead. Truth be told, he was feeling a little excited by the drive. This was a journey he remembered taking a score of times with his parents, twice a year – even, one year, three times – for holidays when he was growing up. He would be wedged into the back of the family Renault with his little brother and sister, his mum and dad in the front, generally squabbling, sometimes in English when his mum was swearing, and then in French when his dad managed to wedge a word in.

It was because of his memories of these childhood visits, to his second 'homeland' as his mother called it, that Jack had set up and organised the road trip for his mates on their last day of school. A secret bond, and for him, maybe a rite of passage, his first solo journey into France without his family. His idea was to head south to meet and stay with the relatives he had spent so much time with when he was growing up; hopefully to work on his cousin's farm and earn some money; and so he could show Milo the region he loved. Bob and Mike were mainly along for the drinking, and to meet girls (so they claimed, but boys have to say that). And to contribute to the cost of the petrol. So much, Jack knew, but thus far he had given only generalisations and some tempting clues to his friends, not the full itinerary and agenda. Jack didn't like to share, on the whole, preferring not to debate, and to retain the power of the surprise, also to leave himself a let-out if he changed his mind.

Clearly, now, things had to change; the romance was draining away, to be replaced by functionality – being on the run would alter everything. Suddenly they were fugitives, not tourists. It did all seem a bit crazy, he was halfway to thinking Bob and Mike were right. All that he could sense coming from the back of the car was tension. He would need to keep these guys calm if he was going to nurse them through it, if he still wanted to go through with it himself. He drove on, leaning in towards the windscreen to follow the central white line, the silence among them broken only by the radio which he tuned and retuned, flipping from country classics to Motown and from pop to jazz. The Leader of the Pack; I Love Paris; Stop! In the Name of Love; Help Me, Rhonda.

The others winced when it got jaunty but didn't have the will to tell him to stop, each of them retreating into their own personal level of gloom, disconnecting from the whole. Bob and Mike, without saying so, had already decided this was nothing to do with them, it was all about Milo and Jack. They were contemplating whether or when they could still reject the guilt and decline the jeopardy.

The road in front and behind was tar-black, lit only for thirty yards in front by their flickering headlights, with occasional flashes from the periodic petrol stations, road signs and floodlit advertising hoardings. They passed a giant cigarette advert, and Jack remembered a battered pack in his hip pocket. He dragged it out, acknowledging that marketing works, and thanking some unknown adman for reminding him to smoke. He fired up a rather crushed fag on the car lighter and passed it over to the back, then lit another which he shared with Mike. Lost in their own thoughts, they ran through the tunnel and onto the main road to Dover, watching their rear and holding their breath every time a set of lights came up and overtook them. These were generally freight lorries on their way to the ferry, with a bit more poke in their engines than the little Morris.

About five miles out from Dover, Jack slowed and pulled the car into an empty lay-by. "What are you doing?" asked Bob. "Don't we need to push it for the boat?"

"The next ferry is an hour. We have to be there half an hour before sailing in order to catch it, and we don't want to be out in the open hanging around in the queue too much. We're about fifteen minutes from the terminal, so I suggest we sort our luggage out, get the passports ready, and take off these bloody blazers for the last time."

They changed their tops, got their money and passports, and got back in the car. "Milo, you should go in the front now you're feeling better, it's more comfortable," Mike suggested.

Mike and Bob got in the back, they'd put their hold-alls between them; Jack restarted the car, and they set off down the hill towards the ferry with Johnny Cash belting out Ring of Fire at full volume.

Fifteen minutes later they turned into the port, nervously looking around to see if there was a reception party. It was one o'clock in the morning, the carpark was vast and empty, and all they saw was a dimly lit row of huts a hundred and fifty yards off with a sign saying 'CALAIS – LINE 6.' No squad cars, no cordon of uniformed officers, no thirty-foot poster of the four of them grinning hideously down with a massive line of type underneath shouting **HAVE YOU SEEN THESE BOYS?**

Jack turned down the radio, told everyone to keep calm and give him their passports and tickets, and rolled the car up to the barrier next to Hut 6. He placed the documents in the palm of an unattached hand waving out of the booth, waited, got them back, and that was that: no excitement. As the passports were returned to him with their passenger labels, a dismembered voice called out: "Keep following Line 6, wait in the queue, the ferry will run about thirty or forty minutes late because of the high winds."

"Shit," said Mike when they were just out of earshot, negotiating their way through the maze of painted lines and numbers towards the brightly floodlit ferry which had its bow open towards them. "We really do not need a delay tonight."

They pulled up behind a single file of around fifteen other vehicles in Line 6 and turned off the engine. This was not an overly subscribed crossing.

"The delay makes no difference, really," said Jack, "if they're onto us any time in the next few hours and know which way we're heading and how, they'll get us either here or when we disembark. I am betting they're not looking for us at all, or worst case looking for one or two of us within three hundred yards of the pub. Not looking at all is my strong view, honestly; they can't possibly have tracked us this far, and they're not going to be randomly mass-alerting all ferries and airlines for a pub brawl."

"Unless it's worse than a brawl."

"Let's just take it steady, one step at a time ... We're doing OK so far."

They settled down to wait, instinctively sinking lower in their seats, though there was no-one to hide from and no point in hiding. Mike and Bob were whispering in the back as Jack checked on Milo, who wasn't looking so brilliant. "I'm just going over to that toilet if we're going to be here for a while" said Bob, opening the door on Milo's side. "I'll come too" said Mike, "it would be good to clear my head as well." He slid over and followed Bob.

"Milo, are you OK?" asked Jack after a few minutes.

"Yep, I will be. I'm just feeling a bit dozy, it's been a big night," said Milo, trying to laugh it off. "I've got a headache and soreness over ninety-five percent of my body, but I'm sure I'll live." He eased even further back and closed his eyes.

Twenty-five minutes later, with Milo sleeping, the sign went up to start engines and move forward. Shaken awake as the car rattled over the metal grid leading onto the slipway, and with all the night's events suddenly hitting his mind in a rush, Milo started up in his seat with a gasp. Luckily the men loading the ferry and positioning the cars were right at the other end of the long bay. Looking round, Milo grabbed at Jack in his panic, "You've left them behind, wait mate, turn round – Mike and Bob aren't back."

Jack put his hand gently on his friend's chest and eased him back. "Chill, Milo, chill," he said quietly "it's all right, everything is OK. Just relax. You've been asleep quite a while. Look on the back seat. You see their bags? No, the bags disappeared when the guys got out. I noticed right away as they left the car they were trying to hide their hold-alls in front of them when they walked off. Like when you get a stiffy on the bus and have to hold your briefcase in front of your groin when you're getting off. Remember Homo Erectus?"

That did get a laugh from Milo, even in these exigent circumstances. Homo Erectus was their code for a magnificently botched biology lesson with a young supply teacher who Jack skilfully sucked into a technical conversation about methods of exiting public transport with what Milo explained to him was called in East End rhyming slang a 'Beg Your Pard-on.' [It isn't, so don't look it up.]

"Grown-up men like us don't take their luggage for a pee," Jack went on. "Plus, if they really were desperate for a leak they could have done it when we were back at the lay-by getting changed. I knew they were never coming back."

Now Jack was easing the car into the space being allocated by the loading man with the paddles. He managed it neatly; oddly it was one of the things that had been worrying him most about the whole process, the prospect of drawing attention to themselves with some schoolboy manoeuvrings.

"But why did they do that?" asked Milo. "How are they going to get back, what will they do?"

Milo and Jack were out of the car now, grabbing their packs from the boot and heading for one of the stairways up into the ferry. Jack made the international 'lip button' signal for 'Shut up,' indicating they would talk on the upper deck.

On the stairs, Jack noticed that there were a few scuffs and scratches on Milo's neck and forehead, nothing too horrific, but he didn't want anyone to notice them, so he fished a cap out of his bag and pulled it on him, down low over his brow, and helped him do up the top of his jacket to hide some of the other marks. When they got into the main lounge area, Jack quickly found them a booth right at the back, furthest from the bar. There were hardly any passengers on the crossing, and mostly they seemed to be settling down to get some sleep. Milo slumped, but from a distance Jack hoped he just looked tired or maybe a little drunk.

"What's going on, Jack, for Chrissake? What happened to Mike and Bob?"

"It didn't surprise me, Milo, and I reckon it will be for the best – hopefully. Think about it, they never really felt they were in this with us, they just got swept up with it. All they got into at the pub was some pushing and shoving, they must be thinking there's every chance no-one even tagged them for it. If they decided going on the run is mad, and could get nasty, they probably realised now would be the best time to bail.... making the sailing would burn their boats, if I can mangle a cliché. Being honest I was pretty sure even before we got to Dartford that they weren't going to make it onto the ferry."

"Selfish cowardly bastards. They're bastards."

"No, not like that, Milo, I don't blame them, not at all. It will be for the best, I promise, provided they manage to get out of the docks OK, or at least don't get caught for the next two hours, till we are clear of Calais. Best for them, and best for us – there's no reason to drag them in, and to be honest we can get farther faster without them. If anything, it was me being selfish to get them involved, they could have just legged it like everyone else.

"And think about it – they're not like us, Milo. They didn't take French for a start. We look French, we talk French, we eat French, we love French. They'd be a complete liability while we're charming our way across the country." His levity fell flat again.

"But," he went on, "it will be a nightmare if they get caught in the docks. If they do, I would reckon the police will find out pretty quickly what's going on, and they'd know exactly what ferry we are on. If they do, they'll call France and the *gendarmes* will be waiting when we get off. Even if they didn't catch us off the ferry tonight, it would still flag up to the police that we're on the loose in France. But if Mike and Bob concentrate, the two of them are smart enough to avoid the cops and get back to London; they'll know how important it is, I am sure they won't let us down."

"You're more confident than me."

Actually, Jack's faith in Mike and Bob was not totally unjustified. At that moment the two of them were crouched shivering in their thin holiday shirts, behind a row of massive rubbish bins, in the deep black space behind the toilets, about a hundred yards from the now empty ferry docking bay. All they could hear was the chilly slaps of the cold waves periodically hitting the stone dock, and the sulky shouts of a couple of dockworkers on nightshift a very long way away.

"Come on, Mike," Bob whispered, "please let's make a run for it, we can't sit here all night, we'll freeze to bloody death."

"Well, we could always put our school uniform back on, it's warmer," Mike joked, trying to cheer him up a little and not succeeding.

They both rooted in their bags, and realised the best they could do was to put another t-shirt on top of the one they were wearing, and then their school shirt on top of that. It was a bit white for night manoeuvres but the prospect of getting spotted, chased or caught in a school blazer didn't bear thinking about, so the options were limited.

The lights in the customs and ticketing huts had been turned out when the ferry left. There were no more vessels till dawn, and gradually all the floodlights around the terminal were being dimmed and switched off.

"There's no-one around, running for it is our best bet," pushed Bob. "Come on, let's go, I can't feel my feet anymore."

"We can't go yet. If we get caught quickly they'll work out who we are and realise Milo and Jack are on that ferry, in which case they'll be arrested as soon as they dock in Calais.

"I wish we'd never got sucked in but I think we should give them their best shot. We're in exactly the same amount of trouble if we get caught now or in two hours. If we can hide that long, then even if we do get caught afterwards, they'll be well away from Calais and we'll have probably done more than they expect of us – Milo especially.

"And it's the best plan for us; if we wait till half past three everyone will be asleep or dozy and we can get out of here. At the moment they're only just turning out the lights, and I bet there are a couple of guards doing the rounds."

Bob was looking grumpy, but coming round to the idea.

"And," Mike continued, "we still have to get out of Dover, or we're going to have a lot of explaining to do. It's bad for us, and also bad for Jack and Milo, they'll know right away we were here for the ferry. For everyone's sake we need to get out of town without anyone knowing we were ever here.

"We're holding lots of francs but not too many pounds, so no taxis for sure. We can either try and hitch a lift, which two blokes looking as dodgy as us are unlikely to get at night; or we've probably got just enough dosh for tickets on the first train. And the first train isn't going to be for quite a while, so no point in running for it now."

Mike was talking like quite the criminal mastermind himself, but Bob saw the logic of it all and reluctantly agreed. However he drew the line at Mike's suggestion that they shouldn't smoke. He lit up cautiously with his head in a bin so the flare would not be visible. He kept his hands cupped around the glow of the fag, grumbling that "It's not bloody World War One, mate." He was about to launch into an explanation of how German snipers operated when Mike, who had heard it from him twenty times, waved a long arm towards him and threatened to place his hand over his mouth. He shut up.

They waited superstitiously till exactly 3.30am, because that was the time they had said, and it had become sacred. At the stroke of it, they put their heads above the bins to see if anyone was around. Everything was black, and still. They stood up and turned round to assess the fence they had to climb to get out of the ferry port.

"OK, mate, time to go – do you have your forged papers, stolen maps and dodgy Czech cap?" Bob began whistling the theme to The Great Escape so loudly into the silence that Mike lunged at him and this time actually did clamp his hand over his mouth. "Jesus Jesus Jesus, you utter twathead, please just shut up and get over that wire, before I shoot you myself."

Bob tossed his bag over, then nimbly went up and over after it; then Mike, more clumsily. He was a big lad, not very light on his feet, but he finally managed to pull himself across, dragging his hold-all with him at the same time. The fence clattered and shook, sending a tinny clang around the vast empty carpark, ringing, to the ears of the boys, like church bells on a Sunday morning. Instinctively they both ducked down behind the wire; pointlessly, as it was made of mesh that anyone could see through. Luckily no-one was looking.

They could now see that they weren't outside yet, they'd landed in the employee area, home to the customs officers, border guards and sailors, which formed a buffer between the passenger waiting area and the outer perimeter of the docks. They would need to cross that, climb one more fence, and they would be in the road outside, on civvy street.

They spent a few minutes getting their breath and composure back and reviewing the scene. For 3.42am the staff carpark was distressingly full of vehicles; were there really that many people around? Then they twigged that most of the cars must belong to the crews of the ferries out at sea, not to sinister relays of border protectors tirelessly hunting them down. No more excuse to delay. They proceeded to scuttle, running bent at the hip like an army under fire, all along the side of the fence to the far corner, then turning a right angle and heading towards the end of the next section of fence maybe a hundred yards away where freedom lay.

Try as he might, Mike could not now clear his brain of the earworm Bob had planted from The Great Escape, and inside his head he was humming da da, da daaah da da da; da da da daaah da da da da. Just as they had in the cinema, his hands were periodically making the feverish gear-changing movements of Steve McQueen on his stolen motorbike as he twisted and turned the machine more and more frantically trying to jump the fence. Before sliding into the barbed wire. Not a great omen.

But it was too late for harbingers of doom. By now they had reached the far corner, and they simultaneously released the hollow breath they had been holding... nothing had happened, no shout out of the darkness, no blinding torch in the face from an unseen guard, no-one complimenting them on the quality of their spoken

31

German. Thirty seconds later they had repeated their fence-climbing act, and frankly that was that; sorry for the lack of excitement. They were out, and suddenly strolling along the far side of the unlit road that ran round the docks towards the still brightly illuminated town in the distance. Mike was now humming The Great Escape out loud. Smiling in the dark, Bob joined in.

With the salt in their nostrils, like jolly sailors on a spree, thumbs tucked into belts (metaphorically), they took a brisk and bracing walk along Marine Parade, clicking their heels and tossing their tam-o-shanters, dancing On The Town past the spilt bins of over-flowing chip papers, crumpled cigarette packets and piss-filled beer bottles. Joy in the jetsam of a seaside dream, this was the part of the story that Bob would never forget, the bliss of being out and free before the streets were washed and tidied. Other than them, nothing was moving, except a couple of dawn lorries rolling past in the other direction, arriving too early for the morning sailing. Drinking deep the sea air and almost wishing they had stayed on the trip, they reached Dover Priory Railway Station after half an hour, just in time to get tickets for the 4.30am train, the first to London. They made it with two and sixpence to spare.

A handful of workers came onto the platform while they were waiting, so they hung back against the wall at the far end and read a plaque on the brickwork commemorating the death of stationmaster Edward Walsh. In 1868 he had been murdered by eighteen-year-old railway porter Thomas Wells, who had taken it badly when he was told his work was not satisfactory. Wells was hanged for his crime. "One day they'll put one of these up for us," joked Bob. Not for the first time that night, Mike didn't laugh.

On the train the boys got their choice of corner seats, burrowed back into the cushions, and were asleep in minutes. They completely missed the coming and going of early morning passengers – cleaners, day labourers and factory hands – embarking and disembarking as the train crawled slowly up the Kent coast, through shipyards and the great maritime towns of the Medway. They slept innocently, they seemed to have not a care in world: as Mike had said earlier to Bob, "Mate, this is really nothing to do with us…"

They woke up as they pulled into London, and changed onto the underground, spending sixpence each on a ticket to East Ham. When they arrived, they walked two hundred yards down the hill to have breakfast at their favourite café, which, given their by now virtually exhausted funding, consisted of tea and toast. And there they made a quick decision to go on holiday after all.

Each of them had, as instructed by Jack, left a note for their parents to say they had gone to Yarmouth for an end of term celebration. In fact, half the kids they knew, both at the boys' and girls' schools, were doing the same, and had booked around twenty caravans at two of the biggest seaside camps in Yarmouth. Mike's cousin was going, and Mike knew he had a space in his caravan.

"Because" he told Bob, "he's not that popular, and he got dumped by Tracey last week, she had a better offer. He was begging me to go."

So, they temporarily divided, headed to their respective houses, and when they got in explained to their parents they'd been left behind the previous night when the rest of the lads went up the coast, so had stayed with Mike / Bob. Now after a quick bath and change, they were going after the others on the next train. Honestly, no-one seemed to care, even when they begged for some cash.

For fully two weeks of drunken hooliganism in Yarmouth, no-one connected Mike and Bob to anything, and, to their credit, they told no-one about their aborted adventure, though it could be that their discretion was less about fidelity and more because the tale reflected badly on them in so many different ways. When they eventually came back to London they just melted back into their new life over the following weeks, which meant job hunting and some temp work. And that's where we leave them: Mike and Bob, they had the chance to be great but had not the courage to be loyal …. the price they pay therefore is expungement of character.

FRIDAY

Jack and Milo on the ferry remained cloaked in the shadow at the back of the lounge. Throughout the vessel the lights were dimmed as most of the passengers were napping fitfully for an uncomfortable two hours. Milo periodically stretched his neck and rolled his head back and forth. He claimed he was fine but had some soreness and pain in his back and shoulders and a quite decent headache. Jack fed Milo a couple of aspirin from the first aid pack in his bag and twice went to get them coffees from the sleepy barmaid. All quiet so far, and soon they would be off the ferry and through the port, onto the main road out of Calais and then headed south. Jack was breathing shallowly the whole time; he wouldn't be able to relax properly till they were deep in the French hinterland.

While Milo dozed, Jack got his old maps out to remind himself of the route. He remembered his mum and dad arguing every year about which way to go: either the quiet pretty route from Abbeville to Amiens then down slightly to the west of Paris (to the left, said my mum, holding the map a foot from her nose); or on the big road heading for Bechune then right into and straight out of Paris. It wasn't a difficult decision: given his lack of driving skills, Milo's condition, and the general desire to keep their heads down as long as possible, it was to be the road less taken. That way had generally taken six or seven hours when he did it with the family, depending on who got hungry, who needed a pee, and how the ancient motor performed (and how many times they got lost, which they found remarkably easy to do on what was essentially a straight road all the way).

"What's the plan then, Maestro?" said a drowsy Milo, watching his friend folding and unfolding the maps. "Time to reveal your secrets." Jack had made a big issue about keeping their route and final destination a mystery – something he was grateful for now.

"Let's just say we're pointing south for the first five hundred kilometres and we'll be where we're going by nightfall. And we're running towards something, not just running away."

Milo shook his head from side to side again, snorting: Jack couldn't tell if it was because he objected to him spouting nervy nonsense, or because his headache wouldn't go away.

"So, Jack, we are now distancing in kilometres are we?"

"Indeed we are; no more yards and miles for us. Within the territorial waters, we're French travellers, moving and measuring only in metres."

"I shall be careful to comply."

"I rely on your adherence, *mon ami*. How are you feeling? Are you going to be up to driving us off the boat?"

Milo looked dismayed. "Yes of course I can," his mouth said; but Jack only saw, 'Arghh, no. Please don't make me do that,' in his face.

Jack didn't mind driving; he was actually amazed at the amount of confidence he seemed to have generated over the past six hours. However, he was worried about slipping up and drawing attention to themselves as they drove out of the dock, or being asked the wrong question as the driver, or being pulled over by the border officials and not having the right pieces of paper. He was annoyed with himself now for spending the last half hour thinking about the hundreds of kilometres from Calais when he should have been totally focused on the first five hundred metres off the ferry.

"Maybe I'll do it, Milo, if you'll let me? I am feeling bright, and I need the practice for my driving test." That got the weak smile it barely merited, but at least he was trying.

The bell rang to alert drivers to descend to the vehicle deck. The boys gathered up the maps, zipped their bags and stood up – Milo flinched in pain and put his hands onto the small of his back as he rose, obviously hurting, but OK to move and walk. "Careful, mate," said Jack, "we've just got two flights, then you can crash in the car – we'll make it fine, OK?". "No worry, I'll get there. I'm definitely on the mend." Milo grinned valiantly and leaned a little into Jack, and they supported each other down the stairs, where Jack was able to help him into the passenger seat without anyone noticing any odd movements. Jack got into the driver's seat, got comfortable, and flipped open the glove box; he took out the passports and put them on his lap.

Five minutes later the sign went up to start engines. Jack fluffed it the first time, told himself not to panic, and got it started at the second attempt. After a minute the van in front of them moved off, and Jack followed. They drove about two hundred metres before the queue pulled up at the border check, where there were about five vehicles in front of them. Jack went to his lap and got the passports ready: there didn't seem to be any special checks going on, and two cars and two vans moved through quickly, leaving Jack to pull level with the window in the hut. He passed the passports to Milo, who hid his pain and delivered them into the outstretched palm of the border official. He took them, inspected them with a glance, wrote down the names, stamped an empty page in each, handed them back to Milo, and waved them on using the uniquely French movement that is employed when even a shrug is too much effort.

They pulled away, and after another three minutes they were out of the dockyards, on the open road, and following the sign for Abbeville. As they hit the offramp, Jack started chuckling gently, building quickly to a laugh, so much he could hardly watch the road, and Milo, without really knowing why, joined in. When they finally ran out of laughing, Milo said "Blimey, that was scary – I am not really sure why it's so funny, must be the adrenaline rush we heard so much about in bio."

"No, look at the passports, mate," said Jack, at his most cryptic and smug. Milo had them on his lap; he opened them, let out a yelp and sat up in his seat. "No no no – what did you do, you bloody madman?" The two passports he was examining belonged to Mike and Bob – or in terms of the names actually used in the passports, two boys called Michael and Robert.

"How did you do that and why would you – what's the point?"

"Well, my friend, the How is easy: Mike and Bob omitted completely to ask for their passports back when they surreptitiously deserted us. Perhaps they thought it might give away their scheme to betray us. Therefore, I had them handy.

"For the Why; it struck me in the moment that if the English police initiate a special border alert, the hue and cry will be in our two names, Jack and Milo; not Mike and Bob. So if we enter France as Michael and Robert, and Jack and Milo never come into the country, their enquiry will come up blank with the French authorities."

"But what if we'd been caught with the wrong passports!" shouted Milo, "It would all have been over, we could have been arrested right then."

"Look, I just felt the risk was small, and the benefit is huge. Did you see how little interest that border guard had in actual guarding? Think about it. It's not even dawn yet, the border guy is half asleep, he sees two boys and then he is holding two boys' passports in his hand, he's not looking for a problem. Plus, he was like a hundred and fifty years old, and old people think all young people look the same, you know that. And he had super-thick specs. And we do look a bit like Mike and Bob, in a small car on a dark night. He could hardly see anything different from where he was sitting.

"The main thing is now they have a record of different people entering the country, not us, so if there's a manhunt, the London police will stay searching in England – in a phrase, my dear boy, we're home free!"

Jack was well pleased with himself, there was no doubting that, and his gamble had paid off. Milo, once he calmed down, realised their lives were now likely to be infinitely easier for the next day or two as they drove down France hopefully without half of Interpol in hot pursuit. He exuded a trickle of forgiveness, while trying at the same time to give off a slightly hurt ambience.

"You could have told me."

"I didn't know I was going to do it till the last minute, I didn't want to lock in the plan in case I decided to go in another direction. Plus, if you had been caught and tortured you might have given me up – I don't think you have a big tolerance for pain, you hated that bit in Lawrence of Arabia."

"Most amusing."

"Keep Bob's and put it in your pocket; give me back Mike's."

"But Mike is better looking than Bob."

"I am not sure I've ever given that any thought. But now you mention it, I agree, so that's why I should have Mike's passport, *n'est-ce pas évident?*"

Milo rolled his eyes and gave it to him.

"Right," Jack banged on, ludicrously gleeful at the appropriation of the 'most handsome' passport, "we carry these, as this is now our cover. I am putting our own passports in the back of the glove compartment, there's a gap there I can wedge them in, so they're there in case we ever need them, OK?"

Milo was nodding 'OK' but given his current state of aching and exhaustion he probably would have nodded 'Yes' if Jack had said he needed to have a limb amputated because a wooden leg would improve their disguise.

Jack turned on the radio and tuned to a pop station, where they came in halfway through I Want to Hold Your Hand. Milo perked up. They were through, on the road. Jack kept tuning, shouting,

"Fuck the Fucking Beatles," which he chanted for a while, Milo joining in, the two of them laughing again. "Fuck the Fucking Beatles." The radio next landed on Cliff singing Summer Holiday, and they were off, singing their hearts out, their arms round each other's shoulders as they swayed back and forth.

Half an hour later, they had made sufficiently good progress to reach the wall of despondency that exists beyond the wave of hysteria.

"Hold up, Jack, we need to talk about what happened ......"

"For God's sake, what do you want me to say?"

"What, it's a banned topic now?"

"No, but there's nothing gained in rehashing to no purpose, is there? Look, in our universe – which is no bigger than this car right now – we're frightened witless, that is why we're behaving so weirdly. We are pumped full of some enzymes or whatever and guilt and regret and we're scared for our lives and our futures. We're headless, trying to believe we're grown-up enough to do this, kids who know nothing, not even that they know nothing. OK?

"But, in a parallel universe, where others see us without knowing us, we're cold-blooded killers on the run, ice in our veins, socio-pathic, uncaring, calculating. We're glad we did it, ripping off our shirts, flexing our biceps, showing our stabby tattoos, shouting at the moon with flecking blood on our lips.

"So quick answer, without thinking, A or B, which seems most likely to you?"

"Can I check first, you want to stick with flecking blood?"

"Yes, I am sticking with flecking."

Milo didn't want to choose A or B, he didn't have the energy left.

He realised how tired he was. If ever he had possessed any such vitalising enzymes, Jack's monologuing had drained them from his body as expertly as if Dracula himself had plunged his teeth into his neck and steadily sucked them out. Only a slight exaggeration.

"Excellent," went on Jack, ignoring the fact his audience was now fully comatose, "so your answer is A – good choice. WE'RE NOT PSYCHOS.

"Now we move on to part two of the argument. On Planet One, we're a band of desperate villains and we set out with blades and cudgels knowingly to club down and cut open innocent schoolboys, just for hell, for the goddam fun of it.

"Or, on Planet Two, we're minding our own business, having a nice time talking to girls, sipping a beer, nibbling salted peanuts, celebrating significant events, commemorating slightly unique achievements, and then wham!, we and our loved ones are attacked, and we are forced to defend ourselves.

"Quickly, without thinking, is it One or Two?"

Jack, as he was pontificating, had manoeuvred the little car into the slower lane, an equal distance between two lorries that were trundling along at a fixed speed. He was very happy doing that, it took away the need to make decisions about steering, speed and overtaking, and gave him time to breathe and think. He felt protected. He had worn out his ranting, and, reluctantly acknowledging that Milo's eyes were tight shut (much more tightly than anyone really sleeping), he deflated himself, relaxed, and withdrew into contemplation.

"It's choice Two this time, just so you know."

Even while he was rattling away, Jack knew Milo was right. You can't simply reason it away. You can't make it right through rational thought and argument. He sensed Milo had already been replaying his images from the pub; you can't repress those, deny them, make

40

them disappear. And they probably weren't pictures of things he had actually seen; they were reassembled records that would eventually become the authorised version of his memory.

Jack felt additional guilt because he was more worried about himself and his friend than about the boy on the floor. He had been grateful when Mike and Bob disappeared because it left him fewer people to worry about. Mike and Bob were dead to him now (even Jack winced at the unfortunate turn of phrase), but most likely they would have been anyway after this holiday. There was very little holding their friendship together, looking beyond the ending of the school routine, and disregarding drink, so a single, perfectly reasonable act of betrayal could sever it easily, and had. Now it was just him, Milo and the boy on the floor.

He found himself praying for the injured lad, and for himself. It couldn't end up like that. He decided the boy could not be dead, and determined that if he prayed to an unknown god and said words in a certain order, he would be OK ......

it was just a scratch, he was just winded, dust him off, pick him up ....

it was just a scratch, he was just winded, dust him off, pick him up ....

it was just a scratch, he was just winded, dust him off, pick him up ....

He made his mantra for half an hour and stayed between the lorries. He changed the words just a bit now and then, because they were just the first phrases he had thought of, they didn't feel like a proper spell, and he wanted to improve them; but then he got scared, superstitious, and went back to the original. Eventually his chanting created a world where as long as he didn't know the boy was dead, he was still alive.

"Milo," he said, shaking his friend awake, though he knew he wasn't asleep, "Milo, we need to make sure we don't see any newspapers, or hear any news bulletins, OK?"

"OK, mate, whatever you say," said Milo, totally uncomprehending, but without the current strength to ask why, or the energy to extend the conversation.

"Great, yes... this is the 'No Look No Listen' pact – it is solemn, just remember – sacred." Milo grunted and turned his head towards the window.

Jack did more kilometres, still between his now beloved companion lorries, and decided he could turn on the radio as Milo was probably still only pretending to be asleep and might enjoy some music. Tuning randomly, he laughed out loud when he came into Del Shannon singing Runaway.

Jack began to think about Maggie. He missed her already. He wanted to talk to her about what had happened. I have a bit of a confession to make at this time. You'll remember it was implied earlier, something along the lines of 'Maggie was really interested in Jack. He was less interested in her. It was a friendship, more than a romantic attachment.' Did you get all that?

Well, to be honest, now, I should say that is not really true and I wish I had not led you to believe it, if I did. I think I wrote that because I was swept away with Jack's excitement about the night, and the trip, and that was what he had in his head and what he wanted to believe if only a little bit, just for a while.

That might sound confusing, unless of course you are a seventeen-year-old boy about to take a secret rites of passage journey, and unless you want during that trip to feel you are totally liberated from everything in your short past life, either bad or good, tedious or exciting. If you are that seventeen-year-old boy, then it makes perfect sense.

Maggie and Jack had been friends for ten years, since junior school, and romantic friends for three or four years. Their romance was lovely, really; mainly about novels and poems, a little bit of music. Thick jumpers on cold walks and small gifts of chocolate and crafted verse. Not something to look back on in detail, maybe, but special at the time. They had never been lovers, because Maggie said she was a bit too young. She really meant, but did not say, even to herself: 'I love this boy, but there is something about him I do not quite trust yet, and I do not know which way he will grow.'

And guess what, she clearly knows her stuff, top marks to Maggie for instinct there. A boyfriend who buys secret ferry tickets is clearly ticking the 'don't know' box and placing himself into the 'somewhat unreliable' column. So, anyway, I apologise for only giving Jack's side of it and reporting things that are not unequivocally accurate.

At that moment Jack joined me in feeling remorse for his fecklessness. The summer trip had seemed to be such a great idea, then he tried to justify it to himself by pretending he was fancy free … he had been a complete tosser. It was yet another thing he would need to go back and repair, if possible; then, with a bit of a jolt, he realised that it might not totally be in his hands anymore. He wouldn't blame her if she never wanted to see him again. He really wished he could talk to her right now.

It crossed his mind for an instant that he might be able to get away with telling her that the decision to go to France only happened when they had to go on the run. To his credit he didn't consider that seriously, but what we are dealing with here is a half-formed hero, there is no doubt about that. Of course, there was the other reason for the trip, which would have been difficult if Maggie was around, and which he didn't want to explain; sometime in the future he could tell her about that, she might understand.

"I'm hungry, Jack, can we get the food out?"

"What food, do we have stuff?"

"Yeah of course, I thought of everything, though I packed for a fun trip, not for survivalism," Milo stretched, definitely beginning to loosen up and feel a little better. "It's a picnic, not military rations."

"I love a picnic! You're a proper marvel, my friend. What have we got?"

"Scotch eggs and French Fancies."

"Ha ha ha. What, no tinned pilchards and beef jerky? What about Kendal Mint Cake…?"

They both burst out laughing. This was one of their running jokes. After they discovered that Edmund Hillary had once lugged the stuff up Mount Everest, they insisted that the kids in their hilarious pastiches of public school stories – and I include in those The Famous Five – always had to take Kendal Mint Cake on their parentless adventures to catch international jewel thieves. But still they didn't have a clue what it was; and they couldn't buy it in Green Street Market.

"None of the Kendal Mint, old chap, sorry. Pull over when you get a chance, it's all in the boot. I'd like some fresh air too, for a minute, I'm feeling a bit sick."

Reluctant as he was to shed the protective cover of his guardian lorries, Jack looked out for a lay-by. He went past one that had a couple of cars in it, and pulled into the next, which was empty. It was coming up to 5.00am, they were around sixty kilometres from Calais, and there was a hint of pink light coming up in the sky, though still very little traffic. The country around was flat as far as they could see, which was not a great distance, broken only by ranks of tall straight trees along the sides of the road and thick bushes around the edges of the lay-by, which from past experience Jack knew were less for decoration than to provide unofficial wayside lavatories in the French way. He remembered his mum shooing him into the undergrowth when he was tiny; he hated it, proving, as he said at the time, much to the cute amusement of everyone:

44

"I really am English." It became a family joke. Yes, nothing dates harder than a family joke.

Milo was holding his side and groaning periodically. Jack was worried that he was still suffering, but Milo said, "No, really, it is easing up a bit, I am just going to milk it for a while. But those bastards really stuck the boot in, thank God you got over my head, you probably saved my life."

Jack was pleased at the thought but shook off the compliment modestly. "It was nothing, my friend; although I believe in many cultures you would now be my manservant for life, I am going to consider waiving this clause in your case. Do you think anything is broken?"

"I don't think so. My ribs are really aching, but it's likely just bruising."

Milo opened the boot and dragged forward a big cardboard box. Releasing the top, he began to unpack it, taking an inventory as he did so:

- 4 pork pies

- 4 mince pasties

- KP nuts, salted, 16 packets

- 8 Scotch eggs

- 1 box of plain crisps, 24 packets

- 8 sausage rolls

- 12 lemonades

- 2 boxes French Fancies

- 1 box of Tayto's cheese and onion crisps, 24 packets

"Blimey," said Jack, totally in awe. "We can go on the run for a month."

"That is a seductive prospect."

"What does chef recommend?"

"I think we should eat the pork pies first; after twenty-four hours in the boot of the car they'll kill us for sure."

"Let's keep them then, they can be like a cyanide tablet; if we get cornered by the *gendarmes* you can force down a pork pie and shout, 'I'm Innocent, Innocent You Hear!!' then fall to the ground writhing, with foam coming out of your mouth."

"Most amusing, I'll eat mine first to avoid the temptation."

"I'm guessing," mused Jack, "that your mum didn't help you pack, given the absence of fruit and green vegetables."

"Sad to say this is all nicked from the pub, but she owed me two week's wages, so I don't feel too guilty. Remember, I thought I was stealing for four."

"Ah, good for Bob and Mike playing Captain Oates, they've doubled our chances of survival…"

"That didn't help Captain Scott, Jack, if I may say so; one might suggest it only prolonged his suffering."

They fell quiet, munching on their picnic thoughts. Neither said anything till they had each polished off a pork pie and a Scotch egg.

"I've got another treat, Jack; I think you will like it."

"Ha, surprise me – did you also pinch a bottle of whisky and two hundred fags?"

"Well oddly I do have two hundred fags, but this is much better than that …. look at this."

Milo lifted up the carpet in the back of the car and pulled up the flap that hid the spare tyre. In the top of the hidden compartment were some tools and something flat and oblong, wrapped in a dirty rag. Milo picked it out, shut the compartment, laid the parcel out and unwrapped it, to show a pair of number plates.

"What the hell?" said Jack. "You're travelling around with a change of number plates?"

"Ha ha, my mum got me the motor from a mate of my uncle, it's well dodgy. You remember Ellis, the guy from the Patron's Bar with the green check jacket and weird flat cap who ruffles my hair when I'm not looking?"

The so-called Patron's Bar was a small snug room in The King's Hind round the back of the main bar, open to only fifteen or twenty of Alice's oldest and most disreputable customers. Those guys lived there, and they spent so much they kept the whole enterprise afloat. When Milo was sent in occasionally to serve food and drink it felt like he was entering the hallowed halls of the University of Criminology (courses there being focused on practical application rather than theoretical detection and prevention). "Don't hang around in there, Milo," Alice would laugh, "unless you want to graduate in Pentonville."

"Ellis had some losses on the gee-gees and left himself short, so he gave mum the car to pay off his bar bill. Touchingly it became my school-leaving present. Anyway, unless the fake plates were meant to be part of my coming-of-age gift, I think he must have forgotten they were in there. I only saw them when I checked the spare yesterday to get ready for the trip."

As he was talking, he had already taken off the back number plate and replaced it, and in another two minutes he'd done the front as well. "My brother taught me," he said, only very slightly embarrassed. "Now we are totally anonymous, even if they had been able to connect that motor to us, which I doubt."

Jack was not sure this dodge would make as much difference as Milo believed (he often thought that when someone other than himself had a clever ruse). Was there a point in replacing an old number with a new number if no-one knew the old number in the first place? He didn't say that to Milo because he was quietly chuffed – this was something that bonded them. Now they were co-conspirators, a decision had been taken by someone else, an idea contributed, and that felt good. Historically, they never hugged, so he punched him on the arm instead. It was a bad idea since it landed on one of Milo's best bruises, and he grimaced and rubbed it gingerly.

"Nice job," Jack continued, undistracted by Milo's discomfort. "As I have often remarked, being a member of one of London's premier crime families really does have its benefits."

"Well yes, Jack, it does," said Milo, playing along in his best Cary Grant, "but with great privilege also comes great responsibility: it means one must always be planning one's next bullion heist, or seeking the opportunity for a fancy caper on the Riviera." This was said with a little ornate bow that Milo gave when he was happy with himself, or when Jack was happy with him. Jack was very pleased to see it, as the first sign that Milo was beginning to take the edge very slightly off the horrors of the previous night, and also that his sides must be feeling a little less sore.

"More snacks, guvnor?" said Milo, rooting in the boot for the crisps. "You know what, I think I might have a cigarette," said Jack, feeling for his lighter and pulling out a fag.

"Will you join me, old boy?"

"I will indeed."

They smoked quietly for a while, watching the light break, and seeing the countryside spread wider around them and the road before stretching out further and further. Then they both had a pee in the bushes; Jack was sure he recognised the spot from his childhood.

"Time to move?"

"Yes, I reckon so, are you ready to have a drive now, Milo?"

Milo didn't look so sure, so Jack took the driving seat again and turned on the engine. Milo got comfortable in the passenger seat and they pulled away, slotting again between a couple of friendly lorries in the slow lane, and shaping their bodies for the long haul.

"When do you think you might be ready to reveal our mystery destination?" asked Milo, after another half an hour.

"Yes, I suppose it is time," Jack replied, "but you have to promise not to tell anyone." Milo did a fake double-take at the empty back seat to get a tiny laugh from both of them. "Who were you thinking I might spill the beans to?"

"There are three destinations, Milo, and this is important, serious, so no mocking, OK? I shall be sensitive on the subject."

"Understood, my delicate pal. I shall be gentle."

"Generally our all-purpose direction of travel is towards a town called Vierzon, then we go a bit beyond. You know my dad's extended family live in France, and they're all around there, there must be well over twenty families in the clan. I know it well because up till a few years ago I visited with my folks for our holidays once or twice a year, sometimes more, to stay with the relatives. We're going to start with my cousin Jean, he's around eight years older than us. He runs part of his dad's farm and has his own separate place on it, a few miles outside of the village, very quiet.

"I spent months with him when we were growing up, I used to follow him round like a puppy. My thinking is we can stay with him and get a breather, he can keep us under cover for a while and we can get the lie of the land."

"You reckon he'll aid and abet a couple of outlaws, just like that?"

"It is not like England, Milo, not even the bit we come from. The villages are tight, not criminal as such, but no lovers of law and they do things their own way. Listen, we'll have to see, right? It's not guaranteed, but family is everything to the people there, and I am their family, and you are mine."

[Sitting next to him, Milo blushed bright red. Jack knew.]

"The chances are very good," he went on, "and if he takes us in, then he should be able to give us some work if and when the coast is clear. Being honest, that is kind of how I envisaged the four of us spending the summer, just drinking wine and working in the fields wearing big straw hats…"

"Jean grows sunflowers, of course, and beetroots and huge red onions, I used to help when I was a kid doing all sorts, they still used horses when I was little."

Milo realised that Jack was fuguing to dull his worries and kill time, so he let him meander on for a while about his French memories, then reined him back in.

"It sounds great, Jack, though I am glad you didn't mention the beetroot picking to Mike and Bob when we were planning this jaunt, as I think they probably wouldn't have signed up."

Jack laughed, "But they have shown so much resilience, how can you suspect that!" Moving into his best agricultural twang (starting somewhere north of Worcester and ending well south of Bristol),

"There's nothing wrang with a bit of 'ard labour my lovel."

Milo started a laugh but realised it didn't really warrant it.

"So, Maestro, that is Direction One of your original Three Great Holiday Objectives. What else is there in the web you weave. I'm worried this is sounding a bit goal-driven for a fabulous summer getaway, was there to be any actual fun involved?"

"Look in my hold-all and see what you see," said Jack, indicating the backseat with a nod of his head.

"I can't reach back there, mate, my side's too sore."

Jack made a complicated manoeuvre to keep one hand on the wheel while he reached back with the other to grope for his bag on the back seat. He grabbed the hold-all and dumped it onto Milo's lap.

"Ah," said Milo, "the magician's pouch, let us see what secrets it reveals."

The top was books. He brought them out one by one.

"The Great Gatsby…. good choice, no surprise there, but unless we're driving to West Egg it probably isn't a clue.

"To Kill a Mockingbird – outstanding! Again, unless we're loading the car onto a tramp steamer in Marseille heading for Mobile and a riverboat up the Saint Stephens, that again is not what I am looking for.

"Aye aye, Catcher in the Rye – same again, wrong continent, and not sure about the choice on that one.

"Then we have several envelopes labelled Mags, dad and mum – shall I look inside those?"

Jack shook his head.

"Bundle of francs, two packs of Park Drive, matches. This tells me that wherever we are going will involve expenditure and heavy smoking. Three pairs pants, three pairs socks, three sleeveless shirts, shorts, jeans and toiletries. We will be wearing clothing. I am getting warm, right?"

Jack nodded his agreement.

"OK, last three items. The Sun Also Rises ….. oooo could be. Then we have the same book twice – Le Grand Meaulnes in French, and The Lost Domain in English.

"I think I am red hot now. Clearly there are two potential scenarios.

"First, and in my mind most likely, we are going to re-enact the entirety of The Sun Also Rises. This will involve:

- Hanging out in Paris

- Picking up an escort and taking her brazenly to several bars and parties

- Going to a spontaneous dance and being unpleasantly derogatory about homosexuals

- Riding round in taxis with a beautiful woman with whom I can never consummate my love

- Then off for a spot of trout fishing in the mountains with a gobby guy who mistakenly thinks he is bloody hilarious

- Into Pamplona for the bullfighting – aficionado à gogo

- Bullsplaining away like a barroom bore, beloved of the locals, being the only foreigner who truly understands

- Helping m'lady shag a boy matador

- Getting beaten up by m'lady's jilted suitor

- Picking up the pieces and watching a policeman's baton jiggle up and down"

Jack was frowning, trying to be annoyed. On Hemingway, he had been wrong; he had been a big fan at fifteen; then on rereading and study in his mature years, he'd decided that quite a bit of it was fakery and phony. Hemingway, like the rest of us, despised in others what he feared in himself.

Milo saw his pain. "OK OK, park that one. So, second guess, we're going down on a treasure hunt for this Lost Domain – is that it?"

Seeing Jack look at him out of the corner of his eye and smile, he knew he'd hit it. "It is, isn't it! I guessed it. We're all going on a book hunt! So what is that all about anyway? I chose L'Etranger, I obviously got it wrong."

Jack laughed. He could have stopped him long before, but he liked to hear him rattling on, and it was making them both forget. Milo was shy and self-deprecating, and spoke like this only with Jack, sometimes with Maggie, but otherwise he allowed himself to come across as the East End bartender's boy, perhaps a little crude, even a bit stupid. But the truth was he was top of the class in English, and second in French; and the boy who beat him in French cheated by having a French dad.

"Yes, your second guess is correct, *mon ami*. We are heading for the Lost Domain, or something similar! And I will introduce you to the fantastical mystical world of Meaulnes the Wanderer and the Secret Estate he finds and loses. I cannot believe you have never read it, you goddam existentialist."

They both laughed and each spat out of their window; for some reason existentialism creased them up and made them spit satirically.

53

"This is a proper book about finding and losing aethereal girls, attending magical children's parties, being bold and piratical beyond our years, being irresponsible and selfish beneath our years. Mainly about the loss of something extraordinary and the lengths you will go to search for it and recover it."

Jack was genuinely passionate now and was striking out the beats of his rant with his left fist on Milo's right knee. Milo flinched internally each time his bruised leg got hit but did not complain because the pleasure in the passion was greater than the pain of the punch.

"For a rites of passage story," Jack continued, still rapping out the tempo of his argument, "this book is the same for French kids as The Catcher in the Rye is for Yanks and Brits – except it is not phony, it is good. Ha ha ha ha ha ha. Not even GOOD [whack], it is COMPLETELY [whack] GREAT [whack] and MARVEL-LOUS [whack], MAGICAL [whack], SINCERE [whack], and AUTHENTIC [whack]."

"Blimey, Jack, I get it!" said Milo, squealing and shuffling his knees towards the door and outside Jack's radius of emphasis. "No more adjectives for Chrissake, my leg can't take it."

Jack laughed. "Jean's house is in the actual Meaulnes landscape, I spent months as a boy on holidays there exploring with him and the other cousins. The book is his bible ..."

"OK I get it. You are such a romantic! But actually, that's two for the price of one," said Milo, "because clearly going to Jean's and seeking 'Le Grand Meaulnes' domain are really the same thing in the same place. I am excited for us both.

"What about the Third Thing?"

Jack went quiet for a moment, partly coming off his Meaulnes high, but mainly because this would be the first time ever that he would reveal his biggest secret. This was another occasion for him to be grateful that Mike and Bob had decided to bale; this felt intensely private and he was struggling even to share it with his best friend alone.

"Milo, don't go mad, but I want to look for my dad."

"Wooooowwww. Thanks for telling me, mate!" Milo was shocked, he had not seen that one coming.

"How are we supposed to find your dad, he's been gone for nearly three years, I thought no-one knew where he'd gone?"

"But I think I do know. Look in that envelope you found earlier that says 'dad.'"

Milo went back into the hold-all to fish it out. As he was searching he said to Jack, without looking at him, "Are you sure this is a good idea, Jack? How was this ever meant to fit in with a summer holiday? Didn't your mum get everyone out hunting for him before?"

"Just open the envelope, Milo, and read what's in there. It's the letter my dad left me when he went, no-one else has ever seen it."

Milo opened the envelope, flattened out the page inside, and looked gingerly at the neatly handwritten letter.

"Are you really sure you want to share this, Jack, this feels a bit overpowering."

"Just read, Milo."

Dear Jack

I could start with "This is the hardest letter I have ever had to write" or "I am so sorry to let you know," but there isn't a good or easy or acceptable way for a father to tell his son he is leaving him.

I don't want to burden you at fifteen, and I know whatever happens next you'll hate me, but my life has become unbearable to me over the years, and now you, Georgie and Frank are older, I'm going, I am so so sorry.

I'm heading for France and I'll stay with some relatives for a while, I'll be around there and I'll try to let you know where I am from time to time.

I love you son, and I am sorry – but I can't go on the way I have.

Dad

"Jesus, Jack, you mean you never told your mum about this?"

"She had her own letter, Milo – she didn't share hers with me, and I didn't tell her about mine."

"But what if this would have helped her?"

"It was special for me, Milo, the last thing he left was this, for me. I just wanted to keep it sacred."

"I am not sure what you want me to say now, Jack. I'm your friend, I want to help you, but this seems like crazy stuff for us to be getting involved in. Was your dad OK when he wrote that, he sounds desperate."

"Mum was worried, we all were, but for me at least I knew he had a plan and part of it involved family. My dad had two brothers there, though one is dead now; or he could be with uncles, or cousins, or nieces or any of at least a dozen other relatives. I knew he would be looked after; and I know I was probably wrong, and selfish, but I thought if he wanted mum to know anything, he would have told her. What he told me was for me, that was all he left me that was mine.

"Of course, I was worried, we all were. He hadn't been himself for a long time. Mum said the week before he went she found an old suitcase hidden under the stairs packed full of envelopes. They all had stuff in, some really thick, and they were all sealed, but they weren't addressed, they were blank except for numbers on them. From 1 at the bottom of the stash to 490-something at the top. There were nearly 500 envelopes, and when she asked him what they were he said they were part of a project he was working on, then lost his temper, started crying and told her to leave him alone.

"After he left a few days later, the suitcase was gone. He'd taken the envelopes, a spare set of clothes, a few photos and books, and the car. He'd paid off the mortgage before he went without telling mum, and he'd put thousands in her bank account, she didn't know where it had all come from."

It was nearly 8.00am now, and the roads were filling with traffic, especially heavy freight trucks and light commercial vans, with smaller cars weaving in and out of the slower vehicles. They had left Amiens behind, and a sign said they were a hundred and twenty kilometres from Paris.

"So did you or your mum get word from whoever he went to, and stayed with?"

"A bit. We've not been down there since he left – nothing un-friendly, it is just there has been no time or money for jaunts since we became a single-parent setup. But mum has contacts, and calls people regularly to see what's happening. And I swap letters with Jean, he's a bit outside the village, so he doesn't see everything. He told me dad did turn up, came and went for a while, but he hasn't seen him for a long time and didn't know if anyone else had. My mum tried various uncles and cousins several times but got the impression they were holding back information or knew more than they were saying. Let's say that is typical of the region; no-one wants to be unhelpful, but the natural inclination is not to cooperate."

Milo opened a bag of crisps, and offered one to Jack, who instead took the whole packet and balanced it on his lap. Milo smiled to himself and opened another. They both crunched without tasting or noticing, while Milo tried to ingest the unexpected information from his friend, piling it on top of everything else that had happened.

"Well, I have to say this trip is classic Jack, Jack. Do you agree? I can see I didn't need to worry about self-interest when I left you planning away quietly by yourself.

"To be clear, what we're doing is driving down to the middle of France to stay with your cousin for a working holiday; which also coincidentally provides an opportunity to explore the countryside where your favourite book is set; while we try to find out from your extended, expanded and pathologically reticent family whether they know anything about your dad's movements and whereabouts that they are prepared to share.

"Am I roughly right?"

"You have forgotten Fleeing Justice."

"I thought that was taken for granted. And that is a latecomer, not part of your original motivation."

"Well in that case, yes, your summary is very accurate *mon ami* – in fact it sounds most logical and sensible when you describe it like that, so many carefully-patterned layers of interlocking benefits. You should be proud of me, as I am of myself."

Jack was clearly unabashed. No surprise there.

"For the newly added dimension of evading the law, this is a huge bonus; there is no better place in the world we could have chosen to hide out now, to lay low. If we get there safely.

"Let's pray the police won't be interested in us, that nothing bad happened, and that that they don't even think of us being in France; but if they do ever decide to sniff around down there, those people are not lovers of the cops, and they are fiercely protective of their privacy and their own blood."

Milo knew it was futile to protest against Jack's selfishness, other than to point out that if they hadn't potentially killed someone then his utterly solipsistic vacation itinerary – a voyage around himself – would, when finally revealed, have been really irritating. Sadly, it turned out that he was right: now they were on the run it was a prospective lifesaver. For them, of course, but not necessarily for the boy on the pub floor.

He had learnt from experience many years ago that it made for an easier and more agreeable life if he accepted Jack's self-centred choices graciously, and also that sometimes, perhaps more often than not, they worked out well for both of them: so that's what he did.

"OK Jack, I'm Spartacus," said Milo, which was their shorthand for saying he approved the plan and that he would stand up with Jack and share any responsibility.

"No, I'm Spartacus," said Jack, which in this context just meant "Thanks mate."

"Do you want to stop for a break?"

"We'll need fuel before we get past Paris, let's break when we do that. I reckon about an hour. OK?"

"Sounds good," said Milo, "I can wait for my next Scotch egg."

"Just remember when you're casually indulging yourself with discretionary egg-based product that there is a clock running on those pork pies…."

"Yes, sorry, I'd forgotten it was a question of pieorities."

"Pieorities, yes. We definitely do not want any porkrastination."

"Ah yes, jelly good, never pig off till tomorrow what you can pig on today."

"Now you're scratching a rind, my friend."

"Pork pie eaten when it's sunny, Makes your tummy very runny."

"So the poet says. But I thought we agreed no pig-and-pie-based rhymes and puns? We should never have started it. For crust's sake, my friend, we've embarrassed ourselves, our families and our school."

"What school is that, old boy, don't you recall we got sent down for scrapping with the Townies...."

It was an old joke in their patter, but realising what he'd said, Milo fell silent. This wasn't Greyfriars after all. He had a debilitating wave of anxiety, didn't move for a while, and eventually it looked like he had really dropped off to sleep this time.

Jack turned the radio down a little and tuned idly till he found a French channel playing Piaf. *Je ne regrette rien.* If only that were true. He drove down past Beauvais and stopped for fuel without waking Milo. He put on his cap before he got out of the car and kept his head down as he filled the tank, making sure he faced away from the attendant, who, truthfully, could not have been less interested. He paid, superstitiously avoiding a glance at the newspaper front covers, then jumped back in the car and drove out. **AVEZ-VOUS VU CES GARÇONS**. *Non.*

He pulled over in a small lay-by four hundred metres on from the gas station so he could have a cigarette and study the map without being watched. He was trying to remember one of his dad's famous routes going around Paris to avoid the traffic and the city. It headed off west and down to Cergy, then round west of Versailles and then south. On the map he followed the larger and smaller roads of different colours with his finger, then got a pen out of his bag and wrote some numbers and a couple of names on the back of his hand. Those side routes seemed crazily counterproductive when he was small and desperate to get where they were going, but they were useful now. He remembered his mum saying, "Why are we going so far left Mac?" "We're going west darling, not left – this is international navigation not directions to the cemetery." Why cemetery? Strange sense of humour, my dad. That became even more obvious later.

Jack reckoned it was three hundred kilometres to go now, give or take, and at the rate they were driving – lorry speed, tucked into the quiet lane – it could take four and a half or five hours. Discretion was more important than speed, so if they stopped somewhere deserted for a lunch break, they could schedule the rest of the journey to arrive at Jean's after he'd finished work, when his farmhands would be gone for the day.

With the tank full, Jack drove on steadily, Milo snoring a bit now. On the radio some cool jazz sax, maybe Ben Webster or Lester Young, but after a while it felt as though it was sending him to sleep, so he looked for something a bit more poppy. Every hour, at one minute to the hour, he turned the radio off for five minutes to avoid the news. Superstition. When he did that it reminded him to say the catechism under his breath:

it was just a scratch, he was just winded, dust him off, pick him up ....

it was just a scratch, he was just winded, dust him off, pick him up ....

it was just a scratch, he was just winded, dust him off, pick him up ....

Beauvais to Cergy was just over an hour, then he pointed towards Rambouillet and drove for another hour till he was twenty kilometres away from the town, eventually pulling into a temptingly empty lay-by in a section of the road surrounded on both sides by thick forest. Milo woke up as the car came to a halt; surprised by the giant surrounding trees, he looked at Jack quizzically.

"Where are we?" he asked drowsily.

"Don't worry, mate, we're not in a fairy tale."

They both got out and lit cigarettes, and Jack showed Milo on the map the progress they'd made, and the route for the next section – basically straight down to Vierzon, about two hundred and forty kilometres. They didn't want to rush it, so currently it felt as though they were timing it right; there would be a further stretch of driving on small roads after Vierzon, but that was fine, they wanted to arrive in the evening, not in the afternoon.

They cracked open the boot, sat on the tailgate, and munched miscellaneous meats accompanied by a side of crisps and washed down with lemonade. "French food," said Jack with elaborately simulated salivation and an accent wearing a beret, "I have dreamed of it sooo long."

The early afternoon had grown chilly, but the break was doing them good, so they found extra shirts in their bags to add another layer, locked up the car, and started off up a path that led away from the lay-by into the woods. People obviously parked up here for a little local hiking as well as trans-national snack breaks. They came up to a sign:

RISQUE D'INCENDIE

Interdiction de Fumer du 1er Avril au 30 Septembre

They both immediately put out their cigarettes.

Then Jack laughed, "I bet we are the first people ever to take any notice of that warning. So much for the outlaw life, Milo, I am not sure we are really cut out for it."

The fresh air and the stillness of the forest hit their chests with a shock, like entering the sea on a hot day and realising too late the water is freezing cold. It was the first time since they had left the pub that they had been out of sight of the car or the ferry or the road; separated from the symbols of their flight they were washed over by normality.

Among the great uncaring trees they lost their concentration and fell off the tightrope. Milo started crying. "Sorry Milo," ventured Jack, not accustomed to gentle talk among men, "this is crap. What are you thinking?"

"As a pretentious person, I want to say that I am weeping for the end of innocence. But given where we are now I think I need to mention other causes: 'messed-up holiday,' 'miss my mum,' and 'did we kill him?' are currently my top three fugitive anxieties, mundane as they are, probably in reverse order. Oh, also, going to prison for the rest of our lives."

"First, Milo, as we did already discuss, maybe when you were not feeling so bright, it was him that came at us with a knife .... OK we got into a tussle, but we had cause, and it was just pushing and shoving till they started the kicking. Then they pulled the blade! Surely, anything after that is self-defence. We were just trying to protect ourselves and make him go away."

Milo wandered off the dirt path into the forest undergrowth, kicking leaves and cracking twigs to hide his snuffles and cheer himself up with some noise. Jack followed and put his arm round him.

"Honestly, we don't even know that anything is wrong, he might be less injured than you, if you think about it. Someone shouted out he was hurt when they were halfway out the door, they didn't know. We could probably put an end to this in twenty minutes if we made a call or decided to open a paper."

"We're not doing that, no way."

"Of course, my friend. We have the No Look No Listen pact,

63

which is sacred."

Jack dropped back. He was getting tired now, he had been keeping everyone's spirits up for a night and most of a day. He wanted to cry but realised he was able to choose not to, which surprised him, and pleased him. It felt like cheating: deriving most of the benefits of crying without actually having to produce the tears.

The sun was dropping lower and shone through the trees. Jack watched as the light and the trees formed the pattern of a henge; ancient and holy. He called Milo to turn round, pointed, and made the sign of Jesus arms, palms up: feel the beauty; embrace the peace. There is a life for us beyond the human mess we've made.

They came together and walked silently on the forest ground slowly towards the light for five minutes. Then the sun went behind cloud, and the epiphany was over. They returned to the path and headed back to the lay-by.

"That was spectacular," said Milo, "positively druidic, we must make a note to come here for the solstice."

"Yes, I had no idea that was going to happen," Jack replied. "I certainly didn't choose this route for the sacred sites. I should probably confess at this time that I only brought you into the forest because you are the sole witness against me."

"Ah, you are cunning. That was my plan too; how sweet we had the same thought! With you gone I would be home free, and I could blame everything on you without fear of contradiction."

"I imagined that only one of us would walk out of this wood alive, and the secret of the Schoolboy Slayers would be buried forever in a shallow grave."

"Don't worry, there will be other opportunities. You need to watch your back, my friend, no-one is to be trusted. Now, shall we get back to the car? I do need a legitimate fag and I can't bear the thought of setting fire to this magical place."

"*Moi aussi, mon brave*, but I intend to light up two metres before we pass the sign to prove my criminal credentials. I spit at the law."

"I think it is more of a guideline than a law, to be fair, but I too will demonstrate my contempt for authority, whilst of course honouring my own personal woodland code."

After the cigarettes, more pies. By this time Jack would have killed for an apple, or even a tomato. Life on the run: if the cops don't get you the rickets or the scurvy will. The lay-by was still empty, which gave them the confidence to go separately into the woods for 'personal travel preparation' as Milo amusingly euphemised it.

Finally, they were back in the car and ready for the last leg. Milo, though feeling quite a bit better, didn't want to try driving yet, so Jack started the car, they pulled out, and he looked to find a couple of lorries so he could continue his favoured tactic of lurking unobtrusively in the slow lane. It was harder to do it now, as the traffic was a lot thinner, and there weren't as many trucks in the afternoon. Gradually the roads south were emptying, though there were a lot of vehicles moving north towards Paris and the Channel ports.

"How about a game of Phony Bits to kill the time?" said Milo.

"Oooo good call – what did you bring, I've shown you mine."

Milo, reached round to the back seat to pick up his bag, still feeling some soreness but pleased to realise he was improving. "Well, given we had the same exams yesterday, I have some of the same books as you, but I also have a couple of excellent extras in here, and some more in the boot for later.

"So, let's see – we got Huck Finn, we got Lord of the Flies, we got The Grapes of Wrath that adds to your Sun Also Rises. And we both have Mockingbird, Gatsby and Catcher…."

"OK – rules?"

"Usual rules. First person chooses the book, the next one has to find the phony bits. You can score three points per book, then the next person can score three if they find extra bits or can choose the next book. Shame there are just the two of us, but we probably won't find any more players locally. Mockingbird is exempt for the first two rounds."

Mockingbird was a sacred text, not to be derided. Plus, it was the ultimate test of the game, as there wasn't much in it that they wanted to, or dared to, call phony.

"Who's going first?"

"You call the first book, as you're driving"

Jack thought for just a moment, he wanted to play hard but fair, no point in making life impossible, and the game was more fun when they got on a roll.

"OK let's start with an easy one, I'll pick Catcher."

"Thanks, man, that's appreciated." For some reason, Milo hated Catcher in the Rye; he'd just never taken to it, never believed it, and had often said to himself, but never out loud, 'That book is a waste of words.' He picked up Jack's copy rather than his own, out of a spirit of fairness, as his own copy was marked and scrawled over and he knew it too well. He feigned thumbing through studiously, though he really didn't need to in order to find the passages he wanted. He started with:

"First, the goddam hotel with the perverts and morons. So he, a schoolboy, gets a hotel room in New York, fine; then out of his window – like in Rear Window – he sits and watches from another room in the hotel as a distinguished grey-haired guy gets out a suitcase and puts on a bra, lingerie, stockings and high heels, and prances around.

"Frankly, this did not happen. He would pull the curtains, for a start. Not only that, it is meaningless. It makes no point, it is fake, phony, could not happen, did not happen.

"Second, IN THE WINDOW ABOVE he watches a man and a woman taking liquid into their mouths and squirting it all over each other again and again. So-called sex games – curtain open again. What about the optics and angles, how can he see everything going on in both these rooms. IT DID NOT HAPPEN, it is phony. And there is no follow-through, what happens next? He can still see, presumably, but stops reporting?"

"Calm down, calm down!" said Jack, laughing at Milo's increasing stridency.

"Listen," Milo went on, "the scene is fake, the setup is fake, the narration is fake. This is written by someone who is trying to create a version of degeneracy but has no experience or understanding of what it is. These are pitiful pervy pantomimes reproduced by someone who has researched them in badly written pornography. If you want to show that New York, modern life, mankind, is corrupt, depraved, sordid, don't do it with a made-up clipping from some feeble sleazy mag, there surely is plenty of genuine material to work with."

"All right all right! I accept your claim on this. Are you expecting that to be two points, or just the one, given those bits run into each other?"

"That's two points. My third, let's see......" Milo ruffled the pages again until he found what he was looking for. "Ahhh, the whimsical conversation with the New York taxi driver, about where the ducks from Central Park go in the winter, when it is sooooooo cold. 'I wondered if some guy came in a truck and took them away to a zoo or something.'"

Milo suddenly clutched his stomach and yelped, and Jack stiffened with alarm thinking maybe some of his ribs really had cracked and popped out in the kicking he'd taken. Milo wound down the window and stuck his head out, making the most horrendous retching noise, but when he came back in, and turned around, Jack finally relaxed, realising he was joking. Milo continued to alternatively place two fingers from each hand in his mouth in sequential rhythm, retching and gurning, shouting, "Where do the ducks go, Jack; please, please, where do the ducks go?"

"OK, Milo, I get it, I get it, don't clutch at me while I'm driving."

"But my wankometer is quivering madly, as they say in the seminar at The Cambridge University."

"They do indeed say that, m'lad, they do indeed," said Jack, suddenly sucking Leavis-like on an imaginary pipe and stroking the ear of a faithful literary labrador.

"But then they also say: JD Salinger shall not be mocked by boys who have not written so much as a laundry list."

Milo had written plenty of poetry but didn't see why he should have to have it certified by a higher authority in order to compete in a comedy take down. "If you can only criticise when you know more or can do better than the person you're roasting, life will be a lot less fun – that is an impossible standard. Isn't the satisfaction achieved by denting your better heroes; couch lizards pricking try-hards and do-wells?"

Jack shrugged. "I think respect for *il miglior fabbro,* or any *fabbro,* is a kind of superstition, to ward off devils."

"That's how the Guilds were formed, you know that. Also, you know there are only the two of us here in the car, right, so no devils will be criticising your laundry lists in retaliation. Now, moving on from this pretentious toss-pottery, how are you scoring me?"

"A full three, I cannot deny you, but no bonus for puking out of the window."

"Miserly! So, my choice of book now, and I choose The Sun Also Rises. How are we going to play while you're driving?"

"I'll try to remember bits, and you'll have to look them up. Start with the last paragraph, about the policeman's baton going up."

This was well known to them both, and before even looking it up they were creased up with laughter, like – well I guess like school-boys giggling in the back of the class, to be truthful.

"Yes, we have a conveniently impotent fellow in a cab with his lady, discussing sexual competence, and a policeman raises his sizeable stick to stop the traffic, jolting the car, and throwing them together. Terrible image, terrible writing, and not just a misstep, the whole book ends on the crap metaphor, so much rides on it, 'scuse my French, oh dear Lord."

"Well on the basis of Salinger's laundry list, do you think you could do any better?"

"Yes, I reckon I can. My laundry list is: one bloody cummerbund; two bandanas, one red, one green; fourteen golf socks, left foot only; and four silken ties for m'lady to bind my wrists and ankles."

"Well it is a bold list, and intriguing, but I meant can you do better than Hemingway's metaphor."

"Ah, I see. Well, let me think... Yes. They are driving past the military barracks, where the crack troops of course are drilling, and as he says 'Oh, Brett, if only I still had my penis,' twenty soldiers in a firing squad simultaneously shoot bullets into an inflatable model of Brigitte Bardot. Boom boom boom."

"Or or or," said Milo, "they're driving past a French bakery. The boulanger gets the settings wrong on the pressure cooker and just as Jake says to Brett 'It's damned annoying not having a nob, old girl,' a vat of confectioner's custard explodes, ripping open their cab, tearing off their clothes, and covering them in thick yellow cream. THE END."

"My God, how did Hemingway miss that one!?"

"He went for the lazy option. So, one point scored, two more phony picks please from TSAR."

"Before that," said Jack, panicking rather, "can I just be clear I am not mocking Jake for his injury. I am mocking Hemingway for his baton."

"Jesus, Jack, as you have said yourself, this is just the two of us here in the car, you don't need to show me what a lovely sensitive guy you are, Maggie can't hear you."

"I'm just saying. Don't mock the afflicted, it must be horrendous for that to happen. I had a recurring dream when I was about twelve that I chopped off my willy with scissors. I swear when I woke up many mornings I would startle like a shocked frog, a massive heaving chest of breathless fear, and I'd check my bits with both hands before I thanked God I still had them."

"Thanks for the share, brother, that means everything to me – if it makes you feel better I will sign a certificate that you did not mock a prickless protagonist."

"A dickless dipsomaniac."

"A cockless columnist."

Milo did not mention to Jack that when most of the boys were going through the change he had still had a tiny penis. It scared him, and boys laughed at him in the changing room, so he stopped going into the showers. He dealt with it alone for a couple of years, thinking his life was over before it had begun, and then a badly overdue surge of puberty changed his body. Now, though in fact no-one had yet come close to seeing or touching his late-blooming member, or indeed shown any interest in it whatsoever, he rehearsed confidently their compliments when it finally happened.

But the time of the small penis haunted him; he wasn't ready to use it as an apposite anecdote, even when he was bonding with a best friend in a murder conspiracy. What if Jack had made up the lurid tales of auto-penectomy in order to entice him into loose talk and confession? Milo could relate to Hemingway's thoughts and feelings about the hopelessness of love in a sexless body because he had had the junior version and had for a long time believed he would never be able to sleep with anyone. So he possessed empathy: it wasn't stopping him joining in a giggle at Jake Barnes's lacking baton, but it did at least make him conscious of his own potential for cruelty.

"Can we move on?" he said after the period of introspection. "Name your second."

"OK my second is in chapter three, I think. It is when Brett comes in for the first time and Jake Barnes says, 'She was built with curves like the hull of a racing yacht.'"

Immediately they were in fits of laughter again, like little kids shouting 'knickers' and running away.

"Is that literally the worst analogy of all time?"

"No, it's much worse than that."

Ha ha ha ha, they couldn't stop, Jack almost decided to pull off the road to avoid having an accident. They had an arm around each other, the tears cascading from their eyes.

"WHAT WAS HE THINKING!!??"

"Quick quick, for a bonus point do four better Hemingway versions of the same metaphor: GO!"

"She was built with curves like the boxing glove that knocked him

71

out the night he threw the fight, before it struck his face just below the eye but above the highest point of the cheekbone."

Milo did the 'so-so' sign of the flat hand rocking slightly back and forth. "OK for a warmup."

"She was built with curves like a pair of the brave trout fighting for breath in the leather pouch carved with a pattern typical of the region."

"Yes, getting there."

"She was built with curves like two bottles of the harsh local wine which he had tied with a string around the neck and lowered to cool in the icy mountain stream."

"Better."

"She was built with curves like the curves in the sand made by the hooves of the bull as the bull stared at the matador in the hot sun and asked, which one of us will die today?"

"OK nailed it, bonus awarded. Move on; third passage please."

"It's tricky to go for specifics, the whole thing is phony in a way, the whole atmosphere," said Jack. "The problem is as soon as someone shouts 'I am not a phony' you think right away, 'well I might not have thought you were, but I sure as hell do now.' And when they look round the room pointing, going 'you're a phony, you're a phony, you're a phony' then clearly there is need for examination, investigation and revelation. It is the same with Salinger really."

Milo smiled to himself. "Not a worry for you then that we play this game, Jack?"

"Not a worry because we do it in the spirit of humility and self-awareness. We believe in lessons to be learnt. Plus, as you say, we have no laundry lists to be accused of faking or embellishing –

we are literary and novelistic *tabulae rasae*."

"Ooooo listen to the scholar!! Back to Mr Hemingway if you please, your third accusation?"

"It is a bit feeble after the others, but I am going for Limpia Botas."

"Que Señor?" asked Milo, using a fancy accent.

"Limpia Botas...... around page 60-70 .... Boot Cleaners to you; Shoe Shiners."

Milo rummaged and found. "Got it."

"OK, so at this point you have the 'hilarious' double-act of the alcoholics, Mike and Bill, doing their stand up, sit down, fall over routines. You got my inverted commas on 'hilarious,' right?"

"I did indeed."

"Another time we can discuss why drunkenness in Mr H can be a shorthand for everything from wise and funny to sexy and strong."

"Amazing stuff – no-one ever appears pitiful, wretched and obnoxious till they actually stop boozing. We digress."

"We do," said Jack. "Anyway, it is just a trivial droplet in a sea of tosh, but around that page apparently they are ragging on the local boot boys – perhaps we can assume 'poor people' – by getting them in to repeatedly clean their shoes. As I recall the drunk Mike says, 'This is the eleventh time he's got someone to clean my shoes. Bill is such an ass!' Hilarious, side-splitting, crap... it never happened, and the worse thing is, why pretend it had happened for comic relief when it is nasty, condescending and not at all funny. PHONY."

"But it is great writing, is it not? The cadences!"

"Ha ha ha yes, the cadences! All hail the God Hemingway who

gave us permission to use the same word three times in the same sentence. You know the day after TSAR was published sixty-five percent of the thesaurus publishers in New York filed for bankruptcy."

"Only sixty-five percent? The others just weren't watching the ticker tape."

They took a moment of quiet contemplation. Jack suddenly realised that they had been enjoying themselves, it was like a holiday after all, but only because they were wildly suppressing reality.

Reading his thoughts, Milo said, "We forgot for a moment."

"Yep, we did," replied Jack. "But we don't have to slide all the way back down the snake now we have remembered. We agreed, he's Schrödinger's boy: so long as we avoid the news, avoid the papers, he is neither living nor dead, he is in the same state that we left him in."

"Good old Schrödinger. How many lives has he preserved? How many deaths has he delayed? Humanity owes that man a huge debt."

Jack decided to make a confession, nervous for once about Milo's reaction to one of his ideas. With some difficulty he assumed a modest tone.

"Please don't laugh at me, I didn't tell you, but in addition to Schrödinger, I have been keeping him alive with a mantra. If you just keep saying it nothing can change."

"That sounds magical, my friend, this is a fantastic concept. Can I assist? Tell me the spell." Milo thought 'I quite fancy the role of sorcerer's apprentice,' and then, 'I suppose that's why I've been playing it.'

"More of a kind of prayer? An incantation? I hope you're right about the magic, I want it to be a holy plea, for sure. This is how is goes:

it was just a scratch, he was just winded, dust him off, pick him up ....

it was just a scratch, he was just winded, dust him off, pick him up ....

it was just a scratch, he was just winded, dust him off, pick him up...."

Milo shifted uneasily in his seat. He of course immediately knew he was going to have to criticise Jack, and, as well as being against his own better nature, that seldom-if-ever sat well with his friend.

[There was an occasion when Mr McGorry handed Jack his English essay with an -A and suggested helpfully that there were one or two things to discuss. Jack replied coolly "Please go ahead sir, I always welcome positive criticism." Milo saw what was coming, and fled to the toilet without permission, vaguely finger-signalling incontinence. The class called him Milorrhoea for a month, but he felt it was well worth it.]

"Blimey, Jack. Sacred chanting as a life support system, that is a totally brilliant inspiration. But as you're asking...." [he decided at the last minute not to leave any room for confusion] ".... that is a completely crap mantra.

"I'm so sorry to say it. That is definitely not a mantra that is going to keep anyone alive."

Jack was defensive. "It came to me from the Universe. I thought it was the right thing, to accept it spontaneously, without question."

"Destiny allows for some editing, my friend. Sacred words of enormous portent have been mysteriously granted to you by A Greater Power, but knowing you as I do, you can improve them. I think we agree, this situation demands our best efforts."

"Go on then."

"Me?"

"Yes, isn't that what you were suggesting?"

"No, clearly I was recommending you."

"Well I guess it's your turn to outdo the Universe, given you don't like my version."

Milo rolled his eyes, but 'sulky Jack' had never been known to waiver, so the decision was final. He sat and thought for a while.

"OK, how about:

O My Brethren, pick him up, raise him high, heal his bones.

O My Brethren, pick him up, raise him high, heal his bones.

O My Brethren, pick him up, raise him high, heal his bones.

What do you think?"

"Not bad off the top," Jack praised it, somewhat reluctantly, "but I am still nervous about changing."

"It is OK, we can amend it once, honest; the cosmos smiles on progress, but not on farting around."

"All right, that's it then, we're done. It's better, it will help."

They drove on for ten minutes, chanting in unison, in a good rhythm, and they were filled with hope.

O My Brethren, pick him up, raise him high, heal his bones.

O My Brethren, pick him up, raise him high, heal his bones.

O My Brethren, pick him up, raise him high, heal his bones.

"Pie?" asked Milo.

"We've only been going an hour since the last pie, mum. We don't have to eat all the pies before we get there, do we?"

This was more a question than a rejection.

"Pork pies must go today, that is the only rule."

"We'll have one more break, in an hour. I need to look at the map anyway. Want to play more Phony?"

"No, I think I am Phonied out for now," said Jack. "Also I think if two kids in a car want to play 'Pretentious Bits' in twenty years' time, it will start with an argument to decide who will be Milo and who will be Jack."

"We could have that debate right now," Milo responded drily.

"But we can't both be Jack, my friend."

"Not even joint billing then."

"If it was up to me, but you know how it is – call my agent."

"Pretentious Bits … I love it, and I love I am in it, even if I'm not the co-star apparently, or even the supporting cast in an ensemble of two. But is Pretentious Bits how we want to be remembered?"

"If it is a choice between 'do you remember that pretentious twat' and 'wasn't he the infamous knife-slayer,' I am going pick nauseating banter-boy every time."

Suddenly too tired even to point out the false dichotomy, Milo eased himself back into the seat and let his eyes close, aching, but used to it now, so no whimpering.

"If you want a proper snooze we could clear the back seat?" suggested Jack.

"I'm good," said Milo, "it would probably hurt more to curl up at this stage. Ignore me."

Jack went to the radio, keeping it quiet, and tuning till he found some jazz. He couldn't recognise who it was, but he determined it was cool, and he let it play. It was a high-risk decision because when the track finished the announcer would say who it was and if it was someone who wasn't cool he was going to look foolish. Fortunately, it turned out to be Dexter Gordon. Another lucky escape.

There were no lorries now to adopt for protection; they were completely alone for large stretches. It made him nervous that they were out on their own, as though his superstitious attachment to various random *camions* had really safeguarded them. He found himself constantly checking the mirrors and side-roads to see evidence of *gendarmes*, despite the fact they had not seen a single police car since Calais.

When he thought about it, he wasn't really sure what the point was of trying to spot the police; they were hardly in a position to outrun them or evade them if they were recognised or followed. Unless maybe they pulled over to the side of the road and ran desperately across fields like in North By Northwest (terrible name for a film!), though remarkably that would also involve the *gendarmes* employing a flying unit to track them – naturally enough at the moment that seemed eminently possible.

Or they could flee into a thick wood, of course, if they were motoring through a highly forested area at the time the police closed in on them. What if Milo stumbled over a tree root and broke his leg, so the bone showed through the flesh? 'I guess I would just have to carry him to safety,' he thought, quietly proud of himself for the bravery, loyalty and strength he would show.

He skipped the stop they had discussed, as Milo was sleeping soundly and the road signs were beginning the countdown to Vierzon. He knew they had to have a break at some point to do the route planning, and it was best to do it before Vierzon so they could decide on the way in and out, or round. He was going to find a lay-by but at the last minute took an exit signposted to Theillay; he remembered the name, he had been there with his parents, a tiny town not much more than a village, with a café and a railway crossing. He really felt the need for some coffee. As he pulled into a parking space Milo woke up, wondering where they were and why they were stopping.

"Theillay," said Jack. "I've been here before, but I have a horrible feeling I have botched it slightly, we might have overshot. Let's get a coffee and look at the map."

They crossed the road to the café and sat outside in the late afternoon sun. The café had some tree shade and half a dozen impressive planters with cheerful flowers. "Blimey," said Milo as he was gradually coming back to life, "if you take away the bruises and chanting, this is just like a regular holiday." Jack tried a laugh which didn't quite catch.

He ordered the coffees in his perfect French, getting a warm smile from the waitress, who was charmed by his accent, thinking these were highly empathetic English – a rarity. Plus, decent-looking young boys, just a bit older than her own son, though the smaller one was worryingly scuffed around the edges. Jack asked about food; he had been craving *pain au chocolat* since they landed, but it was late in the day. She said she had some left, and would warm them up for them, to make them perfect. More smiles.

Jack spread out the map, and immediately swore mildly under his breath, *en Français naturalment*. "Argh, I brought us too far, we could have come off at Salbris."

"Where are we actually heading then, not Vierzon?" asked Milo.

"Sorry, yes, Vierzon was just my shorthand, we're heading to this place," he pointed, "La Chapelle-d'Angillan."

"I see it," said Milo, "so it looks like we've come down a junction too far."

The waitress was back and placing their coffee and *pains au chocolat* on the table. She'd heard what they were saying.

"It is easy enough to get back." She leant over and pointed. "See, don't turn here, take this one."

Jack nodded his understanding and gave her the full wattage in gratitude. "Thanks so much, that's excellent, it is great to have local contacts." She laughed politely and left them to it; Jack might have overstepped. Milo looked at him, shaking his head sadly.

"Don't fret, old boy," Jack said, choosing to misinterpret Milo's disappointed look for a comment on his route-finding. "It's not the end of the world, the coffee's OK, and so is this fancy bun, and this café is very nice and very relaxing. We would never have had this if I had remembered the way."

"This coffee is absolutely amazing."

Milo generally tried to avoid revealing *naïveté* to Jack, but this was the most extraordinary thing he had ever tasted. He had never been to France before, and the coffee he had got used to in England over the past few years was powder and hot water – nice enough if you didn't know about the other, but, as it turns out, a completely different substance. This was like Dr No after The Saint; or Elvis versus Cliff Richard (sorry Cliff). And best of all, he realised he could get this ambrosia whenever he wanted now, and he never had to go back. The pillars of adulthood were being erected around him.

Jack nodded about the coffee, "Agreed, it is incredible." Going on a riff now, "I reckon drinking a coffee like this must give you the same feeling a vampire countess gets when she sinks her teeth into a virgin lover. Same texture, same temperature, same rush of visceral power pumping suddenly around the bloodstream unlocking the ancient secrets of the universe."

"Blimey," Milo said, "you read my mind, that's almost word for word what I was thinking. So, what's at La Chapelle? Is that the end of the road for us, partner?"

"Nearly," said Jack, happy that Milo was interested…. pleased to sense a slight relaxation in his mood. "Shall we have another coffee?"

"Brilliant idea, let me do this." Milo decided to let the waitress off another round of Jack's familiarity and went into the café to order the drinks. Jack heard an interchange, and some laughter, a genuinely happy sound, and Milo came out with a smile. Jack pulled the quizzical 'Tell me' look, which Milo chose to ignore.

"What's the programme for the rest of the trip then?" Milo asked as he put the coffees on the table and sat down.

"Once we get closer I am going to have to root around a bit, my cousin's place is a bit of a backwater maybe four or five kilometres outside La Chapelle."

"Inform me please about this La Chapelle and its *environs*?"

Jack went into Tour Guide personality, using one of his very best comedy voices. "Firstly, and most notably, in any local or regional guidebook, it will tell you its main and possibly only claim to fame is that it is the birthplace of my hero Alain-Fournier in 1886."

In response to Milo's eyebrow and angled head query. "Sorry, Milo, I thought I said. Real name Henri-Alban Fournier. He's the author of Le Grand Meaulnes, which he wrote in 1913. He was killed in

1914 after joining up to fight in World War One. Meaulnes was his only completed book.

"Second-of-all, the tourist highlights – it is tiny, the population I would guess is less than a thousand. It has a château and an old church; I think from the 1400s.

"Third, more importantly for me, in addition to my cousin Jean, our whole extended historic family lives in La Chapelle and the villages and country around. My sincere desire is that Jean will give us shelter in our present uncertain situation.

"And fourth and last, obviously my dad comes from around there also, along with his clan, actually slightly to the south of La Chapelle on the road towards Bourges. I am hoping I might get a scent of him."

"<u>We</u> might. Together." said Milo.

Jack was affected by the comradeship; he reached over and touched Milo gently, not on the hand, just above the wrist. They looked around. Evening was coming on. A few people were coming into the café and ordering wine, some with food. The newcomers all sat inside the café, at tables round the walls, or on stools at the bar, talking to the owner.

Milo and Jack both used the washroom and having received pleasant thank-yous and come-agains from the owner and waitress, headed back to the car feeling fantastic, to be honest, after their first French encounter had proved so charmingly uneventful. No-one had noticed they were on the run; they were the celebrated invisible *desperados*.

Milo said, "I could have a go at driving now," and Jack laughed, "Bloody typical. Too late now, mate, I reckon it has to be me because I will be guessing routes and trying to find some very small tracks from memory. Anyway, don't be a goal-hanger; I've done all the hard work and I'm taking this baby home…"

"Ha ha ha. How are we for time?"

"We're good. I want to get through La Chapelle without being noticed, find Jean's place, and arrive after his workers have gone home, and before he goes to bed. It feels like people are already drifting away from work here, and La Chapelle is not much more than half an hour, maybe three-quarters, so as long as we don't get completely lost, I think we're in danger of getting it right."

The road to La Chapelle-d'Angillan was straight, about thirty-five kilometres through woods with lakes and water regularly on either side. As they were passing through a town called Neuvy-something, Jack saw a sign for 'Presly,' suddenly realised where he was and took the road indicated. They didn't need to go all the way into La Chapelle – it was actually the road the waitress had kindly pointed out. Presly was about twelve kilometres, and they were there in just over ten minutes, on an empty road. At Presly there was a sign for Etables-l'eglise which was a few minutes, then a sign for a turning that would take them back towards La Chapelle – they had been taking a half circle, skirting the town. Jack took the turning, saying, "Jean's place is before we get into town. The family live all around these villages and in La Chapelle. Jean lives on his own out here, running a piece of the farm and forestry business."

After another few minutes they came to a side road on the right. Jack said triumphantly, "This is it," and was about to turn in, expecting a farm road, not much more than a dirt track. But as he put on the indicator, they both saw at once that this was a large entrance with a nicely made road surface, and above the opening was an imposing and rather beautiful carved and decorated archway carrying a huge banner that proclaimed:

L'expérience Grand Meaulnes

"What the hell?!" said Milo, with a pantomime drop of the jaw.

"Indeed...," said Jack, totally at a loss, "...what the bloody hell is that?"

He sat the car in the middle of the road for a minute with the indicator still on, till a French country motor (shall we say 'battered 2CV with rust trim') came swinging round the curve behind and nearly rear-ended them, screeching to a halt with its horn blaring and the driver gesticulating comic-book style. Jack finally made the turn, just to get out of her way, and she pulled off with a silent shouty swear and mandatory waggy finger.

The boys edged down the road around fifty metres till they came to a fork. To the right, a barred gate saying '**Entrée interdite – personnel uniquement**.' To the left another banner and arch, this time with the message expanded to embrace a genial come-hither and a confident international tone:

Bienvenue * Welcome * Willkommen

L'expérience Grand Meaulnes

"Oh, my Lord," said Jack, "this is either a piece of marketing genius or he has completely lost his mind. I wonder if my uncles know."

As it was easier than opening the gate to the right, Jack rolled the car through the arch on the left and under the banner, driving slowly onto a field round which he had once raced a mule; the same field that once served as the football pitch for their famous England v France football matches. It was now labelled 'Parking,' so they parked.

It was beginning to get properly dark as they emerged from the car. They lit cigarettes, as was traditional after any car journey of more than ten or twelve minutes in France in the 1960s, and looked around.

"The whole place has been cleared and tidied," said Jack, in awe. "No-one bothered when it was just a farm. Or a football pitch for that matter. There was a caravan here" [pointing], "a broken-down tractor there" [another point], "and we had our goalposts here" [again]. "And actually I seem to remember a tree with a treehouse in that corner, but that might just have been in a book I was reading while I was here."

"Swiss Family?"

"No, I told you, they all come from round here."

"Boom Boom."

"I see the small barn is labelled **PAYMENT AND COSTUMES**, so I am guessing that is now a part of whatever this Experience is going to be," he was pointing to a newly painted structure in the corner of the carpark with a massive sign on it, "we used to camp in there when it was too wet to sleep outside, and we used it as a fort and castle when we were battling."

'Blimey,' thought Milo, 'isn't this all sounding a bit idyllic? I never had any Irishness to go home to, what were my parents thinking?'

Jack, finishing his visual tour of the newly promoted parking area, now nodded generally towards the gated path for the *personnel uniquement* which disappeared up the hill. "A few hundred metres up there, that's the farmhouse, where Jean lives."

"So, we're not going up there, *copain*? Is it because we're not *uniquement* enough?"

"I think it might be because we are not *personnel* enough actually. But the main reason is that I want to have another smoke and a pee before facing my cousin."

But even as he was reaching for his flies, they heard the distant slamming of a door in an unseen house. And soon after that a very big dog came straining down the path, making an extremely large racket, which announced the arrival of a really huge man being pulled along behind him on a rope.

For the general purposes of comprehension, from this point please note, reader, that with some small exceptions, all dialogue spoken in French will be rendered into English – it is for your benefit, and yes, I know, many of you are clever and sophisticated people who can translate for yourselves.

For this convention, the only guidelines you have to remember are these: whereas Jack is bilingual and understands everything, Milo (who has just finished his A level) has good, but by no means perfect French, so some things will be hidden to him; and Jean and the rest of the French cast have only very small English, therefore anything that is actually spoken in English is unlikely to be completely understood. You will also encounter a young German man, and it is a safe bet that he knows everything – or he thinks he does, anyway.

OK? So, let's move on.

The figure being dragged along on the lead shouted, "Excuse me, we are not open yet, I am sorry, you cannot park here. The facility will open next week, and we will be very pleased to see you then."

"But we desire the Grand Meaulnes Experience immediately, sir," Jack cried back, overlaying his perfect French with a heavy English accent. "We cannot possibly be denied till next week. We have driven at high speed all the way from London, England, in enormous anticipation. In London, no-one is talking of anything other than the opening of the Grand Meaulnes Experience."

The man with the dog stopped about twenty metres from them: for a few seconds he was flattered, excited and delighted; then, as reality hit, he was confused, perplexed and annoyed; and finally, as they say, the coin dropped.

"Jack, you absolute fucker."

"Hello Jean, very nice to see you too xx."

[Where they appear, x's represent kissy noises, mainly used ironically.]

"I'd give you a hug, but I'd better get rid of the dog first or he'll have your balls off."

"But he knows me well, cousin."

"That was his dad, Jack, this is Young Hector; I doubt Old Hector passed down his bizarre reluctance to castrate you to his kids, so you'll have to start again with this one."

Talk of dads reminded Jack, guiltily. "Jean I was so sorry to hear about your dad last year, Terence was a great man. I am sorry I didn't come to the funeral."

"You're a kid doing exams, Jack, I didn't expect you. I really appreciated the card; it meant a lot, and the sentiments. Oddly I found when he died that people who didn't know him that well generally liked him a lot. But anyway, enough of that! Come up to the house now. Who's your pal?"

"This is my close friend and travelling companion Milo Kelly."

"Good to meet you, Mr O'Kelly, any friend of Jack's is of course deeply suspect."

"You too," said Milo. He had caught hardly any of the cousinly banter, but understood the last part, when they were talking more slowly. He'd decided not to offer commiserations as he didn't know anyone involved.

As they walked up to the farmhouse, Jack tried to clarify for Jean the difference between Milo Kelly and Mile O'Kelly; but, as Jean said, perfectly reasonably, it was already too late for that. "I hear what you're saying, Jack, but it's stuck in my head now, I'm always going to struggle with it." Jack rolled his eyes, believing the darkness protected his mockery; but there still came the sound of an amused slap on the back of a curly head.

When they got to the building, Jean pushed Hector into his large enclosure, which had both an inside and outside space, explaining to him that he couldn't come into the house with the rest of them while he had the English guests. Hector glared at Jack and Milo for getting him exiled – there would be ground to make up there.

Jean's house was an antique. Milo could not see much of the exterior in the dark, but coming inside was like entering a fairy tale, maybe Hansel and Gretel. The whole of the ground floor was a single room, which gave off the smell of being a dwelling shared by man and beast – he looked into the corner shadows for chickens, goats or pigs, but nothing was moving in the gloom.

The walls were stacked from floor to ceiling all the way around with things on and off shelves: jars, books, clocks, boxes, tools, lamps, photos, paintings, firearms and fishing tackle. Books more than anything.

On the left as they came in was the kitchen area, with a range lit and a couple of pans on the top. There was a huge wooden table taking up most of the floor space on that side, with seven or eight chairs around it. The tabletop was covered in books, papers, bottles and glasses, but there were no dirty dishes, Milo noted; the place was scatty and scruffy but not dirty or desperate.

To the right was the living area with a sofa and a couple of huge armchairs, all covered in old, embroidered blankets and quilts, lovely but rather frayed.

The floor throughout was stone, a couple of small rugs barely covered a quarter of it.

Jean went to the table and began clearing space, piling up the books, moving the papers, taking away the empty bottles and used tumblers; then replacing them with full bottles and clean glasses.

"Come and sit down, pour some beer, I guess you are old enough now!" said Jean. The last time he had seen Jack he was thirteen or fourteen, maybe having the odd sip, in the French style for kids.

"Have you been driving all day? Are you hungry, you must be. Why didn't you tell me you were coming?"

"Well, to be honest, it was all a bit of a sudden decision, we only finished school yesterday," said Jack, slightly glossing over the controversial parts for the time being. Milo raised an eyebrow on the basis he'd had his ferry tickets for this Sudden Decision for over two months.

"Finished school, Jack?" Jean was genuinely incredulous. "You mean finished, or finished?"

"Finished, yes, for good."

"Wow, seriously? It seems only yesterday you were out there missing the penalty that allowed France to proceed to the final of the World Cup against Germany." Suddenly Jean was laughing uproariously, very relaxed, it all seemed quite normal. "That was so English." This apparently was the cue for yet more uncontrollable mirth. "What happens now?"

"Well, I am not turning professional, so don't worry about that, West Ham wouldn't have me."

Jean went to the range and stirred the contents of the pans, asking, "Sausage casserole, OK? There is cabbage and I have some potatoes baking; lucky there's enough for three because I was cooking for tomorrow as well."

"That," said Jack, "sounds bloody marvellous." Milo nodded vigorously, too shy yet to start talking.

"You must have some thoughts – what happens now you have no more school? Knowing you, you have a plan?" While he was talking, Jean was adding fresh herbs and last-minute magic to the pot.

"Actually, Jean, we were hoping we might stay for a while, maybe in the barn somewhere, we wouldn't get in your way. We'd be very happy to work if you need anything doing."

"This is very strange," said Jean, adopting a deliberate and serious tone. "To be honest, normally I would probably find it a slight liberty to have a little cousin turn up out of the blue with his hand out begging favours after ignoring me for two or three years. That could be thought by some to be irritating and hurtful, you might possibly understand that?"

He managed to sound quite stroppy, but his lips were hiding a smile. That was Jean's way, Jack recalled; he lived alone and was clearly not well-trained in the social graces, nor bothered by the lack of them.

"But as it happens, I do need some help now, so you could be in luck, depending on what you are really prepared to do. Maybe it will be you doing me the favour instead."

"Jesus, Jean, you're not planning a bank heist are you?"

Jean looked baffled, then got the joke.

"Ha ha no nothing illegal, well not completely anyway. Let's get the food out, then I'll explain."

Jean brought the dishes to the table, and plates and cutlery. He served them and poured each of them a large glass of beer. "What do you think of it, Mile? I make it myself, we all do round here."

"Very nice, Jean," he said, the first time he had spoken, slightly unsettled by the change of name, but assuming it was a French thing. "Genuinely, brilliant beer." Unlike real coffee, beer was something Milo did know a lot about.

Jean nodded happily, pleased with the compliment, he could tell right away that he and Mile would be firm friends.

"Now, let's eat, and I will tell you all."

90

Quite a while later, the excellent food was gone, a second and third beer had been poured and drunk, and Jean had been talking largely uninterrupted for over an hour, much to his own embarrassment. He was uncomfortable being the centre of attention and wary about being a bore. But he had plenty to tell Jack, and as his visitors seemed strangely reluctant to say anything themselves, he had to fill their void in any case.

He had decided to go back and start at the beginning by updating Jack on the family: who had been born, who had died, who had got married, who had moved. Due to an ever-expanding head-count, there were now over thirty close relatives living within a twenty-kilometre radius; it was no small feat to remember all this, let alone relay it all in a meaningful and memorable manner. Milo had to hide a smile when Jean was forced to get out a very worn, hand-sketched family tree to make sure he hadn't forgotten anyone.

One thing he steered well clear of was any mention of Jack's father – that was most definitely for another day, when the boy was rested and ready. Jack was just as careful not to ask. Sweetly, Jean tried to keep his thumb over Jack's dad's name when he was showing them the family tree but succeeded only in covering it with a sooty smudge.

Building his narrative, Jean moved on from relatives to talk of farming and the economy, with diversions into politics and Charles de Gaulle. Things were not so good on the farm and in the forestry business, Jean had been worried for some time about the family company and how his uncles, aunts and cousins were running things. He was lucky to be out on his own, doing his own thing, though frustrated that he didn't have more say in the grand scheme of things, let alone some control over strategy.

He admitted he had had some setbacks of his own, including a bit of a disaster in the end with the snail farm. Jack interjected at this point, "God, I remember it, that was great, wasn't it? Mind you I recall plenty of quite painful mornings on my knees helping you catch them, then ferrying them around the country in that awful van with the holes in the floor. What went wrong? I didn't know you didn't have that anymore."

"I overcomplicated everything. I went up a blind alley with the flavoured snails, to be honest.

"Snail farming is incredibly competitive, prices are cut-throat, and the top restaurants play the suppliers off against each other. It was me that got the family into it in the first place, my baby, so I really had to make it work. In fact we put a huge amount into it, but it just wouldn't break even, because people wouldn't pay enough.

I had this idea to add value and make us different to the other farms. I developed a system to infuse the snails with flavours by feeding them with different foods. I had parsley snails, apple snails, lemon snails, onion snails and several more. Basil was good, but very seasonal. It definitely got the attention."

"Blimey, Jean," muttered Milo, strongly suspecting some of those variants were fabrications, "that's pure genius."

"Sadly not," said Jean, with kindly bitterness, "for several reasons.

"First, they were almost fifty percent more expensive than the normal snails, because of all the special attention, corralling, hand feeding and so on. Flavours had to be kept apart, no merging, this was hard. Then people didn't want to pay the extra. I had one chef who took one of our economy common snails, dipped it in strawberry jam and ate it in front of me, saying 'I respect your expertise, and enterprise, but if I want strawberry snails in my Two Star restaurant, this is how I will do it on the cheap.'

"Second, I didn't allow for the quality of the kitchens we were selling to. The basic snail diet approximates to eating crap; basically, therefore, if you serve fresh snails to a diner you are feeding them an exquisite little parcel of shit. Chefs are trained to clean and blanch the snails to get rid of the faeces and grit, everyone does it slightly differently, usually it involves different combinations of salt, vinegar and boiling water. Then they add back flavour with classic sauces.

"However much I tried to explain to them that our snails were imbued with fresh pure flavouring already, they cleaned them anyway, much too religiously, and then complained that they weren't getting any of the extra taste they were paying for.

"And third, some of the flavours were ahead of their time, and I can assure you with the evidence of some unpaid invoices that the world was not ready for pineapple snails. Trust me on that.

"Ultimately the scheme destroyed our reputation and relationships, and there was no profit to be had in the glut of bog-standard *Cornu aspersum*, so we had to close. I won't mention how much we lost, but that was not the end of the catastrophe.

"We loved those snails, they were like family to us. Admittedly, I refused to pay to have the stock professionally removed, but it was also because we wanted to give them a great send-off. The lads and I got drunk at the closing-down party, and we threw open the cages to let them run free. It was so moving, there were many tears. But they proved to be ungracious bastards, and by the time we woke up from our hangovers the following lunchtime all my uncle's kohlrabi tops had disappeared. It took me two years to pay him back for that."

"Argh," squealed Jack, giggling his head off. He knew his cousin of old, and his weird sense of humour; undoubtedly some of this was comedy confection, but he couldn't guess which bits of his story were true and which were embellishment. "Bad luck mate – it's tough being a farmer."

"Yes, and even tougher being a dickhead," laughed Jean, a little maniacally.

He explained he had been no more than scratching a living with beetroots and lumber, always on the edge and worrying, so he was always searching for something to add value. Other things had been attempted and failed. He was still trying to find another way to make money: he used the expression "diversify the income streams" and he'd clearly been reading a book on this.

At last, he came to the *denouement*: realising that the lads were flagging after the snail tales and fearing they would drop off before he could get to the most exciting part, Jean accelerated the conversation. Sadly he had to miss out several important points about farm wages and crop rotation in order to jump quickly to the subject in hand.

"So, my latest creation," he heralded with a mental drum roll, trumpet fanfare and courtly flourish, "is something I call **The Grand Meaulnes Experience**."

This announcement did not get quite the excited reaction he was expecting: the boys looked a little blankly at him. "Yes Jean, we knew that bit, we drove under the sign."

"Two signs actually," said Milo. This was only his fifth comment of the night, and this time they looked at him as though he had intruded into a private family argument.

"Please just tell us, I beg you, before we drop unconscious on the floor, what is the Experience? And what do you have in mind for us?"

"Right. The Meaulnes Experience is the fulfilment of any child's or adolescent's dream about the book, the domain, the adventure. Or adult's of course! In fact, everyone...

"It can bring to life the fantasy of anyone who read the book last week, or who read it thirty or forty years ago, and who wants to experience the events, revisit the feelings they had, or reimagine the lost world of childhood."

The English boys were hooked and awake now; Jack looking

94

knowing and excited, and Milo looking equally fascinated but a little puzzled. Jean picked up on the difference.

"You don't know the book, Mile? Jack does, we did nothing but read it and look for locations one summer. OK, so, if you really have had such a bad education, then you need to catch up quickly. Start by thinking of Le Grand Meaulnes as a kind of iconic rites of passage book for the French teenager, like, what do you think, Jack, Huckleberry Finn?"

"In terms of the cultural importance to kids it is as significant here as books like The Catcher in the Rye and To Kill a Mockingbird. Milo and I talked about some of that on the way down."

Jean nodded; Jack and he had often discussed it. "Mile we don't have time to do the whole plot now, but I have English and French copies, you can read it over the next few days I think? It is about three, maybe four, young characters, growing up, losing and finding people, and places, and romance, and how they handle those situations. You're going to love it; I am very jealous that you have never read it."

Milo nodded nervously, it felt as though he was being handed rather a heavy burden. "So what is the Experience? A celebration of the writer, or the book?"

"It is not a museum. There are already two of those, one in La Chapelle where Alain-Fournier was born, and one in Epineu-il-Le-Fleuriel, the site of the famous schoolhouse in the book. I do wonder if we can have a centre here one day for visiting parties of schoolchildren – the merchandising opportunities could be incredible – but that is for the future.

"For now, the Experience is more of a living thing and an entertainment in the atmosphere of the book and the time. It is a real-time reliving of a day in the life of Meaulnes, at the château, during the period of the wedding. In the main edition, it is the story between pages sixty and seventy. The second day, at the celebrations, before they find out...."

"STOP," shouted Jack, thrusting his hand forward to grip Jean's arm and knocking a glass of beer over on the way.

"What the hell!" Jean yelled in shock, jumping up and backing away. "Jesus, what's happened?"

"Nothing," said Jack, "sorry. Sorry about the beer. It's just that we've told you that Milo hasn't read the book yet, and you are about to spoil it."

Jean looked at him for a long time, as though he was mad, and then gradually started laughing, laughing more and more till his whole body was shaking, and Milo and Jack did the same.

"Bloody fool, but I completely understand, that is the only decent excuse for chucking a perfectly good beer that I have ever heard."

They were all sitting down again now, and Jean recommenced.

"OK so we stick to pages sixty to seventy, which cannot do too much harm, and you, young man, better get the book read as soon as you can because people are going to be testing you on it, and who knows when someone will whisper the ending in your ear?

"So, for the Experience: being honest, I am not a hundred percent ready yet, but I could not resist putting up the sign. It is a great sign.

"Many of the preparations are finished, and the rest are planned, but a lot of things need a tiny bit more attention.

"We will generate the interest and the visitors by having a boy or girl – actually your younger cousins, Jack, who are on school holidays – standing at the two museums in costume and handing out leaflets. Thankfully the museums are quite friendly, just slightly wary, but we have to get them onside. I think Madame

Malpense at the main museum could be a great supporter once she is convinced. She believes she owns the brand of Meaulnes in the region, which could be frustrating, but if she likes what we do, it could be the making.

"As well as tickets at the museums we have leaflets to leave at all the information and tourist centres, and all the hotels and boarding houses around the region, from Vierzon to Bourges. And we have someone working on the telephone to advise and make advanced bookings.

"So, relying on having some customers, we expect them to arrive on the road you came down, pull into the carpark, and we charge them thirty-five francs per person. We are limiting ourselves to forty people per day, so once we have allocated that number of tickets to the first passengers who come, we have to put up the sign in the carpark saying 'Experience Complet,' I've had that made."

Jack giggled, a little drowsily, "So really, the first item you have produced for your infant business is a sign saying, 'SOLD OUT.' I love that Jean; you're not lacking in confidence at least."

"Ho ho, cousin, of course you must have belief. Anyhow, once they have paid, everything is free after that. First, they go to the wardrobe department..."

At that point Jean raised his head from his beer and extricated himself from his passionate speech long enough to realise the kids really were nearly out of it. They were looking at him steadily, but with the glazed eyes of those who externally are desperate to appear completely fascinated, while they've been asleep internally for quite some time.

"Ah sorry, sorry, I am keeping you up and boring you: enough enough – we can finish this in the morning. You boys have had a really long day. When did you leave home, anyway – what ferry did you get? Where's the marmalade your mum promised, we can have that for breakfast? How is she? You should have brought her with you!"

He was rambling a bit while he was clearing the table, he was tired too: it wasn't too late, not even 11.30pm, but as a farmer he was up at 5.00am or 5.30am every day, so he was used to going to bed much earlier. He moved to the other half of the room, beginning to think about blankets, and preparing to show them where they were going to sleep. While Jean was occupied with this, Milo, who by this stage was getting distinctly worried, looked at Jack and made the international shrug-with-arms-forward-palms-turned-slightly-up sign for 'What the hell, mate, are you not going to tell him?' If they didn't say anything, the moment would pass – they needed his help, it would only get worse tomorrow.

Jack did a single shake of head from side to side, indicating: 'Not yet, we will talk later, and I will explain.' Jack, thought Milo, is in denial, even worse than I am.

They looked at each other, then looked up at Jean, finally noticing that he had been standing there watching them for a while.

"Feels like we have all got some stories to tell," he said, waking up. "What's going on?"

Jack scowled at Milo, like a schoolboy who had been snitched on for cheating. It was the first time since they had been running that he had felt the least annoyance or disappointment in his friend, and even as he experienced the irritation, he let it go. This wasn't Milo's fault, and Milo was right. At some stage they were going to have to tell someone what they were up to, get some help, and try to begin to turn things around. Jean was a really good place to start.

"Yes, well we do have a confession of sorts. Can we have another beer please, Jean?"

Jean got a fresh bottle; brandy this time, as he sensed they were going to need some fortification. They settled back down, and Jack began to talk, assisted from time to time by Milo chipping in. The brandy was helping, now giving them a definite second wind. After about half an hour, including a few missed turns and dead ends, they managed to get the story all the way from East London to Jean's house. The only thing they forgot to mention was Jack's dad.

"For Christ's sake," said Jean, hitting the table, "what the hell do you think you're doing, Jack, this is all utterly mad."

He finished another glass and poured again for all three of them.

"If I've got this right," he went on, "I see you walk out of school for the last time, in full uniform, straight into a bar; two hours later you get involved in a knife fight in which a kid may or may not have been badly hurt, or worse; instead of calling your mothers and waiting for the police you flee the country in a Morris Minor using false passports and fake numberplates; the police in two countries may or may not be in hot pursuit of you; and now you want to lie low on my farm like intercontinental gangsters on the run, completely implicating me in your criminal conspiracy..... All this, and you're ONLY BLOODY SEVENTEEN."

"Actually," said Jack, looking at the ancient clock above the fireplace, "I think I am eighteen now." The hands were at one minute past midnight.

"Jesus, it's your birthday? Really? What else could happen..."

"You're not eighteen yet in England," said Milo, helpfully.

"Oh good, so I can't be tried as an adult in East Ham for at least another fifty-eight minutes."

"I think that's aged sixteen, isn't it? You've blown that one, we could both be on death row."

"My friend, congratulations, I believe that is *literally* gallows humour." They reached out and shook hands.

99

Jean looked on, speechless. Luckily he couldn't understand most of what Milo was saying, unless Jack translated – which he had done from time to time, but not completely reliably. And Jack was doing the irreverent stuff in English, showing off for Milo how cool he was.

Obviously, Jean had not had quite as much time to take it all in, or to adapt, so he was immediately more horrified and anxious than Milo and Jack. It was also the case he was not only older but also had some experience in watching the police in action, observing and being around petty crime and some slightly more serious stuff. He realised that those two had not even begun to consider the possible consequences of the position they were in. It also felt like in the telling of the tale the two youngsters had gradually started shifting some of the weight and responsibility for their situation onto him, the older man, as children do to adults, so suddenly he was the one left with blame to apportion and choices to make.

"Do you swear to me Jack that you've told the truth. They started it, they pulled the knife, whatever happened was an accident?"

"I do swear, Jean, on my mum's life." This was a serious oath, both in France and in the East End of London, so Jean looked him in the eye and accepted his word.

"Right," he said "time out now. I have to think, and I need to decide what to do tonight, not in the morning, because by then I suspect a lot of options will be closed."

Jack and Milo looked at him hard, rather in awe of this very clear thinking and mature tone.

"I am going out into the yard with my brandy and my cigarettes. I will let Hector out and take him for a short walk. While I am out I will think. I'll come back in half an hour or so, I will be whistling Happy Birthday To You if I think I have found a solution.

"If I am whistling Hit the Road Jack, that will be the signal that you should collect your things in silence and return to your car. Does that make sense?"

Jack and Milo looked at each other, and then looked back at Jean. They nodded in unison. In the context of the last twenty-four hours, this seemed eminently logical, thoroughly reasonable and entirely responsible.

"I will need to be careful," Jean said to them as he was putting on his jacket. "Hit the Road Jack is such an annoyingly catchy tune, who knows I might end up whistling it without thinking.

"Have one more drink; you can smoke inside, but don't set fire to anything – remember you are not having a very lucky day."

Jean enjoyed walking Hector late at night, and this time was no exception, despite the distractions. The huge young mastiff loved to lollop around the field and shout and lunge at a few random movements in the hedgerow without any serious intent. Jean cherished his last drink and smoke each night with Hector while they sat together watching the moon do absolutely nothing.

Now he had to handle the problem of these English boys, which was also an issue of family duty and the bond of blood. Jean's family were not out-and-out criminals; any criminality was never a goal, but always a by-product of tribal protection and survivalism. Traditionally they had little respect for the *gendarmes*, and the police steered clear of them. They had a code, and the code put family first. Jack was only fifty percent French, but he was one hundred percent family – that is the way it worked.

In truth, Jean had known very quickly what to do – because it would help the lads, and also because it would help him. Everyone could be a winner here. Jack and Mile, he realised, had been thinking no more than a day ahead, maybe two. They had no clue beyond. He had a plan that would see them through at least four months – to them, this would be a lifetime. He would be saviour and genius. The real issue would be the time beyond, and the rest of their lives, but they were at least creating some space to think about that later.

Jean returned Hector to his enclosed run but left the gate to it open, putting him on the ten-metre lead so he wouldn't savage the boys accidentally if they went wandering around the yard in their sleep. He went quietly to the house door and opened it softly, not bothering to whistle because, as he had anticipated, the two boys were fast asleep, Mile on the sofa, Jack curled up in a chair. He put a rug over each of them, gently.

Jean fished the keys to their car out of Jack's pocket. He grabbed a torch off the table by the door and went back outside, walked down to the carpark, and started the little Morris. He drove it out of the carpark, muttering about the wrong-way-round gear stick and pedals and fluffing and stalling it quite a few times, thankful there were no other cars on this particular piece of road. He opened the farm gate, drove through, shut the gate, then drove past the house and another four hundred metres or so to a group of decrepit farm buildings. The car went all the way into the back of the lower area of a small barn, and Jean took the boys' bags out of the car, which was then quickly covered with a tarpaulin, some vegetable boxes and fertiliser bags, and finally he pushed some rusty old machinery in front. He grabbed their hold-alls, and by his torchlight found the set of stairs leading to a room above. There was a put-you-up bed already in there, where somebody had been camping out a while ago; Jean would find another one later, together with any other bits and pieces he could think of to make it a bit more comfortable. There was no power, but there was a tap downstairs.

Jean walked the distance back to the house enjoying one last cigarette for the day, and shushing Hector as he went past. He threw the butt into the yard, took his boots off outside, opened the door silently, checked the boys weren't choking on their own vomit, and crept up the stairs in his stockinged feet (as they say in the best yarns) and straight into his bed. He mainly slept in his clothes, as many single men do, and only cleaned his teeth on Tuesdays, Thursdays, Saturdays, and on special occasions if he felt there was more than a thirty percent chance of kissing someone – so maybe every other year for that. His last act before closing his eyes was to set his alarm clock for 4.15am, an hour earlier than usual.

Jack and Milo slept downstairs like the proverbial careless cubs. Jean, having allocated himself roughly three hours slumber, didn't use a minute of it: he lay awake, fretting and ravelling plans. That's what I mean by the young offloading their guilt on absolutely any random adult they can find.

SATURDAY

At 4.30am Jack and Milo had their rugs simultaneously pulled off them; by the time they came to life Jean was back over in the kitchen, making coffee, heating milk, warming bread, and putting preserves and butter out on the table. Neither of the boys knew immediately where they were, but Jack worked it out more quickly. Both of them had experienced those gorgeous few moments of sweet innocent holiday excitement before they remembered they were killers in hiding and their young lives were over.

"4.30am, Jean, really?"

"Sit down and have your coffee, both of you. We need to talk. Eat first, we've got half an hour to get sorted."

The refreshed bread and homemade jams and butter were all delicious, and Jean's coffee was robust to say the least.

Jean was still at the work surface preparing food; it looked as though he was making a picnic for around eight people and putting everything in a large basket. Once he was done, he came and sat with them and poured them all another coffee.

"OK I did some thinking last night, and this is the way I see it. First, you should know, I don't believe anyone has been looking for you in France yet, not round here anyway, because I would have heard if the *gendarmes* had been asking questions. I say 'yet' because you have only been running for a day and a half, and the police may not have joined all the dots yet, about where you are, and family connections. It feels inevitable they will come sniffing around some time, though, agreed?"

Jack and Milo nodded, but Jack said, "It could be a while, Jean; we left notes that we were in Yarmouth – that's the English seaside. It just depends on what happened to the knife boy, and how seriously anyone is hunting. If he wasn't really hurt, it might be no-one is looking at all. It could be in the end they only come looking for us because they think we are missing and in danger – we don't know enough."

"I don't have a radio, and I don't get a newspaper," said Jean. "I don't even have a radio in my truck. You've left a mess in England, that's for sure, we just don't know what kind, or how bad.

"If I go asking around, it will be all over the area in ten minutes – people are smart here, and I have enemies as well as friends.

"If I try to call anyone in England, who knows what will happen; if I contact anyone it would be for only one reason, that you are with me here, right? If I get the wrong person, or someone is being watched, it will give the game up.

"It feels to me, and I hate saying this, that I have to join your cult of superstition for a while at least and live without knowing."

Jack and Milo were still quite dazed, and a bit in awe of the grown-up's train of logic trying to make sense of such a stupid situation. They just kept nodding. Honestly, they were desperately relieved to learn that Jean wasn't quite adult enough to turn the whole package over to the police to sort out. But this was all mainly governed by tribal rules; there were strict guidelines, albeit they were frustratingly never written down. Whatever version of the code you had adhered to, and it is an indisputable fact that various schisms, streams and branches had formed and reformed over the centuries, Rule One was always '*Pas Des Gendarmes.*'

"So," Jean went on, "my suggestion is we take this a couple of weeks at a time. That means, phase one, we hide you today, and then you join the circus."

"What?"

"Yep, that's the plan. Come on lads, who hasn't dreamt of running away with the circus – you might be the first people who have actually done it!"

"Franz did," said Jack, smiling, "when he was hiding himself."

"Yes he did," said Jean, "but I think our circus will be a bit better."

In Le Grand Meaulnes (and I now forewarn you of a spoiler, but you have had many chances to break off and read the better book, I advise you again to do that), Franz is the pampered son whose fabulous wedding celebration is in progress when Meaulnes stumbles across the magical château. He is jilted, and in his humiliation and despair he attempts and fails suicide before starting a travelling show, moving from town to town, featuring fire-breathing, animal-taming, feats of dexterity and all manner of circus skills. Always seeking and never finding.

"What are you talking about, Jean, please make it simple, my head is throbbing," said Jack, taking another spoon of the most delicious raspberry jam he had ever had – Jean was going to make someone a wonderful husband one day.

"OK," said Jean, "but we need to speed up, we have to be out of here in twenty minutes. My workers will be here before 6.00am, we need to be away by then. You haven't been here for a few years now, Jack, and none of the current crew would know you, but they notice everything, and they'll wonder and gossip if they see a couple of random boys wandering around the yard with no explanation about when they arrived or where they slept. And they can always smell English, which makes it even more perilous.

"Anyway, your situation is this, if I can summarise. You do not want to find out about the boy who is hurt, though you are fearful; you believe sincerely that you are innocent, but you do not trust the police to examine the case fairly; you need a place of safety where no-one knows you, but you need support from someone you trust; you need a roof, work, and a disguise. All right so far?"

Jack and Milo nodded – they found themselves doing that quite a lot when Jean was speaking.

"Last night I put your car in the barn up the road and covered it. I have a room above the barn that you can use today, we need to carry that bed over in a minute." He nodded to a folded put-you-up he had placed by the door earlier. "We will also take the food basket and a bucket. Your bags are already in there, I think by the look of it you have books, paper, pencils, things to occupy you today."

"What's the bucket for?" asked Milo, his first contribution of the day.

"You will not be moving out of the room all day, so you imagine what it is for," said Jean, with a grimace that became a smile. "Think of it as a rehearsal for when you are in prison."

"Now the ideas part. I said last night, I am having some problems getting the Experience going. I've been let down by a couple of students I hired, so I could at present use some workers who will do whatever I ask without being difficult. For the jobs I have in mind, you would need to dress up, do a bit of circus stuff, some acting, some boating, moving people around, dancing with guests, possibly singing (do you play any instruments?), serving food and drink occasionally; actually I suppose that is lots of things really. How does it sound?"

Jack and Milo looked blank, scared and acquiescent in roughly that order. "We're up for anything, Jean, we're here to help," Jack said, a bit unsurely.

Jean laughed. "You're here to hide, Jack, let's not fool ourselves. But helping or hiding, I don't think we have too many alternative choices. However, I do appreciate the energy and enthusiasm, we can certainly use that and it will perhaps help to gradually take your minds off your troubles. If you agree, this is what we should do. We'll get you set up at the barn today, you need to be sure to stay quiet, and out of sight, that's critical to everything. Meanwhile, I will tell the team here I am expecting two kids from Paris to come and fill in for the two students who left, and that you will be arriving tomorrow.

"Tonight, when everyone has left, you can come back here for a shower and a meal, and we'll talk about the jobs, I'll give you a proper briefing. For today, you can do me a favour. I want you to take this book about the Harlequinade, study it and learn all about it."

Jean handed Jack a very beautiful old volume, large format, in an elaborate dark-green embossed case, depicting Pierrot and Columbine on the front embracing, in a lozenge with a lovely floral border. Inside, the book was highly illustrated, and on a quick look though, Jack saw it was a history of the drama which also described several different versions of the play and included pictures of costumes, great artists of the past, and scenery and backdrops from famous performances.

"Actually, you could even start thinking, while you have a whole day to yourselves, about a short version of Harlequinade and how we could put it on. Maybe you clever guys can help me with that. The Harlequinade has always been an important part of the plan, and we have tried rehearsing and staging it in all kinds of ways, but I am getting nowhere with it and there is only a week to go. The kids are keen, but not trained actors, and we are running out of time to learn lines and practise any complicated stagecraft.

"Anyway, for the rest of the plan. As I said, providing it's all clear, you can come back here tonight for dinner and we can decide then where the safest place is for you to sleep. Then at about this time tomorrow, 4.30am or 5.00am, I am going to drive you into La Chapelle and leave you there to walk around for a few hours. Then I'll send someone in in the van to collect you, and you can tell them you've just arrived from Paris on the bus on the way to work here. If we can pull that off, then you can fit in with the team, have a job to do, and disappear into some new characters for a few weeks. No Englishmen.

"Sound good? OK come on, we'd better get going."

Collecting the bed from beside the door, Jean went outside, un-chaining Hector and putting him on his leash while he waited for the boys to follow him. Hector already seemed much more comfortable with them, but Jean knew that was mainly based on his observation of Jean's affections; he wanted Hector to be walked by Milo and Jack, sharing the lead, so he would begin to bond with them directly. The four of them walked the four hundred metres to the barn and then up the stairs. There was no trapdoor; the stairs just came straight up to a hole in the floor. Jean welcomed the lads into the room, like an anxious estate agent, nervous about their reaction. They were fine, they were hardly awake yet, and, as Jean had already pointed out, none of them really had too many choices, so there was no point being too picky, or complaining. They put up the second bed, sorted their bags out, and sat down. Jean pulled over a backless chair, the only other piece of furniture in the room, and sat with them.

"So, are we OK?"

"It's fine, Jean, it just all takes a bit of getting used to…", said Jack. "I don't know what we can offer on Harlequinade, but of course we'll try. Whatever else you have in mind, we'll give it a go, so long as you don't need us to be juggling and eating fire by next week. Your plan seems really sound; my only question is about Milo."

Milo and Jack looked at each other.

"My French is slightly rusty but if I take it steady and don't try to do anything daft I will be back up to perfect in two or three days, so no problem; and my accent definitely passes for Paris. So, no worry with my new history.

"But what about Milo ... he's just done A level, he's best in class (other than me), but it's schoolboy French, he can't be a spoiled sophisticated Parisian adolescent on a condescending work vacation, everyone would see through it in a minute."

The three sat silent, Jack was right, of course. After a minute, Jean hit his knee with his palm in best-ever "I've Got It" style, and said, "How about this. Mile is an American exchange student who has come to Paris for six months to live with you and perfect his French.... Good? No Englishmen! Your families know each other, your parents spend holidays with each other and so on – you can do the back story better than me."

Jack and Milo loved this and were mentally well into it already. Milo was reliving the many golden summers Jack had spent languishing in his hammock at the Long Island house, reading Scott Fitzgerald and William Faulkner as the night dimmed and the lights came up over West Egg.

Jack was recalling the time the boys slipped out for forbidden jaunts to hidden haunts in New York City; spending long evenings prowling the Manhattan jazz clubs, crawling from bar to bar making witty conversation with girls from the top schools in their delicate blazers – violet, candy stripe, elegant *Eau de Nil*, a rather fragile fuchsia.

Jean saw them spiralling off into reverie and realised these kids did not need any assistance with their fantasies. "OK OK, that's agreed, excellent. You can refine it today, but I will give the basic tale to the troops, and you will be expected by them tomorrow. Now, I'd better get back to the farmhouse before they start arriving for work. I'll come back tonight to get you when the coast is clear, but till then, please mark my words, it is crucial you do not leave this room, you do not make too much noise, and you do not show your heads at the window. JUST DON'T, all right."

"Yeah yeah, don't worry, we get it."

Jean left. The boys looked at the bucket. Milo spoke first, "OK you can have a pee, but if you attempt to shit in that bucket you will be dead before your pants touch your knees, is that understood?"

"Yes, couldn't agree more, old boy, it's 'corks up' time today. But as Jean said, we might need a different strategy if we get banged up for fifteen years." Really not funny. They both grimaced. Think before you speak.

For now, they settled into their camp beds, and their bodies immediately reminded them that they had only had five hours' sleep in the past thirty-six. Any worries they might have had about how to fill their endless hours of imprisonment quickly and quietly dissipated, as they both fell into a deep slumber, entirely facilitated by the fact that Jean was now taking care of things. That really is how sleep functions.

Milo woke around lunchtime. By his watch it was before midday, but then he remembered he hadn't adjusted it for French time, it was one o'clock. "Blimey, I am hungry." He said it out loud and then repeated it slightly more loudly with the express intent of rousing Jack, so they could eat. It worked. Again, both of them had a blessed few seconds of knowing where they were [holiday... and exciting...] but forgetting why and how they had got there [running away... and potential killers...]. When the facts came back this time, perhaps it was incrementally not quite as bad. Maybe because their problem was now shared.

Certainly their picnic cheered them up, Jean had done them proud. He'd got some fresh-ish bread from somewhere, which was still delicious, and he'd included cheese, ham, boiled eggs and some suspicious-looking but actually fantastically tasty pickly things. For dessert there was fruit and some hedgerow-flavoured homemade conserve that was pure heaven.

"Boy, this is the life," said Jack, maybe trying to be ironic, but coming off quite sincere, to the extent Milo just nodded enthusiastically. With the picnic laid out in front of him, Milo felt like a minor character in the Famous Five; the scruffy urchin who normally got paid off with "an ice" and a bit of patronising head rubbing; but who this time, because his bravery had been so crucial to catching the smugglers, had received a generously caste-blind invitation to the table set by the farmer's wife with a groaning High Tea as the handcuffed villains could be observed through the window being loaded into a Black Maria by the forelock-tugging local constabulary. Yes indeed, he thought, "This Is the Life."

After they had finished the first pass at lunch, and as they were tidying away the remains into Jean's baskets, intending to return quite soon for another graze, Milo said, "Oh Jack, there is something I was meaning to say."

"Oh yes, old boy," Jack said warily, "and what might that be?"

"It's this, Mr President," said Milo, standing up, using a bottle as a microphone, and starting to sing in a Marilyn Monroe lisp, "Happy Birthday Mr President... Happy Birthday To You..."

"Arrghh argghhh, Milo, that is so fucking weird, stop it. Stop it now. STOP."

And then they were rolling around on their beds, laughing and screaming. "This is the weirdest fucking eighteenth birthday in the absolute history of mankind." Then they remembered they were supposed to be silent.

"We'll make up for it another time," Milo whispered. "You can nominate any future date for celebration once we get everything sorted out."

They lay still, gradually calmed, and smoked a cigarette each. Jack was thinking of all the things he could be doing right now, on his birthday, if everything wasn't so completely messed up. Oh well … can't dwell on it; he'd been telling Milo that, and he had to keep showing an example.

He reached the Harlequinade book out of his bag and started to look through it, stopping at a few pictures, before going back, scanning the contents page, and then beginning to read the first chapter. After a while he asked, "What do you make of this, mate?"

"Honestly, I am clueless," Milo replied. "I've seen pictures of these characters in books and on adverts, I have read references to Pierrot and Harlequin here and there. I have no idea what they do in the drama, they seem like mummers or the gospel plays, everyone is aware of them, no-one knows much about them? Why do you think Jean is so hung-up on it?"

"According to this, I reckon a lot more people than you'd think will know about them," said Jack. "Particularly people of an older generation, all over the Continent, but specially France and Italy.

"Jean's interest will be because these figures or characters like them appear in Meaulnes; at the wedding celebration at the château, and also when Franz has his travelling circus."

He stopped talking abruptly and went back to the book, lighting another fag. Milo had already reached for Jack's English version of Le Grand Meaulnes and started to read himself. He could use the time to investigate this purportedly magical world he was becoming entangled in, as well as keeping ahead of the spoilers.

After forty-five minutes Jack let the book fall onto his chest and decided to have a pontificate.

"If he is trying to create the perfect experience, a special atmosphere, the personalities of the Harlequinade definitely feel like they would be wonderful additions: they are colourful, emotive, evocative, expressive, and symbolic of a time and place."

'Blimey,' thought Milo, 'he's well into this. He hath prepared for me a speech…'

"They are also easy to create; like clowns it is mainly traditional costume and heavy make-up. And acting the characters should be simple too, because it seems like there isn't a great amount of dialogue to learn and say in most versions. And they can represent so much more than the simple drama you see before you on the stage – archetypes, universal truths, like bringing elements of the subconscious to life."

So saying, and seemingly inevitably having begun to claim owner-ship of the project, Jack lay back firmly grasping the Harlequinade book and raising it once more to his eyes. Milo briefly toyed with the vomit sign, but had no-one to share it with but its inducer, never an easy one; so he decided to be rather impressed instead, and perhaps a little charmed, and a tiny bit irritated too.

In his adventures and collaborations with Jack over the years, Milo had learnt to look out for the moment which always came sooner or later when Jack unconsciously decided to stop sharing, grab all the tools and resources, and do whatever he wanted, with no further consultation. Milo recognised that this point had been reached already, remarkably early on, for this Harlequinade plan. It was Jack's now. Always one to take a hint, and currently short of energy to fight for co-billing, knowing from experience it would in any case be pointless, he returned to his book.

After another half an hour, Jack pulled over his bag and sorted out a notebook and pencil and started periodically making notes. He asked Milo what page he was on, to much mirth. "Jesus, Jack, it isn't kindergarten – we're not have a reading race."

"I'm just interested! Let me guess, page 67."

"48."

"Woow, slow, bro."

Milo simultaneously shrugged and tossed his head back in the classic sign for "Sod off and let me read."

Jack had always been like this with books. Who read the most; who read the fastest; who read the best; who read the most exceptional, remarkable, least discovered, most sensational. Milo tended to read two categories: things he liked to read; and things Jack told him to read. He lit a cigarette and passed one to Jack. He noticed they were getting a bit low, he needed to get some from the car later.

Jack had told Milo two years ago, at the start of the French A level curriculum, to read Le Grand Meaulnes, and for some reason, unusually, Milo had dug his heels in and gone his own way with the existentialists. Before he'd even spent twenty minutes with the book now, Milo had realised he'd made a mistake. He had enjoyed his time with Camus and Simone de Beauvoir, though they had never quite welcomed him into their wilful world as intimately as he had imagined; but within a handful of pages he fell in love with the romanticism of Francois; and of course, the youthful hopes, dreams and adventures of the boys in the school were a hundred times more relatable than the cynicism of the Parisian sophisticates.

Next to him, Jack was being equally inspired and entranced by the antique tales of *commedia dell'arte*, Harlequinade, pantomime and circus. Sometimes he wrote things down, sometimes he called over to Milo, half comment, half quotation, not really anticipating any response.

- "For centuries all pantomimes ended with a Harlequinade, they were two parts of the same performance, transforming halfway through the evening."

- "Hey, mate, this is funny – guess why it used to be mimed? Because most of the actors playing the parts in London were French refugees, and couldn't speak English, so it was easier to do a play without dialogue."

- "You've heard of Grimaldi, right – the first great clown? He invented himself in Harlequinade and changed all the parts while he was doing it. You wouldn't have any circus clowns without his innovation."

- "Harlequinade started back in the 16th century and bits of it were still being performed when this book was published at the beginning of the 20th century – that's amazing isn't it, something so completely simple entertaining so many different audiences, who would turn up to see it again and again. Why don't we know more about this stuff?"

('There won't be much I won't know soon,' thought Milo, amused at his friend's new passion, but trying to focus on his own book.)

The room Jean had put them in was huge, maybe fifteen metres by ten metres, with a floor of wooden planks. For the furniture, there were the two beds and a chair – that was all. Along one wall there were some small piles of dust and rubbish where someone had once swept half-heartedly and couldn't be bothered to finish. The bare plaster walls were only about two metres tall and then joined a sloping roof; there was no ceiling, so the roof comprised the underside of the tiles that here and there kept out the rain. The peak of the roof above the floor was high, perhaps seven or eight metres. Heavy dark stains on the floor indicated half a dozen areas where the roof had stopped trying to fight the weather and water had regularly leaked in.

Light was provided by glassless windows cut out of the triangular area of brick at either end; on a hot day like this they made for a delightful draught through the room, but it would have been uninhabitable in winter. As the afternoon waned the light dropped gradually, and in order to be able to keep reading, the two boys chose separate ends, without discussion, and began to move their beds closer to the windows, moving further and further apart in the process. This amused them, and Jack began to bellow his *apercus* about the Harlequinade more and more loudly, in strange voices and made-up accents, with fits of laughter on both sides.

Then to their horror they simultaneously remembered they were supposed to be secret, silent and unseen – Jack put his hand over his mouth and did the big eyes in remorseful pantomime horror. He then broke a second rule to save the first by scuttling to the window to see if anyone was outside, within hearing distance of the raucous English yells. Milo did the same at the other end.

But neither of them was tall enough to see out, so Jack came back and grabbed the backless chair, took it to his window and stood on it, very cautiously putting his head round the edge. Thumbs up – no-one in sight. Milo did the same at the other end, with the same result, just an empty yard outside, no-one around the barn, and deserted fields beyond.

There was a great deal of relief, genuine, because they could have blown it, and Jean would have been furious if they had let him down. They resolved to stay close, and speak quietly and infrequently from then on.

So Milo dragged his camp bed the length of the room and positioned it under the other window right next to Jack's bed; now they could converse in lower than normal tones when and if necessary. Even as he was doing it he realised there was never any possibility that Jack would have pulled his bed to Milo's end, but it didn't irk him. 'I am not at all irked,' he thought, smiling. 'I bet I am the least irkable person in France.' He was sorry that he couldn't share the claim with Jack.

While he was dragging the bed he disturbed a couple of the rubbish piles along the side of the room. "Hey, look at this Jack," he called in a stage whisper, "Wrigley's Spearmint Gum... this pack was made in Wembley, some Brit has been around here before us. And an old Park Drive packet – so I deduce a British person, who was trying to give up cigarettes and failing, stayed smoking in these charmingly-appointed apartments while on holiday in France sometime in the past..." [looking at the added layers of natural dust settled on top of the original broomswept dust piles] "...few years." He did not get a rise out of Jack, who was too busy assimilating theatre history and formulating stage directions under his breath to engage.

Only once did they stop what they were doing to talk about the fight and ask each other whether they thought the boy was OK, what did they think might happen, did they believe Jean could pull this off. Then they chanted the mantra together for fifteen minutes, Milo respectfully on his knees, Jack refusing to move from the bunk:

O My Brethren, pick him up, raise him high, heal his bones.

O My Brethren, pick him up, raise him high, heal his bones.

O My Brethren, pick him up, raise him high, heal his bones.

For the rump of the afternoon and into the evening, Milo read Meaulnes, sometimes with excitement, sometimes a little disappointment, now and then with despair. Some of the choices being made were not smart, 'Who knows what you would do in those circumstances,' he thought, charitably. Then he conceded he might conceivably have made some not-so-smart choices himself over the past day or so.

Jack in the bed next to him had put down his book and was now writing furiously in an exercise pad which said **LIT CRIT Jack du Lac Class 6E** on the front, and which, handily for the current project, seemed barely to have been troubled at all by actual schoolwork. Milo knew perfectly well what Jack was up to. He was creating the scenario for the Meaulnes Experience Harlequinade, as Jean had proposed. As predicted, he did not want to solicit ideas or suggestions, he wanted to do it all by himself. He didn't want to share the credits or have any disputes about ownership. 'All right,' thought Milo, 'it's his way. We'll find out all about it later.'

Milo realised the light was getting too bad to read. He called out quietly, "Hi, Jack, I can't read any more. What about Throost? Do you want to do a rehearsal?"

Jack and Milo were creating a play about DH Lawrence, called Throost. They hadn't finally decided whether it was straight or satire. For a normal performance their required cast was going to be thirty-two players, with an additional small brass ensemble to do some musical interludes, hymns and bawdy ballads. They envisaged it opening at the Nottingham Playhouse.

In the event they ever took it to Edinburgh, or did it in a smaller space, there was a budget version in which they played all the parts themselves and Jack whistled the tunes accompanied by Milo on a tambourine.

"Shall we start then, lass," said Jack, immediately getting into character as Paul Morel, in a rich, treacly Nottingham brogue using a dark brown tone he was particularly proud of.

"'Appen," said Milo, playing Miriam in a voice very similar to Paul's, but cast an octave higher.

"Shall I throost, lass?" said Paul.

"Aye lad, throost."

"Shall I throost higher, lass?"

"Aye lad, throost higher."

"Keep thy heels up, lass, or thy'll bang against t'wall."

"I will, lad."

"Shall thee go farther, lass? Shall I keep thee there, or throost higher?"

"Let me go, lad, I'm wasted and lank with thee. Enough swinging for me, it's thy turn now. Shall I throost, lad? Shall I throost as hard as thee?"

"Aye, lass, throost."

"I hope you're not throosting that girl too hard in there," said Jack, entering as Mrs Morel, using the same voice as Paul, but thirty years older.

"It's me throosting him, Mrs Morel," said Milo as Miriam. "He loves to throost me, though, when it's his turn."

"Bloody throosting," said Milo, coming on grumpily as Mr Morel Snr., "we never had no bloody throosting in my day, we were all down't pit at ten-year-old doing summit bloody useful."

They stopped when they heard a sound from downstairs. The light was almost completely gone, they couldn't really see as far as the top of the stairwell. The boys held their breath and peered through the dark trying to pick out any movement. They were both presuming it was Jean but went still and silent just in case. And in fact, it wasn't Jean.

The head that crashed up into the room through the stairwell at twenty kilometres per hour was huge, black and covered in spikey hair, with bulging eyes and a long bright red tongue flicking in and out of the sides of its hideous mouth.

"Hi, Hector!" cried Milo, reaching out a hand bravely to pet their new-found brother…. "There's a good boy!"

Hector was obviously a quick adapter and having now met and sniffed the lads on a couple of occasions, and watched the way Jean had looked after them, he had decided they were members of his family and he was bigheartedly prepared to forgive the night's banishment they had cost him. He had two basic settings: 'watch yourself' and 'loyal till I die', and they had moved seamlessly from one to the other. There was only one minor drawback to the physical bonding this new affection engendered. Earlier in the afternoon, Milo had had the genius idea of putting the pee bucket halfway down the stairs, for privacy, and because it was beginning to smell.

Hector had thoughtlessly tipped it all over himself on his way up and was drenched from nose to tail in urine. This he was joyfully spreading as he ran excitedly round the room, shaking himself and spraying the walls. Now he was leaping up and rubbing himself against Jack and Milo to generously share the last of the friendly fluid with his new buddies.

Jean followed up the stairs a minute after. "Everyone OK?"

They generally agreed they were a little pissy but otherwise very happy to see him. "You can come back and sleep here later, but you might be better off on the chairs again at the house?" They nodded, 'yes please.'

"OK, pack up your things then, if we're not coming back. I can sort out the beds and bucket later." He'd stepped over the upturned pail on the stairs, and even as he said it he was regretting his misplaced generosity in not telling Jack and Mile to clear it up themselves.

Jean had been very cautious, so it was more than an hour after the last workers had left. The sun was gone, and though it was still a quarter light, the full moon was rising in an indigo sky as they walked down the path. Hector howled on cue, and was confused and annoyed to yet again be left out in the run, even though they were all brothers now, weren't they? Certainly they all smelt the same.

Inside, the farmhouse was cosy and welcoming after the bleakness of their dayroom, and there was a delicious smell of chicken in the oven. Once more, the lost boys experienced the dissonant feeling of happiness overcoming them, knowing it was inappropriate, understanding it was selfish and insensitive not to be scared and guilty and worrying every minute about the condition of the lad in London, but having a moment of peace.

They dropped their bags by the door and Jean motioned upstairs saying, "I think everyone would appreciate it if you had a shower. There are a couple of towels on the rack."

Jack went first, grabbing his bag, and was back in less than ten minutes wearing a set of fresh clothes. The temperature of the water in the shower felt like it had been calibrated by Jean to deter lingering, both in himself and others. Milo did the same, and when he got back they took the same places at the table as they'd had the previous evening, while Jean finished chopping up some salad to go with the chicken and potatoes that were nearly ready. He had some wonderful Ella Fitzgerald playing on the worst turntable Jack had ever seen – it still sounded great. "April in Paris, whom can I run to?"

"A drink before we eat… did you like the beer last night? I've got local wine if you prefer, though I didn't make it myself," he said, smiling.

"Beer please," they said simultaneously, which was the right answer.

"So, before everything," said Jean, pouring three glasses ready for a toast, "we have one special thing to do, and that is to wish our friend Jack du Lac, *Bon Anniversaire*. I am sorry this has been such a rubbish day for it!"

"Hear hear," said Milo, "I mean for the Happy Birthday, not for the rubbish bit."

"It was never rubbish," said Jack, conscious he was close to crying. "I have been with you two, which makes this really special, and I suspect one day I will look back on this as the most memorable birthday of all."

"Bravo!" Jean shouted. "That's my boy!" Now it was Jean and Milo's turn to tear up.

"So, leaving aside this magnificent celebration, how was your time in the barn, did you manage not to make yourselves obvious?" Jean spotted the guilty glance they gave each other. "OK, what happened?"

"Nothing," said Jack. "I realised at one point I was speaking a tiny bit loudly in English, so we looked out of the window to make sure no-one was outside – the coast was clear."

"Jesus, you two – do you not get how serious this is?"

"Well, it obviously takes time to get used to being in hiding, Jean, we didn't even think about the noise, I am really sorry."

"It's OK, I made sure all the workers were a couple of kilometres away clearing undergrowth where we're felling trees in a few days. Lucky I did by the sound of it. In any case, they would come to me if anyone was worried about trespassers in the barn, so we're OK, but you guys really really need to understand the risks we're taking, and be careful, please."

They made "We promise we will" grin-grimaces and nods, while Jean went back to finish the cooking.

"The picnic was fantastic, by the way – thanks so much. Actually we still have some snacks in the back of the car, and I need to check if we have cigarettes. Can I get into the car?"

"I'd leave it now if that's OK," said Jean. "You should move around as little as possible, even the night has eyes here. And it took me a while to camouflage the car, so let's not disturb it till we really need to. Anything fresh in the boot of the car will have gone off in the warmth today, I reckon, and I've got a pack of cigarettes you can take for tonight – you can buy some more in the morning?"

"No worry, Jean, that sounds fine," said Jack, "we will locate Brutus de Tabac tomorrow." Milo burst out laughing.

Jean looked confused. "It's Bureau de Tabac."

"No, we definitely want Brutus."

While Jean was bringing the food to the table, Jack launched into an explanation – he enjoyed telling it, it was one of his favourite stories, and he had polished it through much rehearsal.

During a tough but basic lesson when they were in their first year of French, their friend Bob, not a star scholar, but normally relatively solid, had been called to the front of the class to do a vocab test on Types of Shop. He had no problem with Boulangerie and Boucherie, and was even unfazed by the more exotic Magasin de Bonbon; but when it came to Cigarette Shop he had a brain freeze, panicked, and came out with Brutus de Tabac.

The creation of Brutus resulted in ten minutes when discipline was abandoned, and even Mr Ellis lay quivering on the floor [in Jack's version] as hysterical laughter rolled in waves around the room. "This," he said later in the staffroom, "is why I came into teaching."

Brutus soon became a beloved figure around the school, featuring in jokes, skits and essays. His finest hour was appearing (actually played by Bob) as a cigarette seller at the Senate during the school's version of *Julius Caesar,* with the classic throwaway "Sorry, mate, I'm not that Brutus."

As Jack was finishing, Jean, clearly somewhat less amused than the English boys, who were still in merrimental fits at this stage, said out loud, "Jesus, I had forgotten quite how young you two are...."

Abashed and aggrieved, and with Milo ducking his head in cowardly fashion to create a little distance, Jack had to struggle not to come out with the addendum "True Story." When you have to revert to "True Story" you know two things – first your provenance is seriously being questioned ["never happened"]; and second your audience reaction has been flat at best ["and not funny anyway"], to the extent you are now forced into trying a recovering flourish with a kind of desperate verbal exclamation mark. "True Story" is the ultimate signifier of the playground fail.

He was disappointed with the response, normally it was his star turn. Evidently he had practised it so much it sounded phony now.

Maybe you needed to know Bob. Or maybe it just didn't translate too well. Anyway, he sensed that if he tried to explain to Jean just how hilarious he was being, it was likely to make him think he was even more of a dick, so he decided to let it be. Sometimes you have to know when to walk away.

The food was spectacular, especially appealing to a pair of hungry kids who had been locked up all day. A huge roast chicken covered in fresh herbs and sitting on a deck of roast onions, garlic and baby carrots; new potatoes with mint; and some greens that Milo had never seen before which looked so luscious and delicious he even momentarily considered eating them. Jean carved the chicken, politely asking who wanted a wing or a leg, just like a proper host who had actually invited his guests. "OK let's get down to some business," he said, when they all had a plate of food in front of them.

"Updates first. To make sure nothing was happening we don't know about, I drove up to my uncle Luc's this morning to say hi, and over to my uncle Marc's afterwards. If anything was brewing in the neighbourhood those two would know. They mentioned nothing about the *gendarmes* coming out to see anyone, and no one has had a call from your mum or anyone in England.

"For the Experience, this afternoon I met up with the team. There are the three remaining students for the acting, stewarding, costumes, customer service and so on – basically your colleagues, you will be doing all the things they do, as we discussed. Then two local chefs who essentially work for me most of the time, they are going to do the catering. They're brilliant, and they've done plenty of big events and festivals in the past, they'll run their own team of cooks, waiters, etc. as needed. I trust them completely.

"Then my mum, doing costumes and make-up; and Daphne doing box office and tickets. Daphne is Claude's daughter, have I mentioned Claude yet? He's my main man here, on the farm, a widower since early in the war, essentially he raised Daphne by himself. Claude is also our fixer of all kinds of things, so he's

124

involved with everything I suppose. In addition to all the above, I have quite a few of my own farm and forest people helping out in various capacities such as building bits of scenery, organising laundry, that kind of stuff.

"For music, I am trying to get Madame Jestique, I will tell you more about that later, it is not certain. Having her on board would be a huge advantage."

[Jack thought he remembered that name but didn't want to break Jean's flow by asking.]

"I told everyone when we met that the last two members of the team would arrive tomorrow from Paris, a French lad and an American boy who is staying with him on an exchange visit for the summer. So, you are expected, and you are not English – never English.

"I have decided Claude will pick you up in the van at Bourges station tomorrow at 10.30am, just after the train from Paris arrives. I know I said La Chapelle before, and the bus, but I checked it out today and none of that works, that was silly. La Chapelle is too small, the bus is too intimate, the timing is wrong, the transport connection to Paris is unfeasible, even for poor students. It was a bad idea; Bourges is better, it is big enough for you not to be noticed, and lots of trains come in."

Milo was impressed with Jean's readiness to change plans and criticise himself. This was a reassuring trait in a leader, he liked it.

"So Claude will meet you at about 10.30am, but in case anyone is around watching or taking an interest, you two will be outside the station at 10.15am to greet him when he arrives, saying you were early to the station in Paris, so you caught a train that got in at 9.30am instead. All right so far?"

Milo and Jack nodded, quite impressed.

"We will leave here at 5.15am tomorrow, you will be hiding in the back of the van, Bourges is about forty-five kilometres from here, I will drop you off in the town centre around 6.00-ish and be back here by 7.00am. I've told my workers to go straight to the plantation in the morning so no-one will be around.

"You will therefore have a few hours to walk around, get breakfast, and commune with Brutus" ['So he did get it,' thought Jack, determined not to grin]. "I suggest for form's sake, and just in case, you should please arrive in the *environs* of *la gare de Bourges* at 9.30 so it feels like you could have come on that train. Then have more coffee at the little café there and wait. Claude will be driving the little green Citroen van, I will give you the number plate, Claude will have your description in case you miss each other. OK?"

"Seems like a very good plan, Jean, thank you. Should we have a description of Claude in case?"

"He is one hundred and sixty centimetres tall, the same amount round his chest, he wears a rancid leather cap, and he looks like a man who has smoked one-and-a-half-million cigarettes in his life and regrets that it has not been a great deal more. Will that do it?"

"That feels like he will just blend in with many other men in the vicinity," said Jack, "can he not carry something striking and individualistic, like a bust of Napoleon?"

"Ah but we're in France now; everyone will be carrying a bust of Napoleon. How about a stuffed marmoset."

"A live snake!"

"A cello."

"Please please SHUT UP."

"Sorry, Jean, but in fairness we have each been locked up all day with only an idiot for company, it is not surprising this happens."

126

Jean counted ten. "OK, so now, this is where I will tell you the current status of the Experience, and explain where I hope you will fit in. Will you please calm down, listen, and take it seriously. This is very important."

While saying this, he had started to clear away the empty dishes and he brought back a big platter of cheese and fruit for the centre of the table.

"Up till now, I have invested nearly two thousand francs, which is way more than I expected, and more than I can afford. So I need this to work. By the way, having a couple of extra workers who don't want paying makes a big difference."

Now it was Jean's turn to throw back his head and laugh madly, while the other two looked rather less amused, wondering if he was entirely joking.

"You two have probably lost track of time, but tomorrow is Sunday. We're opening the Experience to the public next Friday, so that is in six days' time. We have less than a week to practise, rehearse and perfect.

"Holidays start in France around now, but vacations get really serious in a few more weeks, when we get closer to August, then this area will be full of tourists and holidaymakers. I need to start earning right away: it is fine so long as I can break even for the next few weeks, we're going to run the show throughout, and worst case it will be great training for when we hopefully are snowed under with customers for the peak season. But then we need to be making maximum income.

"The way I envisage a day at the Experience, and you can help me develop it, is this..."

As he spoke, Jean had gone to one of the larger sideboards and brought back an extremely bulky red folder rather sweetly inscribed on the front, in best jam-label calligraphy,

L'expérience Meaulnes.

He unclipped a folded, or perhaps more accurately concertinaed, document from the top of the wodge of papers inside and pulled it out. As he proceeded to unravel it down the length of the table in front of them they saw it consisted of complete pages along with other fragments and scraps of paper, and in one instance card, all taped together periodically, a bit like his family tree. He unfurled it with a flourish, a little like Howard Carter proudly displaying to the honourable members of the National Geographical Society an ancient Egyptian papyrus that was going to hieroglyphically reveal the secret code to the mysteries of life.

"…These are just my rough notes, remember."

Jack and Milo fatally caught each other's eye and simultaneously screamed with a laugh-like noise they unsuccessfully tried to suppress. Jean thought for a moment about being offended, and then joined in.

"Yes, OK, it looks a bit untidy, I know; but I can't get it typed up or printed, because it's confidential, right?"

"Exactly," Jack agreed, "if this got out there would be a dozen copycats launched before you could utter the words 'completely mad fucking enterprise.'"

They all laughed again, but this time the mirth was accompanied by a play-slap on the back of Jack's head that probably stung a little bit more than he expected.

Jean called for calm, then, taking up his brass letter opener, started to point in sequence to the key items that he had skilfully hidden in the text, indicating that Jack and Milo should follow along as he was speaking:

- Members of the Harlequinade are the greeters, guides and entertainers for the day for all the guests

- Once the customers have parked, proceeded to the Hut and paid (as she is an experienced cashier, Daphne will run this) or presented their pre-purchased tickets, they will go to the costume racks, where everyone gets their outfit for the day

  o Younger men can dress as Meaulnes, or Franz, or Francois, in frock coats and silk waistcoats in the 19th century style

  o Younger women dress as Yvonne or Valentine, with big hats and parasols and ornate wraps

  o Children dress as page boys or young girls in local dress with flowers in their hair

  o Mature folk can dress as Monsieur and Madame Seurel, Monsieur de Galais, and the other older guests or entertainers from the party – or anyone they want!

  o Also there are lots of generally exciting non-specific period costumes and accessories anyone can wear; we obtained a job lot from a theatre that was closing

- There is an accordionist employed to start the day at the Hut and be with the guests at all times throughout the day to play their favourite tunes

- Guests ride on hay wains driven by specialist carriage drivers between the Hut and the landing stage three fields away, assisted by the Harlequinade – I have made flat paths, and the horses are big and slow, so there is no danger to the public. Plus they are beautiful

- I have leased two barges, stunningly carved and painted with reliefs of animals and flowers, real traditional old canal boats. Each can hold up to forty people, and the bargemen will steer them up the two kilometres stretch of river to my uncle's hamlet where there is a jetty owned by our family, then down again, regularly picking up and dropping off customers throughout the day

- One of my uncles owns a huge field there, just where the landing is, and it leads beautifully up a sweeping hill to a slightly ruined house at the top, surprisingly named Hill House, which is also owned by my family. I have been given use of the field and house, though of course they expect me to pay

- It is a huge old house, no-one has lived in it for years, so I've had a crew doing it up, painting the outside, new shutters, window boxes. It is actually a Potemkin, because no-one could live in it, but it looks fabulously grand from the outside

- I have the catering team stationed there. So their job is to create lunch for the guests, laid out on trestle tables. When the customers disembark they take a walk up the bank of the river and into the field, they take their food and have blankets and pillows to lie on while they eat

- The meal is a banquet buffet: spit-roast hog, chickens, salmon, quiches, salads, breads, many cheeses, figs and grapes, sparkling wine, many beers, and a galaxy of gateaux

- There are marquee tents, they are like little circus big-tops, made in bright colours, red and yellow, blue and yellow, where if the weather is bad, entertainers can work and customers can keep dry while enjoying themselves

- If it really pours, people can go into a couple of the rooms in the house which have been done up to a basic standard – there are also toilets and washrooms we've had fixed

- During the buffet we have magicians and jugglers, to go from group to group

- After lunch there is pony racing for the children while the tables are cleared and folded away

- On the terrace of the house, which forms a natural stage, there can be readings from the book, and some scenes are re-enacted – I have an expert coming from the museum every day to give short talks

- Finally, there is the Harlequinade, played by the six characters who have been with the customers all day

- After the play is over, there is a dance on the terrace, with cocktails and macarons. Then the last barge returns, and the hay wains take the visitors back to the carpark."

Milo and Jack were stunned by now. Jean got up and replaced Ella with a very cool Lester Young.

"Blimey, Jean, that is a plan and a half."

"At least two plans, I would say," said Milo, who was distinctly growing in confidence around Jean.

"It feels incredibly bold and ambitious," went on Jack. "Can I speak honestly, cousin; without wishing to reduce the mood, do you think we have the resources to create something so intense day after day – do we need more help?"

Jean had to decide on his reaction instantly: whether to be affronted, to dig in, or to accept the challenge. He smiled. His spirits were immediately elevated simply because Jack had said 'we' instead of 'you.' It felt as though everyone was accepting reciprocal portions of everyone else's worries.

"OK nothing is set in stone, no leaflets have gone out yet, but we need to be quick and get them done by midweek. However it is essential to me that the Experience celebrates the spirit of Meaulnes and that anyone who comes has a fabulous day – a magical day – it must be the best quality, right?"

"Of course," said Jack, "but you still need to make a profit, or you won't be able to keep providing the Experience. Or save the farm. And, generally, it is thought best not to kill your employees in the process. They probably don't believe in being worked to death for someone else's quality experience, maybe that is why you lost some people already?

"Fortunately, Jean, you have two staunch allies now, excuse me if that is presumptuous, and feel free to brand us minions if you prefer.

"And luckiest of all, one of them, my humble self, is newly a world's leading authority, as of this afternoon, on Harlequinade; and also a recognised scholar of Le Grand Meaulnes. And as for my friend Mr Kelly here, well he is a recently graduated student of Business Administration and Management Studies, with Honours."

This was nearly true. Milo's mother had envisaged a day when he might well be running the pub, and she wanted him to understand the basics of cashflow, P&L and the Balance Sheet. Milo loved his mum dearly but was reluctant, secretly knowing he was going to have absolutely nothing to do with the pub and the family business once he got the place at art school that he had quietly yet doggedly been pursuing. But a compromise had been reached: in exchange for an agreement that Milo could choose the three "artsy-fartsy" A Level subjects he wanted to do at school – English, French and Art – Milo promised to do a Business Studies course at night at a local college which his mother paid for. He hadn't actually graduated as yet, so that was an exaggeration, but he had taken a final set of exams and was awaiting the results. Anyway, now, within hours of finishing it, the course was already coming in useful – who would have thought it?

Still snacking on the excellent cheese and grapes, Jean poured more beer, and passed Milo the folder with the rest of the notes and papers. "Here you go then, Mr Business Expert – let's see what you make of it." Milo apprehensively responded by spreading out the sheets on the table and picking out those that were mainly numbers.

Obviously Jean had already worked out that if they managed to get forty people a day, and charged thirty-five francs each, the best daily takings would be 1,400 francs.

"That's a lot of money," said Jean, looking nervously triumphant. "Specially as I worked this farm really really hard last year and ended up losing about 3,000 francs."

The budget indicated that Jean was planning on operating six days a week. Locally it would be absolutely frowned on to try to open on Sundays. Milo broke down the costs Jean showed him into a daily list of outgoings. While he was working, Jean got up, changed the record to Miles Davis, and ground some coffee beans. For the boys, these heady sounds and smells had unconsciously become the way that adults lived, things they hadn't known they wanted, how life was changing.

"OK Jean, leaving aside the money you have already sunk on costumes and signs, your daily costs for the staff, food, barge hire, carts and what you are being asked to pay for the field and house, the pony handlers, the magician, the juggler, the Meaulnes scholar, that all adds up to 1,200 francs every day, give or take. That, too, is a lot of money."

"Yes, I worked it out before, I made the costs add up to a bit less to be honest, but that does look right the way you have listed it. But that's good, isn't it, it means we make 200 francs a day?"

He had been basing everything on staying open for fourteen weeks, from late June through to the end of September. "That is eighty-four days, at 200 francs a day, so, what's that, close to 17,000 francs profit – that is more than this farm has ever made in its history."

"Slow down, Jean," said Milo, leaning over and touching his arm where it rested on the table. He was playing the bad cop and he felt quite exposed in the role, because of the difference in age and background. Jean had the practical experience of running a farm by himself for well over five years; Milo had taken a theoretical exam a few days ago – he didn't even know whether he'd passed.

"You're seeing all the potential advantages, but we need to look at the possible threats and drawbacks. Not to be rude, please understand," Milo was relentlessly polite, "but you can't really run the business on the basis of being full every day – that's sensible, right?"

"I suppose so," said Jean, warily.

"You can work out the risk by dividing your daily cost by the price per person – so the total 1,200 francs daily cost, divided by thirty-five francs per person, it means you have to attract thirty-four people every day to avoid losing money." Milo was certainly hitting his stride now; he was a natural at this, Jack realised, impressed and rather proud.

"You understand, Jean? Every day, it is the last six people, the numbers between thirty-five and forty, that make you your profit; if those six people don't turn up, you're out of pocket."

Jean was definitely looking anxious. He drained his beer and opened some more bottles.

"So," continued Milo, "we need to ask, how realistic is it that we will have a full complement of forty people every time?"

Jean was at the shrugging stage by now.

"Then," went on Milo, slightly on a roll, but not a good one, "we have to look at the bigger picture, what else could affect us?"

Jean wasn't sure if this was a rhetorical question.

"What is the weather like here, does it ever rain?"

"Now and then, like anywhere else. Probably a few days a month on average, the odd summer storm as well."

"Right, so there's your other issue, you are running an outdoor tourist attraction, there is not really any indoor element, and limited shelter. So basically, if it looks like rain, you're going to lose a day's business. The problem is that on rain-cancelled days you'll have no income but your costs go on much as before – you still have the boats, the field, you still have to pay the staff. You might save a few francs by avoiding purchasing the fresh food, but not much, probably very little, because you can't predict the rain too much in advance.

"Your margin is fourteen percent – that's a 200-franc daily profit as a percentage of your daily 1,400-franc sales revenue. It really leaves too little room for error. It means if it rains fourteen percent of the time – that's only twelve days out of your season of eighty-four days – you would make nothing.

"Let me give one scenario, so you see where we are. Say you do well and sell thirty seats every day – I think it would be a great achievement from a standing start. And say it rains six days only between June and the end of September. Does that sound reasonable?"

Jean nodded.

"OK," said Milo, working with his pencil and making some scribbles, "in that case you will lose 18,900 francs in the next fourteen weeks."

Everyone fell silent.

"Are you sure?"

Milo rechecked his figures.

"Yep, it's 81,900 revenues and 100,800 costs."

"Holy shit holy shit. Shit shit shit….. how could I have been such a fool?"

Jean was sitting with his head in his hands and rocking his body, the eternal and ageless body language for "I have been a glow-in-the-dark dickhead. I have been a dickhead so big it can be seen from space."

"Can I make a suggestion?" said Milo.

"Could it be a bit less depressing than the analysis so far?"

"Well, we could look at this the other way. We've just kind of agreed that a rational budget for sales is 81,900, right?

"And we know you would be pleased with 200 francs a day profit.

"So, from that we can calculate that you need to peg your costs at 775 francs a day."

Milo pulled his chair closer to Jean, put the papers between them, and pointed out how he got to the figures.

"What we need to do, to make this work, and take away the risk, is reduce the costs per day down from 1,200 francs to 775 francs.

"Here is a list of all the costs and associated activities. You need to decide and choose what you can do without."

Jack was now just the official observer and the first assistant coffee pourer. Jean even let him grind the beans and make another pot for them, an unprecedented act of delegation. Milo and Jean kept their heads together for an hour, and finally, triumphantly, got the cost to 790 francs a day – "that will have to do, I cannot cut more."

To get there they had lost the hay wains, with their drivers and mighty horses; one of the barges and its associated boatman; the daily Meaulnes expert; the pony racing; two members of the staff; the figs (which for some reason were bizarrely expensive, it could be they were discarded because of a typo); the sparkling wine; the piglet rotisserie (thank Christ for that, thought Jack); and every star in the gateauxy.

"Lots of equine retrenchment there," said Jack. "A veritable abattoir."

"The problem is," mused Milo, "you hire them, but you also have to feed them and employ humans to make them go. It all adds up. Plus, kids on ponies, it's uninsurable, right?"

Jean looked blank – he had grown up on a farm running in and out of whirring machinery and skipping under the hooves of pounding beasts. He had no concept of children in jeopardy, and besides, where are the parents, isn't that their problem?

"The biggest saving by far is the second barge. Each barge can hold forty, but we have a maximum of forty customers, so two boats is about twice the capacity we need. It just means instead of operating an all-day shuttle service, the boat takes everyone up at the same time in the morning and brings everyone back at the same time in the evening. Discipline."

Everyone nodded, wisely, in danger of falling asleep now. But not before Milo had one more inspiration. "I believe it is important to make the full target of 775 francs. To save those last fifteen francs, how about if Jack and I take a pay cut – we're so grateful to you for helping us, I am sure it would be a pleasure."

Jack gave him an evil look for donating his pay without asking. Jean smiled broadly and put a grateful hand on Milo's wrist.

"That is so generous, but I can't possibly allow it." Jack looked relieved.

"Because," Jean continued, "I think we agreed at the beginning, just a few short hours ago, that you are unpaid volunteers. No-one gets paid."

"We thought you were joking."

Jean laughed even louder. "Jack, what is wrong with you? You were virtually born here, you know that no-one jokes about money in France."

"So what's the deal?" Jack asked, not wanting to let it go quite so soon.

"The kids get a few francs for expenses, their travel paid, nothing much, and it is from me, off the books, not a salary. While they are here, everything is paid for, food, lodging, any reasonable requirements including the use of a car if they want. The same will apply for you two. If you look closely you'll see there is no actual salary allocated to any of you in the first place, so sadly it cannot be reduced any further."

Milo and Jack looked at each other, then at Jean, and the three of them just started giggling – what the hell.

"Listen, I can say one thing, which I have also said to the others." Jean was speaking perhaps with a small hint of guilt in his voice. "This is a free holiday for them, and a great adventure; and for you, I am providing the sort of safe haven that would cost a fortune in the criminal underworld, at no charge.

"But I promise you that in the seemingly unlikely event we make any money, more than our gloomy friend here anticipates with his clever pencil..." [he looked very hard at Milo at this point, but possibly there was a wink] "...then I will give everyone a bonus at the end of the season. Is it fair?"

"Fair enough chief."

It was getting late now, and they were tired. But the next piece of business was the Harlequinade, and it could not be let go. So much else had been cut in order to save Jean going bankrupt, now the play had assumed even more importance than its previous pre-eminence in his mind. It suddenly felt the magic of the day might totally revolve around the players and their performance. Jean began to emphasise that to them yet again.

"So I have the costumes, they are fabulous versions in the nine-teenth-century style, we have Pierrot, Harlequin, Columbine, Clown, Pantaloon and Policeman.

"The three students have been here a week now. They have not been able to do much in rehearsal as we have no script, no music, no scenario. So they have been getting free food and lodging up at the Forest Lodge for just hanging out and doing some odd jobs. You were right to guess, the other two students didn't like the look of the place, nor the costumes, nor the things I asked them to help with, so they left after a couple of days. Kids, right? No stamina."

Jack and Milo looked down at the table. They didn't feel ready to comment, perhaps out of some universal loyalty to the concept 'teenager'; or maybe just because they wanted to see how much stamina they had themselves before indiscriminately criticising the frailty of their fallen comrades.

Jean went on to explain that Forest Lodge was a slightly decrepit and now rather spooky old house once allocated to the farm's Chief Forester and his family when the business was several times larger than it was at present. Jean's family had had to sell a lot of the plantation land fifty or so years ago, but they'd kept the house and four or five hundred acres, now running this as a smaller part of their company alongside the agriculture business. As well as the forest on one side of the Lodge, there were a few fields in the front, in the direction of Jean's farm, changing crops from year to year including sunflowers, maize and flax. On the other side of the house, less than thirty metres away, was a sizeable pond, virtually a lake, where Jean allowed favoured local folk to fish for carp and pike; it was also used by the kids in the area as a swimming pool.

Various people had lived in the house over the years, but none of them had enough sense of ownership to repair or decorate it, with the result that now, finally, it was perfect for a student house.

"They definitely," said Jean, "could not make it any worse. There is power and water, at least, and plenty of room. It is where you two will have to stay from tomorrow night onwards, I hope you understand?"

"No problem," said Jack, "we mustn't be seen to be too friendly with the boss!" They laughed. "What was it you were asking them to do that caused them to abscond?"

"Ha, nothing outlandish, I promise. For most of the time up till now they have been assembling and hanging bunting along the sides of the river and at the picnic field. They helped the guys put up signs and got the Hut we're using for the tickets and costumes cleaned up and ready – that kind of stuff."

Did he look a bit sheepish? Something he wasn't telling them? Jack decided he was just embarrassed; under a very tough exterior Jean was essentially a kind man and would have taken it very personally if they left feeling unhappy or resentful.

"So anyway," Jean went on, "for the Harlequinade, the three students have their roles picked, they have been fitted into their costumes. And they have the make-up designed and they've practised putting it on, we copied it from the illustrations in the book I gave you. As I mentioned my mother – that's Bernadette, Mile, more formally known as Madame Terroir – came and did the adjustments to the outfits, and she taught them all about the make-up, she has a lot of experience with the local amateur players. You remember your aunt, Jack? She's not really your aunt, just as I am not officially your cousin of course."

Milo looked blank at this last statement, but Jack nodded to him reassuringly. Familial titles were bandied around rather loosely in the region and were generally indicative rather than prescriptive.

"Of course, we have only one girl player," Jean continued, "so she is Columbine. Her name is Amelie, she comes from Orleans, so relatively local, she is filling in time this summer before going to university for the first time this autumn.

"Her brother, Albert, is two years older than her, he has been in university in Avignon, he's back for summer and wants the work. He is not an actor at all, so he has demanded a part without speech and with very little actual drama – we made him the old man Pantaloon as generally that just needs the performer to shuffle around a lot and dribble."

Jean gave the impression, without saying as much, that he considered this an inspired piece of casting.

"The third one is the son of a friend, or business contact, of one of my uncles: he asked me to find the boy something as he is drifting in France for a year, so I have only known him for a few days. He seems quite a strong personality. He's German, but from close to the border near Strasbourg, I think Baden-Baden or somewhere like that, so he is practically bilingual. His name is Karl and he grabbed the character of Harlequin. My initial impression is that he believes he is the centre of the universe and everything in it, but in fairness I haven't had any trouble with him personally, and he didn't disappear with the others at least. Actually one of those lads who absconded was a friend of his, so I think we're lucky he didn't go too; something held him, but we need to be careful. I would say he is quite a lot older than I was expecting when he was offered to me, I'm guessing roughly halfway between your age and my age."

Jack and Milo exchanged glances. Karl sounded like a prize arse even on the basis of a hundred-word introduction; what fun to bunk with him and join his theatre troupe, they did not think at all. However, there were no choices in this scenario, other than to trust Jean.

"What we have not done, especially since Frederick and Pascal fled the scene of the crime, is have any rehearsals, or discuss a version or a script. I am hoping one of you can take the lead on that, because Amelie, Karl and Albert don't seem well-versed or particularly creative, and I confess myself to be bereft of ideas and inspiration for the drama. I am saying, help me please – maybe this is why the Fates have sent you to my barn."

"And the Muses, Jean; don't forget the Muses."

Jean smiled. "Yes, Mile, the Muses would be extremely welcome too. Let us pray they favour us."

Milo, maintaining eye contact with him at all times, stretched out his arm, opened his palm and swept the extended limb round in a flourish finally shaping an elaborate bow towards Jack. The universal body language for "In that case let me introduce you to my friend; a dramaturgical genius who spent the afternoon furtively scribbling wonderous words of wisdom in a mysteriously under-used exercise book. He will be your saviour this evening."

Jack was just summoning up the graciousness to look slightly em-barrassed at his friend's silent endorsement when he realised they had no time for false modesty. "Yes, I do have some thoughts," he said. It came out sounding rather less confident than he had hoped and intended. He opened his notebook, looked around to make sure they wanted him to talk, and when they nodded, he began.

"OK so a few things we know.

"First, I love the fact you have got the classic costumes, obviously they are perfect for the *atmosphère Meaulnes* but also that is a great period for us to do the Harlequinade.

"After two hundred years the play has had so many versions and styles, staying classic gives us the broad latitude we need to pull this off."

Milo looked at Jean, and Jean looked back … their glance agreed this was sounding reassuringly authoritative and extremely theatrical, though Milo was not quite sure how much of it Jack was putting on.

"Also, typically," Jack continued, "leaving aside the big theatres in cities, the journeyman players toured from place to place giving shows in different kinds of venues, using *ad hoc* stages and platforms – that is perfect for us.

"Finally, because the players were peripatetic, looking for the best and most lucrative locations to set up, they often went further and further afield, playing for festivals and celebrations, often moving from country to country. That meant, to avoid having to translate scripts, and so the audience could understand, very commonly the Harlequinade was a play without words. I avoid the term 'mime,' as you note, in case it causes alarm!"

Mime is definitely a controversial medium in many cultures; Jean and Milo looked a trifle dubious even at the mention of the word but were otherwise so convinced by the confidence of Jack's disquisition that they kept quiet and let him continue.

"Other things we know, at a practical level, are:

- We have a cast with little acting experience

- We have little money to spend

- There are six days only before the first public performance

- We have three players cast, and three to be cast

- We have costumes and make-up for six players

"One thing I needed to ask you, Jean, which is key, is about music – you said there would be musicians at the house?"

"Ha ha don't try to catch me out, I said music, not musicians. It is only Madame Jestique I have been talking to; she is the church and theatre pianist, she does concerts, plays and parties in the schools, and she actually used to accompany the movies in Bourges cinema. You'll be delighted to learn I have finally secured her services. We have a piano, and she can do all kinds of styles, you know, everything from religious to jazz to ragtime to ballads. Actually Jack I think you have met, at some kids' parties years ago; but I believe it was such a long time, and when you were so small, that she will not remember you. Besides, for various reasons, mainly to do with hardly ever talking, she is incredibly discreet, we can rely on her."

"Good grief, old Jestique?! She must be 143 years old, Jean, she was completely ancient even back when we were children. She also played the hymns at Sunday school. And you're right, yes, I remember, at the Saturday morning picture shows. Blimey, good call, if you think she will live long enough. I bet she is cheap too."

"Be respectful, you brat, she is a much-loved local institution, and actually she's around fifty-five years old, definitely no more than sixty; kids always think their seniors are antique as soon as they hit forty. And I pay her more than she asked, because you must never take advantage of decent people who are ageing, especially considering which direction we are all heading. Also, we would be completely lost without her, so we have to keep her inspired as well as healthy."

"OK but this truly is perfect for the idea I have, it could not be better, so long as you like it. Here goes, please don't judge me harshly."

Jack was now flirting with them nervously; he was anxious, never having exposed himself creatively on a project of anywhere near the importance of the Experience. He might also have been feeling particularly vulnerable following the recent painful incident with Milo which he had labelled in his mental filing cabinet as The Rejected Mantra.

144

"Don't worry," said Jean, realising Jack was tense, and trying to put him at his ease, while achieving quite the reverse, "if we don't like it we'll just say."

"But we won't laugh," said Milo, making it worse. It was quite fun for him to see the mighty Jack shiver, and he was loving it, in a nice way, of course, not a cruel way.

"Perhaps there might be some of that Positive Criticism you thrive on. I suppose it is always a bit of a risk, isn't it, when you keep the notebook to yourself: you don't have to split the glory, but you do also retain total ownership of all the bad reviews."

Jack poked his tongue out at him like a twelve-year-old. Milo poked back. Jean rolled his eyes.

"Come on children for heaven's sake, it is after midnight, we need to nail it and get to bed. Frankly, unless it involves macramé underwear, cannibalism and a barbershop quartet, I am probably going to say 'great let's go with it' just so I can get some sleep."

"OK," said Jack, "then I think we're safe, I can cut the barbershop."

"Maybe snip it a bit."

"Or just trim it."

"Worst case tidy it up a bit on the back and sides."

"Concentrate for Christ's sake!!"

"OK, here's the idea. First, for a modern audience, the earliest basic theme of the father banning the lovers from getting married is a bit foreign, so I reckon we can have a more contemporary version of the love triangle, which is still not out of character with the origin story and all the variations.

"For a style, as we favour what-we-shall-not-name-as-mime for practicality – to avoid learning lines, avoid Milo's foul accent, and to get it done in time – then I suggest we merge it with another great wordless medium everyone knows, which is the silent movies. My idea therefore is no actual dialogue, just speechless expressions and huge expansive gesturing. The players can mouth words and make exaggerated movements, just like the silent actors, and we have some sign boards we put up during scenes on easels to set the tone, beautifully designed, like the written 'explanations' inserted into the silent movies. Just a few, saying things like:

Je t'aimerai pour toujours, advienne que pourra

or

Défends-toi ou meurs, porc infidèle

or

Maintenant le vieil homme va les attraper à coup sûr

or

Enfin, la justice t'a trouvé, dans la tombe"

"Yes yes yes, we get it – great signs, can we move on," said Jean, enjoying himself, but looking at his clock. "It is so late now."

"OK, for styling, we have harsh lights pointed at the platform; I am still thinking on this, but perhaps a monochrome colour scheme on the props and backdrops to accent the black and white; and we definitely have the piano playing the mad accompanying music: love music, chase music, dangling from a cliff music, like they had accompanying Charlie Chaplin and Buster Keaton. Fortunately you have already hired the perfect person to do that style – she probably did it for real.

"Well, that's it really; the rest of it I can make up during the week if you're happy with the basics?"

Jean looked at Mile, asking the question with his eyebrows, and Milo nodded enthusiastically.

"It's brilliant," said Jean, "I think it solves all our problems, and the audience will love it too. Well done, Jack."

How easy decision-making is when there is no chain of command or committee involved. That was it, Jack was in charge. He was chuffed; the praise of his older cousin, going back to kids' football and teaching him to ride a pony, meant a huge amount, as did the approval of Milo, though that was generally more of a given.

"That's brilliant!" Jack said, which sounded rather like 'I do compliment you greatly on your judgement, Jean, and your endorsement, Milo; you are men of outstanding wisdom.'

"In that case, Jean, two quick things please.

"First, you'll need to find a rational way to make me the 'Director' so I can create this in a week, people will need to do what I ask.

"And, secondly, I want to play Pierrot; Milo should be the Clown, and you will be the *gendarme*."

"Crikey, talk about taking control, Jack. OK OK OK, it all makes sense, you seem to actually know what you want, and that is ninety percent of genius, isn't it – or something like that. We're on."

They really did have to be up in a few hours, and were desperate for sleep, but suddenly there was one last forgotten task of the night, which had to be done before they met any of the other members of the team or workers the next day. That was to check on the backstories and personal histories of their new identities.

Jean gave Jack a rehearsal of his cool Parisian upbringing, where his parents lived, what they did, where he went to school, why he came to La Chapelle for the summer. They now quickly added the fact that his degree was to be in Theatre Studies, his parents were a director and a choreographer, so Jack had been raised in grease paint, born in a chest of drawers in a Paris theatre dressing room, fed his bottle by the chorus girls while his parents were busy – he could still remember how the feathers on their headdresses tickled his nose as they bent over him cooing, etc. Which was why Jean had appointed him to organise their little effort. Jean would tell the others that since the two students had left because they thought that he and his Harlequinade were a complete shambles, he had felt the need to find a suitable replacement who had enough drama knowledge to take over direction, as well as being a player – it was very lucky for all of them.

And for Mile, he reminded them he was to be an American who speaks a little French. Discussing what part of the USA he might have come from they agreed that his parents were in the cinema business in Hollywood, and they occasionally worked with Jack's parents, and had grown friendly enough to arrange the exchange visit. It felt like it was all getting a bit rich, but it was too late at night to do rewrites.

"We will have a pretend briefing when you 'fake arrive' about what we've been doing, what your roles are and so on. It will seem realistic if I do it all in front of the others. Obviously you will never have met me, but we have corresponded and talked once on the phone. Clearly we cannot plan every last thing out in detail tonight, so much of this we will need to make up as we go along – stay smart. For the personal cover story, just keep thinking about your histories and what you might get asked. It is easier for Mile, if someone asks him a question about Hollywood that he can't answer he can pretend he doesn't understand the French.

"The final thing we need to decide is what to call you? We don't know if there are any news stories or TV anywhere about two kids on the run or missing called Jack and Mile, but obviously you need new names. What will it be?"

Milo chipped in first, for him it was easy, "I will be Scott, please, a nice, plain, easy-to-learn American name with an underlying romantic resonance."

"Bravo, nicely done, it fits perfectly. And for you, Jack?"

"I guess it would be too obvious to be anything from Meaulnes? I know it could not be Augustin or Franz, but could it be Francois? His name is seldom used, it wouldn't leap out. He stands back from the action, comments, organises to an extent. I doubt many customers are going to dress up as Francois, he is not the hero."

"That sounds fine, Jack, your name is as likely to be Francois as anything else. Really the names themselves don't matter as much as you remembering you are not Jack and Mile, don't make any slips. When we have the meeting with the team in the morning, do not forget we have never met before!"

With this final admonition, Jean handed out pillows and blankets, put enough wood on the stove to last a few more hours, and said goodnight, "for at least the next four hours. Some time we will remember to get some sleep."

SUNDAY

At 5.00am Jean woke the two boys. Neither of them had slept terribly well, through a combination of uncomfortable beds and even less comfortable memories. Milo had heard Jack whispering the mantra in the night but had left him to do it for both of them. They had a very quick coffee and then Jean bundled them into the van with their luggage. "You can get a proper breakfast or two in Bourges," he said. "You'll have plenty of time."

Jack and Milo dozed in the back for about forty minutes before the van pulled up, the back opened, and a grinning Jean welcomed them out into a quiet and unobserved backstreet.

"Welcome to Bourges. I can't hang around, just in case we might be spotted. So I am afraid I must now say goodbye forever to my cousin Jack and my new friend Mile," he pulled a sobbing face, "and later I will remember to be excited to meet Francois and Scott, players in our Harlequinade!!"

He mimed "HURRAH" and punched the empty air, doing everything he could to try to lift spirits he could tell were extremely deflated. Then finally he took their bags out and put them on the pavement, left them a cigarette each, bowed elaborately, got back in the van, and pulled away. Jack looked at Milo and Milo looked back.

"What the fuck have we done?"

"Well speaking from my hiding place behind the rubbish bins at dawn on a grubby corner in a seemingly deserted town I had never heard of before this week, I have to believe that whatever it is we have done has been done badly. Possibly it could not have been done worse."

His riff ran dry, losing steam, leaving them both discouraged and depressed as they gazed after the departing vehicle of the man who had shared and then absorbed most of their fears over the past two days. Jean had distracted them with fantastical plans and outlandish ideas, and reassured them, and fed them, and in all ways both aided and abetted them in the most fraternal and *sympathique* ways imaginable. As his van turned the corner and sped out of sight, their hearts plummeted.

The first thing they realised was that in his haste to get away, Jean had forgotten to tell them where they were. They knew they needed to get to the railway station by 9.30am, and it was just touching 6.00am now, so they had plenty of time. Jack knew he did have a guidebook in his hold-all which had a section on Bourges, but, like many, he decided to follow his instinct instead, so they took the direction Jean had taken, on the basis he was probably getting onto a main road, which hopefully went into town as well as out of it. After a five-minute walk, three streets over they came to a sign

150

saying **CENTRE VILLE et GARE 1km**, pointing *à gauche*, and they happily followed the instruction.

They were hungry, and as Jean had suggested, they stopped at the first café they passed. They went inside and parked themselves in a corner table. The owner was in the process of opening up, putting out the trays of brioche and croissant, and to be honest he looked quite unexcited to have two customers at that moment. Jack cheered him up by madly over-ordering multiple pastries in a charming Parisian lilt, and two large coffees with milk. "Take your time, Sir," he said ingratiatingly, "we can see we have arrived when you are busy."

This politeness, and the fact they were quite obviously French, and not English tourists as he had suspected, had the desired effect of encouraging the owner to bring their *petit-déjeuner* quickly, and they tucked into the freshest most delicious croissants they had ever tasted (in Milo's case, there was not a lot of historical competition, but Jack had eaten many hundreds). They ordered a second round of coffees and sunk back into their seats watching as the little café came to life with its constant traffic of morning locals and passing van drivers popping in and out, some picking up a drink to go, others stopping for a brioche and a chat. Clearly the owner was well known and well liked, and this was a popular spot.

"What do you think, Jack," said Milo, "how long do you reckon we can hang here? It's much more agreeable than walking the streets."

"First, I must point out, my name is Francois, and I know nothing of any Jack while we are in earshot. *Tu comprends?*"

"I do *comprends*, pardon *mon brave*."

"So, as regards lurk time in the café, I feel we have another few minutes, then perhaps we should move, in case anyone starts wanting to ask us where we are off to, or just because others have looked at the table in a needy way, and we don't want to get over-noticed or absorbed into someone's memory."

151

They drained their coffees, got their things together, and paid on the way out; a little kindly chit-chat with the owner, who hoped to see them again and again. Though it was not much more than dawn, and the streets had not yet begun to warm, they put on their sun hats and pulled them on low, remembering they were supposed to be incognito, or at least discreet.

They walked on in the direction of the town centre, feeling much better. Before they had left the café Jack had taken the guidebook out of his bag and slipped it into his pocket. He had not wanted the owner to see the English book, as their reputation as "local folk" had by this stage been well established, but he wanted it to hand as they were about to reach the centre.

The guidebook, which Jack now began to read out loud to Milo in a high-pitched nasal comedy voice, stated that Bourges is a picturesque city ["not town," he noted] in Central France, and it is famous for ancient houses which retain the medieval half-timbered style. It has a fifteenth century palace and a thirteenth century cathedral, according to this authoritative text, and there are several museums.

"Is that from The Goon Show?" Milo queried suspiciously.

"Which bit, the half-timbered houses?"

"You know what I mean. The voice."

Jack reddened. It was a sworn oath between them never to quote from, mimic, refer to or in any other way acknowledge the existence of The Goon Show, a BBC Home Service radio programme of comedy skits described as revolutionary by men with pipes, and much beloved by certain sections of the school community and their parents.

"No."

"Not Harry Secombe?"

"No, of course not."

Milo looked at him for a hard twenty seconds.

"OK, I am going to let it go this time. Just be careful my friend."

"Right," said Jack, declining to respond to the implied threat, and anxious to move on, "it sounds as if the cathedral is the place for us?"

And indeed, the cathedral was the perfect aid for conversational recalibration, because it was in sight already, towering above them though they were still probably four hundred metres away. But Milo was not so sure it should be the place for them, given his current guilt and possible state of sin.

"It's fine, Milo," said Jack, casually discounting two thousand years of Catholic history, "it is Sunday morning, it will be open to all, there will be lots of people around, we can blend in. Priests will not point at you and scream 'There He Is, SINNER.'"

"Hopefully there will be singing. Plus, I would like to see the stained glass of Lazarus and Jean d'Arc; and also the Grand Housteau and magnificent nave of which everyone speaks. Oh Oh Oh and also the Astronomical Clock designed by Jean Fusoris!"

"All these things are bound to delight us," said Milo, giving way to Jack's enthusiasm as he so often did. "Trusting your personal assurances about priestly reticence, pray let us proceed at full pace – *à pleine vitesse.*"

"*Oui, à toutes jambes.*"

Feigning cynicism, they were both rather excited to have discovered such a convenient wonder to both distract and disguise them, and when they arrived outside ten minutes later, it certainly did not disappoint. For Milo, this was literally the largest thing he had ever seen.

"It took over one hundred years to build, and the roof alone uses the wood of close to one thousand oak trees – so literally we are standing beneath a forest," said Jack, glossing over and improving nuggets from the guide. "It has been burnt down several times, bits fall off with alarming regularity, it has been invaded, pillaged, and once came within hours of being blown sky high. Every generation feels it knows best how it is really meant to look, so it has been restyled in a seemingly endless succession of designs. It has even changed religion on more than one occasion."

"And yet," said Milo, "here it is, it really doesn't feel like it's going anywhere, does it? Maybe that's why people have been so relaxed about trying to mess it up over the centuries, they can sense they're not even going to make a dent in it. Frankly it is hard to believe it is manmade, it does feel far beyond the scope and scale of humans."

"OK, Milo, look at these guys above the door – that's us! You see Christ there is choosing the sinners and the saved – which side will you be on my brother? It might depend on whether our assailant lives, but surely there can always be redemption even for the killer."

Milo didn't like the death banter while entering this place, not at all; he pulled his cap even further down over his brow and went in through the centre of the five doors, under the stern gaze of Jesus, without looking behind for Jack.

The cathedral was even bigger inside than out. "Taking his breath away" is generally a phony and tired expression, but it was accurate here, because this was something completely outside his experience and comprehension – total wonder. Which of course is why they spent hundreds of years and used half the building materials in Central France making it. To instil in the women and men who enter here a tiny hint of what it feels like to meet God. 'Hello, God,' thought Milo, 'I hope you have brought me here for a reason.'

Jack, choosing to believe that Milo was a little miffed, or tired, or just needed a moment apart, had studiously remained outside, flouncing around with his guidebook, learning outlandish cathedral-based facts, and rehearsing clever things to say later when they were back on speaking terms (he estimated twenty minutes).

"I give you permission to leave me, and really I have many things to do."

Milo, alone, felt an overwhelming urge to do something he had not done for a week; he went to a pew, took down a hassock, and knelt, clutching both hands together against his forehead to pray.

"Please, God, please, let him be alive. I am so sorry I have run away. I am sorry I have not been mortified every second. I am sorry we adopted a pagan mantra. I am sorry there have been jokes and laughter, but you know those are out of terror. Please, God, please let him be alive."

He repeated it several times, augmenting and embellishing, then going back to the simple version. Then he stayed perfectly still for fifteen minutes, trying to totally cleanse his mind of any thought. Finally he got up, nervously looking behind to make sure he had not been observed; and like a man in the street who nearly trips over and does a little skip after, perhaps to show he meant it, or that it was the fault of the pavement, he bounced quickly away up the nave.

Jack was just learning that the inside of the cathedral was one hundred and eighteen metres long by sixty metres wide, and the height of the nave was around thirty-seven metres, much higher than Notre Dame. His twenty-minute limit on regaining Milo's goodwill was well passed, and he had admitted to himself reluctantly that his friend was suffering and really needed this period on his own; but at the same time, being Jack, he was worried and believed that only he could help. Eventually his desire to interfere overcame his resolution to be sensitive, the change of heart not a little inspired by boredom. He went through the doors, a man on a healing mission, ready to comfort and cheer.

He had never seen anything like the scenes inside the cathedral. He had been a churchgoer, and sang in the choir for years, in a small church in East Ham, St Paul's. That was a place of regular worship, twice on Sundays, intimate, monochrome, reverential, respectful, and hushed. What he saw around him now in this spectacular and awe-inspiring space was life, going on, in a dozen places; simultaneously, colourfully and noisily.

In an area to the left in the far corner, fifty metres away, were around twenty-five children, aged possibly between five and twelve, gathered in the pews in front of a young priest and a brightly dressed female helper, reading passages, raising competitive hands to answer questions, then suddenly banging tambourines and breaking into a song. The priest adores the woman, he thought; and this is the only hour each week he sees her. Perhaps it is a tragedy. Perhaps it is just as well?

About fifteen metres further round there were five or six beautifully dressed ladies, their flamboyant Sunday-best dresses covered temporarily with colour-coded aprons, as though they had co-ordinated in advance who would be Scarlet, who would be Mustard, who would be Plum and who would be Coral. They were elegantly lugging huge trugs of fabulous blooms up and down small ladders to decorate a system of vases and holders around the pulpit and choir stalls. Two working men were bringing fresh flowers to them in wheelbarrows, one of them forgetting to take off his leather cap till he was reminded by the eldest of the women, without humour. The decorations were the most extraordinary floral displays Jack had ever seen – mind you till that moment his closest encounter with flowers was the small and rather weary bunch by his mum's bed when he had visited her in hospital. Everyone said those were "lovely."

Carrying on round the panorama, in the choir itself were around ten boys and ten girls, in beautiful black cassocks and pressed white surplices, full regalia for a last-minute rehearsal ahead of the services starting soon. They looked and sounded divine, though their choirmaster didn't agree, stopping them constantly at the same place with a rap of his stick on the lectern, and making them start over and over again. Luckily it was a good bit, everyone was enjoying it, and that delicious trill stuck in Jack's head for the rest of the day, not unpleasantly at all.

Further along, a group of a dozen men and women in their seventies, eighties and probably nineties stood at the end of some pews, leaning on the chairs and talking. Jack thought, 'these people have done this for the last fifty years, every Sunday, gradually they are the last left standing because their friends die every week. And the young leave them to it.' They were chatting, gossiping, occasionally laughing, waving the odd stick for emphasis. And they were blocking the pews so no-one else could get through, keeping themselves the best seats in the house, well earned.

Elsewhere, a superior team of older and more world-weary altar boys was preparing the priest's accessories and fussing officiously around the pulpit, while their eager junior versions, prattling excitedly, spread out industriously through the pews distributing hymn books and orders of service.

Around the door there were a half a dozen kiosks and booths, selling cards, hymnals, models of relics, figurines, artefacts, all manner of Catholic texts, pamphlets, lives of saints, guidebooks and even sweets and drinks – all doing a lively business as it was now past 8.00am and the early-bird tourists were starting to drift in, some stopping to shop before even looking around or realising where they were.

In the nearest corner to the right were the confessionals – four of them, ornate wooden cubicles, beautifully carved with putti and cherubim: all were being used, with queues of penitents already in place; some, obviously with clear consciences, were light-hearted and chattering, while others looked more serious, if not actually timorous, as Jack tried to imagine the events that had brought them there this week. Then 'O Lord,' he thought; then 'No no no.' He had spotted Milo in the line for the confessional closest to him. 'What are you doing there, brother? Literally, no good can come of this; not today.'

157

Milo was next in line, so Jack walked quickly towards him, speeding up as he saw an old woman leaving the confessional Milo was queuing for, and almost breaking into a run as Milo stepped forward and reached his hand out for the door handle. Jack arrived in the nick of time – if you are on the side of the wrong angels – and smoothly grasped Milo's outstretched arm, wheeling him gently but firmly away and walking with him up the aisle like a devoted nephew supporting an aged relative or a kindly nurse persuading a wandering patient back to bed.

The person who was behind Milo in the line, a middle-aged woman dressed all in black, with rosary, head-cover and all the penitential paraphernalia, stood up and called after them.

"What are you doing? Let the boy alone if he wants to confess – why are you taking him away?"

Milo turned his head back, but Jack kept his down and ploughed on down the aisle, not allowing his friend to miss a step.

"Stop," she shouted now, "bring him back and let him see the father."

Jack cursed under his breath, I will not say what, but we know that any expletive in church, however mild, is equal to a hundred swearwords outside. He didn't look up to see how many people were staring at them, but he couldn't stop himself hearing her voice – yes it was shrill, sorry – echoing around the vastness.

"This is the last thing we need, drawing attention to ourselves. What the hell were you thinking, Milo?"

He'd started speaking as they approached the portico but fortunately they'd passed fully through the door and were outside the cathedral, if only by a metre or two, before he said the actual hell word, or who knows what chaos might have broken loose, what bolt might have hit them. As it was, the sudden morning sun did strike them hard and made them blind.

They could not see, and barged into and through a party of visitors, slurring apologies right and left like drunks leaving a bar. Then they were out and away staggering into a dark side street where they leant their backs against the cold morning wall and Milo whimpered, "Sorry, Jack, sorry sorry sorry."

Jack put his arms around Milo, awkwardly, at ninety degrees, hugging neither from front or back, but clumsily from the side. It had been an established fact they never embraced but under the emotional weight of the last few days this was changing fast.

The powers of recovery for eighteen-year-old boys are amazing, both physical and mental; after thirty seconds they pulled away from each other, abashed but repairing already.

"We can talk about it later, if you want," said Jack, "for now, just say I'm Spartacus."

"OK, you're Spartacus."

"No, you say I'm Spartacus."

"I just did."

It was a hackneyed routine, but the familiarity was as soothing as five minutes in an oxygen mask.

"Ha ha ha," Jack did a hilarious pantomime chuckle, including hands moving up and down on his tummy, "so, what I need right now, this absolute second, is a cigarette."

"Hail, Brutus."

"Yes indeed, except I don't think you can hail Brutus, I think you have to seek him."

"I looked for him in the kiosks inside the cathedral, but the closest they had was a tobacco tin in the shape of a crusader's tomb, with a dog curled around the feet of its master."

"Nice," said Jack, "but you're losing focus, perhaps from want of nicotine."

"Not at all, my friend, for here, as I speak, is Brutus."

They had turned the corner and found themselves facing a magnificent tobacconist and newsagent, newly thrown open for the day for their personal gratification. Instinctively they both covered their eyes with their hands, for directly in front of them was an impressive display of the great newspapers of the world, from Die Welt and La Stampa to El Correo and The Daily Telegraph, the latter providing the transfused plasma that pulses through the needy veins of ex-pat Englanders, bringing them back to life each morning with carefully measured doses of two-day old cricket statistics.

"Can we see how Essex got on against Northamptonshire?" asked Milo, wistfully.

"No, do not look, *mon ami*. The bowling figures of Mr Barry Knight are of course of immense interest, but remember, it is the 'No Look No Listen' pact. If you catch even a glance, you will be turned into a pile of dust as the news filtrates your body. Keep walking through the news, look neither right nor left: it is all *tabac*, no *actualité*, nothing but the *tabac*, OK? If we don't look, nothing bad can happen."

"Can *have* happened," Milo corrected, "never let the perfect be the enemy of the pluperfect."

"Who made you the grammar police? Though in this instance I find your wit arresting, and I am pleased to see that your years of learning have finally borne fruit, culminating in this single jest. For you, I fear this may be peak persiflage: the rest of your life will descend gradually into disappointment and despair at the inability to repeat such bantering brilliance. Revel in the

160

moment of your glory."

Eyes covered, they stumbled over the threshold under the bemused gaze of the shopkeeper and headed for the cigarette counter. Unlike England, where the age limit was fourteen, in France it was compulsory to smoke from the morning of your twelfth birthday, so there was no chance of being asked for any form of identification. They purchased six packets of cigarettes and two boxes of matches and made their getaway with the heady joy of gentleman safecrackers shinning down the ivy with the Duchess's jewels stuffed down their trousers.

"Thank you, Brutus," said Milo.

"Oh yes, Brutus has served us well this day. Hail, Brutus."

So saying, they lit up, inhaled greedily, and let out the smoke gradually with synchronised groans of pleasure and satisfaction. Jack mused futuristically that "this is so good it has to be bad for you; I bet in a few years' time it will be made illegal in many situations as increasingly we become aware of the horrible health issues associated with smoking. Soon, children, especially, will be urgently requested not to take it up, and the sanctimonious will begin to describe it as a 'loathsome and filthy habit.' Children to come, and all future inhabitants of planet Earth, I entreat you, do not smoke!"

Meanwhile, in the past, in the perfect, and oftentimes in the pluperfect, Milo took another deep deep drag on his cigarette, and sighed blissfully while giving the elaborate eyeroll he reserved for Jack's wildest forms of fancy.

As he got that lovely 'hot' feeling in his lungs Jack whispered through his exhaling lips, "All the joy of sex without the sex." Milo nodded knowingly, and encouraged a smile to play around his lips, without having a clue what Jack meant. With goodwill, the bond of mutual misapprehension is just as strong as a shared understanding.

The splendidly brassy clock above the fancy hat shop next door told them it was now 9.10am, and they had agreed to be at the station by 9.30am to simulate arrival on the earlier train. Jack consulted the small map at the back of the guide. "OK it is about a kilometre, we'd better move." They went back into Place Etienne Dolet to cross to the road they needed but stayed in the shade around the edges of the precinct rather than walking straight across in the bright sunshine, just in case anyone had noticed them from the ruckus earlier.

Finding the route, they pulled their hats down hard and went for a quick stroll up the boulevard, ignoring the over-groomed dogs and the kids with slicked-down hair being dragged off for Sunday at their grandparents. Their timing was perfect, and they slipped inside the station building just as the 9.30 arrived from Paris, ready to slip out again with the crowd as it disembarked. The descending hoard turned out to be first a travelling salesman, early for the working week, with at least two layers too many of outer clothing for the warmth of the day and three cardboard suitcases for two hands to carry: then second a hundred-year-old woman with a fox collar, a fascinator and a parasol half her age, bearing a Pekinese dog under one arm, who appeared out of the steam like a figure emerging from a Manet. Jack had never seen a parasol and Milo had never seen a Pekinese; this was turning into a day of constant and amazing discoveries.

They cleverly inserted themselves among the throng after it passed through the ticket barrier, and the four of them left the station together, emerging into the bright Bourges morning.

"This looks like a fabulous town, Francois," said Milo, in his best bad French. Jack nodded in admiration of his skilful mangling.

"Ah, Scott, according to my trusty guidebook, this is a city, not a town, it contains one of the most noble and ancient – and magnificent – cathedrals in all of Europe."

"Well I never," said Milo. "That would be truly worth seeing – if

162

only we had the time to make such a leisurely visit within our famously intense schedule."

"*La prochaine fois.*"

"*Certainment.*"

They both used the toilet, as people so seldom do in books, and then took a table at the station café. Sadly, and it gives me no pleasure to mention it, this café, like so many railway station cafés, was not very charming, being rather run-down and ownerless, like the rented car that no-one bothers to wash. Just as it lacked a regular owner it also lacked regular customers; perhaps people in transit are perceived not to need or desire comfort, cleanliness and civility, and if that is the understanding, our little café was very successfully failing to supply those items.

The café had tables both inside and out, so having been careful to secure seats on the pavement with a wide view of the approaches and parking spaces, Jack and Milo lit cigarettes, nibbled at the watery brew the weary waiter brought, and carelessly surveilled, just as if they were waiting for somebody they didn't know to pick them up.

After forty minutes, the same van they had descended from three hours earlier arrived in the little parking area, and a squat man got out. I am not saying small, exactly, because parts of him were extremely large – he had arms like a brick-carrier and legs like an Olympic wrestler. It is just that there was not a lot of body in between, as though the maker had wedged the top and bottom together without much thought for the middle. He had a leather cap that had not been removed from his head since World War Two; a leather gilet over some kind of homespun shirt; heavy woollen trousers that he had pulled on a year or two before the cap; and boots of a type so ill-fitting and poorly suited to his work that they might have been gratefully borrowed from the last corpse he had happened upon.

"You will not have much trouble identifying Claude," Jean had said in the van, "and you might be surprised by him. He is to be trusted, he is a brother of one of my uncle's wives, so a kind of relation. He worked for my dad for over twenty-five years, and I managed to get him to transfer to me about five years ago. He is smart but pretends not to be, and really quite well off, but he would hate it if you guessed that. He's a bit of a local hero round here because of some things he did in the occupation, but don't let on I told you that, he hates that too."

Jack and Milo had already settled their bill, so they grabbed their bags and walked down to where Claude was waiting outside the van, smoking. As they got closer they noticed that, whereas Claude's face and arms were a rich yellow from his decades of outdoor work and hard living, his right hand, and the right side of his face, were a slightly deeper shade, a kind of leathery tan. "Don't stare!" Jean had warned them. "He is so sensitive. Half his face is rather stained from having a cigarette wedged into the right side of his mouth from dawn to night for forty years, working, driving, eating, drinking. The man has been on fire for longer than the tomb of the unknown soldier – he's gradually turning himself into a living block of charcoal."

Of course, as you know yourself, when you are told not to stare, it becomes not only irresistible but inevitable you will do so. Claude laughed out loud when he saw the boys' eyes transfixed on his parti-coloured visage. "I bet Jean told you I am very sensitive about my face?" he rasped, "That's his best joke. Actually thinking about it, his only joke. It doesn't bother me. I don't have any mirrors, and no-one is queuing up to kiss me. I sacrificed my career as a movie star because I wanted to smoke a hundred cigarettes a day. We all make choices, right?"

Claude's voice was different from any noise Milo had ever heard, maybe like a hoover sucking through a wet washing-up cloth, though honestly speaking he had never heard that either. He took a rough guess that it might be something to do with the smoking.

"You guys are earlier than I thought, what happened? And who is who?"

Jack stepped forward. "I am Francois, I am very pleased to meet you Claude."

Claude was looking very hard at Jack. Jack didn't quite know what to do, he shuffled around a bit, maybe Claude was always like this with strangers?

"We started out on our journey very promptly," Jack continued, "so we found ourselves arriving with the first train rather than the second." Jack tried never to waste a lie unnecessarily; avoiding them could cause linguistic contortions, but Claude was not there to query his syntax.

"I am Scott, the American friend," said Milo. "I can say 'My Name Is Scott,' after that it is a bit *comme ci comme ça*."

"I am Claude, as you know. I am pleased to pick you up. Jump in, I will take you to Jean."

And that was that. One minute they were in the van, dozing; Claude smoked three or four putrid cigarettes; and the next minute they were getting out in the driveway of what they knew must be Forest Lodge, being introduced to Jean, and pretending they had never met him before. Really, so far, it seemed as though the plan was flawless.

"It is so good of you to come at such short notice," Jean was babbling, and they were blathering back, "We are delighted to have such an opportunity, we are keen to work hard, thank you so much for taking us on."

Claude passed the van keys to Jean and said goodbye to the boys – it was just the one word. He again gave Jack another really hard look on the way, making sure no-one else noticed his interest. They both thanked him effusively, repeating how nice it had been to meet him, hoping very much to see him again soon, but while they were still speaking the gate had swung closed and his not unfriendly back was halfway up the lane heading on foot towards his next job.

Once the fake greetings were complete for any watching eyes at the windows, Jean walked the boys out of earshot to the gate of the lane, pretending to show them the layout of the grounds and access roads. He took the opportunity to update them on tasks he had completed in the morning, including visiting the stage they were building at Hill House to check on progress, looking at some menus with the caterers in the light of the new budget, and seeing Madame Jestique to confirm the details of her employment.

They completed the walk around the grounds and Jean turned to the boys: "We'd better go in. Are you ready, Francois? Are you ready, Scott?"

Nervous thumbs up.

Jean rang a big bell at the front door to let everyone know they were coming in but used his key rather than waiting for someone to open up. "Hi, all," he shouted very loudly to the whole house from the hallway, "we're here. See you in the kitchen."

Jean led Milo and Jack through to a massive kitchen, with wood-burning stove, a walk-in larder, and a huge table in the middle with at least ten chairs tucked around it. The room was very run down, but had obviously been cleaned scrupulously, and the kitchen tools and equipment all looked a lot younger than the building. It was nice, exciting – indoor camping on a grand scale. Jean explained that this room was the main communal living area, but all of them, including Scott and Francois, had their own large bedrooms upstairs. "It is shabby, but you'll have plenty of space and privacy – you'll need it because you'll all be living on top of each other here for the next three months."

As Jack and Milo were admiring the setup, which they thought to themselves was custom-designed for outlaws on the run – renegade chic – the clatter was heard in the passageway of people coming down the stairs at a variety of speeds. Into the room at intervals came the three incumbents, and here I will introduce them in the order of arrival:

- First came Columbine, named Amelie. Jack and Milo tried not to stare, but it is hard to avoid eye contact with someone you are being introduced to. This was a girl who grabbed your attention, examined it at arm's length between finger and thumb, then languidly put it back in the jar with a bite taken out. She had a mass of red hair, unruly but fabulous, like a pre-Raphaelite model. 'That is enough hair,' thought Jack, 'to fill four pillowcases.' In a thought within a thought, barely reaching the surface, he saw himself snuggling into the pillows, but sweetly. From what Jean had said previously she must be about seventeen, but that looked like an extremely young seventeen. Had she really left school? The same age as Milo, Jack calculated, but obviously considerably younger than his own eighteen years and two days. She had small, perfectly delicate features – to say features like a doll would be accurate, but would give totally the wrong impression, of something static, blank and fixed, when this face was alive, intelligent and dynamic. She said hello to Jean, then looked beyond to the two new arrivals. Milo got a sweet smile and a half-curtsy, before she moved on to Jack and they locked eyes and just held the look for much too long. Jean did not notice but Milo was already thinking 'O Dear.' Amelie was just about to say something when she was interrupted by the next person rolling into the room.

- The second player, Pantaloon, named Albert, was large and heavy, and thumped in, a few seconds behind his sister, a distance I would reckon he had maintained for most of their lives. He had boy versions of Amelie's beauty, which seemed not to work quite so well, leaving him looking a little wan, his thinner hair rather pale, his face attractive but a little weak atop his beefy bones. He looked at Jack and Milo but was not tempted to speak before Amelie; and while he was waiting for her to begin, they were further interrupted by the next player.

- The third and last actor to come in, Harlequin, named Karl, was tall and blond haired – almost white – with blue eyes and chiselled features straight out of the Big Book of Square-Jawed Clichés. He sauntered in, hands in pockets, the very dictionary entry for Confidence; a dark red rich confidence with an intense bouquet that he ceaselessly poured from a great bottle until it spilt over the edge of the glass onto a white tablecloth, making an ever-expanding crimson stain you could never quite remove before finally dripping down and gradually covering the floor. As Jean had mentioned, he was significantly older than the others: maybe twenty-five, thought Jack, uncharitably. What's he doing here?

It was mutual dislike at first sight for Jack and Karl, and not the mild kind. Karl didn't dislike Milo yet, but only because he hadn't spotted him behind Jean. To make it worse, on entering the room Karl moved to the side of Amelie, and as they stood much too closely together, Jack saw the backs of their hands brush discretely against each other. 'Oh Yuk,' thought Jack, 'don't touch her! You can't do that, she's a kid!'

He kicked himself for being late to the party, and would also have liked to kick brother Albert, who should surely have been standing between them but seemed totally unaware of their intimacy.

He kicked himself again, this time on both shins at once, when he remembered that the brilliant draft scenario he was soon going to present made Columbine and Harlequin lovers in the first act. Panicking, he began the rewrites in his head.

Superficially the meeting was all bonhomie. If Jean noticed any tensions between the boys he pretended not to, being a busy and anxious man who just wanted to achieve his end goal without a lot of personnel issues along the way. Everyone was quickly introduced to everyone, and Jean began to get some lunch for them all while they chatted. "Don't expect me to do this every day! It is just a treat to welcome the new guys." He'd brought in some baguettes, salami, cheese and fruit.

"No salami for me, if it is OK, please, Jean," said Amelie, "I'm vegetarian."

"Me too!" said Jack, "What a coincidence!"

Jean and Milo's chins hit the metaphorical table with a synchronised thump which they were surprised the others didn't hear. This was completely brazen even by Jack's standards.

"I cannot stand the thought of the animal suffering," Amelie continued. "I am sure as a farmer, Jean, you must find that rather silly."

Amelie was clearly a young lady who generally expected people to succumb to her charms quite quickly, but if she was hoping Jean would say, "No no no, I find your standpoint absolutely endearing," she would have been somewhat underwhelmed by his grunt of response. What he really wanted to say was, 'As a farmer, as you ask, I tried to kill a pig this morning. I hit it twice with an axe, but it wouldn't die, so I shot it. I sold the corpse to the butcher in La Chapelle so I could pay for the sets, the props, the costumes and for the make-up you will be putting on in a short while.' But that wasn't entirely true, and, in any case, he didn't want to distract the talent with the petty details of their busy impresario's working day.

What he actually said was, "It is a sad necessity that my work occasionally involves a little slaughter." It probably did not come out quite right; sometimes he could sense he was trying a tad too hard with the diplomacy.

"For me, it is about Buddhism," said Jack, whom Milo felt at this stage was either horrendously sleep-deprived or who might otherwise have accidentally consumed or inhaled something wildly hallucinogenic. "I respect the soul of the beast. But, by the sound of it, I definitely do not want to be reincarnated in Jean's farmyard."

This got a bit of a laugh (from all except Karl) and moved them past the tiny froideur between Amelie and Jean. 'This is going to be a tough group,' thought Milo, 'and not just for comedy.' He was tempted to ask Jack to share with the team the latest Buddhist Pork Pie recipes but decided to sit back and enjoy the ride instead.

Jean asked, over his shoulder, in order to hide his grin, "For the vegetarians, instead of salami, would you like me to make you an omelette?" Amelie politely looked to Jack for a decision, but as he had not encountered such a question in all his forty-five seconds of vegetarianism, and as he knew next to nothing about the guiding principles of his new regime, he quickly batted it back to her, "After you, Amelie." She said no, thank you, and Jack concurred, leaving him none the wiser about whether he was officially allowed to eat eggs or not, and rather regretting his snap dietary declaration when everyone except Amelie was served a much bigger meal than him. But it would be worth it, because in Jackworld, their mutual sacrifice would inevitably bring them together.

As ever, Jean's food preparation was outstanding, and they had an excellent lunch which also included dishes of olives and pickles, a jar of artichokes and a tomato salad with a *vinaigrette aux fines herbes* (Jean explained, when asked by Milo). During the meal, the backstories of Scott and Francois were not over-interrogated, though Karl was on several occasions about to ask follow-up questions which were headed off by Jean passing platters or offering drinks.

Everyone made a special effort to communicate with Scott the American, some by speaking slowly, some by speaking loudly, and actually Milo found he could understand much more than he would have believed. Whenever Jack thought he might be struggling, he translated, but I won't bore you here by repeating those bits, as you have enough to put up with already.

When they were finishing the cheese and fruit, Jean served them a deliciously vigorous java. Jack wondered if it was much too robust for Amelie, but before he could say anything his inner dick-alarm fortuitously warned him that a seventeen-year-old girl might not welcome even his own masterful protection from the evils of a cup of coffee. Pondering this lucky escape, Jack was about to light up a cigarette, but Karl, at last with a chance to assert seniority (after all this time!), intervened bluntly: "We have agreed not to smoke in this house, sorry."

Jack looked around the room, as if counting the ballots. "Who voted?" he asked innocently.

"We all agreed," said Karl, glaring at Albert to keep his mouth shut; it was obvious he was the weak link and would just as soon smoke, but also clear he was in awe of Karl.

Jean said quickly, defusing the situation, "I guess it was 3-0, so even if you two want to smoke, it only makes it 3-2. Don't look at me for a vote, I am not living here! I presume, though, it is fine for anyone to smoke in their own room, so long as the door is shut and the window open, all OK with that? Great. And down here, if you want a fag, the garden is only five metres away…"

Jean then went on to make the announcement that there were to be major changes to the planning after losing the two original student actors and following the arrival of *les Parisiens*.

"OK so Francois here, as he has mentioned, has a lot of background and some experience with the theatre, this is one of the reasons I was so happy to offer him the position. Fortunately for us, he has also made a deep personal study into the history and culture of the Harlequinade. So, as well as being a co-worker here with us on the Experience, he is going to be boss of the Harlequinade, OK?"

When Jean said "OK" it was distinctly rhetorical: Karl was about to say something, but even he lost his nerve when Jean placed the "OK" squarely ten centimetres from his divinely sculpted chin.

So, give us ten minutes while I get the lads sorted out upstairs, and then we will get going, all right? We'll see you in the Hall."

Jack and Milo collected their hold-alls from where they'd left them in the hallway, and Jean took them upstairs to their bedrooms.

"Actually there is nothing specifically designated for you," he said, wandering up one of the corridors that led off the landing. "As I recall, this room is empty, this is Amelie's room, this next to it is Karl, and then Albert. And then," turning around and pointing across the central landing to the opposite side of the house, "the whole corridor on the other side of the building is empty, another four bedrooms. So you can take whatever you want."

The corridor ran in a straight line across the whole of the second floor, divided by the hallway in the middle. At each end of the corridor was a shared bathroom and toilet; the bedrooms just had sinks in them.

"Bed linen and blankets are in this cupboard," Jean went on, "take what you need. There is a cleaner who comes in once a week, but she does the kitchen, toilets and hall only; she's not here to clean your rooms or change your beds, but she'll take laundry if you leave it out. All the bedrooms have bolts on the insides if you want to secure your door at night, but there are no locks and keys. I'll see you downstairs."

Jack thought about taking the last room in the already inhabited corridor, for being drawn some reason he couldn't quite put his finger on to being next to Amelie. But he was hampered by last-minute loyalty and forced to agree with himself that he should probably stick with his friend of fifteen years rather than a girl he had known for less than fifteen minutes. 'You're a diamond guy, Francois,' he thought, sincerely meaning it.

The rooms Milo and Jack eventually chose were at the far end of the opposite corridor. They were large, and they had fantastic views over the fields towards Jean's farm, rather than being tight to

172

the woods behind. Without unpacking, they dumped their bags, washed their hands, and headed down to join the troupe.

The room called the Hall at the Lodge was an oddly magnificent chamber, with ornate fireplaces and extravagant detailing. Clearly the forestry managers in receipt of this grace and favour residence had had considerable status in their day; the area was large enough to hold a small dance or a dinner for around twenty-four people. Jack could see that the room and the furniture in it had been well adapted for theatrical use, guessing Jean had done that some time ago to create this dedicated rehearsal space. A dressing, costume and make-up corner had been created at one end, and there was a sizeable raised platform at the other, with some lights above and curtains behind and in front forming a stage big enough for the actors to work on comfortably. There was an upright piano facing the front of the platform, about two metres back, and set below it at floor level, so the pianist could observe the action at all times while playing.

'That's perfect,' thought Milo, 'how does Jean get to all this stuff?'

The student group had found extra chairs and formed them into a circle in the middle of the room, leaving empty seats for the latecomers. One of them had seen pictures of actors in rehearsal, and they sat in circles, so this was very authentic. At that moment Madame Jestique also entered; Jean had managed to book her in for a few hours to meet the complete team for the first time. She arrived with Claude, who had given her a lift and now decided to stick around for the fun. He parked himself comfortably in a chair against the wall from where he could observe the whole room; watching him, Milo thought, 'This is not an employee, he's more like Jean's family.' Everyone politely stood as Madame Jestique was introduced by Jean to the ring of actors, by name only at this stage, not by reputation. Then she took her place at the piano stool, turning it to face the troupe, while Jean remained standing to give a short preamble.

"Good afternoon, everyone; and welcome to the new generation of the Harlequinade!

"Francois, you and I have managed to discuss your new ideas for the play on the telephone over the past few days.

"Would you like to give everybody a brief resume of the new scenario you have brought with you today?"

Jack was not expecting to be the centre of attention quite so quickly; Jean was apparently not a lover of the over-effusive introduction. So, clearly, this is what he meant when he said, "Stay smart" and "Make it up as you go along"; he had only missed out "While you're flapping around in the deep end."

'Here I am, making it up,' he thought, but hopefully did not say, as he rose.

"Thanks, everyone, for listening. I have sketched out a version of the Harlequinade that I am suggesting we work on as an ensemble for the next two days, improvising within the framework I lay down."

Right now, Jack was offering votive blessings to Thalia, the comedic muse, for the fact that he had taken Drama O Level. An essential part of the course, in his view, had been the ingestion of half a ton of jargon that he could regurgitate in a wide variety of voices, tones and timbres in ever-ascending levels of pretentiousness. Miss Prendergast would be so proud if she could see him now. ["Reach deep inside yourself, Jack; use what you find."]

"By Wednesday we should be able to lock in what we have developed. Then, Wednesday night and Thursday will be dress rehearsals of this fully evolved version, with Madame Jestique very kindly working with us all week on the accompaniments, which will be finalised at the same time."

"So," went on Jack, making sure he had retained their attention, "this is the idea. First the cast of characters:

- Pantaloon is a rich old man with a beautiful daughter, Columbine

[Karl barely stifled a yawn at this.]

- He has a guest in his house, Harlequin, noble son of an old and aristocratic friend of Pantaloon's, from a far country

[Karl perked up a tiny bit at "noble son."]

- Pantaloon has two servants, Pierrot and Clown; the first resourceful and clever; the second a hopeless but loveable rogue, devoted to his friend Pierrot"

Jack looked around to make sure everyone was following, while being careful not make specific eye contact or solicit any questions.

"The idea is to borrow from many past versions, while making a show that is relatable and relevant to the modern audience."

Jack was not even sure himself if he was being totally serious at this point. Karl made a gagging motion behind his hands, which Jack feigned not to see in the interests of mature creative collaboration.

"The plot is this. Harlequin is a self-regarding, spoiled man in his mid-twenties, who is being indulged by Pantaloon, a snobbish old gentleman who hopes to curry favour with Harlequin and his father, an old friend and business contact.

"To fulfil this aim, Pantaloon has been allowing his beautiful and somewhat innocent daughter, really no more than a child, barely seventeen, to be courted by the preening narcissist, ignoring their age difference, and not realising that he has no honourable intentions towards her."

Jack was very much following Jean's instruction to make it up as he went along. He was waving a piece of paper in front of him, but it might as well have been blank for all the relationship it had

175

between what was on it and what he was saying. Jean and Milo were both looking a little bemused but trying not to show it. Karl was staring hard at Jack, eye-darts flying thick and fast; but Jack was able to ignore the evil looks while at the same time letting Karl know he had seen them.

"The young girl, trusting her father, and wishing to please him, has received Harlequin's advances, but she is naively confused by his designs.

"Pierrot has for several years been her kind and loyal friend. He is the same age as Columbine, perhaps a year older, and in many respects, though she a mistress, and he a servant, they have grown up together like brother and sister who might one day become lovers."

This hadn't come out quite right, but they all nodded forgivingly, understanding what he meant.

"Clown is Pierrot's best friend, a fellow servant. He is attending Harlequin as his valet during his visit. The cheeky rascal cannot keep his fingers to himself and uncovers on the writing desk a letter Harlequin is writing to his brother, who is at home in the far country. He reads part of it out loud:

"'The old fool is actually helping me to woo his precious daughter.'

"'My game among these peasants is beginning to bore me, but I am intent on picking a little fruit before I return.'

"'I will be back for my wedding to the Contessa next month.'

"Clown, though a *petit méchant*, loves Columbine and Pierrot – they are his family, for he has no other. He is shocked, distraught, angry. Suddenly Harlequin is at the door, Clown drops the letter and leaps out of the window to avoid detection. Landing in a bush, he brushes himself down and runs with the news to Pierrot.

"Pierrot and Clown determine to foil the devilish intent and reveal the monster for what he is. But how?

"Pierrot finds a huge blond wig and takes one of Columbine's gowns. That evening, while Columbine is sitting dutifully with her father in his study, reading to him from his favourite book of sermons, Clown helps Pierrot to dress up as Columbine, with much pantomime play between them.

"As night falls, Pierrot-as-Columbine stands on the balcony of Columbine's room, waiting. When Harlequin comes out into the courtyard to smoke and drink his brandy, Pierrot calls out to him in a soft girl's voice; he looks up, he sees the hair and frock in the dim candlelight, and a finger coming over the balcony beckons him up.

"Delighted with this turn of events, and of course not at all surprised that the girl should desire him, Harlequin climbs up the vine and over the balcony. Entering Columbine's room, he sees a figure in the bed under the coverlet. Again, the finger emerges, beckoning.

"He takes off his Harlequin suit and drops it on the floor; and clad only in spotted knickers, he enters the bed. As he does, Pierrot-as-Columbine jumps out the other side, grabs Harlequin's clothes and runs out of the door, locking it. Outside the door he quickly removes the gown and wig, and Clown, who has been waiting in the passage, begins to loudly bang a gong, shouting 'Fire, Fire.'

"Pierrot and Clown run downstairs and enter the courtyard from one side just as Pantaloon and Columbine enter from the other through the French windows of Pantaloon's study. A passing Policeman, in the form of Jean here, also runs into the courtyard from the street outside, shouting: 'Fire, did someone shout fire?!!'

"Unable to get out through the bedroom door, Harlequin runs onto Columbine's balcony in his spotted knickers and in a panic starts to climb over, before suddenly noticing when he is halfway down that everyone is beneath in the courtyard, watching him. He tries to scramble back up, but it is too late; Pierrot and the Policemen grab his legs and pull him down.

"The Policeman asks everyone what is happening. Harlequin, hands covering his shrunken genitals, rages that Columbine has tricked him, but Pantaloon says his daughter has not left his side all night, and that Harlequin is a bounder, and worse, to be hiding naked in the chamber of a schoolgirl.

"Thus finally, with a little extra business (we can work it out later), Harlequin is handcuffed and marched off to jail by the Policeman; and, of course, Columbine suddenly realises that she has always loved Pierrot and Pierrot has always loved her, and, regardless of Pantaloon's snobbery, we all know it will end happily."

There was silence after he finished, and Jack immediately experienced the terror of the scorned. But then Madame Jestique hammered a congratulatory flourish into the piano, and while the notes still echoed, Albert, Jean, Milo and Amelie jumped up and clapped. And then they all cheered, with Claude joining in the hurrahs from a seated position before even he got up to walk across and give Jack a pat on the back, of a strength which gleefully sent him flying.

The collective response was far more than Jack had expected, so much so that it almost overwhelmed him. So this is theatre. darling! Everyone loves me! 'They were exaggerating, of course,' thought Jack, 'probably from the relief of having a version to work with at last; but if the excitement has the effect of bringing everyone together, well, that is half the job done.'

The last person left seated was the quietly brooding Karl, but when he saw his amigos Amelie and Albert both metaphorically and then literally slapping Francois on the back, he had no choice but to pretend to go along with the congratulations. Leaping to his feet, he switched his features to the 'charming' setting, held his hand

178

out to Jack and said, "What a great farce, I just hope our troupe can do it justice, my friend. I love the slapstick, if we get it right the audience are going to love it. Forgive me if I moan just slightly, I think you have set me the biggest test of all, to play such a nasty guy."

The others murmured in friendly sympathy, followed by a muttering swell of encouragement that said, "If anyone can rise to the challenge of playing a boorish egotistical predator it will be you, Karl." Milo smiled benignly within, knowingly exactly what his friend had done.

Did Jack give Karl the international raised-double-eyebrow sign for "Really? A big test? I'm just surprised you're not complaining about being typecast." If he did, the expression was gone in an instant, no-one else noticed, and even Karl wasn't sure.

"What about the script," asked Albert, in a nervous groan, "we haven't got long to learn our lines."

"No worry there, Albert," replied Jack, "the added magic is that other than a couple of notable exceptions, like perhaps the cry of 'Fire' or reading part of a letter out, this play has no lines, no script, and a very broad acting technique, big gestures and you can be as melodramatic as you like. We could describe it as mime, but don't let that concern you, actually this style is very typical of Harlequinades over the centuries, it is part of a great tradition."

Again, this went down very well, a relief to those who had been scared about memorising blocks of dialogue, and also to those who hadn't had much acting experience: Jack had made their lives a great deal easier, while not spoiling the fun and thrill of doing the show. Making people's lives more contented is a most endearing quality, and Jack loved being most endeared.

"The mime will be in the atmosphere of the Silent Movies. And what is very exciting for me and for all of us is that Jean has this morning secured us the services of the wonderful Madame Jestique to provide the background, the emotion, the dialogue in music, using the style of the old black and white films – like Charlie Chaplin and Harold Lloyd – you recall?"

Madame Jestique fingered eight bars from Safety Last to prod their memories.

"The guy hanging from the clock!" cried Amelie, "My Grandad *loved* those movies. I am a big fan of all those silent stars – what a fabulous idea!"

Praise from this source aroused a warm feeling inside and just below Jack's chest, though naturally he outwardly exhibited nothing but a modest shrug.

"Jean informs me that Madame Jestique worked as a pianist in the movie theatres and pantomimes when she was, if I may say so," he said with an elegant bow towards her, "in the earlier years of her career. She has also performed regularly in this style in revivals and at film festivals – as well as playing in the local churches, rehearsing ballet and dance in the schools. Once Jean agreed the idea for the silent movie ambience, he mentioned she would be the perfect person to provide the music."

Madame Jestique at this stage had had quite enough praise and started paying loudly to divert and distract: a ragtime style, Maple Leaf Rag, jaunty and syncopated. The kids, and Jean, still on their feet from saluting Jack, started gently bopping around; the bopping gradually changed to boogieing; then the boogieing quickly turned into the whole ring of them dancing together, lively, laughing and excited, in jubilant exaltation. A few days ago, everyone's mood had been so low that two people they trusted ran away without saying goodbye; and now everybody was inspired with confidence; they were suddenly engaged in an enterprise that had the prospect of success, the likelihood of enjoyment, and perhaps even the possibility of a triumph.

Milo and Jean span each other round and round, chortling; Jack reached out to Amelie to do the same, but before their hands could touch, Karl was between them, his back to Jack, facing Amelie and taking her by the waist, making it appear he had never even noticed the attempted embrace he had so skilfully frustrated. Instead of joining the innocent abandonment of the kermesse, Karl pulled Amelie into him, drew her head onto his shoulder, and attempted an inapt slow dance, which was awkward and arhythmic. Yet Amelie bowed to his lead and shuffled around with him. Jack, watching, could see she was uncomfortable but flattered; seemingly prepared to trust the older man against her better judgement.

Madame Jestique slowed the tempo and brought the song to a gradual halt rather than a quick stop, so the dancers could unfurl and unravel and fall back into their seats nonchalantly without getting stranded on the dancefloor. If it finished well, they would want to do it again.

Jean clapped his hands to get attention. "I am very happy we're all so positive, this is a new beginning." Everyone applauded with him (except Karl) and stamped. "What I suggest, if Francois agrees, is we take a break now before having an early dinner ahead of tonight's rehearsal. I have arranged some food for our evening meal from the caterers up at Hill House, they're having their own rehearsals today and checking the equipment, ingredients and so on. As I'm going to pick up the food, I'll take Francois and Scott with me, we can have a quick tour of the Hut and the farm jetty on the way, so they will understand the locations and some of the other duties. When we're up at Hill House we can check that the stage and sets work for the new scenario and see if we want any changes to the backdrop and props. If we need to do any work, I'd like to brief the building team as soon as possible. Take some time for yourselves, we'll bring dinner back; we won't be too late – an hour and a half at the most, I reckon."

That said, Milo and Jack followed Jean outside, and they all got into his car, leaving the van in the drive. They lit cigarettes as they pulled away, was Jack's hand shaking slightly?

"All right?" Jean asked.

"Yes, just a bit of a shock to suddenly be running a show. It went better than I thought it would."

"It was great, Jack, I'm incredibly grateful. It almost seemed at one stage like you were completely busking there and changing it as you went along. I can't imagine why" [Milo in the back failed to suppress a hideous strangled laughing noise], "but it worked, and it's terrific.

"Now, back to reality, some details. All of you staying at the Lodge have the use of the van in the drive while you're living here, don't mess it up. There's another set of keys inside, and here is a personal set for you two.

"For housekeeping, I don't know if you noticed, there is a cashbox on the shelf just above the sink, I will put fifty francs in every time I remember for you to buy the things you need.

"And, just to indulge our star talent, Claude, Daphne or I will bring up a box every day of baguette, croissants, butter, milk and wine; it's easier and cheaper than sending you out to do it yourselves because you'll go to the wrong places and get cheated by the locals – and obviously being students you wake up too late."

Jean's farmhouse was less than a kilometre from the Lodge, and as he was chattering away they were already turning into his side road and driving under the Experience signs into the carpark. When they got out, instead of going up towards the house, Jean led them in the other direction towards the small barn they had observed when they'd first arrived; Jack's childhood fort and castle which now bore the sign **PAYMENT AND COSTUMES**. Fiddling with his massive bunch of keys, Jean found the right one, and let them all into a surprisingly large room.

"Remember it, Jack? We're calling it the Hut now, it's the commercial centre for the operation."

"Yes, I was telling Milo we used to sleep in here sometimes; it was falling apart then, and there was a lot more hay and a few more cows. You must have spent a fortune doing it up."

"Building and decorating doesn't cost a lot round here, Jack, especially when you do it yourself."

Directly before them, as they entered, was a reception and cash desk, and on the wall behind was a large sign with an arrow to the right **MEN'S COSTUMES** and an arrow to the left **WOMEN'S AND CHILDREN'S COSTUMES**.

"So this is the point of entry to the Experience," Jean was saying. "You come in, pay here, or submit your ticket, then go to the racks and mirrors to choose the kind of costume and accessories you would like and try everything on. We are still improving the stock of costumes and accessories, but we definitely have plenty to get going. What do you think? Take a look – try it out."

Jean carried on chattering while he worked around the desk, tidying up some papers and generally checking things over. The boys split to the different racks, stunned by the quality and range of jackets, shawls, hats, scarves, boots, gloves, spectacles, cravats and particularly by a completely amazing collection of waistcoats.

"The busiest period will be when the people come at opening time," Jean went on, "that's 10.00am for us and around 10.15am-10.30am for customers, to be strictly ready for the 11.00am start now everyone leaves together. I hope it will be quite good fun for everyone to dress up, to begin to be part of the Experience, to go back in history, to be a child again."

He turned round to emphasise his point and naturally found Jack and Milo doing the tango. Given the choice of a thousand characters, they had adopted their beloved Some Like It Hot; Jack Lemon in a cloche hat, 1920s frilled blouse and feather boa; Tony Curtis in a natty yachting cap and sailor jacket; and they were dancing, rather well, La Cumparsita. Milo seriously fancied himself a Tony

Curtis lookalike, in which fantasy he was tragically deluded.

"Jesus what the hell are you two doing now!"

"Oh, Osgood," lisped Jack sashaying over to Jean and flicking him with the boa, "don't be jealous."

Milo bent double with the giggles and choked out, "You're not a natural blond!"

"I can't marry you, Osgood," Jack whispered loudly, ripping off his cloche and doing a twirl in front of his cousin. "I'm a man."

Then they froze. Jean looked mortified. They'd gone too far.

After a beat of five Jean broke silence.

"Nobody's perfect."

Timing and Deception, the two legs of the comedy stool. He had known all along. The three folded up in a decent wave of laughter, then rolled outside into the sun for a recovery cigarette.

"OK focus now, please boys, we are already running late."

"Well you started it."

"I wasn't the one tangoing."

"You weren't the two tangoing. It takes two..."

Jean looked at them and shook his head, sadly, at the poverty of the humour and the time it wasted.

"Have you actually got any idea what I mean when I say focus?

They shuffled their feet and hung their heads performatively in a vain attempt to simulate remorse.

"As I already mentioned, Claude's daughter Daphne is running the cash desk and managing the Hut and carpark. She already works for me, so of course her participation is free as I am already paying her!" [As his accountant, Milo gave a look that dissociated himself entirely from that theory.] "I guess the best way to understand Daphne's position is Box Office Manager, or Back of House. The theatre, eh? We love it. So, she is responsible for the processing, making sure you lot do your jobs, guaranteeing that every customer is happy with their costume and with the boat trip.

"When we open in the mornings we estimate there will usually be a crush to get everyone ready, so at that time we are asking you actors to assist here in the Hut, and to help get everyone down to the jetty. For this part, you are not in costume, you have pink-and-white candy-stripe blazers and act like tour guides, answering questions, helping people out, leading the way, making sure everything goes on time. Does it sound OK?" [Purely rhetorical.] "When the guests have found their accessories and made characters, they then progress outside..." [he led them out, locking up behind them] "... and we take a nice walk. No riding now I have given up my magnificent horses; the wrangler was devastated this morning to have his participation cancelled. So, on we go, down the riverbank towards the barge with Tommy playing on the accordion – I mentioned him, right? The landing stage is about three hundred metres away, across parts of three fields, I think it makes a lovely walk on a summer day, though being honest Milo I will miss the romantic rocking and rustic smell I had imagined for the hay wains."

['All right, all right, Jean, let it go,' thought Jack, 'I am sure he feels bad enough already.']

"What if it's raining?" Milo asked.

"If there is a sudden shower, we have about twenty very large umbrellas," said Jean, with the triumphant tone of a man who had thought of everything, "families can have one each, and you young actors can hold them up for the old folks!"

185

Milo and Jack exchanged a look behind Jean's back that said, "I am not quite as confident as Jean that everyone loves spending their vacation paddling up to their ankles in rain under a leaky umbrella," but they did notice how well the woodchip paths had been laid, and that the footing was extremely good.

The jetty was pretty impressive. Jean had invested in yet more branding, a sign saying **EMBARK HERE FOR THE MEAULNES EXPERIENCE RIVER CRUISE**. And the whole area was festooned in bunting, fabric flowers and flags that then extended up the river on both banks, brightly coloured and gaily blowing in the breeze, vivid, exciting and joyful.

No barge was waiting to take them on the water. Jean informed them it was arriving Tuesday and was being delivered by river, of course, from the boatyard. "We will have a practice run that day, a complete rehearsal."

They took a stroll up the bank for about two hundred metres; they wouldn't have time to walk the whole of the course and still get back in good time with the dinner. At this point the river was not more than twenty-five metres across and very slow-moving; it had the appearance and atmosphere of a canal, and the tall trees either side often made it feel like it was running through a tunnel. Jean was childishly keen for them to see the fabulous bunting and homemade flowers and the way they had been decoratively pinned, staked, hung, flung, draped, wrapped, twisted and woven into the reeds, bushes and trees on both banks of the river as far as the eye could see. "The students worked on this for a few days, and I got many of my farmworkers to help out also. What do you think?"

"It's mad and beautiful, Jean," said Jack, much to Jean's relief and satisfaction, "I completely love it. You really have a feel for these things – this could easily have been grotesque and inappropriate, in fact it should be; but instead it is magical, totally in the Meaulnes *ambience*." As he spoke, a pair of swans glided by, ignoring them.

"Did you hire those too?"

"No, they come free with the river; but I had them painted white."

They returned to the car, and Jean drove them to a parking space close to the jetty at the other end of the river cruise, where the passengers would disembark for Hill House. It was a short trip, barely long enough to smoke a cigarette, across a small stone bridge, then basically turn right and two kilometres very close and parallel to the river. Pulling up, they left the vehicle, and Jean continued his exposition.

"We won't cruise too quickly in the barge because the voyage with its unhurried and peaceful mood is part of the dream. I don't think we will go much more than three or four kilometres an hour, so we will probably take thirty or thirty-five minutes between the jetties, that feels right to me. We can perfect the timing when we do our practices later in the week, and of course we can adjust it slightly either way when we get a feel for how much the guests enjoy the cruise. The accordionist will come on the boat and he'll choose music of the period, plus I would imagine folk tunes and some classics, and maybe even some evocative current stuff – actually I will leave it to him. I have auditioned him; Tommy is young but brilliant, a student from the conservatoire at Châteauroux, and he has family around here so he is overjoyed to be employed for the summer. All the musicians and cooks are being paid, by the way: it is only you actors who volunteer." [Again he was chuckling while he said this: it appeared to be a subject that was providing him with endless amusement.] "He is very tall, the accordionist; that maybe is not entirely relevant to his musicianship, but I think people like that."

Jack looked quizzically at Milo, with the eyebrows asking, "Where did he get that idea? Is it evidence-based, or anecdotal?" They decided not to open a discussion on the topic.

"Less importantly," Jean continued, "the steering…. We were going to have a bargeman, but I called the boatyard this morning, following our conversation last night, to let them know we just want one boat. Once I reminded them of the route, frequency and so on, they said they are fine for us to hire the vessel without a dedicated helmsman. They know me, I have been there a couple of times for basic training. So, we can steer ourselves, and save another fifty francs a day – how about that Mile, are you proud of me?"

Milo was indeed proud and glowed a little. It made up for the dig about the hay wains; suddenly he was a man of influence, and a force for good.

"On arriving at the jetty here," Jean went on, noticing the effect he had had on Milo, but not acknowledging it, "the customers leave the barge, and can immediately view the whole vista, across the meadow that rises up the hill and flattens off just before Hill House, which is set at the top there, you see? It is a pleasant location, right? I've had the meadow mown, and closer to the house I've had some gardeners tidy up in general, and around the terrace we have pots, planters and window boxes, the theme is all red and yellow blooms, including geraniums and sunflowers, against deep green foliage."

Jean was sketching everything out for them with sweeping arm gestures, and they were in awe as usual of his passion and excitement.

"So, from the landing stage, here, our guests will take a gentle walk along the bank of the river, then on the pathway up the rise; the accordionist will walk along too, playing quietly. Then there, on the flat area in front of the terrace, there are piles of cushions and blankets, and the guests spread them out to make themselves comfortable and prepare to enjoy their picnics.

"The magicians and the jugglers will circulate there, entertaining groups with all their skills and tricks. You actors, still in your blazers, also mix among the customers, making sure everyone is comfortable and having fun, and checking if anyone needs anything, letting them know where everything is.

"Meanwhile the catering team will have prepared the food, and the buffet lunch will be laid out and ready. Plenty of bread, cheese, cold meats and chicken, quiche, green salads, bean salads, potato salads and so on. To drink, there was wine and beer for the adults and lemonade for the kids. And for dessert, fruit, chocolate, maybe tart – but not so many cakes!" Jean winked at Milo, who had cost him his starry gateaux.

"The accordionist will walk around, or sit with customers when requested, playing ballads, arias, 30s jazz standards, and some funny songs for the kids. He has such a great repertoire he can almost adapt every day to whatever he feels the customers would like or what they ask for. The acoustics are fantastic here, the sound travels so crisply and clearly across and down the meadow.

"Gradually Madame Jestique, with her piano a little higher up on the terrace, will take over the musical lead from the accordionist, as the time for the play approaches. We have sacrificed many of the other activities, the pony racing, the readings from Meaulnes, and so on; so we move straight from the picnic to the play, it means the play is clearly the star of the show, even more important than I ever planned."

[Milo looked at Jack, who was careful to avoid his eye this time.]

"While the customers are finishing off their meal and taking coffee, you actors will grab a snack for yourselves and drift off into the dressing room in the house to prepare your make-up and costumes."

While they had been talking (or listening, in the case of everyone but Jean), they had gradually been climbing the slope, hearing the imminent accordionist, watching the impending magician, moving through the destined blankets and bolsters, hovering above the prospective brie and yet-to-be baked baguettes and walking past the future lounging guests, until, finally, slightly breathless, they surmounted the Hill House terrace.

"Wow!" Jack cried out in surprise and delight, "Wow wow wow –

that is unbelievable, Jean! Really, how do you do this?"

What he and Milo were looking at was a perfect little theatre. For the audience there were five rows of crimson velveteen banquettes under a gorgeous, patterned, open-fronted marquee. These were arranged in tiers, each of the rows easily broad enough to hold ten or a dozen customers in some luxury. Then, for the performance, across the terrace, set directly opposite the seating, connected onto the house façade, was a stage with a delightfully shaped, painted and embellished proscenium arch rising eight metres. The stage was about ten metres deep, about two-thirds of which was behind the proscenium and a third in front, approaching the audience, thus giving the option for some action in the round. There was a thick velvet canopy stretched on poles to make a roof running back between the proscenium and the house, and it hung down on both sides to form the walls. The front of Hill House therefore – with a door, two sets of French windows, and two first floor windows, one of which had a balcony – was framed and contained by the arch of the theatre structure and formed the backdrop.

"It's amazing, Jean," Milo agreed, nodding. "This is incredible quality, well done. I have no idea how you organise things like this without a team of fifty people."

"Well, I would like to take all the credit," said Jean, while they were walking and talking and Jack was assessing the stage area and measuring everything with his eyes, "but if you think about it, I probably do have a team of fifty, if you count you students, a couple of dozen people who work on the farm one way or another, full-time or part-time, and then a network of twenty families in four or five hamlets and towns around here. Those include people who have all kinds of skills and experiences. In this case, some of my uncles and cousins did some work in a small theatre in La Chapelle that got shut down between the wars, and our relatives are not the kind of people who like to see things get wasted. We all have barns with space, so storage of, shall we say, found and retrieved objects and materials is never a problem; you have no idea what treasures are hidden in our backyards."

Jack signalled he had seen enough for the time being, so to finish the general tour, Jean showed them the second piano and Madame Jestique's music area on the other side of the terrace where the tea dance would be held each day after the Harlequinade. Initially, he said, they were going to move the piano each evening between the theatre and the tea terrace, but it just felt too clumsy, and bad for the instrument, so now they have two.

They went inside the house, and checked out the two large downstairs rooms inside the house that had been roughly painted and nicely cleaned, for the customers to use as shelter in case of rain; the toilets, the washrooms, and the dressing rooms. When they were inside, Jack and Milo headed up the stairs, and before Jean called out, "There's nothing to see up there, it's not in use," they had already had a quick view of a range of dirty and decrepit bedrooms, almost all with holes in roofs and walls, which, as they were not necessary for the Experience, had clearly not been refurbished for years. Milo noticed that one of the rooms, at least, seemed to have been camped in – the dust had been shifted around a bit, there were some sad-looking blankets on a rusty bed, and, on a broken bedside table, an ashtray with an old pack of Park Drive.

"Is there someone living here?" he asked. Jean looked a little uncomfortable, before saying, "There was, some time ago, but not now; a transient guy who did some odd jobs up here, I let him sleep here for a while. Actually I am just going to give the upstairs a quick check, to make sure it is all locked up properly. If you use that door" [pointing] "it takes you straight out onto the stage – start having a look to see what you think."

As they walked out of the front door of the house, which now led straight onto the boards, the two boys got that thrill everyone gets when entering a stage at any time; the nerves and excitement, even if there is no performance. Showtime!

"Pudden," said Milo; "and Custard," said Jack. They both grinned hugely at the simultaneous thought of the last time they'd appeared on a stage together, aged six. Their infant school teacher thought

191

of herself as a bit of a Peter Brook, and rather than sticking with a straightforward nativity ("So uninspiring") she augmented it with a sub-plot involving artisanal players representing popular Christmas archetypes such as "Present," "Drumstick," "Sprout," and "Bauble."

Bauble was particularly memorable, consisting of Mike in a huge brightly coloured papier-mâché ball covered with tiny pieces of mirror, rotating on the darkened stage as the rest of the class shone torches on him, making him glitter and glint. He sang sweetly:

I am Bauble on the tree
See the lights reflect on me

Bob was Present. He came on in a vast gift-wrapped box, with only his little head, diminutive legs and tiny arms poking out. He did a manic jig for two minutes to Santa Claus Is Comin' to Town, before the class pounced on him and began to rip off layer after layer of paper and ribbon while he sang out:

I am Present wrapped with care
Giving pleasure everywhere
When I'm opened you will see
What is held inside of me

But the undoubted stars of the show were Milo and Jack in the form of Pudden and Custard. Milo was set in another massive papier-mâché structure, more ovoid this time, and painted like a colossal Victorian plum pudding with just his feet out at the bottom and his head out at the top wearing a green knitted hat. Jack was inside a giant blue-and-white-hooped cardboard jug, with handle and spout, that had CUSTARD painted on the side. They danced formally around each other to the music of an Elizabethan galliard, until… but wait… we do not have to describe it, we can see the real thing brought to life.

"Do you remember it, Francois?"

"I do indeed, Scott. Shall we?"

So, the grown boys face each other, and, using muscle memory, throw right leg over to the left, then swing it back in a half circle to the right; then left leg over to the right, before sweeping it back elegantly to the left. Then they dance round each other twice, prancing like the Lords'a'Leaping; until Pudden splits away and moves to the front of the stage, where he falls onto his knees, armless, pulls up his head, gazes intimately into the faces of the audience, and sings:

I am Pudden round and sweet
Full of plums and good to eat

Then Custard does a last cavorting solo circuit of the stage before returning and halting behind and over the genuflected Pudden, crooning:

I am Custard thick and yellow
Splattering this jolly fellow

And so saying, he leans forward, pouring from his spout a cascade of gold streamers, buttercream-coloured paper ribbons and bright yellow tinsel. It brought the house down every night. The secret was a very diluted wash of glue on Pudden that made the custard stick, just enough to look, they thought, totally authentic.

"Jesus, guys, seriously, what are you on? WILL YOU PLEASE CONCENTRATE."

Jean had finished inside and came out just in time to see Jack leaning over the kneeling Milo waggling, bowing and bending his head and shoulders while keeping his arms by his sides. As though... as though what? As though he was tipping an imaginary stream of custard over his friend using a giant invisible jug. Don't ask; just move on.

Jean was now clicking his fingers in front of their eyes as if to wake them, shouting, "Come on, we need to get this done and get back. No More Horseplay."

"Sorry, sorry, Jean, it's OK we were just reliving the great theatrical triumph of our youth." Milo shot up from the floor, honestly rather shaken by the recollection and re-enactment. Everything was slightly weird for the moment.

Back in Director persona, Jack paced the stage back and forth and back and forth for a while in thought; then went to sit in the audience area, beckoning Jean and Milo to go with him, so they could all get the customer's perspective. He took his exercise book and started to make some simple sketches, with Jean looking over his shoulder.

"What we have here is really close already to something we can use, Jean," he said. "I am guessing we don't have the time to make an actual set, right? But really, we don't need that anyway. I am just thinking, in addition to the general use of the features of the house front, we can get by with four areas – the courtyard, Harlequin's bedroom, Columbine's bedroom, and Pantaloon's study. All the other action can be fitted in or around those, or done at the apron edge of the stage, almost in the round.

"So if say we move half a dozen of these larger plant pots here, here, here and around here, then I reckon it becomes the courtyard very easily.

"If we rig up a curtain across here," he was motioning a line roughly halfway between the house front and the proscenium, "then we can pull it and divide the stage, just bringing in a couple of pieces of furniture here and there to create the sets we need.

"The other most important scene is Columbine's balcony, so that is easy, we have it already existing on the first-floor window.

"For the scene inside Columbine's room, we close the curtain and in front we put a bed and a lamp – very simple.

194

"For the scene in Harlequin's room, we have the curtain closed, and in front we have a smaller bed, a chair, some luggage, a desk with writing materials – we show externally that the other window on the first floor is that room, because later Clown will jump out of it towards the audience – we must remember to have a bush and some cushions to break the fall."

"Yes please," said Milo, "could there be many cushions, thank you, of unprecedented plumpness."

"For Pantaloon's study, where Columbine is reading to him, I think we just open the French windows of the house, and the audience can view them in the room from the outside, OK? It just needs a big armchair and a smaller upright chair for the girl."

While Jean and Jack had their heads together, focusing on Jack's pencil as it sketched scenery ideas in his notebook, Milo wandered to the side of the stage where he was partially hidden from them by the upright of the proscenium. Invisible, he lit a cigarette and watched them work, suddenly enveloped by contentment, wondering how they had transmogrified so immaculately into inhabitants of this extraordinary universe.

And then the reaction hit him: how, why, had they been wrenched out of the cosy world of boyhood, the protection of school, for this risky and rather terrifying venture? And with that thought came back the regular recollection of the boy on the pub floor, startling him; the space between memories was marginally increasing, this time he had forgotten for almost an hour. Milo began the mantra.

"OK are we done here for now?" said Jean, calling to them both after a further fifteen minutes.

"Sure," said Jack, "I've got plenty to be going on with, I think we can nail ninety percent of this and handle any small issues that come up tomorrow or Wednesday."

"All good for me," agreed Milo, "I just do the broad concepts so

I am always ready to leave; it's the man with the notebook who dictates the pace."

"Let's just pick up the food from the kitchen," said Jean. "The easiest way is around the side rather than through the house."

They walked on the pathway that ran close to the house on all four sides, taking right angles till they came to the kitchen door which was in the back of the house about five metres along from the dressing room door.

Although he was the owner (or at least the owner's close relative, and the person paying the rent) Jean knocked and waited patiently. After a short time the door was opened by a woman with a man standing just behind her; they were each wiping their hands on their aprons, and when they saw Jean they both then smoothed their hair down with their newly dried hands.

"Julie, Jacques, how are you? Let me please introduce you to our new friends, Francois and Scott. The lads have come down from Paris to work for the summer and they are helping me get the last stages of the Experience ready. Scott is actually a *bona fide* American youth, so I guess we can officially say the Experience has finally gone international!

"Francois, Scott – please meet my cousin Julie, and her husband Jacques. They're completely brilliant chefs, and I am pleased and proud to have them working with us here doing everything to organise and provide the catering."

Everyone seemed very happy to meet everyone else, and handshakes and friendly nods were shared and exchanged.

"I am really sorry to bother you when I know you're so busy preparing," said Jean. "How is it going?"

Julie was a woman in her mid-thirties, Jacques probably five or six years older. He had a diffident air, shy, slightly furtive, as if he assumed everyone knew his guilty secret whether they did or not. She was open-faced, and very beautiful, in a country way, thought Milo, though he would have struggled to explain to you what that meant.

Julie spoke for them both – when you knew them, you got used to the fact that Jacques seldom contributed conversation when Julie was there, and never when she wasn't.

"It's good, Jean, I think we're on top of it. We've done the full menu on each of the past two days, and we invited volunteers from the farm to come and be our test customers. We got all the food out, looking attractive, on time, we stayed within budget, and the people enjoyed eating it. Actually we're pretty happy, if I can say that without the risk of aggravating your superstition."

"Fantastic!" cried Jean, so loudly he shocked himself. "That's such great news!"

"You mean 'such a relief,'" laughed Julie, "it sounds like you really didn't think we would crack it."

"I never doubted you for an instant, not a second."

"Now," said Julie, "for what you really came to ask about – your dinner, right?"

She and Jacques stood back from the door and beckoned the three inside. Down the corridor and to the right was the main kitch-en, and on the table, five large cardboard boxes. All around, the kitchen looked like a battlefield after a particularly bloodthirsty skirmish with a high body count: pots, pans, dishes in piles, dirty dishcloths, ingredients still out, waste food on the counters. Julie noticed Jean looking around, perhaps a little disapproving. "Sorry Jean, but we have only just this minute finished, and it's been a crazy day." Jean made the shrug with the hands in front of the chest, palms outwards, raised. The universal sign for, "Ignore me, what do I know, you guys are the best."

Moving the men and the subject on, Julie pointed to the boxes and described the contents. "It should make quite a feast, it is leftovers from yesterday and today; as we didn't have forty volunteers there is a ton of the best stuff left, something of everything. It is a good exercise, a good experience: you and your actors will be able to taste the whole menu so you will be confident how good it is, and then you'll be able to describe it to the customers when you are helping to serve them."

"I was hoping for that excuse," said Jean, mock serious, "and at the same time we are really hungry, we've got mouths to feed, this smells wonderful, and crucially it is already paid for!"

Everyone picked up one of the boxes, they went outside and put them in the boot of Julie's car, calling goodbye to Jacques as he was returning to the kitchen, "Thanks my friend, this is amazing."

They got in and Julie drove them the four-hundred metres down the hill to where they'd parked Jean's vehicle. They transferred the food boxes, and Jean shook Julie's hand, asking before they got into the motor, "Are you guys going to be OK, it looks like there is an awful lot to do before you knock off, shall we stay and help?"

"No, don't worry, Jean," said Julie. "That is a kind offer, but I know you have plenty enough on your plate. We can handle it, it's all part of the job." Jean gave her a "Thank you" sign. Troupers like her, he loved.

The three said goodbye again, Jean mentioning he would call her the next day to arrange a final meeting before the launch. They pulled away, very excited about the setup, the stage, the backdrops and the food – it had been a good day.

"You guys must be exhausted," said Jean, as the thought finally struck him that he had woken them up before 5.00am and they had been wandering around for well over twelve hours already.

Milo was next to him in the front seat, and turned to check Jack in the back; he'd suddenly flagged and was looking very fatigued. Milo was feeling a little the same, but Jack had been working much more intensively than him over the past three or four hours. Milo realised with a bit of a shock that it was still Sunday, and they had been on the run for about eighty hours with maybe fifteen hours sleep, give or take.

"We need to get him some food."

"Are you going to be OK to do a rehearsal this evening?" Jean asked.

"We'll be fine after a drink and a snack," Jack replied, a trifle groggily, "but maybe we'll keep the run-through to a couple of hours if we can; we'll definitely sleep well tonight."

"OK, but be careful, we can't lose our Director on the first night. I'm sorry also that we're running late for dinner for everyone, I should have got us back sooner. Youth has no patience and does not like to be kept waiting, we don't want to alienate our cast before they're even onside." Jean was only half joking.

He pulled the car up close to the door at the Lodge and shouted for some help to unload. Albert and Amelie came out quickly, as though they had been waiting for them, and the five of them carried the boxes in. Karl was not to be seen, presumably avoiding the 'being helpful' phase of the operation, and Madame Jestique and Claude had gone home during the break.

While Amelie and Albert started to take the small parcels and cartons out of the boxes and unwrap them, beginning to arrange the delicious-smelling food onto plates and serving dishes, Milo and Jack headed upstairs for a quick wash and to change their by now very sweaty t-shirts. Jean had to make a couple of phone calls to follow up things that needed to be organised and ordered after their site visit.

When they finally got into the kitchen for dinner, there were three empty chairs set aside for Jean, Francois and Scott, all at one end of the table, both sides of Albert. Milo looked for the sign that said, "Reserved For The Not Cool Boys." Meanwhile, Karl and Amelie seemed very far away at the Popular Kids end on their own, and all Jack could see from that distance (though Milo and Jean failed to notice) was Karl's canoodling, toe tapping, hand brushing, unnecessary passing of implements and condiments, general simpering and self-satisfied smirking. This was most frustrating and annoying, and reminded Jack to be more punctual for meals in future. Or even earlier.

The main conversation as they entered was all about the food, which the forerunners had been patiently sizing up, politely waiting for Jean, Jack and Milo to join them before beginning to serve each other. It was a fine, fabulous, generous selection; Milo did wonder whether Jacques and Julie had really intended for them to eat it all at once – or whether they'd thought there might be fifteen or twenty of them rather than just the six. The meal included chicken, a large part of a couple of savoury tarts, several loaves, salads, cheese, some cooked meats, salmon, baked potatoes and lots of tiny pots of sauces and dips. For dessert, they had cherries, pears and pastries, with some fantastic custard stuff; no-one could precisely identify it, but everyone had a second helping. Everything was beautifully prepared, and there was a great deal of enthusiastic talk about how much the customers were going to love it. As well as being fed, the team were encouraged and excited.

Of course, Jack was a little hamstrung (should that be eggstrung? cheesestrung?) by his unforeseen vegetarianism. He picked around items he would normally consume with vigour, copying Amelie when he was unsure of the animal or vegetable content of the food, and was quietly chagrined by the fact no-one really noticed or cared. Amelie did not even raise her pool-like eyes to confirm their special bond. 'How long,' he thought, 'before I can change my mind without looking like a dick?' Sadly, he decided, you probably have to give it a couple of years or move to another country and make a clean start.

Madame Jestique returned to join them just at the end for coffee, and, when no-one was looking, she had a bird-like pick at what was left on the table. Her fingers were quick and deft; she wore beautiful black glovelettes that covered the wrist, hand and the base of each finger, but left the tips free to caress the keys, or in this case the quiche. Satin? Milo was watching hard, fascinated, but he was famously poor at recognising fabric types – they were definitely not leather, that was as close as he could narrow it down. He imagined, with surprising accuracy, that they had been given to her by a wealthy admirer in 1928 after a particularly remarkable performance.

"Right," said Jean, picking that exact moment when it was necessary to choose between moving meaningfully to work or giving up the day entirely, "let's do it, shall we? If you agree, Maestro" [said to Jack], "then you can begin the rehearsal while I clear the dinner things away? I see from the scenario that my policing skills are not required until a few moments before the end, so, sad as I am that my prodigiously undervalued acting skills are once more to be hidden from the public clamour, I might as well make myself useful washing the dishes while you stars are polishing your talents."

The other five actors, and Madame Jestique, filed through to the Hall, and as they did Jack started addressing them.

"I would like us to do one run-through this evening, if that's OK, just to get a general feel for timing, to develop some instinct about movements, to find some indications of when and where we will need to change sets, and so on. Madame Jestique, if it is all right with you, I was thinking for this rehearsal you could watch and take notes about what music might be suitable, and when, and what transitions between styles would work out – does that sound good?" She nodded in response and played a phrase on the piano in agreement – Milo suddenly realised that he hadn't heard her speak a single word yet. "Of course," went on Jack, "should you wish to play at any stage I promise no-one will stop you!" Everyone laughed, beginning to relax.

"So, first onto the stage, please, Pantaloon and Columbine."

201

Milo was watching his friend with no small degree of awe. He had stepped into this role-within-a-role with aplomb. He smiled to himself; he had hardly ever used the word "awe" before, and never the word "aplomb" at all, though he had encountered both with delightful frequency in his favourite Victorian novels. Whatever less gaudy words you would prefer to use, Jack was nevertheless completely in his element, commanding the room, demanding attention and respect. I'll stick with "awe."

Jack had no problem positioning Albert and Amelie and moving them around. They responded willingly and with Jack's prompting started to use the broad gestures and expressions from the silent movies. The whole team were having fits of giggles as they experimented with the melodramatic motions and gurning, but within a short time, between them, they had recognisably created the characters of the pompous, fussing father and the dutiful, loving, innocent and ever-so-slightly suspicious girl. Madame Jestique took notes for a short while, but soon lay down her pencil and started running her fingers over the keys, picking out some tunes and themes that immediately felt appropriate. She couldn't resist playing, her effortless facility made everyone smile.

"So next," said Jack, to himself and the room simultaneously, "enters Harlequin. He preens; by some small actions and attitudes he demonstrates his arrogance, his self-regard. The old man and the child do not see through him, they take him at his own face value. The old man shows him respect, and at the same time hopes to gain favours, business connections, and a good word with his father, a man of substance and influence. The girl has never previously met a man of such sophistication, such confidence; she has been swept away. She of course relies on her father to protect her, so because he makes no intervention, she infers that Harlequin's advances must be normal and acceptable."

Unlike Albert and Amelie, Karl did not like Jack pushing him into position and pulling him into different shapes: he even snatched his arm away from Jack's touch in a way that might have been described as petulant in a less friendly environment. Jack noticed

202

this, but no-one else saw it except Milo, who was watching much more closely than the rest, and could see that Karl absolutely hated being told what to do. Milo also realised that Karl's anger was intensified a hundredfold because it was Jack doing the telling and touching.

Nevertheless, Karl was a decent performer, and intuitively had a good understanding of the part and what was needed. Using the larger-than-life movements and old-fashioned facial contortions he managed to create the impressions and effects Jack was asking him for, and he even enhanced it himself with some extra business, getting Pantaloon to pour him a drink then touching Columbine familiarly while the father's back was turned.

"Brilliant, Karl," said Jack, generously, managing to sound about a thousand percent more sincere than he was. "So, if the three of you on stage could move to the back, yes, still facing the audience, thank you, chatting vivaciously without making any sound of course, then we bring on Clown and Pierrot standing on the front edge, consorting with the audience, and sharing their viewpoint, to observe you all and comment, a little bit like a Greek chorus."

Jack and Milo, as Francois and Scott, now entered as Pierrot and Clown. A play within a play within a play – trust me, they were as confused as we are. Feeding off each other they managed to create some simple faces and body language that would clearly inform the audience that

a) Columbine is lovely;

b) Pantaloon is a fool, venal but not evil;

c) Harlequin is a self-obsessed charlatan who means to seduce the young girl;

d) the two of them – Clown and Pierrot – see through all this, and they intend to protect their friend Columbine.

Madam Jestique was having great fun skilfully turning these concepts into music. As well as the accompaniments to thoughts and actions, she was already attaching a little musical signature tune to each character, reinforcing their purpose and personality. Jean, who had finished drying up and was now standing at the back, watching them, was very happy with this; the music was contributing as much as the movements to expressing and clarifying the meanings and motives.

The team continued to work late into the evening, developing and practising gesture and motion; discussing stage positions; deciding which scenes would work against which part of the backdrop, and which props were needed when. There were some frustrating periods, but more often they were all in fits of laughter, particularly when Clown jumped out of the window (quite a few times, actually); when Pierrot simulated the donning of the yet-to-be-acquired blond wig and became Columbine; and when Harlequin was caught halfway down the ivy wearing only what in actual performances would be his spotted knickers. Well, everyone loves a pants joke, right?

Finally, Jean, seeing that Jack was so immersed he would keep going all night if nobody stopped him, clapped his hands, with a mock shout, "Enough. Enough tonight. It has been brilliant, everything I have seen tonight fills me with confidence and personal delight. Thank you so much. But now is the time for rest. In particular, our friends from Paris were up around dawn this morning to get here, they must need some sleep." Jean was experiencing that great feeling you get when you have had a clever idea and someone later says, "You were right all along."

"Thanks so much, everyone," agreed Jack, "I think that was outstanding, a wonderful ensemble effort. We're nearly all the way through, and I've got a whole book of notes, but you seem to remember everything. Unless Jean needs us to work on any other Experience skills tomorrow, I reckon if we rehearse for the whole day we will be ready to run through the complete performance in real time by the evening."

"It would be good to get familiar with the Welcome area and the Costumes either tomorrow or Tuesday," said Jean, "I reckon we could set aside a morning or afternoon – you choose. Then we ought to have a visit sometime in the next few days over to Hill House to talk to the caterers about how they will want us to help them with the customers. And of course, you'll want some practice sessions using the actual sets and backdrops, I'm getting the builders in to do some adjustments tomorrow, so any time after that – you can plan it.

"Now, I would offer you a night cap to end the day, but sadly you are all too young for strong liquors," said Jean. Karl raised his hand to object but Jean failed to, or chose not to, notice him. "However, I have bought a crate of my home brew if anyone wants a beer before bed, and there is a bottle of nice red, one glass only for you Columbine, I promised your father."

Madame Jestique made her excuses, without saying a word as far as anyone could recall, and got ready to leave, with a smile. She had worked with very many professionals in all kinds of productions, but this was special, and fun. Jean signalled her to wait just a couple of minutes, indicating that when he'd got these kids settled he would give her a lift home.

Milo and Jack decided to take their drinks outside so they could light cigarettes, and they found some extremely uncomfortable garden loungers which they were grateful to slump into.

"Don't get too cosy in there," said Jack, "you'll be asleep in five minutes."

"I can't believe how much has happened in the last couple of days. How are we still alive, let alone awake?"

The rest of the cast wandered outside, Jean to have one quick cigarette, the others just to hang out with Francois and Scott while they finished their drinks. Amelie and Albert sank with an orchestrated sigh of contentment into the other deckchairs, while Jean wandered to the edge of the terrace, ten metres away, between them and the moon, drawing deeply on his own cigarette and looking contentedly out across the lake. Karl paced up and down for a time, then came up behind Amelie's chair and leaned over the back of it, possessively. Jack was too tired to be properly annoyed but made a mental note to be rather angry about it in the morning when he had more energy. Again, he noticed Karl had positioned himself so he could not be observed by Jean, and before Jean turned to say goodnight, Jack saw Karl quietly undrape himself from Amelie's chair.

"Don't stay up too late, you've worked so hard, I am so proud."

"Thanks Jean, we really appreciate it." This from Albert, who had hardly spoken all day. Perhaps he was ready to come a little out of his shell.

After Jean and Madame Jestique had left, Albert, surprisingly, extended his new loquaciousness by telling a few jokes, and he was surprisingly good – mainly schoolboy stuff, nothing offensive. Then Amelie told a rather risqué joke about a schoolgirl saying to her history teacher there was nothing she wouldn't do to get a passing grade and him saying great, how about doing your homework. Everyone laughed loudly, not because it was a good joke, but because it was Amelie.

"What about you, Jack, you have any jokes?"

"I only know one, shall I try it?"

They all nodded.

"So, God calls Karl over, and says, 'Karl, I can give you a choice. If you agree to have a shorter penis, you can have a longer life.' 'How much shorter?' asks Karl. 'That's interesting,' says God, 'everyone else asked how much longer.'"

Milo laughed uproariously, because, well, heck, he was still a schoolboy at heart, and someone did say penis; but in all honesty the others just looked a little baffled. "I guess you had to be there," said Jack, almost as peeved as Karl.

After Milo, learning a lesson from Jack's disappointment, declined to engage in the mirthification, Karl was invited, and showed less reluctance.

"When I was crossing the border to come here, the French guard stopped me.

"Name?

"Karl, I said.

"Age?

"Twenty-five, I said.

"Occupation?

"Not this time, I said – though I appreciate the suggestion."

Karl, what a wag! No-one laughed, everyone did that thing where you have half a chuckle ready in a friendly supportive way and then have to choke it back when you hear what has actually been said. They looked at their feet, not just because the joke was old and unoriginal, but also because it was deeply insulting, and they knew someone should point it out. All of them felt guilty, in their own way, for staying silent. 'It is just as well Jean and Claude are not here,' thought Jack, 'or offence would have been taken, potentially with consequences.' But the rest were young and not in the mood for contention, they relaxed, forgave themselves, and moved on.

After the jokes there was a little perfunctory chit-chat followed by a longer period when they slowed into a collective, satisfied hush; then all at once they silently made the decision to retire. Albert, Amelie and Karl moved inside, Jack and Milo decided on another last cigarette. Then with the final big effort of the day they dragged themselves out of the low chairs, taking it in turns to give each other a hand up, and shuffled slowly into the house like hundred-year-olds who had mislaid their walking frames. Finally they pulled themselves painfully up the stairs by the handrails, suddenly barely able to move their legs.

There was a melee on the landing as everyone sorted themselves out, waited for washrooms and divided into their corridors. Milo noted Karl's hand on Amelie's lower back as they all said their goodnights; just like Jack he was unhappy about it, but as elder-brother Albert was walking with them he presumed the situation had some controls. He respected Amelie, and already liked her a great deal, on a few hours acquaintance; a bit pretentious, slightly self-absorbed, but nice, bright, and full of character. But he also knew, and saw, she was in many ways younger than her years, and she might well lack the experience and shrewdness to deal with an accomplished predator like Karl who could get what he wanted while making her believe it was her idea.

After five minutes coming and going to toilets and bathrooms everyone had organised themselves, and with a final "sleep-tight" echoing up and down the halls, doors closed, and absolute quiet took over – the quiet of being in the country, thought Milo again. No cars taking the street corner too quickly; no next door's dog yapping; no baby down the road screaming. And utter blackness outside the window.

After a couple of minutes, Jack slipped out of his room, and knocked softly on Milo's door, entering without waiting for an answer.

"You OK, Milo?"

"Kind of!"

"Yes, me too. Crazy crazy days…. What's this, our third day on the run?"

"Three and a half if you count Thursday night."

"Are you OK with it all?"

"Of course! This has always been my dream, this is how I always hoped it would go: car-warmed pork pie snacks, followed by listless naps in a pee-soaked barn, then finally I merge into the shadows concealed as a jester in a semi-professional historical drama. At last, my destiny is fulfilled: I have become an outlaw mime; a mummer on the run."

"A trouper in trouble."

"A clandestine clown."

"A fugitive thespian…." But Jack had dried, the banter was telling them it was done for the day, and all that was left was wishful thinking and prayers before bedtime.

"Seriously, I guess we are where we are," Milo said, "I can't complain, it's my fault we're here in the first place. Whatever decisions we took, we have to live by them. Do you think we can relax a bit now about what happened, and whether they're after us? If he'd been really hurt, surely we would know, somehow? Someone would have told us, or found us?"

"No news is good, normally; but we've kept ourselves in a vacuum. And absence of evidence is not evidence of absence. We're in a part of France where they don't even get news from Paris for a fortnight; news from Britain will come next year… Of course it is wonderful to think he's OK, and we can keep our lives, what unbelievable relief and joy it would be if he's well and healthy, but it is too soon to stop the mantra, right – join with me, brother, in saying it.

"O My Brethren, pick him up, raise him high, heal his bones.

"O My Brethren, pick him up, raise him high, heal his bones.

"O My Brethren, pick him up, raise him high, heal his bones."

Milo realised they were both clasping their hands in front of them, like small boys kneeling at their bedsides in supplication before slumber. "O God, please look after my mum and my dad; please make my penis grow; let me score a goal Saturday; oh and please save the stab boy in the maroon blazer."

"Right," said Jack, "don't dwell on it, I'm off to bed, we should both take advantage of a full night on a proper mattress. Night, Milo, sleep well."

"Night, Jack, sleep well."

Jack opened the door quietly and slid out, aiming to slip silently back into this own room and sleep the sleep of the unjustly-accused-yet-exhausted.

It was either good, or rotten, luck, depending on your view, and you will probably work it out later, that at that exact moment Karl, having waited what he considered to be a frustratingly discreet amount of time, was knocking lightly on Amelie's door, clad only in what Jack interpreted as a rather skimpy dressing-gown, with his hand on the doorknob, ready to push it open.

Jack, across the landing, gave Karl the full-on corridor-to-corridor stare from roughly fifteen metres that demanded: 'What the hell do you think you are up to?' Karl gave Jack a return look that said: 'Hold on while I formulate a physical and emotional response, because I cannot immediately decide whether I want to demon-strate guilt, anger or triumph.'

"What the hell do you think you are up to?" Jack asked, after a few seconds of stand-off. He'd thought it, and now he'd said it: it really was very rare for him to do it in that order, normally it was speak from the hip and construe the meaning at a later date.

Karl's first reaction was to put his finger up to and over his lips in the international sign for, 'Can we please at least agree not to make a racket and wake everyone up?' What he actually said, in a rather ludicrous stage whisper, was: "Whatever I am doing, it is nothing to do with you."

Instinctively Jack realised the best tactic here was to make some noise, so he delivered, at slightly higher than normal daytime volume, the best response he could come up with at short notice, "Karl, I fear that's not your door, old boy."

Milo was opening his own door to see what the noise was, and when he heard Jack's bizarrely pompous tone he started laughing, thinking he must have wandered out into the middle of some horseplay. That was an appropriate response to the language, but not to the situation. For a rare moment in their relationship Jack glared at him, but immediately turned the look into the facial expression plus tiny shake of the head and finger half pointed at the lip that indicated: 'You haven't understood the situation, you are on my side, shut up for a minute.'

However, Milo's manic laugh had already added to the increasing commotion, and Albert was next into the corridor, ruffling his hand through his hair and pulling the waist band of his drooping pyjama pants up over his stomach. "What's happening guys, we all need some sleep."

Jack looked at Karl and shrugged out his palms, "Karl will tell you – I am sorry I woke everyone; I was just trying to help."

"Help how, what's going on?" said Albert, now concerned and suspicious, looking pointedly at his sister's door, and Karl's proximity to it, in fact his hand actually still on it. Karl stared back at him and suddenly couldn't hold back his contempt.

"Jesus, it's none of your fucking business what I do, fatso."

There was a rush of silence as the others realised what he'd said. Albert looked straight down at the faded and worn carpet. His

211

cheeks were stricken crimson with anger and humiliation, the burning red of spanked flesh. He knew with complete certainty that he would say and do absolutely nothing except fold his arms self-consciously over his belly while the blood pounded in his head.

Immediately after Karl had blurted out the playground jibe he realised he'd crossed a stupid line. "I'm sorry, I didn't mean that. It's late, we're all tired out and there really is nothing going on that anyone needs to take such an interest in."

Albert didn't move. He couldn't fight back, but at least he wasn't going to help him by saying it was all right. Karl shuffled his stance, looking round for help without catching anyone's eye. Milo thought, 'He's never felt a moment's real embarrassment in his life, this might be as close as he'll ever get.'

The stand-off was becoming excruciating. It was then that Jack (and if you had asked him to explain why, at exactly that moment, he would have looked blankly at you) decided to bail Karl out.

"Look, apologies again, I feel this is all my fault. Karl's had a couple of beers as we all have, I know he didn't mean to be rude, I am sure he's defensive because I put him on the spot. I just saw him out when I went to the toilet, he obviously forgot which room was his, so I was pointing him in the right direction – right, Karl? I'm so sorry to disturb everyone and this got out of control!"

Milo decided at this point that he had been right when he burst out laughing the first time: Jack's exposition was a) palpably false and b) let a wriggling foe off the hook. This was completely out of character for his friend; an inappropriate kindness which was both strategically feeble-minded and counterproductive.

At the same time, in Jack's head (thoughts after words, so back to the norm), motive was retrospectively filling in the gaps in his reasoning and informing Jack why he had done what he had:

- For Jean's sake, Jack did not want to blow up the whole team less than a week before the launch of his new business. Jean had already lost two people, and had been lucky enough to replace them, but Karl had been teetering, and if he lost more now, for any reason, it would delay the whole project, and he was losing money every day till it opened – it could ruin him.

- For their own sakes, they had come a very long way, and they certainly didn't want to draw unnecessary attention to themselves. Ending up in a public play is one thing, but at least they would be in heavy disguise. They definitely didn't need to provoke any unfriendly or hostile scrutiny.

- He wanted to warn off Karl – his move had achieved it. Maybe the main benefit was that he had alerted the rather slow-on-the-uptake brother... surely even Albert would not believe Karl was innocently trying all the wrong doors.

- He wanted to protect Amelie – he had done that for to-night. Admittedly that was not a lifetime immunity from the disease that is Karl. Also, was he protecting her from Karl, or from herself – did she even know he had saved her? Was her immediate reaction going to be relief or annoyance or, oh my yuk, frustration? Perhaps she won't even thank me until, in twenty years' time, as a mature woman, she'll express effusive gratitude on a badly written postcard sent from another country with tear stains and insufficient postage.

One motivation he did not consider or analyse was that he wanted Amelie for himself. Did he? What about Maggie? He never thought about it, honestly, because tonight he decided to attribute to himself only the best of intentions.

OK, time for bed, we can wrestle these issues to the floor tomorrow or the day after. 'For tonight,' thought Jack, 'my work is done.'

Back in reality, amongst the group assembled in the corridor there was collectively an outward acceptance of a narrative that everyone knew on some conscious or unconscious level was nonsense. Amelie never emerged at all – wise girl.

This was the point where Karl could have brazened it out, could have said, "Yes I am going in to Amelie, what of it? What business is it of yours? She is expecting me, it is what we both want, and she is old enough to make the choice."

He didn't, which meant that Karl knew it was wrong, it didn't matter whether Amelie had agreed it with him or not. And if Amelie wasn't aware, and he was just taking his chances at her door, then that was much worse.

Even if Karl had persuaded himself that it was a morally permissible diversion, he clearly recognised his actions were sufficiently questionable that he chose to avoid defending them after midnight in the hallway wearing a green silk shorty kimono appliqued with topless women in the more socially acceptable guise of mermaids. He certainly didn't intend to engage in debate about his intentions with the anxious older brother in front of a pitchfork-ready audience of jealous antagonists, but at the same time he was furious with himself for going nastily over the top in closing him down, he could have easily done it casually, smoothly. That wasn't going to help his plans and now he'd have to triple the future charm to get him back onside.

Anyway, for now the new Parisian boy, for a reason he could not fathom, had provided him with an exit strategy. The others were too fatigued really to want to continue imagining motives for his wandering, Albert was dying to get out of the corridor and lick his wounds in private, and they were all of them desperate for sleep. So, he took advantage of Francois's get-out-of-jail card and mumbled.

"Of course, so sorry: as Francois says, this building is so confusing, I'll find my way around it eventually."

Everyone leapt at the chance to placidly nod their agreement, mutter their goodnights again, and disperse. None of them had any trouble finding their bedrooms. Before he entered his own, Jack took one last glance back down the corridor and caught Karl glaring at him as vengefully as Satan cast out from paradise.

And all our five actors did sleep then, heavily in every case, but not immediately, or happily, in some.

Amelie had, despite anybody's suspicions, already been asleep, very peacefully, for some time. In a romantic novel, they would have said 'blissfully unaware.'

Albert lay awake for ten minutes wondering whether and how much he should worry about Karl's attentions to his sister. He despised himself for not being braver while deciding he would rather not be. In just a few days he had developed quite a hero crush on Karl, who was in so many ways everything he dreamt of being, so he had been especially mortified to get a glimpse of what Karl thought of him. He would have to work even harder for his respect.

Karl was sleepless for less than four minutes, during which he briefly considered touching himself while thinking lasciviously of Amelie but then decided instead to use the time more satisfyingly to formulate a plan to eliminate and annihilate Francois. He would defeat and destroy him, and also his ridiculous sidekick if necessary, for justice and for honour, or possibly just for fun. He didn't include Albert as a victim of the new project only because he'd forgotten about him altogether. When he dropped off, Karl slept with a smile on his face, not exactly a look of innocence, let's call his expression contentedly malevolent.

Milo lay awake for twenty minutes, fighting sleep to relive every hour that had passed on the journey since the glass was thrown at The King's Hind. He wished life had not become so frightening; he thought of the boy on the pub floor; and he began an extremely crucial prayer, which he drowsed off halfway through.

215

Jack spent half a moment considering – perhaps humorously – whether he should sleep curled up like a defence puppy across Amelie's threshold, then drifted off instantly. But he woke sitting up gasping ten minutes later, and then again ten minutes after that. Finally, he slept, dreaming of himself running headlong through a sinister tunnel of decorated trees that appeared endless, pursued by a handsome man in a white shirt stained red who was waving a knife at him and gurgling blood up from his throat and mouth that flecked in droplets all over his chin and collar. Jack himself was chasing a shadowy figure in front that kept eluding him; every time he got within shouting distance he cried out to him, but the man covered his ears, shook his head and ran more quickly. Here and there he passed pretty women at the side of the path: he wanted to stop for them, but each of them waved him on, like watchers at the great race urging him to outrun his pursuer and spurring him on to overtake his quarry.

MONDAY

When he officially awoke, the sun was shining into his room, and the first thing he realised was he had no curtains. Then he gave some thought to where he was, and why – the sudden rush of wretched reality that had become the routine three minutes into every new waking day. From where he lay, or just by easing himself up a little, he could see across the fields; some dark green, others yellow with sunflowers, and one blue-tinged from a crop he did not recognise. It was utterly beautiful.

In the far distance he could see smoke coming from the chimney at Jean's farmhouse. That made him feel quite cosy, though as soon as he thought of Cousin Jean he got anxious about what had happened the previous night. Would Jean get to hear about it – should he tell him first, rather than waiting for him to possibly get a different version from someone else? Of course, this was a question for Milo. So he got dressed – realising belatedly that he had nothing clean to wear, and actually not many clothes at all – and went next door, knocking before trying the handle.

Milo's room was empty, so he set off towards the stairs to look for him. Before he reached the landing, Milo came out of the wash-room, naturally wearing exceptionally small swimming trunks.

Jack laughed, loudly yet silently, at the extraordinarily white matchstick legs, bony chest, and tiny briefs.

"This is a winning combination, *mon frere.*"

"Laugh away, Spartacus, because you are coming with me," whispered Milo, not at all offended by body mockery, and tossing a pair of trunks to Jack. "Jean left us a stash of odds in the bathroom, here are yours."

"Arghh," cried Jack, bending backwards and putting in a twisting sideways leap to avoid catching, or even being touched by, the flying swimsuit.

"Noooo ….. lost property!"

At school, if you forgot your kit, or deliberately failed to pack it, hoping to get a pass for P.E., Mr Mills would direct you igno-miniously into the unused staff shower where there was a seeping tea chest containing a fermenting soup of shirts, shorts and socks deserted by unwashed generations of stained and psoriatic thirteen-year-olds. The rumour was a second-year boy developed buboes on his unfilled scrotum after being forced to do cross country in a gangrenous pair of abandoned Y-fronts.

"Oh for heaven's sake, don't be such a baby there, young Maester Francois," said Milo in his best matronly tone, picking up the swimsuit and pressing it into Jack's reluctant hands. He was still *sotto voce*, and when Jack gave the question mark eyebrows 'Why are you whispering?' Milo pointed to his watch, which indicated 5.40am.

"Oh, eek."

Jack slipped back into his room and changed into the minute costume. They grabbed towels from the cupboard, let themselves out of the kitchen door, and headed to the lake, a relaxed and enjoyable stroll of roughly twenty seconds.

In the daylight, on his ultra-white frame, Milo's bruises and welts from the fight at The King's Hind stood out alarmingly.

"Blimey, mate," commented Jack, "how does that all feel – you've been living with pain, I am very impressed!"

"Getting better all the time, thanks for asking, Doctor. I found some ointment in one of the bathroom cupboards that I have been most liberally applying."

"Random medication! Respect your courage, brother. It wasn't the tube labelled Karl's Bum Cream was it?"

"Ha ha ha. No, I shouldn't tell you, but that's his toothpaste; he just writes Bum Cream on it to stop people stealing it, but he said you can use it whenever you want."

"He's a gent."

"You misjudged him."

They'd arrived at the rickety wooden jetty that reached ten metres out into the water. Several planks and bits of railing were missing, and it had a couple of dilapidated rowing boats tied up to it. They walked warily to the end and placed their towels onto the decking.

"Now what?" asked Jack, looking suspiciously at Milo.

"The traditional next step to achieve what we like to call 'a swim' is to physically enter the water," Milo replied.

Jack observed the lake. It was sunk into the landscape like an elliptical font in a church nave, serene meniscus, ready to be broken, quietly willing to transform. Superficially inviting, and yet much thought should be given before leaping in. I don't know when or how we humans developed the extra sense that allows us to look at something and know whether it is hot or cold, but Jack had it, and the mental thermometer he'd popped scientifically into the water was hovering around 'bloody freezing.' He certainly didn't need to put a toe in.

He opened his lips to deliver a brilliantly witty retort, but you will never hear it, and nor did Milo, because he had already pushed him, and the banter turned to bubbles rising to the surface from Jack's shocked and open mouth a metre under the water.

As Jack shot up, spluttering and coughing, he heard Milo cackling with glee. At the same time, Milo, appreciating that till wet he was intensely vulnerable to retaliation, leapt off the jetty over Jack's bobbing head, in a mighty bomb.

They were having fun.

When they realised that, it reminded them both to be serious, and they felt guilty. They looked at each other and said the mantra three times, crossed their fingers, and for a moment felt nervy and sad. Then Jack splashed Milo; Milo pulled Jack down; the tension broke again and they struck out in a synchronised breast stroke across the lake.

The lake was around sixty metres long and thirty-five metres wide – probably about the scale of a competition pool, thought Jack, though he had never seen such a thing. Without taking soundings all over – Mark Twain, he thought – Milo guessed that there weren't many places where they would be out of their depth if they stood up. It was completely surrounded by ranks of reeds and grasses that flowed off the banks and into the water. From the surface level, inside, you could see where the birds were making nests among the stems. Milo expertly identified them as "duck type," following his years of birdwatching in the park.

Around the edges of the lake, every fifteen metres or so, were little areas cleared of the reeds, almost like small beaches allowing access to the water, which were used by authorised fishermen setting up their stands for the day or night. One side of the lake was only fifteen metres from the woods, the other side, beyond the reeds, flattened off into a kind of meadow, then a hedge before you reached the fields.

Jack and Milo swam half a dozen lengths, slow and peaceful, tranquil in the space between the dawn and the day, before Jack let out a cry of angst, suddenly standing. "Oh my God, Scott!"

Milo, startled, did a 360-degree reconnoitre, saw no immediate dangers, no *gendarmes,* no men with guns, and called back, quite panicky, "God's sake, Francois, what's wrong?"

Jack put his head deep into the water, pulled it up, arching back, shaking the pond out of his hair like, thought Milo, a rather manky Afghan Hound confidently believing it was Best In Show.

"We're exercising! For Chrissake, man, we've swum three hundred metres already – what were you thinking! What happened to the inertia treaty, to the high standards of indolence to which we hold ourselves?"

Whether to strangle or chortle, thought Milo; finally deciding on neither, writing it off to stress, he literally (yes!) took his friend by the hand and led him to the jetty. "Do not fear. I have the antidote."

Pulling his towel towards him, he unravelled a corner to reveal a pack of Park Drive and a box of matches. "The serious swimmer's drug of choice."

"And to think I was getting worried about you."

Still standing up to their chests in the lake, they lit two cigarettes and inhaled very very deeply.

"Got to clear that clean air out of our lungs, Scott."

They walked out towards the centre, till only their heads were out of the water along with one hand each, holding their cigarettes at an exaggerated and ostentatious angle like 1930's poseurs in a Berlin nightclub.

"This," said Jack, with feeling, "is the best smoke I have ever had in my life."

"In my whole life," agreed Milo, "all seventeen years of it. And there will never be another like it."

"Well, you never know," mused Jack, "they say the first cigarette after sex is very special."

"But I am going to give up smoking when I am twenty-five, and I really doubt I will have had sex before then."

"Of course, you're right. So maybe it will be the cigarette you light when you eat your first mango, or after winning the luge in the winter Olympics."

"Both are more likely than sex, for sure. I did once see a mango in the fruit museum. But those other cigarettes you conjure, enticing as they are, cannot rival this cigarette, which will for ever after be designated in my heart as 'le beau feu en l'eau.'"

"So romantic, *mon frère*, perhaps we should keep the butts of these remarkable cigarettes and put them in a finely-crafted glass case."

As they were chatting and bantering, they had floated and bobbed back from the centre to the jetty and they were standing under the shadow of it, relishing the last drag of the best-ever smoke, enjoy-ing the view over the still and silent pond with the reflecting sun now reaching slowly across it towards them. As this last delightful minute of calm waned, and just as they were reluctantly beginning to pull their bodies out of the delicious weightlessness and back onto the landing stage of reality, suddenly something heavy, dark and powerful flashed so close above them that it brushed the hair on their emerging heads before shattering the pond a metre beyond them and sending up a massive plume of water which hung for a moment in the air before crashing down on Jack and Milo, blasphemously extinguishing the greatest cigarettes ever smoked.

"What the hell," shouted Jack, startled and confused. His hands and arms went automatically over his head for protection as instructed in the class at junior school on "What to do in a nuclear attack." Then Karl's head bobbed up out of the pond a metre away, laughing uproariously. Galvanised by shock, Jack reflexively pulled back his arm and launched a punch straight into his mouth, turning his fist and locking his wrist at the point of impact, just as his father had taught him. It struck Karl well and true and made a very satisfying thwack, like a gone-over pear dropping two metres onto cobbled stone.

But Karl was stern stuff, and Jack realised in less than a second that he had a serious problem on his hands, because Karl was not a boy, he was a man, and he just shook off the blow – the best punch Jack had ever delivered – and came back at Jack with his fists flying. He was much bigger than Jack, and stronger, but Jack did have some boxing skills and Karl in his anger was flailing rather than aiming. So as long as he could block and duck the roundhouses Jack had a chance. Karl caught him one on the side of the head, but it glanced off; Jack kept his nerve and got a tasty jab into the eye – this time Karl yelped. He came back even harder, and Jack was getting worried.

Then from the sky came down a mighty paddle, as if a wooden lightning bolt had been thrown by Zeus himself from Olympus.

"What the fuck is going on," shouted the *deus ex machina*, on this occasion a demi-God named Jean, who had been arriving in the drive with a tray of croissants when he heard the palaver in the pool. Placing his baked goods on the table on the terrace and picking up an oar from one of the boats as he walked down the jetty, he'd chucked it – like a caber, I would say, rather than a javelin – between the fighting youths to break them up. As he said later to Milo, "there was no way I was going in the water in my clothes just to pull those two fools apart."

The boys froze and said nothing. Jean dragged them both up onto the jetty where they stood shaking like soaked and quivering schoolboys in the headmaster's waiting room. They were clearly in shock, both of them, and Karl had two lumps, one on the top lip, and the other under the right eye which was changing colour as Jean watched. Jack was physically unscathed but looking white and drained: he wasn't a fighter, had hardly had even a minor scrap in his now eighteen years, but suddenly he'd been involved in two serious unsolicited affrays in less than five days.

Karl and Jack neither looked at Jean, nor at each other, but stared fixedly ninety-degrees sideways like a pair of novelty bookends on the discount table of a tacky gift shop: The Pitiful Pugilists.

"Well," said Jean, "I am waiting – what happened, why are you guys brawling? You hardly know each other."

Again, nothing.

"I can't have fighting here. If you worked for me in any normal capacity on the farm and you were caught assaulting each other at work, for any reason, you would be instantly dismissed. Tell me why I shouldn't sack you right now."

Jack was about to say, "Because I'm your cousin and also you cannot run the Experience without us," but retained enough sense to bite his tongue. His other choice was to say, "Due to the fact Karl was going to abuse Amelie last night and he's got it in for us because we stopped him," but again, so much to be thought through before he wanted to go down that road.

In any case, his moment was lost, and Karl, typically, had decided to speak first.

"Horseplay," he said. Actually he used a German word, "*Pferdespiele*," which for some unfathomable reason Jean understood.

"Horseplay my arse."

[Milo was coming close to losing it. He bit his lip almost to the blood to stop himself completely cracking up with laughter. He sensed it was inappropriate, and Jean wouldn't appreciate it, so he gradually sank the lower half of his face under water where the ensuing giggle bubbles would hopefully be mistaken for a little innocuous flatulence.]

"He bombed us, Jean," Jack chipped in, "I over-reacted when I went to splash him back and went too far, missed the water, caught him on the chops – really my fault, I was way too excited. Karl, I am so sorry, you can have a free hit whenever you like."

Karl nodded in comradely appreciation and was about to take his free punch right away before the coin dropped that Jack was making a joke at his expense to convince Jean they were both OK with each other.

"No free punch necessary, Francois," he said, U-turning midway through the motion. "Actually, I believe it was my fault, I bombed you out of the blue, too close, and too hard – it must have been quite a shock, I can understand why you were both scared." The last said with a little underhand relish.

Jean was not taken in at all by all the fake camaraderie, sham apologies and *pferdespiele* nonsense, but he didn't want to – really could not afford to – fire these boys on whom so much was now riding. Also he loved Jack. But he had to say something, and he had to make sure this didn't happen again, or an already overly fragile situation was likely to crumble very quickly.

Jean gestured to Claude, who had arrived with him in the car and who was standing at the land end of the jetty, watching, smoking of course, and, like Milo, trying to keep the amusement out of his expression, which was much easier in his case due to his face's nicotine-impaired flexibility.

"Take these two idiots up to the forestry please, Claude, and put them to work today. It is a big Time Out, and a chance to think. Not the planting, the hard graft. Give them a sandwich for lunch, but please, I don't want to see them till dinner time if you can bear it."

Claude nodded, without hiding his lack of enthusiasm for taking on the city boys wardenship and becoming executioner to Jean's over-expeditious judge. Jean ignored Claude micro-posturing as old friends mainly do, he didn't need to explain himself or justify himself, he wanted the boys taught a lesson, tired out, and kept out of the way for a day to cool off.

"Make sure they take chunks out of the trees instead of each other.

"Karl, Francois, you've got five minutes to get dressed and get to the car – we'll see you tonight, and when we do, we never talk about this again, and it never happens again, OK? Also, we cannot lose a whole day's work on the play, so we will have a rehearsal tonight after dinner, agreed?"

He turned away without waiting for an answer, he really wasn't seeking an opinion.

"Scott, with me please, I need to check the fence down the end there, you can help me. On second thoughts, go and put some trousers on first, and be back in five minutes. We'll have breakfast afterwards."

When Milo returned, he had done that thing, in his panic to be quick, of putting on dry trousers over a wet swimsuit, so damp stains were already beginning to appear all around his waist and upper thighs. Jean pretended not to notice, and they set off down the field side of the lake, heading spuriously towards the broken-fence excuse to have a quiet chat.

"What's happening with Jack, Mile, I'm worried. He turns up here, agitated like I've never seen him, telling me he's been in a terrible fight in London, totally out of character apparently; now three days later I find him going full-on Rocky Marciano with someone he barely knows, supposedly over some ill-judged water play."

Silence sat flat on the pond, the wind blew the reeds, Milo found the peace deeply comforting and the presence of Jean totally reassuring. He had not experienced much contentment for a great many months, since before he had started revising so hard for the exams which had somehow diminished into nothingness in the past few days. Far from upsetting his equilibrium, Jean's concerns and questions calmed him, quietened him. Because someone else cared, because there was a grown-up who was trying to understand and help them; it was an immense relief to be with a man who could insert an oar between two grappling bodies and pull them apart like an axe splitting kindling.

He entered a reverie, he sensed Jean by a kind of emotional osmosis, not listening particularly. He didn't understand all the words, but the sentiment and the question were obvious. He processed it slowly, and equitably decided not to answer.

"Mile, you need to tell me. If I know, whatever it is, I can probably help in some way. If I don't understand, I am going to get it wrong and make things worse. I am not asking you to grass on your pal."

Milo looked across the glass-blown lake to the trees beyond. A single bird rose from the tallest pine and spread its huge wings only twice to bring it down to the water, where, to Milo's surprise, it plunged sleekly through and under the surface rather than crashing straight into the crystal glaze. Magic. It got inside without breaking it.

"Mile, will you bloody listen!"

Milo turned his face up to Jean and smiled innocently, suddenly, guiltlessly, now realising he was going to tell him what had happened between Jack and Karl. Or, in fairness, what had happened between Karl and the rest of the crew. In some ways, a confession; in some ways, a distraction.

As he told his story, Jean became increasingly agitated, while continuously querying, "Are you sure?" "Did he really?" "Did you see that yourself?" At the end of the narrative, Jean commented, "So really, nothing happened, do you agree? The suspicion is this was the first attempted visit? The assumption surely must be it was by some arrangement?"

Milo, by his silence, did not dissent to the first two questions, but with a slight cocked head expression indicated he could not concur with the third, and that the inference was by no means indisputable: "Don't blame the victim." Jean explained slowly that he wasn't looking to scapegoat Amelie, or put any blame on her, but to assess the facts so he could decide how culpable Karl was. There were some areas of grey.

"So why is Jack even involved, Mile?" he asked, though he suspected he knew the answer before he even put the question.

"You know Jack. It's a mixture of chivalry and kindness, and envy and libido. Plus, didn't you sense for some reason he and Karl took a massive instant dislike to each other – that's just chemistry, right?"

"I didn't especially like Karl myself, the first time I met him," agreed Jean, reluctantly, "with some people, they're hard to like, but Karl falls into another group, they're easy to dislike. Oddly, from what you say, I did miss out on spotting anything between them, but honestly, I am so busy at the moment, and so scared of losing my shirt on the Experience, my radar is way off. I saw nothing between Karl and Jack, and I've also never noticed anything at all between Karl and Amelie, though I have been around them quite a few times.

"I wouldn't want to protect Jack unjustly, though he's family. Nor would I want to accuse Karl of anything unfairly just because it is easy to blame the bloke no-one likes. I am conscious of needing to be decent and impartial, for the good of the whole team. You know also, I am very nervous at the moment about rocking the boat for the Harlequinade, we have only a couple of days, not enough time to find and recruit more replacements."

Jean and Milo had stopped walking as their cautious conversation eventually got to the nub – even a slow-moving stream will eventually strip the flesh off a dead rabbit. They had turned in towards each other instead of pointing directly ahead, and Jean was waiting. Milo was still in his shy fugue but also perfectly at ease. That may have given him the confidence to raise the last point.

"Jack is under a lot of stress, I think, Jean. Obviously because of what happened last week in London, but also because he's missed his dad in so many ways for the past three years – things he keeps to himself – and now he's got a sense he might be near him."

Jean nodded. "Yes, that's been the part we've all been avoiding, isn't it? I can't pretend I am surprised." It was his turn now to play the dead bat. "But there's not much to say, other than we can help him through it. And of course we can keep him busy and take his mind off things. That goes for you too, my friend; let's get back – we'll see how we can repair the day and move you on busily."

When they arrived at the kitchen, Jack, Karl and Claude were gone, and Albert and Amelie were pecking nervously at some *pains au chocolat* they had mysteriously found in a box on the terrace. Milo sat down and joined them, while Jean began to pace around, clearly a little agitated. Amelie looked worried and Albert looked at Amelie, a pointed gaze which in the best brotherly tradition of undying familial loyalty and selfless protection was intended to demonstrate to Jean, "This really was not of my doing: regard her and all her works!"

Jean realised that, much as he hated confrontation of any kind, he needed to address the issue with the three of them, and did so first shyly, but then, in his stride, more boldly, shaped by genuine concern, affection, and, frankly speaking, annoyance.

"I don't know in detail what personal matters have been fomenting here…" [trying to cover up for Milo, unsuccessfully] "…but I have a broad idea, and I am extremely disappointed to discover it. I believe you all to be nice kids, great kids in fact, or I would end all this now, regardless of cost. I am *in loco parentis*; and you know I take that seriously. You are not – none of you – as old as you think, so you have to put some trust in my experience. Rules are needed, and they have to apply to the young and the charming as well as to the rest of us. Just so it is absolutely clear, the rules for the Lodge are: respect everyone; no fraternising beyond friendship; always manners; always decency; always kindness. OK?

"This is the last we will talk about this, but you cannot now pretend that it is OK with me, so I am hoping and requesting that you please respect my business and my wishes. It may be that you think I am too conservative, and that nothing untoward or illegitimate has been close to happening – in this case, I would like you to trust my judgement over your own, even if I am wrong.

"Amelie, if you would like to pack your things, please, I am going to drive you into the village and you will stay with my sister Caroline for the rest of the season. She is a wonderful woman, she has a very stable husband, Marc, and two gorgeous infants, twins. Actually they are my nephew and niece." [Amelie had got there just ahead of him in working that out.] "It will, I know, give her great pleasure to have a guest," [Jean's uncertain tone completely belied the confident nature of his assertion.] "so you will also be doing a generous act, especially if you do some small tasks for her." [This sounded very vague; clearly at this stage he was making things up.] "I can assure you she will make you extremely comfortable, she has a lovely home, and she is a superb cook. I will arrange for you to be picked up and dropped off every day by Claude or one of the others.

"Albert, Scott, please get in the car also, we will all drive on to the Experience together once we've dropped Amelie's things off and introduced her to my sister. As Francois and Karl are labouring in the forest with Claude today and won't be back until this evening, we cannot have a rehearsal until tonight, so instead I would like you to work with Daphne and do some practice sessions with her around the **PAYMENT AND COSTUMES** hut. Finish your breakfast all of you, and gather your things together, Amelie, I will make some telephone calls and see you all outside in twenty minutes."

After seventeen minutes the three sheepishly filed out of the house, Amelie struggling under the weight of two enormous suitcases while Albert politely held the door open for her. Milo took one of them, and they heaved them into the trunk, which Jean had left open. Everyone tried to catch no-one's eye, and succeeded, just bundling themselves into the car with Milo in front and the siblings in the back. For some reason he was not quite sure of, Milo was as keen to avoid Jean's gaze as the others. 'Surely I am the only totally pure participant in these sleazy events,' he thought, looking around to banter with a non-existent Jack. Hmmm.

Jean spoke as he drove. "Daphne will be arriving at the Hut shortly. You know she's in charge of the payments and tickets, and you Harlequinaders will help her get the customers quickly through the system. One of your main jobs is to help customers choose their costumes and try them on – we can't have too many delays now we are only having one barge, it will have to leave promptly at the fixed time. So please mainly tell people who are trying things on how great they look and that it will fit with a little tug on the waist. But of course make sure also they have the time of their life.

"Today you can also pick up your candy-stripe blazers, that's what we'll all wear when we are helping people in the entry area and on the boat, and also once the boat arrives at the Hill House jetty, and we walk up with the guests. We will give that part a proper test later in the week when we have the final dress rehearsal. OK?"

Frankly, no-one was in much of a mood to respond, and definitely not to quibble or question after having been dressed down like a bunch of shifty schoolkids half an hour before: it was misery made only more painful because it was justified. If Jean had said, "Today the plan is to strip to your underwear, smear your bodies with goose fat, and swim the length of the river sucking up any unsightly animal excrement with drinking straws," there would have been only a mumbled, "OK, Chief" in response. Jean's code of behaviour was not modern, and had exaggerated the strength of his criticism, but it was the same code that made them respect him and they hated themselves for having let him down.

As he was posing the distinctly rhetorical question, Jean pulled the car up outside a sweet little cottage just on the verge of the first village they had come to, about three kilometres from Forest Lodge. "Stay here, please, just for a moment," he said, as he jumped out and took the side path round to the back.

They waited in the car, completely silent. Milo got the impression Albert and Amelie were angry with him, but he honestly could not be bothered to engage with their mood, or to defend himself, or explain. Besides, he could also tell that Albert was equally annoyed with Amelie, and Amelie was annoyed with both the boys. There were no winners at the moment. The atmosphere was becoming unbearable, but thankfully Jean came back after five minutes, presumably having spent one of them saying "Hello" to Caroline, and the other four telling her a potted version of what was going on at the Lodge and asking for help.

"OK, Amelie, come in and meet Caroline, let's take the bags, she is absolutely thrilled to be hosting you here." Milo had no idea whether this was sarcasm or a slightly desperate type of enthusiasm, but now it was just him and Albert in the car, and the silence got as lumpy as cold gravy. Luckily, Jean and Amelie must just have said "Hi" inside and dropped the bags because they were quickly back in the car. Then Jean tuned the radio to some crazy holiday pop, She Loves You, Yeah. When he started singing along the tone shifted instantly. "Let's have a good day now, move on, do some useful work."

"Thanks, Jean, for everything," said Amelie, surprising all of them. "I like Caroline, she's really lovely. I'm very happy to be with her."

This cheered Jean enormously, a signal from Amelie that she was onside, that probably she regretted the position she had been in, that she was very happy not to dwell on that.

At the **PAYMENT AND COSTUMES** hut the kids all met Daphne for the first time. She was Claude's daughter; small, the same height and original build as Amelie, but much more robust, and of a very different character. Positive, busy, chatty, confident, dark, pretty, with bobbed brunette hair, she was already behind her big desk, organising papers, stamps, pens and copies of the Programme.

"Good morning, Daphne, lovely day – how are you getting on?"

"Hi, Jean, good morning. Yes, OK, I think we've got things mainly under control, the only issue is the cash register, which is still not working properly."

"Did your dad have a fiddle with it?"

"Not yet, he keeps promising. Is he with you now?"

"No he had to take some bad boys for a day's tree felling, he's not that happy to be honest."

Daphne laughed. "Dad's a strange choice for a prison guard, they'll come back bigger reprobates than when they left. What did they do?"

"I'll tell you later," Jean mouthed, motioning to the listening ears of the three youngsters with a finger on his lips.

"Let me introduce you please to sixty percent of our Harlequinade (if you don't count me). This is Albert, our Pantaloon; here's Amelie, Columbine obviously; and this is Scott, an American from Paris, who is Clown. Scott speaks French quite well, if you go very slowly and occasionally point to things. The two missing lumberjacks are Karl, who is Harlequin, and Francois, who is Pierrot. Francois is Scott's host in Paris, so they have come down here together for the summer.

"As Karl and Francois won't be training with you today, we'll have to bring them over for another session as soon as we get a chance; sorry for the double distraction Daphne."

Daphne gave the gesture for, 'No problem, Jean, you are the boss, and in any case I do not mind.'

Daphne came out from behind the counter and shook hands with Albert, then Milo, with whom she sensed immediate amity, and finally she gave Amelie a hug, two air kisses, and a look that said, "You and I are going to be good friends, though you will take a while to get the hang of it."

"Now," said Jean, "I need to get up to Hill House to check on the scene changes and talk to the cooks and the laundry people. I will be back to pick you up at the end of the day."

"Don't worry, Jean, I'll run them back when we're finished."

"That's really kind, Daphne, thanks so much.

"Now, while you are here, Daphne is in charge, you please will do all she asks, and anticipate and complete many other useful chores she does not yet know she requires to be done. Have a good day, all, and everyone remember, as I will, to forget the issues of last night and this morning. We now have a clean start – let's concentrate on having some fun and doing a great job." Jean was one of those natural leaders who liked to speak simply from the heart without too much forethought to get tangled up in; generally this worked pretty well, and sometimes it could be truly inspirational.

After he'd left, Daphne gave them the grand tour – they had all been to the Hut before, but only as part of a general look around, this was the first time they'd seen the arrangements close-up. Daphne showed them the basic workings of the cash desk and the method they were using to record the sales, issue the tickets, and account for the receipts. "The last thing we need to sort out is this wretched cash till," she said, "my dad reckons he can fix it, but he said that about the tractor the week before it killed Jacob."

They all looked a bit shocked at her callousness.

"Jacob," said Daphne, the smile on her lips amplifying into a loud laugh, "my dad's best cockerel. After dad patched the tractor up, Jacob was panicked by the noise it made and flew straight into the engine casing when it was running. Cooked instantly. Don't worry, we did not waste the corpse."

Amelie blanched.

"Thank God Francois is not here, Amelie," piped up Milo, noticing her reaction, "he places an amazing spiritual value on all forms of life."

Daphne looked blank at this odd comment, and a tiny bit miffed, in her good-natured way, that her own rather funny story had been undercut by some over-stretched banter. But the tour must go on, and Daphne shifted focus to taking them in detail through the racks of costumes, explaining all the different options for men and women of all ages, and for children, and even toddlers. They tried some of the costumes on themselves and were surprised and excited, as Milo had previously discovered, to see how just putting on a couple of items created distinct new personalities for each of them as well as a charmingly coordinated period ambience for the whole group.

Questions were asked and answered: about welcoming procedures; issues in the carpark; how to collect tickets and receipts; how to manage the fittings (there were three curtains at each end making 'cubicles'); and where customers could leave their possessions and clothes if they didn't want to take them up to Hill House or secure them in their cars (there were a few lockers, and non-valuables could be lodged also with Daphne, but it was not to be encouraged as it would slow them down when they got back at the end of the day).

After three hours Daphne called them together. "Lunchtime now, but one last duty this morning." She wheeled a clothes rack out from the back and took off its cover; there were a dozen beautiful pink and white striped blazers hanging on it.

"One for each of the actors and Tommy, tailored specially, and some spare jackets to be used by the rest of the team when needed.

"For you, Amelie and Albert, they are already fitted and finished by Jean's mother; your names are on them. The same for Karl. Then there are two she made for boys called Frederick and Pascal. Sadly it seems they will not be needing them now. So, my dream is that they will be roughly the same size as Francois and you Scott. What do you think?"

Milo took off the Pascal blazer, a little generous for him, but the Frederick was perfect.

"Lucky for us, yon Frederick was a shapely youth, wiry, yet with an understated strength."

"Good to know, Scott," said Daphne, laughing, "it doesn't look too loose, and we can always have it taken in if you wake up less shapely tomorrow. If we have to, we can adapt one of the extras for you."

They were all thrilled with the jackets, a badge of belonging, and some of them wanted to keep them on, but Daphne suggested, sensibly, as they were unique, it was probably best to leave them at work and change each morning when they arrived.

Then she locked up the Hut and the four of them piled into her bright little red car. Milo had no idea what it was but his first, incorrect, guess would have been a 2CV. She drove them at about 85kph into one of the local villages, where she screeched to a halt outside a serviceable-looking eatery, which of course turned out to be owned by a member of Jean's clan. Functional on the outside, inside was all charm and intimacy, and they were made to feel like family – everything had been covered by Jean, with his usual thoughtfulness ('How does he find the time to do that?' Milo mused yet again).

Amelie had an omelette with mushrooms, Daphne also, and the boys shared a casserole that Milo believed to be among the four greatest things he had ever eaten. He couldn't work out all the ingredients, and they were never given a menu, but he recognised some kind of bacon, some fabulous beans (haricots?) and pieces of a fowl, most likely chicken, but possibly a smaller bird, that melted in the mouth with the consistency of peach flesh, not meat as he had previously encountered it from Sainsburys on the Barking Road. 'Oh Brave new world' he thought, 'that has such *poulet* in it.'

After the main course there was a small slice of *tarte au poires* and then cheese. 'Life on the run, just gets better all the time,' mused Milo, as they were served strong small coffees with tiny almond biscuits. 'O my Lord – and Jack has lost the chance of learning that an omelette is vegetarian as well as losing the opportunity of sharing one with Amelie. I will tell him later what he has missed. Poor boy.'

"Do you get to do this every day, Daphne?" Albert asked, part joking, and assuming this was a special one-off occasion.

"Actually, this is the second time only!" Daphne replied. "The other time was when Jean brought me here to persuade me to take this job, just two weeks ago. You should know, unlike the rest of the tribe, I never sought to mix family life with business. I have returned here relatively recently – for a while, I escaped!"

Suddenly realising she was talking, she shut up and stirred her coffee self-consciously. Milo said gently, "Do please go on, we'd love to know the rest of that story."

"Well, it is not so very much, and honestly I am not really accustomed these days to speaking about myself. But as you ask, I was the first girl in this very large extended family to go to university. I went to Toulouse, and after I graduated, in Chemistry, I was recruited to stay and work there.

"I moved in with my lover, who very sadly contracted leukaemia a few years back, and then finally passed away about two years ago – that's when I decided to get out of Toulouse.

"I have been hanging around here since, living in one of my dad's buildings, and helping Jean and dad out with this and that. Then Jean decided it was time for me to have a proper job and got me involved with this – he is very good at interfering in other people's lives, as I suspect you have each found out by now."

"I am so sorry," said Albert, nervously, not quite knowing what to say. Like most people allowed into someone else's sadness, he was unsure how to show sympathy without imposing or making it his own. Albert was conscious he had hardly experienced any setback himself; he had been shielded from anxiety and ailments, never been close to an illness, let alone cared for a dying partner, and had never even seen old age and infirmity. It struck him that Daphne was probably only four or five years older than him.

Daphne tapped him on the lower arm, gently, "Don't worry, Albert, I appreciate your thoughts, maybe I shouldn't have shared, I am not used to being back among so many nice people. It is kind, but I am not looking for any reaction, I told you only so you won't get embarrassed when you find out from someone else."

Sobered, they returned to the car, and Daphne broke the tension with her crazy driving, getting them back to the Experience site even more quickly than the journey out. "You certainly like some speed, Daphne," quailed Milo hiding on the back seat. She laughed uproariously. "But I have told you, Scott, I have nothing to live for, other than the fact Jean will kill me if I let him down." Milo was liking Daphne a lot.

As they arrived back, Milo, Amelie and Albert were shocked to see a line of vehicles queuing up to get into the carpark.

"What's happening?" Amelie cried, ready to be in a panic. "Have we got the dates wrong?"

Again Daphne went for the massive chuckle, her default it seemed in pretty well any situation she encountered (which is great when you think about it, thought Milo; though in time it will be good to discover which are the humorous laughs).

"Don't worry, my dear Amelie, this is all arranged just for you. Jean is keen to practise everything in real conditions, so basically these are all relatives and workers who have been given a bit of time off to come and be customers for the afternoon."

As she was speaking, Daphne negotiated her way past the stream of cars and vans at 60kph and they parked, disgorged, and hurried up to the Hut.

"So this afternoon, my job is just to stand back, to avoid interfering, and to watch you greet, direct the carpark, take the money, issue the tickets, and help choose and fit the costumes."

The kids looked at each other. They weren't ready, but then, these weren't proper customers, so let's give it a go. An accordion started up a few metres away, so close and so loud it made everyone jump; then they all burst into relieved giggles when they realised what it was.

"Meet Tommy," Daphne shouted above the noise, "he's here to practise too."

And there was Jean's two-metre-tall musical student, twirling amongst the throng and playing a fabulous folk jig. He nodded and took one hand off the instrument to wave when the song allowed. "Hi, everyone!!"

"Hi, Tommy!!" they all called back, smiling.

Initially, Albert took the carpark, Milo took the cash register, and Amelie looked after the ladies and children in the costumes. When they'd finished their first tasks, Albert and Milo went on to the men's area and helped them to pick outfits, try them on (briefly, as instructed) and see what worked. This involved quite a lot of 'suits you, sir' and hardly any 'perhaps sir might benefit from a slightly larger size.'

The results were great, much better than they would have expected with only three of them. It was fun, they got all the cars safely lodged, everyone paid roughly the right money (which Jean had given them) and got the correct tickets and Programmes, and frankly, emerging from the Hut, all the customers looked fantastically authentic. And all done in around forty minutes from start to finish. It worked!

And then … they did it all again. This time it took thirty-five minutes, everybody looked fabulous, and there was even some dancing as everyone gathered outside in their outfits.

As a thank-you, the guest customers were then seated at some bench tables and all given a long cold drink – beer or lemonade – and a choice of excellent cakes. Tommy played some emotive ballads to slow the mood and create tranquillity, as he would do every day on the return boat trip, to bring the travellers gently back to earth. They all – customers and servers – thanked each other profusely and slapped a lot of backs. It was exciting: everyone was assured and reassured that this was to be the success of the year and would put the region on the map. Then as the afternoon wore on, the guests gradually drifted away from the Experience to spend the rest of their free time playing with their children, visiting their lovers, or going to the supermarket. And Daphne gave Amelie,

Albert and Milo a last debriefing: small tweaks and tips for minor improvements, tiny suggestions to refine this and that.

"Smile, pupils," she affectionately clapped each of them on the back, and went on cheerfully, "you have done very well! I will happily give your boss a testimonial for you to start work, so congratulations, you get the jobs."

They all laughed and applauded and punched each other on the arm in congratulation.

"Though honestly I don't think there were too many other applicants," Daphne continued. "The hours are long, and the pay is, I am sure, very small, knowing Jean: but I think we are a great team, we will have a lot of fun. Also I think we may be part of something wonderful here, if we can bring it off."

So saying, she bundled them into the motor and they shot back to the Forest Lodge at light speed. The kids were really happy and all of them had fallen for Daphne in a big way, Milo thinking, 'She is one of life's irresistibles.' Jean was waiting for them in the drive ('How does he always know when we're coming?' thought Milo), and they all went to the door together, including Daphne, who was corralled in for dinner and to watch the evening rehearsal.

As they were entering, Claude's car pulled up, and he jumped out, followed by Jack and Karl; the others turned to welcome them. Claude gave Jean a shrug with his palms and wrists rotated, and rolled his eyes, a complex combination of signs indicating 'I really wish you had not asked me to do that, boss, but it is over now, I drilled them for you, they've paid their price, and here they are, I hope ready to move on.' Jean nodded his respectful thanks back to Claude, and also, with a small angled upward jerk of the head, invited him to stay to dinner with his daughter, as a well-earned reward.

When they got inside and started to wash their hands in the kitchen and gather round the table, Jack bowed his head to Jean, supplicatory, demonstrating appropriate remorse.

"How did it go, Francois?" Jean asked him. Everyone turned to observe.

"I very much enjoyed my intensive course in lumber technology." He held his hands up facing outwards, so that Jean and the others could see his blisters – the palms were a fluorescent red never previously observed in nature. "Today we completed the practical section, I can only hope that the theory test is less painful…"

"He did well," said Claude, putting his arm round his shoulder, "I reckon once they showed him the ropes he cut and cleaned two or three trees on his own, quite impressive for a novice. And his greatest achievement, he never lost a single finger, that's very unusual for someone on their first day in forestry."

As he said that Claude held up his own left hand with its back facing them all, creating a missing finger by folding a digit inwards in the noble tradition of a million dads down the ages; and the table laughed as dutifully as all those dads' kids have done for five thousand years. Milo winked at Daphne, "Your dad's a hoot"; Daphne rolled her eyes, but grinned.

And Karl? He was another matter, which Jean, Milo and Daphne had not failed to note. He was quiet and did not want to catch Jean's gaze; in addition to the humiliation of being sent to punishment camp, he had a minor-quality black eye and a red welt above his lip, neither of which were making him very happy. He washed his hands and took an unobtrusive place at the end of the table, between Albert and an empty space reserved for Madame Jestique, who had not yet arrived. Claude spotted Jean watching Karl and raised his eyebrows to him, indicating 'I'll tell you more later, this one did not do so well, possibly a problem.'

Once again Jean had brought the food back from his visit to Hill House ("You seriously finished all yesterday's?" Julie had asked incredulously). As they were all beginning to unbox and lay things out, Madame Jestique entered and took her seat, nodding her hellos to everyone.

"Julie and Jacques were having more practise sessions today and very kindly reserved some of the results for us," said Jean, as he carefully pulled half of a magnificent quiche from its wrapping, flourishing it as proudly as if he had cooked it himself. All around the table there was similar flaunting and joyous whoops as the containers were emptied and the food was unveiled, another magnificent banquet, and they were all very very hungry. 'Blimey,' thought Milo, yet again, 'how does he do it!?'

When they had worked their way through many delicious courses as far as the coffee, which was paired with a huge box of colourful macarons that made them all smile and whimper, Jean said "Francois, perhaps you are thinking of starting soon? With your approval, while you are working, I have something I think it might be fun to introduce to the show."

Jack did a little surprised look that Jean liked. He hadn't consulted with him about the idea, and he was pleased that Jack was feeling proprietorial about his Director role, and still totally engaged, not resenting his day in the woods. Jean gave Jack a 'Trust me' glance with his eyes and brows: he didn't want to get into it with him in front of everyone as he was feeling too clumsy to pull off the subtleties of the stranger-boss right then and worried he would reveal himself as a cousin with a bright idea rather than tenuously maintaining his pretence of being a figure of authority. He nodded to Jack to take the lead, and Jack spoke out immediately: "That's a great thought, chief, let's get going while it is still light. We've plenty of the evening left, and we need all the rehearsing we can get. I do think it is appropriate for me to apologise to the team for having to work late tonight, I think you all know I am largely to blame for disrupting everything today, I am sorry to the whole team for that, and I will do my best to make sure nothing like that happens again."

Everyone at the table, with the exception of Karl, nodded their appreciation of the speech, and several rapped on the wood to demonstrate their approval. The team was back together. They went through to the Hall and Madame Jestique took her seat and started a few bars from Debussy's Suite Bergamasque. The others took their places for the opening and subsequent scenes, with Karl looking more than a trifle shop-worn, and more broody and grumpy than ever.

While they were working on the raised stage at one end, Jean was at the other, undoing a huge carry-all he had brought in from his car and pulling from it an old-fashioned canvas bag more than a metre long, covered with buckles, interesting little pockets and handy leather straps. After quite a bit of fiddling, being rather grateful that everyone was occupied and not watching his clumsiness, he got the canvas unravelled to reveal a strange and gorgeous object. The bottom was like a beautifully polished teak extendable artist's easel; the top some sort of shiny brass, wood and glass device from early in the century, a gadget which to the others looked like a short, wide telescope or possibly a long-lensed early camera.

Jean, attempting to assemble and erect it, was by now tangled up like the comic postcard of the man on the beach being strangled by his own deck chair, with the caption "Help Me, Missus, I Can't Get It Up." Everyone had gradually stopped acting in order to observe this phenomenon more closely, and the rehearsal had ground to a halt while the performers were collectively having a massive fit of the noiseless giggles.

In the end this rather conveniently helped to break the ice for Jean's big reveal. "So," he said, eventually noticing that everyone was watching as he finally fixed the last screw in place on the wooden tripod and checked the brass top was locked on with all its cogs and handles in place and facing the right direction, "this could be one of the finishing touches for the plan, subject to Francois being happy with the result.

"I have tried it out once, but we might need to experiment. Believe it or not, this contraption has been in my uncle's attic for the past thirty years, it is an authentic silent movie projector. He worked in the tiny cinema in Bourges after World War One and kept the equipment after they got put out of business by that bigger place that did talkies and colour."

[Madame Jestique grimaced and played the opening bars of the Funeral March.]

"I tried it this morning, the arc light still works! This model can be hand-cranked or also has a small motor, we can see how it goes, maybe run it on the motor till it fails, rather than having to get in an extra person to crank it."

Jean went to the far windows and pulled the curtains, shouting to ask Scott to please do the same at the other end. They were not thick curtains, and it was still quite light outside, so they didn't make it totally black, but dark enough. Jean returned to the projector, turned it on and got ready to start it up.

Jack was confused about what Jean was up to but couldn't ask too many questions because that would emphasise that the inspiration for this part of the show had come from another source. Luckily, Milo, very aware of Jack's sensitivities in the area of sharing credit, came to his rescue.

"Can I ask, Jean, I am sure it is a dumb question, but what film is it you are going to show?"

Jean laughed. "Not a film exactly. Why don't you start the play from the beginning, and I will demonstrate what I think this might be able to add to the performance."

Jack gave Jean a gracious nod indicating he would allow it, and with a few quick requests brought the starters back for the opening scene. As Pantaloon and Columbine took their positions, and prepared to launch into their roles, Jean started the machine. It made that fabulous evocative whirr that excites film lovers, the rattle and hum that thrills the soul of classic-movie buffs everywhere. Then

244

the bulb came on, casting an amazing sepia-cream light playing across the stage, illuminating it like an old black and white film, and as the internal mechanism continued to rotate and spin, the light flickered with tiny flaws creating occasional ragged grazes and spotting on the cast, like an antique print that had been reproduced too many times.

Everyone was astonished. The result was unimaginably beautiful, unutterably perfect. The whole team burst into applause, clapping hands and stamping feet. Madame Jestique hammered out the opening bars of La Marseillaise. Each of them knew without any doubt that this was the final embellishment that would make the show incredibly compelling. Milo and Jack hugged Jean; Albert hugged Daphne and Claude; Madame Jestique hugged herself alone. But across the room, Jack saw Karl's lunge at Amelie being flicked away with the parrying skill of an Olympic fencer. Oh how his innards chuckled; what joy, what infinite joy. Of course, Karl, turning clumsily like a dog in a tight circle, came around to try her from a different angle, but he had lost too much time, and when he got there he found himself facing Jack's now-intervening grin. Karl's chagrin was complete as Amelie dodged him and joined instead the Daphne dancing nexus while Jack pulled him ardently into his own embrace: "Isn't it wonderful, Karl?" he whispered into his ear, "Are you as excited as me?" Karl pushed him away, muttering something in German that Jack didn't need translated.

Settling back down to work, the next half an hour was a pure delight, as the actors played out a full rehearsal under the dazzling illumination of Jean's new effect. They were able to see where it added, where it had less impact. By fiddling with the speeds, lenses and lights, Jean was also beginning to discover and employ some new variations and effects. It was magic dust and fairy lights combined.

Jean had also brought with him for the first time some of the big sign boards he was having designed in town. They had the most fabulous calligraphical fonts of the 1920s, and elaborately drawn Art Nouveau borders of flowers and leaves. In the flickering movie light they looked magnificent. The signs would stand at the side of the stage and be used to divide the scenes, to give emphasis, to provide explanation, and to add some humour. So far the signs he had made, using new wording from Jack, and still a work in progress, were:

Pantalon prends garde à ta fille!

Harlequin se révèle.

Clown fait une dégringolade heureuse.

Pierrot et Clown jouer les héros d'un jour.

Pierrot est-il plus joli que Colombine?

Harlequin tombe en disgrâce – dans les bras de la police.

The signs looked great in terms of art and design, but Jean was not yet convinced that they had got the concept quite right, there was a danger they were pointing out the obvious without being particularly funny, and also were they talking down to the audience, maybe even spoiling the scenes by telling in advance what was happening? Perhaps some of that was in the timing of when they were displayed. He made a mental note to talk to Jack later about some rewrites; he loved the perfect styling, which was beautifully in tone with the ambience, so he definitely didn't want to lose them.

The rehearsal went really well, driven forward by the adrenaline high from the thrill of the projector. Everyone worked hard, even Karl, though it was noticeable to all that while the rest of the team were enjoying themselves, and it showed in their performance, Karl was both seeping disgruntlement and oozing general resentment.

At the end, as usual, Jean offered everybody a nightcap to say thank you, except Amelie, as normal, whom he considered too young for strong alcohol. Instead he found her some marvellous prune extract (I am not being satirical, it was blissful) to make her

246

feel special, and not left out. Jack and Milo took their beer bottles into the garden once more, so they could smoke, and the others came and went.

Amelie was in the garden asking Milo to tell her more about the pleasure of smoking, "Given that it is the main thing I seem to see you two doing"; and Jack was revelling in the petty power, disguised as noble concern, of telling her they could not possibly supply her with her first cigarette. Milo wasn't nearly so committed to her abstinence, except for the fact he didn't want to annoy Jean, who he guessed would be furious if they encouraged her to toke.

Meanwhile, Karl and Albert had wandered into the kitchen, Karl extending his reparative charm offensive by putting his arm round the younger boy's shoulder, pouring him a beer and quietly teaching him a German student song, the best one, about how quickly the golden years of youth pass, and how hard life is afterwards.

O alte Burschenherrlichkeit,
Wohin bist du verschwunden?
Nie kehrst du wieder, goldne Zeit,
So froh, so ungebunden!

Drifting out into the garden, wistful, melodic, as Albert caught on and the two voices merged, it was quite beautiful.

Jean, Claude and Madame Jestique were sitting in the Hall sharing a bottle of wine that was much too good to waste on the young ones, just unwinding from the elation of the rehearsal. As the song swelled, Madame Jestique admired the musicianship (from such unexpected sources!) and went to the piano to create a gorgeous soft accompaniment; Jean sat back and congratulated himself on the quality of team-building reflected by the note-perfect duet; and Claude just clutched his glass and tried unsuccessfully to disguise the fact he hated anything in German (it didn't matter how lyrical it was). It was idyllic, harmonious and congenial, and therefore, as I am sure you will have predicted, it presented the perfect moment for discord.

"Right," said Jean, heaving himself up, "I think I am off to feed Hector, and make some calls." He never stopped.

Walking out to the garden he mentioned to Francois and Scott that he was off home, and maybe it was time to think about bed, as they all had an early start. He politely asked Amelie if she was ready to make a move and suggested he could drop her off at Caroline's. They went outside into the carpark with the others following them to say goodnight, joined by Albert and Karl, still singing, and Madame Jestique and Claude jealously nursing their glasses.

When Jean and Amelie opened the car doors, Karl, not understanding, stepped forward to also jump in, assuming, wherever they were going, he could come too, and asking where they were headed.

"Not you, Karl, sorry," Jean called out gently, "this lift is just for Amelie, she is now staying with my sister Caroline as I think she was missing some female company, being the only girl stuck in a house with all you *Raufbolde*."

That morning when this decision had been taken, Karl had already left. Jack had too, but he seemed to be taking the news a lot better, to the extent there was quite a large grin on his face. But Karl, learning this now for the first time, looked astounded, annoyed and guilty, all at once – his face could hardly sustain the burden of so many conflicting emotions, but one thing he didn't look was embarrassed.

"That's not the reason, is it?" he asked, "You're trying to split us up."

"Let's not open this up again, please Karl, other than to say there is most assuredly no 'us' in this scenario, so nothing to 'split up.'

"Can we please leave it tonight and talk about it in the morning? We have had such a good evening, let's leave it on a high. We spent all day suffering and then recovering from this morning's brawl, which I believe followed some quarrels last night, so please let's not reopen and revisit all the aggravation now."

"I don't want to be disrespectful, Jean" [here it comes, then], "but I would like to discuss it now because I feel very aggrieved by this. I have come to this out-of-the-way place, effectively to bail you out with your little show, to do you a favour. Now you seem to be implying it is in the better interest of Amelie to be protected from my friendship, which is an entirely ridiculous notion. Can you not see how utterly offensive this is both to me and to her, to be told we must be segregated like children being kept apart in a kindergarten class?"

The kindergarten allusion was perhaps not his finest moment given their age difference; and looking round the circle of listeners in the expectation of finding overwhelming support left him rather disappointed. Jean was staring at Karl, wondering what an earth he could do to stop him making a fool of himself in front of everyone, again. Then an unexpected voice broke the silence and relieved him of responsibility.

"Actually, Karl," Amelie said, as she got back out of the car, "although Jean arranged this change of domestic arrangements, I can assure you it was I who eagerly endorsed it. Given I am a young girl who is suspected of having a surfeit of wants and a deficit of self-control, it is clearly my own weak nature that I need to be protected from. You don't need to take our separation so personally."

So saying, she got back into the car and slammed the door. Jean looked at Karl, shrugged, whispered in his ear, "Let's agree, we shall never speak of this again," and ducked into the front seat, putting his head down quickly to hide his grin.

They pulled out of the drive with a screech, leaving Karl suddenly standing in front of a half-circle of onlookers, each of whom was straining to suppress their triumph, joy, relief or disapproval. The lights from the house flooded the driveway like a sports stadium, and right in the middle of the pitch was the star athlete, Karl, illustrating the unarguable fact that even the best players occasionally take a beating.

He had regressed. Last night he had been a man with a dream frustrated; before breakfast a bullying adolescent; at lunchtime a schoolboy on detention with facial abrasions; and now, after tea, he was a toyless toddler who had dirtied himself in the middle of the nursery. None of the others could bring themselves to look at him.

Karl was utterly humiliated, and therefore, as Claude immediately realised, extremely dangerous. Thinking quickly, he stepped forward, put one of his huge arms around the youth's drooping shoulders, and murmured so that only he could hear, "That's bad luck, buddy, that was really unfair. Let's get away from the kids and get a proper drink somewhere."

Without really waiting for a response, he simultaneously led and pushed Karl into the passenger seat of his van and put the key in the ignition. Before driving off he pushed the cigarette lighter in, pulled out a pack of grizzled mentholated cigarettes, put one in his own mouth (in the normal slot) and placed another in Karl's as the boy slumped, expressionless, in the soiled pants of his own wretchedness.

Claude lit his own fag, then Karl's. Karl inhaled deeply. Breathed out. Inhaled again. Breathed out again. "I don't smoke," he said, as he inhaled for a third time.

"I reckon you do for tonight, Karl," said Claude. "After that it might be a habit you want to review on a day-by-day basis."

And then they were gone: the spotlit field of dreams was deserted. Only the crowd was left, sadly viewing the empty oval and lamenting the end of the drama while pretending they were glad it was over.

Madame Jestique had tired early of the tragedy and had slipped inside to do the musical equivalent of hiding behind the sofa to watch between her fingers: she had opened her piano and started to play. With unconscious relish she had chosen Questa o Quella from the beginning of Rigoletto, one of the most arrogant male songs ever, the cocksure musing of the Duke of Mantua who feels all women should belong to him, even if they are already married to his friends and members of his court. As the shaken troupe of actors drifted back to the old house along the lighted pathway, like extras moving across a film set, the brilliantly conceited music embraced them ironically.

After listening entranced to the echoing piano filling the night, Daphne called out, "That's it for me tonight," and peeled off to her car, humming. Madame Jestique finished the aria, nodded and waved her goodnights, and joined her for a ride home. The others headed quietly to their rooms, currently down to three. "Night, Albert"; "Night, Francois"; "Night, Scott."

After five minutes, Milo popped his head around Jack's door.

"Blimey, chief, that was some day."

"Double blimey, indeed it was. It feels like all days are some days now, Milo – how long do you think we will be able to keep up this pace?"

They lit cigarettes, now conscious that they had a reputation to uphold for incessant smoking: Milo opened the window to ensure they remained compliant with house rules.

"How was the lumbering?"

"I lumbered pretty well for a little'un. The actual lumber guys are maybe four times my size, they pick up the trunks and twirl them like cheerleaders' batons. After the big tree is downed with a single punch, they strip off the leaves with mighty sucks of their cavern-ous lungs, and then they gnaw its knotty flesh with their sharpened teeth to trim off the branches and twigs. They taught me sweary words and how to drink rum. They talked of arcane things and ceremonies from the ancient depths of time. Sadly, I cannot relate these mysteries to you, because I am now inducted as a member of the inner secret glade, and subject to their – our – woodland code of silence. In any case, my friend, you would be terrified to learn our rites and rituals; the smearing with sacred saps, the thrashing with thorny twigs, the binding tight with virgin sprigs. And the sacrifices, my god, such a waste of nubile young lives. I cannot, must not, tell; I believe it is my fraternal duty to protect you."

"I respect that. You have probably already said more than you should."

"You teased it out of me."

"And what of Karl, whom now I will begin to refer to as your nemesis. Did you timber with him?"

"I swung not the axe with my arch enemy, as I prefer to refer to him. Nor did we share the very long saw. In fact, Claude was pretty careful to have us kept apart. Poor Claude, he definitely had better things to do today than superintend two petulant numbskulls."

"I was thinking nincompoops."

"Careful, old boy, it is fine for me to self-stigmatise in an ironic and knowing way, but I am not ready yet for third-party censure."

"Sorry, sport; you seemed to be remorseful, I was merely admiring your self-awareness.

"Jean is worried about you going off the edge. He won't tell you yet, but he's pissed off with Karl and doesn't like him. You, he loves, but he has to be fair, and seen to be fair."

"Well, anyway, I am thinking an objective has been achieved if the fragrant and fragile child has been moved to safety."

"Hearing her tonight, Jack, are you sure she was ever in that much danger? It felt to me as though she was much savvier than suspected about the nature of Karl and his evil ends. I know she's Schröding-er's girlfriend, but the odds are even she was always asleep."

"Also that she was always awake."

"Possibly she was never there at all."

"Yes, she probably wasn't. That enigma is a coin she will never spend. But, taking it at face value, she seems extremely content to be staying away from here, doesn't she? Good for her, she does appear much more independent and self-assured than I was imagining."

To Milo's ears, who knew him well, he was sounding terribly wistful, and saying things he wanted other people to hear, not what he really thought.

"Slightly condescending there, old boy."

"Isn't it allowed these days to say a girl has good and admirable traits without accusations of being patronising? I am just saying that in terms of her role in 'The Affair Karl,' or lack of it, I might have read things slightly wrong, if you can believe it."

Jack looked at Milo, challenging him to answer back, or agree. No response. Milo wasn't going to fall for that one, though he was laughing inside at Jack's woeful attempt at a confession of human frailty.

"But that doesn't exonerate Karl from his dubious actions, his fumbled plotting, does it? I was still right about him, he admitted it, and he flaunted his belief in the right of a man to exploit his power."

"Calm down, Jack! You're literally foaming; chill my pal. Don't confuse Karl with the theatrical role you created for him."

"Do you get the feeling at the moment everything seems louder, broader, more highly coloured, more sinister than it actually is? Maybe it's because our senses are heightened by our own plight; our nerves are tingling from stress, anxiety and the lack of sleep.

"You said it yourself; you've won this: you've protected a nice if occasionally annoying girl who now we suspect did not need protecting; and you have humbled an arrogant, disagreeable and potentially – I stress, potentially – menacing would-be lover before he could damage anyone. You should relax, enjoy the moment.

"Now, can I check, have you chanted the mantra today? That is what we should be worrying about, not a teenage love-spat that might or might not be minacious."

"Oh my word, sir, I love minacious, you've put your finger right on it. For the chanting, no, I have not done it yet today. Both Jean and Claude took me aside at different times for short whispers. Nothing has been heard from London; no-one strange is in the area; my mother has not called or made contact with anyone. No stories have appeared anywhere in the French press or news that they are aware of, certainly not locally."

"This is good, Jack, this is great news, or rather excellent absence of news. Every day that goes by, it is not just about us being safer, but it must mean nothing so bad happened to that kid, right? Or surely we would know."

"Sounds like a good theory, Milo, I hope to God it's right. Shall we chant a while, to make sure?"

"Great idea, let me get something from downstairs."

Milo slipped out of the room and crept downstairs in the dark, not wanting to put on the lights in case he woke the others. Then he realised, only Albert was left in the house, and he was about twenty metres away in the other wing…. he didn't need to tiptoe.

He'd seen some candles in the kitchen drawer so he went for those, edging gingerly around the downstairs rooms till he found the position of the light switches. Finally managing to turn on the kitchen light, he collected five candles, two glasses and the open bottle of brandy, about half full. He went to his own room on the way back to Jack's to fetch another pack of cigarettes. Behind him he decided to leave lit all the lamps and lights he'd put on. Why? He didn't like the dark, at all, sometimes it made him think he was dying; but, on a less morbid level, he also thought he might have to go back down, and he didn't want to be stumbling and staggering round again later.

In Jack's room they poured large brandies and lit cigarettes, then used the glowing tips to light the candles, which they placed in a circle around them on the floor ["It's a pentagram, actually," said Milo]. Milo turned out the main room light. "Very romantic," said Jack, and in the dark, Milo was embarrassed. "OK so now we chant."

"First, can we toast to the boy's health?" asked Jack. "Would that work?"

"I am not sure it can be permanently added to the ritual but calling by name is strong magic in its own right, that can't hurt."

"OK, so it is Bart, right?" asked Jack.

"I was on the floor getting the crap kicked out of me, if you recall, but yes, I can confirm I heard someone shout 'Bart' both inside and also when we got out onto the pavement."

Jack winced at the recollection. "Bart is a daft name, seriously, that was definitely it?"

"I am afraid so, Jack – I think I'd heard of the kid before, in any case, being one of the hard crew from the St Francis prefects, wasn't he even head boy there or something?"

"Do we have to toast him as Bart, or can we use another name?"

"You can't just change his name because you think it's stupid. If you are genuinely going to toast his health, his recovery, his escape or whatever, it means nothing if you arbitrarily used a random name just because you prefer it. You know what you are suggesting is saying a prayer, really, and I think prayers traditionally work better if there is no confusion about who you are praying for."

"But Bart, Milo – it's such a tosser's name."

"Sweet, my friend. Two days ago, you were prepared to make any sacrifice to preserve this kid's life. You were willing to do any punishment, penalty or penance; to spend a life hitting yourself with chains; to give up all the things you love, from bacon sandwiches to The Waste Land.

"Now you are calling him tosser. Nice. What do you think God thinks when you behave like that, do you think he detects genuine remorse in you; sees your sincere sorrow, regret and contrition; recognises your absolute commitment to keep the boy alive?

"What is the point of our elaborate rites and rituals if it is not to get God himself on our side? You must show respect, my brother, you need to demonstrate both remorse and misery."

"OK, Bart it is," agreed Jack with some chagrin, "you're right, you're right. So, we make the toast, then we do the chant, agreed?"

"Yes, good. Would you like to propose the toast?"

"Actually, my friend, I was hoping you might favour us."

Milo was flattered, he even reddened slightly. He indicated acceptance with a gracious bow, and a "Wait one moment" with a gently raised single finger. He went to the window, lit a cigarette, and looked out at the moon. Jack joined him.

After what seemed to Jack like well over half an hour, but which turned out to be five minutes when he checked his watch, Milo signalled he was ready. He went back to the pentagram, sat cross legged within it, pointed to the place opposite for Jack, poured brandy into the two glasses, and passed one of them to his friend.

"Gentlemen,

"Please raise your glasses to Bart, a schoolboy seeking beyond himself for grace. May he boldly cast off the clutter and confusion of adolescence and eagerly embrace the compassion and composure of manhood. And may he stay whole and well, with skin unbroken, powerful lungs and strongly beating heart."

They drank, deeply.

"Wordy, but works for me. Specially 'skin unbroken,' let's drink to that again."

They drank deeply again. Then started chanting.

O My Brethren, pick him up, raise him high, heal his bones.

O My Brethren, pick him up, raise him high, heal his bones.

O My Brethren, pick him up, raise him high, heal his bones.

After a hundred chants, the air went out of Milo, and they felt it was OK to stop. It had been a hard day, and he was exhausted. At last, they had finished all their works and ceremonials and he had earned his bed.

"I've got an idea," said Jack. He was feeling a little heady now, with the spirits and the tiredness, but something had been on his mind.

"No ideas, Jack. The shutter has come down on initiatives today."

"Yes yes, just one more thing. Don't be a woose, this is important."

"What, then?" Asked Milo, wondering even as he spoke, 'Why why why get sucked in, you fool?'

"Well, I reckon we need to get rid of the ties and blazers right now, while no-one is around. They're still in the bags; having them in our possession is a huge liability. And, given you are into rituals tonight, there needs to be something to mark the ending of the scholar's life and to commemorate the rite of passage."

"Would that be the rite of passage from schoolboy to murderer?"

"I was thinking the more stereotypical boy to man."

"OK, fundamentally a sound scheme, but it's late, Spartacus, where can we dump them now? Having them is stupid, but it's worst just to put them in the bin, someone could really find them then. We haven't got a vehicle to drive out anywhere."

"Ah, but that's not what I am thinking. Get your superannuated school uniform, and follow me…."

Milo was too tired for this, but also too tired to argue. He shared the rest of the brandy between their two glasses while Jack rooted in his bag and found his blazer and tie, then they went next door to collect Milo's and headed downstairs. Milo was happy he had left on the lights. Jack led them through the kitchen, picking up a big old empty wicker breadbasket from the kitchen worktop on the way, then out into the courtyard, through the back gate, and down to the lake. Passing the jetty, they skirted the edge of the water and came to the first of the shoreline fishing spots. Jack stopped there and waited for Milo to join him. He placed the basket on a tree stump, and almost reverentially put his blazer and tie into it; Milo instinctively placed his on top. They drank deep of their beakers as a prelude to the rite.

"What now, Jack?" asked Milo. "If we chuck the wicker in the water it's just going to float around unless we find some rocks to weigh it down."

"None of that, sport," Jack replied, fishing in his pockets. He pulled out a little bottle of lighter fluid, and some matches. "Our uniforms are going to get a Viking funeral. Fire and Water. Blazers be Blazing"

"Brilliant!!" said Milo, enthusiastically. "The Norse rituals! I love it.

"Though can I just point out, if you are open to artistic contributions, that actually the vast majority of Viking funerals took place on land, not at sea.

"Even Norse rituals involving ships more often took place on the shore, with the King or noble buried in his ship and then the vessel turned into a burial mound."

"Jesus, Milo, this kind of inconvenient detail is exactly why I don't encourage collaboration. How do you know this stuff?"

"School project, sport. Some of us were paying attention. I did it with Steve Abel, I wrote the words and some poems and performed the rune-casting, and he drew lots of illustrations. We got a B+, and we were told we were only marked down for enjoying it too much.

"At the risk of boring you, the rituals didn't really involve setting fire to very big things. Where there was fire it was more like our own cremations. What I think we are honouring here, if I may make so bold, is your love for The Vikings movie, which we saw together three times starring me as Mr Tony Curtis and you as Mr Kirk Douglas."

"We went there with glee."

"O yes, it was gleeful. We were thoroughly exhilarated."

"Kirk Douglas was Spartacus."

"I'm Spartacus."

"No, really, I mean Kirk Douglas was Spartacus."

"Jack, do you ever get tired of the banter?"

"What do you mean, amigo?"

"Is it natural, the way we speak? Do you think it gets phony?"

"Too clever by half?"

"And sometimes just not funny?"

"Too much of it?"

"Definitely way too much. Where do you think it comes from?"

"When you're in the patter, it generates itself, right? It develops its own energy."

"That's when you're inside."

"Yes, where else would you be?"

"What if you were outside the patter, looking in?"

"I think that might be hard going. Fine for any bits that really are funny, but the pretentiousness, the unlikely wordplay, the wit beyond reason, people jumping in and out of character to make unfeasible jokes – objectively it might be rather tiresome, even now and then a little nauseating."

"Yep, definitely feels like you would not want to be outside looking in."

"Well, I wouldn't worry too much, Milo. You know why?"

"Tell me."

"There is absolutely no-one outside looking in. No-one is watching, no-one is listening."

As he said it, naturally there was a rustle in the bushes behind them across the clearing. They froze, stopped speaking, then for some reason both stooped low. They strained their eyes into the gloom, scanning the small space and the foliage around; if it had been daylight they would have put their horizontal palms above their eyes like the peaks of caps, the globally recognised body language for "I am looking very intensely."

Jack found a branch in the undergrowth and made a half-hearted effort to poke here and there in the bushes and swing it through the reeds and grasses either side of the clearing; he really only started to whack seriously when he was totally convinced there was nothing to find or hit. There was nothing to be seen; nothing to be heard; no more disturbances in the shrubs. After half a minute, they looked to each other for assurance.

"What do you think?"

"Nothing."

"Nothing?"

"There is only you and me."

"Very well. Where were we in the banter?"

"I think we were establishing that Spartacus was not in The Vikings."

"Not even in spirit."

"Let's agree to set Spartacus aside," said Milo, "just for the time being. Spartacus will not aid our ritual. The Vikings will, however, because you will recall that there is a scene of a body being carried down the cliffs and placed onto a mighty longboat that is then pushed out into a brooding fjord while an army of highly skilled archers shoot fire arrows into it, creating a fabulous conflagration. A Hollywood confabulation, all of it, and not with the authenticity of my school project, but much better box office. So, I think that is what you have in mind for our blazers, no pun intended, which is a magnificent concept, but *c'est ne pas l'histoire.*"

"Shall we do it anyway?"

"O we're doing it, for sure. Absolutely. Otherwise the blazer pun won't work."

"Others may revel in such a pun to the extent they let it determine their actions, Milo. For us, it is about the statement. By doing this ritual, we become men. It is also useful of course to destroy any evidence linking us to crimes abroad, but mainly I am thinking of the rite of passage."

"Ha ha, we are Lords of the Flies, are we?"

"There will be no ashes, though." Jack sounded frustrated.

"Not out at sea, no. Sorry my friend."

"In which case we can't make a paste from the incendiarised residue of our fallen fabric and paint our faces in the style of a crazed martial cult."

"A bitter disappointment, I agree."

"Anyway…" [Jack was off on a William Golding riff now, which in Milo's experience could take some time, unless he managed to impose discipline] "…the Lord of the Flies guys are just adorable rascals compared to our own universe of grizzled villainy. They went rogue only once, circumstantially; whereas we're in and out of roguery time and time again, sometimes even of our own volition."

"OK, shall we get the show going?" Milo, spoke firmly, to get them refocused. Though delighted by the enterprise in general, it was clear he was cast as the sidekick for the venture and would not make the shortlist to light the flames.

"OK, OK, but it is not a show, Milo, please respect the rite. Shall one pour and the other light?"

"It is not a flambé either."

"I opt for the matches as they are my matches, and this is my idea, OK?"

"I can't dispute the logic of the playground philosopher. Pass me the vial of liquid fire in that case."

Milo poured the fluid all over the uniforms and stood back. For a moment he expected Jack to light a match, but instead he stepped forward, lifted the basket, took it as carefully to the waterline as if it held the baby Moses, stepped fifteen paces into the lake, up to his waist like a preacher at a country baptism, and placed the basket in front of him, where it floated, gently.

Jack inwardly sighed a breath of relief as he had been worried his big moment would be humiliated by sinking, or even just lurching a bit. As the basket bobbed in front of him, and Milo stood venerationally on the shore as solemn and excited as any pagan awaiting the transmogrification of his King to a God, Jack finally reached the matches from his top pocket, took one out, struck it on the box, made fire, and dropped it into the uniforms.

Flames flared up, so fiercely and quickly that Jack took a rapid pace back, lost his footing, stumbled and fell backwards into the shallows. The movement pushed the basket Newtonianly out the other way, into the lake, and it floated off rather more swiftly than Jack had intended on its last journey as he thrashed around in half a metre of water. Instinctively Milo ran towards him, then realised Jack was laughing hysterically, not crying in pain. Too late to stop himself, Milo was already in up to his knees, and Jack grabbed his legs and pulled him over. The two boys rolled and wrestled, shouting and laughing, staggering deeper, then proudly rising up together in the hip-high water to watch the ancient magical scene as the basket slowed and drifted into the centre of the holy pond crackling and spitting with the reverential flame of holy relics consumed by sacred fire.

Milo was just noticing that Jack was missing half an eyebrow when....

"WHAT THE FUCK? WHAT THE HOLY FUCKING FUCK DO YOU TWATS THINK YOU ARE DOING NOW?"

It was Claude. On the shore. Shouting, and swaying.

"I told you, didn't I?? I bloody told you, but you wouldn't fucking believe me, I bloody told you."

This was Karl, also shouting and swaying, and additionally slurring.

When Claude removed his supporting hand from Karl's collar in order to point at Jack and Milo, Karl stood for a few seconds, concentrating extremely hard on staying upright, before losing focus and falling in slow motion flat onto his face with his arms by his sides, making the meaty slap of a prized suitcase being dropped three metres onto concrete by a disenchanted baggage handler.

Milo felt sick.

Claude made the sign of two hands suddenly covering the mouth combined with eyes being rapidly enlarged which everywhere in the world says 'Whoops,' followed by 'It wasn't me.'

Jack laughed maniacally: two more blackeyes for Karl.

"Serioushly boysh," Claude shouted, clearly only a little bit more sober than his prone pal. "What the hell is going on? Don't answer yet, help me get this body to bed."

Milo and Jack paddled out, soaking wet, looking mournfully over their shoulders at the still-burning clothing and the fire they had been enjoying, now all to be abandoned. Jack reminded himself to come back in the morning to make sure the job was properly done.

Claude realised for the first time in his life that he was extremely tall, it was a wonderful feeling. And he was certainly aware that he was completely in control of the situation. Yet for some undefinable reason, despite his height, and his dazzling leadership skills, he couldn't quite get his arms high enough or his aim clear enough to grasp portable parts of Karl rather than just thin air. After a few attempts that fell short, or missed the mark, finally Milo and Jack intervened and picked up Karl, establishing him in a roughly upright position between them. Balancing him tenuously in the middle, they lurched off slowly in the direction of the house with Claude in tow managing to stay off the floor by gluing his forehead against the seat of Karl's peach-coloured corduroy trousers and walking approximately in step with him.

"How did you get back here, Claude?" asked Jack, trying to cover some of the social awkwardness with small talk.

"Drived. In. Van," said Claude.

Jack waited to see if there was a Rest. Of. Sentence., but Claude felt he had probably relayed the nub, and took the opportunity to have a breather.

"Did you chaps have a nice time?" asked Milo.

Jack started laughing. He laughed and laughed. Milo caught it and started laughing. Then they were in hysterics, and began to double up, trying to free their arms so they could hug themselves with laughter, but Karl locked onto them and was doubling up with them, and then all three were madly bowing up and down like synchronised footmen obsequiously greeting a rapidly disembarking charabanc of randomly assorted trans-European aristocrats.

Claude caught it too. He had no idea why anyone was laughing, though it was irresistible, but then his head lost contact with Karl's backside in all the cackling hilarity, and as the three others eventually managed to squeeze themselves into the house he was left in the courtyard, bent double, hands on knees, head lolling up and down, shaking, barking, hooting and then screaming at the moon with laughter. What a night. It seemed to sober him up a bit, so he reached into his leather waistcoat for cigarettes and a lighter and flamed up a fag, something he had been desperate to do for twenty minutes.

Inside, Milo and Jack dragged, pulled and pushed Karl through the halls and up the stairs and down the corridor towards his bedroom, having to carry him now because he had ceased completely to co-operate. They felt like contestants in one of those strange traditional races that involve moving a hog-tied husband or an unfeasibly large sack of flour up and down a steep hill to win a flitch of this or a wheel of that. Milo was seriously flagging now; sadly he didn't see a triumphal bacon and cheese sandwich in his own immediate future but the thought of it reminded him how long it was since the last meal. He wearily shifted his hands to Karl's ankles to get a better purchase on the leaden load, and noticed, as they went past Albert's unlit room, that the door was open and there was nobody in – what was that about?

In the stories and the movies, you'll recall people put drunks to sleep carefully, removing shoes, trousers, shirts, maybe even slipping them into their pyjamas. Not so in real life: an inebriated body is a dead weight that is just too bothersome to be gratuitously shifted around, specially by companions who have also been drinking, or who are tired, or who frankly just don't like the inhabitant of the intoxicated corpse.

Thus, Jack and Milo flung Karl onto his bed, judo style, using his own momentum to bounce him the last two metres. He landed face down.

"What do you reckon, sport, face up, or face down?" mused Jack.

"My mum's quite an expert on this, actually," Milo noted proudly, suddenly remembering he missed her. "Someone she knew died sleeping drunk on their back by drowning in their own vomit."

"OK, so we turn him over," said Jack, moving towards him.

Milo began to protest, before he realised that Jack was joking. Not bad for this time of night! They pulled Karl closer to the edge of the bed, turned his head to the side, and put the waste bin under his mouth.

"He should be safe like that. But we could at least draw an Adolf moustache on him?"

"Oh, and you were doing so well for a minute," said Milo. "Obviously it is in many respects a brilliant idea, worthy of serious contemplation, however I believe the current thinking is that Hitler tashes are considered offensive even in a humorous context, and we would be in danger of embarrassing our generous French hosts. Also it cannot be done with a ballpoint pen, and I fear we have no marker, so I suggest instead we leave on a moral high and go and check on our other ward. I also wouldn't mind drying off some time."

Turning off Karl's light, they wandered out into the corridor. Milo saw that Albert's door was now closed, and there was a strip of light showing along the bottom. More mystery.

In the kitchen they found Claude, who had somewhat miraculously managed to put together a pot of coffee, and who was on his fourth cigarette. He had the proper drunk's instinct for self-preservation and had proudly sourced without human intervention the two great fundamentals of life.

"Hi, boys," he said, almost perfectly. "Sorry about everything. Thanks for looking after Karl, I think he is very drunk."

"You're not looking so brilliant yourself, Claude," said Jack, feeling a little cheeky, and also reckoning Claude owed them one for hauling Karl upstairs.

"It has been a rough night, my friends," said Claude. "I took that lad to my favourite underground drinking club, I thought if I could get a few big drinks in him, slap his back, make a huge fuss, maybe even introduce him to some females his own age, or a bit older, then it would help calm him down, divert him, and stop him being such an utter arsehole.

"But he got very drunk very quickly, he started pushing people and shouting in German; then he was singing old German songs – those songs are really not very popular in this region. I admit, after a while I took a few drinks myself, just to cope with the martial music. Karl was swaggering around, and periodically, because I was the only person who he knew, and everyone else hated him, he would come and cuddle me. Then he progressed to hugging, singing, and strutting at the same time. However much I tried, I couldn't help appearing to be with him. The end of the story – we got kicked out, and my membership has been torn up after forty years, so thanks for that, everyone. Stop laughing for fuck's sake, Mac, I can see you sniggering you old bastard."

That got Jack's attention.

"Who's Mac, Claude?" he asked, an edge in his voice.

"Oh shit," said Claude, hitting himself hard on the side of the head with his non-smoking fist. "Sorry for the slip … it is just, you really remind me of your dad, Jack."

Jack and Milo looked at each other, wondering what had just happened. No longer Francois, then, and with a completely reconstructed family tree to boot.

"Chrissake, Claude. You knew who we were? All this time??"

"Yes of course. Sorry."

"Would you like to explain?"

Claude made the traditional face for 'Do I really have to?,' realised he couldn't think clearly enough to get out of it, and started.

"First, you are the spitting image of your dad, who happens to be one of my oldest acquaintances.

"Second, you don't remember me, but I actually met you on quite a few occasions when you were much younger, I even gave you a lift in the car a couple of times. Your hair was a completely different colour then.

"Third, I've seen your dad several times in the past year, and given the state he's been in, it would stand to reason that at some stage someone from London would come out to look for him. I've been thinking for a while it might be you, because the word out is your mum has given up. So you weren't totally unexpected.

"Oh, and one other thing of course."

"What?" asked Milo very intrigued now.

"Jean told me who you were before he asked me to pick you up at the station. But he also asked me not to let you know I knew. He's a complicated bloke."

But Jack was ignoring this bit of strangeness and zoning in eagerly on the comment Claude had thrown away earlier.

"You've seen my dad, Claude? When…? Where…?"

Claude looked cagey, his head was clearing enough to realise he had said too much, and he looked left, right, and left again, like a character in an animation searching for a way out. But no cartoon door appeared, no window opened, not even a poorly-drawn trapdoor for him to open and dive into. Instead he remarked that Jack had moved his face purposefully to a position about twenty

269

centimetres from the vacant grin he had cunningly assumed.

"Claude, I know you are in there, so turn off the idiot smirk and talk to me please.

"I haven't seen my dad for three years, and we have all been worried sick about him – mum's had the police involved, and a lot of people are convinced he's dead."

"Jean told me not to say anything, Jack. You'll get me shot."

"Too late now, Claude. I don't want to get anyone in trouble, but I have to know this. I can smooth it over with Jean."

"Wait," said Claude. He stood up shakily, went to the door a bit unsteadily, then into the courtyard. 'Fresh air,' thought Milo.

After a while Claude climbed up onto the garden table. He lit a cigarette and stared into the distance. Milo and Jack looked on, thinking 'He's lost it completely.'

Time passed. Then, beginning to regain his confidence, Claude climbed back down and wobbled back in, announcing, "OK Jean's awake, I can see his kitchen light on." So there was some method in his craziness, at least; that was quite a relief.

He went to the phone, dialled, waited till it was answered, then said, "Sorry, boss, I need you up at Forest Lodge, Jack's onto me." There was some indiscernible shouting at the other end, then a pause during which Claude said nothing, but looked warily at the handset; then some more unintelligible yelling, while Claude remained silent, trying to edge himself behind a potted plant that was much too small to provide adequate cover; then finally a distinct *merde* that could be heard around the world, followed by the crack of someone slamming down a phone five hundred metres away. Claude gingerly put the receiver back into the cradle on the second attempt, trying and failing to look nonchalant, and said, "Jean will be here in three minutes, then we can all talk, right?

Shall we have a drink? I am suddenly feeling dangerously sober."

Claude poured coffee for everyone, including one for future Jean, and a generous tot of brandy to go with every cup. By the time he had finished serving, Jean was cleaning his boots on the mat, then he was in the room pulling up a chair. Hector was with him – neither of them looked very happy.

"Dick!" he said to Claude, "What's been going on?"

Claude launched into a lengthy mumble which covered all the events since Jean had left earlier; including Karl's initial devastation (Jean nodded to show he had seen Karl's reaction to Amelie's speech even before he'd taken her off); the mammoth healing drinking session (Jean grimacing the question, 'I can see how you got there but what were you thinking?'); the singing and expulsion from the club (Jean's head in Jean's hands); finding Jack and Milo setting fire to the pond (tabbed to revisit later); Karl being carried to bed (thumbs up); and then, muttered, scrambled, slurred and whispered, Claude's tentative admission that he'd blabbed (he said "nearly blabbed") about Mac.

Now Jean was looking just at Jack.

"I am so sorry, cousin," he said. "This was about conflicting and irreconcilable loyalties. You know my dad loved your dad; he originally pulled me into this so-called conspiracy before he died. He didn't know half the things Mac was into, it turned out, but he had made me promise to look out for him. It was fine till you got here, then I realised I was probably going to have to let one of you down, it just took me a little while to choose – to put it crudely."

"It's not a 'so-called conspiracy,' Jean!" said Jack. "This is like the whole village plotting to dupe the stupid English kids. One of the reasons we're here is to look for clues about dad, given everyone in England has been so scared about what's happened to him, and you knew that, and you lied to us."

"That's not fair, Jack. If you look back over the transcripts you will find that I didn't lie, I just didn't say."

"Technicality!!"

"OK, fair cop on that, all I mean is that everything was done in good faith, to try to help everyone – no-one wanted to mislead anyone."

"Maybe. So prove it now, please just tell us everything."

Jean sat silent for quite a while, looked at Claude, and drank his brandy down in one. Reaching to pour another, he realised the bottle was empty, went to his secret alcohol store in the larder to get another, and topped everyone else up as he returned to his chair. That bit of routine business had given him the time he needed to gather himself.

"OK. Around about two years ago, perhaps a bit more, my dad got a call from the *gendarmes* in Orleans. They said they had someone in the police station, and he'd given dad's name as next of kin. It was an old guy who had been sleeping rough, stinking, starving. They'd found him half dead, he'd been beaten and pissed on by some students, they'd also tried to set him on fire but he was too wet. He was refusing to go to a hospital. One of the policemen was a military veteran, and saw his tattoos, he was trying to help him out of brotherly respect, so he called and offered my dad a chance to pick this character up, no questions asked."

Jack was white at this stage, staring ahead and shivering. Milo put his hand on Jack's hand, and Jean put his arm round his shoulder.

"Are you sure you want to do this?" said Milo.

"As long as the story ends up with him still being alive, I am OK," said Jack, "can you please cut to that bit, Jean?"

"Yes, he's alive, Jack, that's the good news."

"Great," said Jack, his shoulders falling forward in relief, "in that case, give me another brandy, and get on with it."

Claude poured more drinks, just small ones for the boys this time, put another pot of coffee on the stove, and generally fretted around the kitchen tidying and pacing. He persuaded himself he heard something in the hall, so he opened the door, put his head around the corner to check, had what he considered to be a quick sortie to the bottom of the stairs, but saw nothing moving.

Jean went on. "Dad collected me in the middle of the night and we got to Orleans at dawn. We found the police station and located the friendly policeman who took us to the cell where your dad was locked up for his own safety. I don't want to scare you, Jack, but you're asking for the truth, dad and I were totally shocked, my dad was even crying a bit because+ your dad was in such an awful, dreadful state. Emaciated, filthy, cut, bruised, clothes stinking and torn, hair singed, no shoes. All he had with him was an oversized brown suitcase, locked, he hugged it to his chest like a sick baby.

"The police guy helped us get him out of the back door and into our car. We brought him all the way back here fast asleep. Dad asked me to take him, so we could keep it absolutely secret, and no-one else would know. That seemed perfectly natural and logical at the time, I am not sure why now, but it is what dad wanted, so I did it.

"Mac stayed for several months with me, living in the barn where you guys spent the day when you arrived. By default, I became his nurse. Dad I think genuinely wanted to take responsibility, but as he lives in the middle of a dozen families, if it was to be kept clandestine, it seemed the weight of it all fell on me. Of course I chose also to bring Claude into the circle, as a best old mate of your dad's from their youth, it was a great decision because honestly I could not have managed without him, and your dad would not have pulled through without him. I may have nursed him and nurtured him back, but Claude bullied him, and that was much more important.

"For the first few days he just lay on the bunk without moving, he wouldn't even get up to pee in his pot. We had to wash him by hand, clean him up every few hours, like a baby, feed him by spoon with blended chicken soup."

"Christ, Jean," interrupted Jack, "didn't you get a Doctor?"

"Honest, Jack, I wanted to get medical help. But Mac refused, and screamed and shouted – it was the only thing that animated him. It wasn't only him, my dad wouldn't let me, because he didn't want him hospitalised, or probably institutionalised. That's not the way we do it round here, it's not like England.

"Then also there was all the complexity of you and your family, and why he was here, and whether he was even legal here, we didn't know anything."

"Surely you could have let me or mum know that you'd found him?" said Jack, sounding really upset.

"No, Jack, we couldn't. Your dad wouldn't let us, he went crazy. He was saying all kinds of stuff, we didn't have any idea what was happening in London, your mum had contacted everyone months before to say he'd run off, but no-one knew the story. You have to remember, he's one of us, Jack, he comes from here, if he comes back here we're gathering round him, right? Isn't that natural, the right way of things? Isn't it what you would want us?"

"Not if my mum is going mad with worry."

"Well, everyone here loves your mum, Jack, she's extended family, but, when it comes down to it, Mac is our blood. God, it sounds primitive saying that, I'm sorry.

"And the other thing round here, I know this is archaic, is don't get between a man and his wife.

"Of course, no-one is impressed if someone walks out on

their family, but you have to presume it is a choice they have a right to make. And it didn't feel like we should be judging, or second-guessing: all we were trying to do was heal your dad and keep him alive, finding out the history and motivation was second on the list. Perhaps if we'd ever reached that stage we could have taken things in a different direction."

"Mmmph," spat Jack angrily, "I think largely this is bull, my friend," then more calmly, "but we can discuss that separately another time. Please continue the story."

"As I was saying, Claude and I looked after your dad when we brought him back from Orleans. He was nearly three weeks in the barn before he could even get up. He had nothing with him at all, no clothes, nothing, just the suitcase which stood in the corner, that he would never open. First it was sleep and soup, then gradually we introduced solid food, cigarettes and brandy. Other than shouting No Doctor and No Kate he didn't say anything for days; then he gradually talked a bit without really telling us much; eventually he asked for books and so on. But it was ages before he could get up and walk around. We took it in turns to be with him, but it got too much to do the twelve-hour shifts as well as running the farm, so with my dad's approval we also got Daphne involved. She was living in Toulouse, she lost her lover to leukaemia just before this all happened, so she'd moved back here and was a bit lost. To be honest I think watching Mac for those long shifts gave her back a sense of purpose, it helped heal them both."

"Can you fill in a gap for me, Jean? Dad disappeared from London three years ago, but you got the call from Orleans a couple of years ago – what did he do for the missing year?"

"It's not a hundred percent clear, Jack, Mac never really opened up about it entirely, though he said a few confusing things when he was delirious. From what we could gather, it seemed like it took him quite a while to get out of England, he came to France without papers, helped by some of his old secret buddies. So he is undocumented here, as far as the authorities know he doesn't exist.

"It appears from things he said when he was ill and burbling that when he got to France he came down here and hung out secretly for quite a while without letting any of the family know; for months, maybe a year and more."

Claude had been pacing around and getting flustered. The new coffee was brewed, and he served them all a cup, even heating a small pan of milk, a sure sign he was feeling guilty. He clearly wanted to be part of the conversation, but without actually talking or drawing attention to himself.

"Why wouldn't he contact you if he was here?" said Jack. "That makes no sense. I always suspected he would come here, but so he could be with family, if he was having a breakdown or something and wanting a safe place to hide out. But why would he come here and not tell anyone?"

Jean looked at Claude, who looked back at him.

"Madeline," Claude grunted.

"Who?" Jack asked.

"Madeline," said Jean. "Jack, are you sure you want to know all this stuff?"

"You honestly don't, Jack," said Claude.

"Just tell me," Jack replied. "Frankly, how bad can it be, if he's alive?"

"This is serious, Jack," said Jean. "This goes right back more than thirty years. Did your dad ever tell you what it was like for him here then, what it was like here as a kid?"

"Nothing other than the stories we got when we came here for holidays, about local landmarks, quirky old relatives, that kind of thing. Dad's always been a bit secretive about the past, I always presumed it was about him being a drinker, then giving up, that seemed to fit."

"OK so you know he was a drinker, we all were back then," said Claude, picking up the story, "but your dad was the prince of boozers, putting it bluntly. I and my brothers tried to rein him in, but he was wild, in the end we had to let him go his own way. You know he'd lost his dad in the first war only a year or so after he was born, and his mum couldn't control him.

"Your dad was a different guy then, Jack, you understand that. He was angry, and being honest, he was violent too.

"Then a great thing happened to him, he met a girl, Madeline, who was sweet and kind, and he fell in love, and she changed him almost overnight. Contrary to what you read, a woman can change a man it seems."

"I think romances do generally say the love of a good woman can change a man, Claude."

"Well, we must be reading different versions. Anyway, Madeline always was an amazing girl – I was at school with her, we were both a few years younger than your dad. Massive red hair piled up, spilling all over; wonderful voice; lovely kind personality." Claude sounded wistful, was it just the nostalgia of lost youth?

Jack looked at Jean to see what he thought. "I've never met her; you'll need to take his word for it."

"Trust me, if you ever see her, you'll agree; still now at fifty she has a special quality about her. So, your dad was swept away, and I guess she was too. Mac said they met at a young farmers dance; I always suspected there was more to it than that, but anyway the way he told it by the end of that evening he was already in love. The story was that he walked her home and kissed her once and then was outside her house the next morning to leave her flowers – crazy stuff he had never done before.

"He stopped hanging out with us, which frankly was a big relief, and he stopped drinking, which closed a few of the local bars. Every evening he walked out with Madeline, in an old-fashioned courtship. He started reading again, writing terrible verse, working like a maniac."

Jack was open mouthed. No kid really wants to hear about what their parents did when they were young and foolish. And specially no child wants to hear about past and previous lovers of their mothers and fathers.

"I had no idea about any of this. How is this relating to my dad coming here a couple of years ago?"

"He was looking at her," said Jean.

"You mean looking for her?"

"No, Jack, literally looking at her. This is the bit you don't want to hear, but I guess we are going there.

"It seems most of your childhood vacations were organised to facilitate the surveillance of his lost love.

"In fact, it appears every time you came here on holiday your dad was stalking Madeline."

"What are you talking about, Jean? That's mad."

"Over the years there were reported sightings on several – well, many – occasions by various members of the family. Late at night, someone crouching, lurking, hidden in what you might call vantage points in the woods and places like that, watching her house.

"She married a few years after she split up with your dad, and she has three kids: she and her husband farm a difficult piece of land about six or seven kilometres north of here. The guy she married,

Hugo, was also one of our gang in the old days, frankly a nasty piece of work.

"When Mac was here with your mum and you kids, there were rumours, stories, that he would go out at night, presumably when you were all asleep, drive around, end up near there, and just hang around, watching."

"Holy shit, Jean, please don't say that," said Jack, really distressed now. Milo put a hand on his shoulder while he took his brandy down in one.

"For Christ's sake, Jack, you asked me, you insisted – do you really think I want to tell you all this? But there is big stuff to deal with here; in order to handle it, if you really want to find him, you are going to need to know."

"Carry on."

"OK, a handful of people had an awareness of what was happening, very tight family, but we kept it to ourselves, there was no evidence of anything, a lot was gossip. Your dad was a war hero, he is blood, and we had all been impressed by the way he had sorted his life out after such a tough start and how he had packed up the booze and built a lovely family. It had taken several years for him to be accepted back here once he started bringing you for visits, but he had worked at it.

"Now people were worried, but at the end of the day, no-one was hurt and no-one was sure. Obviously, there was a concern about your mum and you and your brother and sister. I guess no-one really wanted to confront it, no-one was close enough to Mac to talk to him."

"So what then?"

"Well, nothing then really, no-one said anything, people got a bit reluctant to invite your dad anywhere. We don't know if Madeline was in the least aware: in those days she and her husband were rather outside the village life, they didn't have many close relations and were pretty isolated then, so it is more than possible they knew nothing about any of this at the time. I hope someone would have said something if they had thought there was any danger, but it seemed, how would you say, harmless, if not innocent?

"What we did notice was you stopped coming, frankly a lot of us were a bit relieved. Also, news stopped coming from London, no-one was much in contact, and no-one was keen, not because we didn't want to know about you, but we wanted to take a little time off from Mac.

"Now we know you'd stopped coming because Mac had done a runner, but we didn't find out about that for a while, and genuinely when we did, when your mum contacted everyone, we had nothing to contribute because no-one had seen your dad recently or had any knowledge of his whereabouts.

"As we said, we only found out later, when your dad was delirious and spewing all this stuff out, that after he got out of England, he came here. He changed this story plenty of times, but one version was that he camped up in the forest for months, probably close to a year, maybe even more. He has survival skills, and the biggest skill of all, as far as I can see, is that he didn't really care anymore, certainly not if he lived or died.

"At some stage we do know he made a few camps deep in the woods, and some hides around the edges. He used a deserted ranger hut and ruined outbuildings. He fed himself on God knows what, there is a stream up there for water, and he brought equipment with him, waterproofs, sleeping bag and so on, for the winter. Obviously he was dragging his bloody suitcase around, whatever that is about – I used to wonder what's in it: looted treasure, religious paraphernalia, guns and knives, who knows. Do you know?"

"It's letters," said Jack.

"Letters?"

"Yes letters. Nearly five hundred of them. Mum saw them hidden, then a couple of days later dad was gone, and they went with him."

"Only letters, nothing else?

"It is chock-full of them, there isn't room for anything else."

"Who are they from?"

"They're not letters from anyone, they're letters he's written himself, fresh envelopes, all in sequence. None of the envelopes is addressed, each of them just has a number on it."

"Blimey." Jean had a look that said, that explains something,

"Indeed, blimey."

There was a general silence, while they all thought, 'What the hell?' They were very tired now, and all at various stages of having drunk much too much.

"Shall I finish, Jack? I think we need to wind it up, then get some sleep."

"Yes please, Jean."

"OK so apparently these hides were all in spots where he could watch Madeline unobserved, so when she was working in the fields, hanging out the washing, feeding the chickens; even possibly into the house, maybe where she was bathing or dressing. Claude and I have been several times to look for him here, and we've broken up these camps when we have been able, but they spring back up.

"This is not savoury stuff, Jack, but no-one knew, and being honest, your dad was clearly not in his right mind. The miracle is, thanks I guess to his army training and whatever secret service nonsense he got into after the war, he was able to do this covertly for so long. He has clearly been a lot more careful recently than when he was doing his nocturnal spins during your holidays. I suspect maybe somewhere in his consciousness there must be an awareness that this has been escalating, intensifying over the years, obviously becoming a lot more serious than when he started off by just trying to get a jealous peek at an old girlfriend."

"What was he trying to achieve by all this?" Jack threw out the question to the room.

Milo plucked up the courage to speak for the first time in an hour. "He was obsessed, Jack. I doubt if he thought through any actual objective. He wanted to know, and then perhaps he forgot how to stop, lost perspective."

"Yes," said Claude, "and it isn't like he could ask around the community."

"Or go to a library and take out a book called The Life and Habits of Madeline," said Jean, risking sounding facetious just to try to break the mood a bit. "Honestly, it doesn't look as though he planned anything bad, there was no effort to make contact that we know of, and as far as anyone's aware there was no attempt at a physical encounter. You could wonder whether it had anything to do with Madeline at all."

Jack was about to ask what happened next, and how his dad had ended up sleeping rough in Orleans, when, they all heard it this time, there was a clear noise from the hall.

Claude made a move for the door, but this time Milo was quicker – he was less drunk and more nimble than Claude, and before Claude had gone two steps Milo was through the door and at the bottom of the stairs, calling "Who's there?" There was no answer, but from upstairs, direction unclear, there was a scuffle, the squeak of a swinging door, and the click of a latch.

The others, including Hector, were close behind Milo. "Did you see anything?"

"No, but there was someone out here, and they're still in the house."

"Albert?"

"Well, not Karl for sure, he was genuinely comatose; we won't see him till tomorrow."

"OK, so either Albert, or a strange intruder."

"I reckon there was someone watching out by the lake, too," said Milo. "That could have been Albert as well, or someone observing us, who followed us inside."

"Yes, that wouldn't be difficult, all the doors and windows are open, and everyone in the house is either drunk or so worked up they're not paying much attention."

"Shall we search the house?" pondered Jack.

"There must be twenty-odd large rooms plus attics and basements," said Jean. "If it is an intruder they're already out of the window by now and across the fields. If it is Albert, he's doggo and if we burst in on him he can pretend he's been asleep for hours. I could let Hector loose to chase around, he would certainly scare the daylights out of anyone he came across, but he doesn't know what scent he's meant to follow so he'll be all over the place.

"It's nearly 2.00am, so I am going to suggest we call it a night. We have a big day tomorrow, the barge is arriving, actually in a few hours, plus we have to keep rehearsing and working on the Experience. I know we are all distracted, but I can't afford to let up. And I can't afford to have this team fall apart, so in the morning we're all going to have to make nice with Karl and Albert because the show must go on, Jack – it really has to."

"We haven't finished talking, Jean," said Jack, anxiously. "You didn't even say what happened when dad was living with you. Where is he now?"

"Jack, leave it now, you've taken a lot in, we can pick it up tomorrow. I'd like you all to come down to the jetty in the morning to help with the boat, if that's OK. Claude will pick you up at 5.45am at the front – that's less than four hours. So you need to get some sleep, we all do."

Jack was upset, but his eyes were closing and he had had a lot of brandy, he was too exhausted to fight.

"One thing I can do for you tonight, Jack." Jean fumbled inside a small bag he'd bought with him and pulled out a large envelope. He emptied it onto the table. A large red notebook, and maybe fifteen or twenty sealed envelopes, unaddressed, but each with a number on the front – not sequential, Jack could see among them 68, 181, 19, 208.

"What's this?"

"Stuff we found in the barn after Mac disappeared on us. One morning we went up with the coffee and bread, and he just wasn't there. All his things were gone – we had got him some shoes, clothes, he had a couple of paperbacks, pencils and so on. And, of course, the wretched brown suitcase. These things had fallen down the side of the bed and he hadn't realised.

"What you said about the letters explains it. I had assumed he had lots of jumble and junk in the case and this packet of letters was just part of it. But it seems this is just a handful of the mass of letters filling the whole thing, they've dropped out while he's been looking at them, or whatever, and he didn't notice.

"It would surprise me if he hadn't missed the notebook, it's like a diary by the look of it. I haven't read it, but I think you should. He's not coming back here to try to recover it, we know that. For the letters, there are about twenty. The highest number on the envelopes I found is 479, so if there are really nearly 500 in the case – and it did look to be bulging when I saw it – then he's probably not going to notice he's missing those unless he gets them out and counts them. I bet it would freak him out if he knew. Anyway, these are yours now, I have been waiting for the right time to give them to you."

"Thanks, Jean, I appreciate it."

"*D'accord*. And now, time for bed. This has been one of the most exhausting days of my life, to be honest, and it must be worse for you, given your time as a lumberjack."

Jack summoned up a smile at least, and Milo joined him. They said their goodbyes, and finally Claude and Jean left, with Jean letting Hector run ahead of him down the pitch-black lanes, while Claude shot off in the other direction, Elvis blaring Return to Sender through the open window of his van.

"For fuck's sake," slurred Jack, desolately, "what a complete and utter shitshow."

"Excellent swearing, my friend," said Milo, admiringly, "that is some impressive cursing."

"Too kind," said Jack. "Can you believe it, Milo? My dad the Peeping Tom, the sleazy lurker, the crazy sinister spooky stalker hiding in the woods watching decent people trying to peacefully live their lives.

"He dragged me down here year after year as cover for his obses- sion, sneaking out on my mum at night while we were all sleeping, it is kind of grotesque, no?"

"Take a step back, Jack, a lot has happened today. Grab hold of the most important thing we found out – your dad's alive, that's fantastic news isn't it? By the sound of it, Jean will have some clues about where to find him.

"And, though I trust Jean, you know there are always two sides to any story, it's never black and white. At the very least it is obvious your dad has not been well, I am so sorry to say that, but if someone is not in their right mind, then there is a question about how much they are responsible for their actions. Let's sleep now, for God's sake, I am about to fall over."

Milo took Jack's arm and began to walk him upstairs. "Last time I went to bed was all of four hours ago – let's see if we can make it stick this time. Set your alarm for 5.30, don't take your clothes off, and don't clean your teeth, that's wasted time if you're not kissing." Jean's rule.

"Sage advice," said Jack, as they reached their doors, "thanks for everything today, sport. I couldn't do this without you."

"No problem. Tomorrow is another day – we ride the boat to freedom!"

"Willie Dickes and Danny Velinski!!"

"That's us, Jack, and I bags Willie Dickes tomorrow when I am tillering us across the border."

"Damn, you're quick. But you can't have the tiller and also get to choose the top name. You don't have to decide now. Sleep on it, Spartacus."

"I will. Sleep well, Spartacus."

And, finally, they went to bed, and slept.

Milo dreamt that he left the house and walked to Jean's to ask for the return of a book of poetry he had lent him. Hector wouldn't let him in, so Milo stroked him behind the ears, until Hector started to sing Blowin' in the Wind in a beautiful baritone voice with crystal-clear diction.

Jean opened the top window and looked out, "That's excellent, Milo," he called, "I have never heard him sing Bob Dylan before, generally he loves show tunes, Rogers and Hammerstein, hits from the musicals."

Hector sang You'll Never Walk Alone to humour his master, and then snatches of Some Enchanted Evening, before returning to Dylan with A Hard Rain's a-Gonna Fall.

"If he is singing Dylan songs, I think he must like you very much."

"He might like me, but won't let me in, Jean."

"Not everyone may enter, Milo. And for those who can, the time must be right. It is OK, Hector will know when you can come in."

"Can I get my Prufrock?"

"I had to change some of the words, I hope it is all right with you. I asked Mr Eliot, he was very pleased with what I had done."

Jean threw down the book, but it floated just above Milo's up-stretched hands, and before he could catch it, he woke up.

PART TWO:

A LAUNCH AND A SWAN

TUESDAY

The sun was shining brightly in through the open window, but more significantly, specifically in respect to the waking of Milo, Claude's leather face was ten centimetres away from his shouting "WILL YOU WAKE UP FOR CHRIST'S SAKE, YOU SAD LITTLE CITY BOY."

The wellbeing benefits of Milo's tiny teaspoon of slumber drained away in an adrenaline-rush of panic before he was even fully awake. But at least amidst the terror he had the involuntary gratification of sitting up so quickly that his forehead struck Claude's nose with a satisfying thunk. It sent him reeling backwards against the wall, where he slid to the ground, hands to his face, a tiny gush of blood seeping through, squealing, "O shit O shit O shit."

Albert and Karl, who had already been woken, broke into the room to see what the kerfuffle was, followed by a quivering Jack, whom Claude had shaken from sleep seconds before.

"That's a big disappointment," said Karl, in disgust, "I thought he had discovered your dead body."

Karl was looking bizarrely fresh that morning considering his condition the night before. Even his face was on the mend. Say what you like about him, but he had amazing powers of recovery. "This is now officially a mad house," he continued, "everything is completely out of control. Is there any chance you could get it together and come down? I'll put the coffee on – somebody in this hellhole needs to be mother."

'There can't be mothers in hell, can there?' thought Jack. 'Or kittens.'

Albert and Karl went down to the kitchen, and Milo helped Claude staunch his nosebleed, wiping unnecessarily hard with rough toilet paper and making him wince and swear.

While they were all engaged, Jack slid down the back stairs and outside on a mission. He slipped through the courtyard and out towards the lake. Retracing his steps from the night before, he swiftly arrived in the clearing where they'd launched the basket and started the fire. Something was on his mind – a nagging thought that they had departed in a hurry and left it burning.

The basket was floating innocently about five metres out in the lake. Jack speedily removed his shoes, socks and trousers, placing his toe nervously into the water simply to confirm what he knew already before rapidly stumbling after it, trying to ignore the icy temperature. He got to the basket: empty. Not even ashes.

"Argh no no no."

The contents could not have disappeared so conclusively, someone had been out and picked up the bits. Evidence. It could be anything from a scorched tie with a name tag still attached on the back to a singed badge with the school motto. Exactly what he had wanted to destroy he had gifted to his enemy – whoever it was.

Putting his clothes back on while he was still wet he wandered dolefully back to the house saying "Damn" at every step to avoid thinking. Fifty-three Damns. Damn Damn Damn Damn Damn Damn Damn. When he finally ran out of Damns by reaching his destination he thought the thought he had been avoiding: 'How could I have been so bloody bloody stupid? Damn.'

He reached the kitchen to find Albert and Karl fussing around with the coffee, which was nearly ready. As he entered, they had their heads together talking earnestly: as soon as they saw him they clammed up. "Morning," said Albert, sheepishly. 'What the hell,' thought Jack. 'The more Karl insults the boy, the more he creeps round him looking for approval. What's he been doing to buy his favour?' Jack knew.

"Had a nice walk?" Karl asked, innocently.

'Shit,' thought Jack, 'they've got it.'

Milo came in at the same time from the hall, leading Claude who was blindly holding a large red and white handkerchief over his nose and eyes. They all took seats at the table. Claude had brought bread and pastries, and Albert got out the cups and filled them from the big steaming pot, pushing a jug of hot milk to the middle for those that wanted it. Everyone around the table except Albert was nursing a hangover: for Jack and Milo, it was manageable; for Karl it was throbbing and sparking; for Claude it was just a normal six o'clock in the morning.

Albert was struggling to hide his smugness at temporarily being so much brighter than the others, but Milo, even in his own stupor, could sense something else was up with him – something sneaky, the kind of pernicious self-regarding excitement that comes from having the currency of information, the power of the secret, that cannot resist drawing attention to itself. Milo looked over at Jack, and saw he was also looking at Albert, and in his case, he knew what the secret was.

After ten minutes silence ruptured only by the munching and slurping of five currently mannerless males, Claude called nasally, "Time to roll boys, the barge is nigh." The effort of talking re-opened his nosebleed, the handkerchief went back over his face, and he slipped the van keys to Milo as everyone piled in. "I'm lying in the back with my feet above my head. Drive to the carpark at Jean's and we'll walk to the jetty from there."

When they arrived Jean and Hector were waiting in the carpark ['How do they always know?' thought Milo], and they all set off together down to the landing stage. It was a glorious summer morning with bright sunlight already, but there was a fresh chill in the air and mist was sitting on top of the river like the smoke in a children's magic show. Halfway along the path they came across Daphne and Amelie sitting on a little bench carved from a felled tree. "You didn't think we were going to let you boys have all the fun," Daphne laughed.

She had picked Amelie up from Caroline's, and now the young girl was seated next to her watching incredulously as Daphne was knitting – knit one, purl one, knit one, purl one – using a combination of remarkable coloured wools. Due to a couple of critical lapses of concentration, what had started off as a one-piece baby suit was gradually morphing itself into a stripy dog blanket for Hector, but she loved it nevertheless.

"You're joking, right?" Amelie's suspicions had finally provoked her to challenge the sorceress. "You're seriously telling me this is how people make jumpers?" The girl was polite, as ever, but totally unconvinced.

Jean set his feet square just by their seat, everyone gathered round, and he launched himself into a description of the way the day would go.

"The barge is being brought up for us from the boatyard, they promised it will be here at 6.00am, so any minute now. The deal is that the guy who brings it will stay on and give you all an introduction and some basic guidelines before heading off. He offered to take us once up to the Hill House landing stage and then back down here again, but honestly I think we will be OK, I can do that. I want as many of us as possible to get the skills so we can be flexible over the next couple of months about who drives it depending on other jobs and so on, also to cover for each other if anyone is absent or ill.

"The boat is a special tourist version, so instead of solid walls, it just has forty seats, eight rows of five, well-spaced, so you can walk up and down the ends of the rows, or even between the rows. It has open sides with a rail, and a nice colourful canvas roof for shade or shelter, which can be on or off, depending on the weather, and can just cover the front and the cockpit, or the whole boat."

Jack and Milo, feeling they had got the gist of it, dropped off the back of the entourage while Jean ploughed on. They had been waiting for an opportunity to swap notes.

"What's the story with Albert?" Milo asked, "You looked a bit worried at his know-all expression."

"Yep, I am a bit. I ran down to the lake this morning to make sure the blazers and ties were properly destroyed, and there was nothing left in the basket. And not the sort of 'nothing left' appropriately represented by ashes and ceremonial detritus. It was completely empty."

"OK so when we heard rustling in the bushes last night, someone was there after all? If anyone cleared out the basket, you're reckoning that might have been Albert, and he put the embers out and got a badge or name tag, something like that?"

"You are ahead of me as always, though I will continue to refer to you as Watson, of course. Yes, that's how it feels, otherwise why would he be looking so pleased with himself? And it gets worse, he had his tongue four centimetres from Karl's ear when I got back to the kitchen, and I don't think it was just to lick out the wax. They're conspiring. They shut up as soon as I walked in on them."

"Jesus, that boy has no shame and no pride. So we're busted."

"I think it must be so. In which case, it is just a question of waiting to see what they do with the information – if they have worked out what it might mean."

"Well, if there was a badge, tag, maker's name or anything in the pockets, the least they'll know is that we're English, and possibly that we're using false names. I can't see how they will guess why we're doing this."

"There's nothing we can do; we just have to wait and see how they play it."

The others had wandered towards the jetty as Jean was speaking, so Jack and Milo had to stop talking and move to catch them up. As they came up to them the team all seemed to be looking at them excitedly, and waving, and Milo found himself waving back, as one does, before he realised they were looking far beyond him and Jack, a hundred metres further, to where the mighty hulk of the barge was emerging elegantly out of the mist, with the boatman waving silently at them. They turned to watch: it was graceful, majestic, moving with no noticeable means of propulsion, perfect and beautiful, with two great lamps on the front like the eyes of a huge unblinking fish that was swimming soundlessly towards them.

The barge turned from black and white to colour as it materialised from the haze. The fantastic carvings of flowers, fruits and small forest animals along the sides below the deck, from prow to stern, were gaily painted in simple vivid tones of red, blue, yellow, brown and green, the smallest elements delicately picked out; and the boat was topped with a brightly striped canvas canopy of red, white and blue, currently just covering the front half of the barge, with the back half left open to the elements. There was a sculpted wooden figurehead on the bow, a full-bodied woman wrapped in a red, white and blue toga, with dark green laurel woven into her red hair. Later they were shown another figure at the back of the barge, a tubby Dionysian in a toga hammered with gold leaf, pink plump face, purple lipped, bald, with his own crown of laurel, and looking, as Milo said, a lot like Charles Laughton in I, Claudius.

And the fabulous finishing flourish, which they saw as the barge drew in to the landing, and the solitary boatman skilfully skipped along the sides from front to back to tie her up to the jetty, was the bold lettering stitched onto bunting hung daintily along the gunwales, both port and starboard, spelling out: **L'expérience Grand Meaulnes.**

"How does he do it?" murmured Milo, marvelling. "How the heck does he have time to plan and organise all these details?"

Spontaneously the whole team clapped and whooped. This was stunning, and people would love it. It had magic and style and created perfectly the ambience of the Grand Meaulnes. Claude clapped Jean on the back with one of his ham-like fists, sending him staggering a few paces forward. Everyone laughed, including the boatman, who had the air of a man who had entered a room and joined in the collective amusement at a joke he hadn't heard and wouldn't understand if he had.

The bargeman finished securing the boat and leapt ashore. They all shook hands and made their hellos; his name was Anton. He gathered them around him and, with Jean's encouragement, got straight into the instructions.

"This is **L'ÂME DE L'EAU**, our finest boat. For the next three months or so, we've agreed with Jean here something we never usually allow, which is to rename her Le Grand Meaulnes. Vessels are pretty touchy about such things, so this is a big deal."

[He was smiling. Jack couldn't work out whether this was meant to be a joke or a genuine piece of soppy seagoing sentimentality; no-one laughed, so no-one would ever know.]

"You're going to be taking her two kilometres up the canal and two kilometres back, and Jean says you will do it once a day, perhaps twice on rare occasions. On that basis you'll need to refuel her around once a month. I have already spoken to Jean about where to take her, what to ask for, and what to pay. There is no fuel gauge as there is on a car, you use this dipstick, and do not forget it; you don't want to be floating adrift with forty passengers, even in such a quiet location.

"The key issue you need to focus on, always, is safety. Safety of yourselves, but safety mainly of your guests – you are dispensable, they will sue your boss."

The boatman's heavy humour and over-rehearsed patter, as well as quickly becoming irritating, were not mixing so well with Jack's hangover – how much longer?

"For safety, rule one, the boat must be tied securely to the jetty when your guests are getting on or off, and the loading and unloading of customers must be done calmly, no rushing, no clustering, no pushing.

"Rule two, everyone should wear a lifejacket. It is ninety-nine-point nine percent likely that no-one will ever need it, but if they fall overboard it will save their life, so a very good rule to follow. Here you see," he said, pointing to a little ledge under every seat, with a lifejacket on it, "they are kept here, and you can encourage the passengers to put them on before you pull away.

"Rule three, everyone on this boat must have a seat, and be sitting, before you pull away, as that is the time of maximum risk.

"Rule four, arms inside the boat when travelling, no-one trailing their hands romantically in the water and having them ripped off by floating logs or getting caught in the tree branches.

"If you stick to those four rules and read them out to the customers before each trip, you will sail easily and safely and have a lot more fun."

Jack believed at this point the man's pompous monotonous drone was beginning to force the blood out of his ears and squeeze the *aqueous humour* out of his eyeballs. He nervously touched his cheeks for fluids; thankfully they were dry, thus far it was all in his mind.

"So, now come onto the boat please, and let's gather forward in the cockpit so we can all see the controls."

As they embarked, the boatman handed each a lifejacket, saying he preferred it while he was on board as it was his job at stake. The cockpit area was on a triangular platform in the bow, about half a metre high, with low walls on each side that joined together in an arrow shape at the very front. The canopy that covered the body of the boat was raised up a metre here in step with the rising height of this little deck, so the cockpit was covered, but the skipper could still look back along the whole length of the boat with no loss of visibility. The cockpit held the steering wheel and throttle as well as the other controls. Anton gave them a moment to sort themselves out. "Everyone comfortable, everyone can see? OK, so this is the starter, once the key is on, press here. Right?"

The engine started, no problem, this was pretty simple stuff. He turned it off again.

"This is the throttle, when the engine is on and you want to go, you push forward like this for more speed; pull back again like this to slow down. All OK? Anyone want to try?"

Everyone was fine without trying. That surprised Jack a little, because who didn't want to drive, even when the engine was off and you were going nowhere? Everyone has sat on their father's lap in a parked car, it is high on the list of memories. No volunteers though, he was guessing everyone just wanted to get this over as quickly as possible, however great the boat.

"And this," said the boatman, never scared, obviously, of stating the obvious, "is the steering wheel. Turn it right and the boat steers to starboard – a lot of people don't know that." There were genuine titters at this stage around the team, they could not hold them back. "And," pause for effect, "turn it left, and the boat will steer to port." Jack let out a huge guffaw, which with quick thinking he evolved into a sneeze. "Hay fever," he shouted from the back. Milo did the same sneeze. "Pollen," he yelped, gesticulating vaguely at one or two innocent trees.

"Now," said the boatman, slightly wary of the nasal heckling, but moving inexorably on, "who can point out to me the brake?"

Everyone was looking everywhere on the control panel, underneath, even checking for a foot control. Jean, who had driven the boat before, and was in on the joke, made himself particularly busy scouring around and fussing.

Finally after what seemed like several hours to Jack (not ordinary hours; hours alone in an unfurnished room, no radio, no TV, no book, not even a jigsaw or a potato to roll across the floor), the boatman gave a mighty fake chuckle, Santa at Christmas in the department store ho ho ho style, and said, "There are no brakes on a boat." Jack, who had cottoned on to the answer early, could not even be bothered to feign surprise. Some of the others were more polite, but you could still hear the thud of anticlimax breaking the silent water, the slowly deflating hiss of punctured curiosity.

"No brakes, the best you've got is to reverse the throttle – in this position – which will slow you enough to pull in and tie up when you're stopping; make sure you give yourself a nice long run at it. And don't aim at anything that will snap if you hit it. We don't recommend that you slam straight from forward to reverse too abruptly as it can cause damage, but also it is not going to stop you immediately, your momentum will keep you going forward for quite a while. So be careful."

There were a few other aspects to the lesson. How to tie up – fore, aft; how to steer straight, how to steer round corners (this another laboured piece of wit; there aren't any corners on rivers); a few tips on daily cleaning and maintenance. Then the boatman announced, "That's it, I have been doing this for thirty years, and now you know exactly as much as I do." A joke or not?

"Mr Jean here has been with me for several tutorials in the past couple of months, so I am very confident in his skills, and in his ability to mentor you. Therefore, I think my day is done, *bonne chance!*"

So saying, he reached with both arms behind the last row of seats, pulled out an ancient bicycle, heaved it onto the towpath, and in an instant was pedalling off, and quickly out of sight. They were on their own.

"Right," said Jean, jauntily, "who wants first go?" Everyone giggled.

Karl put his hand up. "I do." So did Amelie, so did Daphne. Jean did a swift Ip Dip Sky Blue and fate chose Daphne for the maiden run. Karl protested the result, demanded Eeny Meeny Miny Moe instead, and won triumphantly – he virtually did a victory lap of the boat. Daphne couldn't be bothered to argue. Jack made a noise in his throat like a house puppy in the lean-to watching the neighbourhood mongrel taunting it from the end of the garden.

To make it a proper practise, everyone jumped off the barge and went back to the land end of the jetty. Daphne and Amelie, the disappointed volunteers, were designated to be greeters – 'stewardesses,' laughed Karl – on this first trip. They controlled the 'customers' as they got on, and made sure they were handed safely into the boat.

"What about the lifejackets?" Amelie shouted to Jean.

"Personally, I think it spoils the ambience, when we have such delightful costumes and awnings. But he's right, for the nervous, I think it is appropriate to make a short safety announcement before we start the day, and to point out where they are, and that people can choose if they wish to wear them."

Karl then started the engine, and Amelie and Daphne cast off the bow and stern lines. Karl eased the boat away, annoyingly smoothly. They began their slow, steady progress, gliding up the river: Karl hardly needed to touch the wheel. Everyone was entranced, a muttering arose among the crew about Jean's genius, this was going to be another enchanting segment of a wonderful day.

Jack and Milo decided that as this was a practice, and all the customers were actually employees, it would be fine to stand up and walk around a little 'just to get a range of perspectives.' The others did the same, it made for an even jollier holiday atmosphere. At first they all naturally gravitated to the cockpit area where Karl was showing off his steering and handling prowess; his captaincy seemed mainly to exhibit itself in the fussy and gratuitous manipulation of knobs and handles that had never been explained to them as having a necessary function. There seemed little risk in this two-kilometre journey on an empty stretch, and to Jack's annoyance Karl did seem to be a natural commander. A hundred bad U-boat jokes went through his head based on the national stereotypes exemplified in The Rover comic books under his bed. He was a little too old for them now, but they had illustrated his youth. Being born as the war was in its final phases and raised in what you might call a military household probably had not helped his empathy levels – he would need to work on that.

Other than Milo, who liked to see where he was going, and enjoyed watching the action in the cockpit, the team gradually scattered around the boat, chatting to each other about how great it all was, and taking in the view from different seats and angles. As they made their stately progress the barge provided the ideal waterborne vantagepoint to experience, just as intended, the colourful banners and fabric chains and artificial flowers designed by the team in the previous week. They looked glorious in the early morning sun and created the excitement and mood of something old and gay and precarious – simply perfect for the party of the Lost Estate.

A beautiful swan, the same one that had been gliding through their evolving dreamscape all week, was swimming gracefully towards them with three cygnets in tow, on a long, straight stretch, two hundred metres away. Milo saw it second, as he presumed Karl had already spotted it; everyone else was gossiping and looking back down the river. Right or left, thought Milo, pick your side – currently the swan was aimed directly at the centre of the prow. Milo had taken a step forward for a clearer view, and was just half a pace back from Karl, who was standing in front of the wheel, legs splayed confidently, like Clark Gable in Mutiny on the Bounty.

The barge motored gently towards the swan, the swan swam elegantly towards the boat, the gap inexorably closing. Milo, still waiting for the swan to navigate away from the middle of the river, suddenly panicked that they were going to hit the mother and cygnets and he was about to grab Karl by the arm and warn him, when suddenly the great bird sensed the boat was nearly upon them and was not changing speed or direction, and coolly turned to begin shepherding its young out of the barge's way.

Milo recognised that of course the swans were going to get clear of the boat and breathed a mighty sigh of relief. He was about to share a joke with Karl along the lines of 'No swan for dinner, then' when Karl pushed up the throttle to a higher speed and dropped his arm, pulling down the wheel, and swinging the barge to the right, towards the now fleeing swan family. The adult managed somehow to flap away, miraculously pushing two of her children in front of her; but the third cygnet could not react in time, and the boat went right over it.

The barge was now heading for the starboard bank at full throttle with a cackling Karl hanging on to the wheel for dear life. He'd lost control. As soon as Jean had felt the boat change speed and direction he'd turned and headed to the controls. He was too late to stop the cygnet being ploughed under, but he managed to push Karl aside quickly, pull the throttle back to zero, and turn the wheel left, taking it away from the bank, just in time, then gradually back to the centre of the river.

"What the hell do you think you're doing?" he whispered in a shout, fifteen centimetres from Karl's face, not wanting to alarm the others. "Do you want to get us all killed? Do you want to wreck this boat before we even get started – you want to put us out of business?"

Amelie and Albert were in the stern of the boat, gazing back down the river, so they didn't know what had happened. But now the jerking bloody body of a broken cygnet emerged before them bobbing on the surface as its life drained out, while from the bank the mother swan flapped its huge wings and let out a haunting, hopeless scream.

"Oh my God," Amelie cried, turning to stare at Jean, observing him at the wheel, and presuming he had been driving, "what have you done? You killed that poor little bird."

"Deliberately!"

Daphne was yelling at Karl, and thinking Amelie was too. Amelie and Albert presumed that Daphne, like them, was shouting at Jean, because they couldn't see exactly where she was looking.

Jean opened his mouth to start explaining to Amelie that it was Karl not he who had been driving at the time; but then he realised that was going to sound lame and ridiculous, and it might perhaps cause more problems among the team, so he decided just to make progress as quickly as possible and hope the incident would be soon forgotten.

He took the controls himself for the rest of the journey, and in a few minutes they were pulling into the jetty at the Hill House landing. Other than intentionally murdering a beautiful animal, it had been a magical trip. If they could occasionally avoid massacring the wildlife, customers were going to love this cruise.

Things were calming in the boat, but Amelie was still glaring at Jean. Milo and Jack were exchanging notes in the middle row of seats, and Jack determined to take Amelie aside once they got off, to tell her exactly what had happened. Jean had other ideas however.

"OK today is about learning the barge, so let's take her straight back up the river. Everyone ready?" He went on without expecting any answers. "Amelie, can you take the helm this time? Do you want to turn her round?"

Amelie stared very hard at Jean, but he had his back to her and didn't see.

"We can't go back there after what you did, Jean."

Now she had his attention.

"What are you talking about, Amelie? Can't go back where, and what do you think I did?"

"Jean, you purposely ran over an innocent cygnet. The mother is back there crying her heart out. The body is still floating in the water. I don't want to go back there now, and I am not sure I will want to go that way later, or any other time."

She was shaking, her voice was tight and tense, and the bright sun shining through the red, white and blue awning ran down her face like melting ice-cream. Everyone was quiet, even Karl temporarily lost his smirk. Daphne and Albert both took a step towards her, to comfort her, but she bridled and twisted away.

"Firstly, Amelie, it wasn't me that drove into the swan." Amelie looked cynical, but Jean went on anyway. "Secondly, none of us has driven a vessel like this before unchaperoned, so anything that happened was obviously the product of unfamiliarity and an accident of nerves. Thirdly, it is horrible that the baby swan got hurt, but this happens in nature, on the river, all the time – not just boats, also foxes, fishermen and kids with catapults. We can't let something like that damage our enterprise or even ruin our day."

Amelie was crying now, great heaving sobs. She clearly felt it deeply, and yet this also seemed an over-reaction: was there something else going on? Each member of the team had a different view of what was happening, ranging from 'Justifiable if extreme response to a tragic event' to a more old-school 'Genuinely upset but perhaps a little attention seeking.' I will not comment.

Consciously pulling herself together with an expressive handker-chief to her lips and nose, she shook her head at Jean, saying, "Jean, you can say what you want, but for me this is serious, a life has been taken, a mystical animal has been crushed, you can all take it lightly, or laugh, but this is horrible. I really do not want to go back down there, but I don't want to make trouble, or delay the practice, so with your permission I will step off here and walk up to the house to take time to recover myself, while you continue – is that OK?"

This was very much a rhetorical question, Jean realised, because Amelie had already disembarked without looking back, and began to wander off up the decorated path towards Hill House.

Everyone looked at everyone, some stunned, some annoyed, some sympathetic. "OK," said Jean, irritated, but trying not to show it, and keen to move on, "how about you, Scott, you ready for a drive?"

Milo the trouper, pleased to help smooth things over, stepped up and turned the key in the ignition, hoping he was managing to hide his nerves. Albert, supportive of his sister as ever, and looking to Karl for his lead, let go the front rope while Karl let go the back, and Milo engaged the throttle to pull forward gently. As he did so there was a shout from the back and Jean and Milo turned their heads, worried there was something wrong.

It was Karl. He was saying something, possibly deliberately muffled, and as he spoke, he pulled his dark jacket close round, stepped up onto the gunwale, and casually walked off the moving boat onto the jetty with perfect poise, like a figure entering a Caspar David Friedrich landscape.

'You've got to give it to him,' thought Jack, irked beyond telling, 'he's got a sense of style to match his bloody ego.'

'Blimey,' Milo was thinking, at the same time, 'that guy really never gives up – it's as though opprobrium makes him stronger.'

Karl glided off the jetty, striding towards the fleeting form of Amelie, who was entirely unconscious of her follower. Jean knew neither of them would turn round till the boat was out of sight, and he realised Karl had played an almost perfect hand. Albert stood bereft on the stern, abandoned by his sibling and his hero, too late to jump, adrift like Jim Hawkins among the cut-throats.

Shocked like the rest, Milo felt the need to refocus everyone and get back to the job in hand. "How is this Jean?" he said, giving a little throttle and studiously turning the steering wheel about 60 degrees to start to bring the bow round. At each end of the course, around both jetties, they were lucky to have broader sections of river which would allow the boat to turn, but this was, as they say in professional barging circles, the tricky bit, and would require, Milo thought to himself, tightening his grip a little, the mastering of some serious seadoggery.

"That's super, Scott, thanks," said Jean, grateful for his calm steering and tranquil demeanour, such a good influence. "Now ease back on the throttle, all the way back to neutral, then a little reverse while you turn back the steering wheel ... that's right ... excellent ... Now forward again ... and turn the wheel the other way ... brilliant ... and more throttle ... and we're off!"

Milo felt a thrill: he had successfully manoeuvred the boat round with no mishap, impressed Jean, taken the air out of a tense situation, and was now heading back downriver in a beautiful vessel on a glorious sunny day, Captain for the first time. He liked it. Jack could see how elated his friend was, and he was happy for him and for Jean, but his mind was on Karl, and he was staring backwards into the distance at his vanishing shape closing in on the diminutive figure of Amelie. Nothing to be done, unless he wanted to jump in and swim back to her rescue.

Milo was now extremely comfortable at the controls, taking the barge back up towards the farm jetty at a steady four kilometres per hour, using slightly more power, at Jean's suggestion, because they were running against the current on the return ride. After they had been going for ten minutes or so they came to the place where the cygnet had been killed. Everyone was looking for the body, which wasn't there, when suddenly the mother swan came out of the reeds at them, wings extended like an avenging angel, honking like a fire alarm. Milo suppressed his natural reaction to steer away, and kept steady, just pushing the speed slightly higher as the bird mounted up the boat's side, screaming and madly flapping. She didn't get quite the angle she needed to get over the gunwale and onto the deck, and gradually they left her behind, still hollering and howling; she wanted to follow and attack them, but she didn't want to leave the other two cygnets. They were all very shaken, not least Jean, who was wondering if that was going to happen every time they went past.

They spent the next few hours practising on the boat, with Daphne, Claude, Jack and Albert all doing a half or complete circuit, and each of them doing at least one turn of the barge at the end of the course. Only once more did the swan show herself, again not making it onto the deck, though Jean and Claude stood ready to push her off using lifejackets as makeshift shields if she had made it over the side. On the last two runs she didn't appear, leaving Jean to hope it was an end to it.

When it got to lunchtime, and they were arriving at the Hill House end of the route, Jean told them to tie up and stow everything, as he'd arranged with Julie for them to have a meal up at the picnic area. The team got off the boat, slightly shaky on their legs, and slapped each other on the backs, congratulating each other on how well it had gone. "Of course," said Jean, drily, "a magnificent success; if you include gratuitous bird slaughter, two mutinies, and the provocation of a lethal animal into a lifetime vendetta, Blackbeard himself would envy our morning's endeavours."

The whole time they were walking up the path towards Hill House Jack was scanning the meadow and the gardens for the figures of Karl and Amelie, as he had been imagining them, holding hands in the summer house or more intimately intertwined behind the rhododendrons. He saw some wild strawberries in the hedgerow which triggered a recollection from the Tess of the D'Urbervilles they'd studied last year; he recalled the scene vividly from reading the passage out in class, even doing the voices of the characters. He saw Karl-as-Alec holding a hideously engorged strawberry in his hand and pushing it towards Amelie-as-Tess's face…

"… holding it by the stem to her mouth. "No--no!" she said quickly, putting her fingers between his hand and her lips. "I would rather take it in my own hand." "Nonsense!" he insisted; and in a slight distress she parted her lips and took it in."

'That used to be my favourite bit,' thought Jack.

Mysteriously there was no sign of either Alec and Tess or Karl and Amelie in the environs, strawberry-eating or otherwise. But when Jack and the rest of the barge party got up to the picnic area Julie was waiting, cheerful as ever, with hot and cold dishes and some fruit and cheese. After thanking her, and complimenting her on the quality as usual, Jean asked if she had seen the other two coming up earlier.

"Yes, of course," Julie replied, "they came and the lad gave me your message, that we were to let them have the van Claude left here. I made sure it was filled with fuel, like you asked."

Jean looked at Claude, and Claude looked at Albert, who just looked sheepish. Jack was steaming. Milo and Daphne wandered a few yards off where Jack and Jean couldn't see them to have a massive giggle together. "That's classic," whispered Daphne. "Completely brilliant," Milo agreed, conscious of the disloyalty to Jack, but unable to suppress the conspiratorial *joi de vivre* with the person who had become his new best pal. How many people can remember the exact moment when someone suddenly becomes essential?

Meanwhile Jean was suppressing the desire to bawl at Julie, "Why the hell would I give Karl the van to take a girl away in?" remembering firstly, he was much too nice to shout at people; secondly, he admired and respected Julie and would never speak to her like that; and, thirdly, letting his people take vans at short notice was exactly the kind of thing he would and did do.

"What now?" asked Claude, between two bites of a salmon tart.

Albert was sitting disconsolately a short way off and Claude was careful not to let him hear. Jean gave Daphne a polite upward nod to ask her to look after the boy for a while, and she linked arms with him and took him up to the terrace for a calming walk.

"Do you think Karl and Amelie are on the run?" Claude asked, when Albert was out of earshot.

"Jesus, Claude," Jean answered, "they're not bloody Bonnie and Clyde."

"Karl's more like Bruno Richard Hauptmann," muttered Claude, balancing a new cigarette on a pastry-flecked lip in order to light it.

Jack looked questioningly at Jean … "?"

"That's the kidnapper of the Lindbergh baby."

Jack was no wiser, honestly, but got the message from the context. He wasn't laughing.

"They're almost certainly back at the Lodge," Jean went on, "I can possibly understand why Amelie didn't want to hang around waiting for us, given how upset she appeared to be, and her wish to avoid going back down the river. In which case, maybe Karl was playing the gentleman by requisitioning the motor on her behalf."

"And scoring some points while he did it," said Jack, desperately trying not to sound jealous, and failing.

"Wait till she finds out the truth about the swan," said Milo. "That should dampen her fancy."

"She doesn't fancy him," Jack shrilled, almost losing control of his voice, "we know that. Last night she showed him up in front of all of us. Also, where do you get 'dampen her fancy'? We're not doing a bloody quadrille in the Bath Assembly Rooms."

Milo did a twirl and kissed his own hand. Jean politely applauded. Claude chuckled. Jack suddenly realised: 'They are mocking me, because they all presume I am enamoured with Amelie. Or is it enamoured of Amelie? (And why am I using antique language? Is that a symptom?) Am I enamoured? I thought I was a comely companion. Of the chivalric persuasion.'

"I have a girlfriend." This came out of nowhere but seemed to Jack to be an utterly convincing argument and refutation.

"My word, Jack, that is the first time I have ever heard you say that," said Milo.

"This is not a moment for quibbling, it is a time to be bold," Jack replied, testily. Looking at Jean and Claude he asked, "What happens now?"

"Finish your lunch," Jean suggested, "there really isn't anything else to do right now. They're long gone, so we're not going to chase after them, especially as they've taken our only motor up here – we're going to go back in the boat, which was always the plan for us. Claude was going to use the van, but I guess he's relegated to the waterways now as well.

"If they've done a runner, we'll know in an hour when we get back to the Lodge for rehearsal, but I am rather hoping for the more likely alternative, that they will be there when we return, probably having renewed their shaky vows."

Jack pouted. The others all looked at each other, it seemed he just couldn't help himself, it was funny on one level, but a bit worrying on another. "Shouldn't we go now?" he prompted. "Just in case they're in trouble?"

"No," said Claude, "this pear tart is delicious, and I think I have earned one beer before we rush off, no?"

He looked at Jean, who waved a hand magnanimously and said, "One beer, as a compromise, then round up Daphne and Albert and let's get back to the jetty."

After they finished their drinks, they all waved thanks and goodbye to Julie and started down to the river. Jean walked behind with Albert, explaining the situation to him as he saw it, and trying his best to put his mind at rest.

"Of course I am worried," said Albert, in a slight whine that grated on Jean like worn brakes. "You know, my father didn't want her to come, she's not over my mother's death, she's fragile. He only let her sign up for this to get her away from an unfortunate relationship with her music teacher. He told you some of that, right? And you promised you would personally guarantee her wellbeing. You don't really seem to be doing that."

"Look, I didn't expect anyone in the team to be a problem, Albert. Karl is much older than I expected, but you like him, right? He is not a monster."

Albert flushed. "I do admire Karl, very much. But that doesn't mean I think someone his age and stature would be a suitable boyfriend" [he choked on that] "for my sister."

"I thought after last night she made the same point?"

"Since mum died, she can be impulsive, capricious. She abused the music teacher all the time, but it didn't seem to put either of them off. She's vulnerable, Jean, you know this, she was sweet and utterly stable, now she shifts and vacillates."

"I understand, Albert, we will fix this, I promise. First, we take the boat back to the farm jetty, pick up the cars there, and drive straight back to the Lodge. I am sure they will be there; I reckon Karl was concerned about Amelie and grabbed the van to get her back as quickly as possible so she could rest. I am sure after last night, he's got the message about the other stuff, he could hardly fail to." Albert smiled at him, thinly, grateful to him for trying to help.

When they got on the boat they realised it was Albert's turn to be Captain. 'Good,' thought Jean, 'this will take his mind off it.'

But Albert totally bodged the job of reversing the boat and went hard backwards into the bank. Then he panicked and throttled too hard to pull her off, and they would have gone cracking at speed into the opposite bank if Jean hadn't quickly intervened.

"Would you like a breather, Albert?" Jean suggested kindly, and Albert nodded yes, though honestly it had not really been a question.

"Shall I take her, old sport?" Milo asked, stepping up. "Only if it helps."

"Thanks, Scott," said Albert, looking shaken, and grateful, "I really appreciate it." He looked painfully sheepish and a little guilty at Milo's friendly gesture as he handed the wheel over to him. Jack, looking on, suspected he knew why.

Back at the farm jetty, Milo pulled her in gently, and Daphne and Claude tied off the two ends tight. Jean secured the boat, put down the gangplank, and they all disembarked.

"It doesn't feel that safe to leave it here open like this," said Daphne.

"Don't worry, I thought of that," Jean replied, putting his fingers in his mouth and whistling.

Nothing happened, and the team looked at each other blankly. Jean smiled back and waited. Then they heard a thump thump thump down the path, and a joyous bark, and Hector was on them, jumping up, yowling with pleasure, and sending flecks of happy spittle hither and thither. "Oh Christy Yuk," shouted Jack, trying to cover his face with his hands but laughing.

"I left his pen open before the last run, he has been on trust, and see how good he is – yes he is ..." [rubbing the ears]. "So Hector will sleep on the boat tonight. For tomorrow I have got some tarpaulins and a chain and padlock organised for more security. I'll bring some food down for him later."

They walked up to the carpark where they'd left Jean's car when they'd arrived at dawn, which felt like a lifetime ago now. Daphne's motor was there as well. "I am not going to miss out on this," she whispered to Milo, "do you want to jump in with me, and I'll give you a lift up to the Lodge?"

"Great, love it," said Milo.

"Jean, I'll come up to the Lodge in my car, in case there is anything I can do to help," Daphne called out, "I'll bring Scott."

The two cars set off, and as ever Daphne went at it like a Grand Prix driver, so on the three-minute journey they arrived at least four minutes ahead of the others. Milo scraped himself off his seat, and they got out and smoked a cigarette each before the others arrived. In any case, they didn't want to go inside without them, because the signs weren't good - the van was nowhere to be seen.

When Jean, Claude, Jack and Albert pulled up, and Milo opened the door for them, they were all scanning the driveway and the road outside for the missing vehicle. Albert began to look seriously worried. "They're not here, are they?"

"Wait here," said Jean, mainly to Albert, but including the rest. "Have a smoke, I won't be a minute."

Jean went into the house. He looked in the kitchen, then the hall. He went halfway up the stairs and began to shout, "Karl... Amelie... Is anyone there?" No answer, so he continued all the way up into the corridor and checked their bedrooms. No-one. He retraced his steps, down the stairs, shouting again, "Karl... Amelie... Karl..."

311

Then he was back outside, shrugging to the others, and shaking his head. As he did so they heard the noise of a vehicle coming up the road outside, and everyone simultaneously perked up and relaxed, thinking this must be them. But when it turned into the drive, it was Caroline, and she was on her own.

"What's happening, sis?" Jean asked her tensely, as she pulled up and wound down her window.

Seeing his concern she got out of the car, took him by the elbow, and walked him aside, to the end of the driveway by the gate.

"I came to tell you something, but it looks like you're already worried about it? God, Jean, I hope I haven't screwed up.

"Amelie stopped in earlier to change her clothes. She said she was going into Bourges for the evening for a night off. I just presumed she meant all of you together, but I was busy with the kids' tea so I couldn't get into a long conversation. Anyway, something felt off, so I watched her out of the window and she walked back down the road where she thought she couldn't be seen, and got into your van with a young guy, maybe twenty-five years old, fair hair, blue eyes. I'm guessing now it is the bloke you are trying to keep her away from?"

Jean nodded.

"I realised too late they were going on their own," Caroline went on, "heading off into town, so I wondered if anything is up, or if you needed to know – you did put me in charge of her moral welfare, after all. I kicked myself after for not challenging her, I'm so sorry."

"You weren't to know," said Jean. "Thanks for coming over, we're a bit anxious because they took the van without asking – at least the boy did – and Amelie was in a very upset state after we ran over a swan today on the river."

Caroline looked rather blank at this.

"I'll give you the full story when we have more time," Jean said.

Caro indicated by her silence that she could hardly wait for the opportunity to arise.

"Did she give any indication what she was going to do in town?"

"She said she had a couple of errands, cash some traveller's cheques, then maybe a walk and dinner, all a bit vague. As I said, I was preoccupied, I told her not to be back too late and not to wake up the house when she gets in. Do you need me? I ought to get back, Marc is looking after the kids and he needs to get back to the milking."

"Go go, sis, thanks for letting me know, I'll run with it and let you know what is happening – hopefully she will be back for an early night!"

He kissed her on the cheek, she turned and waved to Claude and Daphne, nodded to the unknown boys, got back into the car and reversed out of the drive.

The others all gathered around Jean, "What now?" asked Jack.

"That was my sister, Francois. That's where Amelie is staying. She's telling me she's fairly certain that Amelie and Karl have gone off to Bourges together."

Madame Jestique turned into the drive on her bicycle as they were talking. She decided this was not a circle she would join and rode straight past them, wheeled her bike through the front door into the hall, and a few seconds later they heard her fingering out the Overture to Humperdinck's Hansel and Gretel.

"Good grief," said Jean, "Hansel and Gretel…everyone already knows about our straying kids."

"She always knows everything that happens within a radius of five kilometres, by some kind of small-town osmosis," Daphne said. "And the one thing you can rely on is, she will never tell."

"Mmmm the music can be a slight giveaway if you're in the know," Jean said. "Albert, Claude, Scott, Daphne, would you mind taking the car into Bourges and looking for them? Francois, I think you should stay here, if it is OK, in case they come back, but also to keep the peace and everyone's sanity, as we don't want you causing a ruckus in town" [Jack looked hurt; everyone ignored it]. "And you have some useful work you can do running through the accompaniments and musical ideas with Madame Jestique. Also it is important we have a liaison here who can act as a hub for information – someone who can take phone messages and pass them on. Everyone will phone in periodically to report, and immediately let you know if there is information. I have to be up at Hill House to work on catering, the entertainers and the changes on the stage, but I'll check in too, and I'll come back later."

The assignments were universally approved. Albert and Milo went into the house to change clothes as the evening was coming on, there was a slight chill, and by the look of it a threat of some rain. Daphne and Claude popped back to their houses to do the same and were back in twenty minutes to pick them up.

Shall we stay at the Lodge? Or go to town? Town, of course, that's where the action is.

Claude must have smoked four cigarettes in the half an hour it took them to reach Bourges in Daphne's car and pull up in a parking space outside the cathedral. It would normally have taken forty minutes, but Daphne was driving, and Claude was smoking – it was the dream team. They got out and scoured the parking spaces in the square to see if there was any sign of the van, but no luck. That didn't necessarily mean anything, but it would have been a bonus if they knew they were definitely around.

They decided to split into pairs for the hunt – Albert and Claude;

and Milo and Daphne. They made a quick list of the main cafés, bars and clubs and split them between the two teams geographically. Also culturally, as there were a few dive bars no-one could go into except Claude, and at the same time there were two places Claude was banned from. They would start with the cafés and bars, as it was still too early for the clubs to be open.

They agreed to circle back to the car periodically to report progress. "You have a pencil and paper, right?" Claude checked with them, "So leave messages here under the wipers. And here," passing out some cards, "this is the telephone number at the Lodge for anyone who doesn't have it. Remember, Francois stayed there this evening and he'll be manning the phone. He'll take notes when anyone rings in with news, so we should all call periodically to see if there is anything happening."

"Thanks, dad. Here's a spare set of keys for the car, just in case. If anyone is on to them and needs to follow, then the other pair will find out soon enough that the car is gone, and they'll have to get a taxi back."

Claude and Albert headed off to Le Coq D'Or, the biggest, most famous bar. It had the virtue of being only a hundred metres away across the square, and it seemed to Claude to be the one most likely to attract 'tourists,' or a couple of young kids who didn't know the town and were trying to impress each other. When they arrived, Albert starting walking through the outside tables, dramatically bending over and looking rather myopically into faces in the half-light under the umbrellas and annoying several customers, who glared back: one began to get up.

"It's OK, Pierre," called Claude, warily, over Albert's shoulder, "he's with me, and he's too young to know how to behave in a grown-ups' bar."

The pugilistic Pierre laughed and waved to Claude. He was everyone's idea of a docker, or maybe a miner, rock hard, leather cap, check shirt, scarred face, similar smoking stains to Claude, though not as pronounced, and covering all his face not just half. He sat back down, so Albert could not judge his height, but his chest and arms were massively strong and forbidding.

"Put your pup on a lead, mate, and join us for an aperitif. It's been a long time, Claude, what have you been up to?"

Albert observed that Claude was very nervous around Pierre, he looked uneasy, clearly there was some history.

"Just a quick one, Pierre, we're on a job, but of course a drink would be great. Let me introduce you to Albert."

Albert was fazed, but not surprised when Claude sat down and drew up a second chair for him. It was obvious he couldn't say no to the man. "Are you sure, Claude? We should really keep looking shouldn't we, we don't know how long they're going to be around."

Claude was not nearly as diplomatic as Jean and naturally talked to the boy as an equal, no soft soap. He turned away from Pierre so the man couldn't hear them and spoke quietly.

"Albert, we're all determined to search as long as it takes, we all share the responsibility and we're all worried about Amelie. But there are three ways this could have gone: either they're already back at the Lodge, in which case it's all fine; or they're already on the run, in which case there's probably not much we can do; or they're genuinely here for a night out, in which case we've got at least three or four hours to find them.

"There are only about twenty places they could be, all within a kilometre of here, with two teams out looking. Besides, Pierre knows everyone in Bourges and we're likely to learn more having a Pernod for fifteen minutes than we will by shaking random bushes like kids hunting Easter eggs."

Claude turned back to the table ready to engage with Pierre, who was in the act of signalling "three Pernods" to the waiter five metres away, in the manner of a man who owned the café and most of the town around it.

[In fact, Claude informed Albert later, "He doesn't own the café, but he does receive fifty percent of the profits for making sure it doesn't burn down." "So he's like a fireman?" "Jesus, Albert, seriously? Were you raised in the woods by Snow White?"]

"Who is it you're looking for, guys?" asked Pierre.

"Two students who have been working for Jean on his Meaulnes Experience. One is a German lad in his mid-twenties, about six foot one, slim build, blond, blue eyes, annoyingly dashing, name of Karl."

"Shame my wife's not here, she'd sniff him out like a truffle," said Pierre somewhat morosely into his drink. "Is he the same German lad I heard you were out with last night annoying everyone with your singing, and starting fights?"

Ignoring this – partly through embarrassment, partly through lack of time – Claude went on.

"The other is Albert here's sister, Amelie. About eighteen."

"Seventeen," interjected Albert, "barely."

"Seventeen, barely, maybe five foot three, say forty-five kilos fully clothed, brown eyes, massive frizzy red hair."

"Curly."

"Massive curly red hair."

"OK, I get it, a quite distinctive couple, I would say. What is the worry, have they stolen something?"

"Ha ha, not quite. They took the boss's van under false pretences, but he's prepared to let that go as long as it was for a lark and they get it back before midnight – on the twelfth stroke the princess's carriage will turn into grand larceny.

"What we're more worried about is the boy and girl have a bit of history, Jean doesn't want them going off on their own as he's promised her parents he would look after her, so it is a fatherly interest, if you know what I mean.

"Also you've heard the Experience is about to launch, and there are some entertainments we've set up and rehearsed, and the kids are a key part of it – we can't replace them at this stage so we really need to find them and make sure they're going to play their parts."

Pierre nodded and signalled for a man inside the bar to come over. "Charles!" The henchman (for so he was) had a hat pulled over his eyes, proper gangster style, and a trench coat, in summer believe it or not, though in fact there were some serious specks of rain in the air now. Albert could also see in the half-light his dark glasses and moustache; one unnecessary and the other unpleasant. Charles leaned into Pierre, his ear finally reached a point around five centimetres away from Pierre's lit cigarette, and when Pierre began to talk out of the corner of his mouth the glowing ember of his fag-end danced tantalisingly between the lobe and the auricle. Albert was hypnotised. Eventually, just as the ash was about to fall into the auditory canal, the sinister gentleman pulled back and up, and headed off into the darkening square without a glance back. Pierre noticed Albert's trancelike stare and laughed.

"Don't worry, my friend, I have never deafened any of my minions by fire; speaking in secrecy is a skill refined by my family over a thousand years of villainy.

"Charles will spread the word through our network, Claude; it might save you some time, we have guys in pretty well all the bars. I owe Jean, as you know, so if I can help this evening I will happily do it – specially as for me the effort consists entirely of sitting under this umbrella while you buy me a drink and tell me how

Daphne is doing."

And that is what they did for half an hour, much to Albert's frustration, while the light over the cathedral went out completely, the rain fell harder, and the bats began to flap in the night sky outside the circle of light created by the bars and cafés.

Meanwhile across town Milo and Daphne were doing the job old-school, actually searching for the fugitives themselves by physically walking from place to place and ticking the locations off the list they had been allocated. They had to visit three cafés that would close quite early, six bars after that and two clubs for later. The first café was a blank, as was the second, but at least they had a break for ten minutes with coffee and a plate of frites. Then they had a five-hundred-metre stroll to the next place, which became a bit of a jog when they saw from a distance that a waiter was already beginning to carry inside a few of the chairs from the pavement tables.

Arriving breathless, it was easy for them to see the rather dirty, un-kempt café was completely empty and a few quick words with the grubby manager, grumpy at being delayed an extra five minutes on top of what he considered to be a grindingly hard day, established that no outrageously handsome and stylish young couple had frittered away the afternoon there with canapes, tinkling laughter, jazz piano and champagne cocktails. The man then gave them the number two shrug from the international shrug handbook, the one that means, "Now piss off," rather than the number one shrug that says, "So sorry not to do more for you, you know I would literally do anything to help if I could."

'Those two shrugs,' thought Milo, 'take exactly the same amount of effort. Is it mystifying someone chooses one over the other in any simple social or commercial situation?' He and Daphne discussed this conundrum on the way to the first of the big drinking bars. Bonding. There were some specks of rain in the air, obviously it was going to get worse, but right now, not a bother to their progress.

The first of their late bars was four hundred metres back towards the centre of town, and when they got there it was barely open, the owner and waiters were still wiping the surfaces, putting chairs out and polishing glasses. There were only four or five customers, all inside, some at the bar and some scattered on different tables, drinking a beer and a shot on their way home from work. No girls, no youths, these were the tired middle-aged men who had stopped by to test their daily resolution of having a single round only, just to avoid getting home too early. Some of them would still be there at throwing out time, but they could always try again tomorrow.

Daphne and Milo ordered two small beers as an excuse for a chat with the barman. He was busy, and not keen to talk, and brushed them off quickly saying no-one of that description had been around the bar any time that day. Daphne turned on the charm and gave him one of the cards with the Lodge phone number.

"If you see them and call us in time to come and pick them up, we'll be back with twenty francs for you, that's a promise."

"Might there be anything else?"

"We'll see when we're back," said Daphne with an outrageous flirt that said quite distinctly "Not a chance my friend."

She grasped Milo's upper bicep tightly but not very convincingly in a double-armed embrace, indicating ownership. To do him credit, the guy gave an apologetic smile for crossing the line, and a laugh at her cheek. He liked her instantly, a lot, as virtually everyone did. And he knew Milo was not her boyfriend, for any number of reasons. He would most definitely be on the lookout for the opportunity to leave her a message.

Daphne did not release her grip on Milo's arm when they left the bar, so they staggered and swerved down the pavement like drunk-buddies on a weekend bash. They both started giggling at the same time, and in a few minutes they were laughing so hard that they were bent over double, choking for air.

"So," said Daphne, first to recover, "I am guessing you and I are not taking this mission as seriously as some I could name." She said the last with a massive stage wink and a pantomime flick of the thumb over her shoulder, pointing in some unspecific direction, like a hitchhiker, at the absent Jean and Francois.

"I'll be careful what I say, so I am not embarrassed when his corpse is found in a ditch on the Paris road," said Milo, "but frankly I do not see Amelie as a clear and present danger to Karl's safety."

"And is he a danger to her?"

"Come on, you know better than me. But if you want my opinion, having observed her for a while, unfiltered by Jean's paternal prism, Francois's youthful yearning, and Albert's fraternal frailty, I suspect she's much stronger than they think, she's more mature than they allow, and for the most part, well able to look after herself."

"I don't think you are going to be embarrassed," agreed Daphne. "And having watched the appalling Karl, I would say though he is arrogant, pushy, overconfident in his charms, narcissistic, and has not received nearly as many refusals in his life as he needs and deserves, he is not a physical threat to the girl unless she wishes him to be."

"But she's too young, right? Possibly impressionable?" said Milo. "That's what the others are worried about."

"Yes, a bit. If anything were to happen it would not be illegal, but I know Jean would be mortified. Her mother died, she has lost track, and had some bad experiences, she is going through a difficult period. Jean has personally promised her dad he will look after her, that's what is primarily worrying him.

"For Francois, sorry to say it about your friend, but sadly he is unable to hide his jealousy. In the context of her vulnerability, is there a huge difference in age between him and Karl? I hate to say, it has been pretty obvious what he has been thinking, even if he is denying it to himself. We need to be sure this is about the girl herself, and not about men wanting to decide what is best for women. Or about one boy competitively wanting what another boy has. I want to keep looking so I can make sure the kid is not being manipulated or coerced, beyond that I am not so sure. The sense I got from Jean is that he is just as worried by Karl's general behaviour, what he might be plotting, and whether it could mess up the launch. And he would also quite like to get his van back."

"So, we are humble foot-soldiers sent on a mission with only the sketchiest brief, hardly with information enough to know that what we are doing is right. They do not want us to think too much of the moral ambiguities.

"However, one fact I do know is that we're a bit too early for these bars. They've not started serving food yet, or even finished polishing the tables, all we are seeing is future drunks parking their butts for the evening on their regular seats."

"I've an idea," suggested Daphne, "let's flip the list to kill some time."

Taking the piece of paper from Milo she pointed: "If we turn this upside down and go to the Boucher Sanglant first that will be a two kilometre walk the other side of the cathedral square, it will take us about half an hour through town, which should be about right for them to be open by the time we get there; then we can walk back from there towards the cathedral again, and pick up these other three bars on the way, when they are getting busy. OK?"

"Good plan," said Milo, very happy to have the thinking taken out of his head. "And we can take in some sights as we go – you can introduce me to Bourges."

"Well, it is the cathedral first, well-lit by night, and magnificent – actually we're two hundred metres from it, as you can see."

The rain was now getting more serious, so Daphne reached into her handbag and, after a momentary rummage, pulled out a telescopic umbrella, flourishing it with a hint of the stage magician.

"You have a Knirps," said Milo, delighted.

"Indeed I do, I am impressed you are a student of the brand." So saying, she put it up; it was just about big enough to cover both of them if they were intimate.

"My mum has one," Milo rattled on, "she treasures it, swears by it. I miss her. Plus, of course, it is one of inventions that revolutionised modern life and gave us so many of our present freedoms. Who is not fascinated by a Knirps?"

"Very many people, Scott. Shall we proceed?"

She pointed toward the cathedral, and they headed off, linking arms and leaning into each other with the umbrella above, by now incredibly comfortable in one another's company.

"I'm queer you know, before you get any ideas," said Daphne, pulling him even closer, and laughing.

"Me too," said Milo.

"I knew that," said Daphne, smiling to herself, and then to him, "I just wasn't sure you did."

"Well, I've never said it out loud."

"Thanks, my dear, that is a great honour. I knew we were going to be best friends after about half an hour."

"That's very sweet. I knew in twenty minutes."

"Maybe I knew in fifteen minutes," she laughed again. "Or maybe it is just not a competition."

"Just as well it isn't, because I knew in ten minutes."

They walked on in silence. Milo's heart and mind were racing at a million miles an hour. He had told someone, and that made it suddenly real. He was terrified and elated in equal parts.

"Who did you tell first?" he asked.

"No-one till I went to Toulouse. It is not so hot round here being queer, in case you wonder. France is magnificently odd, in my view anyway; the laws are incredibly liberal, but the people are extraordinarily conservative, especially in our beloved rural areas. In fact we were one of the first countries to do away with many of the laws about same-sex relations, believe it or not at the time of our revolution. Which was when, young man?"

"Ah, a test! Something I feel comfortable with… That would be 1789 to 1799."

"Well done! So what they say about ignorant Yanks, that's not true…"

Milo was getting the impression she was teasing him; in a way he hadn't quite worked out yet.

"Yes," Daphne went on, "in matters of sexual and cultural liberalism I would calculate that Toulouse is about fifty years ahead of Bourges, and Paris would be a hundred years ahead of Toulouse. I am not sure what it's like where you come from in America."

Again, there was a dig there, was she on to him? He was about to remind her that he came from Swinging London, where anything goes, when he caught himself. Firstly he remembered he was Scott, from Hollywood, not London. And second, London wasn't so swinging in any case when it came to same-sex intimacy, given that you could still go to jail for it. In terms of Hollywood queer culture, other than reading movie magazine gossip about hidden relationships and lavender marriages he half-remembered some news about the law beginning to change in some states a year or so before, but not enough recollection for anything more than a bluff.

"I reckon Hollywood is roughly halfway between Bourges and Toulouse, to be honest," he said.

"To be honest," said Daphne, in inverted commas, knowingly, "is that right?"

O Lord, she knows. Milo was immediately ashamed. He had just tried to mislead someone who had literally a hundred and twenty seconds before entrusted him with her biggest secret.

"No, not right, and not honest. I am so sorry, Daphne. Maybe soon we can get a bottle of wine and I can tell you the correct version. I have to be careful, because a lot of my story isn't mine alone, it is shared with Francois."

"So it is Francois and Scott still? That's the story you want to stick with?"

Milo was really conflicted. His loyalty to Jack went back nearly a decade and a half. But here was the chance of a friendship with someone who already knew more true things about him than Jack, after just two days. And arguably he had more in common with her, a real outsider, a kindred spirit; as well as kind and lovely. Different from an infatuation with the tantalisingly-out-of-reach-charmer archetype. Jack wouldn't miss him in the front row, he was already wildly oversubscribed as a love object.

"Cheer up," said Daphne, reading his mind, "he's not that irresistible."

"He doesn't even know I exist," said Milo, fake sobbing, then beginning to laugh. In a minute they were both reeling around in hysterics.

"Don't be daft," said Daphne, when they calmed down and started to breathe again, "that's like saying your Laurence Olivier doesn't know the audience exists – the audience is the only reason he's there – in fact HE doesn't exist without the audience…"

"Or our Johnny Gielgud…"

"… or our Jean Gabin…"

Milo was about to go "your Jean Marais" when he pulled up, frozen; Daphne bumped into him before also stopping dead.

"The van," he choked, pointing straight-armed like a fleshless wraith emerging from a fermenting grave, "We've found it! Hurrah – oh my gosh!!" And there it was, shining in the sky-bright overhead lights of a carpark across the road.

"But not hurrah," Daphne bewailed, sister to the wraith, pointing above the van to the sign that said "**GENDARMERIE.**"

"Far from Hurrah, in fact completely reverse Hurrah. That is the police station carpark. Either the van has been impounded and dragged in after an arrest of some sort, or the driver has voluntarily parked it there while entering the station to talk to the police about some matter they believe to be of public interest."

And even as they spoke – as they say in the most lurid tales – there emerged from the glaring doors of the station the very beautiful forms of Karl the man and Amelie the girl, both looking over their shoulders to finish a conversation with a very keen young plainclothesman, who was following them unnaturally closely, attempting to get near enough to hang tightly on to every word that Amelie was speaking.

Suddenly realising it was pouring with rain, the three figures stopped and retreated into the shelter of the police station's porch. Karl, as if to remind the young officer, and drive his point home for the last time, took out of his pocket a small packet, drawing out of it a square of fabric, holding it so the detective could see, and making the international wagging finger sign for, "Just remember what I told you, what we agreed."

Amelie was watching, and occasionally spoke, but much more reserved, definitely not so animated as Karl. The policeman responded with the intense nodding and thumb gestures for, "I know, I promised, I will follow up, I will find out." He was focused on Amelie more than Karl as he spoke, but Amelie wasn't giving him much back, Karl was answering and encouraging him.

Karl and Amelie then sprinted to the van through the downpour; the lights came on, Karl started the engine, and they began to slowly pull away to the carpark gate. As they drove glacially past the policeman still watching them from the porch, Amelie wound down her window, urged, they saw, by Karl, to say goodbye to the young man.

"They're shameless," whispered Milo to Daphne from the crouched positions they had both instinctively adopted, ducked down behind the closest car.

"He is," whispered back Daphne, "I am not quite so sure about her."

"What was it he was showing him, did you see?" said Daphne, slightly more loudly now the van was disappearing up the road.

"I am afraid it was part of my school uniform," said Milo, deadpan.

"Of course it was," responded Daphne, likewise, "I should imagine parts of your school uniform are under forensic investigation in every *gendarmerie* in France… What the hell is going on, Scott?"

Milo pointed up the road at the departing lights of the van. "Shouldn't we chase them first, and discuss this later?"

"Good point. To the car!"

Milo thought, Daphne is suddenly the heroine of a between-the-wars thriller. He saw her become Audrey Bagot in Red in the Morning, as she coolly tailed a gang of crooks at high speed up and down the highways and byways of Dornford Yates's France while remaining immaculate, unflappable and utterly soot-free. Yes, Daphne was the spitting image of Audrey, except perhaps for the swearing, hitching up her skirt so she could run properly, muddy ankles, getting hideously out of breath within fifty metres, and lighting up a fag the minute they got in the car.

Luckily they had been virtually at the cathedral already, and they were inside the motor in a minute and a half; but in that ninety seconds they got utterly soaked, having had to abandon the cover of the Knirps during their sprint. Daphne wasted no time, other than a second drag on her cigarette, in gunning the engine and hurtling the car out onto the main road. Using language Audrey would have blushed at, which I will not repeat here, she punched Milo painfully in the shoulder and announced that the Game Was Afoot.

Now we'll cut back to the Lodge for a while, with your indulgence, where, for someone who has been left behind, Jack is having an unexpectedly exciting night.

The first part was thoroughly satisfying. He and Madame Jestique had a hugely productive evening, as Jean anticipated. They worked through the storyboard of the play, almost frame by frame, and she gave Jack three or four suggested pieces of music for each scene. Gradually they made the selections, then they had a run through of the whole thing. They worked out that there were a couple of bad transitions which caused clashes, also one section became a little repetitive, another had a slightly bland run. They made substitutions and had another run through. It was perfect. 'Blimey,' thought Jack, 'what a joy to work with a professional. Even if she doesn't say anything.' Madame Jestique had another engagement and played her way out.

Jack was left alone, minding the phone. He looked grudgingly at the red notebook Jean had given him, the one left in the barn by his dad. At some point he was going to have to pick it up. He knew it was now, not least because at the speed things were moving, there might not be another opportunity. Also, it might contain some clues they could use to find him.

Jean had guessed it was his dad's diary, was it OK to read it? Jean had encouraged it, and there were exigent circumstances: Jack decided, though he didn't want to, he had to open it.

He immediately realised, 'This is not a diary, this is my dad's auto-biography.' There was nothing indicating when the text had been started or finished; Jack guessed by the age and tattiness of the book and the state of the pages, some torn out, some loose leaves stuffed in here and there, that the account had been written over a period of many years and evolved and adjusted like memory over time; there were a dozen different inks, pens, colours and pencils used, and even the style of writing changed noticeably as it progressed.

Anyway, the beginning, at least, was quite classical and neatly scribed; Jack started to read. I should warn you, this will be the hardest hour and a half of his life. He will quote here some things from the text, but many he will not want to share, indeed very many he will regret later ever having read at all. Most passages and events he will summarise, and if you want me to guess, I would say you will be shown around a third of the actual manuscript.

My name is Macon du Lac, called Mac since I was one day old, and this is my life.

I was born in 1912 in a small village near La Chapelle-d'Angillan, in Central France. My father was killed in battle two years after my birth in the last month of World War One. My mother raised us on her own: me, my two older sisters and two much older brothers. It was not so desperate as it sounds, there were twenty other women relatives in the villages around, many had lost children, many had lost husbands, basically everyone shared – this was a different time to the time you know now.

I am sure you will not be disappointed to learn I am not going to give you every detail of my life. You do not have time, I certainly don't. I think I might be trying your patience already. Shall I give you a handful of highlights? Not all so high.

So far so good. Mac went on to talk about his education, he felt deprived, he loved to read, to write, but he was not encouraged. Then:

At sixteen I started drinking very heavily. I had just left school and had a farm job with one of my uncles. I was bored, and hanging around with older cousins, who had bad habits – it is nice to spread the blame, but they should have looked after me better, my mother was too busy.

Many stories then about unpleasant acts and vandalism, generally getting in trouble and making a nuisance of himself. Some of this might be excused as the high jinks of youth, but for much of it there is a definite sinister undertone.

… when I was twenty, I met Madeline and everything changed. I tell you now about one moment: we had been seeing each other for three months and had been increasingly intimate – as we would have said then – and now we were sleeping together, in a room I had at the top of my uncle's barn. I remember it being largely full of straw, and the animal smell coming up from below – we were certainly never cold.

I woke one morning with the sun shining in through the curtainless windows onto her face on the pillow, peaceful, beautiful, surrounded by that massive carpet of rich golden-red curls, and the breath was drawn from my body, and I knew a level of pure feeling, utter love, I had never known before, and never since.

Does anyone ever know the best moment of their entire life? That turned out to be it for me.

I vowed to give up drink, work hard, and make more of myself, for her. Maybe to make a life, a family.

Then it all went wrong. Mac became jealous. He got obsessed with Madeline's history, her previous lovers. She innocently told him stories of her past, and he used them against her.

A large part of this first section of Mac's journal was about the Geography Teacher.

Do you recall those intense all-night conversations you have when you meet someone new? A confessional, talking about your past, where you come from, old girlfriends and boyfriends.

We did that a few times, but I know Madeline slowly got wary about what she told me, she discovered that some of my interest was not so healthy, some of my jealousy was retrospective, I was objecting in my head to boys who had touched her long before we met even – how does it work? I wanted possession of something innocent, perfect, untouched – impossible.

Before she got too cautious, she told me about when she'd left school, the leaver's dance, her and her friends all dressed for the first time as adults, suddenly they were women. But they were only fifteen or sixteen, that's how I remember it, anyway.

I think they were dressing up, not dressing; some of them like children wearing their mothers' frocks and shoes and flashy jewellery. She told me that her geography teacher had noticed her, with her little black dress worn off the shoulders. "Madeline, I didn't realise you were so grown-up."

He went on to proposition her. Mac was deeply upset by this. He pretended to Madeline he had moved on, forgotten about it, but he secretly researched the man, collected evidence, discovered a pattern of behaviour, decided he was a sexual predator and abuser, a threat to the young girls he was teaching. His sister Anna helped him, she found and talked to a number of girls from the school that she had known.

Then at the end of the year, sometimes a single day after they had left the school, even at the leavers' dance itself, the story was he would move in, pretend it was the first time he had noticed how grown-up they looked, flatter their eyes, and push for a date. The girls might feel uncomfortable, but he still had the aura of authority and they almost all accepted. He invited them for adult drinks and evenings in faraway locations, he said it would be discreet, intimate, all words to excite a young girl.

He insisted they should wear their grown-up outfits, make-up, high heels. It turned out that, once, one of these sweet girls turned up in the regular little flat pumps they all wore for school. He got flustered and asked her why she had dressed as a kid. "Oh the high heels were my mum's, not mine, she's using them tonight." When he went to the counter for the drinks the bartender started asking questions about who the girl was – it was the last time he chose that bar, he had to find somewhere further out where they didn't take so much interest.

Anna found three girls, two older than Madeline, one younger, who were willing to talk to us. The pattern was the same, he told all of them sequentially they were the most amazing, special, beautiful girl in the world. They all said, he was looking for girls to be absolutely innocent, no previous boyfriends. Over three or four dates he gradually pushed towards sex, always saying how pretty, special, womanly, exceptional, breathtaking the girl was. In the car there would be fumbling, fondling, petting, until the final question was asked to go back to his house so, and they all repeated the same phrase he liked to use, they could be "licked all over." I think we know what that means, and who really does the licking.

Mac and Anna enlisted two of their friends, Andre (who was also Anna's boyfriend) and Hugo, in a conspiracy to bring the man down; so he says; so it says in the text. They formulated a plan, watched him, got ready to trap him in the act.

As it happened, it was then virtually the end of the school year, the leaver's dance was not so far off. As it got closer, it became the centre of the community activity and attention for a few days; preparations were made, dresses were sewn and embellished, family suits were

332

loosened or tightened, even the cars got washed. Everyone got involved one way or another and it was easy enough for us to arrange to drop someone off, or pick them up, or deliver something, so we could be around the school carpark along with a few dozen mothers and fathers waiting, or locals who left a few years before just standing and gawping.

When the dance ended, the kids spilled out, in groups or pairs, chatting excitedly, looking at each other regretfully, perhaps for the last time in some cases. The chaperone teachers were among them, still watching, saying goodbye to the star pupils and the class clowns and the kids whose names they had never quite learnt. Then, there he was at the back, Geography Teacher, wearing a tight-fit bright-red shirt open way down the front instead of his normal button up corduroy, imagining (I reckon) that he looked quite the business. And with him, under his wing, tottering on high heels, a very pretty girl, much younger looking than most, staring up at him as he leaned towards her talking with his head turned so no-one else could hear or see what he was saying. Then he touched her, very briefly, once, high on the shoulder above the line of her dress, and he turned and walked to his car without looking back. She watched him go, all the way, long after he started the engine and pulled out of the carpark. Then she went to join her mother, laughing slightly shrilly as she embraced her, ready for the lift home, turning once as she got into the car to look at the school for the last time as a schoolgirl.

They stalked him, guessing he had arranged a date with the girl, whose name was Fleur.

Friday was a waste of time. We sat in two cars, not in the carpark of the bar, but in the streets either side, covering both exits, and we waited for three hours, but nothing happened.

Saturday it was different. We got there early, two cars again, and we waited for an hour, then they turned up, pulling into the carpark, driving right to the back, into the shade of some trees.

When they got out and walked across to the bar, my heart nearly

333

broke, I swear to you. To me, even knowing what I knew, it looked like a dad taking his daughter out for ice-cream on a Saturday morning, with the girl all puffed up and proud, reaching for her dad's hand, looking up at him in breathless excitement as though she could hardly believe he wanted just to be with her.....

They waited while they had drinks in the bar, then when they came out they followed them to a lay-by.

...... we knew where they were going, this suited us just fine, we were pleased – apologies for that. Andre and Anna had got just in front of them in Anna's car as soon as we could see they were preparing to move off and sped ahead to park in the dark area at the lay-by; Hugo and I followed in Hugo's truck. We didn't need to get too close as we were confident of the destination.

When they arrived Geography Teacher turned his car right to the back of the lay-by, away from passing lights, close into the hedge. Unwittingly they were about fifty metres behind Andre and Anna. When Hugo and I pulled in we were about another fifty metres back from them.

Everyone's lights were off. In the moonlight I could see him adjusting his seat, turning close into her, and I knew the conversation. How she was "special," "different," how she had stood out at the dance, so grown-up, so much more mature than the rest of the girls. He was careful not to mention he had noticed her earlier in the year and had been studying her, checking her family history, making sure there were no strong males in her life to watch and protect her, finding out her mother who loved her was too busy and preoccupied to supervise her closely.

Then he asked about her, "I would love to learn everything about you." And as she spoke, excited at the attention, I could see in the half-light he was gradually moving his head closer, he had an arm around her bare shoulders, just beginning some small gentle strokes, nothing too soon, nothing too quick, this was an experienced seducer, using the power he had built up over years with the girls in his classroom. That's how he got them, beautiful charming smart funny sweet girls who later in life, approached as equals, he would stand no chance of winning; he got them by manipulating them before they had a grown defence, and desperately using the vestigial power he had over them before it drained away in the adult world ....

The three men, according to the book, abducted Geography Teacher, while his sister took the young girl home.

.... Hugo got level with the driver's door, he wrenched at the handle, pulled the door open, reached in, grabbed the teacher and yanked him out, throwing him spread-eagled on the ground face down and sitting on his back, holding his face hard into the gravel. "If you make a sound, I will smash you harder than you could ever imagine. I warn you." The tone, a made-up gangster voice, was enough, the teacher lay deadly quiet except for some snuffling and was it sobbing? My job was rather less dramatic, I slipped the feed sack over the teacher's head, so he couldn't see us or anything else....

Anna's task was more difficult. She also had a stocking mask, though she was careful to show she was a woman, to help to reassure the girl. She had moved swiftly to the passenger side of the car, where Fleur was sitting, just about to scream. She opened the door as quietly and calmly as she could but of course everything was scaring the life out of the poor girl. My sister quickly whispered, disguising her voice (though Fleur didn't know her): "We're here as friends. Fleur, please don't be scared, you won't be hurt, we are here only to protect you."

Fleur was looking up at her in shock, it must have been terrifying, this is the part of the plan I hated but at least we had a woman to calm her. Andre had said maybe a big fright would be good for the girl, to make sure she was more careful in the future, but this was nothing to do with her and her choices, she was the victim and she deserved none of it.

"Please listen and trust me if you can," said Anna. "This man you are with is not what he pretends; he is wicked, he has hurt others, and we want to stop it. Please believe me.

"These men are taking the teacher with them. I am going to get into the driver's seat. You can trust me, I am simply going to drive you home; you have absolutely nothing to worry about. I will say nothing after this, please do not talk to me while we are driving."

She drove the girl home, dropped her without being seen, and left the teacher's car at his cottage, where she had stashed a bicycle earlier in the evening. Then she rode round to her mother's house to make an alibi. Meanwhile, the abduction was in progress, it says in the book:

.... *Hugo had tied the teacher's hands together behind him. We dragged him to the truck and threw him in the back, leaning in to bind his legs, put a handkerchief around his mouth, then we tied him top and bottom to the sides of the vehicle, so he couldn't even raise his head up. Finally, we threw a tarpaulin over him, regrettably covered in horse shit.*

We got in the front and prepared to move, with Andre in Anna's car ready to fall in behind us. We had muddied the registration plates on both vehicles, probably being much too cautious. In convoy the car and the truck headed off into the country. Just like in the movies, when the body in the boot comes back to life, we suddenly heard scuffling, rapping and muffled shouting coming from the back of the pick-up. After the initial shock, and a panic that he'd got free, we checked through the window behind us; there was no worry, he was still tied up tight as a calf. We both started giggling madly with relief and released tension, and after a couple of minutes the laughter got so bad Hugo had to pull into the side of the road because he couldn't see clearly to drive. I virtually had my head in his lap rolling with hilarity.

Then there was a sharp series of taps at the window; we both froze. An official voice called out sharply: "What is going on in there? Gentlemen, please keep your hands where I can see them. What is this bundle moving in the back? Please wind down the window and show yourselves and your identification. Move slowly."

Hugo and I looked at each other. Oh Shit, busted. Should we run?
How would we talk our way out of it… Hugo wound down the
window, there was no-one there. I presumed the officer had gone
to the back to look under the tarp. Then a head shot up like a
jack-in-the-box in Hugo's window, shouting in the fake police voice:
"Surprise, dickheads!!"

Andre – what a card!

After we both tried to swing arms and fists at him in our adrenaline
rush, attempting naturally to take his head off, there was more
laughter, and we spilled out on the hedge side, the three of us hugging
and tumbling over, unable to breathe any more in pure glee. What
Geography Teacher made of this, I have no idea, but if he started off
scared, by this point he must have been beyond any form of known
terror. Or perhaps, I thought, his geography teacher DNA is kicking
in and saying in a stern voice, "You, you, and you; you're disrupting
the class, I am splitting you up, and you'll sit in the front next time."
Yes, that would definitely work: much better than "You look like a
very naughty girl, please see me after school."

"I am sorry, Gentleman," said Andre, continuing in his policeman
character, "but I am going to have to issue you both with a summons
for Horseplay Without Due Care And Attention During The Execu-
tion Of A Kidnapping. Now, please be on your way, and don't forget
to treat your prisoner with the courtesy he deserves."

I remember thinking, just at that moment, 'Anna, you've got yourself
a decent boyfriend for a change.'

They took him to a deserted barn – owned by Claude's father, Jack
was interested to learn – where they hung him up on a rope by the
arms.

When he calmed down, we put on our masks and gathered around
him. He was still dressed in his Geography outfit of corduroy trousers
and baggy tweed jacket with leather patches on the elbows; he'd
clearly thought he needed to power dress as a teacher for his date with

Fleur. Hugo and I held him steady while Andre flipped off the feed sack and undid the handkerchief around his mouth. He immediately began to scream, asking what was happening, why they'd taken him, what had they done with the girl. He obviously had not heard anything Anna said to Fleur at the car, or anything since. He had no idea. Seeing us standing ominously watching him, he started by blustering, then sensing the hostility in us he began to plea to be freed; when we just stood there, silent, that gradually turned into begging for his life. We all took a step back, making a circle around him, looking on quietly threatening while he wept and beseeched us to spare him.

"Do you want the girl, is that what this is all about? Where have you got her? You can keep her, do whatever you want to her. She means nothing to me, just let me go, I won't tell anyone."

Sickened, Andre cracked and shouted, "Shut the fuck up," directly into his ear. "We do not want the girl, we want you. The girl has gone home, where she should be. Look in your heart, and you will know why you are here, Geography Teacher. But we may not kill you, that is entirely up to you."

Andre went rogue and said they would not murder him if he could answer ten questions on his expert subject.

"Don't worry, I am being honest," said Andre, "if you answer every question correctly, you can live – I can't promise anything more than that just yet. Are you ready?"

Geography Teacher nodded, desperate to believe this was just a hideous joke, but failing to see yet how it could be, what it all meant.

"Ten questions. Question One: What is the capital of Peru?"

"Seriously?"

"Is that your final answer, remember your life depends on it."

[By now Hugo was writhing on the floor stuffing his fists in his mouth to prevent his laughter escaping into the soundscape. It appeared Hugo had an odd sense of humour.]

"OK, I'll go along with it. Lima."

"Very good! Question Two: What is the longest river in the world?"

"The Nile."

"Excellent, this is going very well, for you anyway! So many might have said the Amazon, I hate to admit it, I am impressed.

"Question Three: Which is the closest planet to Earth?"

"That's astronomy, not geography. Geography means study of the things on the earth, not space."

"Blimey you have got brass balls now you have finally stopped crying – you are actually disputing with me what I am allowed to ask you? I set the rules, Mr Teacher, you're not in charge here. Try again: which is the closest planet to Earth?"

"Venus."

"Correct – you knew that all the time, why did you try and talk me out of it?"

"It's a question of principle, I am serious about my subject and the way it is taught, and I don't like people getting confused about what it includes."

"You need to be careful, that patronising pomposity might get you killed. Also, don't let's get ahead of ourselves, we will certainly be coming back to the issue of principles later.

"So, Question Four: What's the tallest mountain in the world?"

"Everest."

"Question Five: What currency do they use in Sweden?"

"Krona."

"You're good, well done! You might go all the way!"

"Question Six: What is the largest continent?"

"Asia."

"Question Seven: What is the largest lake in the world?"

"Superior."

"Question Eight: What country did Iceland used to belong to?"

"Iceland was part of the Kingdom of Denmark."

"Very good, very good. Question Nine: What is the smallest country in the world?"

"Vatican City."

"CORRECT! Boy, you do know your stuff, I can't deny that! Just one more question, and a correct answer saves your life – are you excited?"

Geography Teacher was beginning to recover his confidence, he'd decided to believe this was some prank that had gone horribly wrong, and he would end up on top.

"I think I know you boys, right – you used to be in my class?"

In fact, he was partly right, Hugo and Andre had sat at the back of his classroom a few years before, being careful not to learn anything, and lacking even the enthusiasm and energy to disrupt it. But they all knew he was bluffing, he couldn't possibly tell them with their masks and disguised voices, and in any case he hadn't even bothered to learn their names when he was supposed to be their teacher so he was hardly likely to recognise them now through two thicknesses of eighty denier nylon.

"Let's get on, please," said Andre, sensing the change of tone in the teacher and realising his fear of them was dissipating. "Last question to come."

"Make it something fair, not the amount of precipitation in some godforsaken country, or the net weight of the annual Azerbaijanian beetroot crop."

"Ha ha, it is great you've got your sense of humour back! No, that won't happen, actually we have been more than fair, because the last question is on a subject in which you have a very special interest."

Hugo and I were looking on by this stage, mesmerised at Andre's spiel, and wondering where all this was going – we'd never discussed a test, and we certainly hadn't planned on letting the man go without teaching him a lesson.

"Come on then," said the teacher, "let's have it, and get it done."

"OK, Question Ten: Do you think it is acceptable for grown men to have sex with children? More specifically, do you agree it is OK for teachers to have sex with their pupils?"

There was silence. The colour literally drained from the teacher's face completely, just like they say in books, it really happened, blood dropping out of his head into his hanging body; his lips disappeared.

Then suddenly hell let loose, he was screaming, kicking, shouting: "You bastards, you bastards, what the hell is this about? You've got it wrong. Who are you? What are you talking about? You know nothing about me, this is nonsense." And so on and so on, for three, five, seven minutes without stopping.

Andre signalled to me and Hugo with a nod to join him outside. We were all feeling pretty stressed as you would imagine, and we lit cigarettes and breathed the cold night air in some relief. Hugo pulled a flask out of his pocket, unscrewed the lid and passed it around – it was very bad brandy, exactly what we needed. Sadly I was meant to be off the booze at the time, but it didn't seem the moment to be a stickler about that.

"You believe this guy?" asked Hugo. "Not just a creep, also a coward and an all-round dickhead."

"Complete dickhead," agreed Andre. "Nice how his first concern was to protect the safety of Fleur – he's an absolute diamond."

"You went well off script there, mate," I said to Andre, "where did it all come from?"

"No idea, sorry guys. It just hit me and I ran with it. Somehow going in cold with the plan just didn't seem heartless enough; now we've met this guy, in person, and he offered us the little girl in exchange for his freedom, I was inspired to be a bit more cruel."

"It was reasonably amusing, I'll give you that, but can we get back on schedule now?" asked Hugo. "It's gone two o'clock, we're going to need to wrap this up and get it cleaned away before the farmers start moving around."

"Yes OK," said Andre. "I still want to hear him admit what he's done, so we challenge him, like we originally planned. We can get there from here, don't worry, let me do it, and I will wind it up – just remember your parts, and be ready, do you have the tool?"

"Yes, no problem, I have it stashed behind a bale in there, he can't see it."

After another cigarette and another round from the brandy flask we went back to him. The light inside was poor and orange, it took a while when we re-entered for our eyes to adjust, to get the full picture back. I saw for the first time there was an owl sitting on the beam in the corner, enjoying the show: somehow it made me nervous, but the others hadn't noticed.

Geography Teacher had stopped shouting and was looking at us, half terrified, half trying to be menacing. The menace was a bit diluted by the pee running down his left leg; his right leg was dry.

"You're dressing to the left then, Teach?" said Andre, cockily.

"What are you, my tailor?" spat back the teacher, I thought pretty bravely in the circumstances. "You boys have no idea what you are playing with here. Let me go immediately, and I'll go easy, I might even decide to forget about this."

Andre was losing patience now.

"As I recall, your score is nine out of nine. If you get ten, you live, at least – we'll tell you what else happens after that, if we get there. You still haven't answered the last question – is it OK for men to have sex with children, and for teachers to have sex with pupils? I'd advise at this stage that you try to narrow in on an actual answer rather than bluster and blah."

"Well, what is the right answer?"

At this point we all laughed, we couldn't help it really; the tension was a bit much, and now the guy was asking us for our opinion.

"Teacher, do you want to die? For God's sake, it is not what we think at the moment that will get you off the rope – and I would have thought it is fairly obvious what we think, or we wouldn't all be here at the moment, with you hanging on our every word."

The teacher was kicking and spinning again now in his agitation. His throat and tongue had dried out, and his voice had risen an octave and was rasping like a file on metal.

"I mean, what is the right answer to stay alive, you fucker? Just tell me what you want to hear, and I will say it."

"We want to hear the truth, Sir," said Andre, for some reason reverting to his title.

"If I defend my perceived actions and tell you I think whatever it is you are accusing me of is OK, then that is not what you want to hear, and you will kick me to death, right?

"If I agree with you that I think it is wrong, and illegal, then you are going to say that in that case I knew the law and broke it.

"I can't see how I can win here, you have set this up, set me up, to get the result you want."

"Seems easy enough to me," said Andre. "You claim you didn't have sex with any underage girls and didn't have sex with anyone you were teaching at the school. If that's true, then can't you simply say, 'Of course it is wrong for a man to have sex with a child?'"

"OK OK, of course it is wrong for a man to have sex with a child. Of course it is wrong for a teacher to have sex with a pupil. Are you happy now!?"

"Yep," said Andre. "Happy as I am going to be. You have told the truth, teacher, and saved me from having to kill you, which I didn't want to do."

Geography Teacher let out a huge yelp which gradually turned itself into a long sputtering sigh of relief, some colour came back to his face.

"Don't get too comfortable!" said Andre. "You have told the truth, so you will live, we promised that. But you are also guilty, we know that; telling the truth now does not let you off that, nor does it assure us you will not do it again, when you are back out there and subject to urges you seem to be unable to control.

"So, we are going to let you go, don't fret. But subject to two things."

Geography Teacher looked suspicious. "You didn't say anything about that."

"I said we wouldn't kill you if you answered all ten questions correctly. You should be happy! You live! Just two more things to sort out.

"First, you will never teach again. That is non-negotiable. You are not to be trusted around kids, we are prepared to let you go, but it is a big responsibility for us, if you continue to abuse girls, or God forbid do worse, then it is on us. We need to be able to sleep.

"In exchange for our generosity, we demand you leave the teaching profession and do not do anything that brings you in contact with kids in future, that's the deal. My friend here Mr Stockinghead," he nodded towards Hugo, "has a relative in the education ministry, we will watch the registers of teachers in all regions, if your name shows anywhere we will send the police the dossier of evidence and witness statements we have, and trust me you will be in prison very quickly."

Inasmuch as a man dangling on a rope can go limp, the teacher did, slumping, head down, muttering and letting out a moan of anger, and was it regret, remorse? Too late.

"And what is the other thing?"

"Oh, something much smaller..."

Again, Hugo struggled to stop giggling; the guy really had an evil sense of fun.

"I am afraid we are going to need to adjust your equipment, as a kind of insurance policy."

The teacher gazed at him completely uncomprehendingly. Before any understanding could spark in his brain and jump down his spine, in a ballet we had discussed and practised, I stepped forward and

345

grabbed his legs. My job was to hold him steady, and also to block his view, I stuck my head right up against his chest so he could not look down beyond me.

Hugo, behind him, grabbed a pair of shears and a glass container he'd concealed behind a hay bale. Coming round to the front, he raised the shears up into the teacher's eyeline but kept the jar hidden.

Andre took a pace towards the dangling teacher, undid his belt, and pulled down his trousers and pants, which by now were yellow and wet with urine. Both Andre and I resisted the impulse to step back gagging as the teacher began to struggle and defecate. Andre grasped the man's penis, very small by now, and pulled it.

Hugo lowered the shears out of the teacher's sight, and snapped them shut, loudly, sharply, like a guillotine, as Andre pulled hard on the penis, dug in hard with his nails, and let it snap back.

Hugo dropped the shears, and behind the teacher's back he reached into the jar up to his wrist, and pulled out a piglet penis, which he raised quivering up to the teacher's face, so close he couldn't focus on it, he just saw the flapping bloody tube dripping ten centimetres from his eyes. He screamed, puked, evacuated, and fainted – I am not sure it was in that order, but it was definitely all four.

Hugo was in fits; Andre and I were in shock. But we had done what we intended, it had gone really well; other than Andre's mad diversion into the geography quiz, we had stuck perfectly to the plan.

It was nearly 3.00am. He was unconscious. We untied him, let him down, rebagged his head, and Andre tucked a wrapped cloth in his jacket pocket containing the piglet penis. We had obtained it earlier in the day from Claude, who came about it in the general course of his pig-keeping duties. "No, lads, you don't want a grown pig's penis, they're huge, that would be for a farmer; for a teacher who sleeps with his pupils, piglet size is the most you would want."

Then Andre placed a folded message in the teacher's leather wallet *and stuffed it back in an inside pocket; it was formed from cut up headlines of newspapers, the type that only kids and kidnappers make, and said:* **NEXT TIME WE DO IT FOR REAL.** *A nice surprise for him later.*

We tossed him in the truck, trussed him up, and Hugo and Andre drove him off, leaving me to tidy up the barn, lock up, and drive Anna's car back, before getting home to bed. Scrubbing the teacher's leftovers off the floor wasn't the best job I'd ever had, but I couldn't leave that for Claude.

Andre told me they drove about five kilometres to dump him in the ancient woodland, quite thick, but not too far from some roads, and near enough to a stream where he could clean himself up when he woke – I have no idea, now, why we were all so thoughtful, maybe we were beginning to believe we had gone too far.

Anyway, Hugo and Andre left him safe, it was a warm night, he would be fine, they undid his hands; they suspected by the time they left him that he was only pretending to be comatose anyway, but they'd kept their masks on so no-one really cared.

We never heard from him again; he left the region, who knows where.

And the postscript to our adventure? The immediate consequence was that I was back on the booze and I had made a very unfortunate bond with Hugo; after that we were a terrible influence on each other, and sank to very low depths very quickly. Not so much Andre; he stuck with my sister, and they got married and moved away not so long after, up the north, near the Belgian border somewhere, running restaurants and bars in the mining region.

And longer term? Well, Madeline found out what we had done (I have no idea how, I thought we told no-one), and she dumped me. How does that work? Especially when I learnt a couple of years later she married Hugo while I was away in the desert ....

Three things she claimed: first, I had sworn (probably for the sixth or

*seventh time) never to drink again and I had said she should leave
me if I did. Of course, I meant it at the time, but with the expectation of course that there should always be another chance.*

*Second, whoever told her about our caper exaggerated the violence,
and also declared I was ringleader and described me as the most
sadistic of all. Everyone was saying there was an actual mutilation,
a rumour even went round for several weeks that the Geography
Teacher had died. However much I denied it, others, who presumably
could not have been there, were saying these things to the extent that
the police felt they had to get involved and make some half-hearted
enquiries.*

*And third, we had also been having quite a few discussions about
jealousy, about obsession, call it what you choose. Madeline said it
scared her that I would do secret things to people she had told me
about "in good faith." In good faith – where did she get that? I can
see it now, from the distance, poor girl, of course she was right. Back
then, it just felt, on one level, there is a fine line between an attentive
boyfriend and a so-called maniac.*

After Madeline kicked him out ['quite rightly,' thought Jack, 'you
can't argue with it'] Mac got drunker, more pugnacious and more
promiscuous, generally making himself into a huge irritant and
embarrassment to the village and his family. There followed many
anecdotes of debauchery. Jack held his head in his hands.

In this section the writing got more disjointed, it was often just
streams of conscious about fantasies, feelings and hobbyhorses. It
was as though he had really wanted to tell the story about the
Geography Teacher simply and directly, and he held it in for
that, disciplined, and now he took the brakes off. He droned on
[…'sorry, dad'…] about kinds of sex, betrayal, types of jealousy.
Then he refocused on Madeline's past and future boyfriends, what
he wanted to do with them, very often it involved damaging their
genitals by either cutting or hitting with a mallet, which seemed to
be quite a constant theme.

[The phone rang. It was Albert. Thank God, someone normal. Jack composed himself.]

"Hi, Albert, how is it going, any luck yet?"

"No, just checking in. Claude has got us stuck in a café with some kind of outlaw chief and we've had two drinks so far, that's about the extent of my report. I am feeling slightly queasy to be honest, that liquorice drink is nice at first, but on the second round the sweetness gets to you, with the sugar. I think I'll try and get some coffee."

Albert was gabbling.

"OK, mate, calm down. So, who is out looking for Karl if you guys have decided to go on a bender?"

"The pirate's mate and crew," Albert giggled slightly. "Claude says they know everyone in town, and they have a network."

"Let's hope."

Jack had never really had a good chat with Albert. This wasn't the time to start, but he didn't want to let him go. He wanted company, and a distraction, and an excuse to stop reading.

"Gotta go, Claude's waving. Have you got any messages?"

"OK, Albert, thanks – no, nothing my end, you're the first to call in, no sightings, no news."

"Bye then."

"Bye."

Back to the book.

Then one morning, after a bout of several days on the booze and a

*most severe kicking from a gang in Bourges, I woke to find myself
in the back of a car between two of my largest cousins, with another
cousin in the front passenger seat, and my youngest uncle driving.*

"What's happening? Where are we?"

*"Listen, Mac," said my uncle, with genuine sadness and concern, "We
are taking you to the recruitment office, and you are joining the army
today, for the five-year minimum, in the Foreign Legion, you will be
going to Syria and Algeria. It is decided. A very close friend of mine
is the head of the office, he knows we are coming. The recruitment
process is not so simple but I can assure you that you are going to
qualify, there is a small douceur, but he and I fought together so it is
all set for you. This choice is not optional, my friend, this is to save
your life and save our family."*

*And that was it. I went to Tours to be selected, then to the desert for
five years...*

Yes! According to this book, Mac actually joined the Foreign Legion! Really? Well this, as well as some of the other stories, could
presumably easily be checked with Claude. Jack actually felt a glow
of pride here, bizarrely: 'My Dad, The Legionnaire.' It didn't last
long, there were some pungent sketches from the Legion, this is
probably the least scary:

*One night I surprised a group of men from my squad around the
campfire with one so-called comrade – Leonard – entertaining them
by reading one of my letters which had been returned unopened from
Madeline. It had been delivered to his bunk by accident. They were
laughing. I broke his arm, grabbed him round the neck and held the
letter in front of his eyes while I kept squeezing the fractured bone.
I politely requested that he read out the rest of the letter to everyone
before I allowed anyone to call for medical help. No-one laughed at
me again.*

When he left the Legion after five years, the book said he got
selected for Special Services, spy work, then he even worked for de

Gaulle as a fixer – this was beginning to sound rather incredible, Jack was dubious. Mac said (the text said) he ended up liaising with the Brits when de Gaulle was in London in the middle years of the war, doing secret work using his training.

When he was in London it sounded as though he had many girl-friends, there were plenty of stories, some unnecessarily detailed, which Jack tried to skim or skip. And there was a lot of general ranting, it felt like he was going off the rails at that time. Here is just one small example, to give you the gist without boring you with pages of the stuff (it went on and on); this is with the redactions Jack made in his head as he read (I thank him for that, and you should thank me):

"And what about the sex?" she said. "It was spectacular, and I always did whatever you wanted, and let you do whatever you wanted."
And that was true, mainly I made love to her with xx xxxxxx for half an hour, or however long it took xxxxxx xxx xxxx, and then she would do the few movements and moments necessary to xxxxxx me in xxxxxxxx xxxx. Don't get me wrong – extremely exciting, lovely. But really, thinking a couple of minutes of taking my xxxx in her xxxxx could be the same as love? Is that what women think men are? That those few xxxxxxx, xxxxxxx, and pulls could equal the hours and days of dreaming, thinking, saying, being? And when she xxx xx xxxx in her xxxxx, with me watching, yes it was very thrilling, but I was thinking also of the other score of men she had done it to, some of whom I knew; there is nothing very special about that trick, nothing unique to me. You will forgive me for this disposition? I want you to know that I tried, without you, and this is what happens.

All this time, through the ins and outs of various girlfriends and short-lived affairs, Mac was yearning for Madeline, and the past. Jack had to remind himself that by now it was around a decade since he had even spoken to her; but it was clear to Jack from the manuscript that, to Mac, Madeline, in his illusions, was more real than the people actually around him at the time.

If the past is another country, as they say, then that's just geography, you must be able to travel there. If I make that journey, will I be able to find your house, ten years ago, and wait outside with flowers?

Then in the year before the war ended, he met Jack's mum-to-be:

Finally, I met Kate, an East End girl who was travelling up West every day on the District Line to work in the secretarial room in our department. She was cheeky, tough and fun, not on good terms with her family, leaving her friends behind, her mum was dead and her dad abusive and drunk. Sadly, therefore, she was very vulnerable to my manipulation – not deliberate, but it is probably what happened.

It was always a mistake, getting seriously involved, because I was obsessed with another woman (I was going to say "my heart was lost to another"); but I was lonely for friendship, and she was lovely. I never spoke to her of Madeline, never once. Kate and I were similar characters, fish out of water trying to be something we were not born to be, imposters, surprising people who expected less of us.

Soon it was the two of us against the world, and after six months of quite formal, sweet and romantic courtship between the clichéd figures of the exiled French soldier and the huge-hearted girl clawing her way from a tough place in London, we were married in a tiny backstreet church in front of an audience of five. She tamed me, but still I woke at night shouting, not from what I had done in the desert, because that was my job, and my duty; but from memories of the vile things I had done as a drunkard, because that was my choice, and my nature.

Kate and I bought an unobtrusive house in East Ham, near the underground, and she stopped going to work when, within a year, as the war was moving towards its end, Jack came, second light of my life, something to justify the regrets, if not softening them. Then two years later Georgina and then little Francis-we-call-Frank. My job evolved in the late 1940s to something more traditional – less travelling abroad to kill people, more encouraging others to do it for me; looking after their pay and conditions, and furnishing them with excuses and rationalisations for burying the nation's bodies.... These days I think people are evaluated psychologically for these positions, but I think if we had done that back then, none of us would have passed that test, the desks would have been empty. . . .

Jack gave that bit verbatim because some of it was about him, and he felt it was about time he came into it. He had had no idea that his dad was involved in that kind of work, and again wondered if some of this was fantasy. He was shaken by the comments and thoughts his dad had had about his mum. Why hadn't he known, was he totally insensitive? They all lived within five yards of each other pretty well all the time.

Mac had started to go back to the La Chapelle for visits after the war ended. Jack calculated he must have been one or two years old during these passages, so presumably he and his mum had been left home together in London while Mac toured his old haunts and tried to rebond with his family.

At that time I went back to the home villages every now and again, and I can say they respected me; though I told them nothing of what I had done since leaving, in the Legion, and after, they had heard some stories.

Mac recorded that during these trips he began to "surveil" Madeline, often at night.

Madeline was still living locally, so with my training I was able to see her unobserved, and I followed and watched her a few times, nothing creepy, honestly, completely sympathetically. She had married, and had three kids, two boys and a younger daughter. Her husband Hugo was a brutal and faithless man, of course I knew exactly what he was like, more than anyone.

Then, back in London, with an expanding family, the first mention of the letters:

I still wrote to Madeline at least weekly, but I never sent the letters as they might get returned and blow my life up, which I didn't then want. So I hid them in the house.

What I am describing is a life lived with regret. Those of you who have no regret can have no understanding of the daily grind, the exhausting work entailed in managing the guilt and disappointment. But who, really, has a life without regret?

Then later, something more lucid about married life, and the family:

For my children, I had three rules.

The first was positive and pleasurable, for all of them to read a book each week, and if they couldn't choose it, I would do it for them. They had library tickets and we all went together on Saturday morning, it was the same place as the swimming pool, so sometimes we went there after and if we did we had hot sweet tea and margarine toast in a pile. On Friday evening there was a strict arrangement, the five of us would eat supper together then each would speak about the book they had read in the week, before returning it the next day.

Jack smiled. Amid all the pain, here was a recollection of some of the greatest times of his childhood – specially the toast.

The second: no drink. OK, it is hard to impose that rule on a five-year-old, so it is more a question of example of how not to and a demonstration of what happens if you do. Do not drink: alcohol ruins lives – I found a hundred small and regular ways to promote and advertise these messages. When they were in their teens it was made clear to them (against Kate's better judgement), "You have an obsessive gene that I believe is likely to make you an alcoholic if you touch alcohol, and that will ruin your life, bring you low, and very possibly destroy you and those around you." Nothing too heavy.

The third: find one person to be your person and stick with them, stay with them, respect them, love them if you can, never let them go. Do not play the field, do not experiment, do not fall in love and change your mind. Kate was charmed when she heard me teaching the youngsters this lesson. Everyone likes to believe they are the first or the last. They prefer the former but they will settle for the latter.

Some animals take only one partner their whole life – wolves, beavers, swans among them. The Victorians and many other ancient cultures and civilisations had different values to ours, not tolerating divorce, even frowning on remarriage. Perhaps because they believed so strongly in their versions of the afterlife; how confusing, how saddening, how embarrassing it must be to arrive in heaven and have to choose from a range of lined-up spouses which one you wish to spend eternity with...

Jack caught himself nodding, perhaps visualising himself trapped in that very dilemma. Milo might have been more in sympathy with the people stood shivering in the line. Not being chosen for eternity, right? Even more humiliating than being left behind when they're picking the sides for football.

If you leave a partner behind and take a new one, maybe more than once, then this is a recipe for a life of sorrow and regret. Nothing is ever right, you will desire both the past and possibly the future, but the present is always compromised. The truth is, when you travel on, if you are this type, you always leave a little of your luggage behind, and spend the rest of your life looking for it or wanting to go back for it. The bag you leave behind, however small, will always be the bag that seems to have contained the most vital and necessary items....

.....

For over a decade Kate and I played happy families; she believed I loved her, and my confusion came and went and came again with the years, but I was always loyal in my way. And, of course, meanwhile the letters spored like mushrooms in the darkness under the stairs, filling a suitcase which was now bursting with news of a life that no-one cared about, not even the person living it.

We took enormous pride in educating the kids; the books, and music, trips to museums and galleries, the lives of the writers and artists.

All the things that poorly educated people value – you can laugh if you want. Perhaps the most useful thing we did was make them do their homework and we (well mainly Kate) religiously went to all the sports, all the plays, all the concerts.

.....

And we even ensured we forged their bonds with their heritage, taking them back to the home villages in France every year. Kate's family was a lost cause to her, so our children forsook any possible roots in the East End and became solely French by ancestry. They developed strong relationships with their French cousins, uncles, aunts and grandparents: and while they did that, I slid off to spy on Madeline. This is the least creditable part of my history, or maybe I should leave it to you to decide that. Skulking around the fields and outhouses by night to get glimpses through windows, to see the husband with his crude table manners, drinking again, and her children, growing up in parallel with mine, shouting, coming home filthy, refusing to go to school, ignoring and disrespecting their mother.

And Madeline? She was so lovely, so golden, so serene, so patient, so earthy, natural and wild, so full, so glorious, so gorgeously unkempt and untouched.

This was one or two weeks a year, year after year, I was drawn to it, could not avoid it, waited for it, desperately anticipated it, it kept me going. And always I hid my obsession under the excuse of wanting the best for my children, for them to be with their family, to know their country, learn their language and culture. You can have contempt for me – you should – but you will not match the contempt I have for myself.

.....

The letters became the main thing in my life, but as you would imagine, the more time I had to write them, the less I had to write about. I used to be quite proud of the content; achievements, trips, exciting events, the odd complex or elegant assassination, matters of national importance. But now I was running a clerical department: it is hard to write impressive letters about filing, so I went through a period when I was philosophising, it was about ideas, politics, shared cultural experiences. I bored myself very often with these, they were letters to an aunt, or granny, not the kind of material that would excite and enchant a lover, there are definitely more than a few I am pleased I never sent.

There were others that had a lot of love talk, but some of them tipped, over the years, the wrong way, to yearning, begging, frankly moaning. I myself was mildly contemptuous of some of this miserable self-pity, so God knows what a red-blooded lover would have made of it, someone who wanted a strong partner, a Prince. Again, perhaps it was for the best that some of these travelled only as far as the cupboard under the stairs.

Even the remembering became thin: because it turned out that we had actually had such a small amount of shared experience that it was impossible to keep rehearsing those few intimate moments again and again. Also, sadly, memory fades. It just does. The images start sharp and bright and vivid, then gradually lose their focus, definition and vitality and finally become as sepia and stiff as an Edwardian portrait photograph. Eventually you are writing about the recollections of the memories of events; musing upon the long shadow of the action because descriptions of the act itself are faded and frayed.

Suddenly there were two hundred letters, then three hundred, and still I wrote. I continuously had an unfinished letter hidden in my notebook, because each time I finished one, I started the next immediately. I guess they formed an unbroken dialogue (she would say monologue, I think) describing events, thoughts, feelings – not every individual action, of course – for over twenty years. A diary is written for the self, but this was a diary for the other. Emotions, reactions, books, births, baby walk, baby talk. Naturally, as you would expect, I spoke all the time about my children, but mentioning a wife, especially by name, that was extremely infrequent, possibly never.

Now it is, what, two years, three years, since I left my family, since I left England. I try not to think about it, but it is not possible to control that. I have stopped feeling hunger. I have stopped feeling the cold in the winter. Being dirty, that used to upset me, I have learnt not to worry about that. I haven't written much recently in this book. All the time now I write the letters, I do that every day, that is the main work.

So that was it. A life in miniature. Sixty small pages in a notebook. It had taken Jack less than an hour and a half to consume everything his dad had chosen to say about his entire existence.

And frankly, thought Jack, never one to resist making it about himself, I don't exactly have a starring role.

He was beyond shock, about eighty percent of this was new to him, and strange to him. It did cross his mind to ask, is it all true? Parts of it sounded more than a trifle delusional. He would try to check the detail with Claude, or mum, or any relatives who had been around.

He poured himself a brandy and drank it while contemplating his father's life lesson about avoiding all strong liquors. 'Actually,' he thought, 'that was going pretty well till he buggered off. In fact, until he buggered off, I hadn't had a single drop. Plenty since, however.' He drained the glass. 'Good to know about that obsessive gene though.'

And the swan mating principle. "*Some animals take only one partner their whole life...*" Maggie? What was this nonsense with Amelie? 'For Christ's sake grow up, man,' he argued back, 'I'm too young to be a swan, or a wolf.'

Jack looked at the clock. Time was passing, he hadn't got nearly as many calls as he was expecting. The bars and clubs were all open now, there were plenty of places to investigate, but, realistically, were they going to find two kids if they didn't want to be found? Originally it had felt as though he had drawn the short straw tonight, being made to stay behind, but now he wasn't so sure. The rain was getting heavier; other than the horrors of the notebook, this was a better way of spending the evening than trudging the backstreets of Bourges, soaked to the skin, on a wild goose chase.

But the book had left him feeling pretty ill, actually physically sick. He looked at the pile of letters. Did he have to? The only thing on the front of each was a number, so of course he put them in order. He had eighteen of them, the earliest was labelled 13, the latest 479. Then he noticed two were stuck together – 207 and 208 – so it was nineteen in total.

He'd already taken in a lot with the journal. Maybe he had done enough? It was hard going. It would be perfectly fine to stop if he wanted; to think about it, analyse it, regroup, decide what to feel and what to do. Or he could just plough on – there was no doubt he would read the letters; it was just a question of when. And what if there was a clue to where Mac was, or what the hell he was up to? That made it more urgent.

Refilling his brandy, lighting a cigarette – smoking indoors was democratically sanctioned now, given Karl was on the hoof and his vote had gone with him – he was reaching for the envelopes when the phone rang. Saved by the bell…

There was a considerable amount of fumbling and rattling, messing with coins the other end, then: "Hi, Jack, how goes?"

"Hi Milo, I'm glad you called… What's happening out there?"

Back in Bourges, about half an hour before as you may well recall, Daphne and Milo had been pulling out of the cathedral square, starting at fifty kilometres an hour, heading in the general direction of the departing van containing Karl and Amelie. "We've already lost them," moaned Milo, shaking himself like a damp dog to get rid of the surface water, and worrying ahead to what Jean was going to say, and how he was going to face Jack and tell him about Karl and the pieces of uniform at the police station.

"It's OK," said Daphne out of the corner of her mouth, eyes fixed on the night road, "this isn't a big city in America, or Paris, or maybe even London, or wherever you come from. This is rural France, and there is generally only one recognised route between two places. They left the town centre on the road we're on now, the D940, and that is the road north to La Chapelle. They could choose to deviate, they could even decide to turn off completely, but my strong guess and expectation is that having said whatever they wanted to say to the police, they are now heading back to the Lodge to merge back into the team and pretend nothing has happened. So, no reason to believe, really, that they are going anywhere other than 'home.'"

The rain was coming in thick now, and she had the wipers going, not doing a particularly impressive job. While she was talking Daphne was leaning forward to get a better view out. Steering with her left hand, she was lighting a cigarette with her right, meaning she couldn't change gear, so she had to remain above the fifty-kilometre mark as she crossed two roundabouts in quick succession.

"Shall I do that for you?" offered Milo.

"The lighter, or changing the gears? It's done now, don't fret." And suddenly she was up to a hundred kilometres an hour on the badly lit road, and within a few minutes they were able to see in front of them on the long straight section the rear lights of the van, which they were rapidly catching.

"I'll hold back," said Daphne, slowing the car to around eighty, "and just keep them in sight.

"We have another thirty kilometres to go, say twenty minutes. Would you like to usefully employ that time by telling me the truth about who you are and what you are up to? I am pretty sure it won't make me love you any less."

"You can't promise that. Ours might be the shortest affair in history when you find out my evils. What if I am an arsonist, a trainspotter or a child poisoner?"

"A trainspotter would be difficult to accept, you're right. Perhaps it would be easiest if you start at the beginning rather than boasting about your hobbies?"

"OK, this is just us, right? No-one will ever know we have had this conversation?"

"Scott, just tell the story, please."

"OK, not Scott, let me introduce you to Milo." He tried to make a small bow but was constricted by the dashboard.

"And not Hollywood. I am from a place in London called East Ham. I am English, so sorry."

"Ah, so the trainspotting, that's not the worst of it."

"Ho ho. So, also, Francois is not Francois from Paris, he is also from East Ham, his name is Jack, my oldest friend through three schools. He is connected to this area though, he's a cousin of Jean's, and the son of Mac, who was your father's childhood friend."

"I bloody thought so," shouted Daphne gleefully, smacking the dash so hard it made Milo jump. "Claude has been weird around some of this stuff, so I presume he knows. And actually I am fairly sure now you have confirmed it that I met Jack a few times when he was four, five or six years old. He is not nearly as cute as he was then, and his hair, by the way, is a completely different colour, if it is the boy I am thinking about.

"So next questions. Why are you here in disguise, and what's going on with your school uniform?"

"There's the nub. Truthfully, we are on the run, but we are not quite sure why. Last Thursday, which seems like a lifetime ago, was our final day at school, which seems like a completely different

361

world. We finished our exams and went to the pub, which happens also to be my home, as my mum runs it.

"Some bad lads came in and started a ruckus. Jack and I got caught up in it with a couple of friends, a knife was pulled – by them – and one of them fell on it, we think, when we defended ourselves by pushing them off us.

"The four of us had ferry tickets lined up anyway to come down here, so we fled the scene before the police got there, jumped in the car and got to the port. We lost two of our band of brothers there, they had not the courage for the quest."

[Though Daphne rolled her eyes quietly, Milo heard them moving and decided to moderate the Mallory.]

"They weren't driven by the same fears, as they didn't feel like they had really been involved with the fight. The consequence was, we got into France using their passports, so they made a great contribution after all, and no-one knows we are here.

"So the biggest issue is that we don't really know the condition of the boy that got injured, if he did get injured. We ran blind, and we have avoided the news. We were in a complete panic for the first twenty-four hours, then forty-eight; it has faded slightly, very gradually, but it comes back strongly every few hours.

"Jean gave us shelter and saved us, I think. The price we paid was being recruited to his mad enterprise, which has really helped to divert our spirits. And this is where you find us, my dear.

"One other secret issue is Jack's dad – you know him?"

"I know of him," said Daphne, warily. "My dad and him were very tight when they were youths, up to all sorts from every account I have heard. But he was too crazy even for Claude. They made him leave, effectively.

"Then he started coming back here maybe fifteen years ago. I met him once or twice, casually, just to say hi, at the big family meals and gatherings that happen around here every twenty minutes or so. Now it is obvious I was also meeting Jack when he was a toddler."

She stopped, waiting for Milo to fill the gap. She was unsure about what he knew and what he thought about his friend's father and didn't want to say things that would upset or offend.

"Yes, well, I have been hearing some really strange things about Mac since we've been here, so I am not surprised you are trying to be discreet, or at least waiting to see what I say before commenting.

"But one of the main reasons Jack was bringing us all down here, other than the expectation of a summer of wine and fun in a friendly neighbourhood, and some seasonal work, was to hunt for his dad, who has been missing now for a few years.

"Jack thinks this is the place he would come to, and he also believes that people around here would hide him and protect him.

"He understood – assumed – that his dad was a well-loved member of a secretive community that revered and protected him. But when we got here, that began to unravel, so now it looks like he's been leading a double life for the past fifteen years or so.

"I can't say too much about what we've been told in the last few days, that bit really is not my secret to share, but you can always ask your dad."

"I know some of it, Milo, don't worry, you don't have to break any confidences."

"Thanks Daphne. Anyway, Jack's dad, one way or another, has put your dad and Jean in a bad situation, trying to drag them into his weird conspiracy of one. I was there last night when Jack was told his dad's history, and you know Jean and Claude agreed to help

Mac, shelter him and nurse him, and they told us how you helped too, so you know that part.

"We don't know the current truth yet, we sense he is around here still, Jean is about to tell us more, I think. So, that's where we are. We may or may not be involved in a killing in London; we may or may not be being pursued by international law enforcement; we may or may not be close to tracking down Jack's dad, who may or may not be on the verge of something; we are, and hopefully will be still, an integral part of Jean's magnificent and over-ambitious Experience, that is the only good – wonderful – thing that has come out of this. Along with meeting you, of course."

Daphne had gone quiet. A rarity in itself. For a while she disguised the silence by very obviously concentrating on her driving, as she kept the perfect distance between them and Karl in increasingly difficult conditions, now dark black night and a torrential downpour.

Finally, Milo couldn't bear it anymore: "Please say something, Daphne, even if it is 'You're an appalling person and I can't be around you.' Even if it is that we have just had the shortest friendship in the history of mankind, and it is over between us."

"Hardly that," said Daphne. "I was just trying to get my thoughts in order. And in case you have missed it, we're trying to follow these guys in the middle of what now appears to be a thunderstorm. It takes some concentration."

The weather had deteriorated to the level that any cars on the road were slowing almost to walking pace because through the waterfalls of rain on the windscreens they could see only a dozen metres in front of them. Daphne was watching the lights on the van and trying to judge her speed to stay the right distance away. She was worried Karl would pull into the side of the road and wondering what she should do in that case.

Karl made her mind up for her. A parking area with floodlights offered itself to him, a small turn-off at a place called Saint-Martin. He couldn't see much through the torrent, but it looked like it must be a petrol station, the kind with a garage and maybe a café. Karl swung in there in a flash, without indicating, and it was only because Daphne was watching so intently that she managed to swerve in behind them. Their van edged its way across the water-logged carpark to pull up close to the café, while Daphne held back in a parking place near the entrance, trying not to be too obvious. She remembered this petrol station had only one road, used for both entrance and exit, so if she and Milo stayed where they were the kids could not get out without going past them.

"Milo, do you mind getting a bit wet?" Daphne turned and asked him.

"I've never had sex so I don't know what it involves."

"That's terribly amusing, and I am sure friend Francois would banter back brilliantly; but this is Daphne, please concentrate, dear one, I am talking about a mission, not issuing an invitation."

"Sorry. I don't mind wetness of course, so long as it is in a good cause. In any case I am currently quite drenched already."

"Look there," she said, "the phone box – can you get over there and put the call into Jack?"

Milo looked blank, then questioning with the eyes 'why me?'

"Because I need to stay with the car, just in case."

"You mean you will leave without me, if the circumstances dictate?"

"Yes, of course." Straight faced, then laughing. "Love means sacri-fice, am I right?"

"OK, not a problem," said Milo, laughing back nervously, and grateful to have a chance to do a noble feat for m'lady. "Can we finish the conversation when I get back?"

"When there's time, Milo – let's focus on the task in hand."

"Fair dos. What do you want me to tell Jack?"

"You won't have much time. Report that we are in pursuit – you can say 'hot pursuit' if you want to make yourself seem exciting. We think they are probably heading towards him at the Lodge. We are on the D940 about halfway to La Chapelle, the Saint-Martin truck stop. When Claude and Albert hit the road, this is where they should come first."

"They're stuck in Bourges without a car, right, how will that help?"

"Don't worry about that, when he needs to move, dad has friends in all the towns around this region. He'll either get the first cab off the rank or persuade a mate to give him an overnight car. As soon as they make their call to Francois and they learn where we are, they'll find the means to follow.

"Remember also to tell Francois – shall we call him Jack? – that we saw Karl and Amelie at *le poste de police* and that they were showing a *gendarme* your school badge. He is to tell Claude when he calls, and I suggest that Jack tells them from me to go round to the police station before heading back, so dad can have a chat to a couple of relatives and friends who work there, to see if they can find out what is happening."

"Nice plan," said Milo, full of admiration, as he opened the door and leapt out into the storm to run to the phone box.

Ten seconds later, Daphne nearly jumped out of her skin when the passenger door was wrenched open and a soaked figure slumped in. But it was just Milo, back again.

"I need change," he said, dripping.

Daphne creased up with laughter, "In that case it is *plus c'est la meme chose*." She rooted round in her bag for a purse and thrust it at him. "Don't spend it all. Do you know how the phone works?"

"We do have phones in Hollywood," Milo threw back over his shoulder, re-entering the downpour.

Milo was bluffing about his phone skills, but after ten wasted minutes and plenty of wasted coins, he and Jack were relieved and delighted to find themselves on the same line at the same time.

"How's life in the cooler?"

"I'm frazzled to be honest. I've been reading my dad's journal, it is all utterly gruelling and totally gruesome; I'm now the one with the white hair. Anyway, enough of that, I'll tell you later, when you see me. I was just going to get stuck into the letters when you rang, so thanks for that, you're an absolute Godsend and a lifesaver. Talk to me, please, like a human. How are you guys getting on?"

"Me and Daphne are getting on like a house on fire."

"Oooh get you, k.i.s.s.i.n.g. the boss's mate's daughter."

"Not quite, dickhead – I will explain the nuances when we have a bit more time. Maybe a lot more time, come to think of it. Now, can you shut up so I can give you the messages – do you have a pencil?

1.   Daphne and I are in hot pursuit of Karl and Amelie, on the D940 from Bourges to La Chapelle, currently we're both pulled over in a kind of truck stop at Saint-Martin, about halfway. They can't see us because of the rain.

2.   We observed Karl and Amelie at the police station. They were talking to a detective. It looked very much as though they were showing him the badge off one of our blazers.

3.   Daphne says: "Dad, go to the *gendarmerie*, locate one of your friends there, and find out what they've been told, and what they're investigating."

4.   Daphne says they need to get a motor then, and when they get on the road he should come first to the petrol station at Saint-Martin. If we have to leave before they arrive, she reckons it is a safe bet they are coming back to the Lodge, but if they change route we'll leave another message.

5.   If you can get a message to Jean, he should come here too, it is about a fifteen- or twenty-minute drive, but thinking about it, he knows that better than I do.

"Is that all understood?"

"Ha ha ha, listen to the man in the military mode. Roger, copy that, 10-4 10-4, over and out."

[You will have spotted that Milo had opted prudently to omit point 6 at this time, which was, 'By the way I cracked and told Daphne we are knife-boys on the run and not sophisticated theatrical interlopers from Paris and Hollywood.']

"Smartarse. You know what it means, right, that they have the badge?" asked Milo.

"Yes I do. Let me summarise the main points as I see them: A) The badge didn't burn, or Albert was out following us, sneaking around in the bushes, put the fire out, recovered it and gave it to Karl. I suspect he might now regret enlisting himself in Karl's service, but we can find that out later. B) Karl has gone running to the police and taken Amelie with him, an unwelcome turn of events in so many ways. C) Amelie seems to have switched sides again, triggered by thinking Jean killed the cygnet and that none of us take her seriously. That's odd and sad.

"Anyway, sounds like Claude can find out at the police station

368

what they have been told and what they are doing, I'll pass on the message.

"As I said, tonight I will have a lot to tell you, from reading my dad's notebook – some things we know already, but there are some truly horrible things about the phony lives we've led over the past two decades, it's awful."

"Jack, I'm so sorry. We'll talk tonight – more brandy required."

"O yes, we will need plenty'o'brandy. Luckily I spotted last night where Jean hides the good stuff, and I feel no compunction in taking it for salary."

"OK Jack, I'll be there for you, and all the others will too. For now, roger and out, the money has gone, let's hope they call soon."

"Good luck, Spartacus."

"Bye, Spartacus."

Milo hung up the phone. The rain was pounding even harder outside the box, so he was reluctant to go back out, but then he recalled he was already soaked to the skin so it didn't really matter anymore. He held his breath (for some unknown reason), jumped out, and sprinted towards the lights of the car, which Daphne had thoughtfully left on. He tugged the door open and sunk dripping down into the seat, panting heavily to enhance the message that he had acted bravely under some stress.

After half a minute, Daphne turned to him sympathetically and leant closer. "Here," she said, holding towards him an unlit match.

"What? That's not going to dry me, but thanks for the thought."

Daphne laughed and waved the match back at him. "This match," she said, "is not for striking. This match is the second stage of the master plan."

Milo, normally quick on the uptake, was too damp to be bright, and his obtuseness staggered himself, as well as Daphne.

"For God's sake, Milo, did you never let the air out of tyres in London? Or are you much too posh for that?"

"Ha ha ha," giggled Milo, the coin finally dropping. "A match? We were definitely not posh enough for that, we used to drive a screwdriver into the wall of the tyre."

"No puncture, Jean would be most annoyed, remember it is his van, not Karl's. We need to be able to blow the tyres back up when we want to. Therefore, I want you to crawl over there without being seen and let the air out of a couple of tyres with this very match. They've gone into the café, you have a clear run, and this relentless downpour affords you the maximum potential to remain undetected."

"But me again!? I seem to be doing all the work while you stay dry. Is it because you are a laydee?" They were both laughing – this manhunting thing was way too much fun.

"No, it is because I am the brains and you are the man of action. Even we in France have heard of your famous James Bond – you seem to be very good agent material. Did Bond let down tyres? It feels like he would be good at that."

"I have seen Dr No. From memory, Mr Bond has a much nicer car than this, and also several sophisticated gadgets that turn into guns, knives and so on – not a matchstick. Nor does he have a partner who expects him to crawl across a muddy carpark in a monsoon. Actually, James Bond seems more commonly to be surrounded by a great deal of glamour. I know you have to begin somewhere, but I don't think he started his career by doing tyre jobs in a provincial petrol station."

"Oh, so we're provincial now, that hurts. Go."

"I am gone."

Back into the flood, Milo abandoned thoughts and hopes of any dryness, present or future, and decided just to lie in a puddle and become one with the carpark. After fifteen seconds of melding into its crumbling surface till he shared its scent and colour he reluctantly began to squirm. Not as easy as you think, if you have not been trained. He found himself pulling to the right and had to regularly correct his trajectory, until finally after five minutes and thirty metres he was beneath Karl's van. At least it didn't rain under there.

He lay for a moment, getting back his breath, pondering for some moments on the accidents of fate that had wrenched him from a thriving East End pub and the bitter-sweet climax of his student days to brandishing a damp match under a rusty Citroen at a rainswept one-night French truckstop. Still, no time for serene reflection, time only for heroic enterprise …

He reached around the back tyre, located the valve, blindly unscrewed the cap, poked the match into the valve, and felt and heard the first release of air. After a minute, he suddenly realised the flaw in his plan, as the bottom of the car slowly descended onto him, starting to press his body into the dirt. He pulled the match out, rolled quickly from under the van, and finished off deflating that tyre from the outside. The rain was so hard now he could hardly see his hands. When that tyre – the back, left – was completely flat he chose a second – front, left – which was also out of sight from the café windows, and did the same again.

Done. Done done done. Milo felt a surge of self-satisfaction, not in a bad way either, not immodest, but entirely deserved. He was a thoroughly useful boy, and he had someone who appreciated that, whether they were prepared to show it or not. They could work later on the blandishments.

He crawled back to the car, opened it from ground level and started to slide in.

"No, Milo!" shouted Daphne in a stage whisper, using the admonitory tone you would employ to scold a retriever puppy who had been rolling in fox poo. "Back!"

Milo looked at her blankly, dripping.

"In the back," Daphne said, gesturing with a thumb over the shoulder. "You're far too wet for the front."

Milo took on at least a further litre of liquid in his hair and clothes while he processed the realisation that she was joking, and finally crawled in the front beside her.

"I did it."

"Good work, Mr Bond, it is a shame your work is secret and the world can never thank you for saving it."

And she reached over and gave him one of those arms-only hugs you give very wet people, or people with contagious diseases. It still felt deliciously warm and loving to Milo, who was floating high on his derring-do. He was revelling in a starring role he had never anticipated. In a world that was fundamentally Jack's, he had thought he would always be the one to swell a progress or start a scene or two. But after a few hours with Daphne, he seemed to have moved from the edges to the middle.

"What now?"

"As long as the rain rains, there is nothing to do. Sadly, they have the café, so we are in the car with no hot drink, but we can smoke instead.

"The timing really depends on when dad calls in to Francois-or-shall-I-say-Jack. After he speaks to him it will take about an hour or an hour and a half to find out everything he can at the police station. He'll have the car sorted at the same time, and it is a thirty-minute drive. So they should be here in two hours.

"Hopefully this rain will keep on for many more hours, it feels like it. If it stops, we've probably bought ourselves an extra half hour or forty-five minutes by the time Karl works out what has happened to the tyres and gets some help inflating them – there is no pump in the van but there will be one somewhere round here.

"If it comes to it, we just go and talk to them and tell them to stay put and wait for Jean, but that's the last resort as we can't tell how they'll react, and Jean is desperate to keep the peace for Experience reasons. For the same reason we need to avoid you and Jack being betrayed by a member of the troupe, as that would also create an impossible situation. What we really need is breathing space for everyone to calm down."

So saying, she slumped herself down in her seat to wait, and Milo copied her. She put the engine on so she could run the heater to begin to dry him out – this was a serious romance. As the rain drummed down harder and harder on the top of the car, they edged slowly together and held hands.

"Tell me, Milo, as I shall have to get used to calling you, as an Englishman, do you eat the freshest baguette first, or the oldest. This is an interesting test, I think."

Milo responded with a blank look. Daphne felt it rather than observing it, as they were sitting side by side.

"It reflects the character. If you eat the oldest bread first, you will always eat everything before it goes off, and you will never waste any, but you will end up with a lot of reheating, refreshing, toasting and generally unsatisfactory compromising. You know about refreshing? Sprinkle it with water, wrap it in a tea towel, bung it in a hot oven on a fierce heat, and hope it will come back to life. Now I have given up the biggest secret in France to an Englishman, I will be shot if anyone discovers it."

"Right," said Milo, wondering if this was really something important, or a party game. He didn't know her well enough yet to tell.

"You get it, right, Milo?" [She liked using the name now.] "You literally never get to eat fresh bread, the way it is intended to exist. You never experience the supreme joy of the perfect hot crust and soft, warm, spongy, white inside, maybe with a melting runny cheese, or a gorgeous strawberry jam. You condemn yourself...."

"Yes," said Milo, "I do see that, but..."

He was going to continue, but left it there, as obviously she was halfway through a thought, albeit pre-prepared. Tried before, on her or someone else. Reheated bread. But at least refreshed specially for him. He waved her on.

"But," she went on, "if you always eat the newest loaf first, what then?"

Milo dutifully but willingly made the needful "what-then?" noise.

"Once that's gone, you have a breadbin full of overlooked stale crust, and rock-hard leapfrogged stubs. You're scrabbling to find an edible rump, with one eye always on visiting the boulangerie. So in exchange for a few nibbles of the delicious present there are many stiff hard bites of the past, Milo, you understand? Milo?"

We love Daphne, you can tell; but Milo had nodded off, which was wise, undoubtedly the best response he could give just then, as "Phony Bits" would just confuse her. This was an echo from the past, a thing Lucy had done with her when they first met, when it felt so new and funny and natural. Daphne was overwhelmed by her new friendship, the first since Lucy passed, and she was trying too hard, and reaching in the wrong direction.

Meanwhile in town, Claude was hanging up the café phone after talking to Francois and getting the new messages. Albert was crowding behind him, trying to overhear what was being said.

"We need to get round to the police station."

Albert gasped and doubled over, then started up and shook his head madly, twining his fingers into his hair in panic. "What's happened? Is it Amelie? Has there been an accident?" He was quivering.

"For God's sake, Albert, calm down, stop it, nothing has happened to Amelie or Karl. Last time they were seen, which was about fifteen minutes ago, they were perfectly safe, and still being a massive pain in the arse."

"Then why are we going to the police station?"

"I'll tell you on the walk round – but I think possibly you can guess. Anyway, I need to just say bye to Pierre and ask him a quick favour, just hang on here for a sec if that's OK."

"Pierre?" asked Albert, but he was already on his own.

Claude was making his way outside and he wove in and out of the tables till he reached Pierre's. Rain was tipping down onto the umbrellas, and Pierre was now the only person sitting outside, though well covered. Claude sat down, leaning forward to avoid the water dripping down from the umbrella rim, and picked up his drink, while he bent very close to Pierre and spoke to him quietly for some time in a supplicatory fashion. Pierre seemed reluctant at first, but Claude spoke again for a while, after which Pierre agreed to whatever it was he was asking or suggesting. Then Claude got up to leave, but Pierre grabbed him by the wrist and pulled him back down again. This time he did the talking, ten centimetres from Claude's face, very intense, a harsh nod, grimace, and finally Claude, staring it out, was barely maintaining his composure. Eventually Pierre let him up and pushed an umbrella into his hands with a bellow of laughter. Claude struggled with it as he rolled off into the wet dark of the square, then successfully erected it as he signalled for Albert to fall in behind him and get under the cover.

After following him in silence for a few minutes at a distance of half a metre, Albert's nerve broke, and he asked, "Please, Claude, tell me what is going on, I think you owe me that – is my sister OK?"

He got an answer he wasn't expecting. Claude spun on his heels, took half a step back to Albert, landing a handswidth from his nose, and thrust his face upward into the boy's. The rain was torrential above them, hammering onto the canvas of their umbrella, making it hard to talk and harder to hear.

"What's going on, twat," Claude shouted as loudly as he could, which really was loudly, "is that the shit balloon you and your German mate inflated and sent to hover tantalisingly above us all, has been pricked. It is full of holes, it is ready to explode, and we are soon going to be spattered from head to foot in steaming, liquid excrement."

"What do you mean?"

Albert was maybe the worst liar Claude had ever come across – and he had known very very many. In addition Albert had, in his own terms, been drinking quite heavily, and was not feeling totally on top of the situation.

"What I mean is, you and Karl have been conspiring against the others, for some reason. You spied on Francois and Scott, right? You saw them do some weird things you did not understand. You found something of theirs, and you ran with it to Karl like a sad puppy with a half-dead bird quivering in its mouth."

Albert stood aghast at this. He was exposed.

"I'll take that as a yes, then," said Claude. "Guilty as charged."

"I'm sorry. I made a stupid mistake, I should never have trusted him, and then suddenly it was too late." The words spilled out, with a hint of a lisp, and Claude realised the boy wasn't going to be difficult to interrogate. No thumbscrews needed, just a little gentle persuasion to keep him on track.

"OK, exactly what happened? Please tell me now, before we get to the police, so I have as much information as possible. I don't want to land us all in it." Claude drew Albert by the arm into the shelter of a twenty-metre buttress on the cathedral wall so they could keep at least some of the rain off while they were talking.

Albert started off anxiously. "Karl hates the new boys, you know that. I didn't really cotton on immediately that it was mainly because he fancies my sister and sensed the pretty one with the curly hair was a rival. More her age."

Claude's expression said, 'please proceed more quickly, with the facts, not the soap opera,' but Albert was too distraught to pick up the subtleties, and Claude realised he would just have to let him talk it out.

"Karl was also suspicious of them. I think that started off because he desperately wanted them to be guilty of something, so he began to search for evidence without anything specific to go on. The other morning when they were out in the pond he went into their rooms and found passports. Not French and American passports, but British passports. The names in them weren't Francois and Scott and the pictures didn't look like them. Also, with the passports, he found school ties, and jackets. They had name tags, but not Scott and Francois. In one of the jackets there was the address of a pub somewhere in London.

"You remember he splashed them in the pool just after that, that was out of triumph as much as anything I think because he had his proof. While he was checking their bedrooms he was keeping an eye on them smoking in the water; he couldn't hear clearly but he reckoned some of their chatter sounded like English."

"Scott's an American, is that so odd?"

"I told you, he was keen to catch them out, looking for strange behaviour; Francois was talking English too, and not with a very French accent. I agree it is all quite flimsy when you make me repeat it. Anyway, by then his suspicions were sealed by the passports, which he assumed were either fakes, or stolen, therefore indicating it must be a serious offence, or why go to those lengths to disguise it?

"So, he felt he was onto them, although he didn't take anything from their rooms, because he didn't want to alert them. But he told me what he had found and enlisted my support while he was investigating.

"The night after, when they burnt all that stuff, I was watching – they made so much noise, it was hard to ignore. After you all came back drunk and distracted them, I saved some bits from the basket, it hadn't burnt nearly as well as they thought. I gave them to Karl and it meant he had evidence he could keep, because they thought they had destroyed it.

"You understand, for Karl, who badly wanted to discredit and get rid of them, this was exciting, and to be honest, I stupidly did get sucked in. I wanted to impress Karl, I'm ashamed to say it. After he got humiliated it just got worse; even more personal."

Claude badly wanted to shout at Albert to get on with it. He was burbling. But he knew if he broke his flow he would clam up or forget where he was, so he just kept nodding encouragingly, as though this was the most exciting story he had ever heard.

"Karl had already called his dad at home in Germany and asked for help; his father is a big business tycoon, apparently he has a network of contacts everywhere. Karl gave him all the names and details, he's looking into it. He doesn't spend any time with Karl but clearly he indulges him in everything he wants."

Claude, never a patient man, calculated he had about another fifteen seconds left of oxygen in the breath he was holding before strangling Albert. Blithely unaware of his proximity to a sudden death, the boy went on.

378

"So now, as to why they went to the *gendarmes*, I am guessing, either Karl has spoken to his dad again, and he has told him something so serious that he needed to go to the police immediately, or Karl was frustrated with progress, wished to show off to Amelie, and wanted to dirty Francois's name further in the process, with her watching."

"Karl and Amelie showed a school badge to one of the detectives," Claude said, bluntly.

"Ah, that's all my fault then."

There was a long pause, the boy was white now, and looking exhausted.

"As for my sister, honestly I have no idea why she got tangled up with Karl again, she told me she was finished with that, but here we are. He is a very charismatic man, and Amelie recently can be temperamental, wilful, she doesn't care about risk as she used to, and she's careless of people's emotions." [This was said with feeling, and Claude guessed that Albert was the one most often at the wrong end of her moodiness and lack of predictability.] "Did Jean tell you our mother died very recently? There have been troubles at home." Claude nodded to indicate 'Yes, I have been informed.'

Finally, Albert had run out of everything, and Claude realised the grip he had on the boy's arm was now the only thing holding him up. He looked at Albert with a great deal of residual disapproval but also with a respect that had not been there previously.

"OK, we need to get on now, you and I are going to discuss this another time, OK?" Albert wasn't quite clear what the implication was, but chose to hope it would be limited to a fatherly word of advice.

They set off again into the growing storm, the man supporting the boy as they walked. The *gendarmerie* was just a few hundred metres away, and as they neared it Claude looked around to see if anyone was watching them. He wasn't going in through the front entrance, there was a path through the carpark that led to a back way in.

"OK I am impressed you have come clean. For now, I need to know you are done with all that, and you trust me, and you are onside – is that right?"

"Yes," said Albert, immediately, looking as though he was sure he meant it.

Claude stared at him for ten seconds, trying to give the impression he was weighing up many alternatives. "Right then; go across the road over there, sit on that wall, wait there and do not move."

"OK. But won't I get really drenched?"

Claude laughed, and handed him the brolly, indicating to him with a grimace and a shrug that he was just going to have to take his chances, and it would help him to prove he was reliable now. He pulled up his own collar over his head. When Albert was safely positioned, Claude turned and went down the path and into the police station.

For many minutes, Albert sleepily kicked his heels. It was good to have a rest; it also felt good to have told Claude what he had told him. As his energy came back, he began to look vaguely up and down the road, not able to see more than twenty or thirty metres through the downpour. There wasn't a lot of traffic, the only action while he was there was an eruption from the front door of the station when three men in blue flew out, jumped into a police car, and screeched off. But as they were not pursuing Claude, Albert relaxed again, with just that normal back-of-the-mind sympathy for whatever poor creature they were going to capture, rescue, or cover with a tarpaulin.

Then after he had been there for twenty-nine minutes, a car pulled up in front of the police station and parked right in front of the main door, squarely in the **STATIONNEMENT INTERDIT** zone. It was a gorgeous lurid blue Facel Vega Facellia, one of the sleekest, chicest, most brazenly arrogant and stylish cars ever produced, though I guarantee you will never have seen one because they came and went in a very short frenzy of design inspiration.

A man climbed out without removing the key, switching the engine off, or closing the door. He put on a wide-brimmed fedora, pulled it down low over his eyes, wrapped a massive oilskin coat tightly around himself, and sauntered off into the torrent without looking backward, forward or sideways. Albert recognised him: it was Charles from the café, Pierre's man.

Before he had strolled fifteen metres away, the front door of the police station opened, Claude came out, lit a cigarette in the shelter of the porch, then walked quickly to the car holding his coat over his head, and got straight into the driver's seat, slamming the door behind him. After five seconds he opened the door, got out far enough to twist round and get his head above the roof, looked over at Albert and shouted, "Well, are you coming, or do you prefer to sit in the puddle?" Albert crossed the road and got into the passenger seat. The inside of the car smelt like a chariot of leather and sandalwood, hand-tooled by ancient craftsmen for a grateful god. They sped off, through town, and towards the La Chapelle road.

Charles had left the radio on playing some kind of avant-garde jazz-accordion music. Claude had intended not to speak, to punish Albert in a petty way of course, but as both his hands were required to navigate the narrow lanes at high speed, and as the experimental accordion began to saw at his brain like a blunt knife on a tin baguette, he squeaked, "Change the fucking station, I'm dying here!"

Albert jumped a foot out of his seat. "Don't shout. You scared me."

"Sorry, lad, that was out of line, but please please turn this fucking racket off, it is blinding me, and driving in this storm is bad enough without losing my sight as well."

Albert fiddled with the knob and landed on some Satie, like throwing a bucket of ice water on a burning man. "Thanks, son, you saved us." And now they were proper friends.

"How did you get this beautiful car?"

"I sold my soul to the devil, son, and it is just for tonight, it is going back tomorrow."

"Do you get your soul back then?"

"Ha ha ha, good idea, Albert, but I think that is gone for ever now."

"Sorry, Claude," Albert was politely apologetic that his new friend was condemned to eternal damnation in exchange for a short-term car loan. "Did you have any luck with the *gendarmes*?"

"Too much to tell you just now, we're only ten minutes away from the meeting place, and I need to focus on the road in the rain. I can say your sister does not seem to have been a very willing accomplice, so on many levels, I suspect there is hope for her yet."

Claude, good to his word, drove into the wave of water without taking his foot off the accelerator. Albert was clutching hard at the seat edges because the visibility was basically zero, even with the headlamps full on. "Don't worry, Albert," Claude laughed out of the corner of his mouth (the opposite corner to the cigarette), "I know this road like the proverbial. We'll be OK. But Daphne wanted us as quickly as possible, and I wasted a bit more time than I hoped in the police station."

Back at the Lodge Jean had come to check on Jack, drop off some boxes of food for supper, and see what progress was being made. Jack gave him the messages; Jean said he knew the truckstop, and as he suspected Daphne would find a way to detain them, he would leave immediately and catch up with everyone there.

Seeing Jack's upset, and the red notebook, and the pile of unopened envelopes, he realised his cousin had had a very tough evening. He raised his eyebrows to ask gently how he was doing. Jack explained he had read the journal but it was too much, and he'd run out of steam for the letters.

Jean felt bad about leaving him on his own with that much sadness. "Come on, come with me, Jack, I could use the company, and I'm sure you could do with some fresh air after being stuck here all night. Everyone's on the road now, so there will be no more messages, you are off duty."

And that's how it happened that Jack and Jean arrived at Saint-Martin at the same time as Claude and Albert coming from the other direction. Their cars pulled up simultaneously either side of Daphne, just like a drive-in movie; and they all wound down their windows and looked at each other through the rain.

As they were saying hello, the torrent began to slow, and visibility, in the floodlights, started to improve, enough for them all to see the door to the café open, and Karl and Amelie come out, arm in arm, looking rather buddy. They put out their hands, palm up, as you do when leaving home on a rainy day, just to see how wet you are going to get, not necessarily to do anything about it. Actually, they thought, this is not too bad, we'll go for it.

Without looking at each other, the six people in the three cars got out simultaneously and stood in a row, two in front of each car, framed in the headlights, thirty metres away from Karl and Amelie. Lost in each other's company, and moving quickly in the lifting rain towards the van, it took some moments before the young couple looked up, and another few seconds before it dawned on them that they had been apprehended.

Karl, who no-one could accuse of not being a scrapper, reacted immediately, really very swiftly, and pulled Amelie, who was still processing her thoughts, towards the van, opening the passenger door and thrusting her in, then sprinting to the other side, jumping in the driver's seat – did we hear a maniacal laugh? – and starting the motor in a second.

In his mind, he then screeched across the carpark, out of the exit, onto the main road, and sped off at high speed, leaving the three pursuing vehicles in his dust. With his driving skills and stamina they could be across the border and safe in one of his father's strongholds in less than eight hours.

But reality was slightly different, as it so often is. In fact the deflated van raced five metres in a half circle on two wheels before producing a shuddering, shrieking crack and juddering to a halt leaning into one of the larger potholes.

"Shit," shouted Claude, "that axel better not be cracked!"

The others just laughed, even Jean, and the laughter doubled when Amelie and Karl staggered out into the damp night, red faced.

"Hello," said Jean. "A bit of car trouble? Can we help?"

Karl reached his hand sideways, feeling for Amelie's, in the hope of some support and strength from his ally; but in front of everyone she was not so bold, and moved her arm slightly away, to avoid his touch.

Jean, weighing up all the ways this could go, with his normal shrewd eye to the future, and his usual erring towards compromise and good spirit, and his forgiving and understanding nature, decided without even getting to the end of the thought, that it was in everyone's interest for him to be generous, cool and pragmatic.

"OK, you two get in with Daphne and she'll take you back to the Lodge.

"Claude, Albert, Scott and Francois will follow you in this fabulous dream car, which I sincerely hope is not stolen."

Claude did a comedy surrender with hands about level with the lower half of the face, jazzing them slightly, which formed the international sign for 'Of course the car is not nicked, Boss, how could you even think such a thing?'

"I'll sort the van tyres out with Dennis over there," Jean nodded towards the garage manager, who happened to be his cousin's best friend, "and I'll be back in less than an hour providing there's no other damage.

"There's food at the house, everyone please just get in, dry off, eat something hot, drink a beer and play nicely. When I get back I want to have a team talk, and I suspect then we will all be ready for bed, so we are going to miss our rehearsal. Which is frustrating, given the day after tomorrow we have paying customers. Tomorrow is now our only chance to get our act together."

Karl held his head higher as he walked with Daphne to the car, he was not about to show any shame, regret or remorse. Amelie looked subdued, shoulders sagged: Jack watched her and wondered what made her go along with things. His lesser-self pondered (unprompted) whether she would go along with him? How far? His better-self said 'Shut up and don't be a dick' and then, up a level, 'For once, please let me be kind because I want to be, just because it is the right thing to do, not because I think it will get me something.'

Their car, thought Milo, was a veritable holiday fun bus compared to the undertaking going on in Daphne's little motor. Poor Daphne. Then he realised he meant 'Poor Daphne because I am not with her,' and felt amused as well as embarrassed.

"Come on then, Scott," said Jack, "tell us all about what has been happening while I have been stuck at home washing my hair and manning the phones."

"I think Albert has all the good stories, right?" replied Milo.

Albert was nervous about talking, and still a little drunk and rather tired, but received an elbow from Claude giving him permission and delivering the sting to get him going; suddenly, like a tractor on a cold morning being struck on the starter motor with a rubber hammer, he was off once more, kangarooing across a frozen field.

"I think you know more than anyone, Francois, as you were in the middle of all the conversations. Anyway, Claude and I sat in a café and drank fancy grown-up drinks with what felt like a gang boss. I did not get the exercise I hoped to from scouring the town.

"In fact, others were dispatched to do our looking – yes, we actually delegated a life-and-death search for a vulnerable adolescent while we imbibed a succession of warmed hallucinogens in a characterful bar. It is the way of things round here! Those drinks, by the way, give you amazing insights and fabulous powers of speech, but you must, I urge you if you try, rest regularly while under the influence.

"Claude and I then walked to the police station in a rainstorm and Claude coerced me into confessing to him, so now I think he wants me to confess to you too, which is what I will do, along with an apology. I am so sorry.

"I have been working with Karl to unmask you. We have both seen your Robert and Michael pretend passports and your Milo and Jack school-tie name tags. I now realise, much too late, that Karl wanted you off the scene so he can hit on my shamefully unprotected sister, so he was grateful for the clues I gave him. He called his dad to get a private agent investigating you, but then couldn't wait so he also took the evidence to the police station – that being the name tags and blazer badge which I treacherously plucked from the not-so-blazing basket. Don't worry, I did draw the line at stealing your stolen passports.

"We then went to the police station to visit with Claude's *gendarme* relatives for a while, but I was not allowed inside, so I sat in a thunderstorm outside and I can't therefore report on those events. And that is where we got to. And I see, we are now home." As he finished, they pulled into the driveway at the Lodge.

Daphne, Karl and Amelie had already been there ten minutes, enough time for Karl to go upstairs and change, again avoiding what he liked to call 'women's work,' leaving Daphne and Amelie to get out the plates and start laying the table. When he came back, the bread had been cut and the food had been plated. He at least deigned to open some bottles of wine and beer before flopping down splay-legged between Amelie and Daphne, not what either of them had intended, as it meant they were all clustered together at one end of the table.

The four latecomers came in, washed their hands, sat at the other end, and almost without warning a meal had begun. At first, there was limited conversation, then for some reason Milo, this being a night of confessional tales, started the story of how he and Daphne had hotly pursued Karl and Amelie; how he crawled across the carpark in the storm; and how he let the tyres down. Suddenly everyone was laughing – even Amelie, and a possibly chagrined Karl. Milo was funny when he didn't try too hard, he had a sweet self-mocking gentle humour quite different from the double-act with Jack.

Jean came in after half an hour, Dennis had been good to him. It was close to midnight. Jean was really delighted if not a little surprised to detect a good mood, especially as he was likely to break it. He had one beer, to settle his stomach, and some bread and cheese, though he knew it would stop him sleeping. *Fromage* was there, so he put it in his mouth. 'One of the things that makes us human,' thought Jean, in the moment, 'is the ability to weigh up so precisely the six-minute pleasure of a piece of camembert against the five-hour torture of a night of insomnia.'

"Right, team," he opened portentously, then realised his tone was too bombastic, so stopped. He considered momentous, aggressive, persuasive; then settled on a mixture of inspirational, patient and ostensibly accommodating. Yes, he thought, that's it. We are way beyond the point of alienation.

"Right, team, here is the news, some will like it, some will not, but we have a show to put on, so please bear with me.

"Tomorrow is the last day of preparation. First thing in the morning we will have the last rehearsal here. At lunchtime we will run the boat again, we have a group of friends and family coming from town to be test consumers, but not just that, also many local dignitaries and people who can influence support for us. So up at the Hill, the caterers will also get a last chance to prepare. Then we have our actual dress rehearsal of the play on the stage – the dress rehearsal we were supposed to have tonight. This is very nerve-racking, I feel I should remind us all of that, without wanting to puncture the mood of the evening. To have our first dress rehearsal on the actual stage before an important audience on the night before the opening is not what we wanted; we are all cutting it so fine. We are charging people for this, which makes us professionals, we are not putting on a show for free here."

"We can do it, chief," said Jack, very very positive. "We can pull this off, we can have a great run."

Around the table everyone nodded, even Karl. Claude and Albert rapped the table, and Daphne tapped her wine glass against the bottle while knocking the ash off her cigarette into a saucer.

"OK, thanks for that.

"But, before we even get that far, to confront that huge challenge, we have to discuss what has been happening here, and how we get past that."

Not so many nods now round the table.

"Amelie, can we start with you? I asked you to stay at my sister's, to stay away from Karl, because it was the cause of general upset, but then you disappeared with him."

Even before Jean came in, Amelie had visibly been leaning away from the widely-spread Karl. By the time Jean started talking, she'd shied further, and now he had finished speaking she was a continent away from Karl while still sitting next to him, so many emotional miles had been travelled in a single sentence.

"I am sorry, Jean, it was not my intention. When you killed the cygnet, I was so upset with you, and with everyone, none of you seemed to care or take it seriously. Karl was the only one to help. I didn't realise we had taken the van without permission, I didn't particularly want to go to Bourges, though I would honestly say I was not comprehensively kidnapped. We had a nice meal, he was polite and attentive, not pushy, and honestly, Jean, he defended you for killing the swan, he's a decent person. He persuaded me you have been under a lot of stress, that it was out of character; and perhaps as there is so much slaughter in your life, which you mentioned yourself, you might be a little desensitised.

"He took me to the police station, I had no idea why till we got there, then there was some nonsense about passports and school uniforms, and Francois and Scott not being who they say they are, which I think we'd all guessed anyway the minute we met them, and which in my view is nobody's particular business but theirs. I was, I am sorry to say, rather pimped out to a young copper to get him to take an interest in 'the case,' if you can call it that. That was not very enjoyable or dignified.

"Then we headed back; the rain made it too hard to drive, even for Karl" [Jack rolled his eyes], "so we pulled in for coffee to wait it out. When we came out of the café and saw you all there, I had no idea what was going on. Scott has been explaining about why he let the air out of the tyres, and that was very funny, he's a hoot tonight, but honestly, we were on our way back anyway, so it didn't achieve much, other than making for a good story, and giving Scott an opportunity to show off for Daphne, of course." She gave Milo an impish 'I am not the only one' glance.

Milo tried to avoid responding to the Daphne tease with anything other than a casual wave and was grateful (as well as slightly disappointed) to see Daphne doing the exact same gesture. He looked at

Jack instead, old habits being what they are. Amelie had a fair point about the unnecessary tyre tampering, but other than that there was so much to unpack here, like a deliciously stuffed stocking on Christmas morning filled with gorgeously wrapped presents to be opened later at leisure. The boys secretly swapped hidden grins and quivered in delighted anticipation.

Jean stood up to take the floor and spoke slowly in reply.

"Excuse my language, Amelie, but if I can be completely clear:

"I. did. not. kill. the. fucking. swan.

"I think I did try to explain that.

"Another person was driving the boat, and steered into and over the cygnet, I am sure accidentally, and I was just trying to get the controls back to make sure we did not crash. That is the only reason I was holding the wheel when you turned and saw me."

Amelie looked genuinely confused but could not miss the fact that everyone else was looking at Karl and shaking their heads, sadly.

"Also, please let me say, on behalf, I am certain, of everyone here, that nobody took your concerns lightly or dismissed your anguish. I believe we are all empathetic enough to agree this was a horrible event, totally to be regretted, and much to be lamented, and your reaction was entirely appropriate."

['OK,' thought Milo, 'that one is buttered thickly enough now, move on.']

"But let's move on from that episode, shall we?" Jean continued, reading Milo's mind. "We have invested so much time and energy on this today.

"We do need to clear the air on something else; I think the time has come for transparency because everyone has collected snippets

390

of everyone else's story but no-one has assembled the whole puzzle, and this is causing discontent, and preventing us from being a strong team."

He looked at Milo and Jack for their approval, they both assented by small nods.

"Karl, I think you need to address the issue of going into someone's room and looking through their things. Also, an explanation of some phone calls informing on your fellows, and the visit to the police station – what on earth were you trying to achieve, and why?"

Jean noticed Karl glaring at Albert, realising some of this information could only have come from that source. It gratified Jean to see Albert staring boldly back.

"And Albert, your involvement mystifies, you could also please explain what you were up to. We all need to be open."

"Well what about them?" Karl burst out, nodding in the direction of Francois and Scott. [Shall we use the *noms de guerre* for the last time?] "They started all this, aren't you going to quiz them? Or do they get a free pass – it's almost as though they could be relatives…"

That knocked Jean back, he was expecting the defence, but not the attack and the knowing accusation.

"They'll get their turn, Karl – but whether they 'started' anything is a matter of debate. Why don't you begin for us, anyway? That gives you a fair chance to make your case, whatever it is."

Karl took a sip of wine, stood, and took another, longer, draught. He looked around the ramshackle room, and eyed everyone in it, all round the table, and did not take a step back from confrontation. Even Claude had to respect it.

"Keeping it short, Monsieur Jean, you know I got on very well with the two lads who left, one of them is among my best friends. I very nearly went with them, but there is some understanding between my father and your uncle, so I had some coercion to remain.

"It seemed quite suspicious to me, and convenient for you, that those two were pushed aside and then a couple of days later this pair arrives. Clearly also there was something extremely dubious about their heritage, and how they so handily turned up. The fact is, it was obvious to everyone that you knew them before, but you were pretending they're people you had never met.

"I make no excuse for the fact I have become fond of Amelie. You chose, I say, to interpret that in a very negative way, as though you know me and my motives, but you really know nothing about me. Your boy Francois," he nodded, insolently, "apparently was immediately your preferred suitor, a position which you created, by the way, that would never have existed otherwise. This annoyed and upset me. My reputation was undermined, my friendship was unfairly disrupted.

"I admit, I became intrigued to find out what the hell was going on, so yes, I did quickly check out their rooms, and found the names on their passports are not Francois and Scott, they are Robert and Michael. Also, the passports are British, not French and American. Being honest, by the way, Monsieur Michael has as much chance of passing for a Frenchman as I do."

"He's Monsieur Robert," Jack said, helpfully pointing at Milo, not willing to give up at this late stage his established claim to the handsomest passport. Karl looked at him, totally mystified. Milo rolled his eyes.

"I think we can all agree that the pictures in the passports are somebody else," Karl went on, "I can assure you, and Albert will verify, that Scott does not look like either Robert or Michael, and neither does Francois.

"I think you already know that when I found the passports there

392

were school jackets and ties with them."

To everyone's horror, particularly Albert's, Karl now started to produce visual aids from a small bag he had brought down with him after changing.

"The badges from those jackets say London East Grammar School. You see...?"

He held the burnt offerings in front of him, displaying them slowly in a circle round the table. Mostly everybody turned away; Jack looked defiant; Claude looked, let's be honest, murderous.

"I think London East is not in Paris, is it? Nor I reckon in Hollywood, America."

Again he went into the bag; this time some fragments of fabric were extracted and held out at arm's length between his finger and thumb. At this point Claude was looking at Jean to see if he could intervene, but Jean was too dazed to respond.

"In the blazers are those sweet little tags always sewn in by the anxious and loving mothers of poor children who cannot afford to lose their cheap clothing. You see...?

"Do these labels say Scott and Francois? No, strangely they don't; so we can presume Scott's mum and Francois's mum, if such women exist anywhere in the world, have never seen these worn-out rags."

More rifling in the bag, and this time, like a rabbit from the magician's hat, he pulled two singed ties. 'This act,' Jack thought, 'is seriously never going to headline at The London Palladium.'

"Do the little tags on these horrible ties say, 'Michael's Tie' and 'Robert's Tie'? Again, oddly they do not. So, I am also thinking Michael's mother and Robert's mother never gently adjusted the knots on these disgusting objects around the necks of their lovely boys on the doorstep before sending them off to the bus stop.

"In fact the little tags actually say 'Jack du Lac' and 'Milo Kelly. You see…?"

He paused for dramatic effect, but no-one reacted; actually, they were mainly looking at the table, seemingly anxious to count the cutlery or check the level in the salt cellar. There were no gasps of surprise or hands slapped on the table with shouts of 'My God man, that's genius; you've got them bang to rights!' Did he seem disappointed? As ever with Karl, he ploughed on regardless, at least placing his relics back in the bag while he did so.

"So, let me try to keep track: we already had Robert and Michael, and Francois and Scott, and also, let's not forget, Pierrot and Clown; and now we have to add Milo and Jack. A bewildering range of characters, do you agree? Whatever you feel about them, it does seem that neither of these two boys settles easily into a single personality. A humorous English person might say we have a Jack of all disguises but it appears he is master of none."

Another pause here for delighted laughter at his elaborately con-structed English witticism, but again the knives and forks came under intense scrutiny instead. 'Pah,' thought Karl, 'too many French here to get the joke.'

"What do you say, lads, am I getting warmer with Jack and Milo? You would tell me if I was getting hot? I am betting those are finally your real names, so you could put us out of our misery."

Karl finished his oration, capping it off with some serious glares: first at Jack and Milo, then reciprocally at Claude, and finally, lingeringly, at Jean who, in Karl's mind, had not only let all this happen, but had actively encouraged it.

Daphne and Amelie were either side, of Karl, out of his eyeline, and escaped his opprobrium; Albert also, probably because Karl had forgotten him already. Claude had long ago fallen into the category 'I really don't care what Karl thinks,' and Jean was in his own world experiencing a small upswelling of panic for the future of the glorious Harlequinade.

Milo and Jack, taking the main force of the attack, were shocked. They suddenly found themselves accused, when they were sure they were meant to be cast as victims. How did that happen? Jack decided to grab the thistle by the balls.

"Yes, Karl, I am Jack, this is Milo. Frankly speaking, it is a huge relief to be able to say that."

"'Frankly speaking' is a strange expression for you." said Karl. "Although there is always a first time, I suppose. Maybe you would like to explain to everyone, as I have had to stand up here, what the hell you two are up to, and what you are hiding from. It seems to me that anyone who fakes passports, creates such an elaborate *netz aus lügen*, and then gets up at two o'clock in the morning to destroy evidence, must have some very serious and damaging secrets to conceal."

"First," responded Jack, standing up, "I confess, I am not Francois, and I am not Robert or Michael, either. My name is Jack du Lac. I actually come from this area, by way of my father, Mac. I do live in East London, England, as does my friend here, and those were our blazers."

Jack looked at Milo. He didn't want to start talking about him and revealing his story without his approval. Milo started a nod to say 'Go ahead,' but then made the other sign, right hand up, palm out, 'Halt', followed by fingers coming backward a few times, like a bird's wing flapping, saying 'Me, me.' Jack sat down, and Milo stood up.

"I'm Milo Kelly, as you guessed. We can't both tell our story, so Jack will speak for me, as he does it so much better. The one thing I would like to say personally, is thank you. Thank you to everyone in this team, for your welcome, your help, your kindness and your friendship. It has been overwhelming. I think we are all Spartacus, right?"

As Milo sat, everyone with the normal exception of Karl stamped their feet and rapped the table in a warm reception of his charming speech; albeit they also looked a little blank at the Spartacus reference. The movies don't travel so quickly around rural France; they just hoped it wasn't another alias they needed to learn.

Jack stood and spoke. "Thank you, Milo, and can I please second those lovely sentiments.

"We are not schoolboys; we finished our exams a week ago – it feels like a lifetime – and we left school. Three hours later we were sucked into a melee in a pub, we didn't start it, and someone pulled a knife. In our attempt to avoid the blade the kid got thrown over, went down. We don't know what happened to him. We're not rough kids. We study art, literature, French, just like everyone, we don't fight. Anyway, we got scared. We already had ferry tickets booked for a holiday and we went to the port without looking back. Four of us started out, including the not-so-mythological Michael and Robert, who we normally refer to, by the way, as Mike and Bob, our schoolfriends. However, by the time we landed in France we were two, because Bob and Mike decided to turn back at Dover before the ferry sailed, though I still had their travel documents, which you found." [Jack glossed over having used the passports, this was not a confessional.] "Our families think we are in England, in Yarmouth, a cold place where no-one will look. I think perhaps Mike and Bob are there.

"We were planning to come here anyway, to work for the summer and surprise Jean. Jean is my cousin. Honestly, I was also hoping to spend time here hunting for my missing father, but that has largely gone by the wayside.

"Since we got here, it has been wonderful to be thrown in with you all, and to be part of the play, and to have a role in the Experience. It has been hard to mislead you with our new personalities as a disguise, but other than that the thing spoiling it of course has been our anxiety about the kid in London and whether anyone was injured, and that is why we chose to be incognito. Of course the boy's condition has been a constant worry, but as the days have gone by it has got a bit better, on the basis we have not heard anything bad, and we thought the news would have found us if something serious had happened."

Milo was relieved when the story came to an end. He seemed to have heard it quite a lot lately and was rather tired of it. Was there anyone left to tell? Maybe he should get it printed up as a broadsheet:

The Ballad of Milo and Jack

so they could hand it out in the street to every passing stranger.

Even as he was musing he realised of course (what was he thinking!) it would have to be:

The Ballad of Jack and Milo

But then, why not be realistic; given his co-conspirator's pathological reluctance to share the billing, even to designate a supporting role, would it not be sensible, and practical, to avoid the issue altogether and cut straight to:

The Ballad of Jack

While Milo was contemplating the publication and distribution of the tale of their epic adventure, Jack had continued to transmit orally.

"Besides that, only one thing has spoiled our stay here, to be honest, and that… " [turning to Karl, looking right in his eye from a metre away] "…is you.

"I thought initially perhaps we got off on the wrong foot, but it feels like there is something that goes much deeper. What would possess you to 'investigate' us, pry into our things, and even report us to the police – how did you get to hate us so much when you hardly even know us?"

"I know people like you, from school, from *Pfadfinderschaft*, from my dad's business," said Karl. "Cocky, arrogant, cheeky chaps who somehow get everything handed to them on a plate and then believe they have earned it. So I do know you; the pet boy being given the play to manage; the golden youth believing he has a right to the girl.

"Remember, it was you who put your nose in my business to start with – you basically accused me of child stealing, and pretended it was to protect Amelie, but everyone in this room could see it was just due to jealousy. You spoiled my chances, and you got nothing. Are you happy now?"

"This is bullshit, Karl. Nonsense. Most people just live with a bit of a slight here and there and the occasional perceived insult without over-reacting bizarrely to get vengeance. It's way out of scale, way out of proportion. What on earth did you tell the police anyway?"

"And what did you tell your dad?" piped in Albert, who till then had been staring mainly at the table.

Karl glared at him. "I provided my dad with the names on the tags, the school name off the badges, the address inside one of the pockets, and the passport numbers and identities in case any of his contacts can turn up some dirt on you, I am not going to lie about that. And as we were in town I did go to the police station to see if there were crime reports from overseas, or any alerts or manhunts. Truthfully, they thought we were a nuisance, they had no Wanted Posters or books of suspects to look through, like in the movies. Just one young cop who offered to help us because he really fancied Amelie. When he asked what we needed, it was a bit awkward because we had no knowledge of a specific crime. We showed him the badges, I know he thought we were mad foreigners, but he was polite and tried to get Amelie's phone number. Luckily she doesn't currently have one, but he might phone here sometime."

Everyone was quiet now. This was the moment, the point where things could tip either way. For Jean, he loved his cousin, but he had a lot riding on the next twenty minutes. In addition to Jack's wellbeing, he was juggling the whole circus; and while he was searching for his much-loved compromise, there were others who were more intent on pulling the enterprise apart, and letting the plates fall. He decided this was the moment he had to take the lead, against his ordinary nature, in order to protect the project and the majority of the people involved; but as he was about to stand and command centre stage, just in those seconds of apparent hesitation when he was finally formulating his thoughts and speech, and therefore vulnerable, Claude had taken to his feet and was already talking.

"... and guess what happened when I spoke to my cousin the detective in Bourges? First I had to describe you so he remembered you had been in there, though you had only left an hour before. You obviously made a big impression. Then he had to ask around till he found some young sidekick – sidedick more like – who had humoured you and interviewed you, to dignify the conversation with that term. He said he could barely understand the point you were making, there is no crime, the suspects, such as they are, seem to have three names each and one is a clown. It was all a bit confusing for them so I was able to help them dispose of it into a bin. One thing I hate..."

At that point Jean, though always polite, suspected that Claude had held the conch a touch too long and stood up, making the accustomed signals to him for 'shut up' with his right hand (finger to lips) and 'sit down' with his left (flappy hand, palm down). Claude graciously ceded the floor to his boss by sitting down rather too quickly and rocking his chair back precariously as he attempted an open-armed 'you're welcome' gesture.

"OK, so this is where we are," Jean said, "I will describe my understanding of the situation, and after that I will state my plan for proceeding."

What he meant was "I am a little blank right now, but I hope to have had some inspiration and ideas while I am on my feet, or I am going to be speaking for a very long time."

"Without wishing to demean or humiliate anyone in this group...," [he tried not to look around while he said this, but inevitably caught the eye of Jack, Karl and Amelie because he was deliberately trying to avoid them] "...I need to clear the air for once and for all. As Jack has told you, he and Milo are known to me, in fact I have known Jack all his life, so I want to apologise for any attempt to mislead. I was aware of their reason to disguise themselves here, but I want to state clearly, they are not guilty of any crime, and as far as we know in any case, no-one is pursuing them, and, also, no-one is hurt to our knowledge.

"I know these to be decent boys, they are the victims here, not the perpetrators. I should point out also Karl, you have gone to the police, you have asked them to investigate. They know of no crime, and, in fairness, they have chosen not to get involved. Can I ask, even as a citizen who believes it is his duty to flag up this situation to the authorities, what more would you expect to do?

"In terms of the group and events here, to my understanding Karl felt he was getting into a friendship with Amelie. He then thought Jack was interfering, for whatever motive. This caused animosity. Albert sided with Karl; no-one can quite work out why. Amelie was flattered by Karl but perhaps did not see the bigger picture. Then she did see it; then she didn't. It is like the magician at the child's party.

"Milo is Jack's friend, and loyal.

"Overall, if I may say, this is just a childish mess, which is a bit sad because all of us are more mature than that and we should collectively be holding ourselves to a higher standard.

"Can I also say, while this has been going on, which feels like ten years, but is less than a week, we have created the basis of a great entertainment. We have produced lights, music, make up, costume. We have learnt boating skills. We have practised routes, tickets, charging, ushering.

"So, my question is, do we want to waste all that over a squabble and some misplaced amorous urges? We have a chance to do something fun, creative, special, maybe even spectacular, and certainly memorable. We can do it, or we can let the work and effort dissipate into the gutter of what I might call irrational desire.

"Also, and I have to say it, you know it anyway, I have bet the farm on this Experience, and I do not mean that metaphorically. If we implode this now, I could lose everything – I've got loans that can only be repaid by the Experience income. I guess you could say that has been very foolish of me, and I would agree, if the loss was due to 'a poor idea' or 'lack of effort' or 'the absence of inspiration.' But to lose everything I have because of an irritating juvenile love struggle seems to be more than bad luck, it seems to be a deliberate act of sabotage."

Jean stopped speaking and sat down. The idea had not presented itself. For once he had no plan. He had listed the problems, but not named the solution. He lifted his beer to his mouth, leant back, and took a big tug at it, almost more than he could swallow; a drop fell onto his shirt, which fortunately was not clean. This was his lowest point.

Jack stood up. It had become the ritual that if you wanted to speak you needed to stand; no-one had suggested or agreed that, it was just understood.

"I want to apologise to everyone here for the way I have behaved. I want to apologise to Milo for taking him on this crazy expedition. I want to apologise to Amelie for my actions, righteous though I believe them to have been.

"Karl, I want to apologise to you, sincerely and profoundly, for annoying you, suspecting you, accusing you, insulting you. I forgive and absolve you entirely for any action on your part, it is all my fault. But I believe we can put this all behind us.

"I want to state clearly, I believe Milo and I are innocent of any crime. I am prepared to do anything necessary to draw a line under any bad feelings and get on with the show."

Jack sank down, waiting for Karl to rise.

Milo got there first. He bounced up. "I want to endorse everything Jack has said. I am sorry for any part I've played in any upset. I desire only harmony, goodwill and to create a fantastic show with the whole team." He bounced down.

He intended it to be a serious and weighty intervention, but it came across as a little chipper. Daphne suppressed a smile, keeping her mouth behind her left hand, while she supportively rubbed his calf with her foot.

Amelie was now back on her feet, also beating Karl, if he was ever thinking of competing for the floor. Perhaps she was stung just a tiny bit by Jean's use of the phrase "irrational" when describing Karl and Jack's desires, while of course mainly wishing to endorse wholeheartedly his general sentiments.

"I want to be an independent young woman, not the apex of some depressing romantic triangle. You didn't let me finish before. If it helps to move this on, you should be clear I am disgusted with you men, including my useless brother, except maybe Jean and Claude who have been kind, and Scott who we now call Milo, who clearly has other interests and has been sensitive and polite."

She looked at Milo as if he were a puppy she was rather fond of but would not quite have the energy to take for a walk.

"I love being in the play. I loved it from the start, and it has improved again, hugely, in the past few days. If we focus, it could be wonderful. That is why I am here, that is all I want to do. I do not want a boyfriend, and speaking bluntly I definitely do not want to have sex with anyone in this room – actually I have a suitor at home, and I quite like him, though he is much older even than Karl, which is another reason I am here.

"I am not a marvellously trustworthy person, but I can be relied on to serve my own interest very faithfully, and right now that involves coming to terms with the absence of the lover I am denied."

[The whole table was completely rapt at this point, astonished that Amelie was revealing herself to be a romantic storyteller of quite hypnotic power. Daphne was thinking 'this is better than Bonjour Tristesse'; Milo, more prosaically, was recalling a leftover Catherine Cookson he had devoured during a rainy caravan holiday with his mother; while Karl, perhaps unsurprisingly, was transporting himself into the world of Anaïs Nin even as he was failing the audition to be its leading man.]

"If I ever wished to flirt," Amelie proceeded, "which I really really do not, either with the stereotypically overconfident German or with what we newly discover to be the loveable Cock-er-ny, or with anyone else, I can confidently swear that the yearning is very well-suppressed. I say, thank God for that.

"Can we not, please, cast aside these petty longings, which will in any case, I assure you from experience, be forgotten in days, even if not tarnished by enactment, and just get on and do a great show – something unique and wonderful that we can all take pride in, and remember forever?"

Daphne played an approving and sisterly drumroll on the table with two butterknives as Amelie daintily retook her seat with half a curtesy and a short but magnificent glower. Everybody else just about managed to restrain themselves from bursting into applause.

It was taken for granted by now that everyone was on the same side, with Karl being the only uncertainty. They all turned to look at him. He managed to stare back at everybody at once, he had an impressive breadth of resentful glare that could encompass the entire population of the room simultaneously.

Slowly he rose.

Jean was holding his breath but being careful to simulate the general signs of chest moving up and down as he didn't want anyone to observe his nerves. He didn't bet much, but his instinct was this one was about to go belly up. Karl started.

"I appreciate the apology, Jack – as we must apparently call you now. I am not sure how honest it is, given your main concern is I think to protect the interest of your cousin here and get me back onside as you can't do without me. But, nevertheless, it is noted.

"The point is, it seems to me the situation is unresolved. You apologise for your behaviour here; that's fine. You explain how you come to be here; very well.

"But still you confess you are on the run from the law, possibly due to the serious injury, or worse, of an opponent in what sounds, however much you gloss it over, like a knife fight. Should we let that go? Shouldn't these issues be cleared up before we decide we are all a happy family?"

Jean decided to end their ancient ritual of speaking only when standing and holding the carved stick, and instead shouted from the pit, up to the young star with the limelight reflecting once more off his metaphorically golden locks.

"Are you in or not, Karl?

"Everyone has been very generous and humble in accepting re-sponsibility for their lapses and genuine in reaching out to the rest of the team. I don't know what else we can do to make you happy. Will you join in? Will you come back to us?"

Karl looked a little pleased with himself, he clearly felt unimpeachable, impregnable, beyond and above sanction, if not reproach. He obviously thought of himself as a gambler who was holding all the aces, some in his hand, some up his sleeve, a fifth tucked into his cummerbund; and like all bad poker players, though everyone could see exactly what he was thinking, he was absolutely certain no-one had the slightest idea.

"The thing is, Jean," he said, still standing, "things are in motion, stones are being turned over, I am not sure I can stop the un-ravelling process. What could resolve this, I would guess, to the satisfaction of all of us, is a single phone call to London, to Jack's mother, whom I believe is some kind of relative of yours in any case. I am sure she would be pleased and relieved to hear from you, and you could ask two, maybe three, questions, and this whole mess would be cleared up, or, at worse, the healing could begin right away – as they say."

Jean was confounded by the boy's arrogance and self-confidence. But at the same time, maybe he had a point. A clean start was needed, Jack believed them to be innocent, perhaps it was time to end the superstition of not knowing. He was about to offer a compromise, and consider making the call, when he was pre-empt-ed by Claude leaping to his feet, walking around the table, and seizing Karl by his lapels. He shouted quietly at him, pushing him back and pulling him forward to give stress to alternating phrases, insistently, rhythmically, not violently – Claude would have said 'for emphasis' – but still giving the impression he was tangoing with an enormous and rather disjointed ventriloquist's dummy.

"Listen to me, you jumped-up squirt. Everyone here has been nothing but friendly and patient with you."

Karl had never felt comfortable around multi-coloured Claude, and now he knew why – he was a very scary man, and also ex-tremely wide. He could not get away from him, or around him; Claude had him blocked in the corner unwillingly playing the manic marionette.

"We've bitten our tongues, made allowances, given you pretty well whatever you wanted.

"How have you repaid us? More importantly, what consideration have you given this beautiful" [pull], "gentle" [push], "kind" [pull], "trusting" [push], "decent" [pull], "generous" [push], "man who brought you here, made you an actor, trained you, and looked after you in *loco parentis*. You have doubted him, questioned him, suspected him, and now you have betrayed him."

By this time Jean and Daphne had managed to react; they had peeled Claude off Karl and were now steering him firmly away from the shocked boy, out of the room, and onto the terrace to calm him down. Meanwhile Albert and Milo went to Karl, helped him reflatten his collar, brushed some tiny flecks of Claude's spittle off his shoulders, and poured him a fresh brandy. Gracious as ever, perhaps understandably this time, he pushed them away, saying he didn't want their assistance.

Outside Jean, Daphne and Claude all lit fresh cigarettes to replace the fags that had been crushed and dropped in the fracas. They dragged very deeply, so the contrast between the hot nicotine and the cold fresh air seared their lungs quite deliciously.

"For God's sake, Claude?" said Jean, not tersely, a bit in the tone of "Not angry, rather disappointed," but also with a marinade of patient old mate.

"I lost it a bit, boss; I am so sorry. That arrogant weasel has been jerking us around all week, for what? What business is it of his if you are harbouring fugitives?"

"It's OK, Claude, you only made the point everyone else wanted to, and no-one got hit. But please, we need to keep him onside, the play's the thing. Right?"

"That's the thing, boss – I say no. No to Karl. And yes to …are you ready?"

"Blimey Claude, are you volunteering for a life in greasepaint? You want the part? Is it you? What do you reckon Daphne?"

Before Daphne could embarrass them all by answering – we will never know what she thought – Claude burst back in.

"No no no, not me, Boss … you. It seems so obvious – Jean will be Harlequin. It is not a difficult role, though you are a nice bloke – not sucking up now – and the way Jack has changed Harlequin he is a rotter, so in that respect Karl actually was perfect and you will have to work a bit harder."

Jean was stunned as he hadn't (Out of modesty? Fear of performing?) considered it for a single moment. And yet, it was immediately clear it could be the right thing, and a way through this.

It would give him back control of the Experience and end the tyrannic extortion of Karl in a single easy action. Everything else was set well and running smoothly, managed and staffed by people he knew and who liked and respected him. Karl was the only rogue item, and Jean suddenly realised if he let Karl go, then life would be wonderful.

It also struck him that since Jack had reformatted the play, without words, with broad movements, pantomime expression, there was nothing to worry about anymore, no need for memory, action, or any basic talent – so no need for stage fright. Specially as Harlequin was now the master villain, and villainy and deceit require less talent to portray than goodness and heroism, right?

"Let's go back in," said Jean, placing his arms around Claude and Daphne, "and see how it plays out. I'm not sure yet if you are an idiot or a genius, but I do request, please, kindly, that you keep your hands to yourself, Claude, these kids are under our protection, even Karl."

Things had calmed down inside to the encouraging extent that every person was sitting in complete silence and attempting with

407

upmost concentration to avoid catching anyone else's eye. As Daphne, Jean and Claude retook their seats, Karl immediately recommenced.

"That was uncalled for, I don't appreciate being attacked, and I am not scared of you, so you are wasting your time if you are trying to intimidate me."

"No-one attacked anyone," Daphne spoke out, "this was a vigorous debate between decent chaps. Let's please get back on track."

"Did you make the call then?" Karl asked, slyly, knowing perfectly well there hadn't been time to make an international connection.

"As you know, Karl, that's not been possible yet. We can definitely get to that at a time that we all agree is right, once we have consulted with everyone, and also when Milo and Jack are ready. This is mainly about their future, not ours, no-one is an accessory, no crime is known, and no-one has even been accused of anything.

"I've been considering what you said, and I have a reservation. I feel things have got completely out of proportion, these animosities. No-one has asked you to do anything underhand or illicit, you have, I believe, no reason to be unhappy here, or to be resentful. It feels to me like all the issues could be settled with a handshake and a willingness to be generous in spirit, and open hearted.

"What do you say? Jack has told his story, and offered his hand, and his apology – will you accept both?"

Karl was surprised that Jean had not caved in. He didn't know for certain, but he had a very good idea how much money had gone into setting up the Experience so far, and he guessed pretty accurately that it was much more than Jean could afford to lose, or even possessed. He determined that Jean must be bluffing, because Karl was certain that if he pulled out, the play would disintegrate, and without its centrepiece the Experience would collapse. Those aces were burning a hole in his sleeve.

He took a long sip of his beer.

"No, Jean," he said slowly, deliberately, "this is not going to work for me. Let me be very clear then, if you will not make the basic call to London, then I am out, I won't play your game anymore."

He sat down, and Jean rose to the speaking position. As he stood he took a sip of his beer, rather wickedly enjoying the feeling that of all the people in the room, he was the only one who knew what was going to happen; that this was the moment when he would regain control, for himself, the team, and the dream.

"Thank you for being so frank, my friend. In that case, I agree to your decision to leave the team, and the enterprise, and I will say goodbye. I suggest if you go to your room, and pack your things, then Claude will accept the well-earned and well-deserved task of driving you to Bourges right away so you can get the night train to Dijon and on to Salzburg. Of course, I'll contact your people and make sure you are met at the other end. And here," he finished, fiddling slightly clumsily in his wallet, "is a hundred francs for your train fare, and to say thank you."

There was silence and stillness around the table: a long breathless silence and a profound, frozen stillness. Some mouths opened and closed, some just stayed shut. No-one moved, till finally Karl himself stood up, very straight, and said simply, "Very well." He pushed back his chair, walked round to Jean, graciously took the hundred-franc note, politely tore it into four parts, courteously placed them on the table, then turned in one movement, striding to the door in five steps, opening it, passing through, and closing it behind him very precisely and quietly, so much more melodramatic than slamming it. They heard his footsteps running up the stairs, and all turned their heads up to listen to the thump of his feet down the corridor above them, and into his room.

Claude stood up next, and also said, pointedly at Jean, "Very well," and left the room, passing through the hall and out into the front drive, where he chose a vehicle. He contemplated the Facel Vega

Facellia, but decided it was too risky in case Karl got frisky and there was damage caused while he had to subdue him. So, he opted for Jean's car, got in, started the engine, and turned on the lights so Karl would see where he was.

Karl came out three minutes later, having packed all his things into a single not-very-large bag. As he walked to the car, Claude leaned over and opened the front door for him, but Karl ignored it and got in the back, sliding his bag onto the seat beside him. Claude leaned over and was just able to get purchase on the passenger front door and pull it to, saving himself the embarrassment of having to get out and walk round the car to close it from the other side.

As Claude told it later (which he often did, in fact it entered his standard anecdote repertoire very close to the top), the next thirty-five minutes were some of the worst of his life, so utterly excruciating that before they got halfway to Bourges his hair was voluntarily tearing itself from his head and flinging itself out of the open window. Karl said only five words the entire trip, which were "Turn that fucking rubbish off" when Claude switched on the radio and the Beach Boys were innocently crooning Surfin' USA. Claude did what he was told, purely to avoid a fight. For the next thirty kilometres all he could feel was Karl's eyes drilling into the back of his neck, and he spent most of the time praying silently that the little psycho wasn't carrying a knife.

When he dropped him at Bourges station he barely slowed the car to strolling pace. The boy got out while the vehicle was still moving and walked towards the ticket office without turning back. Claude's one concession to the appropriate courtesy a host owes to a departing houseguest was to wind down the window, blow a friendly kiss goodbye, and call out in a cheery voice that only Karl could hear, "Good riddance, you scumbag cuntbox."

He laughed outlandishly into the emptiness of the black night as he pulled away, startling a fox with its head in a nearby bin. His first thought was to cruise through the backstreets and round to the square to see if the cafés were open and his friends were around for a nightcap he really didn't need. Luckily everything was dark and even the rowdiest reprobates were slumbering peacefully, so reluctantly he pointed the car back to La Chapelle and started driving.

Meanwhile, back in the Lodge, guess what, the new team was rehearsing, all together, sadly without the music, but with the lights, and not a little laughter. When Karl and Claude had left, there was some initial panic, on the realisation that this was the last night before the dress rehearsal, and they now had a change of personnel. So the impromptu run-through was hastily convened and lasted till 2.15am, fired by the adrenaline and excitement of the confrontation and its resolution.

It felt good, competent, if not yet fully professional, though they certainly missed Madame Jestique, who would have a surprise in the morning. Jean was a revelation, there was no doubt in anyone's mind that he would be an excellent Harlequin. When the yawns began to drown out the giggles, they declared it over, and began to head to bed.

Claude, on his return, had been informed he was now an actor, having universally been voted into the role of Policeman due to Jean's promotion. Accepting with barely contained excitement, he had already been keenly asleep on the couch for an hour. As they had never reached the last act in the rehearsal, Claude's Policeman wasn't called on to make his arrest; instead the rest of the troupe had left him sweetly slumbering, dreaming of his fine farewell to Karl, when they turned off the lights. Milo remembered to fetch him a rug from the loungers, as it could get cold in there at night.

Amelie raised her eyebrows to Jean as they were breaking up, and he nodded. Thus was it tacitly agreed that she was returning to the Lodge with immediate effect. "No worries, go to bed; I already called Caro to let her know where you were, and I'll get Daphne to pick up your things from her place on her way in tomorrow. Your toothbrush will be here in a few short hours." Although Jean completely trusted her protestations of innocence, he still inwardly congratulated himself that, even if she changed her mind, she would not kiss Jack without cleaning her teeth. Maybe you could risk it later in a relationship, he thought, but not a first kiss with claggy breath, even if the bits were vegetarian.

Despite the ultimate protection of impaired oral hygiene, he still took Jack aside and had a serious word with him about not letting himself and everyone else down by trying to mess around. Jack crossed his heart and hoped to die, as you would expect given his and everyone else's statements at the honesty and transparency session earlier. Jean rather enjoyed reminding him of Amelie's definitive pronouncement that she didn't wish to flirt with any Cock-er-ny, "loveable or otherwise."

Milo and Jack met in Jack's room for the close-the-day tradition now universally recognised as The Last Fag. There were, also, the very final dregs from a bottle of brandy they had borrowed earlier in the week. They were both conscious that they had enjoyed the end of the evening (the beginning of the morning), and they had been neglecting their fears. They felt guilty. They spent ten minutes chanting.

O My Brethren, pick him up, raise him high, heal his bones.

O My Brethren, pick him up, raise him high, heal his bones.

O My Brethren, pick him up, raise him high, heal his bones.

Halfway through they had a small argument about smoking during the ritual; Milo had extinguished, Jack was toking between lines. They agreed a no smoking policy for future ceremonials, Jack duly chagrined. Milo thought, 'I am glad we did this just now. We mustn't lose concentration. Just because everyone knows now, doesn't make everything magically right.'

Jean had left his van in the driveway and headed up the deserted road to walk the five hundred metres back to the farm and clear his head in the cool night breeze. When he had gone about a hundred and fifty metres he remembered Hector was at the barge and wondered if he could hear him from there. He shouted, "Hector" and stopped to listen. Nothing, he walked on, but then a minute later he heard the giant paws pounding on the track, and then the great dog and his adoring slime were all over him.

'At last,' thought Jean, 'something normal.'

With Hector by his side, he opened the next gate they came to on the left and started along a shortcut across the fields to the farmhouse. The moon gave them enough light to see the path, but it was periodically snuffed out by the silhouettes of the giant sunflowers either side.

After a hundred metres more Jean stood still and held Hector by the loose skin on the back of his neck, the sign for him to freeze. In the resulting silence, after a minute or two they could hear the scuffles, scuttling and snuffling percolating out of the apparently motionless terrain. He had done this nightly as a boy, living at the farm with his often-drunk dad and unfulfilled mum, creeping out sometimes tearfully, then resentfully, then resignedly to explore every track and cranny of the landscape and gradually map it and make it his own. After a decade of hard times, teetering commonly along the cliff-edge of failure, now was his time, the opportunity to save it, turn it round, shake off the bad memories and make it whole and clean again for himself and the generation after.

When they reached Jean's place they kept walking through the carpark instead of turning right up to the farmhouse, carrying on, much to Hector's chagrin, along the path to the landing stage. When they reached the jetty, Jean checked on the barge. The heavy rain had not helped, he really needed to sort the tarpaulin out. Luckily the boat was well designed to drain off the decks into the river, but in the stern, where there was no canopy, the seats had little pools of water on them, and he would need to get someone to come down in the morning and dry it all off. Jean checked that Hector's bedding was snug and dry under the canvas and made sure he had his water and food. The dog, realising he was back on

413

duty, complained, but Jean gave him his best pat and said, "Shush, old boy, I just need you to do this tonight, and it is only three hours till morning, so not long." When he got up to the farm, Jean flopped himself onto the couch, fully clothed, barely unlacing and kicking off his boots, and was asleep in moments.

Jean did not dream often, but this night was an exception. You remember the discussion we had about the cheese earlier, and there had also been a surfeit of drama and excitement to process.

He was at the table after school doing his homework, and his mother, Bernadette, was cooking at the stove. Music was playing; the *Vorspiel* from Siegfried.

"I thought we hated Wagner?" Jean asked.

"We like this one."

His father, Terence, came home drunk and threw his bag of tools in the corner. They sounded sharp and hard as they dropped. Jean was scared of him, though he was twice his father's size; Terence was so small he had to stand on a chair to reach the table. He began to take Jean's books and put them into the fire under the range.

"Dad, I need those. Why don't you use the wood? I cut it for you, just as you like it."

"You haven't done it right. The books are better than trees for burning. We should keep the wood."

Caroline came in and asked what they were doing.

"I'm making the fire hot," said Terence, "your mother needs to cook, so we can eat. No-one makes the fire properly."

"Why are you using books, dad?" Caroline asked.

"We need to keep the wood. The books burn very well."

"I can cook without the heat," said Bernadette. She started to drag the charred books out of the range with a wooden soup ladle; it was too short, and it caught fire, so she burnt her hands. She put the pages in a bucket of water then took them out and placed the blackened fragments on the table by Jean, still smouldering.

"I hope they are OK, son. Will they be OK?"

"They're fine, mum, thanks for doing that. I can put them back together later. I love you."

WEDNESDAY

When the sun came in through the window just before 6.00am, Hector was back, tugging at his sleeve. Jean laughed.

He laughed at the dog and also laughed because he recalled the dream, and that he had told his mother he loved her, which he had never properly done in life. That was new.

Realising he had rather romantically yet inconveniently left his vehicle at the Lodge in order to wander home in the moonlight, Jean took Hector back to the barge, then got an old bike from the shed, rode two kilometres back in the wrong direction to pick up his box of croissants and pastries from the cheery boulanger and then back to the Lodge to wake everyone up.

Claude he rocked with his foot till he fell off the couch onto the stone floor, shouting "Fuck," which always was his first word of the day, but generally not till he'd looked in the mirror.

"What are you doing, Boss, can't I sleep here?"

"You have slept, Claude, sorry, in the past tense. Now it is morning. Sleep is behind you; day is in front. Let's call it showtime."

They pottered in the kitchen together, well-choreographed old friends making coffee, boiling eggs, cutting bread, warming pastries, then Claude went into the hall with the traditional makeshift gong of a wooden spoon and saucepan, and banged the hell out of it, chanting with a little arhythmic dad-prance: "Boss says showtime; boss says showtime; boss says showtime; boss says showtime."

Somehow this morning the light was brighter, the dawn was lighter, a smell of grass and flowers permeated the house and filled the air with sweetness, cute squirrels and adorable fieldmice danced playfully along the edges of the shelves, and tiny bluebirds flew in the windows to land tweeting cheekily on Claude's little leather cap – all because Karl was six hundred kilometres down the track.

The new mood was shared by the others as they came down, the first to arrive – Milo and Jack – merged into the jig, linking arms with Claude and Jean to dance around the hall in a delightfully clumsy foursome, then reeling back into the kitchen and collapsing into chairs around the table where they were soon sleepily joined by Albert and Amelie. A honk outside, and the screech of braking tyres, announced the arrival of Daphne and Madame Jestique, who joined them round the table and completed the party. The croissants, coffee, butter and eggs had never tasted so good.

As they cleared away, Daphne and Albert helped Amelie in with her much-travelled luggage, and Jean called out, "OK, to the cars in ten minutes, bring warm clothes and anything you need for the day, we won't be back here till tonight." Everyone looked at him questioningly.

"I've arranged for this morning's rehearsal to be at Hill House. We missed last night's dress rehearsal on the real stage while enjoying the hunt and hot pursuit of young Karl" [Amelie dropped her head and hid her eyes for a moment, grateful for Jean's kindly editing]. "If we rehearse there this morning, instead of here, that means when we do our last dress rehearsal tonight on stage we will at least have had one attempt *in loco dramatis* to get to know the place."

[Jack gave Milo the wise old nod, 'in loco dramatis, he made it up, I like it…']

"They are expecting us up at the Hill. We'll work till before lunch, then we have to go to the ticket shop, we have our test consumers arriving around 12.00. That's our last real-time live practise with actual people. They're people we know, or friends of friends, and they're having the complete experience today, so we meet and greet, fit them out, take them to the boat, float them up to Hill House, and get them to the picnic area. The magicians and jugglers will all be there to do their jobs, and the caterers also. Then after the fun and games, we will do the final dress rehearsal, with critics!"

"Showtime, then," said Jack, looking around. "We'll be ready."

Everyone went upstairs to pack a small bag for the day. Jean grabbed the technical equipment they would need, and a big duffle of props and costumes, and put it all in the back of his car. The others came out, Claude locked the front door, rather pointlessly as he then put the key under the upturned flowerpot by the porch which might as well have had a little sign on it saying "Burglars: Please Use These Keys To Avoid Damaging The Paintwork."

With initial panic, Claude suddenly realised the Facel Vega Facellia had gone from the drive. Then he remembered, that was the plan, they'd already come and picked it up; if it had still been there he would have been in trouble. Perhaps his soul would be OK after all.

They took two cars and a van on the basis they would need flexibility later in the day if they had to split up. Daphne, Madame Jestique and Amelie; Jean, Milo and Jack; Claude and his new best friend Albert. They were all nervous, but excited, and ready to go.

They pulled up in the little carpark behind Hill House and Jean showed the cast the dressing room where they would change, which had a separate smaller room for Amelie. Claude and Daphne took Madame Jestique off to check out the positioning of the piano by the stage; Claude could come back later for his costume, as

417

Policeman was only on for the last scene. In the dressing room, Jean rustled inside the duffle bags and handed out the costumes which were wrapped separately in tissue paper. He told them to get dressed and that his mother would be in in a moment to check on them and help them with any last-minute adjustments. He was halfway out of the door, already calling out some more instructions to the scene movers, caterers and jugglers who were hanging out smoking in the courtyard, when he suddenly remembered he was in the play, and rather nervously turned back to get changed with the others.

He was anxious that four of the six actors, who had joined the cast in the past few days, were trying on their costumes for the first time; only Albert and Amelie were in outfits that had been properly fitted for them. That at least was fortunate because those were the two characters – one very large, one very small – that probably needed most professional measuring, nipping and tucking.

For the rest, Claude's costume was no problem, being an all-purpose loose police outfit, with helmet and stick-on moustache, that would fit virtually anyone. But the other three were officially winging it by putting on the costumes the day before their first performance. It helped of course that the outfits were traditional baggy pantomime garb – Clown, Pierrot and Harlequin – and the characters did not either need to, or particularly want to, be sleekly sewn into their suits. As it happened, Jack and Milo were much of a muchness in size with the two students they had replaced, and Jean was around the same height as Karl, though maybe ten kilos heavier.

They got dressed quickly in the boys' room. The popular perception through history and literature is that all boys in all changing rooms enjoy teasing and pulling at each other, flicking with towels and so on, with a lot of good banter. In my view, and from experience, after the age of seven this is no longer the case; men much prefer to take their clothes off and put their kit or costume on as discreetly, quietly and instantly as possible, head down, and catching no-one's eye. But that is just my opinion.

418

When Amelie came out of her cubicle in a tight-fitting bodice and tuille skirt, they looked away and at the floor – she was a comrade now and after last night's talking-to they wanted to avoid sensual thoughts, to the extent that their concentration on looking the other way just made things stressful. Albert, of course, did not think of his sister in that way, and gratefully broke the tension with, "Jesus, Sis, can you actually breathe in that?" Jack found it harder to hide what was going through his mind until Jean slapped him on the back of the head muttering, "That phase is over, dickhead, everyone got bored." Jack looked at him quizzically. Jean took him by the arm, pulled him aside and reminded him.

"We discussed this less than eight hours ago, do you have the memory of a goldfish? This may well be your rite of passage, but it is not hers, she has made that quite clear. Karl has not been sent away to clear the way for you. You have duties and a goal; Amelie is a test and an accomplice, not what you're here to seek."

Milo, listening without eavesdropping, nodded sagely in agreement. He detected in Jean's diatribe hints of Jung, traces of Mallory and, what was it, a little drop of Tennyson? In his mind it spoke of courtliness and chivalry, solitary nights of vigil on the chapel floor preparing for the trial, a celibate knight, far removed from the feckless seductive troubadour charming his way into m'lady's chamber. He would mention that to Jack later, he felt it would go down rather well.

'How useful,' thought Jack, wryly, seeing Jean and Milo exchanging knowing looks, 'to have my own motivation and purpose dissected right in front of me.' He decided just to nod sheepishly and give the baby thumbs-up.

Jean's mother, Bernadette, was now in the room, and looking at Jack. "Don't I know you, young man?"

"Yes, Madame Terroir, I am Jack, Mac's son, I stayed with you for several holidays about eight or nine years ago."

"My God, so you are. Your hair is a completely different colour. And now you have reemerged as the boy who was meant to be pretending he came from Paris and blew it completely by getting obsessed with a young lady, am I right? Maybe you really are your father's son."

Was there anyone in the room who wasn't analysing him? And was his secret life the talk of the whole of Central France? There was a lot here to unpick for Jack, but before he could go at it with his mental snipping scissors, Bernadette pulled out her actual shears and started snapping around his neck and groin, somewhat threateningly.

"Shh shh, Jack, don't move or speak, I need to adjust you quickly."

And out came needles and threads: a little pull here, and push there, in out in out, and she slapped him on the bottom, saying, "You are done, my gorgeous one, now run away please." Jack, propelled by the momentum of the heavier-than-necessary hand on his butt, staggered into the courtyard gratefully, without a backward glance.

Milo was next, and he was dispatched in five minutes. He fitted almost perfectly, and he had no loose ends to interest Bernadette. He she chucked on the cheek, squeezing the peachy flesh between her finger and thumb with a pantomime cackle, pretending he was Hansel in the tale: "You need a bit more fat on you, my lovely." He skipped out rather willingly to join Jack in the sunshine and they both borrowed cigarettes from a loitering Albert.

"Mum, for Christ's sake behave yourself," said Jean, when they were inside on their own, "you're such an embarrassment!"

"Ha ha ha," Bernie guffawed delightedly, "maybe I'm doing it deliberately, we are in the theatre, beloved, not the cathedral – I thought we were meant to be loud and temperamental."

She fussed around him more than the others, some side-seams needed to be quickly let out and then re-tacked to hold the extra bulk, but all the lengths were luckily OK. "This will hold you for this rehearsal, then I will adjust it properly this afternoon, so you are ready for tonight. Clearly you are, how can I put it delicately, fatter than the German boy. He was delightfully trim, gorgeous really, though I wouldn't trust him with my neighbour's eggs, as they say. I am quite amazed to be honest that you're doing this, we couldn't even get you to the school performance of the nativity when you were ten."

Jean recalled it; he had been cast as the Third King, the guy with the Frankincense. He hadn't wanted to do it, not at all. And he remembered, it came back to him for the first time in years, that he had been so frightened of the stage that he had shut his fingers in the door when they were leaving to go to the performance. He hadn't made much of a job of it, in fact was not badly injured, but had managed to ham it up enough (acting, my darling!) to get a bandage and sling big enough and impressive enough to demonstrate conclusively that he was in no fit condition to carry a heavy box of aromatic resin across the desert. His place had been filled by Petit Thomas, elevated at the last minute from Fourth Shepherd to the eternal pride of his parents.

With an under-the-breath *merde* he also recalled that his humiliation was made complete by being allowed to sit in a hero position in the wings of the stage to watch his classmates acting, before being called out at the end, when they were accepting their applause, for a special range of cheers for "the brave Jean, who rehearsed so hard for his role but got injured just before the play tonight and could not take part." Everyone shouted their approval loudly, except, when he looked up, his mother, who was sitting silently on her hands and stabbing into his heart a sharply frozen glare that said, "I know what you did, you little coward." He reached his hand out and put it onto her shoulder, old now, and said: "I love you, mum."

"Oh God not that, Jean," she said, startled.

"You're all neat for now, just piss off and play with your friends. I'll pick up the costume for the final alteration this afternoon.

Remember, don't fuck up tonight. And don't get your finger caught in the door this time."

Jean flushed as he went outside, picking up his bag as he left. Even though it was his mum, he was left with that feeling you have when you tell someone you love them and they don't say it back – you know it? He collected the waiting Jack, Milo, Amelie and Albert and rather than going back through the dressing room and running his mother's gauntlet, he led them in the sunshine around the three sides of the house, ending up at the front, and approaching the stage that way.

"Hang on just a second while I set Claude up with the projector," he said, gesturing to the big hold-all he had carried with him. He took it to the spot beyond the front of the stage, next to the piano and Madame Jestique, and called Claude over so he could show him how to set it up and run it. Given Jean's elevation to the giddy heights of Harlequin, he would be in the action too long and too often to have the dual role of projectionist, so this now passed to Claude. Once he was confident that Claude had the basics, he pointed out some of the other controls, for varying the speed, changing lenses and so on, and gave him his piece of paper which indicated when to change the settings. It was a lot to take in, but Claude was good with machines, even cash tills and tractors when he chose to be.

Jean then went back to the actors, now in the middle of the stage, checking out the marks and the distances between props, scenery, and backdrops. The players definitely had the best view in the house; they realised that from where they stood on the stage they were able to look out over the audience to the grounds running down to the river and the barge, but also far beyond that, out across the landscape for fifteen kilometres or more as Hill House dominated the countryside around. Jean pointed out the Lodge, the church in the middle of La Chapelle, and his own farmhouse. "I can even see Hector sitting outside the front door." A terrible joke, but it made Albert stare hard into the distance before he realised.

The theatre looked fantastic: Jean's men had done an amazing job converting the front of Hill House into a backdrop depicting Pantaloon's mansion and garden, and in laying out and locating the furniture, plants, and tapestries to form the areas representing the rooms in which action would take place. Everyone was very happy. Jean's foreman Julien stood by to watch and take notes in case any more adjustments might be required.

As well as helping the audience to their seats when they came in, and checking they were all comfortable, Daphne was in charge of the easel and the placards with the scene names and mottoes. She was setting it up on the front right of the stage and would wear a simple period dress and bonnet while changing the boards. She was looking forward to it, not least because, so long as she got them all in the right order, it was really the easiest job of the night, and should also get some big laughs.

The actors began by doing one very slow walk-through of the whole thing, not gurning or gesticulating, just moving from place to place to check the timing, the flow and the starting and finishing positions in the different scenes. Madame Jestique gave them just the very basic themes at every point, effortlessly adapting her timing to theirs. Afterwards Jean and Julien discussed a few tweaks and minor alterations that could be done during the day, nothing major.

Then it was time for the first dress rehearsal, they had an hour to do it before heading down to the farm to greet and meet the final group of test customers.

Madame Jestique had warmed up nicely during the walk through, quietly introducing the music she and Jack had agreed the previous night: riffs, tunes, signature themes for each character, action music, romantic movements, songs from the Broadway musicals; tiny quotes from Mozart, Monteverdi and Mendelssohn; bigger sections from Beethoven, Bach and Irving Berlin. She was ready now to pull the whole thing together at full speed.

Claude had spent the time mastering the projector and running it onto the actors in different positions doing various movements during their walk-through. It felt very close to the creative process, which made him excited and slightly scared at the same time. But because of the technical element he was very confident he could handle the job. He'd already spoken to Julien about some changes to the proscenium and structure behind so they could close out the daylight a lot more and the light from the projector would have more impact – Julien agreed it could easily be done, and he would have this team work on it later. So, Claude was ready too.

In the dress rehearsal, Milo thought the play went rather well. He believed himself to be a genuinely objective observer but couldn't be certain.

Pantaloon, he noted, was fussy, obsequious, and neglectful of his ward, which happened to be characteristics rather similar to Albert's own personality. So, while Albert confidently believed he was acting up a storm to pull off his part, in reality Jack's script, albeit unconsciously, had created the perfect performance before a foot went onto the stage.

Jean had more of a struggle, because he was acting against type. He really was, in Milo's entirely unbiased opinion, one of the nicest people he had ever met, whereas Harlequin, as specially designed by Jack for Karl to play, was arrogant, cruel, deceitful and predatory. Luckily there wasn't a lot of actual speech: once Jean got the hang of the sour grimaces and contemptuous gurns, and the lofty disdainful arm gestures, his character changed completely.

Jack and Bernadette had a long discussion after the walk through about Jean's make-up, and by the time of the dress rehearsal, when the make-up went on, his face was altered with some artful touches around the eyes, at the corner of the mouth, in the hollows of the cheeks, that transformed Jean's open, honest and kindly visage into something shifty, self-regarding and spiteful. The magic of theatre.

Amelie was Amelie. Milo hated himself for thinking it, and had no personal agenda for saying it, even privately to himself, but she really was astonishingly lovely, and perfect for Columbine. She presented her character as slight, fragile, naïve and vulnerable. Milo smiled, knowing that in Jack's mind the similarities between Amelie and Columbine were considerable. But to him, the differences were much more obvious – the real-life version had shown herself to be strong, smart and wilful.

Jack was a good actor and had the advantage of having designed the part for himself and being able to wrap himself in it. The only problem he had now was that the adversarial Karl piñata he had modelled, painted and dangled from a tree, was now shaped like Jean, and much harder to hit with a stick. But he would get there.

And for himself – more wiggles, wider gasps, more bending over, louder farts, more eye rolls; he could go broader, he sensed it was what everyone wanted.

Claude had suddenly realised he was also going to be the Policeman, which was a great and hilarious irony. Jean's mum had bought him out the blue uniform and kepi, and once she had rolled up and re-hemmed the sleeves and trousers it all fitted, in a kind of authentic baggy style typical of the small provincial police station. The moustache was for later.

He was only on stage for a minute at the end, enough to handcuff Harlequin and lead him off the stage to prison, and Jean and Claude worked out that he could leave the projector running while he was doing it, so they would not need any more help.

Milo saw immediately that Claude was a complete natural, assisted by the fact that he knew the police very well, and had on many occasions been cuffed and dragged off to the *gendarmerie* himself.

And so the rehearsal was smooth, professional and exhilarating; Madame Jestique was magnificent; and honestly speaking the whole show, from boards, set and projector to actors, costumes and stagecraft could not have collectively functioned more perfectly. At the end, when Claude had arrested Jean and carted him off to the jail against all his protests, the set-builders, entertainers, waiters and caterers who had all gradually gathered around to watch and listen cheered and clapped and stamped. Madame Jestique and Daphne joined the six characters on the stage and lined up to give their bows and curtsies, just like a real performance. They tried to look cool but in seconds they had broken ranks and rolled into a circle linking arms around shoulders and bouncing like kids, roaring with laughter.

"OK, OK," shouted Jean, much too loudly in his relief and adrenaline joy, "we need to move, we have to be back at the farm in forty minutes, I've arranged a quick coffee and baguette, leave the costumes with mum. Are there any more notes for Julien?"

There weren't. They stripped off in the dressing rooms, back into their civilian clothes, and Julie by then had laid out a table for them in the picnic area below the terrace with bread, butter, cheese, meats, eggs, juice and coffee. "Ten minutes only, you stars!"

Milo had to give Jack a kick when he saw him reaching for the ham with his tongs. "That's made of pig I think, mate," he whispered, "you need to stick to the dairy end."

Jack exhaled awkwardly and glanced longingly at the array of cooked meats. After some hesitation, he finally stood up with his glass and tapped lightly on it with a fork. Everyone looked up.

"I have a small announcement. Not as your Director, not as your Pierrot, but as your friend.

"As you know, Francois, the sophisticated Parisian, was a long-term vegetarian. But he is gone, we feel his loss…"

[Faux sighs and fake sobs from the troupe at the departure of their compadre.]

".… and Jack, newly joined from London, is not. Sophisticated.

Or a vegetarian... I am deeply ashamed of my subterfuge, but my passion for vegetarianism was only a colourful element of my incognito personality. And I am desperate for ham. Please pass the platter."

Much mirth from Milo, Daphne and Claude. General bemusement from Albert. Sad and admonitory shakes of the head and eyerolls from Jean and Amelie. Jack noticed nothing; he was back once more snuffling in Pork Paradise; readmitted to Ham Heaven like the prodigal carnivore he was. Then he lit a cigarette. As I say, things were very different then.

After the high-speed lunch they bundled into the three vehicles and shot down to the farm, with Daphne leading the way. They'd cut it fine, there were already a few cars in the carpark and people walking around, some looking at the river, some waiting by the Hut. Today's customers were not totally tame, to use Claude's slightly crude phrase; these were volunteers and friends of friends, but objectively distant, and Jean had insisted that a token fee was paid – this time ten francs – so that the clients had some investment in the process and would therefore be more critical and demanding than if they were getting everything free like the customers at the previous practice. There was also a group including people like the Deputy Mayor, the Librarian, people from the museums and the other tourist attractions that Jean had invited because they could be very helpful in the future.

Jean and Claude headed down to the landing stage to make sure the boat was ready to go; Jean had remembered to ask a couple of his farmworkers to take mops and clothes down to get the wetness off and they had done a great job. They decided to have the canopy up over the front half of the boat and the cockpit, but to leave the stern end open for those passengers who preferred the sunshine. Overall, it looked fabulous, they were excited and modestly impressed with themselves.

Daphne unlocked the Hut and the rest of the team went in quickly, Daphne closing the door behind them with a quick sign to the customers, one finger held upright pushed forward and back very politely, but firmly, which in every corner of the world says, 'Please give us a minute.' They all got their striped jackets off the rack and put them on, turning to admire each other, with twirls and flourishes.

"Showtime!" Daphne called in her best Jean impression, and they were on, before they knew it.

Daphne took her place behind the ticket desk with Milo hovering around her to help. Albert and Amelie went to the costume racks. Jack, by the door, pulled back the bolt and threw it open, and the first customers trickled in as he went outside and walked down to the carpark to make sure everything was in good shape. He was delegated simpler outdoor duty because he'd missed the indoor training day.

The rest had practised well, they felt confident, and things went slickly. The customers came in, naturally flowed to the desk, where Daphne took their tickets, if they had prepaid, or took their money, if they had a reservation or if seats were available. Milo helped answer any questions, and when they were finished at the desk, with their pass in hand, he directed them to the appropriate rack or assistant to select and try on outfits.

After fifteen minutes the Hut was getting crowded, as more were coming in than were leaving, but it was anticipated, and not uncomfortable. Jack was back now, having had the great pleasure of putting up the **Experience Complet** sign on Daphne's instruction, and he was watching, and quickly learning what to do to help Milo, Albert and Amelie. It was understandable that many of the customers were slow, experimenting to create the perfect outfit: it was their special day, and in general (not so much today) the customers were paying a lot for their outing, so Jean was keen to emphasise to all the team that they had to give the guests the time of their lives. Eventually, after twenty minutes or so, a steady stream of satisfied customers began to exit the Hut fully garbed, and there was a nice even flow of incomers and leavers, till suddenly the last of the forty visitors was being assisted.

Outside the Hut the student accordionist, Tommy, had arrived and was beginning to play, very gently, a selection of traditional folk tunes, some great old songs from the music halls and a medley of delightful overtures from Offenbach and the nineteenth-century comedies. He really was close to two metres tall, maybe ten centimetres taller even than Jean, towering above everyone, so as they milled around him some of the smaller visitors came precariously close to having their heads squeezed into the flashing bellows pumping and dancing across his colossal chest. "Lucky this is a slow number," he said to a wide-eyed little boy, "or I would have taken your nose home with me tonight."

As more of the fully costumed customers left the Hut, Albert was tasked to hand to each of them one of the smart little brochures Jean had had printed. These were sheets of glossy card printed on both sides and folded in half to make a very nicely designed pamphlet which Jean referred to as 'the Programme.' On the front at the top the Programme had a sepia picture of Hill House taken from the landing jetty, very romantic and in period; and underneath it there was a map of the whole course they would take, highlighting all the major stops, features and locations. Inside on the left page there was a synopsis of Le Grand Meaulnes, explaining how their special day was an homage to the wonderful world created by Alain-Fournier, also with little biographies of the main characters. Jean had written these pieces himself, and he was very proud of them. On the right side there was a timetable of where they would be and when, and what they would do there, plus menus and descriptions of the cocktails they could order at the tea dance. On the back was the story of the Harlequinade, so if anyone missed anything they would be able to follow the wordless play; and a list of the players' names, which miraculously was up to date despite the last-minute changes to the actors, though still, of course, using the identities of Francois and Scott, as Jean said, perhaps a little tongue in cheek, 'to avoid any confusion.'

Jean, leaving Claude to make the finishing touches to the preparations on the river, had made his way back to the area outside the Hut where everyone was congregating – Jack took him his striped blazer, and there he stood, their Captain, regally attired. He was now mingling with the costumed customers, complimenting them on their taste and style. Here was a perfect Meaulnes (and another, less charismatic, hiding in a second group ten metres away); here two Frantzs together, who had decided not to argue it out or take it in turns; here an older lady, he guessed as Madame Seurel. She had brought with her a tiny dog, currently in the charge of her beautiful red-haired companion, that was yapping very cutely on its lead with a delicious peach-and-green striped bandana tied around a neck no bigger than your thumb. Here were two Valentines and here two Yvonnes, the taller of whom was saying loudly, dramatically, to delighted applause from her friends, "We're two children. We've been foolish."

Jean by now was truly giddy: he wandered among the characters, shaking hands, introducing himself, sometimes, with permission of course, making a minor change to the angle of a hat, or the tightness of a neckerchief, all the time thinking, 'This can't be right, this is too perfect, this is exactly what I dreamed.' Best of all to his eye were the fabulous silk waistcoats that he had sought out so assiduously. Every man over sixteen without exception had selected one, whether or not it quite went with their total get-up, because they were drawn inexorably to the rack of them by their sensational colours, textures and designs. Bright red dragons, lurid green bamboos, yellow and blue parrots, pink roses on a black background. What a time to be alive, that had such garments in it.

As the final outfitted customers emptied the Hut, Daphne and the crew, magnificent in their striped blazers, followed behind the last of them, and Daphne pulled the door closed behind her and locked it, using a key that hung on a chain around her neck, which she then pushed down inside her chemise.

A young American Frantz was marshalling a large group of characters against a background of lime trees for a photograph, though it would have taken Monet himself to properly record the mixture of people with their many-coloured parasols, the incongruous but fashionable feather boas, the top hats, bonnets, collars, shawls, frock coats, waistcoats and scarves. He insisted that Jean and the team join in, then shouted, "When I count to three, all shout 'Meaulnes' as loud as you can. One ... Two ... Three ..."

"MEAULNES!!!"

Then they burst apart laughing, like an exploding firework; forming and reforming into smaller groups of three, four, six, eight customers as they were gently shepherded down onto the river path, along the side of the meadow in the direction of the boat.

The visitors were excited. They knew they were the first people to participate in the Experience, they were the innovators and the gatekeepers, almost part of the creative development. As they moved together down towards the jetty, the accordion set a jaunty tempo. They walked in time, some linked arms, and the music had the secretly adventurous among them dancing tiny jig steps and executing surreptitious little twirls.

When the barge came fully into sight, there was a collective cry of excitement and the pace quickened. The taller Yvonne remembered in her haste to shout "This time we mustn't get into the same boat. Farewell, don't follow me!" and the whole party cheered and clapped.

The striped blazers edged towards the front so they could efficiently co-ordinate the embarkation, point out the lifejackets, give the other safety advice and comfortably seat the clients, following the routines learnt in the practise drills. It worked brilliantly, and they counted exactly the right number of passengers, so the ticketing process was happily effective. They had a system.

Jean took a special moment with Amelie, who had been doing an exceptional job amusing and charming groups of passengers and was now in the stern having made sure everyone in her area was seated for cast off. "Thanks for a great job this morning, Amelie, I hope you're feeling OK?"

"Thanks Jean, I am. Actually I was hoping for a chance to apologise to you personally about some of the events of yesterday."

"And I to you, Amelie. I know the swan incident was very upsetting, and I apologise for that."

"Everything feels better today. I'd love just to move on."

"Me to." They had one of those half hugs dads and daughters adapt to after puberty; hardly any body contact, but plenty of affection.

Jean had delegated the driving to Claude, as he was going to do it most days while Jean gradually focused on other things. Daphne and Milo let go the rope at the back, and Jack and Albert untied the front, and they were off. Claude accelerated very smoothly away from the jetty, and Tommy eased from a little evocative Debussy into a rousing rendition of Charles Trenet's chanson classic La Mer, which immediately had everyone singing.

Claude quickly took the barge up to the peak "speed" of four kilometres an hour, then allowed it to slow down slightly. The river was bathed in sunshine, and the warmth was lifting off the top of the water in a fine mist. The banners and colourful fabric and paper flowers woven into the foliage, trees and shrubs on both banks looked glorious. It was perfect.

And then, of course, it happened.

Midway up the course, cruising serenely, they were yattering, and passing around some cold lemonade and a bowl of cherries, when suddenly out of nowhere – well actually out of a hollow tunnel in the undergrowth flanking the river – a great white ghost appeared, lightning fast. It flashed across the water and was halfway up the side of the boat before anyone knew what was happening. By the time Jean realised it was the swan, it was all too late.

Gigantic wings rose above the stern of the barge blocking the sun with their shadow, draining the light and colour from the picture.

The mighty bird hovered above the passengers, then lifted, flapped, dipped and precisely bent its serpentine neck to place its beak perfectly into the waist of the lovely auburn woman and pluck the puppy from her quivering lap.

Jean grabbed the boathook by instinct and leapt towards the swan, but by then the great bird had straddled the side of the barge and was back on the river, whence it turned to face the boat, wings spread triumphantly like the angel of retribution, with the squirming dog hung yapping from its beak swinging on its ridiculous little pink-and-turquoise scarf.

"Poupet, Poupet!" screamed the Madame Seurel, hands on the rail, losing her bonnet over the side. She turned to her copper-haired companion, "Why did you let him go?"

The lady haplessly charged with nursing Poupet on the trip, dressed anonymously in the period style, was, Jean noticed now, more mature than he had previously thought, in her late forties, probably, and her red hair slightly greying on closer examination, but utterly stunning. She clasped Madame Seurel dramatically, as though to prevent her diving in, "I am so sorry, Madame. It was all too quick."

'What a voice,' thought Jean, as he watched the two women, frozen, hovering with indecision like passengers on the tipping deck of the *Titanic* wondering whether to risk all on the faltering lifeboat below. The older woman came back to life and made another feeble movement towards the rail, shaping more to drop into the water than to dive, ready to sink beside her pet rather than expecting she could save it.

"No, no, Madame. Your skirts. The current." The soothing entreaty proved sufficient deterrence. The elderly lady paused in her act of daring, and instead of leaping herself, she turned back to the passengers on the boat to nominate a champion, calling first to her dashing son Francois.

"Francois, please save him. Please!"

Francois, who didn't know her, looked at Another Francois, hoping he might hop over the side and be a hero for them both: but instead of answering or even moving, the Other Francois just turned to the Closest Frantz.

Frantz didn't catch his eye. "I'm probably not the Frantz you mean," he intimated with his reticence. Instead he made a pointing gesture to Charismatic Frantz. "He's more the action man." It did appear that none of Madame Seurel's close relatives or their friends was keen to risk their lives for Poupet.

But wait, here was a Meaulnes quickly taking off this hat and neckerchief, what's this? For a second everyone thought he was going in, but this was just a gesture to distance himself from the drama, saying, "I am not Meaulnes, you fools. See, I am Martin, who works for the post office at La Chapelle." Dropping the accessories in his lap, he held his hands palm up in front of him, his mouth creased, his neck compressed in a shrug: "This is me, everyone knows I am not the man for an emergency, not what you want at all."

This all happened in seconds, during which Claude was one of the first to react. He had spotted the first incursion, and though he wasn't aware of the politics of courage displayed and denied at the stern end of the boat, he could see the gloating swan, and he observed the captive dog, so he cut the engine quickly to arrest their progress as much as possible. In the body of the barge, Jean, realising no-one else was going to do anything, had his boots off and was half out of his jacket and a quarter over the rail. But just before he could spring, a dark figure emerged out of the swan cave, and in one movement crossed the bank and dived full length into the river.

Now everyone in the boat, having reared away towards port when the giant bird climbed the side, moved over as a single organism to starboard so they could see what was happening and view the fate of little Poupet. The boat leaned one way and then the other, beginning to pitch noticeably, but the vessel was too substantial to be destabilised beyond the point of a gentle rocking motion. The same could not be said of the rather frailer rail, which was not built to have forty people hanging over it: it began to creak precariously with the distinct danger of tipping most of the passengers overboard. Jean signalled to Jack at the far end, and Milo halfway up, and the three of them quickly began to call everyone to stand back, peeling off the odd gawper who wasn't listening.

Meanwhile, in the water, the swimmer surfaced just two feet behind the swan. The huge bird, triumphant in vengeance, was swinging the screaming dog from side to side like a spiteful boy with a stolen doll, threatening to smash it. Except the swan was not bluffing, it was just enjoying and prolonging its moment of retributive cruelty. Its attention was totally on the boat and its occupants, especially on Jean and Claude, who it clearly recognised. It was honking and flapping so loudly that nothing could be heard outside the circle of its exultant cacophony.

As they watched, mesmerised, the swimmer took two powerful strokes which produced the momentum to fling himself up and out of the water: he landed on the swan's back, between its outspread wings, with both arms around its neck.

Suddenly feeling the danger, the swan reared up, straightening its neck, and turned its head rapidly to defend itself. As it did so, Poupet was flung from its beak like a pebble from a sling. He landed two feet behind the stern of the boat as it continued to drift, engineless, up the river. Jean had already run to the back, and with Milo holding him by the belt as he leaned far out, and by reaching with the boathook extended as far as possible, he was able, just, to claw up Poupet by his bandana before he went under for the third time.

A cheer went up. Poupet! Saved!

Attention quickly returned to the swan and the man. The engine was off, but the boat was relentlessly drifting away up the river.

Reversing the engine would not give sufficient power to halt it, and there was nowhere to turn. So, it floated on, now twenty metres, now thirty metres away, and the crowd moved round from starboard to aft to keep the battle in sight, converting the pitch into a very slight yawl. And magically, the struggle they were viewing became increasingly mythological as the distance between the audience and the scene steadily extended into the past.

In the age-old battle between avian and human, usually there is only one winner – from slingshot and snare to pistol and poison: but this time the enraged and tormented bird did not perceive itself to be the endangered species. Did the mysterious man perhaps expect when his hero work was done to slide off the swan's back without injury to either party; call it quits, now the dog was safe; recover dry land; and head back into obscurity? If so, the swan had other ideas. It had lost a cygnet: having now been denied a dog of equal weight on which to prosecute its vengeance it was happy to exercise its righteous spite on larger prey if necessary. Perhaps this was even more satisfying – an adversary its own size.

The swan turned violently, surprising the swimmer and throwing him off; then it mounted him, spreading and flapping its wings. The man was pushed under the water, and the swan thrust forward, covering him, holding him down. With a massive effort, the man, grasping a swan leg in each hand, shot to the surface, and twisted and rotated the bird till their positions were reversed and the swan was upside down and fully submerged and the man was astride its belly holding it under. His teeth were gritted and he let out a triumphant war cry; it felt to those who could still see them that even from the first moment of contact this had been about more than just rescuing the dog. There was no surrender.

By now the boat was eighty metres downstream: Jean thought again about diving in and swimming back to help but knew that by the time he could execute the plan the struggle would be over one way or another. Claude restarted the engines, feeling the quickest way to help would be to head to the turning point to get the boat around. Meanwhile all they and the rest of the passengers could do was look helplessly on as the boat, now back under power, quietly glided towards a bend in the river and the increasingly distant struggle continued, first with the man on top, then the bird, then the man again, till finally they were out of sight.

Madame Seurel removed her costume shawl in frustration. As she had already lost her hat, she was now, as if by magic, revealed to be Margaret Malpense, the Manager of the Meaulnes Museum in Bourges. Jean had realised earlier who it was, but the stark unveiling suddenly brought it home to him: "Why did it have to be her?" This was a lady who had immense power to help the Experience succeed; or to allow it to fail. She was holding Poupet herself now, using her relinquished wrap to gently pat the little dog dry, as he shivered, shuddered, whimpered, snorted and coughed miniature droplets of river water from his tiny nose. And while she dabbed she chanted a healing, soothing mantra: "There there, Dougal, you're safe now, don't fret my love, there there."

The accordionist started playing The Swanee River. Daphne was closest, and whispered harshly, "Fuck's sake, Tommy, not that one – anything else, it's not a bloody joke." With a deeply apologetic nod to her, paired with a guilty grimace, he moved seamlessly onto the Barcarolle from Tales of Hoffmann, an eternally delightful, calming pleaser of crowds, perfect to settle things down again, yet with a barely detectable hint of the sinister, no?

So Jean looked at Claude and Claude looked at Daphne, and all three put their heads in their hands. This thing with the canine could not be worse. Well, unless the swan had actually eaten the dog, of course. Madame Malpense was fundamental to the whole Experience, both in terms of her blessing of the enterprise, but more essentially in respect to her promotion of the operation in the museum, the sale of tickets, and the generation of hard cash which would eventually – after everyone else had been compensated for goods and services provided – save the farm.

Claude shook his head and gave a shrug to Jean indicating he had absolutely no idea what to do except carry on as though nothing had happened. Jean went and sat next to Madame Malpense and Poupet and began to murmur his apologies and ask solicitously after the welfare of the traumatised pup, reaching out a gentle finger to touch and tickle its tiny ears. Madame Malpense looked up at Jean; was it contemptuously? Or was it a blanker look than that, because she hadn't put on her glasses after taking off Madame Seurel's pince-nez? She continued to rub Dougal while Jean continued his placations and her stare stretched further and further away. She didn't ask him to leave, but he wasn't sure she could hear his pacifying blandishments.

Claude now had his full attention on the river and navigating everyone to the Hill House landing stage without any more incidents. Daphne pulled Milo and Albert to her and quickly briefed them on the situation with Madame Malpense, instructing them to move among the guests to reassure and, where necessary, comfort them. Jack was leaning over the stern with half a dozen of the other passengers, vainly trying to see what was going on behind them, but the man v. bird battle was no longer visible. Jack had an ominous anxiety about their saviour's safety, an unsettling feeling of panic; but, with no particular evidence, most of the others seemed to be persuading themselves that the hero would have had no problem freeing himself from the bird's embrace and making it back to the bank.

Everyone up and down the boat was chattering and murmuring about the event, calming down from their collective shock. As Daphne and Milo scanned the crowd it was evident that they were broadly falling into three claques.

The first group were turning their adrenaline into humour and struggling to supress giggles and chuckles behind Madame Malpense's back because her silly little dog had been snatched and half-drowned. After all, it was safe now, if a bit dazed, so no harm done, and the sight of the tiny animal being shaken around by its natty fashion scarf in the beak of a giant bird was rather hilarious, in a cartoon kind of way. In terms of assessing risk, this group posed no hazard to the future of the Experience that a few free drinks wouldn't conclusively quash.

The second group was more of a worry. There were older women who clearly sympathised with Madame Malpense; some younger couples with untethered toddlers in hand ["What would have happened if it had taken little Zouzou?"]; another dog owner – there but for the grace of God; an Yvonne who had been sitting right next to the companion when the dog was snatched, whose thigh was still wet from the swan's beak. This group was looking unsettled and potentially unsatisfied with the safety and quality of the service. Still, thought Daphne, we can probably calm the storm with money back, free tickets, and some special treats – so long as the rest of the day goes well.

The third group were thinking of the bigger picture, looking backwards, seriously wondering if a man had drowned (or, in one case, a little out of tune with the rest, horrified that a man might have murdered a swan). It was a small group, but the most likely to want to publicise the issue by calling for help and sending out a search party immediately after they reached the jetty. These were the people who would push the event into the local news, potentially harming the reputation of the Experience and damaging business. Daphne was conscious that Jean had got some local dignitaries here, influential people, and that was not helping her stress levels.

It wasn't long till Claude slowed the boat down and gently nuzzled it into the docking point. A Meaulnes standing next to Jack called out "What now, what about the man in the river?"

Jean was still whispering quietly to Madame Malpense, so Daphne spoke up:

"Ladies and Gentlemen, thank you so much for your patience and courage."

[There were some titters, also a few mutterings of discontent.]

"Once you disembark, members of our team will show you the way

439

to Hill House," she pointed expansively up towards the building, which was in clear view, "and walk up with you to the picnic area where there is a lavish and indulgent buffet laid out, all you can eat, and your entertainment will continue. Everything is included free, of course, and because of our drama this morning, to say thank you for your goodwill and composure, there will be complimentary bottles of champagne, and double portions of ice-cream.

"Right now, the senior crew will return downstream immediately in the boat to find the hero who saved the life of brave Poupet and make sure he is safe, dry him off, and bring him to the party. Can we have a round of applause, finally, for Madame Malpense and Poupet her plucky pup?"

"His real name is Dougal," cried out Madame Malpense. "Poupet is just his stage name!"

After a pause, everyone tittered; then laughed with gradually growing confidence; and finally clapped loudly when they sensed that Madame Malpense was rather revelling in the reflected glory and even joining in the mirth. Her companion held Dougal aloft to receive his share of the plaudits and adulation. An unnamed extra in our tale, unprompted by Claude, sang out "Three Cheers for Dougal," and after the Hip Hips and Hoorays were called and responded, the tension broke; cordiality and kindness broke through suddenly like the sun on a cloudy day; and amiability reigned forthwith.

Milo dropped the gangplank, while Albert and Jack tied the boat up fore and aft. Daphne and Amelie marshalled the passengers and helped them safely and calmly to shore, collecting any lifejackets that customers had decided to put on and forgotten to take off. They then followed the customers onto the landing stage and began to point them to the path. Everyone followed the track along the bottom at river level for two hundred metres; it was closely planted on either side by the most gorgeous camellias and rhododendrons loaded with buds and heavy with early summer scent. Then they turned sharply to the right, beginning the gentle climb up the hill with the actors walking among the customers, beginning conversations with the different groups, and steadily putting everyone at their ease.

Meanwhile Jean and Claude untied the boat, fired up the engine once more, and elaborately turned the vessel in the narrow space. As soon as everyone was out of earshot, Claude turned to Jean and asked, "The swimmer - was it who I thought?"

Jean replied, "Oh yes indeed." Nothing else was said, and the two focused on getting the boat back to the scene of the drama as quickly as possible.

On the way up the hill, Daphne, as the last of the adults, had taken charge. The customers were safely conveyed to the picnic area, by now in a relaxed mood. Milo had been sent running ahead to warn the caterers of the special circumstances, and ice buckets full of champagne bottles were already being added to the tables, with waiters now preparing the flutes and turning the wine in the ice to chill it more quickly. They began to pop the corks and pour the champagne as the groups of visitors arrived, handing a frosted sparkling glass to each guest over the age of fifteen as they reached the plateau, and younger ones too, if they received the parental nod for half a flute.

The magicians and jugglers, all dressed like circus performers, gathered round to meet the incomers, quaintly archaic, looking, exactly according to Jean's plan, like the entertainers from a Victorian funfair – like the eccentric touring company formed by Frantz in the book. They helped disperse the customers around the picnic area, assisting them in finding comfortable cushions and rugs, settling them down. Tommy was performing throughout – he could certainly play. Not only that, but he had the most extraordinary repertoire of tunes mixed with the seeming ability to launch into any piece that was requested by a customer whether he knew it or not.

The striped blazers explained to the guests how the buffet worked, and what was available. People began to queue at the tables, waiters helped serve them and took dishes to the more elderly clients who found it hard to get down and up too quickly. The artists circulated from group to group doing tricks with rings, scarves, giant playing cards and artificial flowers, one sending a dove flying into the sky from inside his hat; the jugglers were tossing more and more balls, swords, plates and clubs higher and higher into the air, never dropping a single one. Jean had chosen only the best in the region, and they had been rehearsing for a week off and on around the picnic site to make their acts perfect. The beautiful marquee tents - little big tops – stood by in their vivid colours, blue and yellow, red and yellow, with their canvas fronts tied wide open, in case anyone preferred to sit inside, or ready if the weather turned against them; but as it was such a glorious day, everyone, customers and entertainers both, preferred to stay outside.

Milo and Jack looked on at this in some wonder, never having seen the entertainers practising, and not having dreamt for an instant that they would be so magical and marvellous – it was enchanting. Yet again, Milo found himself thinking of Jean, 'How the hell does he do this? It's uncanny.'

Daphne, while also enjoying the spellbinding performances, was looking anxious, but trying not to show it. "What's up?" asked Milo. "These jugglers are just amazing; you must be happy?"

"Of course, they're brilliant, I've seen them working a few times, I knew what Jean had up his sleeve."

"So what's the worry? Anything we can help with?" It was the first time they had had a chance to talk together since leaving the river.

"I'm just thinking about what happened on the water, how it will impact us."

Jack and Milo nodded; it had also been buzzing in their heads since they got off the boat.

"But look around, Daphne," said Jack, "the champagne, the buffet, the circus tricks – they're all working wonders, everyone is having a fantastic time."

"Yes, it is fantastic of course," she responded, calming slightly, "you're right. But I am still concerned about the man who went in to save the dog – crazy guy, taking on a swan, they're bloody terrifying! Also, don't forget we've got to put on a play in a very short while, and Claude and Jean are kind of crucial to the numbers, so we need them to make it back in time..."

Milo and Jack agreed. Jack gave the half shrug, just top of the shoulder, hardly any arm, a slight turn of the wrists, that says, "I completely understand, but that is a situation outside our control, so we'd best just press on with what we are doing." Milo realised it was a bit more serious than that, maybe they needed a Plan B.

Queues at the buffet were decreasing as most of the visitors were now back on their rugs and cushions enjoying teeming plates from the feast. Julie and Jacques had truly surpassed themselves for this first real day of operations. The days and days of practise, experimentation and refinement had culminated in perfectly balanced tables heaped with the ideal Meaulnes mix of breads, pies, tarts, fruits, meats, cheeses, eggs together with a dozen other delicacies of the period. Even one or two cakes were creeping back onto the menu, Milo noted, intending to check the budget later.

After another half an hour the team began to select a few bites for themselves while they had the chance, and they slowly moved towards the terrace. They enjoyed the entertainment from a distance, still assisting occasionally if any of the customers had a question or a request. Madame Jestique had arrived and was sitting at the piano already. At a cue from her, Tommy began to wind down and fade out as she gently started at the keyboard, very quietly, playing in the background, sublime Chopin and Ravel. The afternoon stilled and set itself, and the audience finished their double ice-creams and gradually began to relax back into their pillows.

"Come on," said Daphne, eventually, "dressing rooms, it's time for make-up and costume."

Now Amelie, Albert, Jack and Milo were all as nervy as Daphne. Having put on a brave face about Jean and Claude when they were quite confident they would return in time, suddenly there was a growing realisation they actually might not get back, and there was the tiny beginning of a panic. It was Daphne's turn to steady the ship.

"Keep calm, team. If they're not back in time, I'll man up – literally – and play Harlequin, I know all the moves, and I can put on a hat and bind my bosom."

She was steady at heart, for sure, but also currently marching them up to the dressing rooms at an astonishingly quick pace, chattering very loudly, largely to herself, breathing very heavily, and failing to catch anyone's eye.

"In the loose costume," she went on, "and with the audience's respect for the traditions, and their general knowledge of the archetypes, we can just about pull that off, I reckon.

"For the projector, and changing the chapter boards, there is always one of us off stage, so we'll have to take it in turns to keep the props and the lighting going – we can do it. And as for the Policeman, well, we'll just have to busk that when we get to it – there is over an hour till we get to that point, so God willing at least one of them will be back by then to do their bit."

Everyone else, trailing in her wake, nodded agreement – even those who couldn't hear what she was saying. People love it when someone steps up. At the door to the changing rooms, they were greeted by Jean's mother, holding their outfits, and looking out for Jean.

"Hello, Bernadette," called Daphne so confidently that everyone within earshot was immediately aware something was horribly wrong.

"Where the heck is he?" asked Madame Terroir, "not hurt his finger again, has he?" She chortled, slightly madly. Everyone else looked blank.

"Here's his costume. I've spent all bloody day letting out the hems on these motleys and I'm still not sure they'll hold his lava flows of quivering fat. We need another fitting."

Daphne was about to be surprised by the motherly abusiveness, before realising she really was joking. Clearly everyone was on edge, and it was beginning to show.

She joined in the laugh. "He's off sorting out something on the boat, they'll be here soon."

"Yes, I did hear. I think everybody's heard. An avian dognapping and a Man v. Swan water-wrestling death-match. If that is a daily feature of the Experience cruise you'll be famous throughout France. You might not have any customers though."

"Thanks, Bernie, that's very reassuring. I actually think we got away with it on this occasion, but if there are difficult times in future it will be good to know we can lean on you for support and encouragement."

Bernadette had given Amelie, Albert, Milo and Jack their costumes, indicating by thumbs and winks that they were all perfectly ready. They went through to put them on and check, and to start making up.

When they were finally on their own, Bernadette whispered to Daphne, passing her the Harlequin costume: "OK you want to try it on, right? On the basis he's likely not going to make it, you'll be taking on the role, and we might need to take it back in again, waist-wise you're more the size of the German lad."

"I'm flattered."

"You should be. He was a truly awful boy, you could tell that the minute he walked in, but what a body. Ugly within, exquisite without. If I may say so, I wasn't at all surprised that Jean had employed him. My boy is tough in business, but when it comes to dealing with human nature, and judging character, he is utterly clueless."

While she was talking away, as much to herself as to Daphne, she helped her wiggle out of her day clothes and pull the costume over her head. It was around ten sizes too large for her in most places, but when she put the belt on, it pulled it in nicely, and with a few pins and tacks Madame Terroir could see it could be fitted to Daphne quite simply, the work would take twenty minutes.

She then rummaged in the big box labelled Oddments and Accessories behind the dressing-room door and pulled out half a dozen wigs that had been used in the past four or five parish shows – some pantomime dames; Joan of Arc, which had also been used for Gaspard de Besse; a powdered judge still giving off fumes; a permed 1920's flapper; The Little Prince – lots of standard stuff. Finally, near the bottom she found the one she was looking for, Evil Tavernkeeper. This had been used in a kind of Sweeney Todd rework in which the sinister landlord of an isolated inn developed the practice of slaughtering wealthy customers and feeding them in pies and casseroles to his other guests. The wig had a beautiful fleshy shiny bald crown with a surround of wispy hair and a couple of dangling sideburns that then needed to be glued to the cheeks. Having wiped off some blood residue with a hanky touched to her lips, Bernadette spent ten minutes fussing over the seated Daphne, flattening her hair, squeezing, tucking, pulling and fitting, then finally trimming and gluing down the side whiskers. Then another five minutes with some very basic make-up, whites and greys, easily creating an older more cadaverous visage. ("This is just to give an idea; we can primp it up later.")

The result was absolutely fabulous in execution, utterly hideous in appearance. Daphne was transformed from a sweet and rather cute young woman to an unpleasant though distinguished and slightly threatening mature man who was most definitely too old and too predatory for the naïve, delightful and trusting Columbine. A different take on the character! But it would work.

Madame Terroir, finally satisfied with her work, patted Daphne on the shoulders, saying, "Hang on, petal, while I get the mirror." She returned with it, bringing it up from behind, reaching over her and placing it into her up-reached hands, so suddenly there was the face right in front of her, twenty-five centimetres away, scary and foreign. Daphne started and squealed – half play squeal, half real squeal – loudly enough that the others ran in from next door to see what the fright was.

No-one actually shouted, "Who are you and what have you done with Daphne?" but they were taken aback – in a good way – and impressed in equal part. This would work.

"Have we given up on Jean, then?" asked Jack, cagily.

"Not yet, but we need to be ready in case, don't you think? Jean would want the show to go on; really, he needs the show to go on, it has to."

Everyone nodded. Jack looked apologetically at Daphne / Sweeney / Ancient Harlequin, saying, "Sorry, Daphne, I wasn't suggesting we shouldn't be ready, and I wasn't disparaging your willingness to step in, or your obvious talent. I guess I was just feeling superstitious and hoping my cousin wouldn't be missing out."

"I completely understand, Jack. I am not pushing myself forward, I can promise you that. It was bad enough losing Karl, in terms of the acting talent obviously, not the man who possessed it; but losing another Harlequin a day later, on opening night, would, as you say, be extremely remiss. So, we'll fight till the last second to hold for Jean, but when the bell rings at 4.00pm, if he's not here and in the clothes I am wearing, sadly I am going on, that's all I am saying. The make-up here, and fitting, are to check it all works, and to save time later, when we might run out of it. As you can see, I have to play the character much older to hide my youthful

447

femininity…" [Daphne and Milo both cracked up slightly at this, and tried and failed not to let Jack and the others see them sharing the joke] "…so later, if it does come to it, we might quickly need to discuss some small tweaks to the tone and action."

Jack nodded. "Agreed, if we have to, we'll change the emphasis, it can be done."

Checking his watch, Milo realised it was 3.25pm already. In twenty minutes, Madame Jestique would be playing some agreeably gentle yet jauntily expectant "Come in and sit down" music, and the audience would gradually be entering into the theatre space, full of excitement and anticipation. Although everyone in the team was trying to remain bullishly confident about Jean, he suddenly knew it was all bravado; he realised at that moment that he was the only one left who honestly thought Jean was going to make it on time.

In the classic theatre all the real thespians have their time-honoured and thoroughly adorable routines and rituals before a performance. The exact journey to the theatre; precise positioning of ornaments and knick-knacks; the strict order of taking things off and putting them on; who must and must not visit; things to be said, things to be avoided. In the Harlequinade, no such affectation exists. Harlequinade was performed by wandering groups of journeyman players, constantly on the move, always adapting, ever changing; taken from small town to manor house, from village square to country fete; everything for the show was piled high on the back of a cart, with the actors walking beside to avoid tiring the horse. A job, not a vocation; a living, not a calling.

Thus was it now with our ever-shifting, always-evolving troupe of recent strangers and untried volunteers. Endlessly adjusting, ever transforming, replacing members of the cast even as the audience was being welcomed at the door. ['O God,' thought Daphne, 'who is getting everyone seated if I am in here trying out a butcher's haircut?'] At various times over the past week they had been full of excitement and confidence; now, half an hour before the opening lines, and in the absence of their leader and inspiration, they dried, they froze, they totally lost their nerve.

Bernadette, with lots of experience in amateur dramatics – albeit from behind the stage – sensed what was happening and began to set them immediate tasks to distract them. First, she helped Daphne out of the costume and back into her civilian clothes so she could start making the quick adjustments she needed to do on the Harlequin suit.

Secondly, she took Daphne's mind off the scary acting bit by reminding her about managing the box office. "Daphne, Julie's here, she's finished feeding the customers and clearing away, and she's asking if there is anything she can do to help – do you want to instruct her about welcoming the guests into the theatre and getting everyone seated?"

Daphne did indeed want to do that, she had been worried about it, so she and Julie went briefly into the courtyard and had a cigarette while Daphne explained what was needed – Julie was a very quick learner and had been in the high-intensity catering business long enough that nothing much fazed her. She shot straight off to do the job.

When Daphne got back she saw that Bernadette had, thirdly, organised the team in pairs to finalise their own make-up. Albert and Amelie; Milo and Jack. As they were rapidly running out of time, she had shifted them round so each couple was simultaneously applying the slap to their partner opposite, this causing a good deal of reciprocal hilarity, exactly as she has anticipated. Each pair had a small table between them covered in the greasepaints, and they were working industriously, with Bernadette hovering over them making suggestions and putting on some detail and finishing touches.

"Sit down," she said to Daphne as she walked back in, "and I'll finish you off. Sit still, no laughing, no fretting, no fussing. And don't try to kiss me, you horrible old letch."

"OK, just wait one minute while I check the river again."

"No worries, just try these trousers on first, I think they'll be OK now. Stripey knickers on first, remember! I can work on the jacket while you're gone."

Indeed, the comedy underpants were, appropriately, much too baggy, but the trousers did fit very well now, once they were gathered copiously at the waist by the stout belt; the length was perfect, the hems were beautiful. Keeping them on, somewhat clashing with the spotted Harlequin undervest she was already wearing on top, Daphne skipped back through the house, out of the front door, and onto the stage, which she crossed to stand on the leading edge from where she could see directly in front of her the first five or six early birds who had taken the best seats in the theatre. They looked properly confused; was the show starting? Who was this character? Why was no-one here yet?

The sight of the audience momentarily triggered the stage fright that Bernadette had worked so hard to calm, but Daphne had no time for it now, she was deliberately and self-consciously looking way over their heads to the river four hundred metres below, to see if the barge was back yet. It wasn't, but she didn't give up immediately, she decided to wait and watch for the count of one hundred, and then it would come into sight. And when it did come into sight, around the bend in the river, within that count, then Jean and Claude would run up the hill and get there in time to get dressed and made up, and everything would be fine!

Daphne braced herself at the stage front, a flat hand held at a right angle against her forehead above the eyes to form a shield against the sun and the reflected bright light bouncing and flashing off the water below. A plucky pioneer staring out across a virgin land portentous with unseen mysteries.

When her count reached thirty-five, with no boat in sight, she suddenly recognised that she had been feeling a tugging sensation scratching at her right ankle for some time. Looking down, she saw it was one of the Meaulnes from the boat, currently in the audience, who had approached the stage and was now below her in the pit pulling gently but insistently at her Harlequin trouser leg. She realised that for half a minute she had been repeatedly hearing, but successfully suppressing, the supplicatory mantra: "Excuse me, sir..... Excuse me, sir.... Excuse me, sir..... Excuse me, sir...."

"Me sir?"

"Yes, you, sir."

Daphne recalled she was currently a man. This was a compliment to Madame Terroir's make-up, and on balance it was a very good thing that she had been taken for a bloke.

"How can I help you, Monsieur Meaulnes?"

Meaulnes also simpered a little, revelling in the collegiality of being submerged into the fantasy.

"I was just wondering, have you started?"

"Started what?"

"You know... we're all wondering if the play has started. I thought it was starting at 4.00?"

"It hasn't started, don't worry. We'll start at 4.00, just as it says in the Programme." She spoke a little deliberately now, maybe it was the disparity in heights, she wasn't normally a rude person, but she wanted desperately to shake him away from her leg, and she began pushing him off with her other foot, as if he were an overexcited poodle.

"You're not a man!" he said, after a while, as though this was an earth-shattering revelation.

"No."

"But the play hasn't started?"

Daphne was flustered now, discombobulated by the rather persistent young man still busily worrying away at her trouser cuff. Having lost count at thirty-five she decided it would be fair to start again at seventy. "Seventy-one, seventy-two, seventy-three, seventy-four." She had paused her surveillance of the river, but now, as she counted again, she nervously looked up to check once more: still no boat.

In her mind she saw the barge speeding unfeasibly quickly around the river bend, screeching to a halt at the landing stage, and a stranger leaping ashore, sprinting away down the riverbank with Claude in hot pursuit. In her imagination, Jean vaulted to the shore from the still-moving vessel with a huge white bundle clutched in his arms like a giant baby, as, partially losing and regaining his footing like an ice dancer, he sprinted up the hill, shouting as he got within hearing distance: "A Vet, a Doctor – is there any kind of physician here? We have an injured swan, it's life or death."

But the truth was, no Claude, no Jean, no mystery man and no wounded swan. No barge. No Harlequin, no projector, no Policeman. "Ninety-six, ninety-seven, ninety-eight, nighty-nine...... [last look] .... one hundred."

Always scrupulously honourable in the strict adherence to personally delineated superstitious parameters, Daphne looked away from the river exactly as she counted one hundred. There was to be no reprieve. In the best tradition of showbiz, she had been plucked from the ticket booth to star in the show.

Her foot scraping hadn't worked, so resisting the temptation to ironically kick out at the Grand Meaulnes, she gave him a rictus smile and appealed to his dramatic sensibility. "You will see me again shortly, *mon brave*, and all will be revealed – that is the beauty of theatre. If you can free my ankle, I will waft gracefully back to my dressing room where I will finally prepare myself to come back and thrill you."

Truthfully, it was more of a stomp than a waft; on her way, lifting an arm and waving without turning round, she said goodbye to the embryonic audience, now around twelve in strength, and then disappeared gratefully back into the house, where she threw herself into the arms of Madame Terroir, all but sobbing.

"They're not coming."

"Don't worry, dear, you'll be fine. I've seen all the others, and trust me they're no great shakes, you'll be upping the talent quotient considerably. Here, try this."

Daphne looked up to see what magic was being waved before her and found a very small bottle of brandy five centimetres away from her lips.

"All of it," said Bernadette, answering Daphne's unspoken query.

Outside, suddenly the doorway darkened as the covers were pulled over the proscenium and stage, and flickering lights were turned on by Julien's men. Madame Jestique was gradually accelerating into her work with a medley of sections from famous overtures: from Rossini's Barber to Richard Rodgers, from Mickey Mouse and Mozart to Metro-Goldwyn-Mayer.

"OK, jacket on, Daphne," instructed Bernadette. It was perfect and hung expertly over the gut and belt area to create an old-man's shape, disguising the ruching that was holding the trousers in position. Quality work in the time.

"Excellent, now let's finish the face." Bernadette worked quickly and expertly on Daphne's make-up. A lot of yellow in the background, a lot of grey and black in the details and line, and suddenly Daphne was looking in the mirror at an even more grumpy fifty-year-old man who was showing every decade of his age.

"Oh dear. Are you sure I can't be young and beautiful?"

"Ha ha, looks like that ship has sailed, darling. Have you talked through the changes needed in the role? You're going to have to be the father, not the son."

"OK – Jack!!"

Daphne called loudly enough to be heard in the next dressing room, but not outside by the audience. Madame Jestique was about to launch into the music for the first scene, so Bernadette sidled out to warn her to busk it for another five minutes, and then she positioned herself behind the projector, ready with the ON button when given the sign. Inside, Jack joined Daphne; she showed him the costume and make-up and they quickly discussed tactics. Once they'd agreed, Jack prepared to address the team as Director, and called them together.

"OK, everyone, Jean and Claude are not coming to our rescue, so we're on our own. As you can see, Daphne is transformed." She swept her hands up and down herself and circled a flat palm in front of her face to illustrate, "View my visage."

"I am now Harlequin," she said. "As you have also noticed, I am fifty, not twenty-five."

Jack continued. "So we're saying now the play is about a father contemplating marrying off his very young daughter to one of his wealthy contacts, an older man, in order to save his family business. It doesn't need much tweaking in our playing, though of course Columbine will be much less accepting of the situation, and much more disgusted by her father's behaviour, even if she still feels at some level drawn towards doing what he wants."

"What about the letter I find?" asked Milo. "Is that still going to be OK?"

"Yes, it is to his brother, so he can still be discussing taking advantage of the girl, the new marriage to the 'Contessa' might seem less likely at his age, but why not!"

"What about the boards?"

"They're on the stand, in order. There is always one of us off stage except at the very end, so we do it ourselves as we come on and off, just stay alert."

As they were speaking, the music slowed again, ending the circle of its holding pattern, and asking the question for the third time, are you coming out? The assembled throng had been delighting in the music for quite a time without being conscious of the delays behind the scene while the cast re-sorted itself. Fortunately, Madame Jestique was expert not only at getting the audience into an excited and expectant mood, but also keeping them there.

"It's time," said Jack. "We have to go. Everyone ready?"

"Yes," said Daphne.

"OK, then please let's have Pantaloon, Columbine and Harlequin on stage." And so saying Jack put arms around at least two of them, and took them to the door. When they reached it, Jack signalled outside to Julien to turn off the lights; the three starters took their places in the half-dark, and then Jack nodded to Bernadette to turn on the projector, Madame Jestique launched into the music for the opening scene and suddenly they were off… there was no stopping it.

Jack and Milo stood together to the side of the door so they could watch without being seen. These were nervous moments. For Jack, he was the tortured creator, putting his reputation on the line, baring his soul to the audience, but at what risk? For Milo, he was anxious for his friends to succeed, and more than a little stressed to remember his own cue and to hit his first mark.

Both of them knew how important it was for Jean that the play should be a triumph, so they were also desperately trying to read any clues from the audience. As the lights went down and the music went up, the movie projector began to whirr, creating the impression of an old Chaplin film, and the crowd spontaneously oohed and aahed; the theatre came alive before the actors even started playing. The reaction could not have been better.

After that, it went so smoothly! I don't know what you were expecting, but it was all so simple, so dramatic, so archetypal, just as a Harlequinade should be, they could not and did not put a foot wrong. The feckless and feeble Pantaloon pimped out his perfect daughter to a doubly distasteful Harlequin played magnificently by the sleazily sinister and aged Daphne, and the innocently cunning Clown and Pierrot conspired heroically to save her.

The audience got drawn more and more into the play, they cried out, they laughed, they booed. When Clown did his immense and perilous leap from the window, landing awkwardly on elbow and bottom, they gasped and put their hands over their mouths in fright; quite rightly too, because Milo had missed the cushion and landed on a bone he would rather have avoided. He was hurt but too much of a trouper to show it, either to the audience or his fellow cast members.

When Pierrot and Clown created their scheme to trap Harlequin, the audience shouted and heckled with glee; when Jack began to dress up in his massive frock and voluminous wig, the air was rich with wolf-whistles and ribald suggestions shouted from the back row, and titters and tut-tut-tuts from the front.

And when the seedy and despicable Harlequin finally shimmied down the ivy in his spotted vest and stripy shorts, they screamed and hooted their approval as he dropped into the arms of the Policeman in the form of a rapidly uniformed Bernadette, who had come on to the stage way before her cue and arrested the dirty old man several minutes early. No-one cared that Harlequin was carted off too soon – this was an area of France where rough and summary justice was universally appreciated and exceedingly popular.

And so they found themselves – Amelie, Albert, Jack, Milo, Daphne, and now Bernadette, joined by Madame Jestique – bowing and curtseying in a line behind the limelight. Laughing, clapping themselves, putting arms around waists and necks, as the audience whooped and stamped and the projector continued to whirr and click and throw its flickering light and shadow at them, illuminating their grinning, relieved and jubilant faces like kids at their first camp holding torches underneath their chins. It was a magnificent triumph.

After their third return for yet more applause, they left the stage for the last time, ran into the dressing room, and hugged. This was the life! And just at that moment their minds, of course, created the image and fantasy of touring the show, growing from regional popularity, moving to national prominence and on to international stardom. Then another thought hit them simultaneously, more of a realistic concern – where were Claude and Jean? Worse too, where was the boat? They had a challenge on their hands if they had to get the customers back to the Hut without it.

The schedule now was that the customers left the theatre area and moved to the terrace at the opposite side of the house, where they would be served tea, coffee, special drinks, snacks and little cakes by Julie and her team. Madame Jestique had a second piano round there, so she could continue to play for them, and she was joined by a young girl on the guitar and an extremely old violinist, with whom, as a trio, she commonly gave small concerts and played at tea dances and family parties. They did a very good Hot Club of France, also some trad jazz, Ella, Frank, Edith Piaf and Charles Aznavour – all the classics and crowd-pleasers. The youthful guitarist was prodigiously talented; a microphone had been set up in front of her because she also did the vocal parts, using many different voices and styles. Tommy had no intention of being left out of this ensemble, not least because he had decided the guitarist was the most beautiful girl he had ever seen; so with a polite and pleading nod of application to Madame Jestique, paired with the joined palms of thanks for her kindness and understanding, he pulled up a chair, made the three a quartet, and prepared to try to win the guitarist with his flashing teeth and floating fingers.

The audience departed their theatre seats and headed to the tea area with great good humour and excited chatter about what they'd seen. Julie had been ready to serve more champagne if there was any residual unease about the Swan & Dog incident, but that seemed all forgotten for now, so she quietly pulled a sheet over the ice buckets and made a "No, not needed" sign with a raised finger on a quietly waving waist-high hand to the waiter to stop him popping the corks.

The customers were all impressed with the tea terrace. Jean had been reading a book about Singapore and had fallen in love with the idea of a "Raffles Effect" here, for no reason other than the style of it, and maybe the fact it was roughly the right period. It could just as easily have been Toulouse-Lautrec or Aubrey Beardsley. So the guests indulgently sank into cushions on rattan chairs, surrounded by parrot screens, divided by miniature palm trees in giant Chinese vases.

The tea interval was designed both as a pleasant last chapter in the entertainment and as an opportunity for the actors to clean off their make-up and change back into their day clothes and blazers ready to take the customers back to the boat. However, as happens to all things in Jean's universe, it had gradually swollen beyond its original conception, from a minor halt and tempo control to a vast and elaborately carved and embellished staging post, with an atmosphere, pleasure and purpose of its own.

So, when twenty minutes later the refreshed and speckless Harlequinade team turned the corner onto the terrace they encountered a dozen couples swinging to a very upbeat version of Charles Aznavour's Je T'attends. The dancers were being lazily observed from the perimeter by multiple editions of Grand Meaulnes characters laying back contentedly on cane-woven sofas and loungers, watching the action while nibbling serenely on perfectly-shaped gaily-coloured macarons, each delicately embellished with a GME logo. You know of course what Milo thought when he saw this for the first time: 'How does he do it; how does he find the time?'

Coffee and three different types of tea were being served by Julie and her team, together with small sandwiches, biscuits and mille-feuilles. For those wishing for a stronger drink, there was the cocktail bar, festooned along its back with bottles of many shapes and colours on mirrored shelves. Wine and beer were always available, plus a collection of famous mixed drinks decorated with swizzle sticks and umbrellas. The cocktail menu was to change every few days, the selection this evening being Gimlet, Martini, Whisky Sour, Daiquiri and Pink Squirrel, which could be ordered, by the less experienced, using the descriptions and ingredients lists provided in the Programme. Milo had blanched at the cost of the cocktail bar, but Jean had dug in his heels, knowing how important it was to send home the customers in the best of good spirits. ["And besides," Jean had said, possibly with a wink, "liquor is one of the things we definitely know how to get hold of at a good price."]

The far end of what had become the dancefloor contained the small circle of five young kids, hands locked together, that is found at every village fete, wedding and celebration, giggling, spinning each other and tumbling out of control at a speed and rhythm joyfully unrelated to the velocity and cadence of the music being played. 'This is good,' thought Daphne, 'a good time is being had by all.'

On the bad news side, Jack, Milo and Daphne had all quickly visited the stage on their way from the dressing room in order to check the view of the river scene below, and there was no vessel in sight. At the dance terrace, Daphne gestured to Albert, Amelie and Bernadette to engage with the customers, join the dance, and help Julie and her team keep the ambience going, mouthing and gesturing, "We need to buy some time while we sort out the boat." Madame Jestique, she knew, was a trouper and would just keep playing till she asked her to stop.

Milo, Jack and Daphne walked back around the corner at an unobtrusive pace, specifically designed not to worry the guests, to a discreet distance where, unobserved, they could hold a private conference while smoking heavily.

"What do you think has happened?"

Daphne threw the question out to herself as well as the others, sucking deeply on her first cigarette since the play. The boys shrugged hopelessly, releasing intertwining streams of smoke.

"Perhaps the man was injured and they had to take him to the hospital?"

"Maybe, but it was a couple of hours ago, you'd think one of them could have taken him in the van and the other one could bring the boat back?"

"Maybe he was dead and they had to call the police?" Jack suggested.

"Again, being cynical, I know he's a hero and all, but dealing with his corpse would still be a one-man job. And dad's quite skilled at handling cadavers, so I just don't think it would hold them up that long. Plus I don't believe Jean would allow fishing a body out of the river to stand in the way of business, specially as today's run was already causing concern. Actually, now I think of it, they could be off hiding the body somewhere to avoid the bad publicity, that might take two of them."

Jack and Milo looked genuinely shocked.

"Jesus, boys, I'm just joking. Don't lose your sense of humour when we need it most."

"Christ, Daff, that's cold …. anyway, we're all speculating, I can't think what would stop them, but it has to be something serious, right? The big question is, will they make it back at all, and when do we start panicking about how we get the customers back to the Hut tonight?"

As they were speaking, they were all looking back down the hill towards the river, superstitiously praying that their collective anxious glances would magically conjure up the barge. Nothing happened there, but at the same time, in another direction, through the faraway gates and up the long driveway, they saw a strange vehicle approaching. It was difficult to pick it out in the gloaming, but as it got closer, first they saw it was yellow, then they saw it was huge, and finally, when it was two hundred metres away, they realised it was an extensive and highly ornate traditional charabanc, motorised.

"Oh my Lord," said Daphne, "what the hell is this?"

They watched mesmerised for the two or three minutes it took for the open-topped coach to crawl up the last part of the hill, achingly slowly, and finally come to a halt in the parking area of the house several metres away from where they were standing.

"Georges!" shouted Daphne. "Is it you, after all this time? What the hell is this you're driving? Where are the horses?"

An extraordinarily old man got down extremely sluggishly from the driver's bench, leaving a young boy sitting holding onto the manual brake with some concern. He began to hobble towards them, using a stick, holding an oversized hat on with his other hand, shuffling so that one foot barely advanced on the other. They decided to meet him *en route* rather than waiting the hour or so it was going to take him to reach them.

"Hello, Daphne, my dear, such a long time!" he said as Daphne put an arm around him and pecked him on the cheek. "You know my grandson, Henry?"

Daphne didn't but waved enthusiastically at him as though they were lifelong comrades. 'O God,' she thought as she did so, 'please don't take your hands off that brake to wave back to me.' She didn't have time to remark to herself, 'That boy cannot be more than thirteen years old,' because she had other things on her mind, and Georges, in any case, was now literally pulling at her collar to keep her attention.

"I had to get rid of the horses a dozen years ago – maybe just after the last time I took you on the school trip, little one. I had Guinevere converted to motor then, the worst mistake I ever made. We still make a living, but it is not the same. Anyway, enough chit chat, what's the job?"

"Job?"

"Yes, Claude called me and told me to come up here and report to you, that you needed us. He said it was urgent and important and I should stop drinking immediately and get behind the wheel – you know his sense of humour! Well, of course you do, he's your father. Anyway, I had had a few, so I took the precaution of bringing young Henry to help me with the basic steering duties."

"Georges, did he tell you anything else – like where he is and what he is doing?"

"He just said he can't make the pick-up you are expecting, and you'll need me, Henry and Guinevere. He'll talk to you later when he's able."

Daphne looked at Jack and Milo, not sure whether to be nervous or relieved.

"Thanks, Georges, I think Claude has booked you to take our visitors back down to where they have left their vehicles at Jean's farm. Can you do that?"

"Of course, my love, that's what I do. Are you going now, or later? I can put up the canvas top if you like."

"No, that's probably not necessary, it is a mild evening, and I think we would like to go in fifteen or twenty minutes at the latest, I will double check that. How many does the charabanc hold?"

"Well, that usually depends where we're going, how far, and if it is up or down hill. It is not like when I had the horses, we could go anywhere then and we never had to worry about fuel or power. This engine I got sold is weak as weasel piss, it was that little shit Dennis at that crooked petrol place in Saint-Martin, you know the one, I am amazed it has lasted this long, I've had to take it back to him at least two or three times."

Daphne was getting just slightly impatient with Georges's exorbitant torpor, though she was working very hard not to show it as he was apparently going to be their saviour. Also, she didn't want to overtly appear ungrateful because he was notoriously sensitive and could just as soon turn the bus around and leave. He was rumoured to have left a large party of pensioners paddling in the Cher at Montrichard, driving off huffily and taking with him their shoes, socks, purses, wallets, bottled beer and packed lunches, because one of them complained they'd arrived at the beach two hours later than promised.

"We have forty people here – say forty-five with staff – who need to get down to Jean's farm. Reckon you can do that?"

"Daphne, this coachwork is Daimler, fifty-odd years old, the last of the giants. Aside from the driving station we have seven benches, each can hold nine children or seven adults. Forty-five is no issue unless we have to go uphill. However, the way to Jean's farm as you know is almost all downhill, with a bit of flat, and a small bridge. We can just about squeeze over the bridge. The biggest problem will be keeping the speed down when we start off down this hill, but fortunately we have young Henry on the manual handbrake, and we can control it. So basically, yes."

Daphne had another glance at Henry, scanning him a bit more conscientiously this time but still not being able to detect a lot of hair on his chin. His arms also appeared possibly a little on the thin side to be singlehandedly restraining a two-and-a-half-ton coach with the additional weight of forty-five well-filled souls. But beggars cannot be choosers, and the slight risk of careering crazily down the hill and plunging headfirst into the river at breakneck speed seemed preferable at that moment to sitting on this terrace all night with her fingers crossed promising forty increasingly fretful special guests and local dignitaries that their barge really would be back any moment.

"Thanks so much for coming, Georges, and you too, Henry." Once Daphne had decided she was in, she was all in, and that meant indiscriminate flattery whether warranted or not. "You're heroes and saviours. I'm going to start getting people together in a while, they're just having a bit of a dance while we wind up the entertainment. Why don't you get yourselves a cake and a drink – I mean obviously a coffee, or soft drink, given how narrow that bridge is – and make yourselves comfortable while we corral and cajole?"

She was only a third of the way through that last sentence before Henry was out of the cab and heading for the cake stand. Georges followed him, but a betting man would say he was unlikely to be in a position to make a dent in the macarons, or even reach them, much before Christmas. Milo took pity and went to fetch him a couple of cakes and a small coffee, then he and Jack had to collect a chair for him also, which ended up in the middle of the path about five metres from the bus. Rather miraculously, Henry managed, from a cold start, to swallow two éclairs and find a rather dazzling partner before the last dance. The lucky girl was one of the Yvonnes; blonde, extremely pretty and at least thirty centimetres taller than him, the basis for which unlikely pairing you must enquire of the universe.

Daphne went back into the dancing throng and signalled to Albert and Amelie, asking them to start to circulate and nudge people towards finishing their fun as they were winding up the event. She spoke quickly to Julie, to make a request; and then went to Madame Jestique and whispered in her ear to make the next song the last dance, explaining the situation with Claude, Jean and the timely charabanc. Picking up an empty wine glass and tiny fork, she tapped, loud as a bell, got part of everyone's attention (without stopping them) and called out, as Madame Jestique's trio cum quartet muted their sound, "Ladies and Gentlemen, the next dance will be the last, and then after you have gathered your things and made yourselves comfortable for the trip, we will be boarding a beautiful historic Daimler coach for our journey back to the carpark to collect your vehicles. I hope you are having a wonderful day!"

"What about the return boat trip?" called Franz Three. "I thought we went back via the river?"

"Ah a number of things conspire against it; not least, we are leaving much later than we thought, and we want to get you back quickly. The charabanc is completely of the period and an authentic finish to our entertainment. I firmly believe that Georges our driver once chauffeured Monsr Alain-Fournier himself and will have many stories for you! And finally, we have complimentary champagne for each of you in the coach, a splendid way to travel through such a balmy summer evening."

As she finished her impromptu speech, the trio quartet quietly began La Vie En Rose, the dancers held each other ever more tightly, the sun began to settle and the sky created just enough pink to make life and the lyric perfect. The customers were very happy with the bus, it had great ambience, it saved them the walk to the jetty, and every one of them suspected that in reality the boat was cancelled because of *l'incident du cygne*, as they were calling it. In any case, all of them were extremely contented; this day had by far exceeded any expectation they'd had – it was somehow magical, even when it went wrong.

The Piaf song echoed its mournful optimism out across the hill down the valley and over the river while the dancers danced the last dance, wistfully embracing their partners, nestling necks, and softly pressing gentle lips in sweetly-smelling hair. Such a blissful day, would it ever be repeated? The song finished; a moment's silence, movement stopped, and then spontaneous applause, all for all. The customers collected purses, lighters, cigarettes and hats and headed for the coach.

Now the charabanc, as you probably know, is the most practically designed vehicle ever for egress and ingress, having a separate set of doors for every bench, on both sides. So in the case of Guinevere, there were seven doors either side, not even counting the door for the drivers. Getting the passengers loaded would barely have taken seconds if not for the extra time taken in amicable disputes and amiable squabbles amongst fresh acquaintances who were jealously trying to manoeuvre themselves next to their dance partners and new best friends. Once they were settled, Julie's team brought out the trays of champagne and passed glasses among the guests, "Enjoy, enjoy! You are our best guests ever!"

The Harlequinade team spent some moments before embarking hugging Bernadette and Julie and venerating the extraordinary Madame Jestique with deferential gestures from a respectful distance. "Thank you, thank you, thank you – we could not have done it, it would not have been the same, it would not have worked at all without you!!" Then hilariously, all realising simultaneously, and all shouting at the same time, "See you tomorrow, when we do it all again!"

Milo calculated quickly in his head and reminded himself that for Jean's plan of fourteen six-day weeks it meant over eighty days like this, with hardly any rest between them except Sundays. Was that even possible? Would they live that long at this pace? Maybe once they got into more of a routine, and if the swan stopped attacking the dog, and if the right cast turned up at the right time, and if the boat came back on schedule, it would all be a bit less stressful and a bit more manageable. But how exciting it was, this acting, and being part of something.

The last people to board were Georges and Henry in the front (with Henry's new-found Yvonne rather inexplicably sitting between them); Daphne, Albert and Milo were on the front bench just behind them but facing backwards; and Jack and Amelie were on the last bench of all, in a position to look forward over the whole group and make sure everyone was safe. Some passengers remarked what a beautiful couple they made; Jack preened, and Amelie pretended not to hear.

After some minutes of fiddling and fussing with a check of the controls, Georges started the engine. It whimpered so feebly that the passengers giggled nervously and shuffled in their seats. Could that frail-sounding antique really drive a coach of this size? Was there going to be another manic chapter in this day of strange incidents? Thus far the Experience has taken them to places of romance and adventure, where charm, excitement and nostalgia have thoroughly transcended practicality, comfort and security. Now everyone is glowing, but tired; if there was to be a choice offered at this point, to sacrifice further quaintness and eccentricity in order to achieve a boring, uneventful journey to the farm carpark, I believe the cry would go up for dullness please. But the die is cast already, and the bus starts.

Guinevere edged forward, swinging very slowly around the turning circle in the carpark in order to point towards the long road sweeping down the hill to the exit. Of course, as is so traditional in coach departures as to be absolutely compulsory, everyone in the charabanc waved to everyone they were leaving behind – the musicians, the caterers, the waiters, the jugglers, magicians, Julie's crew, and cleaners just arriving who have seen nothing of the entertainments. "Goodbye, goodbye," they waved, and called, "Thank you for everything, for a wonderful day, and I am sorry you are not coming with us, but you will be our friends forever." The sky was striped red and grey, quite beautiful, with the tall surrounding trees in silhouette, everything utterly still and soundless except the pathetic whining of the coach engine and the evening birds flying solely and in groups from tree to tree, demeaned to be disturbed by the pitifully delicate motor.

Georges seemed to be in a fugue state, eyes blank and locked at some point several kilometres in the distance. Milo looked at Henry questioningly and Henry looked back with a thumbs up motion indicating, 'perfectly normal, he's in the zone, always like this when he's driving, all the greats go inside to a special place to practise their craft.' Slowly very slowly under Georges's somnambulant navigation, Guinevere crept to the end of the carpark and left the level, edging herself onto the gentle slope beyond. Almost immediately she picked up speed; 'That's quite quick,' Daphne thought, given how much more precipitous the incline would become over the next five hundred metres.

Others sensed it. Bottoms tensed up and down the benches, and hands reached out to clutch neighbouring wrists. Tommy tried to lighten the mood by playing the chase music from the Keystone Cops, and a few hardy souls laughed along with him. Young Henry, who, on closer observation, Daphne decided, was a particularly small seventeen rather than a mature-looking thirteen, reached for the manual brake with the agonising sluggishness inherent in his family genes, and languidly began to apply power. Nothing much happened, to be honest. Daphne was about to jump over and offer assistance (for which read: take over the stick and use it) when to her relief the Yvonne, sensing the risk, added her hands and weight to the lever and tugged on it with the arm-strength of a veteran miner. Consequently Henry, inspired by a desire to a) show off to the girl and b) not be humiliated by his putative sweetheart in front of everyone else, redoubled his efforts. His strength, honestly speaking, even on a very good day, was only equal to half a miner (if that is the unit of powerfulness we are employing), but at least the brake now had two willing bodies pulling on it; with some grating and even a few cartoon-style sparks, it progressively began to fulfil its function, and Guinevere began to decelerate reassuringly. Henry looked up at Yvonne, and Yvonne looked back at him, and fate determined at that very moment that they would be together for the rest of their lives. Which could of course be either a handful of seconds, or six romantic decades, depending on whether they can get the brake to work.

"My name is not Yvonne," she whispered.

"That's good," he replied, not having the vaguest idea what she meant. "My name is not Curt. Is the idea we keep guessing?"

"Can we do this later?" Daphne asked. "If you two don't concentrate we will all die in around four hundred metres time. Do you need more hands?"

"We're OK," said was-Yvonne, "my Gran told me there is no job of any value that cannot be managed by four hands in unison."

"Was she in a three-ton steel trap hurtling out of control down one of the steepest hills in Central France while she said that? If not, I think context can be important for some of those old sayings."

The speed gradually picked up again. Georges had had his leg extended pressing hard down on the foot brake since they had left level ground, there was nothing more to give there, so he was out of the game. Daphne decided she could no longer remain patient and delegate her future to two sweet, distracted kids flirting moonily over the sole means of preserving life, so she rolled over the barrier onto the driver's bench and threw her extra weight onto the brake shaft. That made three miners in total (if you are following the collier-based maths), because she was not messing around. Guinevere slowed significantly. The mood of the whole bus lightened for a moment, and a huge collective sigh of relief was exhaled by the passengers, but it wasn't to be the last of the rollercoaster.

In front of them the slope got steeper and stretched out and down through the gate out of Hill House till it reached a junction at which it was generally thought preferable to halt before turning onto the public highway. They were currently within the last two hundred and fifty metres before the gate, where the incline was steepest, and the charabanc was again accelerating at a rate that first worried the passengers and then the actors; only the drivers seemed to remain oblivious. Daphne dug an elbow into Georges, pretending it was accidentally caused by her efforts on the stick, and managed to rouse him from his intense performance-enhancing reverie.

"What's going on Georges, are we all right?"

Georges blinked as though he was shaking himself from a healthy sleep, perhaps dreaming of days out with Genevieve long ago, behind the horses. Where were the horses now? Not to worry. "It will be OK," he told her, through lips flattened by the onrushing wall of wind.

Daphne was unconvinced, especially as Georges looked suspiciously as though he was fumbling for a non-existent buggy-whip; she prompted him for a little more detail. He answered grumpily, because she was wasting his time, it was all too obvious.

"We can steer the bus and hold the line till the road evens out, no worry, we're not out of control. We just have to hope there is nothing on the public road when we join it, because we won't be able to stop and check for traffic."

"Jesus, Georges," Daphne shouted as loudly as she could in a virtually inaudible stage whisper, trying not to panic the passengers, "your definition of 'not out of control' is a little broader than mine. Generally I like to think the definition of 'in control' would be that there is more than a fifty-fifty chance of avoiding a fatal crash at a minor intersection."

"I'm not enjoying that tone, young lady," Georges coughed out waspishly, "remember I am doing you a favour here, I can just as easily take the bus and leave if you're not a hundred percent happy with the service."

Daphne, Albert and Milo looked at Georges with what started as a confusion and turned into strangled mirth when they realised the pointlessness of the threat. Milo mouthed silently to the others: "Don't walk off the job now, Georges, or we'll all be screwed."

Henry had been watching this, feeling slightly impotent as the weakest man on the brake. He was increasingly annoyed with the 'act-tors' as they wasted time teasing and blaming his grandpa. "Pointing fingers and doing sarky banter is not actually helping us, you know," he said, quite grown-up, "maybe you would be better pulling a bit harder on the stick, looking after the passengers, and letting Georges concentrate on saving us."

Milo felt a pang of guilt immediately. "You're right, Henry, I apologise." He leapt the barrier himself and became fourth man on the shaft, hands right at the top for maximum leverage, legs coiled and feet locked against the back of the banquette: his focused, directed, whole-body force made an immediate impact. "Nice thrust," whispered Daphne. "Thank you, Ma'am," Milo sniggered, before wilting under a withering gaze from Henry. "Jesus," Henry sneered, "can you guys not see we're in danger? A fancy quip isn't the answer to everything."

'Fancy quips,' Milo thought, but did not say, 'do not save ships.'

The charabanc was now less than a hundred metres away from the gate. They had passed the very steepest part of the drive, but they were still careering at a troubling speed. The passengers were uniformly braced for impact, screaming like fairground riders, alternating from hands in the wind above their heads to eyes peeking between crossed fingers. But Georges was looking cool. After seventy years of driving, the more sophisticated vehicle handling skills may have deserted him, actually some time ago, but his aim was still true. Form is fleeting, class is timeless.

He had never had a moment's doubt he would navigate the quite narrow gate at extremely high speed without clipping the brickwork on either side. His anxiety lay sixty metres further on, because he knew at this point there was no way they could halt the bus at the junction with the public road, they were going straight onto the highway, not even looking right and left, there being no point.

So for drama: I would like to turn your attention to a beautifully decorated horse-drawn hay wain (actually one of those eschewed by Jean) which was trotting down the road close by. It was piled high with children from the local orphanage, wearing plaid shirts, colourful scarves tied cowboy-style around their necks, the odd Stetson, playing the ukulele and harmoniously singing "The Surrey with the Fringe on Top" as they returned home from a perfect picnic paid for by a very generous local philanthropist, their best and only annual outing. Luckily, this cartload of parentless five-to-twelve-year-olds was fifty seconds away, and they would only see the dust on the horizon as the monstrous coach careered onto the highway without so much as slowing down. Drama! No Drama! That is the way fate works.

And how about, from the other direction, four very grand lady friends who were proceeding at a sensible speed on the road that passes by Hill House in their fabulously luxurious nearly-thirty-year-old future-classic Talbot-Lago T23 Four-Litre Baby Cabriolet, making their way home from a day out visiting ornamental gardens, languorously lunching, calling on a dear friend for tea, and generally enjoying the open top and the cool breeze blowing through their hair on a warm day. Yes, older people like that too, and the ladies were certainly that. They had owned the car for three decades with never a scratch; in fact, thirty years without even coming within half a metre of another vehicle or a static obstacle of any kind. Had they been two hundred metres closer, just a few seconds nearer to the junction when Georges came hurtling out onto the road across the whole carriageway without stopping, on two wheels for long moments leaning at an unfeasible angle that felt like it would never come back to the horizontal, careering madly on both sides of the road towards them, then there would have been a head-on collision, and not only the four ladies but also seventeen passengers on the charabanc would have been killed – including Milo and Daphne – with the rest all variously injured; from cuts, scrapes, grazes and bruises, to three amputations and one unlucky soul trapped in a coma for four years.

But it didn't happen. By fate, these ladies saw from just the right distance the runaway bus swing wildly round the turn and swerve madly back and forth across the highway as it sped towards them; they braked as quickly as they could – quality, well-maintained mechanism – and as they slowed they pulled over to the side, just in time. While they screamed and threw their hands over their eyes Georges finally wrestled the wheel of Guinevere straight, pulled her back onto the appropriate side of the highway for someone moving in their direction of travel and missed the apprehensive gentlewomen at what he considered to be a rather comfortable margin. Again Drama. Again Destiny! This might have unexpectedly been the last page of the book, but we go on…

Instead of tragedy, we have had great good fortune; so much so that it went completely unnoticed by the Meaulnes Experience customers. They all went "Woosh" as they went through the gate; "Weeeee" when they raced round the corner and across the junction on two wheels; and "Wowww" when they fell back shudderingly on all four tyres; just as if it was part of the entertainment, another exciting exploit on this crazy marvellous day. Georges looked so cool at the wheel throughout the incident that everyone behind him believed he was in total control of affairs rather than comprehending that he had retreated into a self-protective trance and had been blissfully in denial about the extent of their peril.

Leaving the Talbot-Lago T23 Four-Litre Baby Cabriolet and the four magnificent ladies quivering in her rear-view mirror, Guinevere now eased down a gentler incline that continued for a full kilometre of straight highway and finally reached the flat part of their journey, the road here parallel to and around thirty metres from the river. Improvising, Tommy had gone quickly into Je Ne Regrette Rien, which helped everyone release their held breath, and they began laughing, chattering and slapping each other on the back. What larks! The song had a particular significance at that moment for Daphne, who a few seconds before was sure she had killed them all.

The bus slowed steadily, to the extent, finally, that her engine actually had to do some work to pull her along, which was not its favoured function, frankly speaking. They chugged, they stuttered, they virtually ground to a halt, but Georges summoned all his skills and experience and kept her going till they reached the ninety-degree angle at the river crossing. Turning left sharply, losing the speed they had, they rolled up, and nearly over, the little humpbacked bridge, and there, naturally, they became wedged halfway; so the front end of the charabanc attained the side of the river they were eager to reach, while the back end remained stubbornly on the side they were hoping to leave.

Quick-minded as ever, Jack shouted: "We're stopping here for a moment for photographs. See the sunset and the magical light over Hill House; make a souvenir for you and your family of this enchanted moment." And indeed, many went to their bags for cameras, as it certainly was a gorgeous and seldom captured view.

Daphne and Georges were whispering with Milo and Henry. Georges had a short temper for such a slow man, but was equally quick to forgive and forget, helped by the immense shared emotional relief of them all being still alive. He was back in treasured gramps persona, and Henry, who always took his lead from him, was similarly mollified.

"Don't worry, my dear," Georges was saying, "we'll soon sort this out, I wouldn't let my favourite girl down. Henry here can run to Jerome's farm" [he pointed somewhat vaguely with a moving finger that scanned the compass horizontally from south-by-south-west to east-by-south-east with a vacillating vertical trajectory indicating anything between fifteen metres and four or five kilometres] "and get him to come with his tractor and pull us off."

"Push us off, Grandpa;" corrected Henry, "he'll be coming from this direction, so he won't be able to get across the bridge to pull us."

Georges entered a reverie during which his mind set off by tractor from Jerome's farm and slowly drove down a series of backroads before finally arriving at the rear of the charabanc. After about ninety seconds he arrived, saying, "Quite right, Henry, back end it is. That's not as good for the coachwork, if he's pushing, we'll need to get some fenders, do you think the boatyard might have something we can use?"

Milo suddenly realised there was a burning pain growing in his upper arm and glanced down to see it was Daphne's hand clutching him more and more tightly, her grasping fingers cutting off the blood and nails breaking the skin. Raising his gaze to her face to ask her perhaps to ease off, he saw her lips were white as she bit them to stop herself screaming. She had been a hero of the day, saving it in a dozen ways, now he needed to intervene in timely fashion to stop her final contribution to the Grand Meaulnes opening day being the spontaneous slaughter of two generations of the region's premier charabanc dynasty.

"OK," he said, briskly, in his clipped junior officer tone, designed to diffuse tension and brook no denial when ordering troops into the line of fire, "sorry, Georges, we don't have time to wait for the forthcoming farmer in the faraway tractor or for the collection of bulwarks; the passengers have been through a lot today, their cars are parked a hundred metres over there, and we want to get them off home. What I am going to do, of course with your agreement, is evacuate the bus by helping everyone over the benches and out the front."

So saying, and rhetorically assuming the approval, he signalled to Jack and Amelie at the back to start moving the customers forward, and Albert and Daphne began to help the closer guests over the benches. Along the length of the sides of the charabanc the low walls of the bridge were still too high, and the bus wedged too tight, to allow the passengers to open the doors and exit. But at the very front the doors on both sides were clear of obstruction and could be thrown wide, so if they could get them that far it was simple for everyone to disembark very comfortably on the destination bank of the river.

Daphne called out: "Sorry, everyone, we can't get the bus started, but as you can see over yonder" [she pointed to Jean's farm gate, with the last rays of setting sunlight picking out **Bienvenue * Welcome * Willkommen**], "we are just a few metres from the carpark, and it is a mild and pleasant evening, so we end with a gentle clamber and a short harmonious walk before we reluctantly disperse and depart this day forever."

The passengers, by now quite reconciled to the madness of the event, and largely unaware how close they had come to life-threatening injury in the past fifteen minutes, accepted yet further strangeness in perfect part, and climbed up and down over the benches like young recruits on an obstacle course; the young aiding the older, the humans assisting the pets. Special attention was paid to Madame Seurel and Poupet, who might as well have been in a litter, given the way the two of them together were passed reverentially above the seats from hand to hand.

What could happen next, the guests wondered, in the short stroll to the cars? Would a dragon swoop down and snatch a toddler, or painted elephants appear to carry them to La Chapelle in cushioned hathi howdahs? None of the above. But in terms of additional jeopardy Daphne thought she saw a figure in the shadows of the carpark, in the outer radius of her vision; a red flash indicating the drag on a cigarette, the shape looking like Jean's sister Caroline. In this context a sinister-enough apparition for her; it could only be bad news, she might prefer the dragon after all.

While thinking these thoughts she had mindlessly been receiving and passing on customers one by one, till finally everyone was out who was getting out. That left only Georges, Henry and the Yvonne who had yet to disclose her name still on the bus. The Yvonne had come with a group of friends, and was happily waving goodbye to them calling, "I will stay with Henry for now, see you later, don't worry." They looked sceptical, and unsure what to do. "Do not worry, *mes amis*," not-Yvonne sang out laughing joyfully, waving her arms in the air, extending them as high as they could reach, spinning in front of them, once, twice, before incanting her entire Yvonne phrase book in a single burst, like an impetuous tourist.

"We're two children. We've been foolish. Farewell, don't follow me!"

Then she and Henry turned as though a starting pistol had fired for life; like Olympic steeplechasers they hurdled the benches one by one in reverse aiming for the back of the charabanc, which was still lodged on the approach side of the river, where there was an open door, right at the end. They reached it and exited in a single leap before jogging off up one of the many different paths that Georges had indicated were the best route to Jerome's place.

[Though Georges in the interim had changed his mind: he shouted after them in an urgent voice so creaky Daphne could hardly hear it from five metres away: "Not that way, youngsters, that's completely wrong, you're heading for Victor's, he won't lend you a bloody thing."]

By now, the first customers had wandered back to the carpark and Hut, and Albert and Amelie were marshalling them into a loose chattering group rather than allowing them to get into their cars. As the others caught up, and everyone now congregated, Daphne hailed everyone, cheerfully:

"I hope you have had a wonderful experience today, and I thank you for being such an extraordinary audience, such amazing comrades – we started the day as strangers, but I believe we end it as friends."

Daphne stopped as some clapping started, and it grew into applause with shouts and general calls of appreciation and *bonhomie*. Looking over the crowd, she saw the figure in the half-dark was indeed Caroline, who was coming towards her now, making the global gestures for 'Wind it up' (hand cranking motion); and 'Get on with it I need to talk to you quickly' (razor hand across the throat, naked sock puppet yapping hand). Daphne gave her a 'Sorry, just a minute' sign, and went on with her speech, at increasing speed.

"And now, before we part, we have one more duty and one more pleasure."

As she spoke, she fished out the key round her neck and undid the padlock.

"The duty is to kindly please collect your outfits and accessories; you just need, if you would, to drop them in these laundry bins and we will sort them out later – the hut is open for anyone who needs a little privacy behind the curtain.

"And then the last delight of the day is to make our award for the best character, the best member of our party. It is just a bit of fun really, but the prize is worth having – it is a free ticket to come again whenever you want."

Everyone cheered again – who doesn't like a competition?

Meanwhile Caroline had now actually joined the customer crowd, at the back of their excited circle, jumping up and down and making more and more urgent gestures to Daphne. "Hold on just one more minute, I promise we're nearly there," Daphne signalled back (palms up in surrender facing outwards; head rocked back and forth between them).

Speeding up, she went into a huddle with Milo, Jack, Amelie, and Albert to discuss the contenders, and, showing fairness and a proper intensity of adjudication, they looked up and around quite a few times to indicate the wide range of candidates and the breadth of their deliberations, before finally breaking out, all with the expression indicating "This has been the hardest decision of my life, without question."

"And the winner is, I guess actually it is a joint first place, which we have never done before" [small laughter, but genuine] "Madame Seurel and Poupet!! Or should I say, Madame Malpense with Dougal."

I think everyone in the circle knew that this result had been greatly influenced by a desire to make up for the attack on Dougal although it would be cynical to suggest the team hoped it might help to diminish the likelihood of a reckoning or retribution later. But generously, except for the vainest of the Franzs, who had bought his own pair of period gloves with him especially, everyone cheered with a vigorous Hip Hip Hooray; and for her part Madame Malpense certainly gave the impression that she considered the award was well earned and completely justified. She revelled in the applause and simpered appropriately when Daphne reached deep in her bag and pulled out the free entrance pass. Everyone made yet another even louder Three Cheers before applauding generally once more – the day, their companions, themselves – and continuing to clap as they helped Albert, Jack and Amelie put their costumes and accessories into the baskets and gradually drifted apart, chattering their goodbyes, exchanging details, "We'll meet again," "You made my day."

Now Daphne could at last focus on Caroline. In fact she could ignore her no more, given Caroline had grasped her by the collar of her blazer and was dragging her into the limes. Milo was dragged too, as he clung to Daphne's side (a position, she realised while choking, he had increasingly been adopting as his own) and she grabbed him by the wrist for support.

"What's up, Caro?" asked Daphne, finally able to look properly into Caroline's eyes as they crashed into one another and the trees and knowing immediately something serious was about to happen. Caro nodded toward Milo with a question mark; she had seen him at the Lodge but never spoken to him. "It's OK, it's Milo, he's one of us."

"Jean's been stabbed, Daphne, it's really bad.

"I tried to call you at Hill House but you'd left so I shot over here to intercept you. I got called to the hospital an hour ago by your dad, he's still with him."

"Jesus, Caro, what happened? How bad is really bad, he's not dying?"

"It is that bad, kid. Claude wanted me to tell you personally so you can inform the boys, especially his cousin. I'm going to take you to the hospital right away."

"I'll take you, Caroline, it will be a lot quicker. Give me one minute and your car keys."

Daphne and Milo went over to the clothes bins, where Jack, Amelie

479

and Albert were working; Jack immediately knew something was wrong by their tense walk and avoidance of eye contact till they were a metre from his face.

"Is it Jean and Claude? What's happening?"

"Jean's at the hospital, Jack," said Daphne, "he's been attacked. My dad's OK as far as I know. I don't have any more information than that yet. You and Milo go and get in my car, I'll lock up. Wait, give me your blazers first, we'll leave them in the bins to be cleaned, all of us." Amelie and Albert added theirs to the top of the pile. "I hate to think what's happened to Jean and Claude's," Daphne continued, a little in shock, "but frankly that is the least of our worries.

"Amelie, Albert, please leave the clothes bins outside the Hut here when you close up. Here's the key, please bring it back for me to the Lodge. Jean has arranged for a cleaning team to come and collect the laundry bins and they'll wash and press everything overnight before tomorrow's customers come in the morning." [Milo said to himself, stupidly, 'He thinks of everything, all these details, even when he's in hospital.']

"Thanks so much for everything today, you've been brilliant. I would like you to take Caroline's car when you finish, here are the keys. Please head back to the Lodge and leave the car in the drive with the keys in. Get yourselves some food and rest, I'll call when I have information."

The siblings nodded anxiously, worried about all kinds of things, but mainly concerned with not slowing Daphne down.

"No problem, we'll handle it. See you later – please give our love to Jean and Claude, I hope it is all OK." A clumsy ending, but there is no easy etiquette for those 'I'm sorry your friend got stabbed' moments.

Daphne ran over to her car, Caroline was in the passenger seat, Jack and Milo in the back. She started it and shot off from a standing start at forty kilometres an hour, screeching shamefully around the line of customers' vehicles that were still waiting in a queue to exit onto the road. The four of them in the car involuntarily covered their faces and heads with sweater, bag, jacket and hand, in an embarrassed attempt to prevent the clients from recognising that the queue-jumpers were their erstwhile guides, the ever-courteous employees of the Experience.

Once they hit the road, Daphne floored the accelerator flatter than ever before, and they quickly hit maximum speed. Sadly that was only around a hundred and twenty kilometres per hour in her motor, but they might never have made it alive if she could have gone faster. The hospital, even at that rate, was about fifteen minutes off. "Tell us exactly what happened, Caro, what did dad tell you?"

Caroline made a sign to Daphne that perhaps she shouldn't talk in front of the lads in the back seat. It wasn't one of the advanced-level symbols, more of a generic 'hands in front of face palms outwards tiny waves' that can mean anything from 'Not now' to 'Get out quickly before he sees you' or 'There's an awful lot of smoke in here, can I open a window?' In any case, potential translations were irrelevant, because Daphne had her eyes in the headlights watching the road and was not looking sideways.

Caroline tried again, her tone intended as a verbal clue, "Shall we talk at the hospital when we have more time?" spoken in a heavy tempo designed to send out subtle signals for silence. But Daphne had her mind elsewhere and was not prepared for subtlety, again missing the cue. "We've got ten minutes, Caro, come on, we need the information before we get there so we at least have a clue what to do."

"She wants you to shut up," chipped in Milo from the back.

"She has something to tell you that she doesn't want us to hear," Jack joined in. "Please just tell us, Caroline, is Jean dead?"

"No, no, no boys, not dead, honestly. He's badly injured, but I promise when I left the hospital, what, about forty-five minutes ago, he was breathing. It is serious, though."

"So what happened? How can it hurt to tell us?" asked Milo.

"They're not kids, Caro, whatever it is, they are going to find out some time, so you might as well share."

"OK if you say...." But she did pause, still not sure this was the right way. Then...

"Your dad stabbed him, Jack."

"Christ, Caro, you shouldn't..." Daphne started, then stopped, on the basis it had been her own idea. "Sorry... and sorry Jack, so sorry. Jesus, what the hell is going on around here?"

Jack was in shock. "How would that happen. Why? What has my dad got to do with anything, no-one has seen him for months and then he pops up to stab the man who saved his life?"

"Claude says he was the man in the river when you were on the boat, the man who fought the swan."

"Oh God," said Milo, "that was it – I could tell Jean and Claude suspected something when they let us off and went straight back down the river."

Caroline went on, "Claude wasn't surprised you didn't recognise Mac; he's changed so much. When I saw him myself half a year ago I didn't know who it was till Claude said, and even then I didn't know whether I believed him or not. You know, Jack, he's not been well at all, he's not what you remember."

"But how did he stab Jean? Why?"

"They went back in the boat, they would have had to go anyway, whoever it was who went in the river; but they were pretty certain it was Mac. They were going to make sure he'd got out of the river OK and also to see if the swan was all right and they hadn't killed each other. When they got level with the swan's nest they tied up and got onto the shore. They found Mac having a fit, he was tearing up the bird. He'd either drowned it when they were fighting in the water, or strangled it on the shore, and now he was butchering it with his knife.

"Claude said they both approached him, trying to calm him down. It seemed like Mac thought they would be pleased he'd killed the swan, so he was confused when he could see they were scared and horrified. Claude says that the ground on the riverbank was treacherous, and as they approached, Jean slipped in the guts and mud and stumbled towards Mac. Mac panicked and put his hands out in front of him, but the knife was still in his hand. Mac went to push him off, and the knife hit Jean below the throat and went in his chest as he was falling. Then Claude got between them and tried to hold Jean up, it sounds to me like he had to push Mac away though it was confused because he got quite a few injuries from the knife himself on his hands and arms. Anyway, Mac staggered back, and then ran. Claude couldn't follow, he had to tend to Jean.

"Claude couldn't get Jean back on the boat by himself so he just hauled him up onto his back like a coal sack and jogged up the bank till he got tired, then walked, then staggered by the sound of it, till they got to the farm, and Jean's car."

"He's strong," said Daphne, loving her dad.

"Luckily."

They were pulling into the hospital carpark. Jack and Milo had been silent in the back, traumatised, and if it hadn't been pitch black by now Daphne and Caroline would have seen just how white they'd turned. This, coming on top of everything; more knives, an attack on someone they loved. Both of the boys were trying to work out a way to be to blame, especially Jack.

483

The lads tipped out of the car, only a two-door model, so stumbling slightly as they emerged into the carpark, and rather unsteady. Daphne caught one, and Caroline the other, maybe because they were older, a bit more experienced at pain and fear, they were calmer and firmer. In two pairs they walked slowly to the door and into the hospital foyer. A tall nurse behind the reception desk recognised Daphne straight away from school; waved nervously; and ran round to give her a hug first, then Caroline. Daphne panicked because she couldn't remember her name, but it appeared they had been great friends.

"No change, don't look so worried, nothing has changed. Doctor says Jean is pretty stable at the moment. He's got a nurse in his room at all times, as well as your dad, Daphne, who won't leave his side as you know, he's there now."

"Did the Doctor say what he thinks is going to happen?" The question came from Jack, who couldn't contain his anxiety or restrain his need to be involved. The nurse didn't know Jack and looked at Caroline for approval to talk to him. She nodded "Yes."

"Doctor doesn't like guesses, but I heard him talk to Senior, and he said it's 70-30."

"In favour, or against?" Milo asked, panicking.

"That I didn't hear, sorry."

Jack was about to comment on the rather useless, very possibly misleading, and horribly frightening nature of this imprecisely overheard statistical information when Caroline squeezed his arm, shaking her head; they all made their polite thanks instead. The nurse was trying to be helpful, and they definitely needed to have as many friends on their side as possible.

"Can we see him?" asked Caroline.

"Family can go in, but quietly, one at a time, and please don't wake him or expect him to talk. Claude will need to come out first as I really do need to make sure Jean is not disturbed. And please, only five minutes each. Come with me, and I will take you round to him."

When they got to the room the nurse padded quietly in in her soft-soled pumps. Claude was beside the bed in which Jean was laid flat, standing over him like a carved knight guarding an ancient tomb. As the nurse whispered to him, he turned his head to see Daphne at the door and came out to embrace her intensely. He looked grey and drawn, ten years older, and both his forearms were swathed in fresh bandages between elbow and wrist, with the left hand also bound, across the palm and around the thumb.

He waved to all the visitors, relieved to see everyone and to be able to end his solitary vigil for a while. As he said later, "It was exhausting having to keep Jean alive by myself." Claude looked guiltily at Caroline, apologetic. He was also taking the blame: he couldn't quite work out why he felt culpable, and nor could she – maybe just the normal regret that his friend got more stabbed than him.

"What's the latest, dad? The nurse said stable but seemed a bit confused about the prognosis."

"The Doctor has just been in. He treats me like an idiot – probably correctly – like all medical men he assumes we can't understand the most basic descriptions and explanations so there is an awful lot I can't get out of him. He won't be pinned down on percentages with me, but he did say Jean is 'stable,' as you heard, and if he stays stable like this till tomorrow morning his chances are positive. So it seems the risk is all about the next five or six hours.

"He said, I think, that they don't want to open him up if they don't have to because there is a strong danger that would just make things worse, so they are currently watching closely and waiting. They've been testing everything, he's not bleeding inside that they can see, and they are assuming on the basis of what they're observing that the knife missed the organs and arteries, as far as

I understand him. So, 'all his vital signs are satisfactory,' to quote him, and the things they are looking out for are changes to blood pressure, breathing, pulse. As you can see, he's hooked up with half a dozen tubes, and there is a nurse around the room the whole time, and the Doctor has agreed under a bit of persuasion to sleep in the hospital tonight."

"Thanks, Claude," said Caroline, "you're a bloody hero. I'll take a shift now for a couple of hours, I have spoken to mum, and she's coming soon, and my uncle, I reckon there will be five or six family here before long. Daff, I'll get one of my uncles to drive me over to the Lodge when I'm leaving, to pick up the car – can you make sure they've left the keys in when you get back, and I won't disturb you.

"Claude, you take a break with the guys and get some coffee and something to eat and some sleep if you can. Jean needs you all to keep the Experience going, you can't do the official opening tomorrow if any of us fall apart now. Call me in a few hours, if you can get through the receptionist here, and I can keep you up to date."

"Come on, dad," said Daphne, "Let's try the café out front. We can get a brandy to go with the coffee if you like and have a smoke."

Caroline went in to take over from Claude, deciding on a chair by Jean's side rather than standing. Her brother looked terrifying, tightly wrapped in crisp white sheets up to his waist, and with pipes and tubes in his chest, mouth and nose. His face was the same colour as the sheets and the walls of the room – Caroline was looking at the world in monochrome, not even the blood was red. She settled down to her watch.

Outside the others walked back through the hospital carpark and crossed the road to the little café. It was small and intimate, and most seats and stools inside were either occupied or too close together, so Daphne suggested they should stay outside and sit at a large table on its own, where they could speak freely. A waiter came out, Herve, known to Claude, of course, so five minutes were spent discussing his bandages, which they now discovered to their surprise were the result of Claude having spilt a pot of boiling coffee. "You know what they're like when they get to his age, Herve," Daphne said with a wink.

He took their orders, it was easy, the same for everyone – brandy, coffee, bread, omelette – and went back inside, whereupon they lit orchestrated cigarettes: flip pack; remove fag; strike match; light end; big draw; long exhale. If synchronized smoking ever becomes an Olympic sport, we're seeing a podium performance right there.

"Tell us what happened, dad. We had a version from Caro, so weird – obviously Jack's terrified about his dad too."

"I will, but quickly, tell me, how did the day go? Honestly, it was all Jean could mumble when he was on my back, rambling about the Experience and would it be OK?"

"It was great, dad, we did Jean proud, and you. Everything was perfect except the swan and the dog. The food was wonderful, the music was incredible, the play was fabulous – if I say so myself, having been promoted suddenly to a starring role."

"You did Harlequin?" He almost smiled before remembering where they were.

"I did indeed do Harlequin, in a way I think we can agree he has never been done before.

"Obviously the antiquated coach you ordered came within seconds of killing us all and got wedged in the bridge, so thanks for that, but presumably we're not making the Ride Of Death a regular feature. The customers went away truly buzzing; Jean has got a massive hit on his hands. Now your turn please."

"Well first," Claude said when he got going, "did Caroline tell you who it was?" He looked so hard at Daphne to avoid looking at Jack that even if the boys hadn't already known who it was they would have immediately guessed.

"Yes, dad, we know that bit, you can tell us the whole story, Jack's been warned."

"OK, well when the swan took the dog and the figure went in from the bank, Jean and I both suspected it was Mac, but we'd drifted past the scene of the fight before we could be sure. He's changed so much, but at least we'd seen him since, which the rest of you hadn't. Mac's not the man he was – sorry, Jack – he's let his health go, he doesn't eat properly, his hair is grey now, though there is still plenty of it. He's still a mighty scrapper, mind you, so I wasn't surprised when we saw him on top of the bird, but it didn't shock me either when the swan fought back. I really wanted to help him but we were too late, we couldn't stop and we couldn't turn round. That's why we dropped you all off, then went back as quickly as we could. When we got there, there was nothing in the water, so we managed to pull in and park the barge by the swan's nest. We tied it up the best we could to the trees, thinking we wouldn't be there too long. Daff, you'll need to find it in the morning, it's about midway between the two jetties.

"So then we went onto the bank, Caro probably told you this bit, right? But maybe not quite how awful it was."

At that point Herve reappeared with the drinks, so Claude resorted to a couple of deep puffs to pause the tale while the eager waiter emptied his tray and organised the coffees and glasses, leaving the whole bottle of brandy for them in respect and recognition of Claude's reputation and out of regard for the pain he must be experiencing with those kettle-related injuries.

"For some reason Mac was just tearing the bird to bits all over," Claude went on when the waiter was back inside. "He was covered in blood, and the blood on him was flecked with the swan down and feathers. When we got onto the bank, he was holding a wing in one hand and the head in the other. It was truly hellish."

Claude at that point became aware that the sharp clip clip clipping on his shin, which had he suddenly realised had been going on for some time, was Daphne kicking him under the table. Looking up from his story, through the brandy glass, he finally caught her eye. She was frantically signalling to him to shut up, nodding towards Jack, who was sitting with his forehead on the table and his hands in his hair, shivering.

"Jean tried to go to Mac and help him," Claude went on, but talking to Jack now, and gently. "I was too shocked, but Jean just wanted to stop him and hold him, I think. Mac panicked and held his hands out in front of him, but the knife was still in his hand, and then Jean was falling."

[Milo noted he was using the same phrases he had used when he told the story to Caroline, like he'd been rehearsing a version he liked in his mind and was sticking to it.]

"I don't really know for sure how the injuries happened, it almost looked like Mac reached out to catch Jean and the knife was in his hand. Then I got between them and tried to hold Jean up, and I think Mac was trying to help, but the knife was still there, and that's how these happened."

He held up his forearms and revolved them one hundred and eighty degrees, as though to exhibit the full extent of the hidden wounds.

Daphne and Milo had exchanged quizzical looks during the last part of the narrative, both believing Claude was refining the narrative, or at least putting the best possible light on it, because it felt intentional that it was sounding vague. 'I wonder if he's going to say "True Story,"' thought Milo.

Claude, sensing their suspicions, lit another cigarette as he finished speaking, though his previous smoke was only about halfway down. He was relieved to have stopped; he was contented enough with the picture he had created; and in any case he was so tired he was almost past caring. He would have liked to lie down for an hour, perhaps a little more. As his match flared the light flooded up brown and black into his madly coloured face, then strangely turned into blue, a tone even Daphne had never seen on her dad, and she looked around to see where that could be coming from. She saw a police car was pulling into the hospital with its lights flashing, blue lamps revolving on its roof, sending alternating waves of indigo, cobalt, ultramarine around a wide radius. Jack had a moment's fear and looked at Milo, who was already looking back at him. The colours and the flashing reminded them where and when it happened and the thing they were running from. More knives.

So suddenly, seemingly for no reason, the four of them were up and walking away, Daphne barely remembering to leave a twenty-franc note before they were round the corner. They got about thirty metres up the back road before she said, "Hang on, what are we doing? Have we done something wrong?"

"The hospital automatically has to call the police if there is a knife wound or gunshot," said Claude, who was shaking his head, and sounding very groggy now. "I don't know why they need the lights and kerfuffle. It's typical for this lot, after an emergency call they hang around in the police station for an hour picking their noses and then rush to the scene at top speed with the lights and sirens going."

"Sweet talk, dad, one of those looked like your nephew, I'll tell him how much you appreciate his work. Anyway, does that explain why we are flitting off into the night?"

"We're not talking to them, I'm not anyway. And I am the only witness. Jean will probably forget I was there, and he won't remember anything whether…" Claude's speech was slurring now, he wasn't going to cease talking but he was certainly going to stop making sense quite soon.

"Jack and Milo definitely do not want to get involved, or me, and you don't know anything unless I do… really we would be useless unless we accidentally misdirect them ...... we could start a wild goose chase... but we all know the swan did it."

He was sort of chuckling, but rather hysterically; Daphne couldn't decide whether it was the shock, the painkillers, the exhaustion, or the three large glasses of brandy taken quickly on an empty stomach that were knocking him out. Probably a combination of the four. She was worried, and her first thought was to get him home and in bed, not to take him back into the hospital, and definitely not to go on the run.

The three cops had strolled inside now, without a glance around, so the scene was clear. Daphne signalled the team (leader style, keeping her back to them, right arm up and rotating like a one-armed man doing front crawl) to follow her. They broke cover and made their way to the two cars walking so exceedingly normally that anyone watching would have known immediately they were guilty of something. Milo and Jack were directed silently to Daphne's car and Daphne and Claude headed to the van next to it, which Claude had driven to the hospital as an ambulance for Jean. Daphne whispered, "Meet you at the Lodge, I reckon it is best to make dad safe and comfortable there tonight."

Milo drove and he and Jack arrived at the Lodge fifteen minutes later; Daphne had checked the keys were in Caro's car and was now finishing a cigarette standing in the driveway with Claude sitting in the passenger seat of the van with the door open and his legs out. Albert and Amelie had come out to greet them, looking anxious, relieved to see Claude, but shaken by the sight of his bandages.

"Where's Jean?" Amelie asked.

"He's in the hospital," Jack replied, solicitous as ever with Amelie and wanting to be the one to inform her. "He's hurt badly, but stable now, the next few hours are critical, but it is looking better all the time." Where he got the last bit, Daphne was not sure, but a positive spin was not the worst thing at the moment to keep morale up.

"Have you eaten?" asked Albert. They were about to say they had, when they suddenly realised they hadn't – they'd scuttled off before the omelettes had arrived. "No worries," Albert said, "I've got baguette and cheese and eggs, I'll get the coffee on, and sort it out." Everyone looked at everyone – good old Albert! Here was a boy who was growing up in dog weeks.

They all went through the house to the kitchen, with Daphne and Milo each carrying half of Claude and Jack and Amelie ahead of them, side by side, comforting each other. The mood was naturally sombre. It lightened just a little as the coffee and food began to arrive and the rather good omelettes were rapidly consumed, along with a bottle of wine, but nothing was going to be right till Jean was safe. Daphne was thinking, 'This should have been a great, great night, but here we are, one of the most wretched ever.' Jack was thinking about his dad, totally confused, finding out something worse every day, wondering what had happened to make him such a scary miserable wreck.

After half an hour Daphne, who had been offered and accepted the role of leader now without any query or even discussion, stood up. She didn't need to wait for silence as the conversation around the table had been gradually fading for some time.

"OK, everyone, listen up, sorry to be boss, but someone needs to be, I guess. It's late now, I am going to suggest we all get some sleep. Claude and I will sleep here tonight, there are plenty of beds and I can get that sorted in ten minutes. I don't know why but it just feels better to be together.

"Normally we are going to need to be down at the Hut by 9.45 or 10.00 to get everything ready for the customers, but, apologies, tomorrow I want to aim for 8.30 sharp because we need to move the boat back to the landing stage and get it ready, and we need to get the clothes hung up, the tickets ready and so on – we left in a rush. I reckon we can sleep till 7.45-ish and then a quick breakfast and get on the move – I want to shoot back to my house in the morning to get changed, anyway.

"Up till the last moment, as we all know, today was fantastic. Well, apart from the whole incident with the swan and Dougal, which we could not have anticipated, or done anything about – except perhaps Karl not running over the cygnet in the first place. And obviously the lack of brakes on the charabanc could have been a problem but did anyone really notice?"

"Yes," said Amelie, Albert, Milo and Jack in concert.

"Anyway, setting that aside, let's aim for tomorrow to be exactly the same in the main part, we really started well, fabulously actually, and, if we keep it up, word will keep spreading, and business will keep growing.

"We're doing it for Jean, now. If we lose faith and continuity, it will all be over. We have momentum, and we need to keep the doors open. Dad, do you think you will be OK for tomorrow?"

Claude was looking well beyond groggy by this stage. Milo calculated he had certainly had over half a bottle of brandy and a large glass of wine since they had left the hospital, which may have contributed, though in more usual times that might just have been the starter fuel in his carburettor. After they'd waiting a while for him to answer, Claude noticed that the conversation had stopped and lifted his eyes to discover all of them watching him. After another while he realised this might be the cue for him to speak. He hauled out of his short-term memory the question Daphne had asked, what was it? Was he OK for tomorrow? Of course he was OK for tomorrow, and he said so, using an individually developed communication system of grunts, winks, grins and dribble that made it perfectly clear, Oh Yes.

"Right," said Daphne, "let's maybe revisit that in the morning for the full transcript, but for now I am translating that as a forceful declaration of positive intent.

"Is everyone else OK? Any worries, any questions?"

"Will it be the same cast for the show?" asked Albert, usefully.

"Why not, we did well – actually great – didn't we? Obviously Jean won't be back, so I will do the job again; and I thought Bernadette was a brilliant Policeman. I reckon we managed OK with the boards and the projector, but if Claude is up to it, he can take over some of that."

"It's hard to think, while Jean is in such danger. Should we wait before we make too many plans?" Another very sensible question, this time from Amelie.

"I agree, Amelie, but I think the approach we have to take is to be prepared and expecting to do it, so we're properly ready. Of course, we'll keep in touch with the hospital, if things get worse for Jean or we have bad news, we will have much more important decisions to make. Once we've finished here, and I get dad to bed, and the rest of you get settled, I will call the hospital to see if anyone is answering."

At this point Jack made small signals aimed only at Milo and Daphne to tell them that he wanted to have a private conversation concerning something else. They didn't have too much doubt about what it would be. Daphne took Claude upstairs, quite slowly as he was a little shaky, and beckoned Amelie and Albert to help her support him. Collectively they got him up to the landing and Daphne indicated with a nod that they were going to take him into Karl's old room, where the bed was still made up. Daphne pulled back the counterpane and blanket before they gently dropped Claude, who was essentially comatose at this point, onto the sheeted mattress; then Albert and Amelie left Daphne to undress him.

"Goodnight, Daphne – what a day it's been!" said Albert.

"Goodnight, Daphne." Amelie added a kiss on the cheek as she passed her.

"Goodnight, *mes enfants*. I can't tell you how proud I am of you both today. Let's pray Jean is well overnight, and then we will do it all again, for him, tomorrow."

Daphne heard their two doors closing as she took off Claude's boots and debated what other garments he would appreciate having removed by his daughter – deciding he would prefer none at all but taking his jacket off anyway. She was going to leave it at that, and just pull the covers over him, when she was shocked to find his waistcoat and white shirt were completely stained red up and down the left side above the belt of his trousers. She panicked, and was about to cry out for help, when she saw the source was not a wound, but a knife stuck into the waistband covered with blood. She removed it gingerly, finger and thumb on the hilt, to see that the blood was dry on the blade, as it was on the shirt too, and this was obviously the weapon Claude had taken from Mac. She slipped it into the inside pocket of her jacket. Then she calmed her breathing; suppressed a sob, because she didn't have the energy to waste; pulled the top sheet and blankets around her father, deciding she didn't have time to worry about them getting spoiled just now; rolled him up a bit like a plump Claude crepe; gave him an unconscious kiss on the forehead; turned, rose, and left, switching the light off and quietly closing the door behind her.

Before going back downstairs she went to the landing linen cupboard and collected some sheets, blankets and pillows and took them into one of the empty bedrooms, just throwing them on the bed for now, she could sort it out later. Then she went down, through the empty hall and kitchen, picking up a tea towel on the way, and out onto the back terrace where she knew Milo and Jack would be waiting for her, smoking. Jack pointed to the cigarette packet and motioned with his matches, and Daphne nodded gratefully, but first motioned to them both to get up and join her. She led them out to the lake, and around to the well-trodden first fishing spot.

"OK, boys, this is where we truly cross the line. What we do now, we will never talk of again, between ourselves, or others – you understand?"

They nodded without knowing in the least what she was about to suggest, trusting her absolutely.

She pulled the knife out of her pocket. Milo put his arm out immediately, rolling up his sleeve, assuming they were all going to cut themselves and draw blood to seal this secret pact. Jack was a bit more squeamish. "Seriously, do we have to?"

Daphne started laughing for the first time since they had had the news.

"You utter dicks, I do forget it is only a few weeks since you kids were reading swashbuckling tales under your bedcovers.

"This is for disposal, not for a secret blood-bonding ritual. It is the knife your dad used, Jack."

"Argh. You sure this is OK?"

"Oh yes, I think it is. I think it is for the best. Here, Milo, you wipe it with the towel just in case, then Jack you chuck it in. Then we are all guilty."

The first run through did not go well. Milo wiped the knife, then passed it to Jack who politely took it by the handle, thanking him. Daphne had to point out that now they had saved Mac and Claude by making Jack prime suspect, as his were now the only fingerprints on it.

The second run wasn't much better, Milo wiped it, and gave Jack the whole bundle, with the knife wrapped in the cloth; but Jack, put off by the loose tea towel, bungled the throw, and it only went into the shallows about three metres in, they could see the towel bobbing in the water and the blade under it glinting in the moonlight.

Now Milo and Daphne were both beginning to crease up, they couldn't help it. This was the least competent criminal conspiracy ever. Jack was on the tipping point between priggishness and joining in the laughter, when he noticed they were looking at him, waiting.

"What?"

They said nothing, but both nodded towards the towel.

"Why me?"

"Because you duffed the throw."

There was no point arguing, so he stripped off his socks and shoes and rolled up his trousers. It was almost a daily routine for him now. He retrieved the cloth and weapon with no further mishap, wiped the knife again, wrapped the tea towel tighter around the blade, and this time lobbed it well out, close to the middle, where it plopped and sank in a thoroughly satisfactory manner. As he was paddling back to shore, Milo and Daphne clapped ironically and made pirate noises of arrrrproval. The three of them in a circle held out and clasped their right hands, stared into each other's eyes, and renewed their vow of eternal silence.

They drifted back towards the house and settled in the loungers, all in a line looking out at the moon hanging over the tops of the trees. With their cigarettes well lit, Milo set the difficult-conversation-ball rolling with a slightly weak, "What a day!"

"Yes indeed. One to remember, I would say, though I doubt we will have time for carefully crafting our diary entries," Daphne responded, helping the ball to gather momentum. "How are you feeling, Jack?"

"I think I would be feeling better if my estranged father hadn't pulled the head off a swan, stabbed my cousin, and melted back into the jungle."

"Yes, silly question, sorry."

"I just wanted to talk about what might happen now? Well, really, what do you think did happen, and what does it mean?"

"I think the first thing *not* to worry about," said Daphne, in a tone trying to reassure him, "is the police. That's presuming you don't want him caught."

"I don't think I do," replied Jack, though not as emphatically as she was expecting.

"Well my dad and Jean won't talk to them, we know that. Nor will Caro. No-one else knows except our group here. Honestly, even if the police did try to get involved, Jean is not going to support any attempt to make a criminal case against Mac."

"OK but he's out there, what's he up to? Why did he do what he did, and is he likely to do anything like it again? Are we putting people in danger by not turning him in?"

Daphne looked round at Jack impatiently, tired now, not that he could see her in the dark, and snapped, so he could hear clearly the testiness in her voice.

"We don't turn in our own, Jack. I don't know what it is like where you live now, but remember where you come from. The police are only sometimes our friends – and those occasional friends are generally our relations first and *gendarmes* second. Here, if we want something sorted, we sort it ourselves. If we want something cured, we find our own medicine.

"I know you are stunned and horrified, and worried, but I promise we will handle it tomorrow. Tonight, you must sleep – we all must. Tomorrow, Claude will be able to work out where your dad is, because he and Jean have been out to find him several times previously, they know most of his haunts. Honestly, I don't believe Mac can get in any more trouble tonight, and if no-one bothers him he won't hurt anyone. Left to himself he just steers clear of everyone and watches what he watches – Jean and dad told you about it, right?"

"Yes, but I still haven't had time to get used to the idea that my dad had thrown his life away and deserted my mum and our family because of an obsession he has with a woman he went out with thirty years ago. Now he's escalated to killing animals and slashing people who are trying to help him – why has that happened?"

"These are fair questions, Jack, I agree. If there is a reason, we'll do everything we can to find out. Sometimes things aren't what they seem. Maybe not everyone is always responsible for everything they do. Listen, we are all on your side; tomorrow will be a new day for this, I think we have to sleep now, because we've got another big day."

"They all seem big now." Milo said, quietly.

They all fell silent. A bird flew across the moon – the same one he'd seen when he was walking round the lake with Jean, a lifetime ago. The three of them coordinated their last drag, choreographed the last blowing of smoke, simultaneously pushed back their chairs ready to rise. As they did, the phone rang out into the night, louder than a fire alarm. Jean had rigged up an outside bell, which was perfect for people in daytime who were in the pond, or out for a walk, or working close by, but a nightmare after dark, when it scared the life out of anyone within a two-kilometre radius and petrified the wildlife in the neighbourhood, hunted and hunter alike.

They all went in quickly, and Daphne was first to the phone. She listened and mouthed to the boys "It's Caro."

"Yes."

"Yes."

"Yes."

"Yes."

"Of course."

"O my word."

"Yes."

"We're going to."

"Yes, OK, good idea. Talk then."

She hung up the receiver, and stood where she was, thinking.

"Well?" asked Milo. "What's happening?" asked Jack, speaking at the same time. "How is he?"

"Sorry," said Daphne, collecting herself, remembering where she was, possibly on her last legs, but not letting anyone see it.

"Caro says he's the same, stable; he hasn't woken or spoken. The Doctor is relatively positive while emphasising he is not giving an opinion. He says the longer he is stable, the better, if there is no relapse before morning, that's a very good sign."

"What else?"

"The police came in and stood in the doorway to Jean's room. The nurse wouldn't let them go in and bother Caroline, and when the Doctor was called he told them Jean was totally out of it, and in serious danger, and could not be interviewed for many days – if he made it that long. They grilled the Doctor about the wounds, he told them he had no idea how Jean came by them, but, yes, they were made by a sharp implement. They asked about the person who had brought him in, and the Doctor told them it was Claude – he couldn't really not – and that he'd gone home to sleep. Luckily as far as Caroline could tell, from what she heard, the police weren't aware of any injury to Claude, and didn't ask anything along those lines, and the Doctor didn't volunteer any additional information."

"Do you think the police went round to Claude's house?"

"Maybe, but we'll find out tomorrow – for now, let's call it a win, keep all our fingers crossed, hope they don't turn up here, and get that sleep."

The three of them looked at the dirty plates, the empty glasses scattered across the table, the broken bread, crumbs and half-eaten egg and said "Nah" in unison as they headed unsteadily up the stairs.

The boys fumbled their way into their rooms and collapsed into their half-made beds. After fifteen seconds, with one last gargantuan effort, Jack got back up and staggered next door to Milo.

"Mantra," he said; one word.

"Yep," Milo agreed. They started.

O My Brethren, pick him up, raise him high, heal his bones.

O My Brethren, pick him up, raise him high, heal his bones.

O My Brethren, pick him up, raise him high, heal his bones.

O My Brethren, pick him up, raise him high, heal his bones.

O My Brethren, pick him up, raise him high, heal his bones.

After five lines, they were both asleep, curled up on Milo's bed.

Meanwhile Daphne, iron disciplined, refused to compromise her standards, and insisted, to herself, on a properly made bed. She popped the pillows into the pillowcases, stretched the sheets stiff, tucked the blankets in and fashioned immaculate hospital corners. Then she stepped back and admired her beautiful handiwork, before slowly falling face forward on top of the whole thing with her clothes on, fast asleep before she hit the surface.

In a dream, she rose fully clothed and wandered back out to the lake. She sat on one of the tree stumps on the closest little beach and lit a cigarette. Lucy and the nurse from the hospital came and sat on a log next to her. Daphne was surprised to see the nurse, but not Lucy, she saw her all the time.

"I thought you were going to give those up?"

"That was before you died."

"Who's your friend there?" asked the nurse.

"This is Lucy," said Daphne, "from America. She is my lover. Lucy, this is Jean's nurse, I was at school with her."

Lucy reached over and touched Daphne. "I am from Toulouse. And I am not your lover, remember, because I am dead."

"Have you forgotten my name since school?" the nurse asked Daphne.

"You are Marthe."

"I am," said the nurse, smiling.

Daphne passed the cigarette round and they sat quietly, waiting. Then Milo came out of the lake carrying the knife and handed it to Daphne.

"What's that?" asked nurse.

Milo, Daphne and Lucy all laughed. "It's a secret."

Milo looked at Lucy. "I didn't know you knew."

"Yes, Milo. I know everything."

Daphne threw the knife back into the water. It was a great throw, landing perfectly in the middle of the lake.

THURSDAY

Five hours later the house was woken by the phone ringing again. Relentlessly. It was probably five minutes before the six of them realised what the noise was, and another five before any of them accepted the responsibility for answering it. Most of them felt it should be Daphne, given she seemed to have put herself in charge. Here surely was an opportunity for her to show her leadership skills by making the noise stop. But she was furthest away, had gone to sleep last, and had been most tired. So in the end it was Claude who did it, on the basis he was grumpiest, most nauseous, had normally already been up for two hours at least by this time, and he'd wanted to pee for quite a while so he wasn't really enjoying the lie-in. He assumed it was Caroline, and before he reached the phone he had shaped his mood to receive good news. Yes, it would be good.

"Claude," he shouted, miscalibrating his modulation as he picked up the receiver so that the loudness of his own voice made him jump. Over-moderating the tone then much too much in the other direction, he whispered through a drunk-dry throat, "How is he, darling?"

"Your friend is doing well," said a strange voice, in fairness with a degree of humour, "if I can presume I am talking to Monsieur Claude Nuage?"

Caught flat and too fuddled to react quickly, Claude did the unthinkable, and confessed it was him. Daphne came in as he was acting flummoxed, raised her eyebrows and pointed to the phone. Claude shrugged desperately and mouthed "police" as he knew a

503

copper a long way off, even when it was just a voice on the phone.

"Excellent," the stranger went on, "I was expecting to talk to your daughter or one of your employees to get information on where I could find you, but this makes it so much easier. I am Inspector Leopard of Bourges police station, actually I am pretty sure we have met several times before, do you recall?"

Claude shrugged again, then realised the policemen couldn't see him.

"I just need to ask you a few questions, Claude, about what happened yesterday, so if you would be so kind as to wait where you are for half an hour, I will come to you."

"I have to be at work now, can we do it later?"

"How much later? Your boss is in the hospital with a life-threatening injury; for his sake it would be excellent if you can help us as soon as possible. The faster we get the best information, the quicker we can investigate the incident properly."

"I don't know anything that could help. I presumed it was a working accident, I didn't see anything."

"A working accident, are you serious? From the description of the wounds the Doctor has given us, this really could not be an accident of any kind. Jean's sister cannot say much, only that you got him to the hospital and you are not a suspect – obviously we have to talk as a formality so we can rule you out and so you can help us find whoever did it. How did you bring him in if you didn't see what happened?"

"He was on the floor, bleeding, I assumed he had fallen onto something."

"Come on, Claude, you reckon you came across him at random? We know you were with him all day – you were crewing a barge

504

together a few minutes before, someone saw you. Did you have an argument?"

"Listen, you're barking up the wrong tree, Inspector. I would never hurt Jean even if I was drunk; and we were both sober."

Daphne began bobbing up and down, trying to get Claude's attention, then grabbed his arm, waving her palm in front of his face, signalling for him to shut up. "You're talking too much," she shouted silently.

"Just wait there, Monsieur Nuage, please – I am on my way. We need to talk, it is for your own interest to do so."

"Honestly Inspector, this is nothing to do with me, you know everything I have to say. I have to get to work now, but, tell you what, I'll pop in sometime very soon and catch up with you – OK?"

As Claude put forward this agreeable compromise the Inspector was saying something insistent, perhaps advancing his own alternative plan again, but Claude put the phone down, firmly, without slamming, and then lifted the receiver off again so if anyone rang back it would sound as though it was engaged. Cunning.

"Argh."

"Yes, dad, argh – why did you even answer the phone?"

"To make it fucking shut up, Daphne, excuse me for swearing, but I have a most terrific headache and I wanted the noise to go away. Oddly, I was not expecting to be confronted by my own personal manhunter on the other end of the line. I thought it would be Caro or one of the uncles telling us Jean had had a good night."

"Is he coming?"

"I don't know; as you heard, I told him it wasn't convenient, but I have an inkling he might only be further inspired by my reticence."

"Is he coming from Bourges or somewhere local?"

"Not sure. I think he's from Bourges nick, but he didn't say where he was. He did say thirty minutes."

"OK, so that would be our clue, right? We'd better get moving.

"That's my girl, let us indeed flee and save our own skins; but we can leave the kids here to eat some croissants and look dumb, OK? Just for fun?"

"We have limited options, none of which will be fun. Go outside and wait for me."

Daphne was already dressed as you will recall, and so was Claude, so both were ready to go. Daphne bustled up the stairs to rouse the youth, beginning to wonder why she was not only tangled up in all this but also apparently now in charge of organising it. When she got to the landing she stood her ground and shouted, extremely loudly: "Out here, everyone; immediately please."

Short of yelling "FIRE" she couldn't have expected them to move any more quickly than they did, and then she realised, guiltily, that from her tone they must undoubtedly be expecting some bad news from the hospital.

"No no, it's not that. No news about Jean yet this morning, and I think that's fine, personally. But, just to let you know, the police are probably coming here in the next few minutes to talk to Claude about yesterday. He doesn't think that is a great idea, and said so to them, but you know they can be like children when it comes to getting their own way, so they may just turn up. He and I are therefore going to get on with some business around and about, you can tell them if they arrive that Claude had urgent work, which has the virtue of being true. We need you to stick around, eat the croissants – which have miraculously been delivered again – and if they come, play dumb."

Albert and Amelie looked nervous, but they were absolutely prepared to trust Daphne and do what she asked.

Jack and Milo, less so.

"No no no," muttered Jack, placing his palms onto his temples, pointy-up figures above, and shaking his head quickly back and forth, like a kid playing cat. "No, Daphne, we can't be here, can we? Who would we be? Robert and Michael, like our passports? Our old friends Francois and Scott? We've been desperados on the run for two weeks, now you want us to sit and wait for the police?"

Daphne paused; he was right. "OK, yes, I agree, of course that's correct – so the two of you get dressed, get what you need for the day, and go out to dad and wait for me in the car.

"And if the two of you," nodding to Amelie and Albert, "could please put on your angel faces ready for the policemen, that would be so brilliant, thank you. Luckily you really do know nothing, so when you tell them you know nothing, your words will be as pure as baby water." Whatever that is, she thought.

Albert and Amelie were reassured to be told they were clueless and grew in confidence. "OK, Daphne, we can pull that off, I'm sure, I have been working hard on my innocence recently," laughed Amelie.

"Can we mention the swan?" Albert asked, like a fretful actor desperately seeking some notes from a brilliant but preoccupied Director – 'What's my motivation, luv?'

"Oh yes," said Daphne, halfway out of the door, "swans are good, definitely go with that. And the dog." Then she was gone.

Daphne, Jack and Milo joined Claude, and they took his car, leaving Daphne's with the key in for Albert and Amelie if they wanted to use it later. Within three minutes the motor was five hundred metres up the road with the four of them in it, carefully heading

507

away from town to avoid going past the Inspector if he was coming from somewhere close.

He did come, but not for another thirty-five minutes, all the way from Bourges. Amelie and Albert had prepared themselves by putting on some day clothes and getting more coffee. Albert was repeating the mini-mantra "Swans OK" in his head. Needless to say it was a disaster, but fortunately, as Amelie and Albert reported to Daphne later, the Inspector didn't notice a thing.

When he arrived at the door the policeman politely stated that he was here to see Monsieur Claude Nuage, who was expecting him. Amelie, who had answered his knock, respectfully responded that he had just missed him because he had had to leave for his work. The Inspector, showing his badge – "I am Leopard" – cordially asked Amelie if he could come in and whether they could answer some questions. He seemed to her like a flexible man, with excellent manners, who was relaxed and friendly, and who perhaps did not worry so much about the formalities of policing. This felt fine.

Amelie graciously welcomed him in, and took him through to the kitchen, where he sat opposite Albert and gratefully accepted a cup of coffee and even half a pastry while he opened his very smart black notebook and took down the details of their names and home addresses.

He started by mentioning he was investigating the episode the day before, when Jean had been badly injured. Then he asked them where Claude was, as he understood he might have been with Jean at the time. Albert and Amelie said that they didn't know, he had said he had to go to work as there was a lot going on, but there were any number of locations where he could be based for a few hours.

"A lot going on?"

"Yes, as well as some people having their regular jobs, we are all involved in running the new Meaulnes Experience, you must have

508

seen the adverts?"

"Oh that, yes, I saw something in town, and I saw the banner when I went to Monsieur Terroir's farm." They looked blank. "Monsieur Terroir – that's Jean – you work for him." Yes of course, they nodded, indicating they were not used to his family name.

"What does Claude do for this Experience?"

"He is Jean's – Monsieur Terroir's – right hand man, as far as I can see," said Amelie, perkily, intimating she was giving away a little more information than she intended. "He fixes all kinds of things."

"Fixes?"

"Oh yes," said Amelie, feeling she was well in charge and could lead the Inspector wheresoever she chose.

"He's a troubleshooter, you know? He makes the problems go away."

"That sounds incredibly useful." said the Inspector, with an intrigued expression, indicating to Amelie that she truly was one of the most fascinating people he had interviewed.

"What do you both do for the Experience, and who else is here?"

"No-one else is here at the moment," blurted Albert, very nervous, making the truth sound so shifty that the Inspector was fleetingly tempted to rush up and search under the beds in the second-floor rooms. "Everyone has gone to work."

"There are four of us living here, all part of the acting team that puts on the Harlequinade at the Experience." Amelie spoke not so much to say something herself as to stop Albert talking. "We do other things as well, helping get the customers ticketed and outfitted, getting them safely on the barge, basic customer service and so on – actually it is a lot of fun."

"Just four of you for the Harlequinade, is that enough? Aren't there more parts?"

"Everyone joins in, Jean plays a role now – or was going to – and we have a musician, someone to do the costumes, other people from around the farm assist with the scenery, there are caterers, and so on…"

"What about the other two who are here, where can I talk to them?"

"I am not sure currently." Albert's tone was sufficiently squeaky to fully convince the Inspector that they were hiding a major conspiracy. This was much more intriguing than he had thought when he set out. In Amelie's mind, Leopard had been about to give them a free pardon and an apology from the constabulary for wasting their time, but even she could see that Albert's clammy cheeks and quivering hands now risked undermining her own brilliant performance if they weren't careful.

"They're boys? Your age? At the police station, they seem to remember an unhappy German youth coming in."

"He's not here anymore, he…" Albert was about to launch into his explanation of Karl's failed exposé of the London lads when he realised Amelie was squeezing his thigh, hard enough to leave a bruise later; he stopped talking immediately, halfway through the sentence; then realising a sudden hiatus might look suspicious, he continued quickly, "…he's gone away. The two others staying here with us are boys, around our age; they are out now, getting ready for today's show."

"Thank you, Albert. Where do you think I might find them currently, and what are their names?"

This second, or was it third, time of asking might have been a good moment for Albert to choke on a croissant or feign a heart attack (or better still have a real one). As the question (not particularly penetrating or unexpected, you might think) was repeated, and the detective was not apparently minded to let the subject go, Albert's big willing face slowly deflated, like a blow-up moon landing on Leopard's sharpened pencil, and his eager-to-help but dying-to-deceive smirk gradually turned from a groundlessly confident smile into the terrified frozen grin of the guilty schoolboy as he desperately struggled to come up with an explanation, which didn't include the lit cigarette behind his back, for the wisps of smoke drifting out of his nostrils.

Fortunately for Albert the Inspector had no wish to torture him, and in fact was rather keen not to alert him or his sister to any suspicions he might have. It would be much easier for him to investigate if they believed he was unsuspecting, or better still, that he was on completely the wrong track. The last thing he wanted was for them to warn other possible witnesses, perhaps even potential perpetrators, that he was pursuing them.

In his long career, he had gradually transformed himself from a diligent, honest and clumsy Constable who pretended to be more successful than he was, to a self-styled maverick detective who almost always liked to appear, even to his superiors, less smart and intuitive than he had become. Posing as a rule-breaker and paperwork agnostic had also helped him disguise, not least from himself, some little slips into casual extortion and opportunistic self-enrichment that occurred now and again, against his better nature. Something was going on here, Leopard could sense it; and when he'd worked out what it was, he intended to turn it to his advantage, especially if it finally gave him some ammunition against the annoyingly charismatic Jean and his team, who were overdue a little cage-rattling. Or, better still, if it was information that was useful to Pierre, he could barter it with him for favours or, God forbid, a little hard currency. Whatever it was, however, it was obvious these two innocents were not at the hub of it, or even on the fringes for that matter.

Which meant that, right now, he had no motive to persuade the kids that he was anything other than blissfully convinced of their spotless ignorance; so even as Albert was struggling, and Amelie was variously kicking, squeezing and elbowing him, sometimes under the table, occasionally in plain sight, Leopard flipped his rather chic notebook closed with a liberating click, and stood up calmly, brushing off a few crumbs, looking the very tiniest bit bored, and saying respectfully, "I am so sorry, I realise I am late for some other business, please forgive me. You have been really helpful, I am so grateful for your assistance," handing out cards to each of them, "if you do think of anything that might help me, or when your housemates return, if they have ideas, do please just give me a call." And so saying, he left, without waiting to be shown out.

Albert looked at Amelie, and Amelie looked at Albert. "Blimey," they said together, "that was close."

Meanwhile, five kilometres away, lost in the back country, Claude, Jack and Milo were driving fast, shouting at each other and smoking heavily. When they left the Lodge, they'd gone to the Hut by a very roundabout route designed to reach their destination without ever intersecting a road the police might have taken from town, like a child's maze puzzle. There they had dropped off Daphne: "One of us has to work," she said, "but it feels like I am the only one who can give a straight stare to a policeman if he turns up, so you probably need to make yourselves scarce. I need to get the boat checked, the costumes sorted, and the till ironed out – there is plenty for me to do for the next few hours. Come back close to starting time, we will hang a feather boa over the COMPLET sign to confirm everything is clear for you, OK?"

"Brilliant idea!" said Milo.

"We'll have a cruise round for a couple of hours," said Claude, slightly sheepishly, "and check a couple of places for Mac, OK?"

"That's fine, I thought you would. How are your arms?"

"I'll live. Slashes are definitely less painful than kettle burns, but don't tell anyone."

"Ha ha. Just don't get in too much trouble, and don't be late back."

"We won't. See you later, you're a hero, thank you."

Jack had spent a sleepless night worrying about his father and Jean, not in that order, and not with the same level of love, but with an equal degree of anxiety. He would much rather have gone over to the hospital to be close to Jean, but failing that it was a relief to him to be able to spend the next few hours out looking for his dad.

So now they had found themselves in a warren of barely navigable tracks in the forest to the north. Claude, despite being horribly hungover and rather sore in places, was behind the wheel, mainly because in theory he knew where they were going and he could hypothetically take them on a tour of Mac's previous hideouts. But Milo was shouting in his ear from the back seat in the vain hope of overriding some of his directional decision-making. "Chrissake, Claude, even I can tell we've been at this junction three times, and you've gone left every time. Don't you think it's time to give right a chance?"

"You dumb kid, have you never heard of Backwoods Blindness? All trees look the same to civilians. I am a lifelong forester. I keep an axe in the boot of my car at all times. I was born knowing things you can never learn about the deep woods. Be quiet and let me think, for God's sake."

Jack and Milo, for all the gravity of their quest, were rolling around in laughter at Claude's notion that a magical axe in the vehicle's trunk would grant the traveller mystical insight into the secret ways through the trees. Then they pulled themselves back to reality: "OK you go where you go," said Milo, "but we've been round in circles for half an hour, and we don't seem to have got very close to anything you've been looking for."

"We've been past that lightning tree three times for sure."

"OK OK, you're wrong, but I will go right, just to humour you

513

this time."

After fifty metres, Claude did begin to recognise the route and realised they were on the correct track; but he didn't want to give the boys the satisfaction of taking the credit, so he kept quiet. He was looking for a forester's hut, more of a shed really, one they'd used for shelter in storms before it got too dilapidated; and, sure enough, after another four hundred metres, there it was, set three dozen paces back from the road, up to its knees in ferns and with ivy all over its top and shoulders, making it almost invisible. Claude pulled the car into the side of what was now not much more than a path and turned off the engine. There was a silence in the back, much louder and safer than the shout of "Told you so" that would surely have sent him over the edge.

"Once, about a year ago, Jean and I found Mac here after some of the farmers had been complaining about him creeping around at night, peeping and stealing things. We found him before they did, and we took him back to Jean's, locked him up in one of the barns for a week or so, fed him, washed his clothes, cleaned him up, calmed him down. Then he got away again. I came out here a few times looking for him, and saw some signs, but obviously he's got other places too."

As he was speaking they were walking towards the hut. Milo and Jack started off stealthily, stooped, moving with knees bent, like movie cowboys sneaking up on the enemy camp, ducking under a fanciful clump of cacti and zigzagging behind a phantom palisade like kids brandishing invisible Colts. Claude meanwhile strolled upright, talking in his normal (loud) voice, oblivious to the theatrically clandestine manoeuvrings behind him.

"Claude," Jack shout-whispered, "get down! Keep quiet! He'll see you coming, if he doesn't hear you first!"

Claude looked surprised, then irritated. "Chrissake, boys, will you stand up straight – this isn't a John Wayne film. There's only one door in and out, which seems to be facing us straight on, so he has nowhere to run even if he wanted. And, honestly, I don't think he wants to shoot me, and if he did, I don't think he has a gun."

If this was a proper book a shot would at that very moment have rung out through a hole in the hut wall, and Claude would have fallen to the ground, clutching his heart, slain by irony, a wry smile playing on his lips as he said: "You got that wrong, my old friend... it will be your last mistake."

But sadly not: what happened next was exactly what you were already thinking. They reached the shed; knocked politely; heard nothing from inside; cautiously opened the door; and found the large single room completely empty. They kicked around the mess on the floor, which was substantial: newspapers, bottles, wrappers, together with the signs of several fires, including what looked like a classically complete collection of charred woodland carcases, from dormouse to badger via weasel, squirrel, stoat, rabbit and what looked like a baby fox.

"I hope he's been cooking that roadkill at a sufficiently high temperature," mused Claude.

Jack and Milo looked at him silently for fifteen beats before totally creasing up, landing on the floor a minute later in tears of laughter, Jack hardly able to breathe. "What are you now, the rotisserie police?"

"It's serious, you twats, if you lived in the country like humans you would have learnt this stuff. Some of these bushmeats have worms and all kinds of weevily crap that can get in your gut and make you blind." [Defensively] "Everyone knows that."

"True Story," said Jack, and the boys were off again.

"Well, it's clear someone's been living here off and on," said Milo once they had calmed down. But there didn't seem to be anything to show how recently the place had been occupied.

"Maybe a lot more than one," said Claude, "it looks like it has been used over time by loads of people. Last time we flushed Mac out of here, another local tramp he'd kicked out moved straight back in. There aren't many places this dry in the woods, great for the winter, for sure."

"Here you go," called Jack from the corner, where he'd been raking through the rubbish with his foot. He was holding up a little blue packet. "His Wrigley's Spearmint Gum – good to know he's still surrounding himself with all the little luxuries of home."

"Look here," called Milo from the other corner, kicking through a pile of screwed-up paper balls. "These look like pages of a diary torn out." He picked up one and opened it out. "Do you think it could be your dad's writing?"

He held the page with the writing towards Jack, who recognised both the writing and the paper from his dad's journal, and just said, "Yes."

"It's from a diary but it isn't a diary entry – if it is I don't think we should read it, right?"

"It's from the same book Jean gave me, and I've read all that, so this is the same deal. Whereas I appreciate your discretion, it's way too late to start worrying about the ethical niceties, this isn't Trollope or Terence Rattigan, we're engaged in a bloody manhunt."

Claude was looking on bemused. He loved these boys now but he had no clue most of the time what they were going on about.

"Just read it, Milo, please – there might be some clues."

As instructed, Milo read the top half of the top paragraph, peering through his fingers, trying not to look, like a kid watching a horror movie a couple of age grades too old for him.

"Jesus Jack, is it all like this, in the book?"

"What do you mean?"

"You know…. sex stuff…."

Jack snatched it from him, violently, as though he had caught him going through private stuff.

"For Chrissake," Milo yelped, leaping a step back, "what was that all about. You actually TOLD ME to read it."

"Sorry. Sorry, Sorry. And the answer is yes. A great deal of the book is very much along those lines, if you have in mind Jane Austen's less literate older sister writing a bit of hard porn on the side."

"Stick to what you know, right? The first rule of successful authorship."

Jack was reading the bit of paper now, and found himself covering it with his fingers just like Milo. Nothing new here. In fact, some of it he seemed to remember, so perhaps he was looking at some kind of discarded first draft, a rejected version that had not made it into the published volume because it wasn't quite terrifyingly mad enough. He looked up from his reading to see Claude watching him, lips pursed, shaking his head, trying to show sympathy and despair at the same time.

Milo, had gone back down on his knees again to search the rubbish, perhaps to hide the fact he was pale and shaking, a little due to Mac's erotica (it is always a little disconcerting when your friend's parents dabble in porn) but mainly because of Jack's extreme reaction; though, being Milo, he was halfway to forgiving him already, and halfway closer to understanding what he was going through.

He started to rustle through the rest of the pile of detritus, picking out a few more rolled-up balls of the same lined paper and smoothing them out, but these were blanks; then there were old newspapers, most recently used to supply warmth rather than information; a torn and mouldy referendum poster for Algerian independence [OUI A DE GAULLE]; brown wrapping paper with a rather sophisticated anatomical outline of an erect penis, ejaculating, as is standard in any structure that provides overnight accommodation; and a finally a restaurant menu for a place called **DESDEMONA DÉJEUNER,** which certainly offered an outstanding range of filled baguettes, and at a really attractive price. Flicking the menu over, Milo found writing on the reverse, worthy of examination. Still kneeling, he called Jack over and passed it up to him as he carried on sifting through the rubbish, while Claude, who was getting bored with what he considered to be the over-archaeological aspects of the hunt, drifted just outside and lit a cigarette.

Jack tried to make sense of the spindly writing on the back of the menu in the half-light of the hut: the handwriting was appalling, tiny, and faint with age, and the language, what he could understand of it, seemed to be a mixture of medieval French and kids' slang.

"I am not sure how much sense it makes without a code-breaking cypher: any thoughts, Watson?"

"I'm Holmes."

"Holmes doesn't scrabble around on his knees, he looks suave and waves the solution around, so obviously in this case it's going to be me."

"You have the solution?"

"I'm still in the suave phase."

Claude, his hangover drumming, and beginning to be irritated by the chatter, wandered back in and grabbed the paper grumpily from Jack's hand. He was clearly more attuned to the writing style and epistolary peculiarities of the region, because he had no trouble at all making it out.

"It says 'Sorry I missed you, hope the fags are OK they were all I could get this week. No gum till next week, I will hide it for you at the normal place when it arrives. Please drink the milk before the brandy.' It looks like it was written months ago. Could be anything, right? Not necessarily connected to Mac."

As he was saying it, he turned over the piece of paper and saw it was a menu.

"Oh Shit."

Milo and Jack were both watching him by now, impressed by his translation of the hieroglyphics. They saw confusion in his face, then a second wave of bewilderment.

"No wonder I had no trouble reading it."

"What do you mean?"

"DESDEMONA DÉJEUNER. It's owned by someone I know. I mean, I know the owner."

Clearly there was more to be said on the subject.

"And that's her writing. I should have spotted that right away."

"And ..."

"She must have written it."

"Yes, we're getting that from it being in her handwriting."

"Actually..."

Claude tailed off, and the boys could see his cheeks would have reddened if they hadn't already been teak coloured.

"... well actually she's a friend of mine, not that it's any of your business. Desdemona."

Milo and Jack looked at each other and, despite the tenseness coming from Claude's side of the scenario they had to try very hard not to giggle. This was like a kid at junior school shuffling around and pretending not to tell while wanting everyone to know. And the name! Perfect, Jack thought, for an exotic lover. (Mainly because, being honest, as Milo had to correct him later when they were sniggering about it, Jack had confused it with Delilah.)

"Claude, you've got a girlfriend?"

This was Jack, unable to stop himself, unsure if it was a question or a statement, but definitely at the incredulous end of the spectrum. He and Milo were testing in this conversation whether they could get away with teasing Claude. He had become, what, an uncle? He might, they were thinking, be tempted to cuff them like a big bear fondly teaching cubs, but that is just a way of expressing affection, nothing worse. They were in for a shock.

"Don't fucking make stuff up," he shouted, furiously. "That's not funny, don't ever repeat that. Dessie is a friend of mine and your dad's, going back nearly forty years, to school. Mac was away from here during the war, but me and Dessie were part of something when the Germans were here, after my wife died. We don't talk about that time, so don't ask. We got close, then broke up, and she's been with Pierre for quite a few years now."

"Who's Pierre?"

"Ah I forgot, it was Albert who met him, not you. Pierre is a local gangster, he runs some crimes. We've sparred a lot: I generally prefer to keep out of his way – most sensible people do. But he did us a favour the other night, well, he did it for Jean really, he respects him, when he lent me and Albert that car to chase Karl."

It struck Milo that Claude was talking way too much if he really didn't have anything to hide. However, the secret, if there was one, was certainly safe with Jack, who had already moved on from Claude's backstory in his haste to shift the focus back onto himself, and his own problems.

"That's fine," he said, "but what do you reckon dad was doing with her annotated menu?"

"I am interested in that too. I can check with Dessie later; it looks as though she's been helping him out without telling anyone. Getting him stuff. She's got a place in these woods, that's probably the connection." Claude was clearly struggling with some feelings at this point, one of which looked like it might have been jealousy, obviously on Pierre's behalf.

"Right," said Jack, getting bossier as he got more stressed, "we can follow that angle in due course. For now, though, while we're here, we could be hot on the track, right? If you've found him in some of these places before, and they're only a few hundred metres away, can't we look now?"

"Two reasons why not," said Claude, giving him the slow down, calm down sign (palms out in front, parallel to the ground, up and down but mainly pressing lightly down). His throat, in fact his whole body, was beginning to feel extremely dry. "Actually three."

As he said it, he left the hut, motioning the boys to follow him. When they were all outside, he pulled the door to, very hard to stick it, and then led them back over to the car. They all got in, with both the boys in the back, taxi-style, to reflect Claude's current displeasure with them, and Claude pulled away, turning the car around to face the way they had come. He drove for about five minutes without saying anything, until Milo finally realised Claude deemed the conversation to be over and was not expecting to elaborate his point.

"Claude, can you please tell us why we can't look for that hide right now? You mentioned three points?"

"Oh that…" said Claude, as though being reminded of a discussion they'd had several months ago with a 'you're not still going on about that, are you' flick of the head and roll of the eyes (both of which he instantly regretted as they hurt his brain, considerably).

He had the radio on, with the magnificent Rina Ketty singing Montevideo and giving it some very serious lung: Claude was wrestling with the age-old dilemma of wanting it loud enough so he didn't have to listen to Milo and Jack, but quiet enough so it didn't pulse like a stiletto spike being driven repeatedly into his skull by a ridiculously muscled and fabulously moustachioed circus strongman. Reluctantly, he turned it down a fraction.

"… Well, the first thing," he grudgingly continued, "is we only just about have time to get back to the ticket Hut before the first customers arrive. You need to work on the costumes and I need to get the boat sorted out or we won't have an Experience today.

"Second, he goes to his hides at night, mainly, to watch over the house when she's making dinner or sitting outside smoking. I don't think he'll be around any of them in the morning waiting to be caught. The best time to look, honestly, I think will be this evening after the show.

"And third. Boys I hate to say it, but I really need a cold beer and two cigarettes before work. I am rasping and gasping."

"You said there was only just time to get back."

"Obviously including the stop for the cold beer. I allowed fifteen minutes for that."

Even as he was saying it, the car was steering itself off the road, as if by some alcohol-enabling magic, into a rather tidy snack stop. It was a neatly groomed grassy area containing seven tables with umbrellas and fourteen benches, and at the far end there was a gaily painted open-sided caravan groaning under the weight of a five-metre-high sign mounted on its roof shouting in yellow, orange and red: **DESDEMONA DÉJEUNER**. There was a second caravan, more of a traditional affair, set behind it at right angles, all green and covered in vines and colourful hanging baskets – it hadn't been moved for a long time, and looked awfully cosy.

"Desdemona's," chuckled Jack. "Dessie's. Jesus why didn't I remember that name! I've been here a dozen times. Dad and mum brought us every year when we were on holiday."

"Yes, they would have," said Claude, "given she's not only your second cousin once removed, or the other way round, or something like that, but also a very close friend of your dad's, as I did tell you when apparently you were more interested in taking the piss than actually listening to what I was saying." Jack and Milo made 'ooo listen to it' faces to each other in the back while clutching their hands over their mouths in a vain attempt to hold back the worst of their laughter.

As the café was currently completely deserted of customers, presumably in limbo between the breakfast crush and the midday rush, Claude took the rather pre-emptory and presumptuous decision to drive right on through the back of the designated carparking area and to pull the car up just a few metres from the serving hatch.

"Three cold ones, love," he shouted through the open window of the car, without leaning over or looking out.

"If that's you in there Claude you can fuck off, and also go and park in the carpark like everyone else."

"No wonder you're so busy, with that attitude," Claude laughed, opening the car door, getting out and beckoning the boys to follow. "We just want three very quick very cold beers, honey, and we will get out of your way. Also, I thought you'd love to catch up with some friends of mine who have been longing to call on you."

The caravan door swung out, and an enormously large lady emerged, almost as big as she was beautiful – Milo had been around the pub

523

all his life and had seen thousands of characters of all shapes and designs come through the doors, but he had never seen anyone half so amazing. Creaminess is such a virtue in a bosom, I mean nothing salacious by it, but even Milo found it hard to remove his eyes, and Claude's clung like love-limpets to the fifteen centimetres of almost horizontal cleavage disclosed by her largely unbuttoned work top. Another twenty-five centimetres above that were blue eyes and blond hair, mainly original. But the biggest thing was the smile, constant, all over the face, in and out of the lines, not just the mouth and twinkling eyes. Milo and Jack were spellbound. They could see why Claude, allegedly, was taking his life in his hands to risk courtship.

As she stepped down she was holding in one hand four icy bottles with their tops already off, and her other hand amply clutched a lighter and a packet of fags, one of which she was wedging into one side of her mouth even as she was speaking out of the other.

"Jeez, Claude, you only come round here when you want something, and whenever you do you virtually park in my living room and then it's 'Drop everything, meet my friends, fetch me beer.' It is not like I've got nothing to do but be oiled, tanned, smoothed and ready-squeezed into my leopard-skin mini skirt just in case you call."

She gestured to the closest table and they crammed onto the benches, Claude next to Desdemona, while she handed out the beers and lit a cigarette for each of them. Despite their whinging earlier, Jack and Milo sucked the cold ale gratefully. "Ice Cold In Alex," said Milo, drawing deeply on the fag.

"Ha ha, remember when we left The Odeon gasping and went straight to the pub. Mum only let us have a cola float."

"Oooh, cola float. Kids get all the best stuff, right?"

A moment's nostalgia. They looked up and found Dessie and Claude watching them like an indulgent mum and dad on a day's outing. They had another drag on their cigarettes to break the parental spell.

"If it's a bit tight for you there, Claude, you can always sit on my lap rather than falling off the end," Dessie laughed, giving him a nudge with her hip. Claude, if you could tell it, was by now red again under all the other colours of his face, and just about hung one buttock on to the edge of the bench to avoid flying off.

"Are you going to tell me what happened to your arms? You know I know anyway, right?"

"Kettle."

"Ha ha ha. You need to be more careful making your cocoa."

"How did you hear?"

"Please, Claude, everyone knows, except Herve, he actually believed you. How bad is it?"

"Me? I'm fine. Scratches."

"I can see that; I meant Jean. That's what brings you here drinking at this time of day, right? Everyone is talking about it."

"Fuckssake!" snorted Claude. "Doesn't anyone bother with privacy in this region anymore?"

"There's no privacy at the end of a knife, Claude, you know that by now: but no-one is talking to the cops, if that's your worry. Only the right people know, so don't fuss – mainly your nephews and cousins by the sound of it."

"Oh, so, that's what, thirty-seven people...? What's being said?"

"Well, for the last few days everyone has been raving about Jean's Experience. Even those who were hoping it would be a massive failure – so, say, half the population – have been impressed by what's been done. Last night then, the word went out something had gone wrong, quite a few people were very happy, and extremely keen to gossip, so there were all kinds of stories.

"The first assumption was a boat accident, and Jean caught up in it and injured. Then it was all about an animal attack – dog, swan, boar, wolf; name your beast. Someone tried to float bear for a while but not so many bought into that one. Finally, out of the hospital came the story of a knife wound, a fight, or attack. One finger pointed at you, Claude, but people 'in the know' connected the dots to mad Mac, a dozen people have claimed to have seen him lurking murkily around the place in the last few months and a couple of them say they spotted him down by the river yesterday…"

Suddenly realising the lads were still there, Dessie gave Claude the raised eyebrows and cocked head, a sign in the local dialect for 'Is it OK to be talking like this in front of the strange youth?' Subtle, but a bit late.

"Well, it is fine to discuss it, Des, as these are my brothers in arms; but I have been very rude in not introducing them yet. This young man is Milo, and this is his mate, Jack. You remember Jack?"

Dessie was desperate to say yes, as everyone always is, but just couldn't do it – she gave the vague apologetic shrug.

"He was here a lot a few years ago – he's Mac's son."

Desdemona blushed deeply crimson over all visible parts – Claude was careful to check.

"Oh my God, son, I am so sorry, I would never have talked about your dad like that if I had known. Truly, he's one of my oldest friends, he used to be one of my best – we were very very close. Now I do see it, we've met – you came here when you were a toddler, and even a bit older? But your hair was a completely different colour then, when you were here with your mum."

"Yes, I've been here, Des, quite a few times, and as you say, many years ago. It's no worry talking about my dad," he went on, trying not to show any distress about what she'd said, "that is most definitely not the worst I have heard and learned about dad in the past ten days. Let's just say youthful illusions have been shattered, for sure – perhaps that's what I am upset about. But he walked out on us three years ago, so I am not sure I was expecting an awful lot of good news when – if – I tracked him down." Jack was burbling, a mixture of exhaustion, tension and being put on the spot.

"It's kind of you to say that, Jack, but I am mortified, so sorry. Whatever is being said, just ignore it, you know what people are like, they love trouble, so long as it is someone else's."

"The problem is this time there's a little bit of truth, Des," Claude said, regretfully, "Mac was at the scene; and he did have a knife."

"O Lord," she said, running her right hand deep into her thick flaxen hair, while she took a deep-drawn drag of the cigarette she had been waving around in her left hand. "He stabbed Jean? What the hell?"

"I think that's an exaggeration, Des. Mac was mainly focused on the swan that had attacked the boat. He'd gone in the water to fight it."

"That was a version I heard but dismissed as mad talk… Seriously, he was fighting a swan?"

"That's probably a longer story than we have time for now. Anway, we went to search for Mac after the river ruckus, we found him on the bank, shredding the bird, Jean stepped forward to calm him down, probably trying to take the knife away, and that's when it gets blurry. I was there, standing a metre away, and even I don't really know what happened."

"So what now?" Desdemona was talking to Claude but looking at Jack.

"We wanted to ask you," Jack answered, as it had been directed to him. "We found a note up in one of the forest hideouts, on the back of one of your menus."

"It's your handwriting, Des, right?" Claude said, a bit shyly, Milo thought.

Claude passed her the ragged piece of paper, guiltily, as though just by finding it they had invaded her privacy. She fumbled in her tiny purse for a pair of minute spectacles that she perched on the end of her nose. It took her ninety seconds to get set up, and three seconds to read.

"Yes, well, I know he can't get the gum anymore, it is driving him mad. I can get it now and again."

"So, it was from you to Mac; you've talked to him?" This was half an accusation from Jack.

"Yes, of course, are you saying there's something odd about that? If you think about it, I am his closest neighbour. Not in the past couple of days, but before that, I've seen him probably once a week, sometimes twice, for months, maybe even years.

"When I say 'seen him' that's not always true, he comes around now and again, but just as often I miss him or he misses me. At first, he was stealing from the bins: I caught him, we got comfortable with each other again and after that I arranged to leave him supplies in a couple of places we agreed – cigarettes, gum, milk, brandy, and food, but I am not so sure he's been eating the baguettes recently, given the look of him."

"And you didn't mention that to anyone?" asked Jack, again a little edgily. Claude was looking on, quite interested too, but trying to signal to Jack to cool it a bit.

"Nothing to say, love. His business is his business. He's had some tough times, he did stuff in the war none of us want to think about, he's been hard on himself before and after. It doesn't excuse anything, Jack, and I am not defending him especially, and I am desperately sorry for you and your mum, who I always really liked. But Mac wasn't harming anyone I am aware of, and people have a right to peace and privacy if they can find it. Besides, our conversations mainly covered the quality of the half-eaten food he'd been lifting from the waste, and then rather terse thanks for the fresh extras I started topping him up with. We're blood, kid, that makes it a simple bond, there are no prioritisations, or hierarchies. If I have that kind of history and attachment with someone, I keep it one on one, it is no-one else's business."

She was looking in Jack's eyes as she spoke, but the message was clearly for Claude, who was staring. He nodded; he wasn't quibbling. Jack didn't notice, but Milo did.

"So, what's the plan?" Des went on to ask. "Is there one? Jean normally does the strategy; if he's flat on his back, he can't orchestrate the hunt for his stabber. I am presuming you are dodging the police, and simultaneously trying to track down Mac so you can deal with this issue yourself and keep the authorities out of it?"

Milo gazed at her, extremely impressed, wondering why she was running a lunch wagon instead of a regional police department.

"I like it here," she said, looking at him, knowing what he was thinking and laughing, "it suits me fine. If we get to know each other I'll tell you about the war and what we all did, and how it exhausted us for normal life."

She paused portentously; Milo nodded seriously. Then she gave a huge laugh and punched him in the arm.

"Of course I'm not going to tell you any of that shit, you daft boy. Claude must have informed you, none of us ever talk about that crap, specially to kids your age. You don't want to carry that around. The truth is, making egg baguettes and concentrating very hard on being twice as large as life – no more, no less – is perfect for me, I want for nothing else. Now, Claude, how can I help you all – that's why you pulled in, right?"

"I guessed that's what the note was all about," Claude replied, trying to recover some ground, "and that you were in touch with Mac, so, yes please, we will want to ask you for help. But right now, we're going to need to run. The customers for the Experience are probably already arriving in the carpark, we need to get the day going, we can't let Jean down, he needs this to work more than ever. But later. You know these woods better than anyone these days, you can give us a hand looking?"

"Yes, I think I know where to search, maybe even some places you don't know yet. When do you want to do it?"

"Tonight? We can't leave it too long, the police are circling, Mac seems like he might be reaching some kind of crisis, it needs sorting right away."

"What time do you finish your acting? Can you be back here say 19.00? That would give us two hours before we lose the light."

"See you then, Des – you're a diamond."

"Listen all of you: no bright colours, wear boots, nothing that makes a noise, no weapons, torches if you have them – I've got spares."

As she was speaking they were in the car, and Claude had the engine running. "Gem!" he called.

"We go back a long way… all of us," Desdemona said it quietly, almost to herself, as Claude was winding the car window up. And then they were on the road, bombing back towards Jean's place.

Meanwhile, at the Hut, Daphne, Albert and Amelie were missing them, and getting worried.

Albert and Amelie had arrived an hour after Daphne, deciding to walk down to the farm to get some fresh air, leaving Daphne's motor at the Lodge. They were proud to reassure her they had completely thrown the Inspector off the scent, and relieved when she was too preoccupied to ask for a full report.

They all had plenty to do to keep themselves busy: firstly, the clothes and accessories had been cleaned and dropped off in the tubs outside by the overnight crew and they needed to be sorted and hung. Secondly, realising she needed to have a plan to protect the main feature of the morning's activity in case Claude did not show up, Daphne decided she must go and find the barge, sort it out, and have it ready. She grabbed Albert to help her, and left Amelie on her own arranging the costumes by character and size and hanging them in the racks.

As they left the Hut and headed down towards the river, Daphne suddenly remembered the bus ride the night before and realised she hadn't checked what had happened to Guinevere. She and Albert swung back a hundred metres to get a view of the bridge, keenly hoping they weren't going to run into Georges and Henry.

It turned out, on the plus side, that there was no longer a charabanc wedged in the bridge. On the minus side, there was considerably less bridge than was previously considered adequate for its purpose. And what little of the historic brickwork that did remain was strikingly decorated yellow with a parting gift of coach paint.

'Oh dear,' she thought, making a mental note to tell Claude to get a team down to repair it and clean up, 'that colour really doesn't go.' It crossed her mind that at some stage in the future a bill for panel beating and paintwork would be arriving from Georges. She might let dad handle that one.

She and Albert then set off to walk down the towpath to where she calculated the boat would be tied up – it would be about a kilometre according to Claude's estimate. Also, he'd relayed the fact it was secured in a bit of a hurry, to some random foliage or trunks, and was left unguarded of course, so she was praying it was still there, undamaged and in working order. After fifteen minutes, slow headway given Albert was not an enthusiastic hiker and because the ground broke up and was soggy a lot of the way after they passed the landing stage, they rounded a bend, and it was there. 'Thank God,' she thought; so, the biggest worry was dispelled, and if it was in working order, and the keys were in it, they were still in business.

When they came into full view they realised it was sitting nearly two metres out in the river, and there was no jetty, so not so brilliant, but with mixed feelings they saw that Claude and Jean had left a rather rickety narrow gangplank linking the barge to the shore. As they got closer they found their feet sinking into the sodden bank, and when Albert looked down to check the footing, he squealed to see his white shoes sinking into a mess of mud, feathers, bloody down, part of a wing, a bit of a beak, some webby toe things, and various other unnameable inside and outside parts of the dead bird.

"I'm amazed the police haven't been here."

"They may have been, there are some different sized footprints, and look, these prints on the barge? Were they there before? If the police had been here they wouldn't have cleaned up, they would just have had a look around and probably created much more mess than when they started."

"Of course… or maybe Jack's dad came back?"

"That's a thought too, though I suspect he got the scare of his life, he's pretty skittish."

While they had been talking, they'd helped to steady each other over the slippery bank and across the plank to get onboard. Albert untied the front and Daphne the back, both of them having to lean daringly out over the rail to reach the knots. Then Daphne started the engine with the keys that had fortunately been left in the dashboard and just as fortuitously not been used by a random boat thief to have it away with their prize. 'We didn't lose this barge,' thought Daphne, overjoyed, but trying not to show Albert her relief, 'what a great day this is.' Once under way they made it to the farm jetty in less than fifteen minutes at a very cautious speed, turned the barge, and tied her up ready for the customers when they arrived.

The front canopy was still up but needed brushing. They did it together quite well and decided not to try to put up the canopy over the back end, but to leave it open. "At least we don't need to worry about being boarded by the swan today," said Daphne.

Albert shook his head, "We're not having a great run of luck. Don't rule out a kamikaze attack from a squadron of motherless suicide cygnets."

Daphne did a cartoon grimace and punched him in the arm. She hadn't realised they had become friends. "That is very good, *mon cher*, but now we have become close I cannot allow the tautology, you understand? Anything but that." He looked at her completely blankly.

"OK, Albert, no time for delightful banter, customers are going to be arriving any minute, I am going to run and help Amelie. Hopefully the others are back too now." Opening one of the cupboards in the aft section, she found a bucket, brushes, rags and cleaning materials. "Could you please stay and tidy the boat up? Run a cloth and a mop over the surfaces? Specially those bits of blood." They looked up and down, there were also some feathers and what looked like bone, so someone had been treading muck from the shore, or perhaps an animal.

"OK," he replied, he was warming up now, he liked Daphne and wanted to please her. He was so much keener than Old Albert would have been – the Experience was changing everyone. He might consider changing his name to Bertie to celebrate the fresh start. What do you think?

"I'll need water, where is the tap?"

Daphne laughed, and threw the bucket over the side, hanging on to the rope on its handle. "All the water you need, Albert, just help yourself." She pulled the rope, drew up the bucket, and handed it to him. "Don't use too much though, we'll need it for cruising on later."

She ran up the pathway to the Hut, scanning the carpark to see if Claude's vehicle was there yet. Nothing. Amelie was still working away on her own, already in her striped blazer, doing very well; she had sorted all the women's and children's racks and was just starting on the men's.

"Thanks, honey, that's brilliant. The barge is fine, your brother is just cleaning it up."

Amelie's eyebrows went up, and she gave a broad grin.

"Who would have thought it!"

Daphne put her own blazer on and turned to the till and reception desk, concentrating on the other small tasks required to be ready for the customers. Then they saw the cars beginning to arrive, and with just the two of them, they felt unprepared and rather rattled.

Most of the incoming vehicles were local, but there was a nice smattering of more expensive motors from farther afield, a couple of foreign plates, a handful from Paris. In the normal course of events, this was fabulous news, not only was it looking as though they would be turning some people away today, given the numbers, but clearly the word was spreading about the Experience, and business was taking off. It was a particular relief to feel that *l'incident du cygne* was not keeping people away.

However, on the downside, they were hideously understaffed; the doors should have been unlocked ten minutes ago, and quite a few of the customers were beginning to approach the Hut and gather around looking restless. Amelie and Daphne went outside, but closed the door behind them, not welcoming anyone in yet. A woman in a red straw hat, dark glasses and a lemon and white halter top, who had exited an Aston Martin convertible with a large dog and a small man, waved insistently at Daphne and called loudly, across five metres and ten people, "Hey Miss … Miss … Miss … do you speak American?"

"I speak English, Ma'am, but I have an American helper arriving here soon who can translate for us if it will help?"

The woman looked quizzically at Daphne, and a number of heads in the crowd looked on interestedly to see how this one would pan out.

"That's so sweet of you," said the American Lady, testing a smile. She didn't believe she lacked a sense of humour, but she found it was often elbowed out of the way by a resolute demand to be taken seriously.

"What I'll do is speak English for a while, and if I struggle with any of the quainter idioms I am sure you will help me out. All I wanted to ask really is when are you opening up? Is there a problem?"

Daphne was smiling now, she couldn't help it. She realised without being particularly conscious of it that she was attracted to this woman, who seemed to have wandered straight off the set of a Tennessee Williams movie. She had that Elizabeth Taylor Suddenly Last Summer look that everyone was trying to copy this season – only this one was really succeeding. Daphne checked out more carefully the companion the Lizalike had unpacked from her vehicle and decided he was not boyfriend material, not even close. Interesting. She had a feeling about Suddenly Last Taylor but, given the current work stresses, decided she'd have to park that for later.

"No problem at all, it is showtime, we're ready to go! Can I please ask everyone with pre-bought tickets to make a line Here; thank you; and anyone who is wanting to buy a ticket now, please queue

Here – thanks."

The customers helpfully complied, while Daphne turned a little nervously and opened the door – the two of them would just have to take the pressure – but luckily as she did so, Albert, warned by some sibling telepathy that his sister was in distress, came hurrying up the path drying his hands on a rag, and jogged the last few metres. Amelie kissed his cheek as he crossed the threshold.

Tommy had also arrived and started to play, which immediately helped to change the mood. The show had started. He began with some jaunty folk dances, ran them into a couple of classic chansons, then rolled on into an Aznavour which got the customers humming and tapping toes. After that he showed off his party trick of asking the crowd to call out any piece they wanted, uncannily always able to play their favourites.

Once Daphne had wedged the door open, the people from the Queue With Tickets were welcomed in, the *billets* were taken (this was the easy bit), and those customers were shown to the appropriate racks of clothes and accessories. Albert worked inside with Daphne, while Amelie now went outside to charm and count the Queue Without Tickets while they waited – this was something they had rehearsed. But progress was slow, and they could tell the customers were getting just a little bit fretful.

Two more customers drove up and wandered over to join the queue, and that was it – forty in total. Amelie, following her training, which she had not considered very intense at the time, popped into the Hut, checked with Daphne, and with her approval went to collect Jean's favourite sign from where it leaned with its face against the back wall. "Here," said Daphne, passing Amelie a feather boa off the rack, "hang this over the corner of the sign when it's up – it is an 'All Clear' code for the boys." Amelie winked back (honestly, she could wink well), this was a very exciting development.

With quite an effort she managed to pick up the sign and get it out of the Hut, and she then began to stagger towards the carpark entrance. A terribly nice young man in a stripy blue and white t-shirt, white sun hat and rather thick spectacles spotted her struggle and daringly left his place in the queue to offer help. Normally he would be much too shy for such a venture, but his timing turned out to be perfect because Amelie was about to be dragged down by the weight of the sign and its metal stand. Helpful Lad was aware he would be no more able to carry it by himself than Amelie, so he signalled with the international symbol of wheelbarrow hands, upright at knee level, that they should share the load. He grasped the legs, Amelie kept hold of the top, and they were off, crabbing across the thirty metres to the carpark, and arriving just in time to erect the stand as another vehicle was entering.

EXPERIENCE COMPLET

L'Expérience est complète aujourd'hui – désolé!

S'il vous plaît venez nous rejoindre demain xx

The car spotted the sign and swung straight back round, giving them a rueful wave, which Helpful Lad returned with a sweet and inexplicably enthusiastic grin. Our willingness to please is unfathomable and precious, but in this case sadly proved a little too dorky for Amelie, who was about to start quite fancying her helper but unconsciously decided instead to trigger her Wet Alarm. While he was doing his waving and grinning, she was fixing the boa rather fetchingly across the top corner of the sign. She turned and was starting to head back to the Hut, with the boy now panting after her like a puppy.

Then another car pulled into the parking area, and did not leave immediately, despite the sign. Instead, it parked, and the three occupants climbed out; Claude, Jack and Milo. They saw the feather boa; big tick. Even so they scanned the landscape for an ambush: who knows, a wily *gendarme* may have cracked the code and festooned a bogus boa. An unlikely scenario, as they could see Amelie standing right by it. Finally convinced the coast was clear, Milo and Jack began to jog across the carpark towards her, while

Claude, a bit stiffer and slower, nursing his pains, trotted gamely in their wake.

As they approached, Helpful Lad stepped forward boldly to intercept them with his left palm outwards – the sign for Halt! – and with his right hand pointing at the sign.

"Pardon, Monsieurs, I am so sorry, we are closed now today, please try again tomorrow, we will try to fit you in."

"Who the fuck put you in charge?" coughed Claude, wheezing from the effects of his twenty-metre run and about to fall to his knees.

"Jeez, Amelie," snorted Jack, not sure if he was joking or serious, "we're away half an hour and you've already got another pretty boy in tow."

Milo was lighting a cigarette and laughing. "Is it OK if I smoke, sir?"

The handsome young lad was now utterly baffled. He looked to Amelie to back him up and rule on their application for entry; and to do her credit she put a kind arm on his shoulder rather than allowing his complete mortification and whispered in her best Bardot, "It is OK, *mon couer*, these are our friends." Whether it was the huskiness, the "*mon couer*" or the mutual possessiveness of "our," she effortlessly won him over, and carelessly gave him the most sensuous moment of his young life, one he would always remember. So all five of them, now a band of brothers, hurried quickly up to the Hut, where on entry they faced the icy blowtorch of Daphne.

"Bloody hell," she scolded in her best stage whisper, "where the heck have you been?! We're trying to run a business here."

"Sorry sorry sorry – you did say come at the last minute."

"Yes OK, well the police have not been around, so we're all right, and it just makes it annoying because you could have been here all morning."

"Sorry, Daphne, we got caught up in the mission, apologies, we're here now, we'll sort it, don't worry," soothed Milo. "Sorry."

"It turned into a mission, then? How did it go?"

"Tell you later, nothing happened yet."

"Who's this?" she queried, looking at Helpful Lad. "He with you?"

"No, he's with Amelie."

"He's not!" Amelie interjected.

Helpful Lad's face collapsed in the kind of depthless despondency that can only be truly experienced by a seventeen-year-old boy who has been intensively in love with the same woman for seven or eight minutes, then summarily dumped.

"I *am* with you."

"No," said Amelie, firmly, "you're not. You helped me erect the stand; it was beautiful while it lasted, but now I need you to be a man, go back to the end of the queue, and try to forget me."

His head dropped, and he pantomimed the desolate drooping of the shoulders. He was about to speak back – perhaps "We'll Always Have Parking" – but under the collective scrutiny of Jack, Milo, Albert, Claude and Daphne he thought better of prolonging his pain and shuffled out in abject humiliation.

"Christ, Amelie, that was brutal," said Jack, who was unconsciously re-evaluating every chivalrous thought he had nurtured about wanting and needing to protect her, and simultaneously also reassessing quite a few of the less virtuous dreams and fantasies he

539

had fostered about their mutual short-term future.

"You're right," Amelie said, looking guilty, "that was over the top. It's been a very hard few days, sorry, I'll look out for him later and make it up. Without encouraging him."

"Always walking the tightrope, eh?" Milo said, aiming to show sympathy but getting a smack on the arm for his troubles.

"OK, OK, everyone, come on, focus, gather round now," cried Daphne, raising her voice slightly. "Where is Albert, where is Tommy? Bring them in....

"Here's the rack, everyone sort their jackets, ok?

"Right, I think we have been forgetting, it does feel like we have been doing this now for weeks, that this is our official OPENING DAY... Yeah!!!"

They all whooped, stamped and hugged each other. After the days of practise, this was the real thing, the first thirty-five-franc Experience. Many of the customers, both inside and outside the Hut, heard her speech, and began to clap. They were the first guests; they were part of it too.

"Let's do it well," Daphne said, passionately. "Let's do it for Jean!!"

The clapping got louder, and Tommy played La Marseillaise.

"Rise up, you children of our country, The day of glory has arrived!"

Everyone sang together that most marvellous and inspiring of all songs.

When the world had calmed, Milo asked Daphne on behalf of the latecomers, "What's the word from the hospital?"

"Nothing yet," she answered, as she had finished ticketing the last of the pre-bookings and the group had a second by themselves. "I am expecting Caroline to come by, I tried the phone earlier but I couldn't get through to the ward."

"What about police?"

"The Inspector from Bourges – you know him dad, right? – did call at the Lodge after we ran. Amelie and Albert are confident they eased his concerns and thoroughly convinced him no crime has been committed, and no criminals or fugitives harboured. They sent him on his way - right Albert? – and since then no *gendarmes* have been spotted in the vicinity. So that's where we are.

"OK, everyone," she clapped, "final focus now. Get your blazers on, and let's start bringing in the Unticketed customers, please. We need to get everyone out on that river."

The clients who had already been processed were having all kinds of fun now, forgetting the delays and getting into the swing of it; choosing characters; trying accessories; some also applying a little foundation and theatrical make-up that Daphne had put out – eyeliner and lipsticks especially. In addition they had the dramatic bonus of the employees bantering, arguing, flirting and gossiping amongst each other in barely disguised whispers. It had not gone unreported in the area overnight that the Experience yesterday had been rather fantastical, including a swan frenzy, free champagne, wonderful food, a brilliant play, and a crazy helter-skelter charabanc ride. Suddenly they felt they were among the team and sharing their secret dramas: it was exciting, clearly this was the place to be, everyone was beginning to anticipate a magical day.

Milo and Jack went out and started to greet and organise the customers in the Queue Without Tickets and show them into the Hut where Amelie and Daphne handled their money and issued them their passes. As that queue dissipated and people milled over to the racks and began their fittings, all the team moved among them, offering advice, alternatives, other ideas from drawers and shelves they hadn't spotted.

Outside the earlier customers who were fully regaled were trying out their characters, swishing boas on and off, doffing bowler hats or straw boaters, buttoning waistcoats from the bottom, then the top, spinning watches, pushing *pince-nez* up and down their noses, holding their sticks from the handle, then halfway up the shaft, all to best effect. Several Yvonnes were naturally flirting with Frantz and Francois, while old folk in faded faux fox collars and tipped top hats were chattering and bowing to Meaulnes and Madame Seurel; dancing children in sailor caps and floral wraps skipped and chased under everyone's feet, tangling madly with two longsuffering dogs on dangling leads that wanted to join in, and tripping over a snooty cat in a velveteen basket that was equally keen not to. Tommy was sensing the mood and adapting as he moved among them; some Merry Widow, some Maurice Chevalier, some more folk dances, some Piaf, some Verdi.

As the last delightfully outfitted customer left the Hut, finishing a tiny application of eyeliner, Daphne followed behind, locked up, and suddenly they were setting off, only a couple of minutes behind schedule. Close to fifty people, costumed and blazered, beginning to wander down towards the riverbank, like the famous scene from Zuleika Dobson, or as if Pierre Auguste Renoir's Luncheon of the Boating Party had come to life and strolled out of the canvas languidly in the direction of Jean's barge. Then Tommy began to increase the tempo and gradually raise the pace, and soon the group was singing and swinging and tripping their way up the path to a Django Reinhardt medley.

Of course, real life never hesitates to interrupt an idyll, so it was no surprise to Daphne when Caro screeched up just as they were proceeding past the wall of the carpark, causing every head to turn. (Well, there hadn't been any upheaval for several minutes, so some were grateful for the thrill to break the routine.) Caroline got out of the car and lit a cigarette, with virtually everyone in the customer crocodile by now watching avidly; her secret signal to Daphne to 'come over for news' ended up being as surreptitious as a farmer trying to imperceptibly summon his best dog to heel in front of a grandstand full of expert judges at a closely contested sheep trial.

Rather than going back to the gate, Daphne lifted her leg over the low wall and luckily navigated the clamber, if not exactly gracefully, at least without an actual slapstick fall. Stumbling slightly into Caroline's arms she grabbed her hand and pushed the cigarette into her mouth as a kind of interim calming mechanism – she was anxious. She remembered to look over her shoulder and signal by the shake of her head and a shooing hand palm motion at waist level that the kids needed to carry on moving the travellers to the barge, no losing momentum.

"Don't worry, Daphne, the news is good."

"You could have called and said that."

"It is only a ten-minute drive, and the phone there is always busy – easier to come, and besides I needed a break as I haven't slept. Bernadette came to the hospital a while ago and I've left her there alone for the time being.

"The danger seems to be past, fingers crossed. The Doctor came in at dawn and checked him all over. Whatever it was he didn't want to happen hadn't happened, so he's more positive now. The chances are with Jean – we can cautiously begin to be relieved."

Daphne hugged Caro genuinely now, rather than using her as a kind of general leaning post. Turning round she saw Milo and Jack had dropped back to the end of the caravan and were almost walking backwards in their desire to keep eye contact, so she gave them the massive double thumbs-up they had been hoping for: they yelped, returned the sign, and span back on their way.

"What happens now?"

"He's not conscious and the doc says he won't be today – I think the idea is that the drugs are going to hold him under for his own good."

"OK, fair enough. We know what our job is, we'll keep the entertainments going and give everyone a great day. I'll come over to the hospital this evening when we're finished. Those lads and my dad are accelerating the quest for Mac, I haven't been told too much about where they've got to yet, but they were out this morning on the trail. Obviously after what happened yesterday things are coming to a head, one way or another. What they'll do if they find him I have no idea. Claude is staying one step ahead of the law himself at the moment, he doesn't want to be questioned, and he's ducking the Inspector."

"Ah the dodgy Inspector! He's been round to the hospital. He seems very calm, that type who believes he should avoid appearing diligent in order to show off how intuitive he is. And pretending to be a little dumb. I gave him a list of five or six places where your dad used to hang out thirty years ago – including his old school, I think. And that garage he worked in before the war. They'll have fun with him if he turns up there, I think Claude was sacked for being overly attentive to the owner's wife?"

"He never did that, but sadly in his younger days he didn't mind people thinking he did. My mother went round there before she agreed to get engaged to him, just to check her out; she said she was really nice, very sweet, soft spoken and kind-eyed, all of which reassured mum that she wouldn't have had anything to do with dad. But we digress."

"We do indeed. You'd better get on. I'm going home for a bath and change, then I'll get back to the hospital and relieve Bernadette – I'll see you after work. Break a leg!!"

"You should be really careful what you say given the luck we're having on this project," Daphne laughed. "I'll see you later, doll." She kissed her on the cheek, leapt the wall, this time really quite athletically, and jogged to catch up with the boat party.

"Well?" asked Jack. "How is he, is everything OK?"

"So far so good," Daphne replied, conscious that at least three or four of the customers were going slowly purely to eavesdrop on the crazy carnival folk. "The Doctor says he's gone past the period of most danger, so they're cautiously optimistic now."

Milo and Jack whooped inside, and arms were lightly punched between the three of them, above the elbow and below the shoulder, in best congratulatory style. The good news was already passing up the crocodile from pair to pair at lightning speed, and some sporadic clapping broke out.

"On the other thing," Daphne said to the boys, dropping her voice to what she considered to be a whisper, which meant the sound travelled only five metres instead of ten, "they're all over the hospital, and I am guessing we can expect a visit sometime today up at Hill House, so we'll have a chat about that when we get off the boat. Be on your guard." They nodded as sternly as any Great Escaper entering the tunnel; who does not thrill at the admonition to be vigilant?

At the front of the line the customers were now arriving at the jetty. Claude had been panicking about the boat, knowing he and Jean had left it in a mess. Daphne had reassured him they had recovered it in time, and that Albert had been tasked to clean it up. Sceptical, he'd raced ahead to check that the awnings were straight, the chairs were polished, and the decks were mopped, and he was amazed at the quality of the job the boy had done – the boat was looking her finest, glowing in the late morning sunshine. He pulled Albert aside as he arrived and virtually hugged him with gratitude.

There was a lot of chattering among the guests, they were loving the Experience itself, and enjoying the costumes, the embellished landscape and the antique magnificence of the barge; but also this extra, the additional frisson of intrigue and adventure coming from whatever was happening among the crew in real life. Jack could sense the duality and romanticised idly, recalling Meaulnes's visit to the Estate when on the surface there was the splendour of the fete, the games, the gorgeous guests, the brilliant and beautifully dressed children, but underneath there was the drama of love lost and found, of abandonment, wandering, exile, a gunshot in the night and the shadow of death.

'Maybe that's a bit moody,' he decided, turning his focus onto loading the passengers, pointing out the lifejackets, giving the safety announcement and directing their attention to the sunshine glinting on the river and the fabulous decorations running up and down the banks as far as the eye could see. Eventually they settled, Claude engaged the engine, they pulled steadily away, and Tommy began to play his evocative melodies as they glided elegantly along.

Without spoiling any surprises, I can tell you now, up till quite close to the end, this day went very well indeed, probably even better than the day before. Which is not to say there were not some oddities and quirks; but let us montage events swiftly this time, rather than going slowly scene by scene, in case such repetition bores you.

It was a gorgeous day, and the river, barge and ribbons and garlands woven into the hedges and trees were displayed to their best. The boat, with the glamorous passengers bedecked in their finery, relaxed, laughing and taking a glass of this and that, looked superb. For his second change of tune, Tommy played La Mer, always the favourite, and most of the company joined in the special song. Milo made his own translation as they went, "Past shiny reeds, white birds and red-roofed houses"; but there was no white bird today, no swan; on the one hand a relief, on the other, a reminder of all kinds of drama, and their friend and chief in hospital.

Much gossip was generated by the sight of an extremely handsome *gendarme* with a very large moustache who was now sitting in the gap on the riverbank by the swan's nest, on a high-backed dining chair, smoking his pipe and looking sternly straight ahead. He did not adjust his gaze nor acknowledge the greetings as every single person on the barge waved to him as they sailed past and called out gaily, "Bonjour, Monsieur!" before breaking up into groups to chatter.

Albert gave Daphne a look that said: 'Better late than never'; she smiled and nodded back: 'Just as well he didn't turn up early enough to confiscate the barge!'

At the Hill House jetty the group disembarked excitedly and began to move off up the slope at such an eager pace that Jack and Amelie had to run in front and circle back round to bring them under control like collies nipping at the toes of a rather expensive and exotic flock. "Let us take our time, enjoy the walk, revel in the beautiful river scene, smell the scent of the flowers, and spot the gorgeous stars and moons embroidered in the trees and foliage." Jack and Amelie laughed together, spinning like May dancers, and the passengers as usual all thought 'What a handsome and blessed couple.' His hand brushed hers, and his nerves were shocked as if he'd grazed a naked cable. Jean was not there to see it, but Milo and Daphne did. Meanwhile the accordion played on, with Tommy moving seamlessly from sea shanties to country jigs, from folk ballads to romantic arias.

The buffet was as always more a banquet, and the sleight of hand men and jugglers excelled themselves in their art as the guests ate and watched in wonder. The highlight was the chief magician getting a small girl to choose-a-card-any-card, which she dutifully did, a little fearful that she might forget it, so he recommended that she showed it – without letting him see, of course – to the rest of her family. He then walked twenty metres to the buffet with her five-year-old brother and told him to pick any one of the melons that he liked. The boy was excited to do it, but also anxious of course that he might get it wrong and spoil the trick. Once he chose his fruit, perfectly round and untouched, and embraced it heavily in both arms, the prestidigitator nudged him gently back and the little lad walked nervously to his family, where the conjuror asked him to pass the melon to his sister, who gravely inspected it, and pronounced it Perfect and agreed it was Unblemished. To the girl's mother he handed a knife, requesting that she cut the fruit in two. As she did so, to the amazement of all (for a large crowd had now gathered around), out fell the Four of Clubs, picked up eagerly by the little girl.

He knelt and looked her in the eye. "Is that your card?" he asked, and don't let any magician tell you their heart is not in their mouth when they ask that question. The little girl looked up enquiringly at her parents, and they nodded. "Yes, it is."

Spontaneously the whole audience erupted with applause and laughter, this was the most extraordinary thing they had ever seen. Of course you must, please, never ask me to reveal the secret of how this trick was done; there is a code that describers of magical illusions must live by.

As the meal began to wane and the guests were resting, some snoozing, the actors ate a little themselves, then drifted up to the changing rooms. Bernadette joined them there, straight from the hospital where she had handed over the vigil temporarily to Uncle Jerome, whom she had rather nervously left in sole charge till Caroline returned. [You remember Jerome of the hard-to-locate farm who had the tractor that Georges wanted to borrow to push Guinevere off the bridge: keep up now, please.]

Bernadette was looking grey and white; the lines in her face which yesterday had emphasised her remarkable good looks were now scratched in charcoal like an antique print dulled under dusty glass. Jean was still "on the mend," she said, but he hadn't woken. Although he hadn't said anything, she knew he wanted her to come to the theatre to make sure the performance went perfectly. All they could do at the moment for him was to continue the Experience success.

And on that note, the performance was, indeed, perfect. The virtuoso actors, the whirring projector, the flashing boards, the megaphone make-up, the classic costumes, the balmy weather, the empathetic and excited customers, and, of course, marvellous Madame Jestique, who added a new overture based on L'apres Midi, all combined to create one of those nights that legendary thespians write about in their biographies. At the end, as hand-cuffed Harlequin was pushed off to jail in a handcart – a new wrinkle from Claude, who was back Policing this evening to give exhausted Madame Terroir a break – the audience stood as one, cheering, clapping, stamping and slinging their hats high in the air. Milo suspected that there was less caution than usual in the chapeaux tossing as the bonnets and boaters were the property of the Experience, but he took it as a great compliment even so.

And then the tea dance, with Madame Jestique's trio (plus the irrepressible and unquenchable Tommy) creating an absolute sensation, all the actors and crew joining in, Julie providing some of the most exquisite patisserie anyone had seen, and a psychedelic array of cocktails, now seemingly expanded, while Milo had per-haps been a little distracted, to a rather broader ranges of colours, shapes and sizes, brandishing feathers, swizzlers, umbrellas and novelty stirrers, arrayed along the bar, quivering like the plumage of a flock of exotic birds perched on a rainforest branch.

Everyone was dancing as wildly as the Bruegels, but Amelie was most particularly enjoying the revels, spinning and swirling be-tween Jack (wishfully), Milo (joyfully), Albert (brotherly), Tommy (tunefully and, with the accordion grinding breathily between them at the height of Amelie's tiny nose, warily), Helpful Lad (of which more later), and several other young men of varying degrees of handsomeness who were smitten and enamoured but also ex-tremely overawed. It is the role of loveliness to be seen, but perhaps not so much to see; and, however attractive, these suitors formed a willing line of the unremarked because she rotated around one after the other without particularly noticing which was which.

However, just as I was writing that, ironically something did catch her attention as she was dancing; a shape out of the corner of an eye, as we say, intuitively alluring to her, and without thinking or knowing she leaned into a flashing pirouette, accepting a gyrating outstretched hand, which then twirled her twice before pulling her close into a heaving manly chest, below a perfect jaw which hosted a mouth as chiselled as a Greek statue, that whispered quietly into her perfect ear, "Hello, Amelie, I bet you've missed me."

"Karl!" she squealed before she could stop herself, so loudly that every dancer stopped and turned.

Madame Jestique stopped playing immediately, instinctively realising what was happening, and her two companions followed her lead. This left just Tommy squeezing out the final spirited notes of Elvis's Don't Be Cruel, till, looking around and observing everyone else was standing stock still, he shyly halted his squeezing and the accordion gradually ceased breathing in his arms, like a gently smothered lamb.

"Well, it is delightful to see you've missed me, babes," said Karl, deliberately using the unwanted diminutive endearment to belittle and unsettle. "I just knew you weren't as happy as the others to see me go!"

"You have a short memory, then. Or just the same narcissistic self-delusion. What the hell are you doing here, I thought you had marched back to Germany in a sulk?"

"Well, firstly, nice talk, doll, I appreciate the instant analysis as well as the sad change of heart."

He was sounding off loudly, ever the Karl, with half the people on the dancefloor staring mesmerised at a spectacularly beautiful youth making himself so ugly. Five or six people – including Jack, one of the waiters, Tommy, Daphne and Madame Jestique halfway off her piano stool – reacted more quickly and moved towards the pair with the various intentions of asking him to quieten down; inserting themselves between them; or, in Madame Jestique's case, giving the boy a stinging slap with her heavily sequinned glovelette. But holding them off with a palm, he continued, relentlessly:

"And secondly, I never went back to Germany at all."

Looking around as though he were the cleverest person in the world to think of this, he said smugly, "I just got off the train at the first stop and came back. Since then I have been spending a bit more time with my friends over there, actually it was those kind gents that invited me to the party."

As he said "over there" he held his hands up high above his head, bent at the wrist with palm and fingers pointing down like a playground bullfighter, and swept them around in a circle drawing attention to the outer circumference of the terrace area behind the dancers. When they all turned round to see what he was indicating, they found that four uniformed policemen had assembled unnoticed (including the Constable from the riverbank with the massive moustache), spacing themselves out around the perimeter, with between them a couple of men in plain clothes, presumably Detectives. Albert recognised one of them as the Inspector from this morning.

"What the hell is this, Karl?" asked Amelie, dropping her volume to a whisper, embarrassed to be caught yet again in the middle of a circle of gawpers with this beautiful, obnoxious manboy. "What have you done now?"

"It is the reckoning, honey," said Karl, without bothering to moderate his tone. "You're a nest of crooks, but you made me out to be the bad guy. Time to turn over the rock and see what's crawling underneath."

As he was talking, the Inspector was making his way through the crowd to the centre, not exactly pushing people out of the way, but not holding back either. He was clearly incensed, and Karl began to smile as he saw him coming, thinking, 'Now they're going to get it rough.' But when the Inspector arrived in the middle it was Karl he grabbed by the upper arm and marched straight out of the ring, his face just centimetres away from Karl's, almost spitting in his anger, and barely restraining himself from tapping his extremely hard head sharply onto the boy's temple.

"I thought I told you to keep quiet and stay in the background," he yelled quietly at Karl through gritted teeth, continuing firmly to pull him away from the crowd and eventually around the corner, out of sight.

"I agreed to look into this only on the understanding you would stop interfering, what the hell do you think you're doing? I took a big risk bringing you here. Don't think we have all turned out here because we like you; frankly my guys can't stand you. You've got us interested in what might be going on, but if we're going to investigate we need finesse, we do not need you seeping across the dancefloor like shit from an overflowing toilet. You understand that by alerting people, if there is anything remiss, you will only send them running?"

I can add what he did not share with Karl; that the local police hierarchy – at least those without actual blood-ties – had been thinking for some years about delving a little into the tribe of Jean and Claude. The current events presented a convenient excuse to dig deeper. Leopard's chief droned on endlessly that, "The joke is wearing really thin now; somebody needs to take a hard look at that busload of supposedly loveable rogues."

Leopard never liked being told what to do, but he was going along with his boss's wishes for the time being because he'd got interested in these kids, because it kept him nicely out of the office and away from his epic backlog of unsubmitted reports, and because he smelt an opportunity for self-gain, whether it be favours or something more solid.

In terms of actual crimes, and real violence, he knew perfectly well that Pierre and his genuinely nasty gang of thugs were the real problem in the region, but he had learnt long ago never to query his boss's preferences for persecution (the chief himself described it as "priorities for prosecution") in this prefecture, as they inevitably dated back to some tribal squabble over a land boundary in 1887 or a timber deal that went wrong in 1905.

Karl was shocked and shaken by Leopard's hostility. Although it was not in his temperament to show remorse or apologise for anything, he was smart enough to recognise the Inspector's genuine anger, and cunning enough to feign contrition.

"Sorry, Inspector, I didn't realise it would blow up like that. I was just saying hello to an old friend, really. Actually, I genuinely thought she liked me." This last wistful comment caught Leopard unawares, and he had a moment of sympathy for the boy, as Karl intended. "It won't happen again, I promise. Look, here I am, back in the shadows already." So saying, Karl reinforced the pledge by physically withdrawing himself into the shade of the house and indicating he would stay there, peering round the corner, while the Inspector and his men did their job.

"Very well, Karl, I trust what you say. Stay here, say nothing. I understand the person you invited – without our permission – is arriving at the train station in a couple of hours. This is tiresome, but I suppose I will see you there; but not before, please."

The Inspector turned and walked back onto the terrace, where, oddly, he realised the music had started up again, and dancing had recommenced. What he had expected to see was his men firmly holding Claude, Jack and Milo in the centre of a ring of agitated observers and waiting for him to get back. He was already planning on calming the crowd and asking for their patience. However, instead there were dazzling swirls of colour, the upsurging tinkle of innocent laughter, Madame Jestique effortlessly accelerating across the keys to outpace the sweating Tommy, and a whirl of dancers filling the floor.

Given that this throng included a mix of upstanding local citizens and wealthy tourists, the Inspector thought better of stopping the revels for a second time. His Sergeant was hanging off to one side, talking in an animated whisper to Daphne, with Albert and Amelie looking on from two metres. The Inspector approached. "What the hell is going on, Pelou? Where are the men we are here to question?"

"I'm afraid, Sir, that while we were all watching you dragging the young lad round the corner, they…. well, they sort of disappeared."

"Disappeared? What do you mean, they were standing in plain

sight in the middle of the dancefloor!"

"When I looked back, they were gone. They melted into the evening, Sir. The men have spread out to look for them, they can't have gone far."

"You'd be surprised." The Inspector breathed deeply for a moment, determined to be calm and professional despite the infuriating use of the phrase 'melted into the evening'; but he did purse his lips just enough to make sure Pelou was not left in any doubt about his disfavour.

"And I am guessing this must be Daphne Nuage, am I right?"

Daphne's first instinct was to deny it, but as she had known Guillaume Pelou for about twenty years – since she sat next to his younger brother in Arithmetic – she reluctantly realised that might be pointless.

"I am. And you are?"

"Inspector Leopard of the Bourges constabulary."

Daphne gave it her best shot but couldn't hold in the laughter.

"Seriously? Like the big cat? You identify your prey, stalk it, and chase it down at sixty kilometres an hour?" She couldn't resist making the leaping cat paws and meowing.

The Inspector looked at her, not angry, even slightly smiling. "That's not the first time I have heard that, sometimes even from people who have made it sound amusing."

What the banter told him about Daphne was more important: she didn't have the fundamental respect for the law that was ingrained early in regular civilians. It was a big contrast to the nervousness and shy deference he had encountered from Albert and Amelie earlier. It showed him something of how Daphne had been raised and said enough about her father to reinforce the feeling that his investigation was not going to be a hunt for the golden beetroot (a much-loved local idiom arising from the tale of Young Jack of Orléans and his hopeless quest to win the daughter of the Grand Duke).

"We have been hoping, Daphne, to meet up with your father. Just to ask him a few standard questions, you understand; of course he is not a suspect in anything."

"It is kind of you to let me know, but I am not sure why you are telling me?"

"Well, only that he was here a minute ago, and now he seems to have evaporated."

"In a cloud of smoke," Daphne said, archly straight-faced. Amelie and Albert sniggered.

"Excuse me, I don't see the joke?" the Inspector queried gently, not allowing himself to be irritated – from long experience he knew patience and general good humour were a much safer path to success.

"My dad is the world's most passionate toker, Inspector. Commonly he cannot be seen for the industrial smog of nicotine fumes he spreads around himself like a cloak of invisibility. Maybe he is standing just behind you."

Leopard managed to stop himself turning around, though he cursed himself for twitching just enough to make the prank work. Again, he chose the tranquil approach, even allowing a tiny flicker of amusement on his lip to aid the moment.

"Well, I hope if the wind blows sufficiently to reveal his location to you at any time you will be kind enough to give him my compliments and let him know I would love the benefit of a short conversation?" He reached into his pocket to find a name card, which he politely handed Daphne.

"I will relay it, Inspector, if I should see him." Daphne had been raised to harbour a substantial degree of gratuitous animosity against any cop who was not one of her cousins, so she was surprised to find she was struggling to find anything particular to dislike in this man. "But he only manifests sporadically."

"What about his young friends, Daphne, how frequently do they manifest? Again, I thought I saw them here just moments ago, leading the dance and choreographing your customers. Did they melt into the same cloud of fog? Did you see where they went Amelie? What were their names again?"

He was staring squarely at Amelie now, and he had twisted his frame just a few degrees so she was forced to look away from Albert when she answered him. If she turned towards Albert it would be obvious she was struggling to come up with a response. She was about to start panicking. Not only could she not remember if there was an agreed version, she also couldn't, in the moment, quite recall what they'd already told Leopard that morning. Had they managed to avoid it altogether? So what could she say now, other than the first things to come into her mind, essentially 'Arrghh' and 'Urrrrr,' which didn't sound too convincing either singly or as a pair.

Then she had one of those flashes of inspiration that only come in the best stories. The Programme. Jean's beautiful booklet. On the third page was the list of cocktails available, including their somewhat lurid titles and ingredients, so that at the afternoon tea this could now be used by the less-knowledgeable customers to choose their stylish beverage with the naughty glee of children in a particularly indulgent sweetshop. I mention this in digression only to explain why there was a copy of the brochure on every table, and this was what caught Amelie's eye now as a possible lifeboat – or maybe more accurately one of those brightly painted flotation rings that hang from posts on cliffs and at the end of the pier or harbour where they are so common that they disappear from perception until there is a swimmer drowning with their arms madly flapping above the waves. As Amelie was doing at that moment.

The third page was the drinks, but the last page was the cast list for the Harlequinade. This meant two things for Amelie: for her good side, smart and resourceful, it provided an immediate on-hand answer to the question that possessed the virtue of having at some stage been considered and approved by Jean and the boys; and for her weaker side, it meant she no longer had to worry because if she simply showed the Inspector the public information available to all, she was neither responsible for the consequence, nor, as they say, a grass. Such a relief.

She reached down to the closest table, nodding with her warmest half-smile to the occupants. She made the gesture 'Pardon' then the pointing sign for 'May I?' followed seamlessly by 'Merci Bien' as their copy of the booklet was in her hand, her back was already turned towards them, and the coquettish smile she'd chosen to use was now quickly closed and then reopened for the Inspector in a more sweetly innocent version.

One of the males at the first conscripted and then abandoned table was Helpful Lad himself, and, too late, thinking she was there again for him, he had half risen to say hello. In fact, true to her word, Amelie had sought him out earlier on the barge to repair his wounds; and she had spent ten special minutes with him, basking him in the solo orbit of her sun, her whole attention on him, looking deeply into his eyes and listening intently to his stories, laughing with an irresistible effervescence even when he hadn't realised he had made a joke. She had even discovered his name, though sadly (or perhaps just as well), it is forgotten to us now. And she had left him there sweetly and gently, making sure she boosted him in front of the friends who were watching, but also careful not to give him any future ideas.

But that was then, with a promise to keep, and this was now, and she had sadly, due to the stresses of the police interrogation, over-looked their bond once more. She was gone in an instant, purpose achieved, leaving the boy gasping in the little cloud of magical dust she had left floating above him. Could it be that by trying to make it better, she had only made things worse? Beautiful people are condemned to walk the highwire, as Milo said, while the rest of us just long to catch them, or hope to see them fall.

Trying to indicate to the other members of his party that this vision who was well known to him had simply been a little distracted, he failed to find a gesture to cover the full complexity of the situation. Fortunately, the interaction had gone largely unnoticed among the men: but it was quietly observed by a rather genuine, unattached, well-matched and charming young woman at the table who was becoming marginally interested in him. Sighing, she saw at this moment that he was not what she had thought, she felt sorry for him, but not in the way that would encourage love. Who knows what might have happened between them for a lifetime if Amelie had not leaned over their table to rescue herself with the pamphlet for Leopard?

The Inspector took it from Amelie, with an upward nod of the head that asked, 'What is this?' "You see here," she said, "in the list of actors in the play – there are their characters and names."

"Thank you very much, Amelie, this is really useful," the Inspector said, quite genuinely, while at the same time failing to eradicate all of the suspicion from his tone. Turning to Daphne he asked, "Are we sure this is the correct edition? Our information is that the cast does seem to change on a daily basis." Dry sense of humour? 'He seems to know a lot more than he should,' thought Daphne, as she reached out for the pamphlet. "Let me have a quick look to make sure you have the most up-to-date version. Ah, yes, it is. You see here it says Clown is played by Scott, the American boy; and Pierrot, it says, is being played by Francois, the boy from Paris."

But even as she was speaking, Daphne wondered if the game was up in terms of the boy's identities. Was Leopard stringing them along? Since he'd spoken to Amelie and Albert in the morning, perhaps even before then, Karl must have been trying to pour his poison in the Inspector's ear; looking at the half-smile on his face, even if he was still dubious about Karl and his theories, didn't it look like Leopard already had an idea who Jack and Milo were? Perhaps he'd just been having a bit of fun, squeezing them one by one to see what came out?

Madame Jestique and the trio were bringing the penultimate number to a close; they had been playing Jailhouse Rock to annoy the police, but honestly speaking no-one had really noticed. She looked around for Daphne because they were getting ready to move into La Vie En Rose as the slow final song once again and that would be Daphne's cue to go to the microphone and make the general winding-up announcement.

Madame Jestique spotted her with the Inspector, and it did not take any intuition for her to see she was flustered and in a little trouble. She nodded to the rest of the band, went into the traditional loud succession of chords that shouted, "Someone is about to make a speech," and they all joined in, making as much noise as possible. At the same time she made a 'Help me' signal to Julie and Bernadette, and they started a round of applause. No-one can resist a good clap, and soon the whole audience was smacking its hands together and stomping its feet, without entirely knowing why. Then Bernadette started chanting "Daphne... Daphne... Daphne... Daphne..." and everyone joined in with that, too, laughing.

Leopard looked around, first startled by the racket, then irritated as soon as he realised it had been deliberately orchestrated to curtail his impromptu interrogation. "Sorry, Inspector, got to run," called Daphne over her shoulder, already on her way to the bandstand, and barely able to disguise her relief ('He's onto you anyway,' she thought). "As you can see, our fans are impatient!"

Winking gratefully to Madame Jestique, she took the mic from the singer and turned to the customers: "Ladies and Gentlemen; all the Yvonnes, Frantzs, Meaulnes, Valentines, Francois and Madame Seurels; and all the wonderful characters and guests of all ages that have combined so marvellously to make such an extraordinary

559

Experience today, our Opening Day. Thank You.

"Now our adventure is nearly done. Julie and her team will come among you in a moment with a last glass of champagne. The next dance from our amazing ensemble will be our last, and then please let us collect our things and take a gentle walk down the hill to the landing stage – accompanied by the gorgeous music of Monsieur Tommy – so we may commence our tranquil river journey back to the farm carpark to collect your vehicles. I hope you have had an enchanting time!"

So saying, she quickly nodded to Madame Jestique to strike up the band, and as the first chords of the Piaf classic hit the air she randomly grabbed one of the more elderly gentlemen from the audience and swung him into a rhythmic shuffle close against her bosom, from which, truth be told, he never fully recovered.

The centrifugal force of the contentedly dancing throng swirled the Inspector and his men gently out of the circle till they ended up clustered on the fringes, watching; whence, inevitably, they were finally joined by an exasperated Karl asking, "What happened? Where are they? Why did you let them go?"

Leopard looked at him, shrugged, decided he no longer wished to humour the youth, and called, "Sergeant Pelou, perhaps you would be kind enough to escort Monsieur Karl to the railway station? I will meet you there shortly." And with that, his back was turned, and he was heading to the carpark behind the house, with just one more meaningful glance across the dancing to Daphne, who, while pretending not to see him, indicated by the defiance of her posture that she had no guilt and felt no fear. He wished he hadn't looked.

The last notes of the dance faded and the revellers moved apart, shyly or boldly, sadly or gayly, then fumbled for their hats and bags before joining together once again for the dreamlike stroll down the slopes in the early evening sun, the first gradual stage of moving back from century to century, from fantasy to verity, from romance to reality. Some wished to stay behind, but the barge was ready, they had to go, and Tommy played some lively tunes to raise their spirits as they arrived at the jetty. Fearing that without Claude, Jack and Milo – in the aether – they were under-numbered and probably breaking all the laws of the ocean, Daphne had enlisted Bernadette to come down with them to help with the customers, and Tommy, for the purposes of the voyage home, was also being counted as crew. Bernadette was clutching the keys to Claude's car, as he had taken hers when they fled the scene. They would swap back in the morning.

So the five of them, including Amelie and Albert, who, by dint of neither having been stabbed nor having gone on the run, now qualified as the longest serving, saltiest and steadiest seadogs in the fleet, safely embarked the tired passengers. Once everyone was comfortably seated and the safety announcement was read, Daphne started the engine, and they pulled away bathed in a fading golden light that picked out the paper and fabric flowers amongst the foliage to create a spellbinding tunnel for the magic boat to glide gracefully through. Gracefully, but not silently, because Tommy, releasing himself unilaterally from his passenger care duties, began to play a haunting piece on his accordion, actually an adaptation he had created himself from a Ravel piano Nocturne, breathtakingly beautiful, superbly atmospheric, and never heard before by a human ear except his own, alone in his studio. It was perfect, it was divine.

And I think there we will leave them, as our story is beginning, finally you may say, at last you may think, to intensify elsewhere. Be assured, our passengers now, after floating mystically, musically back along the river, arrive wonderfully dazed at the farm landing, return their costumes, and cheer long and loud when Daphne awards the daily prize to one of the youngest girls, fabulously dressed from head to toe before she even arrived in period clothes of the most elegant and authentic styling. The Opening Day is done; another great day for the Experience, and all that Daphne and Bernadette can think, as they then head in Claude's car to the hospital, is how pleased Jean would be with them all if he was awake.

PART THREE:
DOWNHILL WITH LETTERS

THURSDAY, CONTINUES

Our action now moves to the railway station, where Karl has been virtually held prisoner by Pelou for close to an hour, waiting for a train he knew was not due for another two.

Every five minutes the young man, pacing back and forth like a polar bear in a sad zoo, asked Pelou the same questions, with varying accumulating degrees of frustration and bad language, to paraphrase: "Why are you holding me?"; "You know it was me that cracked the case?"; "Why can't we go into town and come back later?"; "Why are all policemen so fucking stupid?" The dedicated Pelou, though privately cursing his boss for giving him such a disagreeable assignment with this – how shall we say – loathsome youth, said nothing, and largely ignored him, which only, of course, had the impact of making Karl more irascible.

Time passes in this unbearable manner, punctuated only by the long-suffering and imperturbable Pelou rewarding himself for his persecution with a small dry cake every half an hour, and Karl smoking heavily and drinking the odd coffee. Meanwhile station life moved from the busy-ness of the after-work crowd of office types and labourers travelling home one or two local stops up the track, into the quiet of the early evening, with intermittent trains stopping and starting, and a light flow of excited people off to the bigger towns for the theatre or cinema, or on longer trips to the city, or the capital, or maybe even abroad.

Then, shortly before the Paris train was due in, here was Leopard, pulling up in his official car, parking carelessly right in front of the main entrance and slipping a rather pompous **Policier au Travail** sign onto the dashboard before walking in, leaving the vehicle unlocked. It was one of his strongly held beliefs that no-one in the area would dare cross him. He put his head round the door of the station café and before he even caught sight of Pelou he sensed and saw the tension in the room, the overflowing ashtray, the pile of tiny cake dishes, the empty coffee cups that no-one had wanted to go near to collect; and then his gaze moved to the enraged German boy corralled by an invisible barrier, imprisoned in a corner like a bull in the ring trapped by nothing more substantial than the matador's shape and willpower.

"It is time," he called, not wanting to enter, "come, let's go to the platform, we don't want them to miss us."

Pelou stood to one side and signalled to Karl that it was now perfectly fine for him to leave the bar. Leopard was already half-way across the concourse, and the boy and Pelou double-timed clumsily to reach him like new recruits treading on each other's heels while trying to keep up with an impatient corporal. Thus the three arrived at the barrier to the Paris platform just as the train came to a halt emitting a thick plume of filthy steam. Through the smoke they heard doors opening and closing; a few early souls, late for appointments, came running out, followed by a trickle of passengers holding handkerchiefs over their faces, looking around to get their bearings, some staring hopefully at the three men as though they might be the people there to meet them and whisk them off comfortably to wherever it was they were headed. "Sadly not us," they gently shook their heads back at them.

Then the whistle sounded, and the train pulled away, dragging with it the last vestiges of crepuscular fog. As the visibility cleared, there were just two people left on the platform; both women, one with an extremely large tartan printed suitcase, the other with a kind of scouty canvas rucksack; and this time it was the turn of the three men to look hopeful as the two approached the barrier.

'Are you the visitors we are expecting?' Leopard asked only with his shoulders and eyebrows as they stopped before them. 'Yes, I think so,' came the silent reply, a half nod, and a cautious humourless grin, from a woman who was clearly on the edge of her nerves.

563

"You must be Mrs Kelly?" enquired the Inspector, in his most polite, civilian, non-law-enforcement tone.

The tartan suitcase looked very confused and made it clear not only was she not Mrs Kelly, but she had never heard of such a one – she looked around for another greeting party, suddenly panicked that they were at completely the wrong station.

"Kate, they think you are Alice," said the scouty rucksack, putting her hand on the lady's arm. As she spoke, Pelou realised she was not really a grown-up at all, but a girl, maybe seventeen or eighteen years old.

Quickly pocketing her initial fluster, the older woman began to compose herself and held out her hand to Leopard. "Apologies, are you Karl? I'd imagined from Alice's description of the phone call you were a lot younger, sorry – also a bit more German, honestly speaking. Also, we were expecting to meet one person, not three." Warily she continued, "I'm Kate du Lac, Jack's mum."

Now it was Leopard's turn to be discombobulated. "No, I am not Karl, Ma'am, I am Inspector Leopard of the local constabulary. I thought we were expecting Alice Kelly, mother of the boy we have been told is known as Milo?"

Kate was shocked to hear she was speaking to an Inspector, really that was the last thing she needed. Looking worried now, she thought, 'What the hell is going on?'

"Milo is my son Jack's best friend; we were told the two of them were here together. What do you mean by 'been told is known as Milo'?" She said this with her voice rising in pitch and volume; it had been a long and anxious journey, and it was becoming evident that they had been drawn there under false pretences. "Has something happened to the boys – are they OK?"

"It is OK, Madame, please be calm, I have seen both of the lads very recently and I can assure you they are in good health. Can I suggest, let's go into the café here, where you can have a refreshment, and we can chat a bit more quietly out of the public gaze. I see we've worried you, and that is the last thing I would want."

[Let me mention here that Kate was married to a Frenchman for nearly twenty years and spent up to a month every year in France and has no problem at all conversing freely in the language. But I think you knew that.]

As they crossed the concourse to the café, to the casual observer it would have appeared that the two women were under police escort; and the same spectator would have assumed Karl was in charge, so confidently was he still comporting himself, even after the humiliation of being in custody for the past few hours.

There was no table for five people, so Leopard sat at one table with the two women facing him, and Pelou and Karl sat at a smaller table to the side, turning their chairs so they were facing them like a chorus, or jury. After they were all seated a rather nosy waitress (who of course had been in the same class at school with Pelou, though she was now rather younger than him) spent twice as long as strictly necessary to take their perfectly simple orders, hanging around overfamiliarly till the Inspector decided the pleasantries were over and it was time to begin, and shooed her away, not unkindly. He realised if he left it any longer to start, people would be put at their ease, and that is the last thing he wanted.

"Madame du Lac, would you like to introduce me to your charming daughter?"

Leopard was looking at the girl next to her, but Kate did a classic look over the shoulder to see if someone was approaching. "You worried me, Inspector, is she coming too? As far as I know, she is in England at the moment, probably..." [looking at her watch] "... tucking her brother up in bed and reading him tales from The Victor comic of our Matt Braddock, V.C., Britain's Master Pilot."

Karl looked quizzically at Kate, unsure whether this was some kind of insult, but she seemed totally unaware of him. Pelou sniggered inside.

Leopard, aware he was being teased, and bored already with the joke about the missing daughter, but prepared to go along with it, gave the traditional shrug and eyebrows to say, "OK you got me, now give me the punchline."

"This is Maggie Lovechurch, she is not a relative, she is a good friend of Jack's, and of course she is worried about him, so when Alice could not come, Maggie suggested she could keep me company, and help me."

'That's me,' thought Maggie, wryly, 'nominated without much hope of winning in the category of Least Well-Defined Sweetheart In A Supporting Role.'

"Why did Madame Kelly not come?"

"She is the owner of a business, in England, a large pub – you would say bar, I think."

"Madame du Lac, I do know what a pub is," Leopard smiled gently, "we in Bourges are really quite sophisticated in our own way, we read books, we go to the pictures – some of us have even travelled abroad."

Kate couldn't help grinning; as others had found, the policeman had charm, which mainly came from not trying too hard. "Of course, sorry. Anyway, she holds the pub together, she can't be away at the moment, so I am representing both of us. She's looking after my youngsters while I am here."

"I understand. So, Madame du Lac, can I check, do you mind if I ask you a few questions? This is not an official interrogation, of course."

Kate nodded, slightly nervously. She was automatically and instinctively wary about what she might reveal to the police. "Yes, it is OK, but I am not sure why, I was expecting it to be the other way round."

"Oh, why?"

"Well, we weren't expecting to meet a police Inspector, to be honest."

"Well, I am sorry if I have given you a shock, I promise you I am probably more surprised than you are. Why not tell me what brings you here?"

Kate was perplexed that he didn't know already, but decided he was one of those types who liked to play it a little dumb and pretend he was ignorant in order to get you to drop your guard and confess. Anyway, she was determined to give him only the scantiest information.

"Well, a man called Karl called on the phone to Alice, in England, and said he could locate our boys for us; he said that they needed our help but they weren't hurt and they had asked him to summon us. We believed him because he knew they were in France, though we didn't – we thought they were in Yarmouth."

Two minutes in, and Leopard was thoroughly confused. He mouthed "Yarmouth?" He couldn't help looking at Karl questioningly, and Kate noticed.

"Are you Karl, then?"

Karl did everything he could to a) avoid Kate's gaze; b) evade the question; and c) mentally flee the café. He said nothing, looked at his shoes, and metaphorically put his fingers in his ears, chanting na na na na na na na na.

"Why didn't you say on the phone you were a policeman?"

"I can assure you, Ma'am, he is nothing to do with the police," interjected Pelou fiercely.

Leopard held his palm up to the Sergeant, flapping it down a couple of times, like a strict but kindly teacher waving to a noisy child across the schoolroom, gently, not harshly, to ask him politely to be quiet and keep calm.

"Karl's position here is no more and no less than your own, Ma'am. He is a member of the public, unofficially helping the police with their enquiries."

It wasn't quite true of course that they had the same status, because Leopard found he really liked Kate from first impressions, whereas he had known Karl for, what, thirty-six hours, and had thoroughly detested him for thirty-five-and-a-half of those. 'Still,' he thought, rather sweetly, 'with my years of professional training I have no trouble disguising it.'

Karl was looking more and more uncomfortable, and Pelou now comprehended what had been behind his pacing, smoking and vile temper for the past two hours. The young man had sensed that whatever he had been trying to plot was about to unravel, and he had lost control of the situation. Pelou began to experience an inner glow of childish anticipation like the excitement when they were children waiting for Pantaloon to get his bottom kicked in the Christmas play, knowing it was going to happen way before anyone else did.

[Thinking that reminded him, what had all that nonsense been at this afternoon's performance, with Harlequin getting arrested? That fake cop had no idea how to take a suspect into custody – even from where he'd been standing, about twenty-five metres away, he could see that the handcuffs were upside down.]

The Inspector sensed the same thing as Pelou; Karl was squirming. Leopard had a very good idea why and was not about to let him off the hook.

"Karl, I think you told us that the boys' mothers had contacted the Lodge looking for their lads and you happened to pick up the phone? So you said the boys were there, and that's how you were aware that the mothers were on the way? And because of something the woman told you, you knew the sons were on the run in France after something bad had happened in England?"

Kate snorted, then looked back down at the table. The Inspector went on. "But now we're told you approached these families with a tale about their sons here in France, to encourage them to come here, is that right? Being honest, I have to say this story feels much more likely, it doesn't need three decades of police experience to favour that version. The question then is, why would you do that? Would you like to say what's going on, please – I don't like to be taken for a fool."

Kate by now was looking white, realising she had wandered into a trap; and not even a well-laid ambush, but a shambles she should have spotted five hundred miles away. While Leopard was focusing his scariest glare at Karl, she risked reaching cautiously across the table and tapping Maggie on the hand, signalling "We're in trouble, say nothing, let me do the talking." Raising her eyes, she saw Pelou looking at her, had he seen?

"I am waiting, Karl, let's hear it, please," insisted the Inspector.

"You can't question me like this. I am not a suspect. I have a right to some privacy, why are you asking me in front of them?"

"I thought we were all friends, Karl, all on the same side, just chatting. You seemed to be OK when you thought we were interrogating these guests in front of you? In fact, I think you were really demanding that. None of us wants this to turn into something official, right?"

Karl settled slightly and began slowly to realise that he didn't have so much to lose in this situation. He had achieved some of his desires easily, in the act of moving people around the world at his will to fulfil his plans; and no matter how much he was currently embarrassed, unless the police here were utterly hopeless, he would eventually achieve his vengeance, whether or not they liked him (even Karl was beginning to suspect they possibly didn't, given how often they joked about it).

"OK," he retorted, suddenly full of his old feist, "why not? Here's the full story, and I apologise in advance, Madame, if anything upsets you, you may not know your son as well as you think."

Kate stared levelly at Karl: he did not know her, or he would have probably shut up. Instead, self-importantly confusing her silence and empty eyes with a supplicatory willingness to hear his story, he ploughed on with his usual arrogance.

"I will give the short version. I am – I was – involved, along with several other students and youngsters, with Jean Terroir's enterprise which he pathetically calls the Grand Meaulnes Experience. For various reasons, to do with conditions, payment, lack of organisation, some people left the show before it launched. Then suddenly these two boys arrived to take their place, one claiming to be American, one saying he was from Paris.

Their behaviour was suspicious, and it was clear there was more to it, it was all too convenient and mysterious. Also, I hate to say it" [nodding to Kate and Maggie] "but in their true light, seen honestly through objective eyes, these are not pleasant people."

The four in his audience shifted around with different degrees and types of discomfort, not quite believing that this narcissist was attacking the character of the children in front of their own families and expecting them to agree with him.

"Some in the party decided to investigate, especially after they started causing discord, there was a threat of violence, maybe there was some theft, certainly there was a lot of lying, indubitably there were sexual tensions. Basically both those boys, as you surely know, are troublemakers – especially the one who called himself Francois."

He looked at Maggie, now revelling in this. "I am sorry to say so, if you are the girlfriend from England; but honestly speaking, whether it was the freedom of the road, the romance of France, or the blood on his hands, your lover rather quickly started firing at a fresh target, he is perhaps a little of a lady's man, would you agree?"

Maggie had her head in her hands and was visibly, and audibly, sobbing. She didn't know what he was going on about, with Francois, but was guessing by a process of elimination that he was almost certainly referring to Jack.

Pelou, a kind and chivalrous man who was a father of daughters, was red with rage, and about to do something indiscreet to Karl, above or below the table, when Leopard intervened – not least because he'd realised that he had made a maverick mistake in creating this open discussion forum rather than holding proper interviews, at the police station, under official caution.

"Karl," he barked quietly, with his rather sinister flat-toned politeness, "please, you will stick to facts, cease the embellishment and stop using this as an opportunity for exercising your spite and vengefulness. You are being absolutely foul – I suspect you know that and don't really care – but that's not something we want to be involved with, we're not a tool for you to use. If you don't stop, then I am sure I can find a reason for you to spend half the night in the holding cell while Sergeant Pelou here goes through the law books to make the longest list of charges against you that he can find. So would you prefer to be silent, or would you prefer to civilise your tone now, show some respect to these kind people who have travelled a long way to help us, and continue your story in an inoffensive manner?"

Karl had had his fun, he thought to himself, so he decided to enjoy the rest in a more understated manner, and this he acknowledged to Leopard with a smirk and a brief nod of the head. He voiced no apology, but just went on in a slightly less cocky manner.

"After some particularly bad arguments and dubious events, I was tasked to check them out. I searched their rooms, I have no shame in saying that, and found some false passports and clothes with different nametags, so by now we had a variety of disguises and fake identities. A couple of papers and items gave me some small clues about where they had come from, and which of the names were really theirs.

"At that time, I was particularly in conflict with the boy who was calling himself Francois. He was preying on a young girl in the group, someone I had taken a protective interest in; his advances were not welcome, and I needed to stop that. Of course, it became obvious quickly that this boy was not a stranger at all, or a new random recruit, he was a relative of the boss, Jean. Jean called all the shots, with his henchman Claude, so I stood no chance of straightening things out, in fact I was hounded out when they saw that I was on to them."

Leopard observed from her reaction that this information especially piqued Kate's interest. He interrupted Karl.

"You know them, Ma'am?"

Kate hesitated, then immediately realised that the momentary vacillation had given her away, so she decided she had no choice but to mostly tell the truth.

"Well I guess if it is the Jean that owns the River Farm, then he is a relative of my husband; when I heard Jack might be in this region, it was one obvious place I would have made enquiries, as Jean is a distant cousin of my son, though he is quite a lot older, they know each other quite well."

The Inspector nodded, his good detective gently beginning to weave together unconsidered threads, while his bad cop shouted at himself from ten centimetres away, nose to nose, spittle flying into his eyes, "You complete fool, how did you fucking miss that?"

"And Claude?" he asked casually, straining to keep the eagerness out of his tone.

"Yes, if that is Claude Nuage, then he is also a childhood friend of my husband, though I don't think Jack knows him."

Karl pushed himself back into the conversation insistently: "Do you wish me to continue, I though you wanted to know?"

They both looked at him, and nodded, Kate with some relief at being removed from the spotlight, Leopard a little irritated at having his flow broken, but he could pick it up later.

"Well then, yes, I agree, I was angry to be so unfairly treated, in such a humiliating way – I think that's understandable. So, I called various powerful people I know" [he positively simpered with reflected aggrandisement] "and had some enquiries made. They found I was right about the identities, and they could trace them to the pub in London, as I thought. Then it turned out that my contacts were not the only people making enquiries, they found out someone else was on their case because there had been a bloody knife fight in that same pub a few days before, and the suspects in the attack had fled – those suspects being the lads we were investigating. They are on the run in France, it seems, with the police after them in England, hundreds of miles off the scent. Am I wrong about that, Madame du Lac, it seems strange you did not mention it?"

The Inspector was now realising the magnitude of his blunder. This situation was much more serious than he had imagined if half of what Karl was saying was true; and by the look of Madame du Lac it certainly seemed likely. She looked like she was ready to lunge at Karl, and she was even toying with the sugar shaker on the table as though weighing it up as a potential weapon. That made Leopard wonder a little about the mother – not that he blamed her specially – and in turn without really thinking it out loud, as it were, it planted a seed about the son. Leopard recognised immediately that he needed to end this drama, split the parties up, and finish the job professionally, as he should have done from the outset.

573

"Sergeant, would you be kind enough to escort Karl down to the station? I will come down soon and, if you don't mind, Monsieur, I think it is time we had a proper chat, as you clearly have more to tell us."

Pelou rose, but Karl dug in.

"What the hell do you mean? I've done nothing but help; I drew these people here for you, you should be questioning them, not me; why do I have to spend time at the *gendarmerie*?"

"Our guests must be tired," said Leopard, "they need some rest now."

He was not really looking at Karl anymore, but making an open-handed gesture to the women with arms reaching out from the elbow, palms facing up to the ceiling, ready to catch anything that falls, the universal sign for, "Sorry about all the trouble, about the difficulties you have encountered reaching us; you are very welcome here, what can we do to make your stay more comfortable?"

"Where are you saying, mesdames, if I may enquire? I hope you have something organised? Or perhaps I can help? It would be useful for me to know, if that's OK."

When he asked if it was OK, his tone softly made it clear that he needed to know anyway, whether it was all right with them or not. Kate realised that, and was about to answer when she saw Karl, still stubbornly sitting, and with his ears wide open. She gestured to Leopard that she was prepared to have the conversation but not in front of the boy. Karl glared. Pelou gave him a little assistance in getting up, with a strong hand under his arm that left a bruise later. Shaking it off, Karl finally stood, pink with anger. But the Sergeant had been doing this for a great many years and was already using Karl's upward momentum to accelerate him towards the door. Then they were gone, talking out by the car, arguing about whether the boy would sit in the back or the front. Watching, Leopard knew he had a problem, also he understood that Karl was a soul that would never be happy with anything less than one hundred percent control, there was no compromise. He was surprised the lad didn't ask Pelou for the car keys and insist it was his turn to drive.

Outside the semi-circle of lights in the forecourt it was now fully dark: this wasn't an area of town that had many houses and businesses, just the café, a man doing shoe repairs who left every day at 3.30pm (presumably to avoid an inconvenient evening rush of business), and a florist who opened every other afternoon. There were no taxis.

He turned back to the ladies. "So, I am at your service. There are no cabs, so I will be happy to take you if you would do me the honour. Do you have a booking?"

"No, there was no time. In any case, as we discussed, I have friends and family in the region, so we were intending to stay with some of those while we are here."

"Where are you expected first?"

"Well, not actually expected, as it happens. We weren't able to get through to him before we left, but the person I know best, and who I know has space, is Jean, so frankly we were just going to turn up at his place tonight. Can you take us there?"

Again bad cop was out, yelling into Leopard's ear from a few centimetres, extremely loudly: "Fool, dolt, idiot." She didn't know, and he had yet again failed to join up the dots, an alarm bell should have rung earlier when they were talking.

"I am so sorry, I didn't quite realise how close you were, there is something I should have mentioned."

At this clumsy intimation of doom, Kate immediately looked rattled once more. "What are you saying? Is it Jean, has something happened to him?"

"He is not dead," Leopard jumped in bluntly, aiming at reassurance, and missing badly. He was normally really good at these things, dealing with events and occasions that required sensitivity, diplomacy; he prided himself on knowing what those in front of him were thinking and feeling. This seemed all to have deserted him now. Maybe the English give off different signals.

"So, he is ill? He's injured?" Kate asked, with hardly less consternation than when she thought he might be dead. She received little emotion back from Leopard, though he was quietly indicating concern for their predicament.

"He is in the hospital, he has been badly hurt, but he is now in a stable condition. What happened to him is under investigation, I cannot really discuss it."

"And yet you did! And now you are refusing to reassure us."

"Perhaps the most reassuring thing would be to go to the hospital, would that help?"

Kate looked at Maggie, who had been patiently holding her tongue now for an hour – much longer than she had ever done before. Maggie had picked up the admonitory signal from Kate that silence was still the correct policy, so she nodded acquiescence, sensing the hospital visit was what Kate wanted. Maggie didn't know any of these French characters, and her sympathy currently was the sympathy of a passer-by observing a horrible accident, not someone directly involved in the event.

However, she had grown to love Kate over the years, her boyfriend-in-denial's long-suffering mum, and she was prepared to support her in any way she could. At the same time, she also suspected that Kate herself was at least half a stage removed from full engagement in anything in France not directly related to her son's welfare. Kate was not the blood-related side of the family, she was only rather precariously married into a clan which at times had seemingly shut her out; and Jack had told Maggie that his mum felt very let down by the lack of help from the French relatives, who always seemed to know more than they were telling, in hunting for Mac.

So, Maggie was ready to support Kate as much as she was able, but she was really only here for Jack, and from this initial skirmish, that clearly wasn't going too well. Other than being used as an unwitting sounding board for a vitriolic polemic on his character faults and duplicity, with graphically specific footnotes covering aspects of his infidelity (what joy!), it felt as though her role had been completely subsumed in some greater drama, to the extent she was struggling to get a credit as Assistant Sceneshifter let alone First Girlfriend.

Leopard went to the counter to see if he needed to settle for the drinks but was brushed adamantly away by the waitress with the silent understanding that payment from the police is preferred to be taken in future favours rather than tangible currency. The Inspector happily endorsed the system though he never troubled himself to keep a record of what he owed and couldn't remember any particular time he had honoured his part of the bargain; anyway, he had no time to argue, nor did he have any money on him, when he came to think of it.

"Ladies," he said, trying, but failing, to sound solicitous, "will you please follow me?"

His unlocked car was still crookedly lodged at the top of the station ramp, half-guarded by the assistant from the ticket office who was leaning on the wall by the door, smoking.

"Evening, Reynard," said the Inspector, ironically touching a non-existent peak.

"Night, Inspector," replied the world's least enthusiastic railway worker, unable to bring himself to agree with the policeman even about the time of day.

"No-one's messed with the motor. Got any room for me yet in the force?"

"Not yet, Reynard, but your commitment to watching my car tonight has pushed you right to the top of my recruiting list."

Kate got in the passenger seat, after first making the hilarious tourist mistake of getting in the driver's side behind the wheel. Maggie got in the back, keeping her head down. Leopard slid in, started the car and pulled away in the direction of the hospital. The women, exhausted, dozed on the journey, uncomfortable, uneasy. And when they arrived and pulled up in the carpark, as they emerged from the vehicle, there, immediately in front of them, were Caroline, Madame Terroir and Daphne, smoking and looking almost as though they had assembled there specifically to meet them.

Although Caro and Bernadette were well known to Kate from her annual holidays – Daphne not quite so much, but vaguely – she was still surprised to see them, and they were shocked to see her, no-one had warned them she was on the way. Daphne was equally taken aback to encounter yet again the Inspector she had managed to send packing a few short hours before. The women embraced, in parts, and collectively, because there was no point pretending they were strangers; but as Leopard was listening, they all instinctively knew this was not the time for too much talk besides the natural enquiry about how Jean was doing. Therefore, as we are quite constrained about what Kate can say to Caro, and what Bernadette wants to tell Kate, I think we might as well draw a line under this strand of our history for the time being and resolve it later: let's for now renew the focus on Jack, Milo and Claude.

At that instant, they were sitting in Bernadette's borrowed car, in a lay-by off a road that runs through a very dark part of the forest, arguing (currently relatively politely) with Dessie. She was in the passenger seat, next to Claude, dressed from throat to ankle in camouflage army wear. On her feet, thick oxblood boots laced up to the calf; on her hands, black gloves of kid leather, with protective padded sausages bizarrely set on the upper side of the fingers and thumbs ('Like fetish batting gloves,' thought Jack, fleetingly yearning for the innocent summer cricket of home); and on her head, a dark brown elasticated beanie hat that Milo suspected folded down to make a terrifying balaclava, probably with bloody fangs appliqued around its mouth. Ringing her eyes was smudged black and jungle-green make-up, and she was sporting, bandolier-style, a belt hung with various knives, torches, twines, tapes and compasses. When they had stopped to pick her up from her wayside café the three men had certainly been impressed by her total commitment to the classic night-stalking wardrobe, and Milo and Jack noticed a heightened excitement in Claude's over-comradely greeting, which Des professionally brushed away. Concentrate.

"You don't look properly dressed," she had said to the two boys (Claude, clothed all over in brown as he now was, just about passed muster).

"We had to melt into the evening," Jack had replied, using a special army officer reporting voice he was working on. "When the police arrived at the Experience after the play had finished we were lucky to get away amidst a distraction. We had no time to prepare to the level we had planned."

Milo nodded, trying to keep his face frozen in a losing battle to remain mirthless.

"Look you little sods, this is weighty business, you can laugh at me if you like" [glaring at Milo, who was now really having to wrestle with the sniggers] "but if you want to catch Mac in the woods, trust me, you need to take it seriously."

It wasn't as though they hadn't tried. They had, after all, removed their stripy blazers and stowed them safely in the boot of the motor. But what they were left with had disappointed her. After a little scratchy negotiation – like a school mum trying to get a vest on her son on a cold morning – both Jack and Milo had to submit to pulling on extra-large black t-shirts over their light-toned summer shirts. They had '**Dessie's Dames**' written on them, apparently the

579

required uniform for her endlessly tolerant and unembarrassable waitresses. "Sorry lads, that's all I've got here tonight." Dessie then handed out flashlights, whistles and other bits and pieces to the boys who had, admittedly, turned up hideously under-equipped.

The argument in the lay-by three hours later was about direction. Not just which way to go, but whether or not they were currently lost. They had started out well and found the first two hides that Dessie had marked on her ancient map relatively easily. One of them had been so obscure that even Mac clearly had never seen it, in fact there was nothing to indicate any form of human habitation had taken place in it within the last decade. The next had been used and even had one of the blue gum wrappers which Mac seemed to be employing as deliberate signposts, given he made no attempt to conceal them. Unless he thought no-one would ever come looking for him or was simply beyond being bothered by that. There was no clue as to when he had last been there, or where he might have gone, so they reverted back to Dessie's archaic charts to determine where to look next.

And that's when it started going askew. They had driven around for nearly an hour, missing junctions, choosing wrong turns, and insouciantly using invisible roads that Dessie's antique cartography assured them were not there. Jack and Milo in the back were thinking, this is like going out for the day with squabbling parents, except maybe a hundred times worse, as it is now pitch black, very late at night, and we are exhausted, starving and frankly scared to death of catching dear old dad-on-the-run who has recently stabbed a cousin and decapitated a swan. And Claude and Dessie, in the front, were momentarily saddened to be reminded of the repeated spats and tiffs that occurred the last time their youthful romance was on the wane. Claude reached out a conciliatory hand to Dessie, and she took it reluctantly.

"OK, let's focus."

"Agreed. Let's just head generally towards the Madeline farm," said Dessie, gloves off now, her manicured finger, tipped empathetically with night-black nail varnish, prodding insistently into the map. "There are three places. One on the way, where I know he has been quite often, well located, well hidden, we might as well try it first, it is not too far off the track, we might be able to surprise him.

"If he is closer to the farm, he will be somewhere around the circumference, I am sure now. Either to the north, here, in the fringe of the managed woods with the best view down into the dip of the farmhouse; or to the west, here, deeper into the wild forest, a much better hideout. But if he's there, we have less chance of taking him unawares, less chance of finding him at all, actually; and the stream is quite wide there, running between the forest and the main farm fields. The north is closest and simplest, let's head there second."

The lads' heads were spinning with this plan, but fortunately they weren't driving. Claude, who was, seemed marginally more confident, and set off again, tuning the radio to a station with some American Blues. Dessie reached over and tried to change it: "Jesus, Claude, you're such a downer, find us some Johnny Hallyday."

"No Hallyday."

"What's Hallyday?"

"You've never heard of Hallyday? He's the French Cliff Richard."

"The French Elvis"

"He's not."

"He bloody is."

"No Hallyday."

She messed around with the knob a bit more, and, instead of Hallyday, came up with Itsi Bitsi Petit Bikini.

"Seriously?"

The lads were rolling around screaming with laughter in the back, being small boys.

"Nothing wrong with Dalida, you need to get your head out of the States and the bloody jazz." Then wistfully, "Johnny does a cracking version of that one, too." More howls from behind.

Luckily, they weren't going much farther. Dessie started calling out distances and directions, and they'd been driving for less than ten minutes before she turned round to the boys and said, "We're about one kilometre from the farm of Madeline, I think you know all the stories by now, right, Jack? I am so sorry, but this is the area to look for your dad because, speaking honestly, he has been spotted hereabouts so many times, by various friends and locals. This goes back a decade, maybe more, even when you were here on holiday with your mum, I hate to say it. We have all of us at different times tried to warn him away, and for years we thought it was OK, he was gone for good, back to London, to stay. Then he was back. I am not sure if Madeline knows it yet. Certainly, her bloke Hugo doesn't, or he would be out looking with his gun. You know Hugo?"

Jack shook his head, which was already sinking down with the weight of attempting to excuse, justify, respect, or at least find some way to understand his father. He knew, and remembered, Hugo's name and personality from his dad's memoir, but he chose to take Dessie's question literally, and in any case, it was much easier not to get into that.

"Mac and Hugo were friends in the years after school. Also with Andre, till he married your Auntie Anna and they went up north. You know Anna and Andre?"

Jack shook his head again in the back, on the same basis. He knew them well from the journal, but not from life. Dessie couldn't see him, but proceeded on the assumption he'd said no.

"Well, when I say the three men were friends, they got into

scrapes together, mutually created some deep dark secrets, became renowned and notable drinking partners, and dragged each other down in horrible ways.

"Hugo finally got out of that cycle for a while, and I believe Mac never forgave him for straightening himself out. Specially as part of the recovery process for Hugo was acquiring the same girl Mac had lost when he spiralled out of control.

"Of course, the irony since then is that after the first year of their marriage I doubt Madeline has gone many weeks without regretting her relationship with Hugo, either when he was sober, or specially when he returned to being drunk, which he has been for much of the last quarter of a century. Not much of a life achieved by running away from your dad, Jack, though that's not much consolation for anyone."

Jack was silent in the back of the car, looking at his lap. Milo pushed his hand quietly over and squeezed him above the knee. Claude gave Dessie a soft elbow in the rib telling her enough is enough, lighten up.

"OK, here, here!" she shouted suddenly noticing they were on a narrow backroad she recognised; everyone jumped out of their seat with the combination of the unexpected yell and Claude standing frantically on the brake. 'Good way to change the subject,' thought Milo, gratefully. As the car shrieked to a halt, Claude pulled the wheel over so it skidded into the side of the road. "Jesus, Des, give us a chance."

"This is the place," she said, ignoring him. "The hide will be in the woods, around thirty metres back from the road, somewhere within a hundred metres of where we are now, up or down the road."

"He'll have heard us and scarpered."

"Not necessarily, all kinds of people come along here, drinkers, lovers, hunters. We could just be a couple out for a shag. Claude, do you want to simulate, to put him at his ease if he is watching?"

Jack and Milo put their hands over their ears and started shouting "No no no no make it go away."

"If you're going to simulate sex, do you mind if Jack and I get out of the car first?" said Milo.

"I didn't bring any protective clothing," Jack said, "and I have reason to believe observers could be at risk."

Opening the door, giggling hideously with embarrassment, Milo called to Jack, "Come on, you and I can search down the road this way while they fake the reverse honey trap."

"Can the hunt be long and very far away, please."

But Claude had already jumped out of the front door. "Hang on, Milo, I'll come with you, you don't know the woods, so best to have someone experienced in each team. Jack, you go with Dessie, she can show you the way." Remarkably they all agreed this seemed like a sensible plan. The worry was that they had already made so much ruckus that perhaps it hardly mattered any more.

"Let's work swiftly," said Jack, thinking he needed to get everyone focused again, "as Claude says, Des and I will sweep up this way, you guys down that way, if we're quick we might see something before everything in the area is scared off completely by our racket. We might as well just go for speed rather than aiming for stealth."

They split off into the pairs and did what Jack suggested, picking up branches and beating through the brush at a fast pace, zig-zagging around and among the first few ranks of trees and across the scrubland between the woods and the road, moving down a hundred, two hundred, three hundred metres. Plenty of life was startled in the undergrowth, they heard it scuttling and going to ground; and even more movement in the trees, maybe bats, owls,

Jack couldn't really tell, except he knew none of it was the human they were after.

Fifteen minutes later, four hundred metres down the line, Milo was beginning to think this was a waste of time. He could hardly see Claude next to him, but they had managed, even in the pitch black, to exchange frustrated shrugs, and naturally Claude had held the torch under his face and poked his tongue out like a naughty boy scout at his first camp, sending the boy into a fit of guilty giggles. Then they heard a long whistle, followed by two short peeps. "What does that mean?" Claude asked Milo. "Did I miss a training session?"

"No-one briefed me either, but I am guessing from context that one long and two short is 'Come immediately, a headless corpse has been found in the library with the candlestick.'"

"Let's hope they are gripping *Colonel Moutarde* by his balls. Let's go."

As they spoke they were already sprinting back towards the car, then beyond it, their two splashes of torchlight spraying randomly in front of them giving vague clues about where to plant their pounding feet in the undergrowth. Milo went over once, scared he might have cracked an ankle, but was up instantly, putting weight back on it, and it was fine. However his face and hands were not so lucky; where he'd gone headfirst into the undergrowth he could feel he was peppered with prickles, scratches, spurs and grazes.

They rushed on, and abruptly, ahead of them, to the left, further back into the woods than they were expecting, they saw the flickering of the other torches. They veered towards the pools of light, Claude shouting "Hey hey, we're here, what's happening?" as a warning more than a greeting, just in case there was a hostage situation or a danger of friendly fire.

"Don't panic, guys," Dessie called back, "the trail's warm, but not ablaze – that's why I piped you 'Join us calmly.'"

Milo was intensely irritated, given he'd nearly broken a leg in their hurry. He looked at Claude, wondering how they should have known it was 'calmly': is there an international standard dictionary of emergency whistle signals, like morse code, or semaphore? He knew that in the Canary Islands natives would enjoy a neighbourly chat from peak to peak using little blasts and peeps: maybe Dessie had been there for her holidays. Claude looked back at him, indicating with a wink 'maybe we let this one go' instead of initiating a night-time quarrel about the interpretation of trills. Or toots.

"What have you found?"

"A camp, down in the dip here," said Jack, "a tarp, food jars, newspaper, chewing gum, a fire that's been extinguished, but still hot."

"Did you see anything?"

"No, but there was a commotion as we came up, something large thrashing away and crashing through the thicket, there," Jack pointed "deeper into the wood. It could have been a medium-sized person, or a larger animal, though I am not sure what, boar? What did you think, Des?"

"It was too dark to see, I just got a shadow by the time I got my torch round. Given the fire was being doused, though, I am betting 'a person,' by which I guess we all think Mac, right?"

"There are strange tales hereabouts," Jack reflected, employing a BBC natural history voice he had been working on, "of a herd of wild boar that make fires and rotisserie each other. Do you think it could be them?"

"Most amusing, young sir, and I guess they also chew gum, drink brandy and do the crossword."

"If it is the English gum, dad has left us a trail of that across most of the region; there's not much doubt he's been here."

"So what now?" asked Milo.

"Sense, if that applies to any situation round here, would suggest he'll..." Des was in full flow when Claude, panicking, suddenly placed his hand over her mouth. [He felt: mouth warm, soft and wet. She felt: hand coarse, dirty and rough.] She got the message and shut up.

"Hold on till we're in the car," Claude said. "Noise travels a long way at night, and if it was a person who ran, they could be lurking round listening."

The four of them stumbled back to the vehicle. Claude pushed Milo ahead of him and shoved him into the passenger seat this time, he wasn't sure why. Jack and Dessie fell into the back.

"OK," said Claude, quietly, "let's keep it low. What's the plan?"

"As I was saying when I was so rudely gobsmacked," Dessie launched, "the obvious thing he'll do is move further over to the west, in the foxhole above Hugo's big field. I reckon he doesn't know we know about that one, and that is the logical place for him to set up now."

"Logical?"

"Well, you know what I mean."

"Happily, I don't really. Anyway, we'll get going, then."

"Slight drawback on that, Claude," Dessie continued. "If it *was* Mac that just escaped us, he'll know we're out looking, so he'll be even more jittery than usual. It is not as though we are in hot pursuit, or even want to be: actually we're supposed to be outwitting him by stealth, and bringing him in gently.

"Also, just on the practicalities, he's on foot, we're in the motor. It is going to take us maybe ten minutes to get there in the car, it will take someone on foot well over an hour, perhaps a lot more in this pitch black as they'll be moving slowly and making sure they avoid detection."

"It's past one o'clock," Jack pitched in, "we need to get up early for work. We can't let Jean down, the show must go on. It is really frustrating, but I agree, I don't see how we can achieve what we want tonight."

"Right now, he's got the advantage," said Claude, "he's watching us, probably, the tables are turned. If we did go there and wait, he won't show anyway, and it will be three o'clock before we know it, and then we'll never get through tomorrow."

"Yes, you're right," agreed Milo, "put like that, it makes no sense to keep chasing around tonight, fun though it has been." This said with some irony: his face was throbbing as he ran his hand over the scratches.

"OK," Claude replied. "I suggest either we get up at 5.00am and try again for a couple of hours," there was a chorus of nervous groans from the others, "OK, not that. So, better, tomorrow we leave Hill House earlier, immediately after the Harlequinade ends, and get out here while it is still light. We know there is a chance Mac will be watching the farm then, and he might be distracted, we have a better chance of parking a good distance from the hide, being a bit quieter, and coming up on him while his attention is elsewhere."

Everyone nodded and murmured various versions of 'good plan.'

"That's settled then," said Milo, beginning to feel a bit shattered and bedraggled, "I wouldn't mind a drink and a fag when we get a moment, and then quite a lot of sleep."

Dessie, from the back, had her torch on him while he was turned to talk to them. "O Lord, my love, your beautiful face! What happened, no don't tell me, you took a nosedive running to help us, right? That's my fault, I am so sorry. Jack, get out and let Milo come in the back seat, I've got a medical kit in my belt, and I can start to patch him up while we're driving."

The boys swapped places. Claude started the car, announcing, "I'm heading back to the Lodge, then, right?"

"Drop me off first, love, if that's OK – it's on the way. I'll reluctantly decline the drink tonight, but it will be great to celebrate together when the job's done. Hopefully tomorrow."

Dessie was talking like a dental patient, slurring her speech through the gap left by the torch she was holding in her mouth which was vaguely pointed into her bag as she rooted for the medical supplies. Claude pulled away, and in the front Jack was also fiddling with his torch, trying to light the map he had inherited from Dessie and guide them home. "Don't worry, son," Claude said reassuringly out of the corner of his mouth as he lit a cigarette, "I can take it from here, I don't need a co-pilot."

"He does, Jack," cackled Des from the rear seat, "he really does; better sort it out or we'll be driving up our own backsides again in ten minutes."

The two in the front maintained a barrage of low-level banter about directions and responsibilities. Although Claude wasn't doing it deliberately, not consciously anyway, he was succeeding in annoying Jack so much that he was forgetting how miserable he was at failing to find his dad – he had really thought tonight would be the night. Claude's heavy humour and outright offensiveness were a decent distraction from the general feelings of despair that would otherwise have overwhelmed him.

Meanwhile in the back, while trying to listen to the front at the same time, Dessie had finally located her cache of war-surplus ointments, unctions and swabs and started dabbing at Milo's face. "Oh my poor pretty boy, those rips on your neck look really sore. On the cheek, not so bad. On the nose, pretty superficial. I don't think your looks will be spoiled; the girls will still want to kiss you."

Milo winced, and it was not just the iodine going into the cuts, then he grinned. "Not so bothered about the girl kissing, to be honest, Dessie, but remember I have performances, I can't let my fans down, my skin must be alabaster, unblemished, by the morning. Work your magic."

But of course, the truth was, by the time she had finished, it looked and felt much worse, and the iodine stains, in particular, made it appear as though Milo's face had been used to mop up a puddle of especially thick horse urine. And Dessie's wrapping of dressings seemed, from inside the process, both rather excessive, and completely random. 'I am undead,' he thought, trying to summarise his current state of being, 'I have risen from my sarcophagus in unravelling bandages after being buried alive for three thousand years.'

They dropped Dessie off at her caravan. The field was pitch black, lit only by the headlamps of the car as they wove between the tables to take her right to her door.

"Thanks so much for your help, Des, sorry we didn't crack it tonight."

"That's OK, lads. It is serious work this, you can't expect to sort it out in a second," she was gabbling a little now, with tiredness. "Mac and I go way back, more than you would want to hear, so I am in for the long haul. He's not himself, of course we all realise that: if I can help him, I don't care how much time it will take. Anyway, I have a few creative ideas of my own, I'll explore them tomorrow, who knows, they might be helpful. Keep the shirts, boys, they really suit you, but please make sure you concentrate on dressing properly tomorrow. You'll pick me up here tomorrow just a bit earlier, right, late afternoon, early evening? Whatever, I'll be here and ready whenever you come, one of the girls can do the late shift for me and lock up."

She hugged all of them, then, after exchanging what looked like sideways glances of meaningful regret with Claude, went inside and turned on a light, flooding the area round the caravan with a soft glow, illuminating the window boxes and tubs of colourful plants, and seeming to throw up a cloud of scent from the night stock and herbs, all tranquil and lovely like a scene from a fairytale.

"Night, boys," she said, over her shoulder, through the open door, "I know it is a stupid thing to say, Jack, but try not to worry too much, we're ahead of the police and anyone else, we'll get there."

Jack wasn't so sure, but humoured her anyway with a parting half smile, designed to make her, not him feel better. Milo knew that smile and squeezed his friend's arm in support.

"OK, boys, to the Lodge; brandy, fag and bed... I reckon we can complete the whole programme in about sixteen minutes." They made it easily, except for bed. Having left Bernadette's car in the drive with the keys in the ignition (standard practice, it seemed, for all vehicles), they were all three lying in the deckchairs in the Lodge garden fifteen minutes later, looking up at the moon, drawing heavily on Claude's toxic cigarettes and chewing on delicious stale croissants with raspberry jam between slugs of raw cognac.

"What a day."

"I think I may have mentioned, they all seem to be like it now."

"Tomorrow, we'll find your dad, Jack," said Milo, desperate to end the night on a positive note. "We came really close. And when we do, we can help, I know it."

Claude fetched another bottle from Jean's not-so-private cache, and kept quiet, not just through fatigue, but also from a cynicism he decided would be better kept unvoiced. He poured large glasses, three-quarters of the bottle between them. He didn't want to depress the boys any further, but he was having a feeling he had had on just a few occasions before. Once when he'd let some friends borrow a barn for a stunt he knew was going to end in disaster; then a couple of occasions in the war, watching a futile rail-track bomb fizzle out pathetically while they were being hunted through the bushes by men with bayonets; and another time, waiting for news about two comrades who had unfortunately been captured alive. It was a mood of intense gloom, a premonition of impending tragedy. He had never yet been wrong.

They drank and talked and smoked, and the sixteen minutes stretched further into the small hours. Finally, the boys fell asleep. 'Thank God for that,' thought Claude, 'these kids are really hard to put down.' He draped them with blankets, then over the next hour looked at the moon, thought a lot at first, then rather less, smoked seven cigarettes and drank the residue of the bottle of brandy to ward off cold.

Later, Jack and Milo woke up one after the other, saw Claude asleep, rolled their eyes at his lack of stamina, and staggered up to bed without saying goodnight or covering him. Each attempted the mantra; Milo got through a dozen lines before collapsing, Jack barely made it to two. An hour before dawn Claude finally roused himself, wandered mindlessly into the living room and fell into the sofa, using the last ten synapses he was allowed to carry over from the previous day to pull half the rug over half himself.

Earlier, at the hospital, long before Leopard, Kate and Maggie arrived, Daphne, Caroline and Bernadette, who had agreed to get together there when the Experience closed, had had a conference to decide who would sit with Jean, and when, in the coming two days. They then collectively met with the Doctor to review Jean's prognosis and his schedule for recovery, and what he might need from them.

Jean was flat out still, swaddled, and had not woken. The Doctor explained this was not something to add to their anxiety, the comatose state was now more to do with the drugs he was being given rather than the original injury, and that the stillness was part of the cure. Daphne suspected he was keeping the message simple because he believed that was all they could understand, but she couldn't be bothered to question him, there was no point.

Caro and Daphne were thinking to themselves, and had previously agreed with each other, that this must a terrible ordeal for Bernadette, the mother, watching over her favourite son, much worse than for them. Bernadette, on the other hand, was herself sympathising with the younger women, the sister, the friend; she could see they felt this deeply, they shared his youth, shared his life in the way she had ceased to do many years before. This was raw, and new to them. She knew also that when the young observe calamity they experience the additional pain of fearing for their own mortality, which was not something she was worried about just then.

As a mother, and quite old now, she had the advantage of having been in this situation several times in Jean's life and she knew having made it this far, this was not his time. She did not relate the danger of his death to herself; it was quite simple, she focused only on him. She was worried, of course, but not fearful, certainly she was much more angry than desperate. Angry with Jean, angry mainly with Mac, but angry with this whole mad venture and the crazy world Jean created around himself. When would he settle, level, find a nice partner? She resolved she should tell him she knew, maybe it would help him to calm down.

"What would you like to do, mum, do you want to stay on now, and I can come and relieve you later?"

"That's sweet of you Caro, that would be great, can you come back around half past one?"

They were determined beyond anything else that one of them would be at the bedside when he woke.

"I'll come at 5.00am if that's all right with you Caro," said Daphne. "I need to get some sleep now as the Experience is a long day, we need to keep up to speed, but I can do a couple of hours before work. Then maybe you can come back tomorrow at 7.00am, Bernadette?" It was no problem; Madame Terroir nodded her agreement, and gratitude.

She decided to walk them out to the carpark to get a last bit of fresh air before the night shift. And, of course, that is where, just outside the hospital, the three women wandered into the party arriving from the train station.

Daphne spotted the Inspector immediately: her first instinct was to duck back inside, but it was too late, he'd seen her, and she quickly covered up by going over the top in the other direction, with an enthusiastic bonhomie in her greeting which stopped only just short of an effusive welcoming embrace. The startled Leopard took a step back as he returned the somewhat hysterical salutation; he was becoming accustomed to odd encounters with this very eccentric woman, but she had so far managed to surprise him every time. The other two he had met previously in the hospital, and he bowed a little formally to pay his respects.

But Caroline and Madame Terroir were too distracted to respond to him, looking in some amazement at the woman with him, whom they did know very well. "Kate?!" squealed Caroline, "Is it you?"

"Hi, Caro, how are you, honey?" They embraced deeply and sincerely, old friends from many holidays, and from a few very long late-night telephone calls from Kate to Caro over the past few years asking about life, the family, and "Does anyone know the whereabouts of my fucking husband?"

Caroline was one of the clan that Kate thought of still with great affection, always understanding she would have helped her more if she could, the only problem being, she never knew quite enough. Bernadette joined their hug, cautiously around the outside, hanging her arms like a scarf on the back of a chair rather than really getting a grip, keeping a little emotional distance. "Hello, Kate, it is good to see you – so you heard, then, what had happened. I am surprised you got here so quickly."

Now Kate was puzzled. Was Bernadette accusing her of something, she seemed slightly cool. "Yes, we were at the railway station with the Inspector here when we found out – of course we came immediately."

It became evident to the Inspector, and to Daphne, that none of the group of women in the hug, nor the girl standing shyly a little way off them, knew much about what was really happening. They knew some of the outcomes, but not so much about the means, method or motivation.

"You were at the railway station in Bourges?" asked Caro, "Why?"

"Well…," she looked at Leopard, wondering whether there was any issue in discussing it, he gave a nondescript shrug indicating it was up to her, he wasn't bothered. "We got a call in England from someone called Karl who told us Jack was in trouble here and we needed to come and help him. We were greeted unexpectedly by the Inspector at the station, and then when we mentioned we were thinking about imposing ourselves on Jean, he told us that he was in the hospital, and brought us here. How is Jean – what happened?"

"He stabbed him in the chest, dear," said Bernadette, dryly.

Kate looked blank, uncomprehending.

"He stabbed him, Kate, and came within a millimetre of killing him – that's what happened. He might die yet. Are you saying seriously you didn't know?"

Maggie cried out, not a word as much but a noise automatically understood by every one of them. It was all the more startling as it was the first sound any of them had heard from her.

Daphne's heart went to her. She realised there was confusion and she needed to step in before things got out of hand in front of the Detective. Bernie was accusing Mac, but Mac was dead as far as

Kate was concerned. So instead, Kate and Maggie has both jumped to the conclusion that Bernie was saying Jack had stabbed Jean.

"There may be a danger we're confusing each other. Kate, do you remember me? I am Claude's daughter, Daphne. I can tell you, no perpetrator has been named or identified around here in the stabbing of Jean.

"If I am correct, Inspector," she looked at Leopard, "you are still trying to ascertain what happened, investigations are being made? But the person of interest in the stabbing, whoever it may be, it is certainly not the boy, correct?"

She was using a loaded tone indicating to all the women, 'Be cautious.' She had said enough to remind all those present not to be rash in front of the police, using an ancient code that states, 'Whether you know me or not, we will talk about this later, be quiet now.'

Any misunderstanding had not so much been dispelled as volleyed back into Leopard's court. He hadn't connected the boy to the stabbing at all – should he have? What did these women know that he clearly didn't? What would his bad cop say about yet another Leopard lack of insight? In his perplexity, he fell back on the old police mantra: "I can't of course comment on an ongoing investigation."

Daphne now had her arm out, like a shepherd, beginning to move and shape the group of women from two metres away, turning them and gently pushing them at the same time towards the hospital entrance, subtly leaving Leopard outside the ring, informing him unconsciously he would not be joining them.

"We will look after Madame du Lac and the Mademoiselle, Inspector, and make sure they have somewhere to stay tonight. Thank you so much for your attention."

Leopard was a strong character, but over-matched by the five women now that the resolution had been proposed, seconded and unanimously carried that his presence was no longer required. He panicked, in the moment, and concurred. 'It is very late,' he gave himself the excuse, 'everyone is tired, there can be no harm to wait; waiting is one of my trademarks.'

"I hope it is in order, mesdames, to find you all tomorrow, for some further informal questions. If agreeable, I will be at the Experience in the morning, perhaps you would be kind enough to reserve me a ticket as it seems to be where everything happens."

And before they could answer – given he knew he had no response if they said no – he turned about and headed to his vehicle, hoping to persuade himself that at least he had had the last word. 'If the last word is "slink," or "cringe,"' he thought in an unwelcome flush of self-awareness as he slid into the car.

They stood in the doorway and watched him drive off, then spilled back into the carpark and lit cigarettes, all except Maggie, who had the new-fangled affectation for not smoking. She could even quote several scientific papers that indicated how bad it was for the health, but with an uncanny instinct for the mood of her immediate audience, she forbore.

They looked thirstily at the café; a stiff drink was in order, surely. But the waiter was already outside, putting chairs on tables and cleaning out the ashtrays. "How about it, Herve, time for a round of cognac?" He answered with a cheeky grin she had known since school. "You lot again! You've got a nerve after ordering all that food last night and leaving before I even brought it out."

"I paid though, right? With enough for a tip?"

"Yes, fair enough, and I could see the *gendarmes* arrived at an inconvenient time…"

He left an open space in the conversation for Daphne to start filling with their story, which she graciously declined to do.

"OK, well then … I am going home now, but I will leave you a bottle and put it on Claude's tab. I will even leave you some glasses and an ashtray. Please put the chairs on the table before you go and take the empties with you, or I'll get it in the neck from the boss tomorrow."

Daphne smiled broadly. "You're a prince, Herve, I'll bring the glasses back tomorrow when you're on your own." She gave him a peck on the cheek that made it all worthwhile.

They settled on their table as the lamps were switched off inside, leaving just the soft illumination of the hospital and carpark lights to see by, and then speech broke out, starting with Kate.

"What the fuck is all this about? Bernie, why did you say Jack stabbed Jean? He would never do anything like that."

Maggie noted that Kate didn't mention Jack was on the run from a knife fight in England, perhaps feeling that would unnecessarily complicate her protestation of his saintliness. Bernadette looked perplexed, but Daphne, a little less emotional than the blood relatives, was alive to the situation.

"It is not Jack, Kate, don't worry about that, no-one is talking about him. I had to shut everyone up because the police don't know. My dad was with him when it happened, so in theory we're the only ones who do know."

"Know what? Who did it?"

"Your fucking husband," said Bernadette, not about to pull any punches.

Kate genuinely looked blank for an instant, thinking, 'This is a mistake, I have no husband, this is a relief, it turns out this is nothing to do with me and my family.'

Caroline had placed a restraining hand lightly on her mother's wrist. "Kate hasn't seen Mac for three years, mum."

"Mac's here? He's alive?" Kate was white in the moonlight. She had learnt over the years to cease wondering what it would be like if Mac turned up; long ago she had stopped dreaming he would return and started hoping he wouldn't. It wasn't a feeling she had ever shared with anyone, especially as her two younger children prayed for him and asked her every night when he would be home.

"Yes, somewhere around, living on the land."

"Oh my God, Bernadette, I am so sorry. He's alive, then."

Then she was breathless, and crying, and hating herself for crying, and for letting them see her. Caroline moved her seat closer and put her arms around her. Everyone was quiet for some minutes that felt like hours.

"But why on earth would he attack Jean?"

"Dad says he is not a hundred percent sure it was deliberate. But Mac's lost it, Kate, he was killing a swan, in some kind of episode, covered in blood, dad and Jean tried to step in, the knife was turned the wrong way, someone slipped or someone pushed – who knows?"

Kate was utterly dazed now. There was a new silence, a long one.

"Jesus… Bernadette… Caro… I'm sorry. What's the situation with Jean, he's strong, right?"

"Yes, very strong, and very lucky. Last night was the crisis, it did feel for a while it could go either way, but this morning the Doctor seemed more confident. With every hour, he becomes more stable, the outcome looks much more positive."

Kate was enormously relieved, and suddenly exhausted, her head falling into her chest, her arms crossed in front, hugging herself, she spoke much more quietly.

"You know it's been three years since he left, but even before that he'd gradually lost it, he'd been growing distant, then something pushed him over the edge and he went. I think he stopped wanting to be well. I tried to help him for the final years when he was on the slide to wherever he was going, and I hunted him for eighteen months after he left, but finally I couldn't do it anymore – you know some of it, anyway, because I was calling you. Honestly, it was the best feeling I've had for years when I made the decision to give up."

"Jack didn't give up. He came here to search again," said Daphne.

"Jack's a kid and didn't know what had been going on," Kate replied, somewhat sharply. "Also, I think Jack had quite a few reasons for coming here. For him, finding his father might have been a romantic quest, and I bet a trip to his origins for a summer holiday was part of the dream, with the normal fabulous fiction in his head. But in the end it turned out he was running away from something, not towards it. For me, I was seeking a reason and a resolution – but I am done with that now."

"What's Jack running away from?" asked Caroline. Daphne looked at her lap.

"The last day of school," Kate explained, "he and his mate Milo got caught up in a fight in their pub; another boy pulled a knife, they defended themselves, the boy was hurt. I didn't even know for a few days, I thought they'd gone on holiday in England, then the police came asking questions. When we went to Yarmouth to find him, he'd never even been there. Then the day before yesterday this person called Karl phoned and said he knew where he was, they needed help, and we should come to Bourges.

"When we arrived, the mysterious Karl – who turned out to be nothing more than a spiteful boy on a mission, by the way – was at the train station to meet us, with the Inspector. He was trying to stir up trouble for Jack, for some reason of his own that I am not even sure about, some small slight that seems to have been blown up completely out of proportion. The Inspector actually seemed to be pretty reasonable, I think he dislikes that boy as much as I do, but he's got sucked into this story, and he's definitely intent on finding Jack and Milo. He is aware now of the fight back in London, from Karl, I am not sure how much detail he has, we're supposed to talk again tomorrow."

The group fell silent. After flirting with enmity, they settled on collaboration and sealed the alliance with cognac. Looking for something to say, Bernadette ventured, "Kate, you haven't really introduced your young friend."

"This is Maggie, everyone," Kate spoke up, pleased to be granted a small practical task, "Maggie, this is Daphne, daughter of Claude who was one of Mac's best childhood friends. And this is Madame Bernadette Terroir, mother of Jean, who is Mac's nephew; and Caroline, her daughter, Jean's sister, related to Mac, and therefore also related to Jack, in some cousin-ish way I cannot possibly work out tonight."

There was mutual nodding during the introductions, nice smiles, a hand reached out to touch once, then another touch.

"Maggie is a very good friend of Jack's; I hesitate to define that too specifically."

"Me too," said Maggie, "close friend will definitely do it."

Each of the women had their own version of what that meant, and everyone was slightly different, shaped by their own experience. When locating a boyfriend on the wide spectrum between Utter Dick and Complete Prince they were all aware that it was possible for a single arrow to point to both ends at once; but what they wouldn't tell her, because she would need to find out for herself, was that this was unlikely to be a sustainable situation. Daphne's understanding was closest to the truth, having spent so much time with Jack and Milo over the past few days, and she most definitely wasn't going to comment.

"I am pleased to meet you all," said Maggie, unaware she was the subject of such deep forensic scrutiny on so slight an acquaintance, "I would have hoped it could be in better circumstances."

"Do you want to stay at Jean's?" Caroline asked. "For evident reasons there is no-one there at the moment, but it is what Jean would want."

"If you are sure, then it would be a huge help to us. As long as it is not an imposition."

"Actually you would be doing me a favour. I'm having to go by twice a day to check on Hector and make sure the place is OK, if you're there I won't have to."

"Hector?"

"You'll see. Nothing to worry about so long as he likes you." Maggie was naturally now imagining a hideously disfigured sinister ancient retainer lurking around outside her bedroom, and perhaps hoping he wouldn't like her quite so much.

"In the morning, we said we would meet Inspector Leopard at the Experience, whatever that is. Karl said the boys were working for this enterprise with him before he left or got fired. Can you tell us where to go, how to get there?"

"Don't worry," Caroline responded, "I'll pick you up in the morning and you can come in with me – probably before 9.00am if that sounds OK with you, Daphne?"

"Yes, that's great, you'll all be in time to help then. Given I am also in charge at the moment, ladies, I'll fix some tickets for you so you can do the whole thing tomorrow with us."

Daphne's head was already throbbing with the complexities this was going to cause, but there was no point in attempting to exclude them, or the Inspector. Tomorrow already felt like it was going to be what pulp fiction might describe as The Day Of Reckoning...

"OK then," said Caro, "mum's staying here with Jean for a few hours, I will take you to the farm now, we'll stop off and pick up a loaf, milk and some butter at my place, there's loads of eggs and bacon at Jean's, and coffee and wine, so that will set you up till tomorrow, and we can take it from there."

Cigarettes were finished and extinguished, and they kindly remembered the promise to Herve to take the glassware and put the chairs on the table. Hugs were exchanged, some strangely intense, and some understandably perfunctory. Madame Terroir kept Claude's car and agreed with Daphne she would drive it to the Lodge later and pick hers up. She wandered across the carpark back to the hospital, and they all stood and watched till she was safely in the lobby.

Daphne jumped in with Caro, Kate and Maggie. They went first to Caroline's to pick up the groceries, then to the Lodge where Daphne picked up her car. Caro then drove the Englishwomen down to the farm barely awake and introduced them to Hector. Maggie was gratefully relieved to find he wasn't the intimidatingly lecherous crumbling vampire manservant of her fantasy but initially nervous to discover he was instead an overexcited beast of uncontrollable dimensions. Hector himself was so pleased to see anyone after a day sitting bored in the shade on his chain that he played up and puppied around friskily, noticing as he did so that the young one was quite anxious around him.

Caro demonstrated how and what to feed him and let him off the chain so he could have a run, while the three women sat on the bench outside the farmhouse door; those that smoked had another in the honourably extended line of last cigarettes of the day, taken with an equally last brandy for the elder two, and a glass of wine for Maggie. Then Caro took them around inside. Kate remembered being there a couple of times, years ago, for family meals, mainly outside, with some football and swimming for the kids, even before Jean had taken possession. But she'd never stayed there, so Caro showed them where to sleep, and the rugs and blankets from the downstairs chairs, last used by Milo and Jack, were taken upstairs to make up a bed in each of the bedrooms. Before she left Caroline whistled for Hector, and got him settled in the downstairs kitchen to guard them.

"This is really good of you, Caro, we're grateful, especially considering."

"Considering what?"

"Considering my husband stabbed your brother."

"Jean's alive, Kate. And until he regains consciousness we're not really sure what Mac did. And Mac's not well. And he's not really your husband, so you do not have the slightest responsibility. It feels like he stabbed you too, a long while ago."

Caro was intending to be sisterly, but possibly overshot a little way. Kate turned her grimace into a stiff smile to recognise the attempt at support. Then the women embraced, and Caro drove away, reminding them that she would be back before 9.00am – which didn't feel so long, actually.

When they were alone, Kate hugged the young girl. "Sorry, kid," she said, speaking into her hair as Maggie was a good six inches shorter than her, "you must feel a bit left out this evening, given all this unexpected new weirdness. It feels like you're not getting written much of a part, but I am so so grateful you are here.

"Sorry it sounds like you've got a duff man too; but at least it must cheer you up that mine's so much worse, eh?"

And then they were both laughing, shaking back and forth in each other's arms, while the tension of the last twenty-four hours

604

drained out of them.

"Do you want to talk about it?"

"No, let's sleep."

"Good idea."

Kate's last decision of the day was to give the big comfortable bed in Jean's cosy room to the girl, before taking the bedclothes off the narrowly dispiriting spare bed and going back down the stairs to lie sleepless on the worn tapestry cushions of the knocked-out old sofa, deeply breathing the smell of her son on the blanket with the dog lying comfortably at her feet. Upstairs Maggie also immersed herself lovingly in the scent of Jack, not realising she was snuggling in Milo's quilt.

Kate dreamt she was in the passenger seat of their old Renault with Mac driving beside her. In the back were Jack, Gabby and Frank, squabbling about a game of scrabble they were playing and whether the word therapoda was allowed. Frank knew it meant something about dinosaurs. He was desolate and would not stop. It was his only good score and they rejected it. Jack was adamant.

Occasionally Kate attempted to point out sites of interest and beautiful views of the landscape, canals, picturesque villages. They didn't look. Kate and Mac were arguing periodically about which direction to take, but it was friendly debate, nothing harsh.

And this was all the dream: no crash, no breakdown, no disaster, no arrival, not even a destination, though she knew what it was.

No portent here, no message, no omen, no code, no mysterious meaning we can see; just a small untimely segment of happy memory popping up disturbingly from a long-ago time, which left her uneasy and upset for an hour when she woke.

FRIDAY

In the morning, with another gorgeous day breaking outside across the sunny country, heat rising already before anything much was moving, Daphne was sitting in the white room with Jean. She loved him, and never once let go of his hand. He'd had another steady night, and the doctors and nurses were quietly pleased with his progress. When Bernadette arrived at 7.00am, they hugged and she gave her the good news.

Then she left and drove to the Lodge via the boulangerie. She had mixed news for the occupants, and some difficult requests, so she might as well bring some extra pastries to sweeten the occasion.

She was interested to see her dad's car in the parking space, so obviously events the night before had left him either too tired or too drunk to go home to his own sheets. Predictably, therefore, no-one answered the door to a fairly soft knock. Daphne checked her watch as she fumbled for her key – 7.30am. Maybe she'd been a bit ambitious hoping to find them awake, but she was ready to turf them out of bed. She unlocked the door and went through to the kitchen, leaving the breads, croissants, milk and eggs on the table. The place was a mess, and she was contemplating rolling up her sleeves for a tidy-up when she heard the laughter and splashing from outside.

Gently she opened the back door and walked quietly to the end of the garden, peering through the gap in the hedge over to the jetty and across the lake. Two swimmers, very beautiful, very little clothing as far as she could see. Jack and Amelie. Bobbing and joshing.

'O Lord,' she thought, 'perfect timing. These kids have no idea. What happened to "I wouldn't flirt with you if you were the most gorgeous boy on the planet, I am devoted to an antique music master"?'

Then she leaned further round to get a fuller view, and another swimmer was thus revealed: Milo. Not quite as pretty, but better covered. 'Thank God for that one, we can still keep this simple, and put on a show.' She was relieved, and slightly disappointed in her own lack of faith. She knew Jack had given an oath of good behaviour to Jean; that surely must be even more sacred now.

Further round still, there was a fully clothed boy sitting in a deck-chair on one of the little beaches, covering up his self-consciousness in shirt and shorts, enjoying himself vicariously as so often before.

"Morning, Albert, how goes?" she called out cheerfully as she skirted round behind him. "I don't blame you, mate, that looks bloody cold."

"Hi, Daphne. Too right, it's freezing. I think these three are only in because they're not awake yet, no-one should be doing dares before breakfast."

Milo was standing now, waving good morning. "Morning, Daff. How's Jean?" Jack and Amelie paused their cavorting and everyone waited, some feeling a little guilty as they had forgotten to check immediately.

"Looking good. A good quiet night, and a continuing positive outlook from the Doctor. Good news."

Everyone in the lake sounded their hurrahs and bloody brilliants, stood for a suitable length of time in respectful thought, and finally returned to their water sports. Albert reached out and touched Daphne's hand, the first time he had ever done it, and said, "You must be so relieved."

"Thanks, Albert, we all must. Have you seen my pops?"

"In a manner of speaking – he's comatose in the living room. Under that appalling smelly rug. Honestly, I did try to give him a clean blanket yesterday, but he seemed quite offended. He's rather adopted that sofa in the past few days."

607

"No swimming for dad, then."

"I think it was fifty-fifty. Half of us felt sorry for him and wanted to let him sleep, and the other half didn't want to see him in his underpants."

In the water, Jack was lifting Amelie above his head in a manly fashion and throwing her, which allowed him to visibly demonstrate his admiration of both her girlish lightness and his own rippling muscle. They were giggling, Daphne would have said 'rather nauseatingly' had she been asked, and, seemingly setting aside for the time being any putative sacred vows, they were collectively working extremely hard to create a picture to perfectly illustrate the dictionary definition of 'bloody annoying couple'.

Albert was grateful to Daphne for standing in his view so he didn't have to notice, and Milo was now rather uselessly swimming breaststroke lengths of the lake, about twenty metres away with his back to them instead of casting a protective circle of cynicism and disapproval around his friend. Daphne wondered whether her flirt alert was right all the time, if so, this was really depressing.

"What did you all get up to last night?" Daphne asked Albert, slightly dreading the answer.

"Sis and I helped Julie clear away as they were a bit short-staffed. She made up some food boxes for us and dropped us back here. We really didn't get up to anything, I think we were in bed by half nine, it felt great to have a chance for some sleep for a change."

"What about the others?" Warily.

"Mmmm don't know. I wasn't sworn to secrecy, but I couldn't tell you anyway because they got back after we were sleeping. After they mysteriously melted away into the evening when the *gendarmes* showed up, I did see the three of them get in a car and shoot off. I could say they were looking rather conspiratorial, but I would probably be making that up. Anyway, they weren't back here when we went to bed. I cleaned up before going up, and the kitchen and yard were a mess this morning with plates, glasses and cigarette butts everywhere, and yesterday's leftover pastries were missing, because I had my eye on one, and it was gone." [Wistful pause.] "So, an educated guess is they must have had a few drinks and post-midnight snacks when they got back without tidying after, and your dad decided to stay over accordingly. This morning Jack decided to turf us all out of bed because he wanted an audience for his gorgeous display of stylised water-larks, and here you are."

Well at least nothing irreversible had happened, she thought, though now her mind was on another mission, to find out where Milo, Jack and her dad been in the car and what they'd found.

"I'm going in to get the breakfast ready and make the coffee. Can you bring them all inside in fifteen minutes? We need to make an earlier start today, I'll explain while we're eating." Albert nodded. "And don't worry," putting her hands on his shoulders as she moved behind him, and leaning down to whisper in his ear, "I have replacement croissants … and they're fresh." He giggled and pretended to quiver in anticipation.

Once inside, Daphne put the coffee on to brew, then went back to her original plan of washing up and emptying the ashtrays, making herself feel better about the skivvying by accepting that her dad had made the mess so it was fair enough for the family to clean up. While she thought of it, she went through to the living room and pulled the rug off Claude, quite violently. She was very happy to discover he had slept in his clothes, both to save her blushes, and also because it would take him less time to get ready. Claude swore his normal morning swear, and Daphne mimed putting her hands over her ears in shock.

"Jeez, dad, I don't know what you're thinking, hanging around with these kids. You're not going to get any younger doing it, unless you actually drink their blood. And, you are becoming a symbol of sad corruption, when you could be a beacon of righteousness and virtue just by showing them how to go home to bed at a decent hour, sober."

"God's sake, Daphne, I am not awake, my head is pounding, will you please please please save it up and shout at me after 10.00am, I am planning on feeling a bit brighter then."

"Breakfast. Table. Five minutes."

"How's Jean?"

"He had a good night," she threw back over her shoulder as she marched grouchily back to the kitchen; she didn't generally care so much about her dad's antics, except recently they were happening too frequently, the Experience was giving him too much scope for malarky, and whether he realised it or not, he couldn't keep up with kids a third of his age, even with his drunk's head and experience. She was worried about his health, and it felt like he was spiralling again.

She laid out the bread, butter and jam, and put some croissants in the oven to heat gently. Careful not to cook them, just warm them. She always wanted to be busy, but this work was also helping her to think; this was a key moment, she was in charge, like it or not, and she wanted to get it right. There was a big choice to be made, and she wanted to avoid lying, because she hated not being straight, even when it was for the best.

The pondgoers tramped back in when she was nearly done, leaving wet footprints in the kitchen, cheery, still sleepy, hellos left hanging in the air:

"Morning, Daphne" [Amelie];

"Hi, Daff, thanks for that" [Jack];

"Oh gosh, Daphne, I am so sorry, we should have cleared up before we went out" [Milo, genuine, but also sucking up];

"Give me the cloth and let me dry those up for you, Daphne, you've got enough to do" [Albert];

"Five minutes, kids, we've work to do." She didn't have time for recriminating.

"K."

"Will do."

The coffee was ready, she took it off the stovetop and put it on the table, using a small plate as a coaster having carefully calculated that it wouldn't crack with the heat. She warmed up some milk; normally she felt that was quite a poncy thing to do, but today she was grateful for the extra three minutes to defer the final decision. Then she was set. She took the croissants out, admitting she'd slightly over-firmed them, but the English lads would think that was the French way, and a couple were slightly softer for Albert and Amelie, so she positioned those on the tray closer to where she guessed those two would sit.

They all came in at the same time, and indeed Albert and Amelie did sit where she expected, and they did take the croissants she wanted them to have, so this was suddenly all seeming remarkably satisfactory, perhaps today she had that magic touch. And Milo, bless him, took a slightly cracky croissant and looked as French with it as a man on a bicycle with a beret and a string of onions round his neck. Jack was a bit more suspicious, but in such a good mood he didn't mind when his finger poked straight through the stiff flakes – he squeezed some strawberry jam into the hole and noisily sucked it out, making Amelie laugh and Albert roll his eyes.

Once they had polished off the rather excellent breakfast, they settled into their coffee and asked to light cigarettes. "I am not your parents, or your doctors," said Daphne, rather frustrated, "you can do what you want with your tender lungs, but let's at least follow the rules and do it outside."

Jack was about to make the case that the smoking rule had changed, along with the votes, now Karl was gone, but Daphne anticipated the argument with a four hundred-watt stare that shut him up before he got going. "I have things to say, Jack."

Everyone decided to stay put and not smoke. They all looked at each other with "What will it be now?" eyes and shoulders, but couldn't generally work up the enthusiasm to be anxious just yet, as Jean was stable, the coffee was good, the sun was glorious, and in any case they would know in less than ninety seconds.

"OK, everyone comfortable?"

Indeed they were.

"So, the news is that today, Milo and Jack will get the morning off. Hurrah for that, you say, more work for the rest of us!!"

In fact, Amelie and Albert looked pretty miffed at this announcement. Claude took it much better because he was currently in a high-functioning coma; a special state he had evolved years ago which allowed him to look round and nod at them intelligently while essentially being asleep.

"Why?" asked Amelie. "Can we even manage with the four of us?" Then looking at Claude … "Effectively three of us?"

"Three and a half," suggested Claude, unhelpfully, reaching shakily for the coffee pot, which was empty.

"Well, it's three, because you're not coming either."

"Really, Daphne, that's too thin," Amelie continued, anxiously. "There's no way we can ticket, costume, drive the boat and keep everyone in order with me, you and Albert."

"Cards on the table," said Daphne, sympathetically, "the Inspector is insisting on coming to the Experience this morning and doing the whole thing. That would mean the boys and dad couldn't possibly avoid him, he would be sitting next to them on the barge, there'd be no escape."

Daphne, after thinking about it for half the night, had decided not to go straight in with news that Kate and Maggie were also on the scene. Right now, she couldn't tell you exactly why – it was just her instinct giving her the option to hold on to that information a few hours longer.

"OK", said Amelie, "I get why we have to try, but how do we run it with just us?"

"I made some calls. Tommy will be with us again, and he's now getting used to helping out, as well as playing the squeeze box. I've asked Caroline to support us for the ticketing and the boat trip up to Hill House before she goes to the hospital and relieves Bernadette. So that makes five of us. Julie will help out at the picnic buffet and will put an extra waiter on. Then Bernadette will come up to help with the Harlequinade, and she will come back with us and be crew for the return boat. I reckon we will be OK."

"What about the play?" Amelie asked, panicking slightly. "There is no way we can do it without the boys."

"Good question, Amelie. My plan is this. Claude and the lads will come up to Hill House at the last moment. Bernie will dress them and make them up in the carpark – I am thinking the back of the van. And they'll run onto the stage straight from the carpark exactly on their cue, so no-one in front will see them till they are actually performing. Sound OK?"

Albert and Amelie exchanged looks and decided it would be all right.

"Can I have a drive of the boat today, then? I've not been given a chance yet with the passengers on," requested Albert.

Daphne wondered kindly about the ease with which he could be bought, like a child negotiating the number of sweets it would cost to tidy his room. She readily agreed: "No worries, Albert, I'll pull her away from the landing stage, then she's all yours.

"Now, is everyone going to be OK with what we've agreed?"

Yes, everybody nodded: there were varying degrees of enthusiasm, but at least the head motions were all in the traditional up and down trajectory that indicated a positive response. 'My leadership style,' thought Daphne, 'mainly seems to consist of understated grumpiness, talking more loudly, and the comparative quick-wittedness that comes from not having a massive hangover.'

"OK, Amelie, Albert, please get your things together, we will leave in ten minutes if that is amenable, we need to get going early, there is a lot to do."

The two of them left for their rooms to get packed. Daphne took the opportunity to ask the others, "What were you three doing last night, out looking for Mac, I guess?"

"Yes," Milo, wary of the inquisitorial tone, felt like he was confessing, though he wasn't quite sure what he had done wrong yet, "we had to make ourselves scarce from the after-party, so we took the opportunity to have a drive round."

"I heard you have hooked up with Dessie, dad?"

Ah, thought Milo, it's not me. Thank God.

Claude tried to look up, the epitome of befuddlement on many different levels; his brain was moving in several opposing directions simultaneously, and everything was going extremely slowly. Too slowly for Daphne, who repeated the essence of her question at a higher volume.

"I thought we had decided that you would steer clear of her, dad?"

Now Jack was particularly interested. This recalled quite a few conversations from his childhood and brought back memories. He knew exactly what came next, he could have scripted it.

One: drawling denial

"Well honestly, Daff, I am not sure we did discuss it quite like that."

Two: pointless mumbling

"Besides, I'm your dad, not your child, I don't need you doing a running commentary on my life, it's not dignified... {other random comments tailing off} ..."

Three: sly whining

"She's not what you think, we've all changed so much, it's not like the old days. She's not in that Organisation anymore, she's not been in touch with them for years."

Four: emboldened arguing

"Anyway, I love you for caring, but it's plain wrong at our age for you to be trying to tell me what to do."

Five: simple cunning

"We all know how important it is to find Mac before the police. She could be the key. We should use any advantage we have."

"I think I can guess who is using who, dad. Where did you go, what did you find?"

But at that moment the siblings came back. Daphne didn't want to share the additional dimension of Jack's quest with Albert and Amelie, or get them worried, or sucked into a massive distraction, so she did a shush symbol to the other three, signalling to them at the same time that, without doubt, they would be returning to this subject later.

Albert and Amelie were walking just sluggishly enough to indicate to Daphne that, although they deferred to her plan, they felt it was an imposition. Daphne guessed that while they had been upstairs Amelie had told Albert off for being such a pushover, so he was thinking about taking a slightly tougher stance on some future issue that was as yet undetermined. Daphne realised she would have some repair work to do with these two and made a note to make a proper fuss of both of them during the morning. They deserved it, frankly, they were getting on with it, and, since Karl had gone, they had been uncomplaining and more and more helpful, unlike some others she could name.

She started the charm offensive immediately by putting an arm round each of them. "Thanks, kids, let's get in the car, shall we? And you three, do find something useful to do today, please."

This parting comment was made squarely to Jack, Milo and Claude but was really designed to emphasise to the listening Albert and Amelie that those three were not being let off on some kind of holiday. Underlining it, she continued, "You can start please by clearing all this mess away, washing up, tidying up the kitchen, the living room and the Hall, stripping the beds and organising the laundry for the cleaner. For everyone.

"Don't just sit around smoking, and please make sure you're up in the carpark at Hill House on time for costume. To preserve your anonymity, I'll ask Bernadette to lay on your make-up double thick."

Jack wasn't sure if she was joking or not. It was too late to ask, because they were out of the house; Daphne had already shooed Amelie and Albert into the car, and they were gone. Claude was beginning to come round a bit, so Milo sent him for a shower while they tidied the kitchen and did the washing up. When he returned, they did indeed go to the chairs in the courtyard and they did light cigarettes ["I can't remember, did she say we should or shouldn't spend all day smoking in the loungers?"], while they discussed some ideas for the evening's manhunt.

"If they're up at the House again waiting to nab us for an interview after the play, we need to run straight off the stage and into the car."

"OK so we'll be scouring the countryside for a desperate knife criminal dressed as a Clown, a Policemen and Pierrot."

"Dessie will be impressed. When she said we weren't taking it seriously enough I think she was hinting at dark clothing, not fancy dress."

"OK, so we pack now, dark clothes, so we can get changed in the car."

"And where can we leave the motor?"

"I'll talk to Julie," said Claude, "and arrange to leave the car right outside the dressing room door."

"What a shame for our fans," said Milo, "no autographs tonight."

"OK, so that's a great plan, all arranged, can I sleep now?" asked Claude, desperately. "And can someone get me a glass of beer?"

Jack got him a cup of coffee instead, with a glass of water. Leaving it on the table beside him, he said, "I'm going upstairs for a while, I've got something to finish."

Milo looked at him, 'Letters?' he mouthed. Jack nodded grimly.

Up in his room, he reluctantly grabbed the bundle he had sorted and opened the lowest number, because of course he would do it in order, and started reading again.

What you see here is just the highlights, a selection, quotations. There was worse in them, better in them, but also things Jack didn't want to keep in his head, so he skipped them or skimmed them – there is no verbatim rule.

Letter 13

... after we'd left school.

I followed you, just by chance, if I hadn't caught that glimpse of you in the street, none of this would ever have happened. I remembered you from a couple of years before; it was your hair, that mass of golden copper curls, unimaginable except it was like that picture in the School Hall, you remember? There were only two pictures in the whole school, Jesus the Light of the World at one end and the lady with the holy grail at the other end, with the huge mass of curly gold-red hair that everyone said was just like you.

Romantic people have claimed in the past, it is like a lightning bolt. I think it is really more like the break in a circuit, which stops everything dead, till all the essential elements migrate across the gap in a fizzing crackle of buzzing blue light, leaving the unnecessary behind, starting the power completely new.

After that, you didn't know this, I trailed you a few times. A couple of times when you went to work on the farm, that was to locate you; I followed you two evenings when you met that boy you were seeing. Did you know I warned him off? He was definitely scared of my reputation, so it didn't take much. I justified that to myself by thinking, if he was run off that easily, how much could he really have cared? Besides, it seemed to me you barely knew him.

I followed you once when you waited for him and he didn't come. Then I started looking for an accidental way to meet you...

[Christ, thought Jack, great start, brilliant. He's telling the woman that he got to her by strong-arming her boyfriend, threatening him, and humiliating him. Super. That's an excellent start to any new romance, it's hard to see how it all went wrong from there.]

Letter 19

... when we are together again.

I swear to you my love, I will never touch another drop, I have not had a drink now for five months, although it hurts a great deal, and I sweat and pace, and in any case it is harder to get it here. You can trust me. It helps that I am busy for sixteen hours a day, either training, on patrol, on guard. A month ago they imprisoned my friend for three years because he fell asleep when guarding at night; apparently napping on duty is frowned on.

Also, I have an agreement with my Sergeant – not a Frenchman I should point out - that if he spots me with alcohol, he will kill me. This is not such a joke, as I did see him strangle a youth with his bare hands; the story was that the boy, from a local village, had spied on our base and had given information to the terrorist group, two of our own died consequently. The justice was not decided in any court.

Yesterday the Sergeant offered me a drink himself, from his flask, and when I said, "No, thank you," he said, playing with his holster, "I thought it would be much easier to catch you out."

[This was more like the stuff in the journal. It sounded incredibly far-fetched, although he'd read tales of soldiers posted overseas. As for the drinking, it sounds like this was a good period for that, but slightly pointless boasting to Madeline about it, as SHE'S NOT COMING BACK, DAD.]

Letter 43

... instead of steering clear we went back the following night, a snow-down black winter night, racketing and sliding around the little hamlet on the ice, waving bottles, swearing, leering. As I say, we were big guys for our age – except Claude, of course, whose heart was never really in it anyway – and no-one bothered us, they served us in

the bar, they kept out of our way when we went on a binge.

In fact the only person to stand up to us was a very old woman, long thin grey hair, colourless hair, older than time, tatty clothes, but proud. Later, someone told me she had lost two sons and her husband in the wars, I think Morocco, Turkey and the Great One. She came out of her shabby house and stood square in the road, she could hardly stand up straight, but she did not move out of our way or take a step back, she stood shivering before us, terrified but brave. "You should be ashamed, terrorising these people, go home, you thugs."

"What is your name, widow?"

"Madame Poulier."

I was about to speak again, but Claude took me by the arm and another on the other side, and they pulled me away, Claude calling back over his shoulder "Apologies to you, Madame Poulier, and to your townsfellows, we will get out of your way."

We found another bar, drank a lot more, and laughed it off. But late that night, when they had all left, Hugo and I went back to her house. He waited in the street while I went up the path to the door and hammered on it a dozen times. I could tell she was inside, really scared now, and now her spirit had gone, in the dusty lonely rooms with no husband and no sons to defend her.

And I put my mouth to the letterbox, and I shouted.

"Madame Poulier… I know you hear me … I hope you fucking die."

And that was really what I was then, that says everything. This is a thing that wakes me up at night, shouting in my sleep with shame, sweating with the despair of not being able to correct it. I am so sorry, so sorry. But no-one knows.

[Jack cried and shivered. Despicable disgusting dad. It felt like, some things you do, there's no way back, right? Except a lifetime

620

feeding the poor, bathing the feet of lepers, that kind of thing. The letter shocked him to the extent he threw the whole bundle against the wall and was heading down the stairs for a strong drink. He turned round at the bottom and went back up; no drink, he lit a cigarette, opened the window, picked up the letters, and put them back in order.]

Letter 67

… he showed me a picture of his wife and children. I nodded and made all the good noises and clucking, obviously I had to simulate interest as hard as I could because I was trying to bond with him, he was going to be my informant, and we had to have a complete trust between us.

He made the congenial signs for me to reciprocate, so while he ordered a whisky, and another orange juice for me, I fiddled in my wallet. I had planted some fake family photos in there because I had no intention of showing him actual people who could become targets later. I picked out an image of a young girl that I had cut out of a magazine and mounted on card and said, "This is my daughter, Flora, she is seven next week." He nodded and cooed back just as convivially.

Then I dipped back into the wallet; I flicked past my picture of Kate, of course, and then for some reason I also passed by the fake wife picture I had made myself earlier. But guess who I did pick out? Yes, it was you. The only image I have, when we were twenty and in love, hand in hand, the picture my sister took at my mother's party.

"This is my wife, soon after we first met."

You have no idea of the thrill that went through my whole body when I claimed you. A stupid trick, irresponsible, imprudent and yet – or perhaps because of that – it gave me the most ridiculous pleasure to own you, even if it was just for an instant.

"You are a lucky man," he said, "she is really beautiful."

"And funny, and smart, and kind," I said.

It must have been the way I spoke, he looked at me for a long time, then shook his head from side to side, slowly, and said, "It is dangerous in our line of business to love so much; and if you would take some advice from a prospective lackey, I think in future you should stick with the fake magazine photos, like the rest of us."

Letter 68

... still my head is full of your sex, and images of you...

['When people say, "embarrassing dad," none of them ever imagine anything on this scale,' Jack thought, mentally redacting the letter even as he read it, looking at it horrified between his fingers. 'This is a genuine tsunami of soft-porn sewage. This is the sort of thing you could read out to sex offenders to cure them – the literary equivalent of chemical castration.']

Letter 83

... not heard from you for such a long, long time. I think always of that morning when I watched you sleep, when the yellow sun crept across the sheet towards your golden-orange hair, when you slept peacefully with a quiet smile on your face holding all the love of the night before, and I lost my breath and thought I might die from the feeling. That feeling, I carry with me every day, everywhere; it is the ink I write with....

[For the first time, Jack was caught out. There was no quick dismissal, and he was worried that just by wondering 'What is it about?' he was betraying his mother. He remembered the passage from the journal. Something had shifted all Mac's perceptions in that epiphanic moment. Mac believed it formed him, thought it shaped him, but didn't it just haunt him, and destroy him?]

Letter 91

… I am still pulsing with the perfumed echoes of your love…

[OK back to the commonplace. This one was heavily censored by Jack; in his mind's eye it became a sea of thick black lines expurgating the reedy blue scrawl. There was a lot of this kind of Valentine's-card-motto pappy pornography, and the bits he couldn't avoid seeing, even with his fingers half closed in front of his face like blinds, were the worst he had ever read. The boy rolled his eyes in mortification, not at the content but at the execution, and the fact it ever got written. 'It must mean,' he thought, 'that he never really believed anyone would see it, surely?']

Letter 117

… living in a dream. Do you remember when we talked about London? Just visiting, not living there. Now I am going there, to be with the boss.

So, this was our last night in Paris, and Marco and Patrice wanted to make a flame under the city. Actually, it was not even as though they were going anywhere, it was just to say goodbye to me. I've told you about them often; we have been together five years, we have the same blood on our hands, we've shared things I don't want to think about. Now they were signing on again, and I was jumping off, to something better. They were generous, but also, I realised, they were jealous, and it was making them angry, but they didn't know it yet.

The banter and teasing reached that point of balance between the funny and the cruel, between the affectionate and the insolent. I had learned in the desert, locked up in a scorching airless barracks with two score of crazy guys from the mad parts of the universe, to handle men on the edge, talk them down where possible, or stay out of the target range and let someone else take the heat. But this night in Paris there were just the three of us, and I was the odd man out, and my companions were going back to the desert next day for another five years, so they really didn't care what they did in France on their last night of freedom. I suddenly realised, I did not like these men, and I resented being there, and disliked intensely the fact they thought I was one of them.

We all three were drinking a lot, it was one of my times to be back on the hooch. In one bar, Patrice started a problem with a couple; he made eyes at the woman, made a tongue sign at her, pushed the man, humiliated him. This man was a civilian: he saw there were three of us, he saw our tattoos, and he saw the absent eyes of Patrice watching him. He realised he was fucked whatever way this went; if he fought back, he would be beaten to a pulp and lose the girl in any case; if he ran he would lose her, but without the beating – providing Patrice didn't bother to catch him.

This beautiful red-headed girl was way out of his league, he might never get one like this again; that is what Patrice had seen, this weakness, why he preyed on him. That is what made it fun for him.

The girl was watching too, in a kind of dreadful fascination. You could tell right away, she did not love this man, maybe they had only known each other for a short while, maybe they had known each other too long. Either way, it was almost as though she had no skin in this game, other than the ultimate fear of what three drunk men would decide to do to her once her flimsy protection was gone.

Then I realised, she looked like you.

Then I realised, this could be us.

So, this made it personal. Previously, maybe I was just ready to settle with Patrice and Marco, ready to close the account with them, draw the line. We had reached that point in our friendship, after five years of sharing blood, tears, death and life together, when we mutually wanted to end it with a greetings card printed "I Never Really Liked You Anyway." But now there was also another dimension, because I could objectively see that strange men must desire you and would not care about hurting you to get what they wanted. I decided I could not accept them wanting you or tolerate them harming you.

With a small change of posture, realignment of limbs, crook of the head, suddenly I was indicating, and everyone understood, that I had switched sides. Now we were playing doubles; and like any sporting double with four competitors, you pair the strongest with the weakest and set them against the two middling players. It makes a contest.

Everyone looked at everyone, putting on those grim, manly, unblinking smiles that are meant to demonstrate "I have no fear" and generally illustrate the reverse. For a long minute everybody stared, me and my new buddy versus two hard men from the desert who should not be licensed to walk among the civilised. After a while I thought, perhaps this is not going to happen after all; perhaps we can go on with our stories and beers, and this nice couple can go off and be disappointed in each other in peace.

Then, believe it or not, the lady dropped her handkerchief. Chivalric, I bent to pick it up, and while I was on my knee, Patrice took the opportunity to punch my comrade hard in the mouth, he went down without a whimper. That opened up Patrice's guard, I sensed it, and as I rose I drove the top of my head into his chin, hearing and feeling it shatter.

Now it was just me and Marco; being honest, it was not much of a contest. He was in shock from hearing the crunch and crumple of jawbone, and he only got in one punch before I broke his arm and nose. All over. Marco held it together enough to drag Patrice one-handed out into the night, and I am disappointed to say he never even said goodbye. There's gratitude for all the times I saved his life…

I helped the red-headed girl to heave up her beaten beau, and with him draped between us we staggered out into the street. We found a taxi. I suggested she should take him to the hospital for a check-up as he looked rather vacant; she was about to suggest we should go to her place to make love, but I put my finger over her lips before she could speak. I told her I loved someone else; I explained she looked very much like her, but I resisted showing your photo. For me it was a bizarrely sweet moment.

And that was my last night in Paris, and my last night in the Legion. Lucky for both...

Letter 155

... Today once more I thought I saw you on the underground, the back of you, your gorgeous mass of long red hair, and a beautiful green coat, exactly the style and colour you would want. I could not see you properly so I got off after you, three stations before my own stop, and followed you out. After a few hundred yards I executed a complex pavement manoeuvre to get in front of you unnoticed and turned round so I could walk towards you and see your face. Once again, it was not you.

Many times, very often, in the evenings, after dinner, I take a walk out of the house, and just go somewhere populated, say a shopping centre, or the bus station, to watch the people milling around, passing to and fro, in the hope and knowledge that one day I will see you. I admit that the odds are against you being in England, given you speak no English, know no-one here, except me (whom you quite possibly wish to avoid), and take no vacations – indeed you have never been more than twenty kilometres from La Chapelle as far as I am aware.

Also, if you were in England, why would you be in East Ham, or anywhere close to where I am on any particular morning or evening. But the dream of seeing you is so compelling that I spend many hours sitting in completely random places, smoking, and searching for you in the faces of everyone passing. One day it will be you.

Letter 166

... was one of the things that grew between us, one of the things that began to divide us, made me uncertain. Let me write as though I am a narrator, part of our story, to try to explain one of my, well, let's be honest, psychoses....

I had had a few affairs before you, nothing you would call important, *but you had had two serious relationships (actually three if you count the last guy, the one I scared off – but maybe we won't count that. And four if you count the geography teacher, but we are definitely not including him).*

You told me, sweetly, all about them. The first was the boy you grew up with from the age of five, the boy next door, almost a brother until when you were fourteen, fifteen it turned into something else, and you experimented with sex, and became lovers.

You didn't tell me this part, so I am guessing, sniffing the sheets from a decade later, that you thought you would always be together. So many shared feelings, thoughts, experiences, holidays, events. Wrapped in each other like intertwined shrubs planted in the same pot, stems twisted and knotted by chasing the same circling sun.

For me, when you told me, I comforted myself by thinking, the sex would have been ordinary, fumbling, rushed, selfish, uneducated. But I don't think you cared, because of your singular devotion.

It was meant to be your delightful fate, to be always together, and never to know another: but destiny let you down. The boy changed schools, and when he went to the other place, he simply, obviously, mundanely, met someone else. He had second sex and found there were many other things in life, physical and poetical, and finally, guiltily, nervously, he called it off with you, breaking your heart. At one time I did vow to find him and cut his scrotum, but this was yet another promise I didn't keep ......

The second boy was a little older, more sophisticated. He came from a richer background locally, son of a banker, and destined to become an important financier. You met and fell in love accidentally in a school play, when you were both sixteen, a year after your first big disappointment and heartbreak. At first you were wary and scared, because the pain was still great from your childhood sweetheart, but gradually he convinced you to trust him.

You noticed after a while that you never went anywhere in public;

627

you had beautiful times together, he seemed completely devoted, but you hardly ever met any of his friends or family.

But you were intimate, intensely so, and he convinced you – in fairness not by words, but by tender action – that this reclusive introspection was a reflection of the sacred separate special nature of your mutual passion. You were soulmates who needed no-one else to define them.

Then one night, two years after you had started to see each other, he failed to turn up to meet you in town at the agreed time. You waited for over an hour, then decided you must have got the arrangement wrong, and got the bus back home.

On the doormat was a letter from him – I have never seen it, but let me summarise:

> I will always love you. Tomorrow I am going to Paris, to university. I am sorry I never told you, but I didn't know how. I will never be as close with another. My parents do not approve of my love for you. I must follow the family business, I have to study finance, business and economics for three years and then work in the Paris branch of my dad's bank. I am sorry to do it like this, I have loved you so much, but it is for the best that we do not meet again, a clean break is the only way. I don't know how I will recover, but in time we will heal. Never will I experience again the feelings I have for you.

And so on and so on. And truthfully, though I jump ahead, we found out later that the boy went on to be successful in his father's banking business, mixed with his own, conveniently married quite young the daughter of his father's rival financier, had five children, and became extremely rich. Which, as I say, later, I found extremely aggravating and intimidating – God knows why. Again, I did want to seek him out, track him down, and beat him on the cock with a hammer, but this turned out to be just one more unfulfilled ambition ....

Anyway, so here is the thing, as usual, I am taking a long time to get there.

For the relationships I had had at that time, maybe there were three or four girlfriends, six weeks here, two months there, that sort of thing; and another three or four that were more one-or-two-night affairs. I hope I had been kind but probably not always, especially with some drinking and wildness. But always with respect, I do believe that. However, the linking theme of every one of these affairs was that I was the one who ended it.

I was not ready – once or twice. I had jumped in too quickly – quite often. I was being nice – sometimes. I didn't really care enough not to – that does not sound so good, that sounds, really, horrible, smug and complaisant. Perhaps I am underthinking this.

But, moving on from that, it seems to me, if you are the one who ends things and moves on, the effect is that you are always in control, always exactly where you want to be – even if you hate the way you got there, and regret it, and have residual thoughts and feelings of love and affection, you have determined your destiny and have chosen the spot you're standing on.

However, and here is the point, if you are the one who is dumped, you are not where you want to be. You have not selected the new place; you are not standing in the spot you chose; you are in a location picked for you by others.

So when a lover says to their partner, "You are my soulmate, I chose you, you are 'the one,'" this can only be true if that person always has ended every relationship in order to get to this one, has naturally deselected and discarded all previous partners and now selects this special one, forever.

Because if a lover has been abandoned, not of her own volition, by someone she might have been with forever, someone she loved deeply, trusted, relied on, isn't it only the behaviour of the other that has made her available, that has placed her in the position to be yours, that had pushed her into your arms and let her say "You are the one."

In this case, am I really "The one"?

Or am I just "The one who is left"; merely "The one who didn't dump me"; patently "The one who is here now, hanging around after my first choices passed me over."

Besides also the thought, obviously (the one that you cannot help having): what did they find that was better? Did they discover something that I never found, work out the thing I missed?

Letter 181

… I wonder if you sensed me? I was in the small copse sixty metres west of your back door, just by your smaller barn, where you keep the feed. Don't panic! I am safely back in London now…

We actually had an excellent visit this year. Jack is now firm friends with his older cousin Jean, and Jean is teaching him lots of things that I should have taught him already if I had stayed focused.

Georgina and Frank have a dozen playmates and a score of fields, woods and lakes to play in, where they can have adventures they could never dream of in England. Did you realise that one of yours played a hide and seek game with two of mine one day during their holidays?

Kate and I spent every meal – every lunch and dinner – with different groups of relatives catching up, and we still only ate our way around half the clan. Sweetly, we were getting calls of complaint from uncles and nieces we couldn't fit into the schedule.

And at night, as Kate and I had separate rooms in our cottage, I was able to get out and travel around. Kate caught me leaving on the third night, but of course she is used to my solitary moods, and she assumed I wanted to innocently wander the paths and revisit the abandoned haunts of my youth, smoking heavily.

*What I did of course was to come each night to watch for you, as
I have done for so many years. By the time I normally managed to
reach your farm, all was dark, and everyone was asleep, so mostly it
was rather pointless, but at least for an hour or so every night I was
close to you.*

*But one night, a light was on, there were loud voices, an argument.
For a moment, I considered running to your aid – I could rescue you
at last!*

*Then it went quiet, the door opened, and a carpet of bright light
rolled out across your yard. You emerged onto it, took eight paces,
stopped, put both hands to your head, ruffled your hair, turned, and
laughed. You lit a cigarette, took four drags, very deep, letting the
smoke out soft and slow over ten beats each time. Then you called out,
"Hugo."*

*He strolled out along the strand of light and stood only a foot away
from you; you leaned forward, put one arm around his neck, kissed
him, then you put the cigarette into his mouth.*

*So, no rescue that night… it seemed you had the situation under
control.*

Letter 207

*… like swans, or grey wolves. How is it possible to bear the weight of
our own history, to carry the baggage, like a sack of crumbling rocks
each carved with the name of a long-lost lover.*

*I dwelt on episodes of infidelity, passive or active, dreamed or real.
I imagined a partner faithless in the arms of another, gasping
for their love, ten years before I met them, or ten years after I left
them. I conjured an act of betrayal, maybe not even sexual, maybe
not cuckolding, but other kinds of humiliation, belittling, casual
negligence; coming back late after meeting a past lover for a drink; a
harmless but knowing lie about the timing of an affair some decades
earlier. Just as bad and hurtful, the repetition of sweet behaviour: a*

best-loved poem previously shared with another; the secret walk you also took an age ago; the book bought once before for someone else.

In Hell the whole archive is made available; they turn the key, open the cupboard, and there it is, ready to view as many times as you want. They do not make you watch it, but you can't resist; the moving images of your previous and current lovers with all the other partners you think they had or ever will.

You can see every detail of her nervously losing her virginity to the curly-haired olive-eyed youth on the Bagni di Tiberio who turned out to be a little bit older and a lot more insistent than she'd hoped; then skip to gropes of condescending cummerbunds at shady champagne balls. Fast forward, the dancing years, and you watch her writhing and groaning for endless hours of senseless sex with lines of pumped-up Salsa men and their colossal cocks; then share the pain of anal sex wheedlingly coerced by a bored contemptuous boy who left soon after perfunctorily wiping himself on the sheets she'd dump tomorrow. Then observe the orgasms generously faked for well-known older men of mixed repute; and ski-less jaded weeks with feckless chalet boys she'd then decline to talk about and struggle to forget.

In Hell, we agree, everything you always knew to be true is true, whether it happened or not.

And Heaven? Here's the good bit.

Heaven is the hell of having to choose which earthly partner you will spend eternity loving. We are back with the grey wolf in the afterlife. It might be a gorgeous, intense and passionate relationship from your teenage years, perhaps the first, that died from fear, curiosity and inexperience; or the dream girl in the pool of sun; or the loyal and loving ally of your middle years and family; perhaps someone not even yet dead, whom you'll wait for nervously. Or maybe the girl in the distance, seen once – country dancing with flowers in her hair; getting on a bus on a foggy evening; riding a bicycle with her skirts tucked up – can you pick her?

But what if the one you choose does not choose you?

And what of the ones you do not choose, who do choose you?

Could it be someone you wanted but never had? What about the humans lost and lonely who never had love in life, can they find it in Heaven? What is the chance that someone will choose them back? What are the rules in heaven, what is the partnership etiquette? Can you do a millennium with one person, then five hundred years with another?

What would make me happy, what I dream about, is this: you and I meet on the first day of school aged four, sitting next to each other. We are inseparable ever after. As children we play together, learn to read together, to paint, to sing, to ride bikes together, to walk to school together and home again, and at weekends our parents dare not keep us apart.

As we grow older we do everything together, reading the same books, writing poetry, working on our family farms in the summer, we learn to cook, we explore, we take endless country hikes, we attend school dances as partners and leave halfway through so we can be alone together, laughing about the others.

No drinking, no dalliance, no meanness, no treachery, no lechery, no others, no episodes, no flirting at parties that goes horribly wrong.

Innocence, kindness, love, loyalty, dedication without awareness, commitment without consideration. No promises to make and break.

On your sixteenth birthday we have sex for the first time. It is at first fumbling, in a vacuum, but patience, anticipation, passion, friendship, nurturing, adoration, caring, natural creativity, healthy physicality and giggling visits to the library gradually make it gorgeous and extraordinary, another circle in the magic ring around us.

There is no history, you see, beyond or besides the shared history. There are no cupboards, no skeletons, no buried bones. No separate need so secret and well-concealed that it can never be discovered. We are clean, free, loyal, undivided, no dilemmas, no conflicts, no memories that make us sit up shouting in the night. A single soul, entwined, conjoined, absolutely pure; no traumas, no alarms, no panic attacks, no constant revisiting, no continuous rehashing, no living backwards. Beautiful children, lovers who can only look forward. And this never changes.

There is no rival experience, no competitive orgasm, no comparative penis.

Letter 208

… of course I love her, but I am in love with you. Perhaps it would be better not to name things, give labels to emotions; but that is what I have lived by, my sacred text. You might say, this creates the neurosis, perpetuates the problem, without the constant droning of the text, you might gently let go, even if it took some years; but I might then say, without a code, without the loyalty to a principle, can there be a purpose, some hope of justification, some form of redemption?

Today, Jack came home with great news, he has won a National School Essay competition. He is extremely happy with the £100 prize, but more significantly, the piece is going to be published in a literary magazine, it could be something important for him.

The theme of the essay had to be "Family," and it could be fiction or a memoir. I asked Jack, of course, to show me his entry. He refused, and that worried me. I said, I will see it anyway when it comes out, so there's no point keeping it from me.

I won't copy it all out here, but this is the essence: it is a portrait of a man who starts married life in colourful clothes, arriving quickly home each night; but who then over the years begins to wear brown, come home late, and volunteer for overseas work trips that should be the duty of junior colleagues. The link snaps between the time of arrival in the house, and the taking of meals as a family, and it seems this is the tipping point, not only for the man and his wife, but also with the children. The child narrator (my own son) says, "Perhaps to my shame, it might shock you to know, I was grateful when we stopped waiting for him. The tension, and sometimes even the hunger, were hard to take, because the symbolism of the family meal had become completely overbearing."

The child speculated about the motivations, not completely understanding, and the skill of the story is in the uncertainty about whether the child does not understand, or whether it is the adults who cannot comprehend and express: good writing for his or any age, this is the world of the unreliable narrator.

The theme, if he could describe it more prosaically, is that love drains gradually when washed away by boredom, or a lack of satisfaction, or the absence of dreams; but it disintegrates instantly when over-gulfed by a greater love, whether chosen, imposed or out of the blue. When you stop caring about the detail, or when you start sacrificing the residual good that comes from the habit of the everyday to the frustration and despair that comes from the absence of passion, then the better essence of life is lost to the hollow shape of love. But he didn't get bogged down in turgid explication, he instinctively knew it and told it with simple images. How did he know?

[Jack was sobbing a bit here. He had not realised that his father had seen the story, and had not meant to hurt him with it, just to tell a truth and enter a competition. His mum had encouraged him and helped him by typing it up; they mutually decided not to tell dad as nothing would probably come of it. Now it seems obvious it was a selfish truth released to the nation about his father's fecklessness... At least his dad had chosen to focus on the technical issues, not the content – though Jack hadn't really been aware at all that he had crafted it like that. 'A father's pride,' he smiled wryly, 'identifying some unintended excellence to praise.' Jack thought, also, 'This must be one of the very boring letters he wrote when he ran out of life. At least he had the self-awareness to know.']

Letter 242

… so then Kate had me pressed back against the wall shouting, screaming.

"What the fuck, what the fuck, what the FUCK is going on with you?

"You don't sleep with me, not for years. You don't do anything intimate; you start away if I brush your hand. You pull away, if I try to put my hand on your shoulder to comfort you, if I just go to brush a hair off your jacket.

"You leave the house early to get away from me, you come home late. Now I find out you have been taking trips you don't even need to take. What is that about, Mac?

"I'd know if there was some fucking one else, you don't even have the emotional energy for that, you don't have the emotional capacity anymore, you lack the desire for physical or emotional intimacy with me or anyone else. Tell me I'm right, right – you can't love any more, what happened? Say something. Come on, say something. At least nod if I'm right – you can't love, you have no love, you have no desire, right?"

I nodded.

"Jesus, Mac, Jesus. What the hell. You're good with the kids, I'll give you that, you certainly resemble a kind and dedicated father. They love you – right now, actually, that really annoys me. You're a great fucking father! I should love that, I should be proud of that, I chose you and made you their father, and you do an excellent job, and I hate that, when everything else about you is so fucking fucking fake.

"You are a great father, indeed, but you are a lousy, mean, spiteful, vengeful, tiny-hearted husband. You're crap. You are an absolutely fucking crap husband."

Her aunt finally broke out of the watching crowd, entered our radius, and pushed between us, her back firmly to me, her arms and love reaching out and wrapping around her wrecked and wretched niece, swaddling her like a shivering child in a warm blanket on a snowy day. I swear she lifted her bodily and carried her upstairs, a door opened and closed.

Maybe twenty people stood in a circle around me, looking at me, some glaring at me, some pitying me; no-one spoke. Friends, family, neighbours. Twenty of the most important people in my life, looking at me with sorrow and contempt as I peeled myself off the wall. I feigned looking round with some boldness but all the while I was careful not to catch anyone's eye.

I walked out of the door, shut it behind me, got sixty metres up the road, sat down on the curb and lit a cigarette. The shock hit me, I cried.

I realised I had just walked out of my own house. I had nowhere to go. Bells rang out.

That's a Happy New Year, then.

Letter 281

... Today I have been very ill – or as the English say, "rather ill."

It came on last night, first shivers, then coughing, I am not sure what, but I have been laid up, sleeping most of the day, no work for me. Kate has been so sweet and attentive, running up and down, bringing drinks, soup, sometimes just mopping my brow! And each time she leaves the room, I think of you.

I fell into a shallow feverish disturbed sleep this afternoon, and you were in my mind the whole long chopped-up instant of it – it was all I could do to stop myself saying your name.

This evening I am very much better – "slightly improved" – and in my lucid patches I can squeeze in a bit of guilt. How have I let things come to this? I take for granted a loyal, kind, loving person who has given her life to me and making our children, and I dwell on you obsessively, uncontrollably.

But if I found you now, if you melted in my arms, then the shame at my behaviour over the last fifteen years would be unsustainable. So where is the solution? Sometimes, and strange love letter this is, I dream that one of you will die, and release me to the other. The shocking thing? In terms of pain, and the complete absence of hope, it does not really seem to matter which.

[This was the lowest point for Jack. His tears were uncontainable, his heaving sighs were stealing the air so he needed to remind himself how to breathe. 'He means the dream will die,' he told himself, struggling to remodel the memory before it settled, 'he means that the crazy fantasy world will cease to exist.' But he knew that wasn't what he meant at all.

Then, instead, he said out loud, "Don't collude with this madness."

Speaking to Mac, directly, he said, "You lunatic bastard, can you not see that if mum dies you will have FUCKING NOTHING. It does matter which, it really does, because the other half of the scale, that you think is perfectly balanced, is completely empty. Not even a ghost lives there. And anyway, this is all too late now, because everyone who loved you has given up and gone."]

Letter 312

... today, finally, the only love letter I have from you has fallen apart in my hands. In any case it is so covered in tape that I can hardly read the words anymore – just as well I know it by rote. Now all I can do is keep it in the bag with your t-shirt and the "other letter," the three things that you have touched, the things that smell still of you to me. I am annoyed with myself, I should have made a copy, or at least taken a photo, before it dissolved into fragments. If it is found in future, and someone wishes to know what it says, no codebreaker

will ever be able to make out the words. That letter, because it is from you, written by you, is to me a holy text, blessed by the trust and faith of writing it. Do you remember? I have it by heart:

> Darling Mac, I think this is the first night we have been apart since you told me you loved me three days ago, which is a day totally sacred to me in the calendar of my life. The last two nights we have spent together have been divine, I have experienced feelings and pleasure such as I have never known. You have become gentle and patient, as I knew you one day would. I love you my love, come soon.

Of course, the other letter is another matter, which we will not talk about for now. The t-shirt? You left it in the room above the barn, the day you brought a change of clothes and went straight off to work. You wore it once when we made love, and it is wound tight now, to keep you in; I have only unwrapped it a couple of times in the past ten years, like the shroud of Jesus Christ, so your essence cannot float away.

Letter 333

… about a fortnight now since I have slept properly – since I had the dream I wrote to you about in my last letter.

I said last time I didn't want to talk about the dream, but I am ready now. I have almost stopped shaking: I mean it, for days I shook, and I could not sleep, and I could not think of anything but the dream. I couldn't work, couldn't concentrate for more than fifteen minutes on anything – I could hardly face another person, not Kate, not the kids, or anyone at work.

So, the dream. It was nothing symbolic, nothing mythological. Actually, it was just a movie; I starred in a movie of my own life…

The reel started running when we met again in the farmer's dance two nights later, the first date. We had both said to each other, "Perhaps I will see you there on Friday," and there we were.

639

Then it rolled on: leaving the bar, walking instead of getting the bus, kissing you outside your house, coming back in the morning with flowers before you were awake. I was already in love with you, and here it all was, in a movie that I could sit and watch, absolutely frame by frame.

The next day, both ducking work, going swimming in the river, then eating at the little café outside town. Sleepy afterwards, lying in the sun in the afternoon, drinking a bottle of red in the evening, and taking another to bed, making love for the first time.

I was asleep no more than five hours on the night I had that dream, but the dream itself lasted forty-eight hours. How can that be? I lived frame by frame in sharply focused technicolour the first forty-eight hours of our relationship, and everything was there: touch, taste, vision, colour, music, dialogue, laughter, your hair, your body, your clothes – frame by frame by frame by frame by frame. Something that had happened more than twenty-five years before, and I was dropped back into it, young, strong, vital. And I felt the feelings I felt – I lived the moments.

I woke shattered, quivering. My brain was overwhelmed with the content, I could not turn it off, I would not stop living it, reliving it. I was full of joy, then sadness, then fear of what was happening, I felt I was spiralling in a madness and totally out of control.

For several days I planned to come to you, as though you knew I was coming, because you had loved me so much in the dream, now you would take me back immediately, you had already decided it. I packed bags, bought tickets; unpacked, cancelled; repacked, repurchased.

I made an appointment with Kate to tell her everything; about you, the letters, the dream, and that you wanted me back. She was scared of course to be summoned to a place, at a time, this is not the natural behaviour of spouses. As soon as I said, "I am so sorry to get you here like this, but I have something to tell you," she leaned forward, clutched my wrist, and said, "I know you have cancer, Mac, it explains everything, the weight loss, the lack of sleep, no focus, no work, ignoring the kids, your shakes – tell me please, I can't bear this."

So, at last I was able to give her some good news.

"I don't have cancer, Kate."

Suddenly I felt as though I was in recovery, in remission, I had been cured. I had been given a second chance. We both laughed uncontrollably, celebrating the release of worry and tension.

And during those moments I lost my nerve completely. This loyal abused woman loved me for myself, she cared only for my welfare, and I didn't have the courage or energy at that moment to destroy her, even at the height of my derangement. I unpacked, unpurchased.

"I don't know what it is, Kate, I am so sorry to have been worrying you. I have been run down, I know, I have been exhausted, and at the same time I can't sleep."

Having to make it up as I went along, I carried on.

"What I wanted to talk to you about is that at work, you know I feel lost now, useless. They are phasing me out, the world has changed, the useful skills I had are no longer needed, I am an embarrassment.

"I am fifty soon, and I am scared. I used to be so confident and bold, nothing worried me, anything could be fixed with my hands and head, now I feel powerless. Not suddenly, gradually. I am growing old. I am too slow for the kids, too weak for you, too ancient for my job. Old friends are already beginning to die off. Where does it end?"

She patted my hands, reached forward and put her arms around my neck, pulling me to her, pulling my head against her breast.

"Oh, my love, my poor, poor love. You're so silly. You've been worried and scared, and brave not to say anything, but you know you can tell

*me anything, you know we can share anything, any worry, nothing is
too much for me to bear for you."*

*"When a man grows old," I said, "clearly he doesn't say to his partner,
'I know I can no longer satisfy you,' instead he fears he will lose her,
by means of decrepitude, to the arms of a stronger, fitter, younger
man, who still has teeth, and pees only three times a day instead of
three times an hour."*

*"You're not old, Mac, you're such a dick – not to say I am not taking
this seriously, but you are four times the man that any boy half your
age could ever be."*

*The maths were getting complicated here. You see, from the greatest
tragedy, this was already becoming a joke. I breathed inside a sigh of
relief at having scaled the first ridge of the mountain of deceit, and
boldly decided to strike out for the summit, without oxygen. "You're
so sweet to humour me, Kate. You're right, we should have talked
about this ages ago. And you are so kind and generous to pretend I
am still the man I was, which we both know is not true.*

*"Do you think it could be time for a change? You know I qualify for
quite a decent pension from work; I can leave any time after fifty. I
was thinking of France, going back, to the roots. The sun, a small-
holding, even a small farm. I worked farms for a decade one way or
another, and I can grow, I know animals."*

*Of course, this was the most irresponsible and obnoxious piece of
drivel, and the fact I was prepared to suggest this just to get myself
out of a conversational hole speaks horrors of what is in my mind and
the way it works. I am so sorry. Instead of anything honest, or saying
nothing, I was covering for my mythological secret life and crazy
fantasies by dangling a fresh romantic vision in front of a woman
that ten minutes ago I had been plucking up the courage to destroy.
I had set out with at least the honourable intention of being honest,
now I had doubled up my duplicity and disloyalty by dangling a new
dream I had no intention of ever delivering.*

What do you think of me now, my darling? A man you do not want turns his life upside down for you and in the process dismantles the existence of another woman who does nothing but love him. Is this an age-old pattern, something ordinary, a cliché? Or a unique and very special torment I have invented?

['Every time I think it can't get worse,' thought Jack, 'my father invents a new level of deceit and betrayal. I am running out of words to describe what I think of him.']

Letter 357

…. can no longer have sex with anyone other than you. I appreciate, I have not been with you for more than twenty years, and even I can accept the premise that I am unlikely to have sex with you again in the near future; but that does not seem relevant, it is you I want, therefore I should not have sex with anyone else, it is not fair to them, it is not fair to you. Doesn't that mean I am protecting Kate, at my own cost; and worshipping you with my abstinence?

… I am not at all conscious of why I am breaking my silence on this subject now, except, I suppose, I could admit that this letter is not going to be sent to you, it is going into a suitcase under the stairs. So the silence it not broken, it is merely remanded in custody. Jack has been going on all the time recently about Schrödinger's box, something from his school reading, and I think I have Schrödinger's suitcase, right? When the letters are in there, they are neither read nor unread. Though like most of his school stuff these days, I probably have totally misunderstood.

["You have, dad, totally", said Jack, out loud, with the kind of contempt a world-weary adolescent reserves for the limitless ignorance of a parent.]

Of course, I cannot say to my wife, "The reason I am not having sex with you is that I am in love with someone else," because that confesses to a real madness as well as an imagined infidelity.

Is this heroic, as I often think myself; or pathetic, spiteful and feckless, as I also often think myself?

Heroic, ascetic, pure, saintly and chivalric: or sulky, vengeful, selfish, cowardly and mean.

The infidelity is real, don't you think, if the desire for it is real, and if the outcomes of the fantasy are just the same as they would be from the actual adultery? How is it different?

[Jack was so deep in despair now, any reaction seemed pointless, even his normal supercilious response to frustration and hurt. He wanted to shout at his dad, shake his dad – "Lighten up, it's all in your head." But when what's in your head spills out onto the pavement, as Mac says himself, that's real.

Jack should have been conscious he was receiving ideas and images he would never be able to process or discard. He was watching his father on a long and dangerous descent without brakes, without resistance to the gathering speed.

And the letters… long ago, it seemed, these had stopped being a means of communication, or a link, or attempted connection to anyone. They were a stream of conscious, or more accurately self-conscious, just liquified nerve endings flowing out, splashing out, spattering out unstoppably. They started as a means of holding onto reason and ended as a physical manifestation of losing it.]

Letter 479

… running my tongue down the back of your leg, from your firm soft buttock to the back of your knee, then sucking the back of the knee really hard, but gently, of course, until, inevitably, you would begin to giggle, uncontrollably. Uncontrollably. Then you would wriggle out of my grasp, pull up your legs, fold your arms around them, and look down at me, floundering at the other end, laughing, with the laughter going all the way from your eyes, to your lips, to your chin, to your neck and breast. Uncontrollable giggling, then locked together, then

644

kissing and then lost in each other.

And it all starts with the back of the knee, I said, not even the front of it. You're so easy.

That was the second time, the sixth time, the nineteenth time and the thirty-third time we slept together. In the months together we had sex sixty-two times, and I think I remember all those times, but of course many of those memories may have been created by me over the twenty-five years since. Anyway, I remember enough for the actual memories to spawn new versions, variants, modifications, augmentations, enhancements, improvements and perfections.

I wonder if you think of me, in bed. You probably must. We were young, inexperienced, I suspect we made up in energy for what we lacked in sophistication, expertise, and finesse. As far as I can work out, find out, you have had only one partner since. The wretched Hugo.

(I discount the two who came before me, because they deserted you, and thus expunged – in my humble opinion – the prospect of residual desire and any memory of sexual excitement, how can that outlast betrayal?)

So, it is Hugo. That does not present too much competition, and therefore I have always been very confident that I am the most wonderful lover you have had. I mean, honestly, I have seen Hugo, I have been around Hugo on many special occasions; and you just know he is no great shakes, right? You agree with me? There is plenty of meat pie and rather good swearing, but where is the charm, the passion, the sensitivity? Where is the kiss on the back of the knee?

And the romance, what about that? Not old Hugo, I don't believe he has it. Does he scatter rose petals on your naked thighs; lick raspberry ice-cream from the hollow in the small of your back; cut your hair without permission; write awful poetry and help you to laugh at it; swim naked in the lake in October because you dared him? Do you – did you – wake with him day after day at 5.00am to drink thick coffee, smoke and see the sun rise though a barn window? Did he ever sing badly on the stairs and catch you giggling in bed?

[Jack edited a bit here. Some stuff with champagne, more bits of flowers and so on and so on …. And then that was it, over. Thanks, dad, for finishing with a wretched montage of the world's most embarrassing romantic clichés, which frankly have left me much queasier than the drooling sex talk.]

Jack had never been so grateful in his life for something to be finished. He was too disgusted, angry and exhausted to cry any more for now. He thought, just for a moment, of the five hundred letters. On and on, day after day, relentless.

What was in them all, were there any truths he should really know, father to son?

Luckily, he was now on a schedule of things other people were relying on him to do; so he lit a cigarette and tried to prepare himself to rejoin Claude and Milo. Thank the Lord for Showtime.

Earlier on, around 9.10am, over at Jean's, Caroline had pulled up outside the farmhouse and rubbed Hector's ears as he came out to greet her. He was very much enjoying the attention; having been left on his own for two days, now it appeared people couldn't get enough of him, old friends and new, and he was loving every moment. He particularly liked getting multiple meals because they'd lost track of who was feeding him, though it was hard work keeping the bowl empty enough to maintain the confusion.

"Hi, is anyone up?" Caro called, putting her head through the door.

"Come in, come in, we've been awake for hours," called back Kate, exaggerating only slightly.

"Do you want some coffee?" asked Maggie, eager to help. Caroline had had coffee ten minutes before with breakfast, but as this was the first time Maggie had ever offered her anything, she felt compelled, actually she wanted, to accept. She put on her great morning smile, "That would be lovely, Maggie, thanks so much."

She took a seat at the table and asked with her eyebrows whether they had finished eating. "Yes," said Maggie, gratefully, "it was absolutely lovely, I hope it was OK, we used some of those fresh jams, beautiful, very French." She blushed, realising she had gushed, then caught Caroline's eye, and they both laughed. "Very French!" chuckled Caro, "I'll tell Jean, I am sure that is what he was aiming for." She touched Maggie on the arm, so she would know she was laughing with her, not at her. Now they were friends. She took out a pack of cigarettes and offered her one. Maggie said no, implying with a shy smile that she would hold out just a little longer against the local culture. Kate picked up her own box off the table and offered them to Caro.

"Here, try one of these – English."

"Ah, the national products! I would enjoy that, the English nicotine in exchange for France's fruit conserves. That feels like a barter that has thrilled the generations."

"Is there any news of Jean?" Kate asked, getting the joke but choosing not to banter – not refusing in an unfriendly way, but just not ready yet for the lighter side, even as a means of defence.

"A good night, stable, every day that goes by without going backwards is a step in the right direction, according to the Doctor."

"That's great, Caroline. I didn't sleep very well; this is all such a mess."

"Yep, you can say that again. But no-one is blaming you Kate or thinking any the worse – you and Jack are victims of Mac, just as much as Jean and any number of other people Mac has screwed over, betrayed and hurt over the years."

She wasn't disguising her feelings again, then, thought Maggie, who had noticed the mention of Jack and tried to avoid showing it. Clearly everyone around here has had enough of Mac, but it sounded like the tribal conventions still wouldn't allow them to cast him adrift.

"What's happening with Mac, is anyone close to finding him?"

Caroline didn't especially want to get into that topic as Daphne had warned her off discussing the activities of Claude, Jack and Milo. "I know some locals are out looking, as well as the estimable Inspector. I've not heard anything concrete."

"What about my son, is he OK?"

Again, the shruggishness from Caro, not unfriendly at all, but saying, honestly, *je ne sais pas*. "I know they've been with the Experience a week, but honestly, it is Jean's thing, with Daphne and Claude, I've not been with them, sorry."

Changing the subject, she hoped unobtrusively, "Did you feed Hector? We should get him set up for the day before we get going."

One of Jean's men was tasked with putting meat into the fridge for Hector every few days, so thankfully there was some freshish food for him. Caroline beckoned Maggie over to help her; the girl wasn't terribly keen on handling it at first but steeled herself to cut it up small under her tutelage, put it in Hector's big cold stone bowl, and take it outside where she placed it in the shade next to his water basin. Hector, watching from his outdoor rug, was disappointed to observe an intensified level of personnel coordination that looked likely to restrict him to a more conventional number of meals in future.

Nevertheless, he decided to fall in love again, and show it. He made a grateful sortie at Maggie, culminating in a surprisingly elegant leap that marked her with doting slobber from waist to neck. His second sally was at the bowl, burying his chops in the meat with a yelp of joy formulated to convey his gratitude. How simple his life, but inside, constantly, is the unasked question, "Where is Jean and why did he leave me behind?"

Kate was now clearing away and washing up, so they joined in and helped her, and then the three of them got their things together. "Would you like to take the car or walk?" asked Caroline.

"Is it close then?" Maggie asked.

"Oh yes, only a few hundred metres, over there," pointing. "I think if Hector makes less noise eating his breakfast we can probably hear some of the chatter. The Experience is on the river side of the farm, where the road turns in, did you see the entrance last night?"

"No, it was dark when we came in," Kate said, "and I think we were too far gone at that stage… I used to know this place quite well, but it sounds as though there have been a few developments since then?"

"That there have. Let's walk then, so you can both get a sense of the way the Experience fits in now. I'll take you round the long way so you get a better view of the landscape. I can come back later and collect the car."

They put Hector on the long chain so he could find sun, shade, food bowl and water during the day. His affection for Maggie dimmed only slightly when she had the bright idea of leaving a note under this bowl saying **Chien nourri à neuf heures ce matin**; though he realised all good things must come to an end, he also knew he could eat the note if he got hungry.

And then there they were, three women out for a walk on a summer's morning, two on holiday, one showing them around, and it was like nothing at all was happening around them.

"Oh my God, this is lovely," said Maggie, looking back at the farm, and encompassing the fields and barns with a sweep of her arms, "it must be wonderful living here, this gorgeous old house, the outdoor life, natural living with the seasons – you know what I mean. Does Jean live here by himself?"

Caroline laughed. She liked these ladies, so instead of muttering "tourists" patronisingly under her breath and rolling her eyes unobtrusively, she shook her head wryly and said it right out loud, "Bloody tourists!" They looked at her, startled; she laughed, and so did they, though they weren't as certain why.

"You know the story, Kate, you've been here often enough. Yes, it is countryside, and if you see it once a year, of course it is lovely. For you, it is fresh air and a nice break; for us farmers, dwelling with it constantly, it's too dry for the crops, the ground is running out of life, the Government ignores us, and we're lucky to get more for the harvest than it costs us to plant.

"For those who don't know the story," she continued, turning to Maggie, "Jean lives here by himself, an offshoot of our tribe, but he employs plenty of people to help him. The land isn't great, and it's a hard hard life, not bucolic and adorably arcadian, he's not a noble savage, he's a scrabbler, like all of us. And he has the pressure of three hundred years of farmers coming before him, building it up, keeping it going – he can't be the one to let it slip. That's why he's created the Experience, it is the last of a long line of special projects he's tried to establish to keep the farm going and keep his dream alive. All the others have not worked out so well, sadly. Really some have been rather counterproductive, like the snail farm, the poetry retreat and the honey factory. I think we're still paying compensation."

She burst into giggles at this point, and they're always infectious, though Kate wasn't sure whether they were titters of mirth or despair. They had now come within sight of the Hut and the carpark, with a rolling view of the path down to the river and along the bank to the landing, and finally to the barge at the jetty. The mid-morning sun was glinting off the gently flowing water, the colourful banners and paper and fabric blooms woven into

650

the foliage on the banks were glowing, and the boat was bobbing brightly with its gorgeously painted decorations turning it into a floating flower stall. From somewhere below came the breezy tone of a confident accordion giving out Le Roi Dagobert and then merging it into Il Etait Une Fermiere. Even from a distance, gaily dressed figures could be seen milling around to the music, clearly enjoying themselves already.

"Oh my God, it's perfect," said Maggie; then, realising she had not only done it again but actually increased the effusiveness quotient, she put her hand over her mouth, making big eyes.

"Ha ha," Caro laughed, "don't worry Maggie, I am not going to tease you, it really is fabulous – I love your wonderment.

"It feels like Jean has finally got it just right, the reaction this week has been amazing. Obviously we still have to see if he's making more money than he's spending: I can certainly vouch for the fact that none of us are getting a salary that I am aware of, so he's definitely improving his business technique."

Caroline's diversionary chatter filled their trek and brought them all the way down to the Hut. She was pleased to see there was already a large throng and delighted to observe that the kids Amelie and Albert, standing out in their candy-stripe blazers, were well in control, had the visitors organised into two lines, and were already collecting prepaid tickets. She wasn't so pleased to catch sight of Leopard hanging around under the lime trees at the side of the carpark, but you couldn't say he was unexpected.

She quickly popped in to see Daphne at her place behind the desk. She was allocating the places, and let Caro know she had already remembered to reserve seats for Kate, Maggie and the Inspector. While Caro helped her with the money and receipts, Daphne got Tommy to count the non-ticket queue, and then to take out the Experience Complet sign when she calculated they were full for the day.

Then Tommy was freed up to start the accordion going once more with some country jigs that immediately started a few people bouncing around. Albert and Amelie were helping the final few customers with their costumes, including Kate and Maggie who has nobly waited till last – family hold back! While they were all distracted, Daphne signalled to Caro to come for a chat outside.

"How's Jean?" Caro asked when they were out of earshot.

"No change since you left, not awake. I managed to get the Doctor when he came in, he thinks he's a safe bet, getting stronger as every hour passes. Fingers crossed we're looking OK."

"Fantastic."

"Yes, two days ago I never thought we would get there. What's happening with Kate and the girl?"

"Nothing to report, really, I picked them up and we walked over; they're really nice, you know?"

"I liked them right away."

Caroline nodded, "Kate always was a gem. I guess you can't judge a woman by the man she keeps. It worries me we cut her off when she needed our help."

Daphne has been away during the time of Mac's original disappearance from London, but understood Caro's guilty thought and gave her a 'we should all have done more' gesture, with a sympathetic frown.

"Let's keep strolling down to the carpark;" Daphne suggested, "much as I like them, I don't know what to say yet. I wish Jean would wake up and tell me how he wants to play it."

"It's easier for me," Caro said slightly ruefully, "because I don't know anything, so if I get pinned down, they can't get anything out of me."

"Sorry, sorry, Caro, I didn't mean to have secrets... it was kind of you to offer to fill in without knowing the whole story."

"So it's not just because Jean's out of action?"

"It's also because Claude, Jack and Milo aren't helping on the boat this morning, they're going straight up to the theatre this afternoon. I told them about Leopard coming today... "

"Ah, I get it."

" ...but I didn't mention Kate and Maggie being here."

"Why not?" Daphne's new-found reputation for complete transparency had lasted all of ten seconds.

"Being honest," Daphne was struggling a little with her answer, "I'm not quite sure. It just seemed like the right thing to do in the moment, it feels like Jack and Milo have enough issues, and I didn't want them trying to come down here today. You know the three of them were out in the small hours last night driving round the forest tracks with Desdemona looking for Mac."

"No! I can genuinely say I did not know that, and no-one told me. Claude's not playing the fool with her again, is he? That's poison for him, right?"

"Tell me about it. Seriously, it is the gossip of the neighbourhood – actually the rumour of the region, I'm amazed you've not heard."

"Well, I've been with Jean most of the time, I promise you he said nothing on the subject."

"He must be the only one. I strongly suspect he knows and is feigning catatonia out of embarrassment. Didn't the twins mention it when you were bathing them?"

"Oddly, now you remind me, they did say something about Claude and Dessie sitting in a tree, but I got distracted when they couldn't spell KISSING, so I didn't have time to join the dots."

"You can bet Pierre will have connected them by now, as if we didn't have enough problems to deal with."

"What is it with Dessie and your dad, seriously: a fatal attraction?"

"Jesus let's hope it doesn't go that far."

They laughed; one defensively, one mischievously, both resignedly.

"Apparently she's been dressing them all up as commandoes and dragging them through the hedgerows in the pitch black hunting for the elusive Monsieur du Lac."

"If Dessie's version of a manhunt means going into the woods every night with Claude, Mac can relax; he will never be located."

They'd reached the carpark, and mutually decided to have a couple of drags on a shared fag before heading back up. An extremely fancy car turned in before the occupants noticed the sign, and Daphne did the sweet "Sorry, no luck" sign with one arm held out parallel to the ground, elbow slightly crooked, and a jazz hand at around seventy degrees. Instead of turning straight round and leaving, the car rolled over; the window wound down, and a familiar face looked out and shouted, "This is the second day we have been turned away, are you playing hard to get, Daphne?"

"Pierre? Is that you?"

Daphne was shocked, but tried not to show it. Like Beelzebub, she had named the demon, and he had instantly appeared.

"I wouldn't have thought this would be your kind of thing."

"Everyone is talking about it, I saw your dad the other night, he was raving about it. I was hoping to catch up with him, is he around?"

"Not at the moment, Pierre, can I give him a message?"

"Oh, nothing really, just say I was asking after him. My commiserations on Jean, Caroline, we are all praying for him, you know that. Things seem to be very exciting up here at the moment; I hope your dad is being careful, Daphne. Anyway, we look forward to the day when we can get on the boat!" So saying, the window went back up, the car turned about, and they were away.

"Oh my Lord, what was that about?" Caroline asked. "He's bloody scary, isn't he?"

"Yes, many men round here strive unsuccessfully to appear threatening, but he achieves totally terrifying without the slightest effort. Dad says they're into some frightening stuff now, way beyond the loveable rogue."

"You know what, I wasn't mistaking him for loveable, but it's worth remembering. Good call from your dad to be off today I reckon. I hope he's not dallying with Desdemona…"

They'd turned now and were striding back up to the Hut, Daphne realised she had dallied too long herself and needed to get things moving.

"He's sworn to me that she's not involved with that lot anymore; and he's extremely evasive about any relationship. Whether that would hold up under interrogation, I have no idea."

"With the hot spikes under his nails?"

"That wouldn't worry dad, he's fine with any level of physical pain, he showed that in the war. The question might be more about Dessie holding out: torture aside, she's not the most discreet person in the world at the best of times."

As they reached the crowd, Amelie signalled to Daphne with a thumbs up that they were all done, everyone was ticketed, the right number, all were regaled in their costumes, and Tommy had them all tapping their feet to a medley of jigs and reels. They really were getting very good at this.

Daphne popped inside to pick up her bag and keys, then checked that Kate, Maggie and Leopard were in the group. She was pleased to see that the Englishwomen had relaxed a little once they'd decided to join in the spirit with costumes and accessories. Maggie was looking particularly cute, and Daphne realised she was going to be a knockout when she finally decided to comb her hair, pull her shoulders back, wear lighter clothes and brighter colours, and smile (the same suggestions, oddly enough, that her own mother had written on the fourteenth-birthday card that went on to become life's most neglected to-do list).

Daphne was equally delighted to perceive that Leopard hadn't undermined his status by dressing up – maybe he realised he looked quite enough like a nineteenth-century police inspector without trying. But even as she was deciding this, he put on a bowler hat from nowhere, pulled out a pipe and put it in his mouth, then fished a tortoiseshell monocle out of his top pocket and slipped it in. He turned and gave her a deadpan wink with his other eye. Oh my word, she thought, he's perfect: This Is Not A Pipe.

As she was imagining Leopard Magritte, there was the roar of an engine as a car screeched into the carpark and there was a thump of a bumper as it crashed straight into the **Experience Complet** sign. And there was Pelou getting out of the town's most ancient police vehicle. Daphne could actually remember looking out as a five-year-old through the window of their little house when her dad was taken away in the very same car on Christmas Eve, her grandma crying behind her on the blistered leather sofa. Fortunately, thanks to various familial interventions, he was home again the following morning for a Joyeux Noel which included a *grosse dinde grasse* mysteriously delivered by Jean's father.

Karl got out of the other side, already moaning at Pelou for his terrible driving and the horrible quality of the ride from the *gendarmerie*. Daphne whispered to Tommy and Caroline to keep everyone happy for a few minutes while she sorted it out and headed towards the carpark. Leopard had already set off in front of her, but they arrived at the same time.

"What's this, Pelou?"

"Sorry, sir," stammered the loyal Sergeant, "I tried to stop it."

"You're a disgrace, all of you," Karl was into it already, "the only thing you tried to stop was me having my human rights."

"Please, Karl, will you do me a favour, just while my officer reports, would you be kind enough to go over under that very beautiful tree and wait just for a moment? I promise you it will just be a few minutes."

Karl reluctantly acquiesced.

"Go on, Sergeant."

"We've been in the station all night, I am afraid, sir. We didn't even arrive till midnight, then it dragged on due to the uncooperative nature of the witness, in my opinion." [Daphne, who they'd ignored till then, sniggered into her hand, then kept quiet and signalled she wasn't really there.] "We were in the interview room for several hours, then the witness demanded a meal, that took an hour, then he demanded we arrange a phone call to Germany, and the Station Commander said I had to do that. By the time he'd had his call it was 5.00am and he needed sleep so we let him have a nap in the cell. While he was sleeping the Commander got a call from Germany that made him go white and quiver, and he tore the skin off my back, sir, honestly he did, and told me to treat the boy with kid gloves and do whatever he wanted, but also to make him disappear and not let him push us all around. So this morning when he woke I let him have a shower in the officers' bathroom, gave him a coffee, and then brought him here at his request as it seemed uncontroversial to do so."

While joyously revelling in the "uncontroversial to do so," Daphne was also now itching to get away. She could sense the customers around the Hut were going to get twitchy if she kept them waiting much longer – many of them were looking in their direction and wondering what was happening. Was this the famous Experience madness they had been promised? OK, perhaps she was worrying about nothing, it was just as likely they were enjoying it…

Leopard signalled her to wait please and be patient just for a few more seconds, and beckoned Karl back over. "I am sorry if you had a rough night, Karl, but thankfully it is over, right, and we can move on now?"

"Is that meant to be an apology?"

"Pelou will handle that later, right, Sergeant?"

As ever the kindly policeman looked slightly bemused, and nodded, though not quite sure what he was agreeing to.

"Now we are off, Karl, I hope you have a good day."

"Hold on, I am here because I want to make sure you are pursuing the case. I believe your Station Commander instructed the Sergeant to make sure I had all the assistance I needed today, after he had had a short talk with my father's solicitor." Karl's smirk was broad, and he wasn't trying to hide it.

"We really need to go, Inspector," Daphne interjected, "we have a timetable, if you really want to be on the Experience."

"Can you fit two more?"

"Seriously?"

"The police force would consider that to be a very great service, Daphne, and it would not be forgotten."

"OK, if we have to, but I am afraid two of you will have to stand with me in the cockpit area, as all the seats are allocated."

"That's fine, Daphne. Pelou and I will stand with you, and Karl can have my seat."

Daphne shrugged her agreement. "You will have to waive any coverage from our insurance, of course."

"You have insurance?"

"Honestly I have no idea, but I know if we do have it cops aren't covered."

Leopard popped his monocle in and laughed, while Karl shook his head at them in despair.

They all walked back up towards the Hut, and Daphne gave Tommy a nod from thirty metres away. He struck up an all-purpose hiking song and led the way out, looking back over his shoulder to call on the customers, who willingly fell in behind him, unconsciously swaying gently in time as they wandered down the dappled path through the avenue of limes and poplars to the riverbank. They cooed in excitement as they neared the jetty and saw the gorgeously painted vessel, anticipating the best day of their summer from everything they had heard about it; they began to queue politely to embark, calmly shepherded by Amelie, Albert, Caro and Tommy in their blazers, while Daphne, on board, began to ready the boat. Albert and Amelie were particularly unimpressed to see Karl turning up yet again; they looked at Daphne, questioning, but all she had for them was a shrug, a roll of the eyes, and a nod towards Leopard. "Ask him about it, really, there's nothing I can do."

Caroline was at least able to intercept Karl as he was boarding and make sure he was corralled in the middle of a group of marvellous ladies from the Parish Women's Association, who had booked the day for their annual outing. One of them had already asked Karl to hold her wool as she had her knitting out. They were mothers, not at all fazed by his sulky looks; one mentioned sitting up straight and another suggested that a smile can change your day. When everybody else was comfortably and safely seated and the lifejacket announcement had been made, Albert cast off the stern, Amelie the bow, and Daphne, accompanied on either side by Pelou and Leopard, engaged the throttle. As she pulled away, she beckoned Albert over to take the wheel, as promised, for his maiden voyage. Then, as was becoming the routine, Tommy opened up with La Mer, and anyone who knew the words – which was everyone – started singing (except Karl).

Kate, Maggie, Leopard, Karl, Daphne, even Pelou – each of them had a feeling that today would be the day when something would happen, maybe everything would come to a head. Kate and Maggie had been confused at the Hut about why it was that Milo and Jack were not there if they were working in the Experience. But they did something in the play? So presumably they would be there this afternoon? Every time they tried to grab Daphne or Caroline to ask a question, they were busy, talking to someone, or had disappeared completely. Kate had managed to get Caroline for a few moments on her own, but she had explained that she was only filling in for a few hours before going back to the hospital, and actually knew very little about how the jobs were allocated at the Experience and, as to why the lads were not at the Hut, that was probably a question for Daphne. Maggie tried asking the young boy in the blazer – Albert? – but he just turned a shade of red she'd never seen before and burbled incomprehensibly. 'Either he is a totally brilliant actor,' she thought, 'or he's very very bad at talking to girls.'

Maggie was totally immersed in the stunning scene: she certainly planned to be cool at some future date, but her daily choice at present was breathless enthusiasm. Smiling, she looked over at Caroline, who was supervising at the stern end, to share the joy; and Caroline, catching her gaze, knowing exactly what she was feeling, smiled back and made the madly beating heart sign with her hand on her chest, then looked skywards like Jesus with arms raised, palms up, to say "What a time of wonder this is."

Turning excitedly to Kate next to her, she said in English, in the expectation of being overheard but not understood: "This is not what I was expecting at all. This is fantastical, magical."

"I agree, Maggie, this is completely amazing, who would have thought it!"

"Jean must have incredible vision to have created all of this. Like a theatre Director."

"This feels like the work of an old-fashioned showman more than a Director, like Barnum with his circus? It feels more like a family; one that is totally dedicated to the enterprise and making entertainment. Jean has that knack of attracting loyal followers to help him. I could see the boys would fall for his dream, Jack did anything to please him when he was tiny. Anyway, by the look of the customers, and how they're enjoying it, and the quality of the whole set up, this is destined to be a very big success. It looks like Jean might finally fulfil his artistic aspirations and his commercial ambitions at the same time. Touch wood!"

"What relation is he to you?"

"You know what, no-one really does proper family trees around here. It is not me that's related to him, it's Mac, and he always referred to Jean as a nephew. Jack and the youngsters were taught to call him cousin, but whether that is in any way real or just a handy tag I'm not sure. I definitely used to know all this, but I'll need to get someone to remind me, Caro knows better than anyone, if we can get her to talk..." They exchanged a glance, recognising they were both perfectly aware they were being boxed off at the moment.

While they were talking, a Meaulnes had come and sat down on the other side of Maggie, and had turned purposefully to face her, but as Maggie was still talking to Kate on the other side, he was staring at the back of Maggie's head. Clearly she had taken his interest, and he was waiting for her to look round so he could try a line. Kate, looking over Maggie's shoulder, noticed the imminent unwanted attention. She was aware of what was going on, with a mother's intuition. She realised from some sniggering among the lairy group of boys he had just left in order to move next to them that this youth was a charming yet predatory emissary sent out to see if he could catch the pretty one, probably for a bet. Kate's protective instinct was fully engaged; Maggie was already having to cope with the accusations of Jack's faithlessness, and however brave she looked now, Kate had heard her crying during the night. For herself, Kate had had enough of deceitful, manipulative men to last her a very long time. She eyeballed the boy square on from about forty centimetres and spoke across Maggie.

"Can I help you, young man?" [In French.]

"No, Ma'am" [in embarrassed English; then switching to French]. "I am so sorry if I have appeared rude or intrusive, but you see I am unfamiliar to the region, here by myself, so I was wondering if I could in a friendly way engage with you on such a lovely day and practise my English while being good company."

"Why are you speaking French if you want to practise English?" said Kate in English. The young man, who in truth was very dashing, especially in his tightly fitting Meaulnes-suit, looked entirely baffled.

Kate continued in English, speaking increasingly rapidly, even for her, "We would be perfectly delighted to speak with you in English, but I have a feeling that you are a smooth chancer who just wants to pick up a lovely young English girl to show off to his friends and probably win a few francs. I don't think you speak a word of English, not even, 'Can I kiss your sweet cherry lips and squeeze your peachy bottom?'"

As she was speaking she had begun smiling, and nodding, and the boy had joined in, so by the end of the speech, when they reached the passion fruit salad Kate had conjured from nowhere, both of them were smiling, nodding and giggling, while Maggie was looking on fascinated, not entirely approving, but not objecting either.

Kate eventually changed back to French, and as she spoke Meaulnes's face first lit up and glowed, "*OK, tu es très gentil et assez mignon,*" then crumpled and creased, "*mais nous ne sommes pas intéressés par tes jeux, tu devrais retourner voir tes amis et leur dire que tu as échoué.*"

She switched her focus to Maggie, feeling it was over with the boy, ignoring him now, and speaking English to the girl.

"This is a place Mac spoke about often, they used to come here and swim off that jetty," she pointed back to the landing stage they'd just pulled away from. "Him, Claude, their schoolmates and cousins. They bathed naked here as boys every summer. He brought me down here once to show me, when we were over on one of our holidays."

[He told her, "We shouted poetry at the top of our voices while we swam; my favourite was '*C'est un trou de verdure où chante une rivière...*'"

As Kate was imagining the scene and recalling the verse in her mind, she began to cry, the memory of the visit and Mac's smiling rendition had come so quickly, so unexpectedly. And the boys, in those long-lost summers, once they had all been so young, so beautiful, so full of hope. She was weeping for her dead marriage, and a husband who had come back to life to stab his friend. And for a son who had lost his way.]

"It is strange, Maggie; now I know he is alive, I feel genuinely widowed for the first time." She was laughing, crying and shaking her head, all at once. "I want to scatter the ashes of my dead husband in this river. Right now."

Then she realised, with a start, that the Meaulnes was still there, sitting with them, listening. "For God's sake," she spoke unthinkingly in English, "will you please piss off."

Up until then the Meaulnes had been confused, but might have been prepared, despite the rebuttal, to press on and take his chances. He wasn't yet accustomed to females saying no to his charm and he was working on the assumption that their lack of enthusiasm was due to a misunderstanding. Nor did he comprehend what she was saying to him in English, not one word, good or bad. However, when he saw tears, of course he needed to get away as quickly as possible, and he moved swiftly to the other side of the vessel and pushed in among his friends to sit anonymously. They laughed at him, without sympathy, for failing the dare so humiliatingly.

Leopard, observing that some event had taken place, and seeing that Kate was putting a handkerchief to her eyes, came down from the cockpit.

"Is everything OK, mesdames? Was that man bothering you?"

"Don't worry, Inspector, where I come from we eat jokers like that for breakfast."

Leopard did not really understand the meaning of what she was saying but correctly guessed from context that it was some form of idiom indicating that the women of East Ham could take care of themselves. This he did not doubt; and he noted that the boy himself, who could still hear their conversation (as the Inspector intended), was looking rather white and shaken, whether by the rebuttal itself, the distress he had patently caused, or the resulting ridicule of his friends, it was impossible to tell.

"May I sit?"

"Of course, Inspector, we would be happy to spend what is left of the cruise with you."

Leopard could not see, because he was facing back down the river, that they were just pulling into the landing stage at their journey's end. As he was dusting off the bench and lowering himself onto it, Daphne announced, "Ladies and Gentlemen; Yvonnes and Franzs and Valentines and Meaulnes; here we are at the end of our passage and the beginning of our revels. We invite you to disembark with the aid of our managers."

Albert and Tommy at the back, and Amelie and Caroline at the front, tied off the painters, and began gently but deftly to shepherd their charges to the gangplank, very experienced now in unloading the guests patiently and safely. Kate and Maggie decided to hold their seats and wait till the queue cleared, which left them rather exposed when suddenly Karl was bearing over them, bending into Maggie's face, leering, and asking with mock gentility, "May I accompany you, ladies, on the walk up the hill to the picnic?"

He hadn't recognised, or noticed, the bowler-hatted figure sitting next to them, who suddenly rose startlingly at an angle that thrust his body between him and the young girl, speaking firmly but calmly, less than fifteen centimetres from Karl's face, "Mr Karl, you surprise me, maybe you didn't get the message?" Karl was astonished more than anything that the Inspector – for he immediately realised it was him, notwithstanding the ridiculous monocle – could resist swearing, even when, he was quite aware, he must have driven him within moments of apoplexy. Was there anything that would make him impolite? Should he try? That would be a challenge, but perhaps not right now.

"Hello, Inspector. May I say, I barely realised it was you in such a fabulous get-up, you are truly the heart and soul of the occasion." Karl had not demeaned himself with the childish dressing up, he was not going to play Jean's stupid games. "What message is it you refer to?"

"The message to stay out of our way," said Leopard, through stretched lips, "to stop interfering, and to allow us to do our job.

And to cease to bother our friends here, and the other potential witnesses."

By now, the boat was virtually empty; in fact they were being beckoned by Daphne, as the last passengers to leave, to hurry along so she could close up the barge and get everyone happily onto the charming river walk and up the enchanting hill.

Kate and Maggie were relieved to be able to move away and join Daphne and Caroline by the top of the gangway. Leopard held Karl by the elbow civilly as though to offer him a steady hand on a yawing deck and manoeuvred him straight past them and on to the jetty. The two men walked on and continued their whispered discussion, superficially looking like best friends out on a stroll to anyone who could not see the well-mannered but unrelenting grip that the older man had on the younger.

Pelou, waiting for his boss at the end of the jetty, cleared his throat and mentioned, hesitant to interrupt, that Leopard, who had felt he should adhere to the strictest travel advice, especially as he was so specifically uninsured, still had on his lifejacket. He took it off and gave it to Pelou, who returned it to the vessel and then had to run twenty metres to fall in behind them as they walked on. He was delighted to observe the intimate supervision of Karl without having to participate – he'd had enough of the boy for the time being (really, forever, but he knew he wouldn't be that lucky). He was taken by surprise when Daphne suddenly came up and put her arm through his, saying, "So Pelou, is it all work for you today, or will you have some moments of pleasure?"

Behind them, Kate, Maggie and Caroline brought up the rear of the party, with only Caro aware that Daphne's new-found chumminess with Pelou was entirely so she could further avoid interrogation by the Englishwomen. Daphne was feeling rather annoyed, to be honest, because this had become her favourite part of the day, disembarking the customers on the landing stage, sharing their mood as the excitement built and they saw the scale and realised the joyfulness of the festivities ahead. But now she felt beset and surrounded by threat and irritation. She liked Kate, and she could tell she was going to be very fond of Maggie, and honestly the two of them were the friendliest of the hazards she needed to negotiate today; but they were an unknown quantity, and their presence could easily tip over the horrendously fragile structure she was trying to balance in Jean's absence. And then there was the Inspector, and there was Karl: no love lost between those characters, but they had a collective objective, and they were a real danger to the boys, and to her dad. Let alone Mac. Jesus, thinking of jeopardy, Mac was the worst of the lot, he could turn up anywhere, at any time, with or without a sharp object. How was she going to get through the afternoon...?

So where was Mac? Well, I can show you. This means we'll be changing viewpoint, no more first-person Mac telling you his crazy stuff (do you believe it all?): now he's becoming a character, like everyone else, and occasionally he'll be taking his turn to move the story along. Though you will sense, as Ms Austen once remarked, by the decreasing bulk of the pages yet to come that we don't have far to go, at least not for this volume of the tale.

As Daphne was thinking of Mac, Mac was lying in a hole in the ground under a bush, a long way away from the groaning tables, the gorgeous swaying throng of carefully curated characters and the anticipatory thrill inexorably mounting at their small but perfectly made theatre.

In fact, Mac was sitting unconcernedly in his own filth – in wrappers, gum, empty bottles and toilet paper. He had his coat on, though the late-morning sun was baking down, and he was holding close to his body the old brown suitcase, so full of sealed envelopes it could hardly be closed. His head was above the ground only just sufficiently to allow his eyes, attached to huge antique binoculars, to peer through a gap he had made in the undergrowth which allowed him to command an uninterrupted view of a vast unplanted, unploughed field that sloped somewhat steeply then rather gently down four hundred metres and ended at the little gate and low wall of Madeline's front garden.

Off and on, he had been there a very long time. He had three other hides within two kilometres, one of which viewed the property from the other side, and two others deep in the woods where he went when he wanted to light a fire and cook something or make coffee. One of them was covered, and he could keep warm in it, but someone had been there looking for him, he had an idea who. It was a nuisance that he couldn't go back there for a while, but they never retained their interest in hunting him for very long.

This won't be such an interesting visit that we're making to Mac; really, I can only describe where he is, and what he is doing. I could try to take you inside his head and attempt to show a few of his feelings, but he has moved to a place largely beyond the reach of the writer. You will have to know him from his journal and the letters you read, because currently his existence has narrowed to watching and catching glimpses. Whereas formerly he wanted to persuade (or prove, or show), but the time was never right, more recently his thinking hasn't often gone that far; most of the time it doesn't go very much beyond She and Me and what he can see through the glasses.

So Mac wasn't particularly aware of the discomfort he was experiencing, lying in what used to be a ditch, dirt caking his hands and face, sweltering in the heat but unable for some reason to take off his coat or loosen his contact with the sweating suitcase or take a rest from the incredibly hefty binoculars. Mac had often cursed the heavy field glasses, one of only half a dozen possessions he had retained, one that he had lugged with him through all his wretched travels. But without them, much would be lost, everything would be diminished. He had taken them from a body, there was still something that might be a bloodstain on them which he had never been able to clean off, not even when he had let Jack play with them. He had kept them like a sacred relic, and now he was using them to watch his old friend Hugo, who turned out to be his rival, his nemesis, riding his tractor back and forth back and forth – trucg trucg trucg. Up and down, far far to his left in this massive field, ploughing, presumably ready for a new crop, Mac didn't care, if he thought anything about it, it was, "Hugo's not a proper farmer, and this is not his farm."

Hugo had started the ploughing an hour ago, after a leisurely breakfast, sitting outside in the garden with Madeline and their two youngest, before she took the kids in the car off to school. Something had seemed slightly off to Mac this morning, they didn't normally sit outside before school; she seemed... not nervous... self-conscious? He couldn't quite put his finger on it, but in any case he had enjoyed having breakfast with them. Obviously, he couldn't touch himself, he never did that when she was with the children or Hugo, that was a rule, nevertheless the extra time with her – the unanticipated invitation – had been satisfying, though his mouth had been dry and he would have loved some of that cold apple juice they were drinking.

After they had eaten in the early sun, Hugo had got the tractor out of the shed, topped up the fuel, and fired it up, trucg trucg trucg. While he was doing it, Madeline went inside, up to the bedroom, which he could see into through the window, and she had taken off her robe, made herself naked, for him, and then put on her crisp, white work shirt. This was a very good start to the day, and to make it even better, Madeline would be back early.

Three days a week she taught full days at the school; the other two days she worked at the museum, but on one of those days she finished early and was back at midday. Sometimes on that day – which was today – she would work outside, either with Hugo, or doing something with the hens or the pig, or fussing about in the big vegetable patch on the side of the house. That's why, usually, on this day of the week he would be in the hide on the other side of the farm, just over the river, because the view of the kitchen garden and the hen run was better from there.

Normally when she came home from the museum, Madeline would change from her town-smart white shirt and black skirt into her farmer's-wife-style floral wraparound. From his foxhole on the other side, he could sometimes see when she leant forward to feed the birds her breasts swing forward, wanting to spill out of the loose dress with the ice-cream-scoop front. Just for him.

But he wasn't over there, because last night he had been chased and ended here. He could still see her from here, but it wasn't so intimate, and sometimes she was hidden. But it was good to see the whole landscape, in the bleached pale colours under the intense blue-white sky, the dark trees forming a vast semi-circle around the top edge, the huge field sweeping down to the small house. And while he waited, he could watch the crawling rat Hugo chugging back and forth, up and down, far far away to the left, hour after hour, trucg trucg trucg, till now, what, about a tenth of the field was turned and striped.

When Hugo stopped for lunch, at 11.00am, Mac kept hearing it, the rhythm continuing to beat in his brain, trucg trucg trucg, while Hugo got two chilled beers from the house and sat on the wall in the shade eating his bread and cheese. Mac looked at his own dirty bottle half-filled with filthy lukewarm lake water and spat the dryness out of his throat.

They were closing in, he thought, dully. There had been quite a few near misses over the past few weeks, then the incident with the dog and the swan, then Jean and Claude interfering and the bloody fool grabbing for him. That was a shame, because actually Jean had always been his favourite nephew. He didn't know who it had been in the woods last night in the dark: one smelt very familiar, one of the others smelt like an ashtray – probably Claude. One was a woman, in which case, Daphne? Caroline? Dessie? One was a stranger – did they bring police with them? No, no-one did that. That wouldn't happen, no-one round here ever reported anything, that would be OK, this was old-school. Inasmuch as he worried about it at all, he didn't worry about the police, just the locals with their bloody pitchforks and flaming torches, like any time in the last thousand years.

He didn't dwell on it, but he knew now he was beyond worry. Today was the day. It felt like everything would be resolved. He was ready, she was ready, that was all that mattered. So long as he could show her, then everything would be all right. For now, he was dozing, though he didn't realise it, lulled into a grainy slumber by Hugo, up and down, back and forth, trucg trucg trucg. A line closer every fifteen minutes, now a ninth done, cutting corduroy on the nap, trucg trucg trucg in the beating sun.

Back in town at the same time, Pierre really was quite annoyed. If you had asked him – if you had dared to ask, to his face – whether he was jealous of Claude, he would have given a great laugh and cuffed you gently round the chops like a storybook outlaw, a Pirate of Penzance, an affable scoundrel, gently bearlike, and told you not to be so foolish. But inside, things were brewing darkly. As a gang boss, Pierre had to be careful with his anger; often the expression of even mild irritation could be construed as a death sentence. But, yes, at the fear of repeating ourselves, we have to confess: he really was quite annoyed.

The intelligence of course had come from Charles, who, as we know, each day sucked up the available gossip, aspersion, theory, insinuation, imputation and innuendo of the region and processed all of it together for Pierre like a cheap newspaper to generate and manage his own version of the local truth. As a matter of course, most were happy to agree, to avoid giving offence, and bearing in mind the absence of an alternative, that Pierre's truth was good enough for them to live their lives by.

But sadly, unusually, news was currently circulating that had escaped the ability of Pierre to control it; news that was unpalatable to him, that he would rather not be broadcast. Previously, Charles had not been brave enough to include this undesirable content in his digest; but now he lacked the courage to exclude it. Because it had become common knowledge in the region, perhaps even a given fact, that Dessie, who everyone knows has long been sworn to Pierre, was canoodling with Claude. The general consensus, among those from whom Pierre might personally have sought an opinion on the subject, was that this situation should not be allowed to stand unchallenged.

"Fetch the car, Charlie," Pierre called out, "not the good one, we're going to get dirty this evening, and we might need to set fire to it later." He often made this joke, but was there an extra edge in it today? Charles sniggered at Pierre's quip, which was generally considered to be one of his principal duties, ignored the undertone, grabbed his driving gloves and retrieved the keys to his gorgeous blue Facel Vega Facellia from the drawer.

Up at the Lodge, Jack, Milo and Claude were on their fifth cigarette and third pot of coffee. After he had come back to life, closer to lunchtime than breakfast, Claude had spent a long time on the telephone to Dessie. Jack and Milo could not help overhearing the conversation, given they were too lethargic to get up and move away; trust me they weren't trying to eavesdrop, there was some nasty stuff in there. Milo looked at Jack, who made the fingers down the throat sign for "I want to be sick" (a gesture he had so often provoked himself); there was definitely something going on. It perturbed them to see the old leathery guy they relied on absolutely for curt disdain suddenly turning so soppy. Obviously, there was also the mission to discuss, the main reason for the call, and Claude did that, making the arrangements for picking Dessie up after their show. Then it was the "You hang up first," "No you hang up first" routine, while Milo and Jack looked on, listened in, agog, thinking what do they do when they rub up against each other at night, do the flakes fly? Do the bones crack, and the joints pop? Youth's imagining of elder sex – you don't want to go there. And they're thinking it's anything over forty, not like proper old.

"Dessie's set something up," Claude reported once he had finally replaced the receiver. "She's spoken to Madeline, they know each other from the old days. Madeline apparently did know Mac is around in the neighbourhood again, watching, creeping. It seems that she's been badly spooked recently, and it scares her because the kids are in the house as well. Hugo can't wait for an opportunity to bury a spanner in his head if he tries anything. Hugo knows all the backstory of your dad stalking his wife, of course he does, he was there when it all started. Hell, Mac thinks he's part of the problem, he hates Hugo as much as he thinks he loves Madeline. Look out for Hugo. He'll have sensed enough now to be on edge and he's an exceedingly violent man, I've seen that for myself."

"It's all very well saying they reckon he's around," Jack mused, "but have they actually seen him in the last couple of days? Has anyone reported him?"

Claude paused. It was well to be reminded now and then that the boy was Mac's son.

"They've seen signs and movements, but no-one on that side has had any encounters. Your dad does still have acquaintances around the other side, he gets fed in other places besides Dessie's, there are people around here who owe him. It is hard I would think for out-siders (excuse me) to understand how things work here, old debts get paid, however irritating and disagreeable – it isn't even honour, it is just duty and expectation. And after that, men and women sort things out for themselves. No-one is reporting anyone, but don't always believe that's good – for his own protection it might be better for Mac if the police were all over him."

"Claude, I've been meaning to ask you. Was dad in the Foreign Legion? He never mentioned it to me when I was growing up."

"Yes he was, son. Best thing that ever happened to him, so I believe; and in fact I am proud to think it was partly my idea. Definitely suited him, dried him out, made him strong, and made people respect him again. And from that, he got into the special forces stuff, which I am sure he never told you about either."

Jack was pleased. Pleased to get some provenance for his book. Also proud of that bit of his dad.

"OK, Claude, I have one more question, what's the story about the Geography Teacher?"

"Jesus, Jack, how do you know about that? No-one is supposed to know about that."

"From what I read, everyone got to hear about it... What happened?"

"Trust me, you don't want to know, and even I don't, really. In my view, the person who went round gabbing about that was Hugo, and then miraculously your dad got dumped, and he got Madeline. Makes you think, right?"

Milo looked at Jack, but Jack couldn't look up. So that was all true too, and maybe worse. "Shall we have a beer?" he suggested.

Claude interjected, though the question wasn't to him. "No, too much to do this afternoon, and you're on the stage, so no messing around." Milo had a small smile – when Claude turned down a drink, the game really must be afoot.

"So anyway, Dessie says we're all set for later. OK, Jack, this could be it – will you be up for it?"

"What do you mean Claude? What's the plan?"

"Dessie has arranged with Madeline that she'll be outside her house this evening after teatime. She's told her where she thinks Mac will be, up on the treeline in the last hiding place. Basically, we're going to be there in the woods, watching the watcher; then Madeline will distract him, and we'll nab him."

"Seriously, Claude?"

Jack was not sure whether to be upset, scornful or incredulous, so made a decent attempt to do all three at once. "You're sitting there telling me that you are setting a trap for my dad, and his old girlfriend is bait?"

Claude shrugged. "It will all work out for the best."

"Great philosophy, I will get that tattooed on my butt so the undertaker can share a laugh with his mates when I'm face down on the slab. Tell us, please, exactly how it will all work out for the best, and what is supposed to happen if we do catch him, instead of – as I suspect will happen – wandering around in the dark for hours with our eyeballs full of thorns like last night."

"This is a daylight raid," said Claude, lamely repeating something Dessie had said, "and if we catch him, he'll be safe, right? And so will everyone else. What can go wrong?"

"Nothing" is always the answer to that question in the moment, and "Everything" in the culmination.

"I'm very glad to see you have thought this through so carefully," said Jack, not exactly dripping with sarcasm, but with a decent smear. "Your plan seems to move forwards in increments of thirty minutes. Let's catch the tiger; then we'll work out what kind of cage we need; and after that we can phone around the zoos to see if anyone wants it."

"OK, guys, let's leave it there for the moment," Milo interrupted, reluctant to intervene, but relieved when he did. "It's showtime… we need to get to the theatre. We have a show to put on, at least that's something we can agree on. The rest we can revisit after our first thirty minutes of certainty." They began to get their things together, including packing a change of items more appropriate for Dessie's daylight raid, and headed out to the car.

While this was happening, at **DESDEMONA DÉJEUNER**, though it was well into the afternoon, the last lunch customers were sweeping their hands across the tables to brush the crumbs onto the grass and easing themselves off the benches to wander over to the colourful counter and pay.

"Thanks, Des, that was fabulous."

"Thank you, thank you, so sweet – see you tomorrow, I hope."

Dessie had hinted to the all the diners today as she served them that she needed to get away more promptly than usual, so there would be no lingering into the dusk, as sometimes happened when the brandy came out. With the last guest gone, she said goodbye to the two remaining Dessie Dames, who were stunned but delighted to be let off early for once, and she shuttered the counter herself. Then in a back room so tight she could barely rotate enough to change her underwear, she excitedly replaced her chef's whites with paramilitary attire. Not black this time, because they were hunting by day, but woodland camouflage pants and tunic with a brown leather Sam Browne belt and various leopard-skin accessories, worn on the logical premise that leopards also hunt by day and likewise do not want to be seen. Unfortunately, though she had a mirror, she couldn't get far enough away from it to check anything but her lipstick. For day-stalking she had chosen a shade of burnt sienna: on inspection, she decided that though it blended with the outfit and suited the broader landscape, it looked more khaki than kiss-me, so she rubbed it off and changed to a ruby gloss that she knew from experience completely captivated Claude. [If you asked him, he would deny ever having seen it, and he would be completely unable to describe it.] She had a moment's anxiety wondering, what if her super-shiny luscious scarlet lips glinted in the sun and warned Mac they were coming? 'Maybe overthinking that one, love,' she thought, 'but good fantasy.' Her personal agenda for the evening comprised two goals, extraction and romance, and she aimed to achieve both; the objectives were complementary as far as she was concerned. Catching Mac would very likely secure Claude as well, so she would help the boys, and help herself at the same time. She hadn't changed a shade of lipstick before going out since she was fifteen. Nerves. Claude again, after all these years.

Her arrangement with Claude was now to take her own car this afternoon. He was going to leave his motor in open view in the Hill House carpark, so, later on, everyone would think he was still hanging around there somewhere. She would park her car right by the door to the dressing rooms, and he would lead the boys straight through the house and into it even while the audience was still applauding. Then they would be off before the police and "that twat Karl" (whoever that was) could snatch them all up for an interview. The only slight change she'd decided on was to go early and watch the play. She'd heard a lot about it; Claude was in it; so while she was there she might as well take a look. This Inspector Leopard they had brought in was an old sparring partner, but such a long time ago, would he even remember her? Anyway, she was suspected of nothing, so what did she have to worry about? She smiled to herself as she picked the car keys off the counter and left the caravan. What could go wrong?

At Hill House, the guests were lounging on their blankets, many of them already wondering why they had eaten so much. Among them were Maggie, Kate, Leopard, Karl and Pelou, who, although each had a different agenda – family quest, personal vengeance, official business – had all decided it would be foolish not to take advantage of the magnificent picnic spread while they waited for the action to commence.

Kate and Maggie had tried on several occasions to grab the helpers in the stripey blazers and ask "Where are Jack and Milo?" "Why aren't they working?" "Don't they usually help with this?" and anything else they could think of. But none of them – the red-faced boy, the beautiful girl with the mass of gorgeous hair, the enormously tall accordionist – could say anything. The best they got was, "I don't know, but I am sure you will see them soon." Caroline had gone now; Kate had seen Bernadette bustling in the distance, too far to call out to; the lady in charge of the catering was unknown to them, and much too rushed anyway; and Daphne, well it was sadly clear by now that she was definitely avoiding them. So, sit, eat and enjoy the juggling as best they could.

At the buffet, which was still busy, Julie never normally bothered to check tickets, given that by the time they got up the hill it was unlikely there would be any infiltrators within the nostalgically at-tired customers. But Daphne had given her a quick whisper about Karl as she dropped everyone off and before she proceeded up to the changing rooms, so Julie had been able to embarrass him as he was midway through the architectural construction of a tower-ing platter of meats, pie, bread, cheese, tomatoes and coleslaw, by calling out in open voice, "I am so sorry to bother you, young man, *puis-je voir votre billet s'il vous plaît?*"

Now, I have to mention, normally at this point, even with Karl, I would feel very sorry for him, because this was quite a childish prank by Daphne, and cruelly designed to demean him, albeit, as we have established, he is remarkably impervious to shame. However, I am afraid he has lost all empathy with those around him because he has been doing that disgusting thing of eating over the buffet – pushing in mouthfuls of quiche and salami with one hand, while filling his plate with the other, with the result that his crumbs and half-chewed morsels were showering the elegant mixed salads and ruched cold meats like gravel pattering on a corrugated roof. No no no.

He looked up, startled. "What ticket?"

By now, people on the rugs and deckchairs in a wide radius were observing fascinated, as well as fellow guests hovering around the table who had already been a little sickened by the gluttonous grazer and had been dodging his shrapnel. Were they about to see some of the famed off-script Experience eccentricity? In the background, Tommy was playing one of his best novelty numbers, the Peter Sellers and Sophia Loren version of Bangers and Mash.

"For the Experience, you have a ticket, right? Issued this morning to you when you paid at the Hut, to allow you to enjoy all the food and entertainment."

Karl did that thing you do when you're caught out by someone asking you a question just when you have put a massive amount of food in your mouth. He panicked. Realising too late he was in gullet trouble, he put his plate down, covered his overflowing mouth with his left hand, and began flapping his right hand backwards and forwards in the direction of Julie, making the time-honoured sign for 'Wait a minute, wait a minute, I want to answer but my throat is crammed.' Then he moved onto stage two of his frenzy, trying to swallow too quickly, getting a lump of pastry stuck in his windpipe, and grabbing his own neck with two hands, choking, while he looked at Julie imploringly and gradually turned from white to pink, from pink to red, and from red to purple. The international body language for 'I am dying here.'

"Help he," he tried, and failed, to say, as he dropped to his knees and his head fell slowly forward.

Leopard had been watching calmly from a distance of two metres. He was holding his own tiny plate containing a minute slice of quiche and some lettuce leaf and radish. He was quite hungry, and in many respects he was a greedy man, but he felt compelled always to appear to behave quietly and modestly while on duty among civilians. It was different if he was out somewhere after hours as a guest of the villainy. If you wanted to get away with bigger things, why draw attention to yourself for trivia? He had earlier noted Pelou stuffing a baguette with runny yellow cheese, pitted green olives and ripe red tomato slices, and had been extremely jealous of his Sergeant's bulging sandwich and uncomplicated lack of restraint.

Leopard could have stepped in at various points to ease Karl's pain: either at the beginning, by intervening and telling Julie that Karl was with him, everything was taken care of; or later, just before he started to panic, gasp and choke. He'd chosen not to, sadly, he realised, because he disliked the boy sufficiently to want to see him humiliated. But he'd let it go too far, of course, and now the incident had reached and exceeded the moment when it could have been calmly resolved. He rapidly realised that he had to act decisively or his career would be in very serious trouble (largely as the result of Karl being dead).

He still couldn't bring himself to show anxiety. He forced himself to place his little saucer down gently; took two deliberately serene paces to reach Karl, who was facing away from him, kneeling; and purposefully brought down his two hands in a single fist from above his head, very very hard, onto the crown of Karl's upcurving back.

Out with a cough popped a foetus of chewed buffet the size of a kidney, disconnecting from his mouth with a snapping bungee of saliva. It bounced as it hit the trampled grass and squirmed into hiding like a frightened mouse. Karl started to gasp and wheeze, with relief, and gratitude, sucking in air like a baby tasting oxygen for the first time. He was alive. He looked round, saw Leopard... his saviour .... and started laughing hysterically.

The crowd, after silence, broke out in riotous applause and cried for three cheers. A life had been spared. Yet again there had been a special drama and excitement at the Experience, all the stories were true. Leopard was embarrassed to be the centre of their attention and celebration, especially as only he knew that it was his miscalculation that had caused most of the jeopardy, so he invented a little bit of official business, and excused himself.

First he checked in with the Corporal he had arranged to be stationed at Hill House for the day with two Constables and a police vehicle. Confirming that all sides of the location were under observation at all times as instructed, the officer had nothing further to report.

Then the Inspector went round to the back of the house, knocked lightly, and put his head inside the door of the dressing room, expecting to find no-one, and succeeding. He'd already realised they would be too smart to be there, clearly all three of them were evading him for their own reasons, so he would have to snatch them afterwards. Pelou had suggested interrupting the performance to drag them off the stage, but he had pointed out that they only at the witness stage, these were not suspects, and also it would annoy and upset half the town for no reason. Also, he loved the play, especially the bit where the bobby comes on at the end and sorts everything out. It would be simple enough to intercept them after the finale. What could go wrong?

On his way back towards his group he noticed a couple of local characters well known to him waiting at the theatre entrance: Pierre and his minion ... what was it? Yes, Charles. As he always did when he encountered rogues whose names regularly turned up in lists of suspects, or who were perpetually brought in for questioning, or who, in this case, were the known kingpins of criminal brutality in the region, he nodded in a friendly way, to show he cared.

"Hello, Pierre, good to see you. I didn't realise this Experience would be your kind of thing."

"Inspector," replied Pierre, as both he and Charles politely touched the brims of their exceedingly smart trilbies. "I see they are sending in the big guns these days; I would have thought you were a bit high-powered to be investigating Crimes Against Regional Theatre. You're right about the Experience, I hate the idea, though now I see it, everyone seems to be having a great time." He gave a kind of leer for a grin, his mouth too tight in the presence of law enforcement to show natural pleasure, even if he really did feel it, which in this case was unlikely.

"We are only here for the play, they sell some tickets separately now, we're told we were lucky to get them – I guess we'll make up our own minds afterwards."

"I am sure you have been fortunate, Pierre, and I hope you both have a very enjoyable evening. From my point of view, the crime rate for Central France will certainly be halved for the next hour, and for that I am truly grateful."

Pierre and Charles were halfway through a smart retort, but the Inspector had lost interest and gone, obviously he had something more important on his mind tonight. Annoying as their little encounter was, and sensitive as they were to the insulting inference that he had bigger fish to fry than them, they were pleased to get him out of their hair so they could focus on their objective. Which was quite simple, really – to catch Dessie in the act with Claude and then give Claude the beating of his life. What could go wrong?

Leopard had deliberately turned on his heel immediately after giving Pierre the parting shot, always believing in having the last word with his criminals, especially when his material was not of the top quality. He heard the pair of them saying something, but he didn't turn back. He was five metres away now, and besides, his eye had been caught by the sight of someone suspiciously pulling their head back round the corner of the house. Dessie. It suddenly felt like the whole spectrum of criminal stereotypes was congregated at the Experience tonight, from adorable ruffians to despicable sadists, and Leopard's only worry about that, from the detecting point of view, was that he didn't have a clue why.

He waited and watched, but Desdemona had seemingly scarpered. Was it him she was trying to avoid, or Pierre? He'd hear a rumour that things weren't going so well there; this looked like proof. Definitely something to keep an eye on: he didn't know what made him more uneasy, Dessie ducking Pierre, or Pierre's newly discovered passion for the theatre.

Everyone had calmed down as he was returning to his party. Some kindly older women of both maternal and less maternal persuasion were gathered around Karl, unnecessarily rubbing him in various largely inefficacious places while cooing like a family of pigeons, and the boy, weakened by his ordeal, was responding well for a change, at least not insulting them or fighting them off. If Leopard was concerned about getting too much attention as a hero, his anxiety was quickly quelled, as it was clearly the victim who was soaking up the adulation.

All the other customers were finishing their meals, and revelling in the escapades of the jugglers and magicians. The latter were drawing gleaming silken doves from their chequered sleeves and casting them gently into the afternoon breeze to float like feathered kites. Bliss was about to end, Leopard could sense that, and once he knew, he wanted it to happen quickly. Tommy had been moving on from comic songs about gluttony to mournful ballads about failed courtship and faithless lovers, and then had gradually slowed to a halt and passed on the baton to Madame Jestique, who gently picked it up on the theatre piano with some quiet Satie and Chopin.

As she played, the ten-minute bell rang, and she moved on to one of her lively overtures (was it HMS Pinafore?), signifying to all that the focus had shifted from the banquet to the auditorium and they should begin to prepare for the play. The timing was good, Leopard was still on his feet and he nodded to Pelou to rise and round up their little band of misfits, and shepherd them up to the entry. But the other customers had reacted more quickly, and by the time they had made the hundred-metre journey to the theatre entrance they were near the back of the queue, which meant when they arrived inside there was no room to sit all together and they had to scatter to fill the last few spaces in singles.

Madame Jestique was now playing an amusing medley of her own devising incorporating a smattering of French Chansons, a little comic Donizetti, some jaunty Scott Joplin and a clarinet piece by Artie Shaw she'd transposed herself. Even as they seated themselves, the audience was tapping its feet, shaking its shoulders, and generally getting in the mood; news of the show had by now spread far and wide, and the excitement was palpable.

Round at the back, behind the dressing rooms, and about ten metres away from the house, stood Julie's delivery van, seconded for the evening by Bernadette, which she had pulled up close to the house once Leopard had completed his tour of inspection and left. Using Julie's van was a last-minute decision by Daphne, made on the inspired basis that it was always there anyway, so would largely be unnoticed. Since Caroline had gone back to the hospital, Madame Terroir was released from watching Jean to manage the outfits and greasepaint for the night. She was also excused from acting duty as Claude had now reassumed the role of Policeman, assuring everyone his kettle scars were healing nicely and would not be an impediment.

Thus Milo and Jack were squeezed in the back of the van inching on their costumes while trying to avoid too much intimacy. They still couldn't go inside the house for fear of being grabbed before the play started. Bernadette had opened the back doors of the vehicle, which were facing away from the building, and the boys took it in turns to poke their heads out to be made up. Claude was hunched down by Bernie's side like an overgrown familiar, annoying everyone with unwanted suggestions and instructions – "thicker," "darker," "heavier." He wasn't yet made-up and uniformed himself as Bernadette was planning to do him up once the boys had gone on. Claude wasn't needed till the very end, and meanwhile he also had to take care to avoid being spotted. Inside the theatre, Tommy was on the projector tonight, as it had been decided that Claude mustn't go front of house unless he was on stage performing.

Daphne, Albert and Amelie, in the relatively privileged situation of being pursued neither by the law nor the criminal underworld, were making up and getting dressed in the relaxed surrounding of the actual dressing room. Madame Jestique's playing was subtly changing timbre and tempo, indicating they were nearing curtain up. Daphne decided to go out to the carpark, checking carefully she was not being watched or followed, to let them know it was approaching the time to make their run. The arrangement was to sprint straight onto the stage, making sure no-one had the time to intercept them. Daphne reckoned once the players were on the boards, and the first lines were spoken, not even Leopard would interrupt it till the end. 'Avoiding his attentions at the final curtain will be more of a challenge, but that's a lifetime away,' thought Milo, 'after all, we only worry in thirty-minute segments.'

"How's it going, Bernie?" asked Daphne.

"Yes, they're looking good – provided they haven't accidentally put each other's pants on in there...."

"O har," said Milo, "I think we're both in the same trouser leg, but the show must go on."

"Blimey," said Daphne, "that make-up is jolly thick, you're like a waxwork."

"They need it heavy, Daphne," Claude interrupted, "we don't want anyone to recognise them, right?"

"OK, but don't stand too close to the lights, you'll start to melt."

Although it was originally her suggestion, Daphne wasn't sure she'd meant it entirely seriously, and now she'd seen it she wasn't totally convinced the extra half a centimetre of slap would make it harder to identify them, but she nodded anyway, to humour her dad. "I bet their own mothers wouldn't know them in that."

That was a bad joke, and she had no-one to share it with. This might have been another moment to let the boys know who was in the audience, but Daphne convinced herself that there was no time, the play had to start, they didn't need more distractions than they already had. She persuaded herself that it was her instincts, not her fear, that led her to refrain.

"Dad, a quick word please?"

"OK, let's sit in my car."

They crossed the twenty metres in a crouch and ducked into the front seat.

"I guess you are making a run for it right after we finish."

"Yes, Dessie's going to be out here with her car. The motor will be running as the audience is showing its appreciation, we'll be straight into it and off. We need to get out again this evening, there's a plan and we definitely will bring Mac in. Obviously we're swerving the Inspector, we need a clear run."

"You sure hanging out with her is the best idea, dad, you know what happened before?"

"Let it be, Daff, she's really helping us, and the rest …. Anyway, we'll see, but trust me on it."

"OK, I've got the spare set of keys for your car, do you want me to do anything with it later?"

"No we'll come back for it, we want it here as a decoy. Anyway, you'll need to get the customers back on the boat."

"Good luck, don't get killed, don't hurt Mac – call me later, I'll probably be at the hospital. Now, let's get the show on stage."

They jumped out and hurried across to the van. Daphne put her head into it and called, "Wait for your cue boys; and break a leg!" As an afterthought she reached out a hand and put it on top of Milo's, saying to Jack as well, "Good luck with everything tonight."

She went on into the dressing room to check they were still in the clear and was relieved to see only Albert and Amelie present. "OK, showtime, we're on, let's move it." Madame Jestique was playing the last chords of her opening music; Tommy started the camera light rolling; the background scenery flickered sepia; Pantaloon, Columbine and Harlequin entered; and suddenly they'd launched.

Five minutes later, cued by the change in the musical accompaniment that introduced the themes for Pierrot and Clown, Jack and Milo leapt crazily out of the back of the van, span round, charged into and through the dressing room, and sprinted onto the stage, before realising, once they'd jogged all the way to the footlights, that they really weren't supposed to be running in character, and they definitely weren't meant to be panting and short of breath. Anyway, the panicky entrance got the first big laugh of the night, so the audience obviously loved it.

After that, it got better and better. For the Harlequinade, this was truly the performance of a lifetime, or at least that is what it felt like to be there on that night. Whether it was the emotions among the cast, the secrets and fears they held in the real world, or the newly charged excitements, jealousies, anxieties and passions in the audience, the nerves, dreads and desires, something mixed it all up and the result was a cocktail of brilliant acting and comedy that verged on the extraordinary. Every joke fired, all the slapstick hit home, not a single gag fell flat. The players threw themselves into it body and soul; they were covered in sweat and bruises by the end, but triumphant. And how the audience roared as Claude the Policeman pompously pushed the struggling Harlequin off to jail in his tiny barrow, and Madame Jestique resoundingly struck the final chords that echoed and echoed around the theatre and out across the grounds and down the hill. What an ending!

The cast came back on for applause; left once; came back on again with Harlequin still being pushed in the little cart; then left again. The audience were shouting, clapping and stamping, presuming they would be out for another series of bows; but this time when they left the stage the Policeman continued pushing Harlequin straight on through the dressing rooms picking up velocity, followed closely by Pierrot and Clown, ever more quickly, until emerging into the carpark at high speed with Daphne still precariously balanced in it, the handcart hit a vehicle parked a metre and a half from the dressing room door, crashed to an instant halt, and sent Harlequin somersaulting high onto the car's bonnet.

"Oh my God, doll, are you OK?" the Policeman asked, terrified he had permanently maimed his daughter.

"Get on, dad, I'm fine," said Daphne, slipping slowly off the motor and onto the floor while rubbing her badly grazed arm and checking her forehead for bleeding.

The obstructing vehicle was Dessie's.

"When I said 'right outside,' I didn't mean a metre."

"Shut up and get in, we've got plenty of company already."

As the boys scrambled into the back, and Claude ran round the front to the passenger seat, Daphne looked up from the flagstones at Dessie in the driver's seat of the motor, staring down at her from half a metre away.

"You hurt my dad again and I'll break your bones, understood?" This came across as more threatening than it usually would from the sweet and kindly Daphne, given the sinister, cruel and frightening make-up, the brutally thuggish bald wig, and the stream of blood currently flowing down her forehead and on to her nose and cheek from the accident. Even so, sad to say, Desdemona elected not to be intimidated.

What Dessie said in her head was, 'Silly girl, I was in the Resistance; I don't scare; I can kill with a shoelace, a toothpick or a rolled-up five franc note.' But what she said out loud, as Claude was now sitting beside her, and he could conceivably have loyalties to both camps, was, "Don't you worry, darling, I'll look after him and get him home well before bedtime." Then she cackled madly.

At that moment, two things happened.

Pierre and Charles, who had taken the long route, back out through the theatre entrance and around the three sides of the building, came charging round the corner, and slid to a stop fifteen metres in front of them, glaring at the occupants of the car while they tried to take in and assess the whole picture.

And, at the same time, out through the dressing room came Karl, the first to be alive to the situation, with Leopard and Pelou on his heels (Chasing what? Just Karl? Or had they set him to seek their prey for them like a hunting dog?). Behind them, though not by very far, were Kate and Maggie, probably at this juncture pursuing because everyone else was, rather than with any identifiable purpose.

Dessie froze when she saw Pierre. Claude looked at her and knew right away she had not told Pierre she was leaving him: there had been no mature parting and fond farewells; no carefully curated division of self-admittedly ill-matched souls; no gracious separation of lovers wishing each other eternal happiness in the arms of another. On the other hand, no break-up sex either, Claude assumed, so every cloud...

Claude realised immediately that the failure to notify was extremely bad for their health. Being honest, they had probably been in for a beating anyway, but now the transgression had been upped from 'generally preferring Claude' to 'sneaking around with Claude behind my back' they could easily be looking at a death sentence, or worse. And yet Dessie still seemed unable to act on the urgency of the circumstances, remaining as she did in a state of shock.

Daphne, alert as ever to the various dangers, stood up shakily and started staggering, feigning not to have seen those coming out of the dressing room behind her, and thereby managing to block and trip Karl and Leopard with her inadvertent clumsiness. Good work.

At the same time, she was shout-whispering into the car window, "For fuck's sake, Dessie, pull yourself together and get the hell out of here," while, just for good luck, reaching inside to slap her on the cheek, possibly a little harder than strictly necessary.

In terms of pulling herself together Dessie jolted out of catatonia, shook her head at the smack, and glared at Daphne; then, in respect to getting the hell out of there, she immediately engaged the accelerator and pushed off at high speed.

She pulled the wheel left as she did so, in the direction of Charles, because she knew that Charles would move, but Pierre would rather die than get out of her way. Sure enough, Charles leapt to the side to save himself, and she sped off at full throttle through the carpark entrance and down the driveway. The panoramic tableau she observed in the rearview mirror as she headed down the incline comprised Pierre whacking Charles on the side of the head and knocking off his hat; Pelou staggering into the back of Leopard as they both stumbled into Karl and landed on top of him; and Daphne standing triumphantly over them, unscathed except for her paternal cuts and bruises. Although Dessie hadn't been able to see the play because Pierre was trying to catch her, she now felt she had experienced the best of the entertainment.

"Chrissake, Charles," shouted Pierre, "why did you do that? You've got no balls at all."

"I have balls, boss, and I also want to keep them. Come on, guv, give me a break. Look, if we go now I can overtake them, that piece of crap Des is driving is no match." Charles's pride and joy, the gorgeous, sleek Facel Vega Facellia, was thirty metres away; contrary to best practice we know he had chosen the good car after all. Noticing that the police were brushing themselves off and likely to take an interest any second, they sprinted for the motor, fired it up, and were well away before Pelou, Leopard and Karl could untangle themselves and raise a hand to prevent them.

Pierre and Charles were already on the incline and looking down the hill in time to see Dessie take a left at the bottom. She had helpfully put her lights on, though it was only late afternoon, and the sun was still well up, excellent conditions for them to watch and follow from a distance. The chase was on.

Outside the dressing room, Karl was helpfully shouting and blaming everyone, from Daphne in front of him, to Leopard behind. "I could have caught them, you blocked me, you weren't quick enough, you pushed me over." Through a gap under Karl's arm, Daphne and the Inspector rolled their eyes at each other, finding time in the chaos to share a collegiate smirk through a crack.

"Constable, start the car," Pelou shouted to one of the attendant bobbies, who had been running uselessly across the tarmac in the direction of the long-departed cars, shaking his fist, cartoon-style, ending up with his hands on his hips. The *gendarme* hadn't realised till that moment that he'd been observed by his boss, who was standing behind watching his dysfunction. He jerked around at Pelou's command, saluted for some reason, and jumped into the motor, gunning the engine. Running to join him, Leopard and Pelou were halfway across the carpark before they noticed there were three of them. Karl was jogging in between.

Leopard shouted at him officiously to absent himself, and to stop interfering in police business. But now they were all in the car, Pelou in front with the Constable, and Karl and Leopard sitting in the back.

"I said stay out of the car, not get in. Karl you need to go, you cannot come with us on a high speed pursuit."

"You're supposed to be co-operating with me, my dad said. So did your Station Commander. And I want to be in on the kill once you catch those little shits. We're after them, right?"

"Ah, always I fear the charm in you will fade, Karl, but you never let me down. Please get out of the car, now."

"Never mind the charm," said Karl, responding with a narcissistic simper, and ignoring the rest, "what's going on, we are going after them, right? I'm coming."

"Sir, we're losing them if we don't hurry," said the Constable in the driving seat, summoning the courage to admonish his boss's boss.

The Inspector had a dilemma to instantly resolve. Taking a civilian passenger on a police chase was against all the rules, probably illegal, and very dangerous. But the process of manually extracting an unwilling passenger from the car would lose them so much time they would be out of the game, and Karl clearly wasn't shifting voluntarily. Faced with the high-pressure situation, Leopard called upon all his years of experience, and made the worst decision of his career.

"Damn it, move on, Constable, get on their tail as fast as you can."

'Ha ha ha ha ha,' thought Karl, triumphantly, 'finally I have made you swear,' his yelp of victory tempered only by the mildness of the curse. He had to aim higher.

'O Lord,' thought Pelou, half in prayer, 'what have we done now? Please, God, get us out of this one.'

'It is true then, what they say,' thought the young Constable, 'this guy is a complete cowboy. Lucky this is absolutely nothing to do with me.'

691

The Inspector may have had to go along with the presence of Karl, but he wasn't going to share his objectives or discuss his strategy. That would have been embarrassing anyway, given the plan currently seemed to be limited to "follow that car." Leopard had revelled throughout his career in the skill of "making it up as he went along" and that was what he was doing now. His boss had no idea where he was, his subordinates didn't realise their inquiry was largely off the record, he had a civilian in the car during a pursuit, and if you had asked him at that moment what, or who, he was investigating he would have struggled to tell you. He didn't know if the boys were the perpetrators or innocent victims, or if they might end up just being bait for a bigger fish. He had that nagging instinct there was something serious at the bottom of it all but had no clue what it might be.

Anyway, the die was cast, as they say, and they were on the road now just four hundred metres behind Charles and Pierre, staying a steady distance apart because the police driver was fortunately very well trained in discreet surveillance.

"OK, Karl, as you ask," Leopard said, equivocally, "we're definitely after them. Clearly you are correct about that, though I am not quite sure what number we are in the queue at the moment given how many others seem to be after them too. As for whether we want to catch them, I am not sure what they have done yet, Monsieur, if anything, so we will certainly not put anyone in danger to overtake them. We want to interview them, and if we can, we will, and we'll find out if there is something. Of course, even if there is something, is it something enough to be worth the paperwork?"

He winked at Pelou, who didn't bother to disguise his return snigger. Karl, growing ever more crimson and frustrated, was struggling to interpret the policeman's word salad, his elaborate and meaningless lawslaw. All he heard was, "I will do what I want and I will not tell you either before I do it or after I have done it." He was launching into another moan at the Inspector when the Constable tapped Pelou on the knee and signalled "behind" with a backward nod of the head and a finger pointed at the mirror. Pelou

692

turned, and saw a car following them, about three hundred metres distant. To be precise, Claude's car, one of the vehicles they had had under observation all day.

"Claude seems to be behind us as well ahead of us," suggested Pelou, rather confused.

"Claude himself had the woman Desdemona pick them up," answered the Constable. "So he's in her car at the very front, with the two boys."

"You actually saw that? You looked half asleep when I came out."

"I saw it, Chief, I was chasing her across the carpark, remember? Then the other car pulled out after them, the one with Pierre in it."

"So how come Claude's car is behind us now?"

"You know how it is round here, everyone drives everyone else's motors. Anyone could be in that; one of his friends, the daughter?"

The Constable was a bright young man (shall we give him a name? let him earn it first), but one who had not covered himself in glory that evening, having been caught flatfooted, as you will already have noted. However he was correct with this guess: in fact Claude's car had three occupants: Daphne, driving; Kate, in the passenger seat; and Maggie in the back.

How? Well, when the actors made their swift exeunt through the back of the stage and the dressing room, and Karl, Leopard and Pelou moved quickly to follow, Kate and Maggie tagged on.

Of course they did, because, in spite of the ingenious subterfuge of doubling the thickness of the grease paint, and despite the awfully cunning plan to list the names of the actors as Francois and Scott in the programme, naturally a mother and a girlfriend (yes, I know we're still arguing about that) saw immediately that Pierrot was Jack, and as Milo was never far from him, so Clown he must be. It was in the size, the stance, the movement of head and limbs. Even their gestures, though dramatically adjusted to be the shrugs, winks and bows of Clown and Pierrot and then deliberately rescaled and restated through the extravagant grandiosity of the silent movies, could not disguise or deny the source. It was always a foolish ambition to masquerade their true personalities, though in fairness they could never have dreamed that one of the people they were trying to hide themselves from would be Jack's mum.

And therefore, after the others all tumbled over each other in the rear entrance, and the policemen and Karl ran to the car and pulled away without even looking back at them at all, Kate and Maggie, stranded, looked at each other hopelessly, helplessly, powerlessly. They were so close! They had come all the way from England for this, they'd been ten metres away, and now everyone had gone, and no-one would even give them a sympathetic glance.

Daphne, brushing herself off, was about to commiserate and move on when she realised she couldn't leave them like this. She wasn't a mother, but she had been a girlfriend, and she'd also been the woman left sobbing at the side of the road while the car drove off – several times. Therefore, she qualified, like it or not, as a sister, with all the attendant duties and responsibilities that entailed. She had avoided them all day, and that was bad enough; she couldn't abandon them at their hour of greatest need, and besides, the game was up in respect to the boys' disguises and location; it was obviously no secret who they were and where they were now.

Madame Terroir had been in the dressing room tidying up, and was wandering out, conscious of only a fraction of the twists and turns, but that was already too much for her; with Jean on her mind, she didn't really want to get involved.

"Bernie," Daphne said, taking her aside, "big favour to ask, please. No time to explain, but I'd better look after these two and find out what's happening with dad, it feels like half the region is in hot pursuit. I'm going to run off in the car. Can you supervise the tea dance with Madame Jestique, then take the customers back in the

694

barge with the two other kids, and Tommy, and grab Julie to make up the numbers? Albert can drive the boat, no problem."

"Go, it's done, no worries. But I'm going to insist on driving the barge." They kissed. A very competent, cool woman.

Daphne grabbed her purse with the spare car key, and taking Kate and Maggie in each hand, walked them quickly to Claude's motor. "Get in, we'll go after them."

"You're so kind, Daphne, thanks."

"Thank you, Daphne." The girl was in tears.

All this was done in less than a minute, but still the police car was barely in sight when they got to the carpark gate. Luckily Daphne knew the area better than the Constable and was a much faster driver. Claude's old banger looked shocking: it was rusty, and the bodywork was falling apart, but he loved it and maintained the practical bits rather expertly, so the current engine was much more powerful than the original it had replaced, and beautifully tuned besides. It took her only three or four minutes to rein back the *gendarmes*, and then she sat three hundred metres behind, unobtrusively she hoped, doing as little as possible to show themselves.

Because you are diligent and caring readers, I think you will be worrying about the Experience customers, am I right? Somewhat abandoned, not only by Daphne, but also by Milo, Jack and Claude. Well, fear not. Firstly, they had perhaps the best tea dance so far, brilliantly hosted, accompanied and orchestrated by Madame Jestique's trio (with Tommy, of course, who was by now making a little headway with the fabulous guitarist) and mightily and magnificently catered and cocktailed by Julie and Jacques. Dancing was initiated by Albert and Amelie, who quickly got everyone up and stirred them on the dancefloor, merging and dividing partners into suitable pairs like scientists culturing and coaxing shy cells in a Petri dish.

Extra champagne was given and taken, then half an hour later than usual Tommy played them down the hill with an alternating series of fabulous whirls and magical ballads. He had shyly asked the wonderful guitarist to come with them, as she had never yet been on the river cruise, and she had said yes, equally shyly, and was walking by his side, strumming her guitar along with the accordion. We can name her now as Gabriella, call-me-Gabi. Yes, said Tommy, I will.

The newly suave Albert (whose recent redness of face, we can reveal, applied not to "girls" in general but very much to "Maggie" in particular) and the constantly winning Amelie slipped in and out and between the groups of guests chattering charming nonsense, making them laugh, helping them to join arms and skip together with friends who had been strangers five hours ago. Bernadette at the front and Julie right at the back, throwing aside her apron to be collected later, added some ballast and grounding, making sure everyone knew where they were going, how to get there and how long it was going to take.

At the landing stage, the wheel was ceded to Albert; Madame Terroir had been bluffing. The boy accepted the Captain's duties modestly, while Julie, Tommy, Bernie and Amelie quietly and calmly embarked the guests, making the safety announcement and seating everybody while remembering there would be empty spaces for Leopard, Pelou, Karl, Kate and Maggie as well as Daphne, and they had gained one passenger in Gabi. It felt quite empty as Albert pulled the barge away, manoeuvred her around, pointed towards the farm, and turned on the front headlamps. As night fell, the lights of the boat made solid green walls of the bank-lined foliage, and the waterway became a tunnel they glided through as the river rolled out in front of them like a twinkling sea-green carpet. Tommy began a mournful song about a lass who drowned herself after her lover had been unfaithful, and the customers began scanning the river for the body. Then Bernie shouted to him, much to the approval of the passengers, to pick up the pace, and he and Gabi segued quickly into a brisk and cheerful jig which got everyone dancing away the last kilometre, thanking their absent colleagues for the extra space to twirl. They all agreed, then and later, that this day was better than they could ever have dreamed; and so, with your worries assuaged, let us leave them there, joyfully content in the afterglow, and return to the chase.

Can I remind you where we are? Yes? At the farm, Madeline returned from work and Mac was able to watch through her bedroom window as she changed from her crisp white high collared smart town clothes back into her loose-topped thin summer floral farmer's-wife. Something felt odd to him, but he was too excited to interrogate the small fretting anxiousness at the back of his mind, and just enjoyed the experience.

She emerged from the farmhouse with a great glass jug of beer, so cold the condensation was running down the sides; beautiful amber light beer with a high white head, which she carried to the end of the field where the dutiful Hugo was still rhythmically running up and down, back and forth, trucg trucg trucg. She spilled some of the froth on her breasts as she walked, and casually, slowly spread the foam. Hugo turned off the motor as she approached and licked her chest, laughing, as she handed him the icy pitcher, which he half-downed in a single gulp. Then as she turned to go back, he squeezed her bottom, she giggled and skipped away, he pretended to run after her, then drank down the rest of the beer, got back in the cab, and started again, up and down, back and forth, trucg trucg trucg.

Madeline's mother came over, not so unusual. They fed the kids, and then grandma took them off in the car with her. Mac could not remember that happening before. Madeline came back out afterwards, to work in the vegetable garden, not in the back part but in the side area, where he could see her, skirts tucked up into her underwear as she knelt swinging back and forth on all fours to plunge the dibber rhythmically in and out in and out forcing the bursting seeds into the moist and willing soil, Mac thought.

Up in his fox hole he had freaked when Hugo touched her, stuffing his hand in his mouth to silence himself, then settled down to revel in her solitary pendulation. Watching her, he reached for himself as the afternoon faded into evening, the sun thinning and lightening, turning the sky from buttercup to lemonade.

But I think we are getting a bit ahead of ourselves, we need to go back a little.

Remember again, half an hour ago: the first car travelling in the direction of the foxhole and the sunlit evening farm carried four – its owner and driver Desdemona; Claude, front passenger, dressed as a *gendarme*, from boot to kepi; in the back, Milo, in the make-up and character of Clown; and our hero (did we agree that?) Jack, still in his Pierrot costume, including silken red and white conical pointy hat with three pompoms down the front, secured under the chin with a ribbon, and high enough to be prodding at the roof.

"What happened to getting changed into our hunting gear?" asked Milo.

"Ah, yes, a problem," replied Claude, "We put all the spare kit and changes of clothes in my car, but we ourselves seem to be in Dessie's. I think maybe I let the plan get too complicated."

"Seriously?" said Dessie, incredulously. "You guys are coming like that? How are you supposed to sneak up on a desert war veteran wearing a second-rate outfit from a travelling circus?"

"He's wearing a circus outfit too?" laughed Milo at his own joke, a favourite. "What's he dressed as, a trapeze artiste?"

"Do fuck off, young man, I am trying to be serious. This is a man who can kill with his bare hands, and he hates mime."

Milo used his mime skills to immediately construct an indestructible invisible protective wall in front of himself, and Jack literally screamed with laughter.

"Jesus fuck, WILL YOU TWO BE SERIOUS!"

698

Now it really was like a day out with mum and dad.

"What are we going to do about these ropey costumes?"

"I think they're rather good outfits actually, Des. Jean's mother made them." Jack did this deliberately, seeing how close to the edge he could nudge her. She did not bite.

"Ha ha ha, Jean's mum hates me… so do all the mothers, and sisters for that matter. Now, lightweights, back to the question, please. What part of 'covert,' 'stealth,' 'camouflage' and 'clandestine' did you fail to understand at the briefing?"

"There's always 'incognito,'" said Milo. "He definitely won't know it's us because Claude doubled the thickness of the slap."

"Also," added Jack, "the 'element of surprise.' He won't be expecting to be ambushed by a selection of traditional characters from the Harlequinade."

"He might expect the Policeman, though" Milo chortled. Jack joined in, but Claude and Dessie seemed not to find it funny – Claude reached behind without looking and tried to clip Milo round the ear, every inch the village policeman. He missed by a long way.

"OK," Dessie said, desperate to establish some kind of discipline in her crack forces, "there's a box between you; grab a torch each, a compass and a clasp knife." Jack and Milo did as they were told and stuffed their pockets with paramilitary paraphernalia; Claude just shook his head. "We'll stop at my place in a minute and get changed; I have a range of things you can wear." She was clearly very proud of her woodland camo and oxblood leather get-up and desired to have a whole platoon of beautiful young acolytes dressed up as junior officers in her Praetorian guard.

Jack and Milo stuffed their hands in their mouths again to prevent the two in front hearing their laughter at the mention of Dessie's 'range of things to wear'; the way she said it conjured up anything from gem-studded dog collars to skin-tight rubber slacks. Claude was growing more annoyed with them, and was about to shout, but suddenly had other things on his mind. As he was looking back to the rear seat to talk to Milo and Jack, his gaze wandered between them, and out of the back window.

"Unfortunately, no time to stop Des – have a look behind."

Hearing the consternation in his voice, the two rear passengers turned at once while Des sat up straighter and looked into her mirror. And there, maybe fifty metres away, was Charles's motor, with him driving, and Pierre leaning out of the window, waving a tyre iron in one hand, and making the international sign for 'you will die' – a flat hand dragged across the throat like a razor – with the other.

"I think they may mean to do us harm, Des."

Claude said it flatly. The man in the car behind certainly wanted to hurt him badly, and possibly might wish to kill him, but he wasn't as terrified as he should have been. Perhaps he'd got to the point in his life where he wasn't scared of much, or possibly it was because of what he'd been through in the war in respect to general pain and fear management.

Generally, his rule of thumb was always to avoid a fight where possible, especially with an incredibly violent crime baron with a steel baton, and particularly when he wasn't a hundred percent in the right. But the issue was being forced on them, and besides himself, others were at risk who genuinely did not deserve it, and who weren't as able to look after themselves.

His shortage of fear certainly didn't imply that he thought that he and the crew with him would have any chance in a fight against the car behind, though they had four against two. He had already weighed it up in his mind. He scored Milo and Jack as a zero in a knife fight (or any other kind), and Dessie he rated a fifty-five percent in hand-to-hand (one-hundred-and-fifteen percent with a grenade or automatic weapon, neither of which sadly they had as far as he was aware, though he hadn't been through all her pouches); so they were comprehensively outpowered by the two villains, both of whom, as we've been told, are renowned and conscienceless killers, therefore scoring a hundred percent each. If they got cornered, he would keep the others out of it as much as he could, and take the medicine himself. Obviously, first choice was to outrun them, and there was still a chance of that.

"You did tell him, right?" He asked; but he knew.

"I meant to," said Des, guiltily, "but I didn't find the right opportunity."

"I think he's worked it out, do you reckon? Secrets round here are like sand in a sieve."

"I'm not sure what the point was anyway, in telling him – it wouldn't make any difference. Both of us are going to take a whipping sometime, it's just a case of hoping we have enough limbs and teeth afterwards to move on and feed ourselves by mouth."

"Gosh, that does sound like a romantic old age. Nevertheless, my choice this evening is to defer the beating to another time as we have things we need to do."

"Shall I try to find a way to relay that decision to Pierre?"

"Oddly, you may be in luck, my love, as he is almost within shouting distance, or perhaps you could hand him a note through the window as he draws level?"

"Maybe you should try the whistles," Milo piped up helpfully, "they're perfect to communicate at this distance."

"Does he know the codes, though?" Jack mused, getting interested.

"What would you need, 'It's not you it's me.'"

"I'd go with 'You're too good for me.'"

"SHUT THE FUCK UP." Claude turned back to have another swipe at them. He missed, but they noted he was really getting quite tetchy. "I was contemplating how I might be able to save you two by sacrificing myself, but oddly I have just changed my mind."

Then his gaze drifted back beyond them again. "Hang on … Des, in your mirror, how far back can you see? Back beyond Pierre?"

Desdemona strained up to the rear mirror, which was a little high for her, and could see only Pierre in it, totally filling her view, ever closer. She had better luck in the wing mirror, in which, as they swung round a corner giving her a better angle, she saw a second set of daytime headlights appear a few hundred metres behind Pierre. By this time, Leopard had decided there was little point in subterfuge as they were clearly part of a convoy, so he'd asked the Constable to turn on the blue roof light, but to suppress the siren, as they were following, rather than overtaking (still "witnesses," he kept reminding himself, not "suspects").

"Blimey, it's the cops! I thought you could never find one when you wanted one?"

"Ho ho, maybe our fortune genuinely is changing. For the first time in history I desired to have the police on my heels, and they've appeared! Isn't that like a demon thing?"

"As you ask, no, Claude," Milo answered the rhetorical question, which is always an annoying thing to do. "Most people strangely don't think of the police as demons. In this context I think you might be thinking of summoning Guardian Angels."

"You can summon angels?" Claude was sceptical.

"Most people prefer it."

"So are the angels after Pierre, or us?" asked Jack.

"Well," Claude replied, grateful to get out of the firmament and back to Earth "the *gendarmes* round here – the few who don't work for him – are always after Pierre, that's a given. However, in this instance I have a horrible suspicion that the Archangel Leopard is still trying to get hold of all of us for his interview about various issues, and Pierre, who is after me and Des about the other affair, just happens this evening to have insinuated himself between us."

"So what happens now?" Milo chipped in. He wasn't yet quite as comfortable as Jack appeared to be with the entirety of their situation. He was in a clapped-out motor hurtling through the darkening backroads of a forbidding landscape with his best friend the outlaw and two hugely irresponsible adults *in loco parentis*. The angry bald man in the car behind was periodically coming very close; at one point he had drawn level with him in the back and he'd turned to point a finger gun, which wasn't very pleasant considering they'd never been introduced. There appeared to be significant peril, didn't the others feel it?

'Why not just chill,' he thought, 'stop worrying. What can go wrong?' Well, pretty well everything as it turns out.

Two cars back, Karl was cackling, and not just mad cackling, serious Vincent-Price-level cackling, throwing his head back and letting it rip. "Seriously, a serial sex pest? ... That's precious ... It's priceless..."

Pelou had reached the point where he could hardly bear to breath the same air as this youth. Karl repulsed him. This wasn't a sensation he was accustomed to; he was a kindly and empathetic man in virtually every case. This hatred he had felt only two or three times in his career. One was for a child rapist, another a man who had beaten his pregnant wife to death with a saucepan because his dinner wasn't ready when he came home drunk. Now this German kid had joined his pantheon of horrors, how could you figure that?

Leopard was aware of Pelou's disgust. Personally, he had learnt twenty-five years ago how to blank out the feeling from the business. At the front line, all the time, for the worst of everything, from murders to missing kids, he experienced enormous pain for the first five years of his career, then gradually trained himself to keep emotions for home and detachment for the job. But that didn't mean he had lost the basic human ability to like and dislike, or the capacity to differentiate and choose between a decent person and a really nasty piece of work; so he sympathised hugely with his Sergeant's utter distaste.

"I didn't tell you that to amuse you, Karl," said Leopard, interjecting to give Pelou a moment to calm. "We only told you so you would understand what's going on with these kids, and the father; and where we might end up going. It was meant to make you circumspect, not rapturous. How have you got so much detestation in you for these boys?" "And why are you such a horrible, weird little shit?" he left unsaid.

Was it really just because Jack had embarrassed him in front of a girl he liked? Perhaps because the girl liked the other boy better? 'Jesus,' Leopard thought, 'what would he do if something really bad happened to him?'

"Come on," Karl retorted, barely suppressing his mirth, "you've got to see the funny side. They're a family of seedy criminals passing themselves off as loveable local heroes. Pious judgemental sanctimonious prigs that it now turns out are shielding a creepy night stalker. I love it. And what I love most is that I was right all along, that means more to me than the girl or anything. What's going to happen now?"

Pelou was reluctant to give any information to Karl and clammed up. Leopard agreed with his reluctance, but decided to give a minimal answer, just to keep the peace a little, and also as a means of relaying some thoughts and alerts to Pelou and the Constable.

"Everyone is a witness more than a suspect. At the moment, there is no specific crime charged. This happens around here very often; we can't apply the law because no-one in this region will make an accusation or give evidence.

"So we're taking a softly softly approach, watching, observing, not specially intervening just yet, though we really want to take all these people aside in a quiet controlled environment and have a chat with them.

"Right now, this minute, we're following someone who is following someone else, and bizarrely, if you look behind, we're being followed too. Therefore my biggest current worry is becoming part of a multiple pile-up on an unlit country backroad.

"In the general course, I think the front car is out to find the boy's father and probably to spirit him away somewhere. We would like to share the discovery and prevent the spiriting till we have investigated.

"The second car is I think out to catch up with the first car, and most likely, to do some physical harm to the occupants – this is most simple, an act of jealousy, we all can understand that one. I suggest we would like to get between those two and stop any violence – albeit we can't protect them forever.

"The car behind us I suspect is carrying wives and loved ones. Their main concern will probably be that no-one gets hurt, or if they do, that they will be there to nurture and mend them. In that respect they are not a worry to us, as I believe they're more friendly towards us than adversarial and they welcome our presence to try to stop these situations getting out of control.

"What I would look out for, if you want my prediction, is that the first car will soon try to shake everyone off. They have some idea where they are going to look for the man, they won't want everyone coming in on their coattails, and they have the additional incentive of desiring to avoid being beaten with an iron bar."

And, as he said it, so it happened.

Let's wind back two hundred and fifty seconds.

"What's going to happen now, Claude? What's the plan?"

"Ah, the plan, Desdemona. Well, I have a cascading menu of schemes in my little booklet, one for every eventuality, but I think the strategy for having Pierre fifty metres behind us in a faster car with the police up his backside is in volume two, which I didn't bring with me."

"Funny."

"Yep. However, in the absence of a well-thought-out idea, what I suggest is we do that thing we did when the Germans were catching us up at the bridge in Orleans, you remember?"

"I did think that might be a bit of a one-off; you reckon we can relive the memory?"

"The sharp right into the woods where the road turns to follow the river is in a kilometre – do it there. Put your foot down now and try to get us at least three hundred metres in front before we hit it.

"Boys," he continued, turning in his seat, "listen carefully, no questions. When we get to the bottom of this incline there is a sharp right-hand curve coming up – you can see it there, right? – and as soon as we get round it, Des will be turning the car left, straddling across the road and stopping very quickly. The front of the car will end up pointing at the river, the back to the woods. All of us will get out of the car on the right-hand side and run into the woods, OK? Get out on the right-hand side, and run straight into the woods, remember."

"OK," they both said. Claude looked at them as though to say, 'That was too easy.'

706

"Well, you said no questions." Fair enough.

They were already halfway to the bend and Dessie had the accelerator flat to the floor. Charles had not been expecting her to speed up, so she'd managed to increase the distance between them to well over three hundred metres, maybe three thirty.

Two hundred now to the curve, and Claude turned to the boys, "Remember, right-hand side, straight into the woods. Now brace yourselves, we'll be pulling up very very sharply."

Then they were at the corner, then around the corner, barely slowing. As soon as she felt they were out of sight, Dessie hit the brakes and swung the wheel hard over, and they skidded left to halt no more than forty metres beyond the bend, square across the road, the front end of the car maybe five metres from the riverbank. All four occupants crashed forward then back like dolls in a tipped-up toybox, stunned for a second. Claude and Jack recovered first and threw open the front and back doors on the right-hand side of the car. They jumped out while Des and Milo were now in motion, shuffling across to follow them. In an instant they were all away from the motor and stumbling into the woods, which were gratefully close and thick just there.

Just as they were hidden behind the nearest row of trees the glorious sound of Charles's Facel Vega Facellia came booming round the corner, followed two seconds later by the car itself. The four of them were now all prone, looking back towards Dessie's poor abandoned buttercup rustbucket waiting warily in the middle of the road like a goat grudgingly tethered for a tiger.

It was very much like watching a slow-motion car crash, except at full speed. They saw Charles's face through his windscreen as he straightened his car after the bend and suddenly realised he was twenty-five metres from an immoveable mound of sunflower-yellow metal sitting primly in his path. His eyes expanded wider than his dark glasses, the cigarette hanging from his lips fell ever so gently into his lap, his beautiful hat shot off as his head involuntarily jerked back, and, most crucially, his arms and hands automatically locked at elbow and wrist as he instinctively swung the wheel hard over, like Captain Ahab trying to avoid the whale.

It was probably – certainly – the most brilliant piece of driving Claude had ever seen. When they did the trick to their pursuers at the Orleans bridge, the Germans had ploughed straight into their, thankfully empty, car and died catastrophically in a fireball he would never forget. Charles and Pierre chose the slightly better option of turning quickly enough to bounce off Dessie's motor, side on side, and then to continue straight on into the river in a diver's arc, still doing forty.

Leopard had seen it coming. The Constable had as well, but given he had a lot of ground to recover with the Inspector, he kept quiet, expressed mute admiration at his boss's brilliant intuition and incisive instructions, and allowed Leopard to think it was only his personal genius that was going to get them through this.

"Slow down, quickly, there will be a trap round the bend when we get to the bottom of this slope. It is the perfect place for them. Reduce to a trot as soon as you can, approach the turn at minimal speed, be ready to pull up within ten metres if we need to."

As he spoke, still watching from five hundred metres back, Dessie's car far below them had already made the turn, and Charles's motor was accelerating behind them and disappeared into the curve, clearly believing they were rapidly overhauling the vehicle in front. If anyone in the police car had any doubts about what was happening around the bend, the shriek of metal on metal and the shattering of glass instantly screamed back up the hill to them like the noise of two tanks crushing a very large greenhouse, lengthways.

By this time the Constable had reined the police car back to less than fifteen kilometres an hour, and Daphne in the motor behind them, taking her cue, had done the same. Both vehicles advanced more and more cautiously, and finally edged their way round the curve within two hundred metres of each other, no longer making any effort to conceal their presence.

As the police car made the turn, the first thing Leopard thought was, 'Oh shit, Pierre got away, I've screwed this up,' because all he could see, in the middle of the road, and blocking it completely, was Desdemona's yellow banger – albeit the primrose colour seemed largely to have changed to sky blue. How could Pierre's motor have got past that? He searched the landscape, starting with the woods on the right (was that a movement, something white in the undergrowth?), slowly panning back across the car parked in the middle of the road, and then left towards the river (no space for a car to squeeze through). Nothing. Then, finally, the mystery was solved when his eyes moved on further, scanning fully to the left. Out in the river, fifteen metres off the bank, about halfway across, was the glorious Facel Vega Facellia, blue, sleek, and smooth as a boat. Bobbing, bobbing, bobbing … and very slowly sinking.

The Constable had pulled the police car onto the grassy verge and completely halted; Leopard was already out, standing in the road. Now he could look down and see the evidence: skid marks from the start of the curve, screeching ninety degrees to the left; swinging parallel to Dessie's parked car, so close they crossed over and infiltrated its space; bouncing back off, fighting to stay parallel, and then going on straight into the river, clearly still at great speed, hence the trajectory into the very centre of the water.

This was taken in in a second, now, what to do? Leopard thought very quickly, but the plan – the decision – was already taken out of his hands. Behind him, he heard "clunk, clunk," and then past him, even before he could turn to look, sped the blue uniform of the Constable, in stockinged feet. Leopard didn't even have time to call out before the young man dived off the bank, into the river, and started swimming strongly towards the car.

The Inspector walked over to the embankment to watch. In the car, which now only had its windows above the water, neither occupant seemed to be moving, so Leopard thought, they're unconscious, they must have been knocked out during one of the impacts.

The Constable reached the vehicle in very few strokes, he was a well-trained and robust front-crawler. He cut through the grey-green water, which was moving very slowly here, and latched himself onto the driver's door of the floating motor by the handle: turning round to look at the shore, for some reason he waved, looking like a holidaymaker having a leisurely bathe and turning back to gesture to his friends on the beach: "Come on in, it's great in here."

His boss on the bank was quite stunned and rather shamed by the junior rank's initiative and enterprise. Pelou was standing by him now, with Karl in tow, smirking as usual. "Is this your normal policing tactic, drowning the villains before they can call a lawyer?"

"Shut the fuck up, Mr Karl, please. Do you really have to make everything a joke, even people dying while you watch?"

"You look quite calm yourself, Inspector. You don't fancy a swim to help out then?"

Leopard and Pelou looked at each other, wondering which one of them was going to crack first and knock Karl out. The Constable (was he signalling for help or letting them know it was all OK?) continued to wave while bobbing alongside the slowly disappearing car.

Kate, Maggie and Daphne had carefully parked behind the police car on the grassy bank and left their car to join Leopard and Pelou on the riverbank. The three women, like everyone in such a situation confronted by a waver, all waved back eagerly, then realised his waves were not spontaneous civilian waves aimed at them, but purposeful policing waves; they quickly pulled down their arms and tucked them across their bodies as though they had never raised them at all. They were clearly hugely impressed by the young *gendarme's* dash and confidence, much to the Inspector's secret annoyance.

"Are they alive, Constable?" Leopard shouted loudly, breaking the anxious silence, reestablishing the line of command, making sure these ladies knew who was in charge.

"Neither's moving, boss," the young man shouted back. "They're both out cold. I am pretty sure that this one," pointing at the driver, "is breathing, but I can't see the other one clearly."

"See if you can open the door and get the driver out."

"If I do that, the car will sink more quickly, chief. I might have time to get this one out, but if I hang onto him, then the other one will go down with the car."

"Get in and help him, Pelou," Leopard called to his Sergeant, loudly enough that the Constable could hear, and be aware of the plan. "Then we can get them out from both sides."

"Me, sir?" Pelou responded dolefully, "does it have to be? I'm not that confident in the water."

"Nonsense, man, I'm sure you're like a bloody fish compared to me. Besides, this is your chance, I already have my commendations, I don't want to be selfish, today's the day for Pelou to be the hero, right?"

Pelou gave him a lugubrious look that said, 'I really don't think it is.' He was thinking, 'Am I really going to have to go in? Is this how it is going to end for me, risking my life to save the biggest crook in Central France? Jesus.'

Hearing Leopard and Pelou competing to see who could be the most cowardly, Karl started to laugh crazily – he just couldn't stop himself. You could hear the noise echoing three hundred metres up and down the river. It might well have been the final sound Charles heard before his head went under.

What about our four escapees? After they had lain flat in half a ditch in the fringes of the woods to watch Pierre and Charles come round the corner and fly into the river, they decided it was time to make their break.

"Let's go," Claude urged, "quick, we're never going to have a better distraction."

"OK, looks like those two won't be chasing us any more anyway. Come on, let's get out of here," for some reason Dessie was whispering, "we were going in this direction anyway, the only difference is we finish by foot – luckily we're close. This way." She was off, motioning the others to follow.

"Shouldn't we help them?" said Milo to the three backs as they disappeared further into the forest. "Obviously not then," he mouthed, falling in behind.

Had they stayed a few seconds longer, Milo would probably not have been totally relieved of his conscience by observing the *gendarmes* largely hopeless handling of the situation. But by then they were already fifty metres into the woods, followed into the undergrowth only by the terrifying maniacal cackle reverberating from the riverbank.

"Jesus, is that Karl?" asked Jack. "It sounds like the House of Usher."

"Actually I think you might mean House of Wax," said Milo in a special pedantry persona he used occasionally, and very successfully, to annoy Jack.

"Will you two BLOODY FOCUS," Dessie whispered, "and let's please get out of here."

The wood quickly became less and less penetrable; the trees were close together, and the scrub was compacted between, with no clear paths. They had to force their way through, knee deep in leaves and foliage. Dessie was in front with her compass, not that she needed it, a machete would certainly have been much more useful. The evening sun was now thickening and filling the gaps between the branches. And the birds that had been settling in, quietly assembling for a peaceful evensong, rose before them screaming plaintively at being disturbed.

"Fuck's sake, shut up!" whispered Claude, to nothing in particular, anxious that they were sending a flying, shrieking ribbon banner up directly above their whereabouts. Anyone in front or behind them would be aware of their presence. "He's going to see and hear us coming a mile off at this rate, Des."

"OK everyone, slow down then, we've got half an hour before the sun gets too low, and less than a kilometre to go, so we'll be fine even if we have to tiptoe. And scrunch together now, let's walk in single file as much as we can, instead of four abreast making multiple rackets."

The slower pace seemed to calm the woods, everything relaxed slightly. After they had progressed a hundred metres further, Milo asked innocently, "So what's the plan?"

"Yes, well if that's what you are asking, I can assure you there is a plan this time," Dessie answered somewhat defensively ("Cheeky bloody pup"). "Madeline is disporting herself in front of the farmhouse. Her mother has the kids. Hugo is ploughing the big field, he'll be half a kilometre away and hopefully out of sight; we couldn't let him in on it as he'd give the game away in a second, and anyway he wants to kill Mac, so that would be counterproductive.

"The idea is we creep up on Mac, because he'll be transfixed by her shape and movement under a specially loose blouse posed with the setting sun behind her, glowing through that mass of copper hair. She'll look so good he'll want to lick her, trust me."

"Chrissake, Des, think of the boy." Claude whispered, elbowing her hard, but missing, losing his footing and half falling, catching himself against a tree.

713

"Shit, sorry Jacko. But you know why we're here, right?"

"Yes, don't fuss, I understand." But he was shaking softly, breathing hard, and crying silently like an unloved baby.

"So," asked Milo, understanding the plan well enough to see the holes, and also wanting to cover for his friend, who he could see was suffering, "we surprise him, we take him unawares, what are you expecting then?"

"What do you mean?"

"Well, let's remember he stabbed someone we love around, what is it, forty-eight hours ago. He might still have the blood on him for all we know. If we shock him, could it be dangerous? Aren't we putting Mac at risk, as well as ourselves?"

"He'll run if we surprise him." Claude was utterly definitive. "I don't really believe he intended to shiv Jean, but I think we can be confident he's not going to slash his own son, right?"

'His many years as a student of criminal psychology have not been wasted,' Jack thought sarcastically, as well as, 'It's fine to theorise about filicide if you're not the fili at the point of the knife.'

"Plus," Claude continued, "I took his knife, I thought, though I must confess I seem to have misplaced it since."

Jack looked at Milo, about to say something before Milo reminded him with a small waving palm sign of their eternal vow of silence to Daphne.

"Yes, but other sharp objects are available," mused Dessie, "and in this case he's not going to get surprised by Jack, is he? He's going to get surprised by Pierrot."

They had all stopped noticing that they were still in costume, except Dessie. And she had been bothered only inasmuch as it

714

frustrated her yearning for a camo youth branch to her mad army. But now, as the plan did not involve a night attack, and didn't really even demand much stealth, given Mac was going to be looking the other way, they could wear whatever they wanted as far as she was concerned. Which was just as well, as they were still in full make-up and dressed as Clown, Policeman and Pierrot. Claude still had his moustache on; Dessie rather liked it, so she hadn't told him.

However, looking at Jack, it did bother her that the poor lad had black tears rolling down his white cheeks.

"O Jack, love, I'm sorry. Sorry. I didn't mean anything by it. I am just trying to help. Once we catch your dad, we can protect him, right? Jean and Claude have done it before, a number of times actually."

"It's OK, Dessie, I understand. It's been a hell of a week, that's all. Ten days ago we were finishing our exams and walking out of school for the last time; now we're on a manhunt through the backwoods of France for the long-lost father who put my cousin on life support. This stuff almost feels normal now – one day we'll look back on this and laugh uproariously."

"Shut up, you lot," called Claude from the back, where he was lagging, "we'll be getting close soon, let's calm it down a bit."

They waited for him, he was right, they quietened down.

"Where are we, Des?" he whispered as he came up to them.

"We're about four hundred metres away from the farm boundary, eight hundred metres from the farm itself," she whispered back. "By my reckoning, Mac's hide is straight over there," she pointed, "on the boundary, directly on a line between us and the farm. It is one we know he uses, and I am betting heavily he's there now. We're about five or ten minutes away if we want to do a proper clandestine approach."

They started off again, slowly and carefully, easing their way through, and concentrating now on furtiveness rather than speed. Even though they were moving so stealthily, the birds were back up in the air, screeching. "It's not us," Claude pointed backwards to where they were wheeling and shrieking about three hundred metres behind them. "Someone's following us."

"Yes," said Claude. "And catching up. You can bet that ruckus is the renowned Inspector Leopard."

"I thought he would be heroically hauling crime bosses out of the rushing river?"

Dessie said this with some anxiety in her voice. Claude could not tell whether the concern was about Pierre drowning or about him being rescued.

"Clearly he got bored with saving lives and considers catching us to be of more service to the community."

"He needs to be careful, inundated gangsters aren't going to go down well in town."

"He will have delegated their salvation, trust me. What I am not sure about is how he is tracking us; I didn't take him to be a highly skilled backwoodsman."

"It was the bloody birds giving us away. At least now they're on our side."

"That's what Tippi Hedren thought, too," said Jack, hoping a joke would take their minds off his momentary lapse – though the streaky make-up was a bit of a maudlin reminder. Des and Claude just looked at him blankly, Milo helped out by saying, "It's a movie, I'll explain later, you guys really don't get the films round here very quickly, do you?"

"Spartacus is coming next month," said Des, putting her arm

through Claude's as if to say: 'and my man is going to take me.'

"I'm Spartacus," said Jack and Milo, simultaneously, creasing up very mildly to further blank looks.

"Let's get on," said Dessie, "we don't want whoever's following us to be right on our backside when we reach Mac."

Claude was at least partly right about who was behind them, stomping furiously through the bush, heedlessly sending the birds up cawing and wheeling. Yes, Leopard was there, but he was not alone, and not even in front – that was Karl (of course it was).

We had left them when Pelou was slowly removing his boots, preparing to have one last plea with his boss about not sending him in. Leopard was ready to argue back and reissue the direct order (feeling rather guilty, to be fair, as he was a rather strong swimmer, but was not going to admit it) when he looked behind him and realised Karl was missing. Turning, he saw the lad bounding through the tall grass toward the wood.

"Wait, stop. Where are you going? Come back here immediately!"

"Obviously they've run off this way." Karl halted and span round, holding his ground, with no intention of returning. "You can bet they've worked out where they're heading. If we track them quickly, we'll get them and whoever it is they're after. It is clear the way they went, you can see where they've crashed into the undergrowth. Do you want them, or not?"

With that, he was moving, and in a couple of seconds was invisible through the branches. Three figures shot past the stunned Inspector before he had even weighed up the situation: Daphne, Kate and Maggie. 'Well,' he thought, 'I suppose that's why they're here.'

"Pelou," he shouted to the Sergeant who was shivering in his shirt-sleeves on the bank, "get in there, quickly, or it will be too late. I'm going after this crew to keep the peace – I might still be able to…"

He got lost for a moment, what exactly was it he was trying to do?

"… to police the situation," he finished, lamely.

Pelou chattered loudly, all of him, not just the teeth; like a child about to be pushed into the deep end by its parents for the first time. His accusing look at Leopard was a mixture of the pitiful, pathetic, petulant and petrified. But under the Inspector's steely and merciless gaze, he threw himself, almost backwards, into the river, and was suddenly under the water, then up, thrashing and punching his way like a drunken boxer towards the vehicle. Leopard watched long enough to assure himself the man was relatively safe – 'Actually,' he convinced himself, 'that's a pretty potent stroke' – before turning and stomping rapidly through the grass into the forest.

The others were well out of sight by now. Leopard cursed his uncompromising compassion towards his junior colleague for losing him those vital seconds – his weakness was his humanity. But he soon worked out he would have no problem tracing their progress and direction, because in their unthinking haste they were making a huge commotion. And also launching a cloud of tell-tale birds into the sky, where they hung thirty metres above them, like a giant avian finger pointing down and indicating: "Here They Are." He adopted a rhythm that he calculated would overtake them before they could get too far and settled into it.

At that moment, the three women were eighty metres ahead of him, and Karl was a hundred metres in front of them. For an urban youth, Karl had a remarkable hunter's instinct; he was tracking the actors very accurately, only two hundred metres back from them now.

Claude, Desdemona, Jack and Milo were being gradually reeled in, but only because they'd had to slow down and move more prudently, having estimated, accurately as it happened, that they were now less than two hundred and fifty metres from Mac's hole. Their own pursuers however had no idea of the goal or its distance, so they were not moderating their movements and speed or the noise they were making crashing through the bush. It was altogether an unfair race.

The evening was rolling in, but much more quickly than it should, and Milo realised the change of light was also due to dark clouds gathering.

"Some rain coming."

"Yep, I feel it. Is my make-up running?"

"Faster than you are."

"Oh please, mate, not the Christmas crackers."

"Shut up, you two, radio silence now."

They crept on. The four of them really were moving quietly and slowly now, because they were less than a hundred and fifty metres away from the edge of the woods, and Des knew Mac's hide was about five metres back from the boundary. The spitting rain was turning into something much heavier, which was making the footing slippery, but at least it would help cover some of their noise.

They spread out, proceeding forward in a rank across, each of them maybe two metres apart. Policeman, Clown, Pierrot and a woman in desert camouflage… all of them cut and grazed from falling and fending off brambles. Some small rips and tears in the costumes – Bernie was going to be very annoyed with them tomorrow, and Jean would moan like hell if they had to be replaced.

Another thirty metres forward, and Dessie, positioned a little ahead of the line, raised her right arm scouting style without looking back, to halt them in their tracks with the back of her right hand parallel to and next to her head. Without turning, she whispered back over her shoulder while lowering her hand and extending it forward to point at a specific tree on the forest's edge. "There, under the broken cedar." Jeez, thought Milo, I have wandered into The Last of the Mohicans. Dessie in woodsman's garb is an absolutely perfect Chingachgook.

She walked forward cautiously. The rain had become a downpour now, and the sky was two tones greyer – the light would be gone in twenty minutes. But at least the undergrowth was becoming less dense as they approached the margin, which gave them some sightlines. Something had been rubbing at the back of Jack's consciousness for some time; when they'd stopped, and he had heard it clearly for the first time, he'd realised it was the distant sound of a farm vehicle, trucg trucg trucg, rhythmically going up and down. The tractor.

Dessie pressed on and the other three fell in behind her, following the footsteps she was pushing into the forest floor. Then, of course, a twig cracked; she stopped dead; and, obviously when the rhythm broke, Claude staggered into the back of Des; then, trying to stumble quietly, he fell heavily, and rolled loudly in the crunching leaves.

Twenty metres ahead, there was an equal and opposite racket as Mac, flushed, frightened, jumped up like a meerkat, his head swinging to scan from side to side. His trousers were round his knees, his face crimson, sweating, his penis hard. He tried to hide himself with his hands and pick up his pants at the same time. In extremis, for a second, naturally, he was less worried that he had been discovered than he was embarrassed to have been caught masturbating.

Dessie, ever the mistress of such situations, exploded the tension with a quip. "Don't wave that at me, Mac, I've definitely seen better."

"For Christ's sake, dad…." Jack had no way of finishing the sentence. He toyed with "Put it away," but that would acknowledge he'd seen it. And the other traditional greetings – "You're looking well"; "How have you been keeping?"; "Great to see you, you old tosser"; all seemed rather inappropriate.

But just with the word "dad" he'd said enough. Mac peered at all of them, narrowing in on Jack for a while, trying to see through the make-up, attempting to discount the three or four missing years; then he moved on to Milo, even Claude for a moment, at least discarding Dessie, hoping one of them would speak again, knowing the voice of his own. The rain was tipping down now, and there was a distant rumble of thunder.

"Jack?"

Then, while he was fiddling with his pants, red-faced, the penny dropped, very slowly.

"Dessie, what are you doing here? … Claude?"

Everything was utterly silent, just for a moment, except the distant sound of Hugo and his trucg trucg trucg, turning the soil in the field below, and the slap slap slap of rain hitting the leaves.

His trousers up by now, belted, Mac dipped down into his hole, out of their sight, and emerged three seconds later with a hat on, and gripping his suitcase protectively in both arms, nursing it like a sick calf. This was a moment balanced in time, poised, silently, that could be tipped in either direction by the falling weight of a raindrop.

"Dad, we're here to help."

Then suddenly there was a crash behind Milo and Jack. And Karl came thrashing through the middle of a bush, smashing into the back of them, shouting with surprise as they turned their ghostly faces onto him in the half-light of the woodland shadows.

"Jesus Christ," he screamed, "what the fuck." The scales had been tilted, and so it began.

Mac – confused, embarrassed, scared, longing, desperate, hopeful – was away, moving as gracefully with his monstrous case as Laurel and Hardy pushing a piano up a flight of stairs.

But though he ran achingly ponderously, almost in slow motion, they were caught out by the speed of his choosing, and he was sixty metres ahead of them before they decided to chase him down. They agreed it like a mob: no discussion, no pact, not even looking around at the others, but simultaneously determining to start, mutually taking the first step, collectively crying out some timeless inarticulate hunting call, enough to startle every bird and animal for two hundred metres round to either flee or come and see what was happening.

As they broke through the treeline the vista spread before them, opening out into the massive unploughed field which curved and sloped a full four hundred metres like a beautiful wet painting pouring its pigment down and around into the yard, outbuildings and cottage at the bottom. Dessie noticed Hugo on their left – trucg trucg trucg – was he closer than she thought he would be? Had he changed direction?

In front of the house in the garden was Madeline. She had been on her knees, tilling and scraping, when the rain on her back got too heavy. She had risen up from the planting, taking her hands out of the moist, sweet soil, and brushed them unthinking along the sides of her forehead to tidy her hair back under the bright red headscarf as she scanned the rainswept landscape to see where the noise was coming from. On second thoughts she reached up to the back of her neck, undid the knot in the scarf, took it off, threw it into the basket beside her, and shook out her magnificent thick curls, now a little grey in the rich copper, but as gorgeous as when she lay with Mac those long-forgotten years ago. Why?

She had been searching for the sounds, the movement, but still looked surprised when she finally saw the succession of tiny figures breaking cover at the top of the hill. A hundred metres down the slope already, picking up speed by weight, stepping and staggering out of control, was Mac, clutching the suitcase. Finally, he was going to do it. The land was soaked now, water running down it in rivers, turning to mud under his broken city shoes, squeezing through the holes into his rotten socks and pressing between his toes. Not to worry, he was nearly there. When he arrived, it would all be clear, he could explain. This is what he had been waiting for, he would not fail now, everything would be all right. Off to the side he ignored Hugo's tractor getting louder all the time, trucg trucg trucg.

Closest behind Mac, of course, was Karl, whose momentum had hurtled him right through the static gang and well ahead of the rest. Now he was chasing hard. Why? He really didn't know.

Then, in order:

- The Clown, in very big shoes

- Pierrot, hanging off Clown's belt as the salt tears and rain were blinding him

- The Inspector, a very good amateur runner, who was stepping hard with a long stride, calling out to the two younger boys in front to slow down and let him take control

- The Policeman, losing breath, losing ground, and feebly waving his cardboard truncheon in cartoon style

- Desdemona, dressed in the summer uniform of a battle-hardened desert militia and suddenly from somewhere for some reason flourishing a real pistol

- Daphne, yelling in her head at Dessie, "Keep your fucking filthy hands off my dad," and actually shouting, "Des, put that fucking gun away, you idiot"

- Maggie, but only because she was quicker on her feet and had slightly more appropriate footwear than

- Kate, bringing up the rear, owing to her high heels – no-one had advised her to bring a change of shoes for hunting disused husbands

They were all slipping and sliding in the mud and the downpour, falling and getting up, and still gaining on Mac: but he didn't have far to go now, maybe a hundred and twenty metres. Still the nearest, Karl was only thirty metres behind him. And ever nearer came the trucg trucg trucg, no longer to be mistaken for the distant toil of mechanical labour, now clearly the sound of agricultural machinery approaching at the fastest speed it can achieve in an attempt to join the drama.

Madeline was standing outside the gate to the garden, soaked to the skin, tall and proud, legs apart, firmly grounded feet, hands on hips, looking unflinchingly at Mac as he closed upon her. Nearly fifty now, stunning, beautiful, her fabulous hair blowing and gleaming in the rain; but Mac was running through time, sprinting to Madeline at twenty, racing thirty years back from this grimy sodden sundown to the glow of morning sunshine playing on her sleeping golden curls.

On he came, in his filthy stained coat and ragged shoes caked inches deep in mud; nothing was between him and Madeline but distance now, nothing to protect her. But she stood perfectly still; she showed no fear and did not baulk or blink. His broken hat flew off, he clutched at it, but didn't turn from their fate. Eighty metres now, and Karl was no more than twenty-five from catching him.

It had come down to the three of them: Karl, Mac, Madeline. Mac was less than sixty metres from Madeline and fiddling with the catch on his case as he ran, so he could be ready to lay it at her feet, show her the contents, present her with the 493 letters it contained, each one to her, every one of them a statement of a type of love, a kind of need, a sort of reverence, a strain of adoration. As he fumbled, he slowed, so Karl was only ten metres behind, and shaping himself for a tackle. Karl to be the hero; this was his destiny.

The rest of them? They had stopped, alarmed.

Aghast actually.

Because, from their higher vantage, they could see that Hugo in his tractor – trucg trucg trucg – was only thirty metres off now and gathering speed by the second.

Hugo, enemy of Mac, lover of his lost love, hurtling towards him in three tons of rusty metal with razor-sharp blades rotating in front, threshing like the frenzied mouth of a blood-tormented shark.

Madeline was next to realise, swivelling from the hip like a dancer to face her husband, moving her hand up in front, palm out, 'No Hugo,' but not speaking. He was not looking at her, deliberately. His watery yellow eyes were fixed on Mac, his thin white lips stretched wire-tight in a skeleton grin. This was a moment he had often imagined would come, a chance he would not pass up. And besides, the decision had been made a hundred metres earlier; the speed, the weight, the water and the mud had combined to manufacture an irreversible fate.

Karl did not see any of this: he was simply focused on acting, intent on displaying boldness, and possessed with the chance to hurt the man. If you had asked him why, he would not have known, but the chase had given him permission to inflict pain, and that was an opportunity he relished. So, gambling everything, he sprang the last five metres between them and leapt on Mac's back like Gary Cooper in a bar room brawl, dragging him down and forcing his face into the effervescent earth.

Throwing back his head like a moonlit wolf Karl howls up into the torrent with both hands on the back of the captive head, pushing it further into the mud. In the contact, Mac's case soars high into the pouring rain, flapping open mid-air: scores, hundreds, of white envelopes go soaring and wheeling in the swirling wind, then flutter down, falling and deliquescing like melting butterflies quivering and drowning in the sodden field. When the case lands, it bounces and slides madly across the field; the soaking residue of saturated paper spreads round Mac then flows on further to the feet of Madeline.

Now she does scream: "Stop Hugo!"

Karl hears it, sees it at the last moment, and rolls off Mac. He manages to pluck himself out of the mud, tries to throw himself outside the path of the machine, and partially succeeds. But it is too late for Mac, who, rising to his knees now, stares at Madeline, unconscious of anything but her presence above him and the letters cascading between them. He reaches his hands forward to her in supplication.

Then the tractor hits. First it ploughs the thick leather case, its blades chewing the skin and whatever is left of its contents to bits, spitting the remaining letters out, sending tiny pieces of leather, cardboard, torn envelopes and ripped-up paper flying like confetti. Fragments of desperate love, and flecks of ranting hatred, fly, land and settle, cling to Madeline's body and dangle from her hair.

Then the cutters scythe into the kneeling Mac; they shred his legs, gouge out his groin, mangle, twist and strip the thin left arm he puts out to protect himself. The bulk of the machine picks him up and pushes him across the mud, over the field, sliding twenty metres more to a grinding shrieking halt, made part of metal, part of bone. Mac is too surprised to cry out, then too shocked to scream.

Kate and Jack were with him in seconds: everyone else stood back, partly out of respect, mainly out of horror at his injuries. His wounds were open but had not yet started bleeding heavily. His body was a butcher's window, and from his mutilated and flattened shape they knew that every bone was crushed or snapped, except his right arm, which was still up straight, waving and pointing its two remaining fingers. Kate had done some nursing, but no medical expertise was needed to predict when everything would close down, fall apart, and drain out. Maybe two minutes if he was very unlucky. She looked at Jack. "Go and get her. Quickly." She wanted to give him a task.

Jack barely glanced around as he stood up, but had he looked he would have seen a field littered with other people's stories.

Claude had dragged the laughing Hugo out of the cab and was swinging furious punches at him, mostly missing before he could get his distance. While he was struggling to find the length, Hugo landed three powerful blows on his eyes and nose. Then from no-where, a clubbing fist, holding a gun, flashed past Claude's ear and smashed into Hugo's face, splitting it open. Claude, half turning, confirmed it was Desdemona doing the pistol whipping, and also noted that Daphne was hanging off her back and trying to prevent it. As he watched, Dessie, twice Daphne's size, shook her off like a toddler, and as Hugo fell slowly to his knees with his nose and mouth gaping open and pouring blood, she pushed past Claude and kicked him hard and true in the testicles, precisely using the point of her highly polished boot.

"Chrissake, Des," Claude yelped, "I had that well under control, what the hell are you doing?"

"Jesus, Dessie," Daphne spoke angrily, but quietly, picking herself up, "are you trying to kill him here, right in front of the police? Do you want to drag my dad back to jail with you? Give me the fucking gun. Now."

Further back up the hill, behind Daphne and Dessie, the police, in the form of Inspector Leopard, were currently more interested in attempting to save the life of the young German than in prosecut-ing the brandishing of firearms without a license.

Karl had saved himself but lost a foot in the process. The side blades of the tractor sheered it clean off as he tried to dive away, and now he was cradling it in his arms like a motherless lamb, lying flat on his back, shrieking, as Maggie pluckily braced together what was left of his legs to stop him thrashing and losing blood. Milo, holding little bits of sick in his mouth, used all his weight at the top end to hold down Karl's shoulders, while Leopard, desperately trying to recall an antique training course he had slept through, took off his belt and tied it into a tourniquet just below the boy's knee which he then wound tighter and tighter, using for the turning stick a small expandable cosh he kept handily in his pocket, normally employed for covertly beating bad boys just like Karl.

Madeline was in shock, as they all were, and her horror increased when Pierrot suddenly loomed at her like an escaped character from a child's clownish nightmare; his black eyes, red lips and white face melting together in the rain; his little conical pom-pom hat still tied under the chin but hanging limply from the side of his head; and the gaily-coloured costume all filthy, drenched, torn and bloody. He held out a hand: "Please come." She took it, of course. Pierrot spun in front, leaving his arm behind for her, and walked towards his father. She allowed him to pull her gently.

Kate was talking to Mac. "Stay with me, Mac. We're getting help now, keep strong." Mac was confused. "Kate?" Kate was relieved that he recognised her, pleased, in some extraordinary way flattered.

"Jack's here too, Mac. He's just coming."

"Where is she, is she here?"

"Gabby's not here love, sorry."

"Not Gabby, Maddie."

Kate almost gave herself permission to show her disgust, but it was close now, just seconds really, not much longer to hold out. Jack arrived, and fell to his knees beside his father, revealing as he did so behind him and above him the standing figure of Madeline. In his last moments of consciousness, Mac brought his eyes into focus, looked past and over Jack and stared at her.

"You told him to stop. I heard."

Madeline was frozen, her copper hair dripping, her sopping wet dress so loose and transparent it covered nothing. Mac looked at her breasts. She thought about folding her arms across them, but she didn't move; what would be the point?

"You tried to save me."

Madeline was silent. Jack, maybe to fill the void, maybe from a son's instinct, maybe out of an ancient respect for the instant of death, said for her: "Yes, she tried to save you, she wanted you to live."

Mac smiled and whispered. "I knew it. Read the letters. They're all for you."

And then the blood bubbled out of his mouth, a cough sprayed specks of it onto Pierrot's chalk white face and sent a misting of crimson onto Kate's white blouse where she knelt holding her husband's hand. The grip spasmed as he grasped for one more breath, missed it, rattled and died.

Silence except the rain and some shouts across the field. Mac is dead now. Is it the end of the story?

Not for Milo and Jack. For the others, we can catch up later. But for Milo and Jack, there is more to come. Not great, for Jack, as he has already had quite a day.

Kate was now standing in the rain, present but apart, an uninvited guest at a private tragedy. Unconsciously she was running through a checklist of emotions, vainly trying to find one to fit the occasion. Nothing. Intuition took over, and she inserted her body between Madeline and Jack, and took him into her arms, moving him away from the scene at the same time. She remembered, it was all for Jack she was there, that hadn't changed.

She thought he would be saying, 'Mum, what the hell are you doing here?' but actually it was, "Dad. Jesus, dad, what the hell

729

happened?" Not just now, because he had seen that; but 'How did you get here. How did you step out of the family photos and the parents' evenings and end up in a hole in France with a pair of binoculars and a suitcase full of mad rambling?' She tried to block his view of the body, but he got round her and looked down again at Mac, whose eyes were open to the storm.

"Dad?"

He took off his Pierrot jacket and knelt to spread it over his father's face and upper body. He spoke to him for the last time, bending close and whispering straight into his ear. "How did you get here?" Everyone was watching now, and thought it was "I love you."

He rose up again, his undershirt covered in his father's blood. Almost as though noticing his mother for the first time, as though he had never been away from her, he pushed her gently aside, and confronted Madeline, still streaming inky tears down his dissolving face.

"What is it about?"

He noticed how beautiful she was, and the shape of her breasts beneath the wet cotton. Realising he was staring, he turned his eyes aside, embarrassed. Madeline looked surprised to be asked. She was still confused by the appearance of this wild boy, and the other one in the Clown suit who joined him as he spoke and put his arm protectively around him. Such strange clothes to wear for a death. She did not know them, or the woman, or the girl or the other men. She recognised Desdemona and Claude, of course, who were all still farcically tangled together in a struggle with her evidently psychotic husband and another woman she didn't know. All this madness. Pain shot through her as she thought about her children. Suddenly needing to be with them, to collect them; she shrugged to the boy, said simply "Sorry," turned round and walked towards her house.

Kate viewed her back, hardly able to comprehend that she was just wandering away.

"Wait, where are you going?"

She didn't stop walking.

"Wait, you can't just leave."

Madeline didn't alter her step at all but turned her head sufficiently to say over her shoulder "You understand. This really is nothing to do with me." Kate viewed her incredulously all the way down the path and through the flaking black door. It went through her mind to go and drag her back out, but what would be gained? She would appear vindictive, or look like she cared, when all she wanted was an explanation.

She turned round to Jack and Milo with a "Can you believe this woman?" face on, and found they were long gone. Up on the tree line a Clown and half a Pierrot could just be glimpsed disappearing back into the forest. That was the moment Kate finally started sobbing, great heaving breathless tears, and sunk down, almost wailing now, in shock, in relief, to rest her head on the lifeless chest of her faithless husband.

Up in the trees, Milo was holding Jack, unashamedly hugging. Both were shivering in the rain and cold in their thin outfits. 'Well,' thought Milo, resorting to facetiousness to cope, as ever, 'I am not surprised he has taken it badly; watching your dad mashed to death by a rusty tractor has got to be one of the top three things to avoid in life.'

Looking for something comforting, he said, "At least he died thinking she wanted to save him, Jack, that seemed to be the most important thing for him for at the end."

"Yes, holding on to that thought, while ignoring his son and his wife."

Milo was tempted to say, as often before, "It's not all about you, Jack," but realised that this time it actually was. Mac was gone now, hopefully he did get that few seconds of comfort, but the price for that was what Kate and Jack were going to have to live with forever.

"Sorry, Jack. But if he did get a moment of peace from her not wanting him to die, I'd take that for him."

"I tell you what, Milo, I agree with you, 'not wanting him to die' is really super in itself. But also maybe not the greatest ever expression of love for a dying man who has given up his life and family and twenty years of happiness for you. 'Wish you had lived' is not much reciprocation for an obsession that led a man to put his life on hold and spend two decades writing letters to an empty suitcase under the stairs.

"Most of us have seen indifference expressed more passionately than that."

Milo said sorry. He knew that nothing he said would be right, so he moved them from the emotional to the practical. "What now? Any clue where we are? And why we're here?"

"Good question, my friend," said Jack, "I was about to ask you the same. Wasn't it your idea to run?"

"Argh, must have been mutual. It appears we might have done it out of habit."

"I wanted to get away from my dad." Jack was crying. "And my mum."

"Why your mum?"

"You know, I'm not totally sure. Because she knows. Because it's too sad. Maybe because I also blame her."

Milo didn't quite want to engage with that. "Well, we have also avoided the police."

"Jesus, how long do we have to do it for? Isn't this over yet?"

"Do you want to go back down?"

"No."

Milo realised they were standing in Mac's filthy hole. Yuk. He subtly moved them five metres along, careful to keep inside the treeline so they couldn't be seen from below.

They were out of ideas for the moment, so they lay down for a while and looked over the field; it was very dark now, but as their eyes adjusted they could detect considerable activity. A police car had turned up with three Constables, and in the headlights they could see them interviewing Hugo, Desdemona and Claude with their notebooks out. An ambulance was already on site, with two nurses and a Doctor. The doors at the back were open and, framed in the inside lights, they watched the Doctor and one of the nurses working on Karl, while the other nurse seemed to be doing her best to warm up Maggie and Kate with blankets as she checked them over.

Jack was shivering badly now, and his body was crumpling like wet cardboard.

"What do we do now, Milo?

This was a worry in itself. Jack rarely called Milo "Milo"; and he never asked his advice.

"Fear not, Spartacus, for I have a plan so good I am naming it Solution."

"Solution! This sounds wonderful, Spartacus. Can I presume it involves a helicopter?

"No helicopter."

"Horse?"

"Not a bad idea, but no, no horse."

"A team of bearers?"

"Again, this is inspired, but no."

"OK, I give in."

"Never give in, Spartacus."

"Fair enough. What does it involve, my friend?"

"It involves walking, then driving, then eating, then camping."

"For the others, I am intrigued. For the walking, I am not so sure. Are we up to it? I am freezing and exhausted already. The Lodge, the Farm, they've got to be six or seven kilometres from here, in the dark, and we don't know the way. I don't think we can make it. Maybe we should just go down and hand ourselves in."

"Lost property! Don't be daft, we're not giving in now, what would Mr Mills say?"

"He'd say 'Kelly, if you haven't got your kit, you'll have to do it in your pants.'"

They cracked up with laughter for half a minute, remembering that day; then quietened, both contemplating just how normal, comfortable and safe it turned out school had always been. All the time they were there, they'd had no idea. Ten days ago they couldn't wait to finish, now if you said to them you can go back but you have to start at age eleven and do the whole thing again, they would have said, "Yes please, where do I sign up?"

"OK," said Jack, "we're not giving ourselves in; so what do you have in mind?"

"OK the plan is this. You see down below us a number of people, including – remarkably, seemingly out of nowhere – your mother and girlfriend …"

"Friend."

"Girlfriend, for God's sake, will you please just fucking grow up!"

[Milo snapped just a little, demonstrating it was finally time to let that one go. Jack would never play that card again. They touched each other's heads in the dark, ruffled slightly, and moved on.]

"And you see Daphne."

"Agreed, but what is your point?"

"There was a fourth car in the chase."

"Ah! The mystery of the fourth car!"

"Yes. The smashed car, the sunk car we saw; the police car we knew of; and apparently a fourth car. And the fourth car will be driveable. We have to hope Daff left the keys in; I think it is very likely, because she always does. But we need to get back to the crash site quickly, before anyone else thinks of moving it – let's hope the police and medics keep them all down there for a while longer."

"How far?"

"It felt like not much more than a kilometre, right? Without Dessie and Claude to slow us down, say twenty minutes max, retracing our own tracks."

"Too dark."

"Feel in your pocket."

Jack looked blank, but did as he was told.

"Torch! Thank you, Dessie! But is the trip too dangerous?"

"Don't be a dick, you have been allocated a penknife. Pick up a stick. And if it gets really hairy, I have this."

Jack peered through the dark, to see the gun in Milo's hand.

"Jesus Christ."

"Daphne squeezed it into my grasp as we ran past her."

"She's thinking we are going to have to shoot our way out."

"More a question of hiding the evidence, I suspect. Come on, no time to waste."

Milo heaved himself to his feet, feeling another great wave of fatigue crashing into him; but there was no time for that now. Jack was lying on his back in front of him. Milo stood at Jack's feet, reached forward, took his hand and then straightened, pulling Jack up with him as he did so. With a groan, Jack rose, but shot past the perpendicular and fell into Milo's arms like a stringless puppet. Milo turned him round gently, pointed him where they were going, and marched them both off into the undergrowth, clutched unsteadily together like the last-placed contestants in the world's most pathetic three-legged race.

SATURDAY

"So tell me again, please," Chief Inspector Prudhomme asked Desdemona the following morning, "why did you pull the car up across the road? You must have been aware how dangerous that was?"

The Chief Inspector had been called in from Vierzon two hours after Mac's death, basically as soon as the regional Superintendent realised what a horrible mess they were in. Leopard had immediately been suspended from duty ("So we can have time to clear his name," said the Superintendent, unconvincingly) under suspicion of negligence; endangering the life of a civilian; wasting police time (a first for a serving officer); causing, or at least failing to prevent, the death of a witness / suspect / victim / bystander [to be determined]; running an enquiry no-one had sanctioned into a felony that probably never happened; refusing to enter the water to facilitate a rescue; endangering the life of a fellow officer; and contravening at least ten other regulations of the police code of conduct – you get the drift.

Leopard was angry at this treatment, furious at the lack of support from his superiors, and even more incensed by the choice of the man to take over the investigation of the affair, because Prudhomme had started his career in Bourges, and had once, around fifteen years before, been his assistant. The humiliation was made complete when Prudhomme took over Leopard's office and his notebooks, with only the most perfunctory apology.

Prudhomme spent the night reading everything available and then making local telephone calls till the people he was phoning were no longer awake. What he discovered was bemusing. Normally he would have just called Leopard on the old boy network to ask what the hell it was all about, but the Superintendent's single stricture when briefing him was "Do not under any circumstances talk to Leopard – it's him you're investigating as much as anyone else." Prudhomme wasn't exactly happy with it, but he suspected he needed to acquiesce and start from scratch. He worked till three, woke up the receptionist at his small hotel, got three hours sleep, and was back at his desk with a coffee and croissant before seven, when he made a series of international calls (Berlin, Paris, and, later, London), read some more files, and questioned a few of the Constables who had been at Hill House and the other scenes.

His only false step so far was to make Desdemona his first interview of the morning, thinking it might be quite a soft touch. She arrived rather late for the ten o'clock appointment she had agreed, completely in a fluster and partially in a low-cut leopard skin top. She was ready for a fight, which meant jangly earrings and a fistful of rings like a knuckleduster; but when she saw Prudhomme, and how young he looked, and the peachiness of his skin, she slowed down.

"No, you're not getting it, dear," Dessie put her hand across the table and lightly touched his wrist, like a mum buttering up an unimpressed young teacher on Parents' Night. "We were being followed at high speed. By gangsters out to harm us. I lost control of the car and we nearly went into the river, I just about pulled us up in time. I couldn't get it started again, so we all jumped out of the car and ran to a safe place. It was all on them, love, you see that, don't you?" Followed by another gentle pat.

Dessie had decided this was her main issue, and that little else could stick to her – nothing criminal anyway: so as far as she was concerned the only problem was avoiding a charge of Causing Death by Dangerous Driving. ["Causing Death by Dangerous Parking," she had cackled to Claude, unhelpfully.]

"Why were they out to hurt you, Desdemona?"

"Ah, nothing to do with crime, Chief Inspector, don't worry about that – we've got no connection with the 'underworld'" (this last with an exaggerated wink that terrified the increasingly nervous policeman). "This was an affair of the heart. I am afraid for many years I was a 'known associate' of Pierre" (another hideous grimace, he assumed it was a different species of wink, maybe never before observed in humankind: if he was the one identifying it scientifically for the first time perhaps they might name it *Monocular Prudhommensis*), "but Claude and I recently rekindled an ancient flame, and there you are, the oldest story in the world, right?"

"So he was chasing you in a misguided effort to win you back?"

"That's one way of looking at it, I suppose. Perhaps it could more accurately be described as a spontaneous attempt to eliminate a rival and convince me I had made some bad choices."

"And you seriously were in fear of your life?"

"Ask the others, Chief Inspector, we all were. The kids with us had nothing to do with the affair, but they were in just as much jeopardy. Charles and Pierre were driving about ten metres behind us at what must have been over a hundred kilometres an hour. That's dangerous enough without the additional flaunting of weapons and making cut-throat signals, don't you think? All we wanted to do was run away and hide; you're not looking at an outlaw gang – we're the victims here."

"And yet," said Prudhomme, slowly, "it was Pierre that ended up dead."

"We didn't know that. We were still running from him. That's the kind of man he was, his reputation succeeded him even after his death."

Oh yes, did I not mention that that was the end of the story for Pierre? Let me explain. By the time Pelou had summoned up the bravery to get wet, and the additional courage he needed to actually push off from the bank and get his head under, it was much too late for Pierre.

The Constable had decided he could not wait any longer or they would lose them both; ignoring Leopard's parting plan for a simultaneous attempt, he had gone down solo several times to get Charles's door open and free him from the car, and he eventually accomplished the rescue. Therefore, while Pelou was breast-stroking clumsily out to the beautiful blue motor, now nine-parts under, basking like a polished whale with only half a nostril above the water, the Constable was dragging Charles back past him going in the other direction, reaching the bank, and hauling him onto the shore.

Pelou finally reached the far side of the car, where Pierre was lodged in the passenger seat, just as the roof went completely under. He made one serious attempt to go down with the sinking motor and open the door, failed, and then made two or three much flashier splashier efforts purely designed to illustrate to anyone watching from the bank how heroically he was behaving. He didn't look back to the shore as he didn't want to appear to be checking out the audience: he just hammed it up, puffing away, pretending to struggle with imaginary handles, while theatrically submerging himself and then dramatically thrusting his body up out of the water. When he finally did look over to the bank with an emotional shrug indicating "Impossible, what more can I do?" he was upset to find it was completely deserted except for the Constable who was fully engaged, with his back towards him, in trying to resuscitate the comatose Charles.

Pierre's body was recovered quite a few hours later, about a hundred and fifty metres further up the river, where the car had finally drifted and settled, by a team of frogmen from regional headquarters. When they got his body back to the lab, the pathologist found hardly any water in his lungs, so made the pronouncement that he must have been killed by the impact and was already dead when the car went down. Therefore, he did not drown. Pelou had not been under any censure, but this cleared him entirely of any suspicion that he contributed to Pierre's demise by any form of negligence.

The spotlight fell briefly onto Charles. Prudhomme asked later, during their interview, "Were you driving much too close to Desdemona's car?"

Yes, of course. Charles drew deeply, deeply, on his cigarette, and explained. "Inspector, I am – sorry, I should say I <u>was</u> – employed by Pierre, and he instructed me to drive quickly. Besides, we saw no danger, because the other car pulled away a good distance; we were closer at one stage, not dangerously so I think, then suddenly we were three hundred metres behind. That seemed quite safe till we turned the corner and their car was resting sideways, right in the middle of the road just thirty metres away. I believe we could have been driving as slowly as the vicar's wife and we would still not have had time to pull up. I think we did really well to avoid a head-on crash into it, but we still swiped it very hard, and then we both hit our heads when the car took off. You do understand, I too am a victim. The car was the best thing I owned, ever, the pride of my life, and it is still, at the bottom of the water."

So that was it. Apparently, no-one was to blame. And no-one, except Charles, cared about the blue Facel Vega Facellia, quietly waiting on the riverbed for future resurrection. He had his compensations, though, as in most ways his life was going to improve immeasurably. Working conditions in their gang had never been entirely satisfactory. Pierre, he could now admit to himself and others, had been the most phenomenal bully. He never resisted any opportunity to humiliate his employees, including Charles; belittling them in public time after time was one of his principal management techniques.

[Once, when Charles was out with his own son, they had met Pierre with one of his kids, and Pierre had spoken to him in front of the children so dismissively, so demeaningly, complaining about a failed errand to collect a trivial amount of money from a wretched gambling creditor who it turned out had already killed himself before Charles arrived. Pierre casually clipped him on the side of the head in front of his boy; even now when he thought about it – though Pierre was dead and gone – the blood pulsed in his temple.]

As chief enforcer, he'd been pushed into doing vile things he hated remembering, in fear that if he failed to do them, those same things would be done to him instead. It was extremely stressful. But Pierre was dead now, and Charles no longer needed to worry about slights and insults and torturing anyone who'd got on his very sizeable bad side. He would move quickly and seal off challenges from various members of Pierre's extended family and other henchmen in order to take control of the business. Blood would be shed, bodies buried, but he felt much more relaxed about killing in his own cause, it felt cleaner, and anyway the slain would all be fellow professionals who shared his code and would

741

not trouble his conscience.

So suddenly he was going to be amazingly rich, rich beyond counting – he had had no idea that Pierre was generating such extraordinary amounts of income. He would completely overhaul everyone's terms and conditions, bring in new standards on the personnel front, improve communications, and introduce rules about respectful behaviour, which, as a leader, he would follow scrupulously himself. Morale would soar; and that would be reflected in further improved performance and even higher revenues.

And as an extra bonus, it seemed the police were being taken off his gang. If Leopard had been left alone he would have pursued the mob relentlessly, both to cramp their style and also possibly, who knows, to get some crumbs for himself; but now he had been pulled off the job, Charles miraculously would have a clear run, the new guy was plainly only around for a short while, and anyway, he only seemed to be worried about motoring offences...

So what about Leopard? How does this story end for him? In fact many felt Leopard was the real victim that day (perhaps leaving aside the people who actually died or lost body parts). His instinctive, off-beat approach had sadly come back to haunt him. That style is annoying, we all know that: in fact for those of us who work hard, focus on the details, and have to follow disciplines, there is nothing more aggravating than a self-styled maverick for whom all of life is a form of shortcut. And because of this depth of petrified animosity, maintenance of the intuitive rainmaker role is totally dependent on success. Everyone is waiting to give you the cake in the face the minute your special insight betrays you or your unique instinct mysteriously evaporates. And Leopard, I think we can agree, did fail spectacularly in several key areas that day. Now he was waiting, impatiently, humiliatingly, outside the office he had occupied himself for a great many years, till the night before.

After Desdemona eventually left at the end of the morning, moaning about being too late to get to the café in time for the lunches, despite the fact it was she who had arrived late and dragged the meeting out much longer than necessary, Prudhomme finally summoned the waiting Leopard to come in and sit at his very own desk for questioning.

The first problem seemingly on everyone's agenda was Karl. Prudhomme asked him outright.

"What was he doing in the first place on a 'ride along' with experienced police officers in hot pursuit of a convoy of other vehicles? Why was the boy involved at all in an investigation, and why had it spiralled out of control to the extent that he ended the day with one foot less than he started with?"

And the perplexity, the confusion.

"Could you explain to me," Prudhomme enquired, with increasing frustration, "what crime you were actually investigating? Leopard? There is no file open, no records, the Prosecutor was never informed. There is only the logging of a couple of random conversations, a couple of pages of notes and numbers in your book, one or two phone calls, and a memo that a meeting room was booked on one occasion for an interview that never took place. We have the story of the German boy who says you were in pursuit of the French and American lads, who turned out to be English – but obviously not the owners of the British passports that were discovered. When I asked him why, he came up with a story about his father having told you to do it, because there was some drama about a stabbing in London."

He looked quizzically at Leopard.

"Based on what you had, it all seems a bit tenuous, right? A bit slight to be initiating car chases, terrorising witnesses?"

Leopard was looking at the wall. Prudhomme calmed, and decided to change tack, and lower the tension.

"On the other hand, Desdemona was certain you were simply

trying to arrest Pierre, and that's why you were on his tail. Was that it?"

This attempted to graciously fashion a little chink for Leopard to slip in to make a story. He stared at Leopard for a long time, trying not to blink in time with him, as he knew that was a sign of weakness. Always be the man who sets the rhythm. If you cross your arms, wait for them to cross theirs, don't echo their shape. He was now hoping Leopard would say something to fill the silence he had carefully created, as they taught them at the academy. Later he remembered that Leopard had actually done the same course, a decade before him. In the end, he filled the silence himself.

"I had a very brief chat with the Englishwoman, Kate, and she suggested you were on the hunt for her husband, Mac du Lac, supposedly to interview him in connection with the knifing of Jean Terroir. Was it that?"

Leopard decided to keep his powder dry, he could tell they were only at the first semi-colon in an extremely long sentence.

"And at the same time," Prudhomme riffled through the thick pile of notes in front of him, pulling out some names, "it appears from a statement taken by a Constable on the scene that Daphne believed you were merely attempting to take her father Claude aside for a conversation about Jean's accident (as they call it), and that the whole thing got horribly out of hand. She was the angriest – she says you could have killed them all."

Leopard, having recognised from the tone after a few seconds that his number was already up, said not much at all, in fact nothing. The truth was, there was no truth. For years in the small community he had exercised so much power with so little consequence that he could do pretty well whatever he wanted. This, he realised now – and to be fair, also at the time – made him extremely undisciplined and rather unsystematic. But that never mattered. He followed his senses, surrendered to his intuition. He neglected to investigate any situations he considered pedestrian and refused to follow up leads he found tiresome. He developed his own code, prioritising common sense, self-interest and his own prejudices above the strict letter of the law. Very often, with the general approval and assistance of most of the local *gendarmerie*, justice was summary, and now and again it was brutal.

Now he had been caught out. If the events on the road and at the farm had not turned so sour (he still could not bear to use the bleak language of tragedy to describe that evening properly, even to himself) he knew that in a few days he would have solved all three crimes – the boys; whatever Pierre was up to; and Mac. It all felt like very low-level stuff, nobody really cared that much, did they?

If he could be bothered later he would make the case that, in actual fact, Karl had been foisted on him by his own chief, and it was that imposition that drew him into the story of the English boys, which in turn led inevitably to the sordid business with the father. It was on record, and that was a potential get-out-of-jail card of sorts, if played carefully. But the most annoying thing was he wouldn't have needed it If he hadn't been so unlucky. If he hadn't been accidentally exposed by two freak deaths, a collapsed lung, and the unfortunate amputation of a foreign foot, he could easily have come out of this as the hero. Instead, he was now staring at suspension, transfer, or dismissal.

"Look, Prudhomme, you and I know what happened here, so I don't think you should be getting too much up on your high horse, we've all done it, right?"

Prudhomme looked blankly at him; dismayed, then despairing. He needed a break. "That's certainly an interesting thought. Let's pick it up again tomorrow, shall we, Leopard? And then we still need to address the issue of Sergeant Pelou."

If anything, this was going to be a much bigger problem for Leopard within the police force. As it happened, the Sergeant, an extremely popular officer among his comrades, never fully recovered from the pneumonia, or pneumothorax, or whatever they'd called it. In fact history will relate that he spent years on full pay while working only a few weeks here and there due to a variety of lung disorders; and on retirement he received a generous police pension in exchange for keeping silent about the events of that day and how he had come to be listlessly doggy-paddling towards the failed rescue of a top criminal suspect, while the Inspector, who it turned out was the two-time winner of the police academy's "Deep Water Lifesaver" award, had lingered on the bank and then deserted the scene. Prudhomme would not let this one go.

"I need to finish now, I've got Charles waiting, then some work to do preparing an interview, sorry. I'm going out to talk to Claude later this afternoon when he gets back from the Experience."

Leopard got up to leave, realising he was being dismissed from his own office; this was getting irritating, and it had only just started.

"You're talking to him? That's more than I ever managed. Am I allowed to work meantime?"

"Yes, I can swing that, but just stick to traffic and petty crime for the time being – try not to chase anyone into a combine harvester while my back is turned."

After Charles, and a short lunch, for the rest of the afternoon Prudhomme updated his notes, read more background, met the Doctor from the tractor incident, and prepared his questions for Claude. A Constable had been sent to observe the Harlequinade in case the boys were crazy enough to appear; he knew they wouldn't, but he had to be seen to be doing things thoroughly, no more seat of the pants.

Eventually he spoke to his Sergeant and made some arrangements for later, then he called his driver to take him out to the Lodge. He always got excited about new interviews, he was an optimist, not one of those cynical old cops; but even though he was hoping this might clear up some small parts of the mystery, he also expected he would primarily encounter the code of silence. It would be interesting to see if he could get more.

When they drew up at the Lodge, he left his driver in the car. He knocked at the door, there was no answer, so he walked round to the back, prepared to be very annoyed at having his time wasted. But there was Claude, nursing a bottle of beer, laid out on a lounger that was positioned to look over the lake.

"Chief Inspector Prudhomme? Do come and join me. Would you like a beer?"

"Thank you, no, I am supposed to be working."

Claude gestured to a second deckchair beside him, and the Inspector lowered himself in.

"Cigarette?"

"Not my habit."

"Mind if I do?"

"Of course not, actually I want you to be as relaxed as possible, so you accidentally let slip the information I need."

"Ah, that's what I like! A man with a plan."

Claude fired up his fag. They both smiled.

"How was the Experience today?"

"Actually a bit hard. We are getting quite good at it, but of course every time we get into a decent rhythm something else happens to throw us off. Today the boat, the food, the entertainment, it was all brilliant, but for the play we had to compensate for the boys being missing, so Tommy played Pierrot and Caro played Clown. Sorry, I am already boring you, you don't know these people, I guess I am just saying, you know how it is, the show must go on!"

"Indeed. And on that subject, may I start?"

"Please, be my guest."

"OK, let me tell you where I am. For the young boys, leave that to me, I accuse you of nothing, I am aware they were here under false identities, and I have discovered what they were running from. I don't consider it is anything to do with you, but at some stage I have to have a conversation with your boss about it. They're not here, I suppose?"

This was a longshot, to catch him off guard. Claude looked confused – why would they be there?

"For Pierre, you don't need to comment, I have been made aware he was very possessive about your friend Desdemona, and when you and she reignited your wartime passion he took it amiss. So this is a love triangle, you were passive and actually, if you don't mind me saying, running away."

"That's very hurtful, Monsieur," Claude said, looking intently at Prudhomme for five seconds before cracking into a grin and then laughing out loud.

"Of course I was running, this was a man who nailed the testicles of his nephew to a tree for a minor infringement of gang protocol."

"That is apocryphal."

"I agree, it must have been agony."

"No, it means, mythological. It didn't really happen."

"A fox pulled them off the tree and chewed them for half a day before choking and coughing them up onto my cousin's doorstep. She is the mother of the newly-created eunuch – that's truly mythological, right? This is a magical region. Now my cousin keeps her boy's testes under her bed in a biscuit tin illustrated with portraits of the first ten winners of the Tours de France. Every year on July 25th she takes the tin to church with her and she prays to St Cucuphas that the boy may be made whole. So not apocryphal, not even atypical. And if he could do that to a relative for a tiny transgression, what was on the menu for a man he didn't particularly like whom he had just found out was involved with his girlfriend? That's why I would have been generally trying to avoid him."

"I meant no insult, Claude. Had I been in your situation, I would have probably done the same thing. Not the intimacy, to be clear; just the running away. In respect to the motoring offences, I am pleased – as well as being extremely surprised, between us – to confirm the accusations are all being dropped. Neither Desdemona nor you will be charged, not even with speeding or careless driving. The prosecutors' office around here can certainly produce some marvellous interpretations. And incredibly quickly, too."

Claude grinned, triumphantly.

"Are you sure I can't get you that beer? Surely this is something worth celebrating."

Prudhomme smiled insincerely. "Still on duty, old boy."

Claude came back with a cold beer, and flopped smugly back into his deckchair, trying to get his cigarettes out from his back pocket at the same time and getting his hand caught under him quite painfully. He tried not to show he was hurt.

"So, Claude, that just leaves the one issue for you, if I may. Which is about Jean's 'accident.'"

Claude shrugged indicating, "I can do nothing to stop you, so I don't know why you are pretending to ask my permission."

"That day, you were operating the Experience, and you and the others were ferrying a boatload of customers up to the jetty at Hill House, OK?"

Claude nodded.

"The previous day a cygnet had been accidentally killed."

Claude raised his eyebrows and angled his head very slightly. Was it an accident? No-one thought so. His expression piqued Prudhomme's interest.

"Not an accident? Who was driving?"

"Seriously, Chief Inspector? Now you are investigating the murder of a young bird? What are you, the Avian Homicide Squad?"

"Homicide means human slaying, so that squad wouldn't be called that. Perhaps you are thinking of La Ligue pour la Protection des Oiseaux? I am not secretly working for them though they may well have an interest – they are much harsher than the *gendarmerie*, so be careful."

Claude grimaced at the wretched banter, thinking, 'Come on copper, you can do better.'

"I am just interested in the events of that day, who was responsible, in case we are detecting a chain of motive."

"Karl was steering the barge when the baby swan was run down."

Prudhomme looked disappointedly at Claude, did this mean there was no connection between the cygnet killer and Mac?

"Next day, you were taking more customers in the morning, and the mother swan attacked the barge, am I right?"

"Hard to describe it, really. I wouldn't say an attack on the boat; she boarded us specifically in order to grab the dog, then she left."

"Smart bird."

"Vengeful. There is no doubt it was a deliberate retaliation, stemming from her grief."

"And the man?"

"What do you mean?"

"The man who came from the bank. To save the dog."

"Ah, now we're in territory of a more confidential nature."

"I know who it was, that's public knowledge now. It was Mac. My question was, why do you think he did that – why would a rough-sleeping night stalker…" [Claude winced, and signalled with a flap of the non-smoking hand beyond the wrist that he was not happy with this tone and it was unlikely to be productive] "… involve himself with an attack on an insignificant dog?"

Claude was disinclined to give anything other than a shrug. The Chief Inspector's lapse of decorum had given his silence a protective validation.

"Especially when it placed him at some risk, both of drowning and detection."

More shrug.

"So, this is what I am thinking, after some conversations with others."

Claude looked uninterested.

"Do you want the simple theory, or the meandering speculation?"

Claude looked bored.

"OK, the long version it is. You know Mac was obsessed with the woman at the farm? He had written to her, over a period of twenty years, nearly five hundred letters, all sealed in envelopes, that he kept in a suitcase."

Claude looked indifferent.

"The woman's name is Madeline; you are aware of that?"

Claude looked as though he might not be aware, without saying as much.

"It would be odd if you weren't aware, because a dozen witnesses have not thought it necessary to deny you have been acquainted with her for the best part of thirty years, since close to schooldays."

"Everyone round here knows everyone else – either knows them or is related to them."

"True, but, leaving aside the widespread local interweaving, you agree you know her, and you also know, because you have intervened in the situation quite a few times, that she has been the unwilling object of Mac's romantic and sexual fantasies for three decades. Even when he was married and living abroad."

Claude looked shocked.

"For Christ's sake, Claude, you were chasing him down a hill in an attempt to stop him assaulting the poor girl – none of this is new news."

"Assailing."

"Well, we'll never know, will we?"

"It was fantasy. He lived his life outside her thirty-metre radius. The further he was from that line, the unhappier he became; but he never crossed over it."

"Till the day he died."

Claude bridled.

"Let me take you back to the riverbank. The Experience vessel is gliding serenely down the stream on a gorgeous sunny summer morning. Suddenly a swan swoops out and mounts the boat; she snatches a puppy; she retreats over the side with her prey and re-enters the water. Consternation throughout the barge. 'How do we stop? Can we turn round?' No… But, what's this? A stranger enters the current from the shore. He wrestles the swan for the dog, and the dog is saved. The fight continues as the boat chugs onwards. You recall all this?"

"Of course."

"But who is the stranger, and what inspires him to heroism?"

Claude was once more indifferent. Prudhomme could fool himself that his rhetorical questions were a meat hammer relentlessly softening him, but for Claude they were the twittings of a confused budgie banging its beak on a tiny mirror. He had been interrogated by professionals, those without boundaries, and lived to tell the tale without telling tales.

"What inspires him is not the attack on the dog, Claude. It is the swan laying its head on Leda's lap, no?"

Claude looked vague, this time without any effort.

"You don't know the myth? OK, Leda was a beautiful princess with a mass of curly copper-coloured hair who was in the terminology of the time 'seduced' by the God Zeus in the form of a swan."

"Now you mention it, I do recall hearing about that."

"The auburn-haired woman, you know who she was?"

"This time we are not talking about Leda?"

"No."

"OK. I think you know the answer to your question. Typically, I think that is your style, right?"

"Sometimes. In this instance we both know. It was Madeline."

Claude looked innocent.

Prudhomme, finally, was bored with his own game.

"Mac was stalking the barge, because Madeline was on it that day, as companion to Madame Malpense, for whom she worked in the museum. Do we agree?"

Claude made no sign.

"When the swan sought its vengeance on the barge that killed its child by snatching the puppy, Mac was not bothered by that, in fact I can imagine he had a great deal of sympathy. But... it went too far when it touched the lap of his love object."

No comment.

"He went in the water, not to save the dog, but to punish the swan for assailing his lady."

"Are we done now?"

"Not quite. I was wondering, was it only you who recognised Madeline?"

No comment.

"You were her age, probably at school together, like everyone else? Did Jean or Daphne know her? No? So just you. Why didn't you mention it to them?"

For a second Claude was tempted to tell Prudhomme to stop trying to read his mind, but he decided to bite his lip and stay silent.

"Why did you return so quickly to the scene? What were you worried about?"

Sans commentaire.

"Were you anxious about the swimmer, or the swan?"

Nothing.

"You recognised him straight away, right?"

Riens.

"Claude, you are going to have to talk sometime. You got back, nothing was in the water, you saw the disturbance in the undergrowth on the bank, you stopped the boat, you tied up the vessel, you disembarked, you found Mac with the swan. All this, frankly, is on the record, you have never denied any of this, it is even part of the very slim notes we got from Leopard."

Claude waited.

"The only question I want you to answer is, how did the knife get into Jean?"

"Have you asked Jean?"

"I've been told I can speak to him tomorrow."

"Well, he might know what happened. For me, it was a blur."

"Mac had killed the swan when you came upon him and was mutilating it."

"Who told you that?"

"Let's say it is a common story in the area."

"Well it is also a common story in the area that the man is a hero, he went in the water to save the dog, the swan attacked him at close quarters, loath as he was, he had to defend himself, using a very small pocketknife, and in the bird's frenzy, feathers flew. Blood was everywhere, it was slippery, he skidded, fell forward, the knife in his hand, Jean stepped forward to catch him, the blade hit him. I have heard that version too."

"You want to leave it at that? Will Jean say the same?"

Claude knew perfectly well Jean would say the same because he had already spoken to him about it. Just because Prudhomme couldn't get into his room didn't mean Jean was still unconscious.

"Mac's deceased, Chief Inspector. Maybe no-one did anything. No-one is sure what happened. Is it likely Jean would press any charges? In my view, certainly, there are no charges to press, but if there were, how can you prosecute a dead man? Does any of this really matter anymore?"

"It affects others, Claude. The truth matters. What happened that day also influenced how Mac died, even how Pierre died. We can leave it for now, I may come back to you after I have interviewed Jean.

"One last question, if I may. The boys, you know where they are? I don't suppose they're here?"

Claude looked blank. "Is that a trick question?"

"What do you mean?"

"Didn't you ask me the exact same thing about fifteen minutes ago?"

"Ha ha. You are too sharp for me. Very well. Don't get up, I will find my own way out – is it OK if I wander round the lake first?"

"Pond," said Claude, not prepared to agree anything without a fight. He nodded his permission, but Prudhomme had already ambled off to the water.

He needed the fresh air, and a little peace, and given he suspected Jack and Milo were somewhere about the place, it wouldn't hurt to annoy them by hanging around. He sauntered quietly round the lake for forty-five minutes, lost in his thoughts, then sat on a bench and started to look up a few things in his notebook. Apart from the English lads, what else was there to sort out? He went through his notes, summarising in his mind where he was from a policing point of view.

In respect to the German youth's foot, the boy had put himself in harm's way, he'd been told to stop but chose to go on. However powerful and important his father might be, what trouble can he realistically cause? In fact didn't the German father effectively order Karl into that chasing vehicle?

There was a suspicion that the Regional Super had himself, under pressure from some important third-party, influenced Leopard and Pelou to facilitate Karl's involvement, but there was plenty of evidence they still tried to get him out of the car. Prudhomme decided his report would exonerate Leopard and Pelou for taking the boy with them in exigent circumstances, and he had the feeling that was the result that was anticipated higher up the chain.

Hugo in the tractor was not to blame for Karl's foot, he was basically ploughing his own field when the boy dived in front of him. He decided he would propose a commendation for Leopard and the English girl for saving Karl's life with the tourniquet.

Regarding Pierre's death, this, he decided, was a traffic accident, caused by driving too close. Charles would get a fine, perhaps a suspended sentence for careless driving, with the defence he had been instructed by his boss, who was in the car with him. Dessie was in the clear already, and although he found that more surprising than the light touch on Charles, it was also not unexpected, given cousinly relationships with influential personnel in the Prosecutor's department.

Leopard could not be sanctioned on that one as it was easy to argue that he had had no, or very little, responsibility for causing Pierre or Dessie to drive the way they did. He would have to separate out the issues with Pelou, the bullying, and the tardiness in attempting the rescue, but the pathologist's determination that Pierre did not drown was key here.

And for Mac's decease? With Dessie, Madeline, Hugo – if you dig deep enough there's a conspiracy, there's a death, but is there a crime? Mac for some reason was ingrained in this neighbourhood, a community that seemingly found it impossible to banish one of their own, however vile. But even with the deep-rooted loyalties, it was hard to find anyone in the locale who had much sympathy for his death. The truth? Everyone talks of a chase, but the man was running anyway; running towards the woman, not away from the pursuers.

The conditions were awful, rain, mud – neither runners nor machines could avoid slipping or had any chance of stopping. Yes, he strongly suspected a trap had been baited, but the man was ready to act anyway, things were boiling over; the ruse did not create the offence, it snared the perpetrator. There is a question over the tractor driver, its speed, its position, but this has been resolved, the man was protecting his wife, who could have been under threat of her life from a man who was known to be involved with a knife incident days before. There is nothing here to prosecute.

What about Jean's stabbing? The two surviving witnesses to events were going to say "accident" and there was nothing much he could produce to prove otherwise. If there had been a crime, the offender was dead, and the victim was not pressing charges. Move on.

So, it all came down now to the "boy hunt," which he had been instructed to conduct, the order coming from the highest level, even more entrenched now, it felt, because the lost foot demanded a justification. So that was his focus. As he looked across the stillness of the lake, there was a last moment of evening tranquillity, before in the deep distance a siren could be heard, coming closer. He looked at his watch. He'd timed it quite well, 'They're just a minute late,' he thought.

He turned to face the house; he had a full view of the back and side. His driver, carefully positioned in the carpark, had the opposite view of the front and the other side. So, the whole house was under surveillance, including Claude in his lounger. Prudhomme wanted to watch his reaction as the siren approached. As he suspected, Claude suddenly sat up, looked around, shot up off the deckchair, and was about to run into the house when he suddenly realised Prudhomme was studying him from the bench sixty metres away. He decided to sink back down, nonchalantly, and lit another cigarette with belated *sangfroid*.

'Interesting,' thought Prudhomme.

Two cop cars pulled in, and it took the eight *flics* they disgorged around forty-five minutes to toss the whole place while Prudhomme and his driver kept their vigil, front and back. Claude had looked him in the eye early on, "Are you sure you're allowed?"

"Oh yes, I forgot to mention, I called for warrants last night, we have permission to search Forest Lodge and some other local properties."

For the first time, Claude looked worried. Suddenly he was keen to get away in the van, saying he had to feed the dog at the farm, but Prudhomme politely suggested he might like to remain, in case they needed any help with locks and so on.

"Can I make a call?"

"Perhaps not, Monsieur, let's just sit out here and enjoy the sun."

Early in the search, simply by watching Claude, Prudhomme was certain they would not find the boys at the Lodge but was even more convinced that Claude knew their whereabouts. When his Sergeant emerged into the yard shaking his head, Prudhomme made the traditional joke to Claude that he had never doubted him for a moment.

"You mentioned the farm, Claude, I think you meant Jean's, right? You want to go there now for the dog?"

Claude realised what he'd done.

"No, Chief, it's fine, I'll tidy up first and go down there later – Hector can wait for a while."

"Hector?"

"Jean's dog."

"Ah, I see. In terms of tidiness, I am sure our chaps have left it neat, am I right, Sarge?"

"Of course, Sir. Actually I think it looks better now than when we arrived." Another classic cop joke.

"Great work. Then no tidying needed; we can all go down to Jean's together and feed Hector, how about that, OK? Our warrant does include it, in case you were going to ask. Do you want to walk, or we can give you a lift?"

Claude knew when he was beaten and decided to bluff it out with a bit of hail fellow.

"Let's take a walk, it's a lovely day for it."

Five minutes later found them strolling side by side down the road to the farm, hands in pockets, chatting nonchalantly, with three police cars and nine *gendarmes* trailing in a convoy behind them at five kilometres an hour.

Claude was explaining to the Chief Inspector that the farmhouse had been occupied by the women from London. "You've not met them, I think? One of the lad's mothers, and a girlfriend. The older woman, Kate, is the wife of the man who was killed yesterday. Jean's family were letting them use the house but after the tragedy yesterday, Madame Terroir – that's Jean's mother – insisted they went to stay with her in town, where they can be properly looked after. So the house is empty, which means I will come twice a day to feed the dog."

Prudhomme nodded and made the 'I understand' noise; if he had had any doubt about the boys' hiding place, the sheer volume of unrequested detail Claude was generating to distract him was all the confirmation he needed. They strode up through the entrance to the Experience, with Prudhomme admiring the signage and presentation, asking about the Hut, and looking up the river to see if he could see the barge.

"It's just round the bend, on the jetty. You should come to the Experience next week, you can see everything, I am sure we can fit you in. Actually, I've got time to show you the boat and landing stage now if you like?"

The policeman politely refused the promenade to the barge and gave an appreciative but non-committal nod to the suggestion of the future visit to the Experience. As they unfastened the gate, rather than going through and closing it behind them, Prud-homme swung it wide open, and, to Claude's annoyance, waved the three police vehicles through and pointed them up the hill to the farmyard. They were moving quickly; Claude realised they wanted to make sure no-one could bolt if they saw them from a distance. Prudhomme and Claude followed them at a leisurely pace. No rush for Claude. The evening was coming in, the sun was half gone, the wind had dropped. A lovely, balmy dusk was forming.

"What do you think, Claude?" said Prudhomme, beginning to enjoy himself in spite of the tension in the situation, and despite his perpetual aura of absolute professionalism.

Claude looked innocent. "Think about what?"

"Think about what we'll find when we search up here."

Claude was wondering now what was happening. Two weeks ago he had never met these English kids, but since then, first on the back of Jean's judgement, and then based on their shared experiences, he had formed a deep affection for them both. Actually, love; but he wasn't going to use the word. Why were they being so relentlessly pursued? Ten cops, all out on a Saturday night after a couple of kids? Ten police seen in one place was unheard of, except maybe drinking in the local bar. How had it come to this?

"Tell me what you're looking for, and maybe I can help."

Prudhomme laughed; he couldn't stop himself. "I like you, Claude, really, and that is a generous offer. I would have guessed that if I needed help in an investigation, you wouldn't be in the top thousand or so people who would volunteer, so really you have surprised me. You don't want people around here hearing about this Claude, because I can tell you, between us, they generally hate the cops.

"I think you know why we're here. We're not going away empty-handed this time, so if you really do want to help, and if you want to save a lot of time and possible damage to Jean's crockery, just tell me where we should start looking."

"Sorry, Chief, I don't know what you mean."

Prudhomme laughed. This was the criminal code for, "You've got me bang to rights, but you're going to have to do the work." They were in the yard now, and the three vehicles were letting out nine cops – seven uniforms, the Sergeant, and Prudhomme's plain-clothes driver. The Sergeant looked to Prudhomme for orders.

"Four in the house, if that's OK, Sarge" [the men found it annoying that he was so relentlessly polite, they preferred just to be told], "and I reckon three to sweep these outbuildings." He pointed comprehensively in the direction of the old pigsties, stables and bottling sheds that Jean had converted over the years for the operation of so many failed businesses.

Claude wondered just for a second if they had got away with it.

"And then two to the barn up there." Pointing to the building four hundred metres further up the hill.

Oh.

"They should shoot up in a car, just to be sure no-one's looking out and ready to run."

The Sergeant dispatched two immediately up the road, while the rest split between the farmhouse and outbuildings. Claude was invited to keep Hector quiet. The dog had been trained to bite uniforms at the smallest justification, and on Hector's scale of retribution the current invasion would warrant breaking skin. Claude decided he should give him some food; he put the meat from the fridge out for him without worrying too much about cubing, then diligently changed the time listed on the feeding note, as that had been agreed by everyone except Hector to be an excellent new system.

"OK, boy, it will be all right, Jean will be home soon," said Claude, sitting at the big outdoor table, stroking Hector's ears while he ate, and making sure the lead was well tied. The dog had loved having new visitors and extra attention for a while but didn't want all these strangers clattering around in the house now. He was OK with Claude but wanted his friend back.

"They'll all be gone soon, and we'll have a walk," Claude reassured him, but he wasn't confident, and Hector could tell.

As predicted, the sound of things being tipped out, tossed around, and breaking began to echo out of the house. Claude was annoyed. "Is that necessary? What you're looking for doesn't hide in a cut-lery drawer, does it?" Prudhomme was a civilised man and if you had asked him he would have strongly protested that he didn't like gratuitous vandalism. However he was also a policeman with twenty years' experience, and in all that time he had never attended a search at which quite a few things hadn't been shattered: clearly it was ingrained in him, and the rest of the force, that a crib could not be properly turned over without rather a lot of casual breakage. Indeed, several times he had reprimanded junior officers when property they were searching did not look sufficiently disordered to demonstrate they had investigated it adequately. But this time, sitting with Claude, he was embarrassed. He got up ready to go into the house and tell them to calm it down a bit, but just as he was calling to the Sergeant a whistle was sounded loudly – the Constables up at the barn. Signalling distress or sounding victory?

"Time to go, Sarge."

The uniforms swarmed like shooed flies out of the buildings and into the cars, and in thirty seconds they were all arriving at the barn. Their colleague was giving a thumbs up and a grin through the top floor window – so no distress. They piled in, led by Prud-homme and the Sergeant, with Claude infiltrating the group in the middle, seemingly unnoticed, and climbing the stairs with them. 'Blimey,' he thought, 'this place really stinks of pee.'

Inside the single huge room that topped the barn there was a heartbreaking sight for fans of Jack and Milo. They were sitting sad and small in pants and socks on a pair of wobbly put-you-up beds, with a massive cop silently looming over each of them. The scene was one of utter dejection, seasoned with apprehension and a good pinch of shock.

"What the hell's going on?" Jack tried to summon a bit of fightback as the man in charge approached them.

"I think you know that son," Prudhomme replied. "Do you have clothes here? If so, please put some on, we're taking you down to the police station."

"Why?"

Milo attempted a pure and pious face, but the last ten days had rather destroyed his innocence. Prudhomme turned round and left without bothering to answer, and everyone went with him except the two boys, Claude, and the two original captors.

Claude was angry with himself. It had been his idea to move them to the barn when they turned up at the Lodge shivering at 11.00pm the night before. They'd managed the escape well, exactly as Milo had planned, and found Claude's car where Daphne had left it, with the keys in, and thankfully unguarded by *gendarmes*, who had moved further down the river to the place where Charles's motor had finally settled on the river bed. With a lot of trial and error, Milo had driven them safely back to the Lodge. However, when they arrived, Claude decided that the Lodge would be the first place the police might come for them (he was right about that) and that they most likely wouldn't know about the outbuildings at the Farm (wrong). So he warmed them up and fed them hot food after Kate and Maggie had moved out, and then got them set up in what turned out to be their usual beds in the barn. He also found their spare clothes and got the Clown and Pierrot costumes to Bernie for mending, washing and pressing for the following night – the show must go on!

But, as we've seen, the barn was a terrible idea, and he'd played straight into the detective's hands. This was what sometimes happened when Jean wasn't around. It was a mess up, but too late to worry about it now, he had to concentrate on the kids. Both boys were working very hard to keep back tears, and Claude, with the nodded permission of the closest policeman, went to both in turn, knelt down and put an arm round them.

"This will be OK. Be strong."

"Can you find my mum, Claude?"

"I'll talk to the Chief Inspector now. Don't worry, I am coming to the *gendarmerie* with you, I won't leave. I'll ask him to send someone for Kate."

An hour later, in a tiny windowless interview room in the Bourges police station, five bodies were squeezed in, uncomfortably hot, deliberately so. The two boys had changed t-shirts and washed their faces. Milo's shirt was his Dessie's Dames special edition, which he had sensibly opted to wear inside out. Along their side of the table, Jack was sitting on one end, then Claude in the middle, then Milo. Opposite them were two people: Chief Inspector Prudhomme and a new face.

"This is Inspector Dodson, from the London police," Prudhomme started. "He has an interest in the case and has asked to be present at the interview." He was a bit uncomfortable to be introducing someone he had only spoken to once, briefly, on the phone and met just five minutes previously. Leopard had apparently talked to him on a couple of occasions and exchanged information about the case, before agreeing he could 'come and observe.' By the time Prudhomme found out about the arrangement, the man was well on his way; and Leopard's words had evolved into 'mutually assist.'

The police driver who had greeted Dodson off the train had told Prudhomme he was worried that the Inspector was perhaps a little unwell; he had been walking rather unsteadily on the concourse and seemed to be slurring slightly, though that might just be the quality of his spoken French. Dodson had assured him he was fine, just rather tired after sixteen hours of travel from London, with some very bad connections.

Dodson had been delighted to find the boys already in custody when he arrived at the *gendarmerie*, and when, as he greeted him, Prudhomme hinted that they could manage without his help during the questioning if he was tired, Dodson was insistent on being allowed to participate, "having come all this way to help," and suddenly they had found themselves in the interview room without further preamble.

"As it stands," Prudhomme announced to the two boys and their escort, "no-one has been charged with anything, no lawyers are present – if you want representation you are entitled to request it."

Claude, a man of some experience in these situations, had had a chance in the car to talk *sotto voce* to the boys in the backseat as they were being driven to the police station and told them to say absolutely nothing, not a thing. "Let's listen to what they say, do not reply, and we can call for a lawyer whenever you want. Your mum will be there, Jack."

"Where's the boy's mother, Chief Inspector, you promised she would be present."

"She's on her way, Monsieur. I had a quick talk to her on the telephone to introduce myself, explain the situation, and let her know I had taken over from Inspector Leopard; so she is prepared. We offered a police car to collect her, but apparently your daughter is bringing her."

Claude could sense something odd about Dodson, he wasn't quite sure what. A looseness of attention? Looking slightly in the wrong direction? Refusing to catch his eye? Perhaps it was just that he was English, where they do things differently. He was about to insist that they waited till Kate arrived, when there was a considerable commotion in the corridor outside, and the door was flung open. Claude could see Daphne in the hallway, but she wasn't allowed in, and Kate came through the door on her own. Prudhomme greeted her by the door and politely introduced himself.

She bustled round the table to take an empty chair next to Jack and was about to hug her son as she sat down, when she suddenly noticed Dodson.

"Oh my God, what are you doing here?"

"I could ask the same, you never notified me?" Dodson looked hugely shocked to see Kate, and a bit of something else, what was it?

"You know each other?" asked Prudhomme, surprised.

"Mrs du Lac and I have spent quite a few hours together in London over the past ten days or so as the case has been under investigation." Dodson seemed to be speaking a little wearily and extremely edgily. Prudhomme thought nervously, 'He has had a very long journey.'

"Of course," said Prudhomme, wary now that he was in the room with people who knew a lot more than him – that was never a situation he enjoyed.

[For your reference, by the way: Dodson does have schoolboy French, but nowhere near as good as Milo. Some of the interview is in English anyway, as Chief Inspector Prudhomme's language skills are excellent.

When French is spoken, in the interview and other subsequent scenes, some phrases are translated for Dodson and some for Milo, either by Kate, or Jack or Prudhomme. But we have not slowed down the narrative (it is quite slow enough already) by constantly highlighting and repeating these translated passages – in fact, as ever, you can just assume they took place!]

Kate could have told Prudhomme, if they had had a private moment, that Dodson had been very peculiar in his behaviour in London, and that she had felt almost threatened by him a couple of times, though it was a commonly acknowledged fact she did not scare easily. He had mainly worked on his own, hanging round almost every evening, asking many more questions than the other police officers, and always insisting she must let him know everything, and come to him first with any news. She didn't like him or his

768

style at all, but she had assumed most of this was because he was more dedicated to the case, and more diligent, than the rest of the cops, who came and went rather quickly.

"Would you like to start, Inspector?"

"Thank you, Chief Inspector, I appreciate it."

"Inspector, can I protest before you start. I have not had time to talk to my son at all since I have been here."

Dodson was an old-school copper, he could be polite to his superiors when he wanted something, and civil to witnesses when he needed cooperation, but otherwise he behaved as he wished, and he wasn't used to following too many protocols. He was irritated now because he had not expected to find the mother here and he was very unhappy to see her. Frankly, he had anticipated a compliant local force helping him get what he wanted without having to explain himself too much.

"Mrs du Lac, I think one point to remember is you shouldn't be here at all. I mean in France, not in the room. We agreed very clearly, I believe, that if you had any contact with Jack you would inform me immediately. Also, I thought it was plainly understood that you would not try to hide him or help him escape."

His voice was raised, but he didn't seem to realise it – everyone else in the room was disconcerted by the volume. Right now, the boys were terrified, even with Claude and Kate there. This was much worse than they ever feared – or more accurately, in Milo's case, this was actually his worst nightmare manifestly coming to life. Claude was trying not to show any emotion, but with his long experience of police conduct, he could sense where the British detective was hoping to take this.

"I came to look for him," said Kate, defensively, "I had no contact and didn't have any specific knowledge – I was just guessing."

"I see," Dodson came back aggressively. "Well, it looks like you 'guessed' right. But that doesn't mean we need to make time now for you to talk to Jack and Milo before this interview. You are here in the room now because the boys are relatively young, but they're no longer minors; this actually is a concession, not a requirement. Anyway, they are here to help us with our enquiries, no-one has been charged with anything."

Prudhomme now felt he needed to intervene, not only because he knew the nuances of the local laws in more detail, and intensely disliked Dodson making statements on what was and wasn't acceptable under their jurisdiction, but also because he could sense Kate didn't trust the Englishman. Besides, Dodson seemed to be getting more and more angry, so Prudhomme wanted to give him a chance to calm down; it was looking as though it hadn't been such a good idea to let him join the interview straight off the train.

"Why don't we just proceed cautiously?" Prudhomme suggested softly. "On the basis we need to start somewhere, a less official chat is probably a good way to get going. If the Inspector accepts it, let's agree that if you feel anxious at any stage, we can pause and decide on another course." However he tried to sweeten it, there was still the inevitable hint of a threat.

Dodson was fiddling with his French cigarettes during Prudhomme's speech, not quite able to work out how the local fag packets worked and wishing he had brought sufficient normal cigarettes from London. Claude and Jack both got quite excited about the implied permission to smoke until the Chief Inspector tapped the Englishman on the wrist unobtrusively [they all saw] and gently shook his head. Dodson might have sulked at this if his inability to extract one hadn't already made it irrelevant.

"OK," Dodson started brusquely, "Milo – you're Milo right? Can I start with you?

"On the night in question, when the fight took place in your mother's pub, you had just finished your exams before working behind the bar, is that right?"

Milo looked at Claude, who had advised him not to say a thing. Claude shrugged unhelpfully, indicating his counsel had not changed.

"That's quite a simple question, Milo," Dodson cajoled, "there's nothing incriminating there." Claude was beginning to realise what it was that was unsettling him about Dodson. Definitely a strong smell of whisky coming from somewhere. The room was airless and small, and the fumes were slowly filling it.

"Yes, I had just finished my exams on the evening you are talking about."

"And you were working behind the bar?"

"Yes, I did it often, I was properly registered as a member of staff, like my brothers."

"I know your brothers, as it happens. They weren't there that night?"

"No, it was one of the nights they were helping deliver toys and clothes for the church charity."

"So it was just you and your mum?"

"And a couple of our regular temps. I think we miscalculated how busy it was going to get." There was a "tut tut" and kick under the table from Claude, meaning 'Don't give out unsolicited information.'

"OK, so you were a bit understaffed, and the bar was pretty lively, I heard. Loads of kids from the schools celebrating, right?"

"I couldn't comment on that."

Claude was proud of his protégé; that's better. Dodson glared at Claude. Claude stared back, not at all fazed. But then, his freedom wasn't really on the line. And by now he was certain Dodson was three-parts drunk. That was something he really did have a lot of experience with; although, confusingly, in his world it was traditional for him to be drunk and the cops to be sober. Again, he thought, the English love being different. He caught Prudhomme watching Dodson and realised he had noticed the same thing.

"What was the mood like? You must have a view on that, it is not incriminating to say."

"The mood was great, to be honest. Everyone had finished their exams, school was breaking up, a lot of people were leaving school that day, it was a big night."

"A big night. So, lots of drink?"

"It's a pub."

"Yes, good point, good point. Would you say things were getting out of hand?"

"I couldn't comment."

Dodson did a kind of vague flapping wave between Milo and Jack, possibly indicating he was going to switch the spotlight from one to the other.

"What about you, Jack, could you comment on that? You were there, I think there is no debate about that, right?"

"I was there, I was of an age to be in a pub."

"And what about the atmosphere, what's your view, was it getting loud? Out of control?"

"All the locals were enjoying themselves and behaving."

"Locals?"

"Just saying, the locals were having a good time, the people who belong in that pub."

Dodson was looking very hard at him. One of his eyes was twitching quite violently. In his slightly rambling and rather repetitive questioning, his voice was modulating between 'much too loud' and 'a supposedly threatening whisper that tailed off into the inaudible.' Prudhomme was beginning to look desperate and wondering how he could pause it as quickly as possible. 'Jesus,' he thought, 'maybe I should have helped him light that cigarette.'

"So in that group – the locals, people who belong – you're including the leavers from your school and the girls' school next door, right? But it sounds like you didn't think other schools should be there, that was a problem for you?"

Jack decided to keep quiet.

"If others came in, you would interpret that as a challenge, some territorial thing, right?"

Jack kept silent.

"That's fine, you know. There's nothing wrong with you wanting to protect your patch from strangers, in fact, lots of people would say, 'Good on you.'"

Jack chose again not to speak. He was disconcerted that Dodson was sporadically shouting without realising it and finding some problems with pronunciation; he was beginning to have the same suspicion as Claude, and hoped one of the grown-ups was going to do something about it soon.

"OK," Dodson tried another tack, "let's move on. Can I just check, Jack, how old were most of these kids, would you say?"

"I thought we answered that already; they were school-leaver age."

"You know the legal age for drinking is eighteen, right? When's your birthday?"

Jack looked at his mum. This is what this is about? He could no longer resist the chipper response.

"I can't believe you've seriously crossed the continent to accuse me of underage drinking. The police must be really short of proper crimes."

Claude winced and squeezed his leg. Dodson's demeanour brightened. He was used to cheek; normally he liked it, welcomed it in interviews. Usually it indicated a cockiness, lack of discipline, love of the wisecrack, that could easily result in a giveaway comment or unwitting confession. This kid was really irking him, smug little git. He started laughing; it was really loud.

"Ha ha ha, no mate, no, I'm just pulling your leg on the booze, that's a very good point, well thought, well said."

[He looked around the table, was everyone else enjoying his little joke?]

"As you say, I am not the kind of policeman that travels the world to investigate alcohol misdemeanours. You're quite right."

More issues with diction, another knowing, bleary-eyed look at everyone round the table, another bizarre chuckle; this time was it beginning to turn a little sinister?

"When you say, 'proper crimes,' Jack, what would you be referring to – what counts as a proper crime in your experience, in your life?"

He gave Kate a contemptuous glance, indicating 'I blame the parents.' Jack looked at the table.

"What passes as a minor infringement in Jackland? Obviously there's drinking when you're seventeen, but we've discussed that. How about using a fake passport to enter France? Driving without a licence? Stabbing someone? No proper crimes for me to investigate, right?"

Everyone was sitting up very straight now. Claude's arm had crept round Milo, Kate's round Jack. Kate was about to jump in and ask how dare he accuse her boy, when Jack gave her the 'let it go' sign of the waving outfacing vertical palm with open fingers.

"In fact, Jack," Dodson pushed on, relentlessly, his voice unwittingly raised again, "I have been a bit negligent in explaining what I do do. Like in the proper crimes category. As you quite rightly pointed out, Jack, I am not the kind of copper that trots the globe for youthful drinking transgressions."

Everyone was transfixed now; it was a tough audience, but Dodson congratulated himself on finally getting their attention.

"As you ask, actually I am the very specific kind of officer who goes to foreign countries to investigate suspicious deaths, manslaughter and murder."

And there it was.

Milo and Jack bleached white; and Claude looked at Kate and Kate looked at Claude as they simultaneously called out: "Lawyer."

Half an hour later, Dodson was in the café round the corner nursing a coffee in one hand and a large whisky in the other, with a plate of cold eggs sitting in front of him, untouched. The coffee had been instructed by Prudhomme ("For God's sake, sort yourself out, man, what the hell do you think you're doing?"), and the whisky was a self-prescribed antidote to the caffeine. The eggs had seemed like a good idea at the time, but now it was making him feel sick to look at them as they congealed on the plate.

He wasn't sure why he felt quite this weird; it had been a very long trip, with plenty of time to kill on the ferry and various trains, and a bar in Paris while he was waiting, but he topped up his system all the time on the job in England and it always seemed perfectly fine. Perhaps it's because they all did it together there, and here he was on his own. France seemed strange. He downed the Scotch and nodded to the bartender for another double.

Meanwhile the boys in the police station were downstairs in a cell, trying to pretend they weren't shaken and sobbing, while upstairs in the lobby Kate and Claude were talking, feeling each other out, waiting for Claude's best lawyer to arrive. Claude had a few solicitors: he liked to think of them as a team of all the talents, each a specialist in one of his favoured offences. They were all good, as evidenced by the fact that Claude, though his record was by no means clean, had never actually been incarcerated.

"So, you've been looking after Jack and Milo while they've been taking part in the play?" Kate was incredulously teasing out what had been going on. The fears she had travelled with, of the lads starving under a bush in filthy rags, had been easily dispelled, but otherwise, she thought to herself, her current panic was more than justified because everything that had happened in the forty-eight hours since they'd arrived was so much worse than anything she could possibly have imagined. Her breathing had become irregular, and she didn't realise that Claude was doing everything he could to quietly calm and settle her down.

"Yes, starring in it, to be honest. They're brilliant – you saw it."

"Well, that wasn't what I was expecting, being honest, and I wasn't totally convinced it was them till halfway through. The programme said the actors were called Francois and Scott, I guess those are their stage names, right?" [This wasn't a joke, more of an accusation of collusion.] "But as you know very well, I didn't come for the light entertainment or the Experience, I thought I had come to rescue them. Or at least to be with them, to help."

"The thing is," Claude continued the soft approach, "they didn't know what had happened, genuinely, there was no contact. They believed, I reckon, that after ten days, as no-one had come for them, it must be fine – they were in the process of letting themselves relax just a bit."

"When I left England the lad was alive. Not in great shape; essentially it was intensive care for a couple of days, then it was described as serious for the next few days, but as time passed people were growing in confidence. I went to the hospital every day. How did it go backwards so quickly?"

"Listen, the boys told me they didn't do anything wrong, just self-defence. That's right, right? In that case, we just need to hang in there, get people to see sense."

At that moment, Claude's lawyer came through the door, his Grievous Assault expert, the most appropriate advocate available in the time given, and luckily the best in the region. The one drawback, if you were, for example, to see the world through Daphne's eyes, is that she is Dessie's sister, Cleopatra. Same build, same look (Claude was very fond of her), ten years' younger, and a very different fashion style, being all black suits and white shirts, even on rest days. Maybe Desdemona had sucked all the colour out of that family.

For the somewhat sad and obvious reason that they didn't have many regular solicitors with a handsome bosom, she was a bit of a favourite with the *gendarmes*, and the Desk Sergeant, Toffe, fell over himself with offers of a private room and coffee. He was thanked with a smile. Cleo liked to keep on good terms with everyone, on both sides, whenever she could, but she didn't want to give anyone the wrong idea or encourage familiarity.

"Now," she said, sitting down and gesturing to Claude and Kate to do the same. "Let's see what we can do. Claude gave me some very basic particulars on the phone, including the fact that the English policeman seems to be drunk, but I'd love to hear the boys' story from you, Mrs du Lac, if that is OK."

Kate's relief at meeting Cleo was huge but so was the lump of fear in her throat, making it hard for her to swallow and breathe. She started off in a gabbled whisper. "Thanks so much, Ma'am, please do call me Kate. Would you like me to go from the beginning?"

"Why not. And please call me Cleo. Just take your time Kate, there is no rush, most stories take a lot less time than people think, and we've got half an hour at least before the Chief Inspector wants us again. I'm presuming that is because he needs time to dry out the Englishman."

A small smile between them all, beginning to build the bond.

"OK, so, the two boys are Milo Kelly and Jack du Lac. Jack is my son, and Milo is his best friend. The Thursday before last they finished their exams, it was the last day of their school attendance. They went straight to the pub opposite their school – The King's Hind – to celebrate. Actually that pub is run by Milo's mother, Alice, and he had to help her behind the bar because some of the normal staff were absent.

"Kids kept coming in, not just from their school, but from the local girl's school, and then from several other local schools. Some troublemakers came in from a school called St Francis – they were also boys who were leaving and had just finished exams. You understand, I wasn't there. This history is assembled by friends and contacts who were eyewitnesses, including Milo's mother and Jack's friend, I say girlfriend, Maggie. I'm telling you this just as it was told to me.

"The hooligans started shouting, threatening, and one threw a glass at Milo's mum. Milo jumped over the bar and went at them, to defend her, and the pub, and to throw them out. On his own. Six of the yobs started beating him, so Jack and two others went to his aid. The other two didn't do much, apparently, except holding people back; all Jack could do was cover Milo with his own body to stop them sticking the boot in."

[Claude was puffing up with pride during the narrative. He had not heard these details before, and he was immensely proud of his boys, defending their mum, putting their bodies on the line for a pal: these were great virtues. Then he noticed Cleo rolling her eyes at him and let the air out before Kate could see.]

"Then one of the boys was standing over Milo and Jack, astride them on the floor, and drew a knife. Someone shouted 'blade' or 'knife,' and everything froze, they say. Then, trying to get them out, Jack pushed up off the floor, barging the attackers aside, and dragged Milo away. When he shoved upwards, he jolted the boy with the knife who was straddling them and he flew across the room, where he fell awkwardly onto his own blade. Jack never touched the boy, and never had a knife, and never grabbed or held the knife the boy was waving around.

"Then Jack and Milo and the two other boys, their friends who had tried to help, all ran. They didn't wait, they didn't look back. Everyone swears they would have had no idea if, or how badly, the kid on the floor was injured, they were out of the door too quickly. As it was the last day of school, they'd already planned to go straight on a holiday. We all thought it was to Yarmouth – the English seaside. But the plan was actually to go to France, to come and see his cousin. I didn't work that out for nearly a week.

"A couple of police – Constables, low-level, not Detectives – came and gave our house a once-over the next day after they'd started interviewing witnesses and begun to zero in on Jack and Milo. At that time, the injured youth was in hospital. He was put into intensive care for a few days, then came out of that and was described as 'serious but stable.' The police went to Yarmouth where the kids from our area appear to have booked loads of caravans for a massive party – dozens of them. No-one had a record of who was where, and nobody was saying much. It took the cops quite a few days to work out they were wasting their time, and in any case, I reckon they weren't throwing a lot at it, because right then it appeared to

779

be just a bit of affray, whoever was responsible, and the 'victim' seemed to be improving, or so I was told at the hospital. I heard the police who went to Yarmouth spent most of their time slumped on a bench in their shirtsleeves investigating raspberry ripple ice cream and keeping the local swimsuits under observation.

"So, we learnt almost a week later that straight after the fight, Jack and Milo and their two friends had headed for the port of Dover. When they were there, the two other boys, rather sensibly, turned back, and Jack and Milo crossed the channel on their own. It's now been suggested that they used the other boys' passports, so there was never a record of them entering France. Then they came down here, hung out with Jean, Claude and Daphne, by the sound of it, and got involved with the Experience, putting on a play. In the course of this activity they seem to have managed to alienate a troublemaking German youth to the extent that he eventually grassed them up.

"Anyway, the injured boy was up and down, but I was always told he was improving overall, and it was positive news; and of course everyone has been terrified and really anxious about him, but also worried about the boys being missing. Initially, as I said, the police seemed low-key, then suddenly came back much more strongly, this time a solo detective, the one who is here, who was all over us every day. Finally, presumably due to the strange German lad's resourceful family putting out feelers, the English detective was contacted, discovered the French connection, joined some dots, started asking about Mac…"

[Cleo nodded to say 'I know about Mac, you don't need to explain that bit.']

"…and asking about La Chapelle. One night Dodson asked me, did I know if they were there, did I know who might be hiding them. I honestly said I knew nothing, but then the boy Karl called Alice directly, and that's when we decided someone had to get out here to see what was going on.

"I checked before I left London and the wounded boy was still being described as serious but stable, but with good prospects, everyone thought he was past the worst; now this Inspector Dodson tells us he has died. When I arrived in La Chapelle my husband was a hated but largely insignificant fugitive; I barely came to terms with him being alive before he was ploughed to death in front of my eyes. The last time I saw my son before today, he was putting on a very funny play to great acclaim, then I watched him dressed in circus clothes chasing his dad down a hill, and you know what happened at the bottom. Now Jack is in custody being accused, if my French is still any good, of a murder in London. All in all, it's been a hectic two days."

Cleo looked up, sympathetically. Actually, she had known some of this from various other sources, but they weren't necessarily as trustworthy, and in any case she always found it invaluable to get a variety of different viewpoints, and she had sensed it was really helping Kate's extreme anxiety to take her mind off it by having to describe it.

"It is quite an ordeal; I am so sorry. Let's see what we can do to improve things."

"What can we hope for?"

"It is an interesting situation, in legal terms. I apologise, of course the technical aspect is of no interest to you whatsoever, but it might help us. The complexity is around extradition. We need to establish if they have actually been charged in England in their absence, and if so with what – it doesn't sound like it. Knowing the local *Magistrat* as I do," [Claude hid a smile] "if it comes to that, he will not I think be inclined to be hectored by an English policeman without a great deal of evidence and documentation.

"Ironically, what might be more of an issue is entering the country under false pretences. Of course, that is an offence in France, not England, so it would be nothing to do with this English Inspector. It might be the decision of a local court to ship the boys back to

Dover, they might even if they were unlucky get a fine or a small detention sentence, likely deferred. That might still be the least of our worries.

"Can I ask, do they have passports of their own? Why did they use the other boys' documents?"

Claude answered. "Jack told me, the other two boys did a runner from them in the port while they were queuing for the ferry. It seems all the boys had already given their passports to Jack at the ferry ticket office on the English side, as he was the driver, showing them to the Clerk. The other boys had changed their mind about the whole escapade, pretended to go to the washroom and never came back and never got on the ferry. So my theory is that when they got to the other side, Jack decided to give the official the other boys' papers so their names went into the entry log, and Jack and Milo did not exist in France. They do have their own passports still."

[Claude was back at the puffery again; this time out of delight at the resourcefulness of his protégés. 'Perhaps,' thought Cleo, when she noticed, 'the swelling up is some inverted display ritual indicating to prospective mates "this male is well-qualified for the rearing of criminal youth."' She decided to prick his ballooning waistcoat immediately.]

"So, regardless of the nonsense you have just told me, Claude, which I discard, and never listened to, it seems to me the most obvious explanation here is that Jack fumbled in the dark, had four passports, and inadvertently handed the wrong pair to the border official, who, also in the dark, accepted them and stamped them. It is a pretty natural mistake; anyone could understand that."

As they were establishing the natural mistake as an incontrovertible fact, the door opened and Sergeant Toffe walked in, rather than the most junior Constable in the station, who would normally have arrived on such an errand. Working painfully hard as a serious professional to look only at Cleo's chin, which seemed the safest spot to aim for, he announced that the Chief Inspector was ready to see them now. "He'll see you now," he repeated with a deep sigh as he led the way. Kate looked at his back in bemusement; the other two just shook their heads.

Back in the interview room, the two Detectives and the two boys were already waiting. Cleo led the way in, and when he saw her Prudhomme grimaced, anticipating what was coming. Back in his Bourges days he had known her well and had been badly bruised in the witness box on a couple of cases under her questioning. She was well known in Vierzon, though they hadn't sparred in the past couple of years.

"Good evening, Chief Inspector."

"Good evening, Cleopatra."

Dodson raised his eyebrows at the name, stared at her for much too long, and pushed himself forward in his chair, one can only say salaciously, leaning at an unfeasible angle, and dropping a hint to be introduced. Claude realised he was actually worse than before; the smell was everywhere. Prudhomme recognised the same thing and started to look panicked. How was he going to get out of this?

"This is Inspector Dodson, from London."

Cleo reluctantly reached out a hand and Dodson took it, shook it and then extended his grip so disturbingly that Cleo had literally to scrape him off.

"We definitely don't have anything like you where I come from," Dodson drawled disconcertingly.

Cleo was startled, then charitably decided to assume it was a mistranslation, or some kind of English form of compliment she had not understood, so she professionally elected to ignore it and move on.

"Before we begin, can I inquire, Inspector," asked Cleo, settling herself in the chair between Jack and Milo, giving them a reassuring nod and "Hello," putting her briefcase on the desk, and beginning to take out notebooks, pens and other lawyerly paraphernalia, "what authority you come here under?"

Kate, resuming her seat next to Jack, felt encouraged already; this was the perfect person to have on their side. Jack and Milo sensed the same. The English Inspector looked at Prudhomme in bewilderment: was he going to do anything to shut this woman up? Policemen of his rank were used to being on the front foot. In London he would never have allowed himself to be spoken to like this, specially not by a low-life criminal defender, particularly a female. Prudhomme could see he was about to say something inappropriate and stopped him with a hand lightly on the wrist, indicating he would speak instead. Somewhat miraculously, Dodson deferred.

"The Inspector is here at our invitation to assist in an investigation, in the spirit of neighbourly cooperation between brother police forces."

Cleo paused the arrangement of her desk accessories for a moment and looked up at Prudhomme quizzically. Really?

"That's wonderful, Chief Inspector, my heart is warmed by thoughts of global law enforcement bonding with itself. The fraternal embrace – it is quite inspiring. But forgive me for being precise – is the Inspector helping you with your enquiry, or are you helping him with his? It is rather different, no? When you say you invited him, would it be more accurate to say he asked to come here, and you said OK?"

"You're splitting hairs, Cleopatra."

Dodson was sweating now and fidgeting hotly in his chair; he was used to doing what he wanted, whenever he wanted. His first contact in the case had been Leopard, and he was much more comfort-

784

able with the style of his response, that guy really was all about the result and doing it his own way. They'd shared some pretty good stories about what he liked to call legacy policing. Prudhomme was turning out to be a different prospect, a boss's man by the feel of it; little willy wet pants. He chuckled to himself. Little willy. Everyone wondered why he was laughing and pretended not to notice.

"It matters, Chief Inspector Prudhomme. It seems to me, forgive me for saying, that the paperwork for this interrogation is not quite in order. The Inspector here is not really aiding in a French case, is he? It appears that you are assisting in an English case, as that is where the crime – if any crime happened – is alleged to have actually taken place. Am I right?"

Prudhomme shuffled some papers in front of him. He was uncomfortable. He was a stickler for proper conduct and annoyed with the English detective for putting him in a difficult position. It didn't surprise him in the least that Leopard had got him involved in this farrago, and he made a note to add that to the list of his infractions. It was also obvious Dodson wasn't at all bothered by the bureaucratic no-man's-land they were flailing around in, so as well as being inebriated he was an ethical landmine. But probably the greatest source of his displeasure was that Cleo, whom he generally admired as well as secretly feared, was completely right about the situation, had summed it up perfectly, and probably wasn't going to let it go.

"OK, I am going to take that as a 'yes,'" she went on, "in which case," turning to Dodson, "as you are detaining these lads, I'd like please to see your international warrant."

"Well," said Dodson, finally cracking under the pressure of being nice to a lady lawyer, "I'd like please to see your tits, but I don't think that's going to happen either, is it?"

Chaos ensued. Dodson was mystified – among his mates at the local nick, that crack would have gone down a complete storm.

Claude got up to defend the honour of his girlfriend's sister; Kate grabbed him by the belt and pulled him back down. Jack and Milo burst out laughing before realising they mustn't find it funny and attempting to retract their mirth. And Prudhomme was halfway through remonstrating with his unwanted colleague, their faces no more than twenty centimetres apart, when Dodson suddenly disappeared from his view mid-sentence under the impact of a heavy slap from Cleo, which, taking him by surprise in his highly intoxicated state, sent him reeling. Off balance, he tilted over an inconveniently positioned chair and ended up prostrate on the sticky vinyl tiles with blood pouring out of his nose.

Cleo stood above him, glaring hotly. "That's the way *on sort les poubelles* round here, you pig."

'She's so like her sister,' thought Claude, with a complex mix of emotions we do not unpack here, and another unforced swelling of the chest.

Taking the French outlook, bearing in mind the severity and satisfaction of the blow, an aggressor would, I think, have accepted that the point had been sufficiently and acceptably made, and the situation had been resolved. At this stage, the humiliated abuser would even, I suspect, have risen, brushed himself off, apologised profusely for the appalling lapse in etiquette, thanked his assailant for the well-deserved lesson in manners, and begged permission to resume the meeting in a more decorous manner.

But Dodson sadly didn't see it like that.

He scissored his legs round Cleo's as she straddled over him and levered her down sharply beside him on the floor where she slumped just within his range for a sharp elbow jab into the left eye that left her screaming. Then there followed a vicious heel into her shin, shredding her stocking from knee to ankle and opening up a long bloody gouge. Cleo managed to get one kick into his testicles, trying to defend herself, and some fingernails across the cheek, but it didn't stop him, he was in a frenzy, and raised a fist the size of a pint pot ready to bring it down onto her face. Fortunately, Milo, the closest, was too quick and caught the detective's arm and bent it back behind him before he could land the blow.

At that point it felt like the interview was over.

After Claude and Prudhomme pulled the two apart, and Kate had taken Cleo to the officer's latrine to mop her streaming puffy eye and gashed leg with a dirty towel, Dodson was put in a cell to cool off. The Chief Inspector then made a difficult call to his boss to brief him. On occasion, when the situation warranted it, his boss had been known to have a robust telephone manner; and this was one of them. However, although his ears were red and stinging, Prudhomme managed to get the message across that due to the maverick presence of the English cop (which to his shame he blamed squarely on Leopard), and that man's assault on a French officer of the court, plus the confusion about jurisdiction, and his reluctance to detain the young boys overnight, they had a very big problem, and they needed to resolve it immediately if they could.

Prudhomme's Superintendent, once his anger cooled, which took a few more minutes of steam-letting, finally agreed, and said he would see if he could get the *Magistrat* on duty to attend immediately. This week the judge on the roster was *Magistrat* Dompler, who as it happened is also known in his private moments as Bernadette's older brother Christophe, hence the surreptitious smiles earlier. Please don't get the wrong idea, there will be no corruption here: this is a character revered throughout the region for his honesty. Also, for fairness and good sense, but legendary as well for his unpredictability. He sides only with the facts, and they can go in many directions. Claude did grin when he knew Christophe was going to be called in, but it was definitely not because he thought the case could be fixed; only because he knew it would be fair.

[Claude was one of Dompler's oldest friends, in fact they were in the Resistance together in the war; but such connections are inevitable in the area. If the *Magistrat* had recused himself every time a friend or relative had appeared before him as a suspect, witness, or

787

legal representative, he would never have heard a single case.]

After ten minutes of pleading, begging and emotional blackmail from Prudhomme's boss, none of which had quite the same impact as the thirty-second phone call he got from Claude, *Magistrat* Dompler reluctantly agreed to convene the midnight courthouse (which was handily in the same building as the *gendarmerie*) as *juge d'instruction*. The midnight court was assembled only rarely in Bourges, generally for the aftermath of the more drunken festivals, the rowdier Saint's days, and for the away supporters at the annual football match with Vierzon. A midweek sitting to hear a case against two young English boys was naturally unheard of, but perhaps that was one of the elements that piqued Dompler's interest.

In the course of an hour and a half of preparation he read the files and interviewed the key personnel in succession. First, the *Magistrat* spoke shortly with the boys and Jack's mother, chaperoned by Cleo and Claude. The meeting with the accused boys was held so that the *Magistrat* could briefly assess their characters and the state of their minds to make sure it was wise to proceed.

Then Dompler interviewed the English Inspector and the French Chief Inspector together. Dodson was in a very bad way, which didn't endear him to the *Magistrat*, who in twenty years in charge of the court had seen many hundreds of inebriated defendants in the dock but had never once had an intoxicated cop in his chamber. Dodson, even in his highly-liquored condition, suddenly realised he had strayed into contact with a man who had the power to end his career, and he soon lost whatever was left of his nerve. Under persistent interrogation from the *Magistrat*, the exhausted policeman panicked and told him the truth, something he had rarely in his life done willingly. After getting some contact details from Dodson's notebook, Dompler asked a Constable to take him out for a walk in the cold night air, with the instruction to the Inspector to drink only coffee this time, no chasers. "You are going to be questioned in open court in less than an hour, you understand? Pull yourself together." Dodson nodded, but though the Constable managed to keep him out of the bars he failed to find the hip flask in his pocket.

After they'd left, requesting the Chief Inspector to sit and listen in, Dompler made two telephone calls to England, to the numbers and names provided by Dodson, using his authority as a senior Judge to wake up people who, though very senior, were not quite important enough to refuse a sitting judge. In fact both parties were happy to cooperate once they learnt the situation.

When they had gathered the information, *Magistrat* Dompler spent five minutes quietly talking to the Chief Inspector, explaining what he was planning. In the private chamber he also reprimanded Prudhomme severely for several elements of his own behaviour. He was not his boss; but his opinion in some ways counted for even more. Prudhomme was shaken, but on this occasion didn't try to apportion the blame to Leopard. Finally, Dompler admonished him to keep all their deliberations absolutely confidential until the facts were revealed in court. They could see where this would be going, but nevertheless Dodson had to be given a fair and unprejudiced opportunity to defend himself.

It was nearly 1.00am when Dompler entered the courtroom where everyone had been assembled to stand before him. He had with him his Clerk, and two Constables, just to emphasise, if anyone had any doubt, that this was an official event. The second Constable had just brought Dodson back from his walk; from his demeanour there was no evidence that the Englishman's level of sobriety had increased, but there was nothing more to be done about that now. He was seated at the table normally reserved for the prosecution, and Prudhomme was deputed to sit next to him, notionally to translate for him, but in reality to keep him under control.

Milo and Jack were across from them at a table at the front of the court usually reserved for the defence, facing the *Magistrat* and his Clerk. The boys were drained and white, Cleo was doing her best to keep their spirits up, but this was the hardest moment of their lives. She was currently standing behind them with a hand on each boy's shoulder; she had a sparkling white bandage around her left leg now, from ankle to knee, and her eye socket was gradually changing from red to blue – a hard day at the office.

Kate and Claude were sitting directly behind the boys, on the front row of benches, designated as family. Daphne and Caroline were forming an audience up in the public gallery together with Amelie, Albert and Maggie, all picked up by Daphne from the Lodge.

[Bernadette was with Jean, and in any case felt her brother the *Magistrat* might appreciate it if she stayed away; Dessie had not been informed on the express wishes of her sister.]

Magistrat Dompler then banged his gavel to commence proceedings. Cleo took her seat between Milo and Jack.

"I am very disappointed to have been called out at night to examine such a disgraceful collection of events. Trust me, I am not intending to allow this hearing to be very prolonged.

"I feel the first focus here, from which all other elements will follow, is to establish some facts with Inspector...," he looked down at his notes, "...Dodson.

"Inspector, it feels as though you have made a somewhat questionable trip from England, which requires some explanation."

Milo and Jack began to wonder what was going on. This wasn't what they had expected. They looked round at Kate and Claude, and beyond them up to Daphne and the others – they got the same questioning shrugs, supportive nods and thumbs. Cleo motioned to them to sit still, look to the front and focus on the Judge.

Magistrat Dompler was about to continue, when he looked up and was annoyed to see Dodson slumped in his chair.

"Please stand up, Inspector, when I am addressing you. In fact, will you please step up there into the witness box, so we can all hear you clearly, and you can see and hear me without any confusion."

Dodson struggled to get up. The *Magistrat* signalled to the Constables to help him up the short flight of steps into the box, which was set like a pulpit, rising above the rest of the courtroom, but below the god that was the Judge. When he arrived in the box, Dodson leaned heavily forward over the back of the witness chair, just achieving enough of the perpendicular to satisfy the *Magistrat*.

"If you could rise, too, Chief Inspector." Prudhomme shot up instantly; if at that moment the Judge had told him to eat one of his own fingers he would have called for the mustard.

"Now," the *Magistrat* continued, "Inspector Dodson, you gave some interesting testimony to myself and the Chief Inspector in my chambers. Since then I have personally checked out your information by phoning London. I now consider these facts to be established so long as they are confirmed by you in this hearing."

Silence now throughout the courtroom, what was this?

"Perhaps you would therefore like to make a statement to the court, repeating what you told me, and then answer some questions. Is that OK?"

Everyone was sitting up straight, on the edges of their seats; this was getting really interesting. Dodson lost his grip on the chair-back in front of him, half-staggering before catching it again and pushing himself up and raising his head to look at the *Magistrat*. He nodded at the Judge: OK, he would do as he asked. He proceeded, slurring occasionally, in English with some French words mixed in. Kate and others were translating to those around them as necessary; the Judge understood perfectly well.

"Although I am a senior detective in the East End of London, where the crime took place, and, though the team I am a part of was handling elements of the enquiry, I was not allocated to the case myself, so if I seemed to represent myself to Mrs du Lac at any time as one of the main investigators, that would have been a confusion on her part."

The Judge frowned; that wasn't quite the wording they had agreed. Kate was looking bemused. She'd been conned?

"And the Chief Inspector here, you misled him too?" the *Magistrat* asked.

"I don't think so. I spoke to Inspector Leopard several times. He knew my story when I arranged my visit, he may not have passed it on, I don't know about that. I didn't realise he wouldn't be here when I arrived. I can see the new Chief Inspector may have believed I was the man in charge, but I don't recall saying that personally and there was no time to correct that impression."

Prudhomme looked at his shoes, his face reddening. Obviously the question the Judge was kindly not asking was, 'And the Chief Inspector never bothered to check it himself?'

"Are you in the Murder Squad, as you implied to all these people?"

"Well, yes and no, your honour,"

[Dompler's eyebrows shot up, which was usually all the warning a witness or accused in his court needed that they had gone off message and irked him: Dodson was supremely ignorant.]

"I am connected to the Murder Squad. I used to be. I was on high-profile cases for twenty-five years, and I used to be a lead detective, but because of some issues over recent years I am now on less sensitive and less stressful duties, and because I am coming up to retirement, I usually do more groundwork, door-to-door canvassing, desk research kind of thing."

"So let's just please be clear, Inspector, for the benefit of the whole court. Are you, or are you not, yes or no please, a current member of the Murder Squad."

"Actually not currently, your honour."

Dompler waited.

"So, no, your honour."

"Thank you, Inspector. Now, can you please inform us, the investigation was run out of your police station in East Ham. Were you or were you not allocated to the case, the case of the affray and knife injury in…" [checking his notes] "…The King's Hind pub?"

Everyone in the court – Kate, Claude, the boys, Cleo, the Clerk and the Constables, the friends in the gallery – was hanging on every word in silence; an eyelash falling onto cotton wool would have sounded like Handel's Messiah.

"Not specially … specifically."

"Inspector, for clarity, were you allocated to the case, yes or no."

"I'd say no, your honour."

Gasps rustled round the room, followed by muttering and some conversation. Dompler banged his gavel three times and waited for quiet.

"And why were you not allocated to the case when all your colleagues were?"

"Because I'm related to someone involved in the case. The Station Commander wouldn't let me be assigned."

"And what is the relationship?"

Absolute silence now.

"The relationship is that the victim is my nephew. Bart's my sister's boy."

The courtroom came alive with shouts and movement, people standing, yelling to each other, screaming at Dodson. *Magistrat* Dompler struck his gavel again three times, and held both arms above his head:

"Everyone – please – shut up and sit down."

People settled. He started again.

"So when you spent so much time with Mrs du Lac in London, and when you travelled out here, you were in fact not operating as a *bona fide* detective investigating the case, you were pretending to do so?"

"That could be thought."

There was a giggle in the court, quickly hushed.

"You mean 'yes,' is that right?"

"All right, yes."

"And when you travelled here to France, far from acting in a professional police capacity, actually you were representing your own and your family's interests?"

Dodson thought much harder about the question than was strictly necessary in order to come up with the answer.

"That would appear to be the case."

"Thanks for your candour, Mr Dodson," the *Magistrat* responded, sarcastically, careful now to drop the man's official title.

"So I think we may have got to some truth and understanding. Now, I believe there is something else you feel you would like to say to the court?"

"What was that, my lord?" asked Dodson, promoting him obsequiously, but sounding vague.

"This is where we in the legal world sometimes fall back on the phrase 'You tell me,' Mr Dodson. I believe you wanted to say something about your nephew."

"Oh yes, thank you."

Everyone waited, nothing happened.

"You can carry on," the Judge nudged him.

Dodson nodded, but again paused for a lengthy period as he struggled to get it out. While he did so his body folded slowly down over the back of the chair he was leaning on, which had the effect for those below in the well of court of making him gradually disappear from view. There was a muffled slap-slapping noise, like a saucepan of cooling custard spilling onto linoleum. Then Dodson unhurriedly reappeared and assumed the nearly upright once more, wiping his mouth on his jacket sleeve.

The Judge, from his position, had seen it all, but he had also seen it all before, and was completely unfazed. He nodded to the Clerk to give Dodson the water jug and glass.

"Maybe a rinse is in order, Dodson..." [now he had also dropped the Mr] "...When you are ready, I believe you have the announcement."

Dodson rolled the water around in his mouth, thought seriously about spitting it out, then reluctantly swallowed it, lumps and all. Finally prepared, as prepared as he ever would be, he spoke out, croakily.

"The boy is not dead."

Of course, the Judge knew this already, and so did Prudhomme, but for the others in court, this was a revelation that altered their lives. Everything changed at that moment. The chatter and yelling started again, there were actual cheers, and again Dompler brought down the gavel.

"Please be quiet. Be patient. We are nearly there.

"Now, Mr Dodson, could you please explain why you chose to tell such a vile lie to the police, the accused, their families, and their legal representative?"

"I never said he was dead. I understand they might have got that impression, but you can't blame me for that, can you?"

"That's a matter of opinion. Let's try it another way, then. Why would you want to leave them with that impression, when you could so easily have clearly told them the truth?"

"Being honest..." [Dompler rolled his eyes at this, but said nothing], "...it is a legitimate tactic in the police to sometimes make the suspect think things are worse than they are. It weakens them and can make them more likely to confess, and to turn on each other. That is what I expected. I was sure two soft kids like that would stab each other in the back." Realising what he'd said, he stopped suddenly and had a quiet chuckle to himself, muttering under his breath, "That's a good one, I must remember..."

"DODSON! Please focus."

"Yes, sorry, your honour. So, my idea, my plan was that I wanted them to accuse each other or give themselves up, so I could take them back to England without a struggle. I didn't realise the mother would be here, or these other people..." [His sweeping gesture, encompassing pretty well everyone in the court, threw him completely off balance, and he only just prevented himself from falling out of the witness box.]

"I wanted the French Police to appreciate the heinous nature of the crime, I assumed from my talks with Leopard no-one would stop me taking them. Once they were in England, my family, my friends in the force… I could make sure they got the kind of punishment they deserved."

Although he had turned a shade of white never seen before, and was slurring and bobbing badly now, Dodson in his mind felt he was having a resurgence, evidenced by how loudly and forcefully he was putting across his rather brilliant points. Dompler, not about to accept a counterattack, even an imaginary one, cracked down with the gavel, and addressed the English policeman and, over his head, the courtroom in general.

"Please do not shout at the court, Monsieur.

"Your statement would be all very well, Dodson, except for a couple of things, perhaps three. I will list them, if it is all right with you?"

Dodson muttered politely "Of course," perhaps not entirely recognising the rhetorical nature of the question.

"Chief Inspector, could you please go and stand by the box and translate for Mr Dodson as required? Mind your shoes."

Prudhomme, as previously noted, could deny the Judge nothing at this time, even standing in a pool of warm sick to pointlessly interpret for a paralytic Englishman.

"First, Mr Dodson, you were masquerading as a police official when you have admitted you had no authority, and that rather undermines your interview technique."

Dodson tried to put his face into a "Did I really masquerade?" expression but couldn't quite shape it.

"Second, I spoke to your Station Commander in London by telephone earlier, and he informs me that it is unlikely any charges are going to be brought in this case. He agrees he was disappointed and suspicious that the boys Jack and Milo had left the scene, but plenty of other witnesses have provided sworn testimony that the fight was started by the other boys – essentially your nephew's gang."

Dodson's eyes were dropping bottomlessly now. It wasn't only that he couldn't stay awake, it was also that nodding off was such an attractive method of escape, and so much less effort than his only other idea, which was to start a tunnel through the floor of the witness box with its opening cunningly camouflaged as a pool of his own vomit.

"Dodson, are you in there?"

Dompler tried hard to be polite in all circumstances, but he'd glanced up to see the Inspector looking totally blank, seemingly fast asleep, and found his patience tried. He gave Prudhomme a glare to remind him it was his job to keep Dodson awake; and sent him several signals suggesting how to do so, miming the elbow in the ribs, the slap on the back of the head, and what appeared to be a poke in the eye but was more likely to be a misdirected attempt at a finger in the chest.

"I need to continue. The clock is against us, so I am sorry but I don't think we have time to wait for you to catch up with us Inspector.

"According to the witnesses quoted by your own superior, it appears that the boy Bart produced the weapon; that the actions of Kelly and du Lac were reactive and primarily in self-defence; and that your nephew's knife wound was accidental, effectively he fell onto his own weapon. Your boss told me he had to speak to you because your views on this were not in line with the squad and you wouldn't let it go."

Dodson's whole head was now regularly falling, his chin hitting his chest every few seconds, then bouncing back off it as he half woke and tried to raise his gaze, then dropping again, then jerking up again – I think you get the idea.

"Third, I spoke to the Doctor supervising your nephew's treatment and he informs me that, as we have learned, far from being dead, he has improved so sufficiently that a full recovery can be confidently anticipated. He is expected to leave hospital in the next few days. In that case it makes it even more unlikely there will be any charges, except…" looking at Dodson "…a possible charge against your nephew for carrying a weapon, pulling it on someone in a fight, and initiating an affray."

Dodson's head was down again, his short flurry of self-justification had put the finishing touches to his exhaustion. He was done and could talk no further. The *Magistrat* saw it; he had observed that look many times before.

"Very well, I'll say no more on this aspect. But there are a couple of other things we need to deal with.

"As an experienced officer you may realise you are in a precarious situation. There are a number of things under our law here in France that you could be charged with, but let us focus primarily on two of them.

"The first is impersonating a policeman. I don't know about England, but I can assure you in France this is a serious offence. We have mentioned it already, and you have not denied it happened, but claim there was a misunderstanding. I am not sure this would succeed as a defence."

The *Magistrat* was growing increasingly irritated at Dodson's comatose condition. He had at least hoped to elicit some dread from the detective at the potential charge, but he might as well be accusing the lettuce in his fridge of being too wilted to be included in the salad for all the brain cells that Dodson was engaging in his terror of the court. There would be no judicial gratification here, he should move swiftly to get this done.

"Lucky for you, I have spoken with our Chief Inspector, and we have mutually agreed not to prosecute this charge against you. It would make for a long case, which would not reflect well on policing in general, through no fault of our own force…" [Was there an ironic pause and glance towards Prudhomme at this point?] "… which would be regrettable. Mrs du Lac might think otherwise in England, of course, and that would be her decision to pursue."

No reaction from Dodson. He was off the hook for one of the charges, but without consciousness of the threat there can be no celebration of the reprieve.

"The second and even more serious charge concerns the assault you made on the advocate representing the boys."

Now Dompler was signalling Prudhomme once more with a series of boxing-style 'jab jab' gestures to actively prod Dodson to wake him up. The *Magistrat* was racking his head to find the legal precedents he must have studied in law school forty years ago for interrogating witnesses while they were asleep, or even for trying and convicting defendants while they were unconscious. Maybe it would come back to him later. He considerably raised the volume of his voice.

"Do you not understand, man, that even at a basic level, assault is an offence that warrants a custodial sentence? And the length of that is substantially enhanced if the person you attack is an officer of the court, especially during the execution of their duties? This goes to the heart of the protection of the judicial system itself."

He threw that in to impress everyone, especially Dodson, of the enormity of the situation. Certainly Dompler had the public gallery agog, which made it half worthwhile, he thought, to work past 1.00am; but he was ever more frustrated that his perpetrator was so blissfully ignorant of the whole proceedings. Dodson's befuddlement placed him beyond fear, sarcasm or humiliation – all the arrows in the judicial quiver were blunted against the shield of his catatonia. Dompler was preaching to the defeated; he decided to wind it up.

He beckoned to Cleo to approach the side of his bench. When she did so, they had a whispered conversation, extremely respectful and very intense, which was accompanied by a great many gracious and obliging bobs, bows, nods and curtsies. After a final interchange of civilities, Cleo returned to her place between Jack and Milo, and *Magistrat* Dompler continued.

"Despite the jeopardy you find yourself facing in respect to this extremely serious physical assault, French justice, and its advocates…" [he made another splendidly appreciative gesture towards Cleopatra] "…can be compassionate, even where mercy is not even vaguely merited.

"I have consulted with the Defence Advocate who was the victim of your attack, and earlier with our Chief Inspector, and the consensus decision is that it is not in the best interest of anyone involved to open a prosecution. The court thanks the Defence Advocate for her generosity in not pursuing a charge, which I can inform you is almost entirely due to her desire for you to leave France as soon as possible, to prevent you from bothering her clients any further. And also so she never has to see you again."

Cleo nodded; retribution would be gratifying, but her first thought was for the boys she was representing.

Now Dompler instructed Prudhomme by use of the international sign of upturned palms on arms extended from elbows tucked into the waist flipping up and down as though tossing a baby ten or fifteen centimetres in the air to 'Please try to make Dodson stand up straight for a while.'

The volume in his voice rose another level, so he was almost shouting. "Dodson, if you can hear me, I think you will also agree with me you have not distinguished yourself or your police badge. Your conduct today has been extraordinary, dangerous and utterly ignominious.

"There is a mail train to Paris leaving I believe in…" [consulting his watch] "… just over two hours, and I suggest – actually I insist – you should catch that and get back to England as quickly as you can. Hopefully for your sake you will arrive before too many people have noticed you are missing, though I believe you might be in for an interesting interview with your Chief before you return to work."

General sniggers. Gavel crack.

"Enough of that: the rest of you, you're really in no position to sneer. My recommendation, Inspector Dodson…" [kindly re-promoting him, though as a form of admonishment] "…is that you think hard during your journey about what you intend to say about your adventures here when you return to England. Remember we have witness statements from multiple policemen of various ranks, officers of the court, and my own records of the proceedings, describing your conduct."

Dodson was past understanding what was happening to him now, and the hints he was being given, and was just standing with his hands clasped in front of his bruised genitals. If there was a thought in his head it was as tiny as the cerebral ganglia of a snail wondering when the thrush was going to stop smashing it against the rock. Please make it all finish soon.

"Our Chief Inspector Prudhomme will give you a lift to the train station and wait with you for the train, I trust you will buy him a cup of coffee for his trouble. Do you understand me?"

Prudhomme took Dodson by the arm and led him out. Watching, Claude was reminded of the final scene of the Harlequinade, and greatly regretted he didn't have his handcuffs and little wheelbarrow with him so he could help.

The *Magistrat* looked at the two Constables; the three of them exchanged sighs and eyerolls as he thanked them effusively for attending to their duties at such an hour and dispatched them to their beds, explaining to all and sundry that these fine servants of the court had earned the rest of the night off.

"OK," said Dompler, once they had left, "I will do you the honour now of treating you all as French – even you, Claude." [Some polite laughter in the court at the Judge joke.] "Can I just mention, this is not the normal way of doing business in the French courts, but in the selection of your friends, you boys have been lucky – for a change, by the sound of it – and you have come before me with unimpeachable testimonials."

[He looked at Claude while he said this with the expression: 'If you've got this wrong, whether you are my brother in arms or not, you will do the goddam jail time for them yourself.']

"This is what we will do. For the single accusation my court recognises, which is that of entering France under false documents, Maurice will send your real passports to his contacts in the border force with an explanation of the mistake, so that they can be properly endorsed and your status here can be regularised. Do you have them with you?"

The boys indicated they did not, remembering they were buried in Jean's barn within the secret most hidden compartment of the forgotten Morris Minor, like treasures interred in the tomb of Tutankhamun.

"I understand, but please make sure they reach Maurice tomorrow. The procedures for getting the passports processed will take I would imagine at least eight weeks. Chief Inspector Prudhomme has agreed that this is an acceptable way forward and will reflect this in his reporting.

"You boys are released under the supervision of Claude and Jean, when he is available, at Jean's farm. You will work for them, without pay I suspect…" [A little Judge-joke titter.] "…until your passports come back, at which time you are free to travel in France, or to return home, as you wish.

"For the potential accusations made from England, investigating those is not under my jurisdiction anyway; nothing official is on the record here about that, and I will not pursue it. Again, Chief Inspector Prudhomme has acquiesced to this decision.

"I tell you one thing you should remember. If I thought for one moment you were actually guilty of anything, especially a knife attack, we would not be resolving the issue like this.

"If you want my opinion, I believe you will not hear about this again, I cannot believe Dodson will be in a position to pursue you.

"My impression from his boss is that he will be retiring early. I doubt he is going to tell anyone in England about events here, because if he takes it further the fact he attacked an officer of the court in Central France will be exposed, and I understand that even in England that is frowned on."

[Pause for proper Judge-joke laughter.]

"I also think these points are being strongly emphasised to our departing detective by Chief Inspector Prudhomme as they wait together at the railway station, as it is certainly in the best mutual interest of both of them that the matter is laid to rest.

"Do you have any questions? No? OK, now go, please, I need sleep."

And that was it.

Shortly after, Jack and Milo spilled out into the cold French summer night with Claude, Kate, Amelie, Albert, Maggie, Daphne and Cleo following them a few metres back, giving them a little space to revel, and believe they were free. What a day. When Maggie moved in to hug Jack, she had been in France forty-eight hours and had spent only a few minutes with him, when he was bent over the corpse of a dead father. Amelie had been just about to embrace Jack herself, but quickly stepped back, thankfully unnoticed, when

Maggie beat her to it; she smiled inscrutably as she put her arms around brother Albert instead, who gratefully reciprocated. Daphne and Milo clasped each other like inebriated sailors falling out of a bar, laughing uproariously. Then everyone broke up, reformed and regrouped, like a country dance, and Milo and Jack found themselves clinging together again.

Claude had stopped on the steps to light cigarettes for Cleo and himself. They watched the boys. "It will take them a while. Shall we find a drink and settle everyone down?"

Milo and Jack had been suspected, accused, prosecuted, found guilty, defended, proved innocent, exonerated and released all in twelve hours, after having lived under a cloud of uncertainty, stigma and regret for ten days. The boy was alive. The relief was like fresh air after holding their breath much too long. Then Jack remembered Mac, dead to him for three years, alive for a week, and dead again now, and cried. Milo sensed what he was feeling and held him closer.

Finally, Jack was ready to seek his mother. He found Kate in the melee with her back to him, touched her shoulder, and as she turned, fell into her arms, crying his heart out.

Leaving those two on their own, with a signal to all the others (jazz hands with half-closed fingers and a nod backwards towards Kate and Jack) to 'Let's give them a minute,' Claude began to push everyone else up the road, like a good sheepdog, leading from behind. There was a bar just up the street, on the corner of the cathedral square, with its light still on, and a bored barman idly listening to the radio while he waited for the shift-workers, road-sweepers, street-walkers and night-coppers to come in for coffee and brandy on their way to or from work. Amazed to see an advocate and her clients coming in to celebrate a victory in the small hours, he was ready to be sulky, but warmed to them when they bought him a cognac so he woke up the cook to make some *croque monsieurs* to go with their champagne.

Being honest, I think I am getting prepared to leave them there, my work feels done. The story nearly ended when Mac died, and we have no more to worry about now, with the English school-boy undead, and the drunken detective departed; no drama left, no jeopardy, no mystery, nothing to wait for. You literally know everything I know.

AFTERMATH

Without Mac, the tension died and disappeared in the lives of Hugo and Madeline. Perhaps it was all that bound them.

There were no letters preserved for her of course, nothing remained of them. Hugo made sure not a single piece of paper was collected in the rain, Kate had no inclination to stop him, and Madeline was long gone from the scene.

The next morning, ignoring the police instruction to preserve the crime scene, he got into the tractor and ploughed up and down the killing field for hours – trucg trucg trucg – till every scrap of letter and sign of blood was turned into the soil. Nothing was left of the scent or texture or history of Mac on his land.

In the wake of the event, any prospect of a murder accusation against Hugo, or even manslaughter, was barely considered, and he was almost immediately released without charge when his lawyer easily convinced the regional Prosecutor, if not Chief Inspector Prudhomme, that he was acting only to save his wife from being attacked. The lawyer also pointed out that Hugo had nothing to do with setting the trap for Mac and was in no way responsible for frightening and chasing him. "If anything, the Clown, Pierrot, and the fake policeman should be in the dock. In particular, the person masquerading as an officer of the law in order to trick a victim surely must be held especially culpable for whatever ensues."

When Prudhomme had interviewed Hugo about Mac's death he

covered all the above points, and prodded in some other areas too, about his relationship with Mac thirty years before, and some of the stories he had heard.

"Look," said Hugo, "I haven't spoken to Mac since the mid-1930s. Yes, I have heard plenty of stories over the years of him coming and going, and rumours of some of the things he got up to. Do you think that makes me happy, as a husband? But I think you will agree, I hardly set out with a gun to hunt him down. There are half a dozen witnesses who have sworn to you that he ran in front of me. I was on my own land, in the slowest moving vehicle in the region. It would be impossible for me to plan or deliberately execute such an idea."

Prudhomme had to agree, Hugo could hardly be accused of actively orchestrating it; the question in his mind was more about how much he had enjoyed the sight of his hated rival running straight into his rotating blades. And how hard had he really tried to stop?

"OK, Hugo, that is noted for now. Can I ask about one more thing, something that seems to link you with Mac. Did you know there is a file on you in the *gendarmerie*, by the way?"

Hugo laughed. "That applies, I would think, to pretty well everyone you meet in this region, no?"

"Possibly true. And in fairness there isn't that much in yours aside from youthful drunkenness and a few bar fights. One interesting thing, though, that overlaps with something in Mac's file. You were both brought in for questioning at the same time, about the disappearance of someone called Gervaise Travailler."

Hugo attempted a blank look and shrugged.

"You don't remember? He was a local geography teacher? Went missing?"

"Blimey, the geography teacher, I recall the case, yes, it was the talk of the town for a while. I think it is an exaggeration to say we were 'brought in for questioning.' I think everyone round here who had ever been in his class was asked if they knew anything."

"And did you know anything?"

"Only the capital of Peru."

"What?"

"Geography teacher joke. Sorry, is it too soon? Look, don't you have the transcripts? Though I'm sure I didn't say anything worth writing down. My recollection is the cops at the time presumed he'd moved to a new district at the end of the school year, and because he had no friends or family around here no-one was aware he'd gone, or where he might be. Wasn't it as simple as that?"

"Maybe, yes; that's a very good theory. Strangely though, I can't find any record of where he turned up. Might be interesting to keep looking." They stared at each other for a long time, before Prudhomme closed his notebook.

"What about my complaint against Desdemona?" Hugo said hopefully, pointing unnecessarily at the stiches in his face. Prudhomme gave him the card of the most junior Constable in the station and wished him the best of luck.

Hugo's face was badly damaged: Dessie's pistol had left a deep cut across the top of his nose, running into his left cheek, just under the eye, that would leave a permanent scar. When he didn't get anywhere with Prudhomme, he did take his complaint to the police Constable he had recommended. The young PC was, in the general scale of this chaos, not much interested, and indeed asked him whether he "really felt this was a stone he wanted to turn over." So Hugo went to a solicitor, someone whom he had been at school with, to attempt a civil prosecution of both Claude and Desdemona. Over time he found out that his schoolmate's fees were small only because he was drunk and useless, but by then he had lost the case and several thousand francs, even at the discounted rate. He went to another lawyer to try to sue the first lawyer and discovered that, in a small town, professional rivals prefer protecting one another to picking through each other's dustbins.

But that didn't mean Dessie was off the hook entirely. Public opinion in the area split very evenly between the team of Hugo and the team of Des and Claude. They were strains of different families, separate ancient tribes, and the bloodlines thickened, regardless of the fact that very few locals had much sympathy with Mac himself. So now Dessie, for example, found her business at the café was halved overnight, and Hugo discovered that a previously quite gentle dispute about the timber border with his neighbour's land suddenly escalated into a very serious court case, for which it mysteriously emerged he could not get any advocate within a hundred kilometres to represent him.

Hugo had lost his way as well as losing his money, and his drinking got even heavier. Despite boasting at length about his tractor killing skills to anyone who would listen in any bar he happened to be in, he was secretly ashamed and embarrassed; for a while he could not work out why, but gradually he decided he had been cuckolded by Mac, who, it increasingly seemed to him, had died heroically at his wife's feet. It had not been a fair fight. He blamed her.

It takes us back to the day in question, to the disastrous chain of events: who was really responsible? It was suspected that the Prosecutor did consider bringing charges against some of Mac's pursuers for recklessly chasing him into the machine, but only for a few hours, being then dissuaded by realising he would also need to accuse Inspector Leopard (his brother-in-law) who was present throughout, and as senior official, would be deemed to have been in control.

Overall, the Prosecutor allowed himself to be convinced of – or at least to accept – their collective defence, which was that they started off by attempting to apprehend a person of interest on behalf of the authorities, largely for his own protection, and ended by trying to prevent someone who clearly had diminished capacity from potentially doing harm to another.

Karl, naturally, considered himself a victim of events, not an initiator. When asked why he had tackled Mac, a man he had never met before, and forced his face into a pool of mud, he vaguely claimed a combination of service to the community and self-defence. When questioned about his presence at the scene, and what he was doing there at all, he launched always into the same long rant about Robert and Michael; Francois and Scott; Clown and Pierrot; Milo and Jack. The first Constable who interrogated him after Mac's death was quite unable to keep track of the eight different suspects and even more puzzled about what they were supposed to have done.

Karl's police interview took place two days after Mac died, in the hospital, where he was resting in the next room to Jean, after the operation to clean up the stump of his left leg. His foot was gone. His father was on the way from Germany to collect him but seemed to be in no great hurry. No-one had been to visit him at all except, bizarrely, the young English girl, who was so plain he could hardly be bothered to talk to her, till he finally realised the mischievous potential of what he could say.

What about the discredited Leopard? Prudhomme certainly had some fun tormenting him. This, rather childishly, was recompense for the unpleasant and rather cruel treatment he had received from him when Leopard was his training officer all those years ago – he probably didn't even remember.

Leopard was lazy and tired: maybe he had got into a few shady areas he shouldn't, perhaps he had ceased to respect discipline and his colleagues, and very likely he had become drunk on his own power and the self-image of the intuitive genius detective which at the end he had so evidently proved not to be. But Prudhomme had not been tasked, thankfully he thought, to judge the whole man, his history and his suspect connections: his job was to unravel the day itself, what led to it, its outcomes, and rule on that.

Once Prudhomme had decided that it was not totally unreasonable for Leopard to expect Pelou to go in the water; once it had been determined by the pathologist that Leopard had not deliberately let Pierre die (which was an initial suspicion from several of the senior officers in the area); and once it was reluctantly accepted that Karl's continuing presence in the area, and even in the car, was not solely Leopard's responsibility (so the chase down the hill, led by Karl, could not consequently be entirely pinned on the Inspector), then the charges left to answer were mainly to do with issues of questionable policing behaviour and competence. At the end of the day, low-level rule-bending, selective indolence and misplaced arrogance were not especially encouraged in the force, but neither were they commonly considered to be sacking offences in that parish.

The truth was, Prudhomme had decided quite early on to recommend a minimal punishment for him, two weeks suspension without pay; but at the same time he had a conclusive private chat with the Superintendent, off the record, which eventually resulted in a transfer to a new station in a neighbouring region. Time for a clean start for Leopard, he still had ten years till retirement, and after a rest, he had something to offer with a little redirection under the right supervision. There were some demons to conquer first, but Pierre's death, sad though it was for his friends and family, might prove very helpful in removing future temptations from Leopard's reach.

We should also talk of Madeline on her own, not just as half a couple. What comes next for her?

In the weeks after Mac's death, Hugo twice raised a hand to Madeline while they were quarrelling. The arguments began to happen more and more frequently till they gradually merged into a single continuous exhausting confrontation. Then almost without noticing or being noticed, Madeline had moved back to the village, into her mother's house with the children, and she was working full time in town, splitting her days between the future and the past, between the infant school and the museum. I'll leave the marriage there, but you will possibly have your own views about the destination of that relationship.

Is that the final word on Madeline, the inspiration of it all, the icon, the muse – I think you will be expecting to hear more?

The problem is, she has no backstory here, nothing beyond the veneer you know already. She knew Mac thirty years before and broke with him judiciously for reasons no-one can dispute. She was beautiful, kind, funny and loving but chose to lead a frustrating life with Hugo, an unsatisfying and increasingly unpleasant man.

As far as our story goes, she gave Mac the most wonderful days of his life, but tiny instants really, in the greater context, which he magnified for over two hundred thousand hours through the tortured lenses of nostalgia, arrested desire, sadness, sullenness and sentimentality. And she was the centrepiece of the single most extraordinary moment of his existence, his one true epiphany, when he watched the dawn creep across her pillow and gradually light the flowing, rippling mass of her long bronze-gold hair with a halo like a Rublev angel, that only he could see.

But there is nothing else. Madeline's twenty-five years before Mac's death, and Madeline's twenty-five years after, they're not part of the tale.

Madeline is everything, and Madeline is nothing: Madeline is the most important person in the book, and the least important character in the story. Madeline has a proper history, which someone else should tell, but here, for Mac, she is only a symbol: of regret, longing, and a last attempt to remedy the past. Luckily, he died before he could learn the futility of that enterprise for himself.

There are a few more small details. I was tempted to withhold these for myself, but as you are still here, I think you have earned the right to share. We'll just take it a few months forward, as another tale starts after.

Jean mended well after Mac's death. You will have realised he had been having visitors quietly before the world officially knew he was better; in fact pretty well everyone in the area who was not a policeman had dropped in to see him. He finally emerged from the hospital a few days after Milo and Jack were cleared, not good as new, but serviceable, and with the hope and intention of virtually a full recovery in time. It felt like he had been away for an age, but when he got home to be swamped by Hector, who brought him down in the yard, opening quite a few stiches, much to Claude's amusement, it had only been a week since the stabbing. So, it turned out he really was a quick healer. And then he was back in the middle of everything.

As sentenced, Jack and Milo stayed with him at the farmhouse for the summer to look after him while they all worked hard in the Experience with Albert and Amelie. They had already, they realised, became fast friends with them, probably strengthened by events with Karl and the stupid jealousy, thank God that was over. The friendship was a bond that would last.

Kate went back to London five days after the liberating night in the courtroom. She stayed at Bernadette's in the interim while Maggie moved into the Lodge with the kids. Kate felt she needed to get back to her other children as soon as possible; they couldn't stay with Alice at the pub any longer and survive, given they were subsisting entirely on lemonade, crisps and pork pies. Although she stayed for the funeral, she then went straight to the train station and didn't go to the wake. When she arrived back in London, she named it Day Zero. She had no sadness or guilt, those had been used up a long while before, but it is hard not to have regret for a past that fell so epically short of your hopes and expectations. The fact you thought it was happy at the time just makes it much much worse.

Maggie took a while to get used to living at the Lodge, but then loved it; she was warmly welcomed by Amelie and Albert, who appreciated the company, as it was feeling rather empty with Karl gone, and Jack and Milo at Jean's. It wasn't long – actually about

813

forty-eight hours – before Maggie was recruited to the Experience, working in the Hut, on the barge, operating the projector and later often playing Columbine when Amelie wanted time off. She had to go back to England for ten days halfway through (remember that language school, and the test about the cutlery?), and although her parents suggested she shouldn't return to France, for her, though for the others it was mainly a beginning, she sensed it was the end of something, perhaps a last chance, and she wanted to get back and do it well.

As for Amelie, she had never taken Jack very seriously, truth be told, and was grateful when Maggie reacquired him. Amelie was Jack's thing, Jack wasn't Amelie's, and if there were feelings to resolve it was Jack's problem to handle them, which he seemed to manage quite successfully, without apparently needing to use his conscience at all. Amelie grew to adore Maggie, as everyone does, and their friendship long transcended comings and goings at the Lodge.

At the end of the summer, Amelie went back home, oddly quite cured of the Music Master, in time to take up her place at university in Paris. Albert left with her, to finish his final year in Avignon. But they will be back one day, I am sure.

You already recall that Tommy won the heart of Gabi, the brilliant and beautiful young guitarist; he believed it was with his accordion virtuosity, she thought it was with decency, kindness, height and consistency. They have a future. The inestimable and magnificent Madame Jestique now leads the four musicians (shall we just call them the Madame Jestique Quartet, as it became, rather than Trio Plus One) to what I would have to describe as great success, but their biggest adventures are for another book, we are running out of space for them here.

The same applies to Desdemona and Claude. Their escapades and trials with the boys of course brought them closer, as did, to put it in Dessie's own words, "the delightfully unanticipated absence of Pierre." Let us just remark, for now, that their old love renews and blossoms more strongly than ever. As for their jeopardy, it was over; Claude had no issues with Charles, nor Charles with Claude, in fact they became friends, much, I have to say, to the undisguised disapproval of Daphne.

And what of our heroes?

It turned out to be the dream summer for Jack and Maggie once the pain of Mac's passing began to fade. They were living close by, acting together, eventually sleeping together when Jack crept out from Jean's through the fields at night, with Hector turning a blind eye, and even walking with him to the Lodge a couple of times. It was a summer that would never be forgotten; Jack thought, this is really what I wanted that night in the Hind after the exam, when I knew we were leaving for France. This was my dream.

Shall I tell you what happened with Jack and Maggie after? Maybe not (though it is something I do know). Let's take it this far: Jack got an offer from his second-choice university, in a lively northern city, but not from his first. Maggie got a scholarship to Oxford. There we will leave them, deciding how to organise a long-distance relationship; you will have your own thoughts.

And when Jack and Maggie were receiving their offers, Milo also got his. He was accepted at the best art college in London. Alice was incredibly proud. Although she was mildly irked to have wasted all that money on the business course, it turned out she had never really expected him to run the pub. She got properly annoyed, however, when he didn't come home to London to take up the place. Maggie and Jack, up until the last moment, standing on the platform, expected him to travel back with them, but he decided to defer the offer and take a year out to stay in La Chapelle. Did you guess that? Milo moved out of Jean's, back into the Lodge, when Jack left.

And Daphne? She's away at the moment; in fact she can be observed in New York, ice skating at the Rockefeller Plaza. She's having a passionate romance with the American woman in the red straw hat (remember her? I told you she would be back). They're living in Vicksburg but weekending in New York; as Daphne says, "halfway between Cat on a Hot Tin Roof and Breakfast at Tiffany's." Is this the future for her? Well, she's having fun, and she does like the woman in the red straw hat very much, but she's missing Milo and Jean.

With Daphne away, and when Amelie and Albert go off to university, and Jack and Maggie get on the train towards Paris, Milo, back at the Lodge, is living alone. Claude, Jean, Hector, Dessie and Caroline, they all come and see him, most days, some of them every day, and he eats with them, and often has Hector overnight. He spends his time painting in the open air, listening to records borrowed from Jean and Jestique, swimming, smoking, drinking coffee and homemade beer, and planning and costing out the changes they are thinking of making to the Experience for the next year. A lot has changed for Milo in six months. In the spring, if it goes according to strategy, the Lodge will be full of students training for their roles, and Milo will be their wise old mentor, which mainly, in his mind, will involve teaching them how to brew coffee for the first time and letting them change Ella for Lester Young on the record player.

The Experience of course had been the success of the season, establishing itself in the region as a landmark and tourist destination. They have made money, thanks to the shrewd budgeting, and many of the Experience proceeds are being invested in other projects and in the general business of improving the family farm and timber enterprise. Milo is becoming a truly excellent *Directeur commercial*. It would all be making Jean a wealthy man if he didn't keep giving the money away to any friend, family member or passing stranger who either really needs it or easily convinces him they do.

Speaking of which, of course, the other financial beneficiaries of the triumphant summer were the kids in the cast, who had unwittingly gambled their unpaid salary against the prospect of an end-of-term bonus. Before they scattered, Jean gathered them together for a surprise party, and made the most emotional speech about how he could never have done it without them, meaning deeply every syllable. He then handed out envelopes of cash to each which looked much thicker to Milo than when he had put the banknotes in them himself that morning. As did his own. And Jean did not forget Frederick and Pascal either, sending generous amounts, though perhaps he hoped to embarrass them just a little into thinking, 'if only we had stuck it out.' And even Karl was included, because Jean was a man of his word, always: but sadly, Karl's envelope was returned several months later, unopened, having been redirected more than half a dozen times.

The Experience is closed for the winter, and Jean, with Milo's help, is already working out how to expand and grow next year, and the year after. Ideas are spilling out, as ever, and Milo's job is mainly to catch them and make them smaller, more affordable, buildable, functional and achievable without sacrificing any of the Experience magic. They might consider a café, a shop, a beautiful bed and breakfast run by Caroline, stylish Meaulnes merchandise; everything, of course, of the highest possible quality. Jean has already had ambitious designs drawn up for doubling the size of the theatre at Hill House, and maybe they will try to buy the barge – but there will be no pony racing, and no hay wain, ever; Milo won't allow it, even if they could afford it, out of a healthy superstition. Let's leave it there for now, there is plenty of calculating for both of them to do.

So, what of Mac? It looks like we will end with him after all. Mac is determined to have the last word.

Five days after he died, his funeral took place in the small Catholic church in La Chapelle. Jean had organised most of it; Kate had helped of course, but she did not know the traditions or where to get things, so she couldn't do that much. Jean arranged for the service to take place at 8.30am, because most of those attending were involved with the Experience, and he didn't want them to miss work. 'Mac won't mind going in early,' he thought, 'he was not a keeper of regular hours, and he definitely won't want us to lose a day's takings.'

817

Everyone you would expect attended: Jean, Claude, Daphne, Madame Terroir, Caroline, Dessie, Cleo, Julie, Tommy, Gabi, Amelie, Albert, Maggie, Kate, Milo and Jack. Leopard and Prudhomme both came in and stood at the back, on opposite sides of the church. Jean could have drummed up around another forty or fifty, all of them fairly close in blood, and most of those had contacted him to ask him if he wanted them. That's how they put it, "Do you want me to come?"

He discussed it with Kate, and they decided if someone said, "You don't need me, do you?" they were probably best excused from parade.

"Let's keep it small, then. Let's just have the people who can find a reason to care about what happened."

Did I mention Madame Jestique was on the organ? She played some Bach as the mourners entered, Sheep May Safely Graze, which was breathtakingly beautiful. During the service she played two hymns; sometimes with small groups in big churches these can sound sadly sparse, and that was the risk, but Jestique did everything possible to compensate. Tommy joined in on the accordion, which filled the room with music, and the team took pride in singing their hearts out, for Jack, for Kate, for everyone, with the total lack of inhibition that comes from being bonded as a family.

For the rest of the running order:

- The vicar didn't say much: Kate had asked him to keep it short, and to make sure he did she'd refused to provide him with all the normal loveable anecdotes to quote.

- Jack, hating himself for his cowardice, had, claiming nerves and distress, opted not to give an address at all.

- Claude, as the person who knew him first and longest, had earlier been given an invitation to do a reading or reminiscence, but felt that he had said goodbye to Mac a few years before, when there was still a bit of Mac left in Mac. His peace was made, and he had no wish to resift it.

- Kate just said no, she had no intention of speaking.

- So of course, in the end, it was Jean who stepped up, regardless of their wishes or otherwise, out of kindness as well as embarrassment, to fill the void and give the wretched man some poor and simple words to send him on his last journey.

In the end they all agreed that he did a wonderful job, it was very moving, though perhaps more remarkable for what it left out than for what it included.

The service ended with Beim Schlafengehen from the Four Last Songs by Richard Strauss, with Madame Jestique playing and Gabi singing; it was truly exquisite, and everyone wept, for Mac and themselves. Even Kate broke down… who wouldn't? But she was angry too, that Mac had been granted something so utterly lovely. Jean pointed out later that if everyone's funeral had to reflect the life they led, Mozart wouldn't have bothered writing his Requiem.

The coffin was placed in the grave in the small cemetery next to the church, with everyone gathered around. Tommy played Amazing Grace at the graveside, then walked everybody out of the graveyard with Non, Je Ne Regrette Rien. Really not the best of choices, thought Milo, looking at Jack. If ever there was a family with *regrette* eternally embedded in its genes it was this one.

It had been too soon to organise a headstone. Besides, Jean knew it would eventually be him that sorted it out, so why not wait and get a free run at it without a lot of input and debate. In the end it was months later when the tombstone was erected, a beautiful piece of pure white marble with elegant black lettering. Included in the text was what Jean considered to be a moving and appropriate epithet from Le Grand Meaulnes:

Here Lie I, Macon Du Lac

A Soldier of this Region

1912–1963

~ Je Suis Rentre Tout Seul ~

Milo warned him, but he would not be told. So, when Jack next came over, and visited the cemetery, there was the anticipated ruckus. Jean solved it typically by having the stone pulled up so that the stonecutter could add at the bottom some additional words by Jack, in English:

A Father in His Finest Time Loved Greatly By His Children: Jack, Georgina and Frank

When it was re-erected, all agreed it looked quite good, just a very slight squidging at the base to fit in the extra lines; even Jean finally accepted it was an improvement.

After he'd left them to it, not at all sulky, the two boys – well, men now – lit cigarettes, and stood for a while, just being together again, remembering what had happened that summer, looking at the stone like a punctuation mark, the last act for Mac.

"I'd say, as a tip," said Milo, "maybe don't get your headstone designed by a man you tried to stab to death."

"Definitely one to remember," Jack replied, "you could be making a grave mistake."

"Seriously, old boy, we're leaving it at that?"

"How about, 'Always Bury Your Differences Before You Bury Your Friends'?"

"I like it, it has a genuine greetings card feel to it – but we're not digging the stone up again."

"Perhaps we could just add it on the back?"

"In magic marker."

"OK but try it in washable ink first because you're bound to mess it up."

"What about your mum?"

"I asked her if she wanted to be included. She declined."

"Sorry."

"I was relieved – there really isn't enough room so I would have had to leave Frank off."

They left arm in arm; there they were again, back in the day, two friends crossing the road to the pub after their last exam....

And as it turned out Mac didn't rest *tout seul*. Every few weeks there were fresh flowers on the grave. No-one knew or ever saw who was leaving them; everyone had their own idea.

A few months later, Milo was on the phone to Jack in England and mentioned the flowers were still coming. Jack laughed.

"Remember when the croissants used to turn up every day and no-one knew where they were coming from?"

"Ah, you suspect a mystery baker?"

"Or A Greater Power."

"Isn't A Greater Power behind everything?"

"You agree, then. Or it could be me, of course; I may be paying someone to do it, just to perplex you."

"One of the two then. That narrows it down."

He was rolling 'perplex' around his tongue admiringly; he might have gone for 'perturb' himself.

"Everyone misses you, Jack."

"I'm always with you, Milo. And also here. Schrödinger's best mate."

Milo hadn't thought about Jack as his best friend recently. It made him sad he had said that. Isn't friendship diminished if you have to name it, grade it and qualify it? Or perhaps that's not true, perhaps friendship is so precious you do have to claim it, squabble about it, compete for it. Jack was competing, who would have thought it?

"Come and see us soon, Jack. We all love you."

"Bye for now, Spartacus."

"Bye, Spartacus."

Jack hung up, and Milo was left with that feeling we've all had: 'I wish I hadn't said "I love you" when you didn't say it back.'

Then he started laughing.

"Well played, Spartacus. Well played indeed."